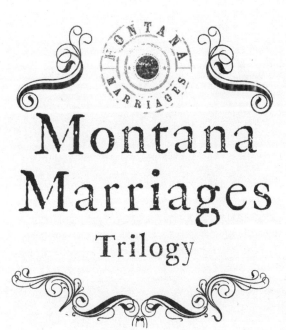

Montana Marriages
Trilogy

MARY CONNEALY

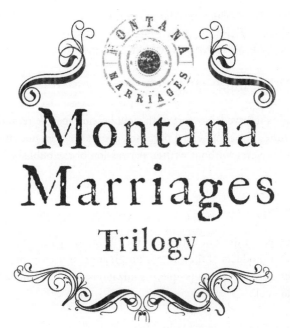

Montana Marriages Trilogy

BARBOUR
PUBLISHING

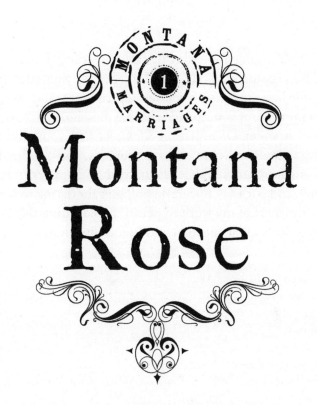

Montana Rose

DEDICATION

I wrote *Montana Rose* shortly after reading Janette Oke's beautiful, classic romance, *Love Comes Softly*. I wanted to explore that same basic premise: a widowed, pregnant young woman in desperate need of a husband who has no choice but to marry a virtual stranger. Of course, in *Montana Rose*, as in everything I write, there is mayhem, disaster, comedy, and gunfire. I can't seem to control myself. For all the years of wonderful reading pleasure, and with my sincerest apologies for daring to compare even a tiny part of my work to hers, I'm dedicating this book to Janette Oke, a great spiritual and literary inspiration.

CHAPTER 1

Montana Territory, 1875

Cassie wanted to scream, *Put down that shovel!*

As if yelling at the red-headed gravedigger would bring Griff back to life. A gust of wind blew Cassie Griffin's dark hair across her face, blinding her.

For one sightless moment, it was as if the wind showed her perfectly what the future held for her.

Darkness.

Hovering in a wooded area, concealed behind a clump of quaking aspens that had gone yellow in the fall weather, she watched the hole grow as the man dug his way down into the rocky Montana earth.

Muriel, the kind storekeeper who had taken Cassie in, stood beside the ever-deepening grave. If Cassie started yelling, Muriel would start her motherly clucking again and force Cassie to return to town and go back to bed. She'd been so kind since Cassie had ridden in, shouting for help.

In a detached sort of way, Cassie knew Muriel had been caring for her, coddling Cassie to get her through the day. But Cassie had gone numb since Muriel's husband, Seth, had come back in with the news that Griff was dead. Cassie listened and answered and obeyed, but she hadn't been able to feel anything. Until now. Now she could feel rage aimed straight at that man preparing the hole for her beloved Griff.

"I'm sorry, little one." Cassie ran her hand over her rounded stomach. "You'll never know your daddy now." Her belly moved as if the baby heard Cassie and understood.

The fact that her husband was dead was Cassie's fault. She should have gone for the doctor sooner, but Griff ordered her not to. At first Griff had been worried about the cost. He'd shocked Cassie by telling her they couldn't afford to send for the doctor. Griff had scolded Cassie if she ever asked questions about money. So she'd learned it wasn't a wife's place. But she'd known her parents were wealthy. Cassie had brought all their wealth into the marriage. How could they not afford a few bits for a doctor? Even as he lay sick, she'd known better than to question him about it though.

Later, Griff had been out of his head with fever. She stayed with him as he'd ordered, but she should have doctored Griff better. She should have saved him somehow. Instead she'd stood by and watched her husband die inch by inch while she did nothing.

Cassie stepped closer. Another few steps and she'd be in the open. She could stop them. She could make them stop digging. Refuse to allow such a travesty when it couldn't be true that Griff was dead.

Don't put him in the ground! Inside her head she was screaming, denying, terrified. She had to stop this.

Before she could move, she heard Muriel.

"In the West, nothing'll get you killed faster'n stupid." Whipcord lean, with a weathered face from long years in the harsh Montana weather, Muriel plunked her fists on her nonexistent hips.

Montana Rose

Seth, clean-shaven once a week and overdue, stood alongside his wife, watching the proceedings, his arms crossed over his paunchy stomach. "How 'bout lazy? In the West, lazy'll do you in faster'n stupid every time."

"Well, I reckon Lester Griffin was both, right enough." Muriel nodded her head.

Cassie understood the words *lazy* and *stupid*. They were talking about Griff? She was too shocked to take in their meaning.

"Now, Muriel"—Red, the gravedigger, shoveled as he talked—"don't speak ill of the dead."

On a day when Cassie didn't feel like she knew anything, she remembered the gravedigger's name because of his bright red hair.

One of the last coherent orders Griff had given her was, "Pay Red two bits to dig my grave and not a penny more."

Griff had known he was dying. Mostly delirious with fever, his mind would clear occasionally and he'd give orders: about the funeral, what he was to be buried in, what Cassie was to wear, strict orders not to be her usual foolish self and overpay for the grave digging. And not to shame him with her public behavior.

"Well honestly, it's a wonder he wasn't dead long before this." Muriel crossed her arms and dared either man to disagree.

"It's not Christian to see the bad in others." Red dug relentlessly, the gritty slice of the shovel making a hole to swallow up Cassie's husband. "And especially not at a time like this."

It was just after noon on Sunday, and the funeral would be held as soon as the grave was dug.

Cassie looked down at her dress, her dark blue silk. It was a mess. She'd worn it all week, not giving herself a second to change while she cared for Griff. Then she'd left it on as she rode for town. She'd even slept in it last night...or rather she'd

9

lain in bed with it on. She hadn't slept more than snatches in a week. Ever since Griff's fever started.

She needed to change to her black silk for the funeral.

Cassie wanted to hate Muriel for her words, but Muriel had mothered her, filling such a desperate void in Cassie that she couldn't bear to blame Muriel for this rage whipping inside her head, pushing her to scream.

"Well, he was a poor excuse for a man, and no amount of Christian charity'll change that." Muriel clucked and shook her head. "He lived on the labor of others 'n' spent money he didn't have."

"It's that snooty, fancy-dressed wife of his who drove him to an early grave," Seth humphed. Cassie saw Seth's shoulders quiver as he chuckled. "Of course, many's the man who'd gladly die trying to keep that pretty little china doll happy."

Cassie heard Griff's nickname for her. She ran her hands down her blue silk that lay modestly loose over her round belly. Fancy-dressed was right. Cassie admitted that. But she hadn't needed all new dresses just because of the baby. Griff had insisted it was proper that the dresses be ordered. But however she'd come to dress so beautifully in silks and satins, there was no denying she dressed more expensively than anyone she'd met in Montana Territory. Not that she'd met many people.

But snooty? How could Seth say that? They were slandering her and, far worse, insulting Griff. She needed to defend her husband, but Griff hated emotional displays. How could she fight them without showing all the rage that boiled inside her? As the hole grew, something started to grow in Cassie that overcame her grief and fear.

Rage. Hate.

That shovel rose and fell. Dirt flew in a tidy pile, and she hated Red for keeping to the task. She wanted to run at Red, screaming and clawing, and force him to give Griff back to her.

But she feared unleashing the anger roiling inside her. Griff had taught her to control all those childish impulses. Right now though, her control slipped.

❧

"A time or two I've seen someone who looks to be snooty who was really just shy. . .or scared," Muriel said.

Red kept digging, determined not to join in with this gossip. But not joining in wasn't enough. He needed to make them stop. Instead, he kept digging as he thought about poor Cassie. She'd already been tucked into Muriel's back room when he'd come to town yesterday, but he'd seen Seth bring Lester Griffin's body in. He couldn't imagine what that little woman had been through.

"When's the last time she came into our store?" Seth asked. "Most times she didn't even come to town. She was too good to soil her feet in Divide. And you can't argue about fancy-dressed. Griff ordered all her dresses ready-made, sent out from the East."

Everything about Cassie Griffin made Red think of the more civilized East. She never had a hair out of place or a speck of dirt under her fingernails. Red had seen their home, too. The fanciest building in Montana, some said. Board siding instead of logs. Three floors and so many frills and flourishes the building alone had made Lester Griffin a laughingstock. The Griffins came into the area with a fortune, but they'd gone through it fast.

"That's right," Muriel snipped. "*Griff* ordered them. A spoiled woman would pick out her own dresses and shoes and finery, not leave it to her man."

Seth shook his head. "I declare, Muriel, you could find the good in a rattlesnake."

Red's shovel slammed deep in the rocky soil. "Cassie isn't a rattlesnake." He stood up straight and glared at Seth.

His reaction surprised him. Red didn't let much upset him. But calling Cassie a snake made Red mad to the bone. He glanced over and saw Muriel focusing on him as she brushed back wisps of gray hair that the wind had scattered from her usual tidy bun. She stared at him, taking a good long look.

Seth, a tough old mule-skinner with a marshmallow heart, didn't seem to notice. "This funeral'll draw trouble. You just see if it don't. Every man in the territory'll come a-running to marry with such a pretty widow woman. Any woman would bring men down on her as hard and fast as a Montana blizzard, but one as pretty as Cassie Griffin?" Seth blew a tuneless whistle through his teeth. "There'll be a stampede for sure, and none of 'em are gonna wait no decent length of time to ask for her hand."

Red looked away from Muriel because he didn't like what was in her eyes. He was through the tough layer of sod and the hole was getting deep fast. He tried to sound casual even though he felt a sharp pang of regret—and not just a little bit of jealousy—when he said, "Doubt she'll still be single by the time the sun sets."

Muriel had a strange lilt to her voice when she said, "A woman is rare out here, but a young, beautiful woman like Cassie is a prize indeed."

Red looked up at her, trying to figure out why saying that made her so all-fired cheerful.

Seth slung his beefy arm around Muriel with rough affection. "I've seen the loneliness that drives these men to want a wife. It's a rugged life, Muriel. Having you with me makes all the difference."

Red understood the loneliness. He lived with it every day.

"She's a fragile little thing. Tiny even with Griff's child in her belly. She needs a man to take care of her." Muriel's concern sounded just the littlest bit false. Not that Muriel wasn't genuinely concerned. Just that there was a sly tone to it, aimed straight at Red.

Red thought of Cassie's flawless white skin and shining black hair. She had huge, remote brown eyes with lashes long enough to wave in the breeze, and the sweetest pink lips that never curved in a smile nor opened to wish a man good day.

Red thought on what he'd say to draw a smile and a kind word from her. Such thoughts could keep a man lying awake at night. Red knew that for a fact. Oh yes, Cassie was a living, breathing test from the devil himself.

"China doll's the perfect name for her," Muriel added.

Red had heard that Griff called his wife china doll. Griff never said that in front of anyone. He always called her Mrs. Griffin, real proper and formal-like. But he'd been overheard speaking to her in private, and he'd called her china doll. The whole town had taken to calling her that.

Red had seen such a doll in a store window when he was a youngster in Indiana. That doll, even to a roughhousing little boy, was so beautiful it always earned a long, careful look. But the white glass face was cold and her expression serious, as if someone neglected giving the poor toy a painted-on smile. It was frighteningly fragile. Rather than being fun, Red thought a china doll would be a sad thing to own and, in the end, a burden to keep unbroken and clean. All of those things described Cassandra Griffin right down to the ground. Still, knowing all of that didn't stop him from wanting her.

Cassie got to him. She had ever since the first time he'd seen her nearly two years ago. And now she was available. Someone would have to marry her to keep her alive. Women didn't live without men in the unsettled West. Life was too hard. The only unattached women around worked above the Golden Butte Saloon and, although they survived, Red didn't consider their sad existence living.

"You're established on the ranch these days, Red. Your bank account's healthy." Muriel crouched down so she was eye level with Red, who was digging himself down fast. "Maybe it's time you took a wife."

Red froze and looked up at his friend. Muriel was a motherly woman, though she had no children. And like a mother, she seemed comfortable meddling in his life.

Red realized he was staring and went back to the grave, tempted to toss a shovelful of dirt on Muriel's wily face. He wouldn't throw it *hard*. He just wanted to distract her.

When he was sure his voice would work, he said, "Cassie isn't for me, Muriel. And it isn't because of what it would cost to keep her. If she was my wife, she'd live within my means and that would be that."

Red had already imagined—in his unruly mind—how stern he'd be when she asked for finery. *"You'll have to sew it yourself or go without."* He even pictured himself shaking a scolding finger right under her turned-up nose. She'd mind him.

He'd imagined it many times—many, many times. And long before Griff died, which was so improper Red felt shame. He'd tried to control his willful thoughts. But a man couldn't stop himself from thinking a thought until he'd started, now could he? So he'd *started* a thousand times and then he stopped himself. . .mostly. He'd be kind and patient but he wouldn't bend. He'd say, "Cass honey, you—"

Red jerked his thoughts away from the old, sinful daydream about another man's wife. Calmly, he answered Muriel, "She isn't for me because I would never marry a nonbeliever."

With a wry smile, Seth caught on and threw in on Muriel's side—the traitor. "A woman is a mighty scarce critter out here, Red. It don't make sense to put too many conditions on the ones there are."

"I know." Red talked to himself as much as to them. He

hung on to right and wrong. He clung to God's will. "But one point I'll never compromise on is marrying a woman who doesn't share my faith."

"Now, Red," Muriel chided, "you shouldn't judge that little girl like that. How do you know she's not a believer?"

"I'm not judging her, Muriel." Which Red realized was absolutely not true. "Okay, I don't know what faith she holds. But I do know that the Griffins have never darkened the doorstep of my church."

Neither Seth nor Muriel could argue with that, although Muriel had a mulish look that told him she wanted to.

"We'd best get back." Seth laid a beefy hand on Muriel's strong shoulder. "I think Mrs. Griffin is going to need some help getting ready for the funeral."

"She's in shock, I reckon," Muriel said. "She hasn't spoken more'n a dozen words since she rode in yesterday."

"She was clear enough on what dress I needed to fetch." Seth shook his head in disgust. "And she knew the reticule she wanted and the shoes and hairpins. I felt like a lady's maid."

"I've never seen a woman so shaken." Muriel's eyes softened. "The bridle was on wrong. She was riding bareback. It's a wonder she was able to stick on that horse."

Red didn't want to hear any more about how desperately in need of help Cassie was.

Muriel had been teasing him up until now, but suddenly she was dead serious. "You know what the men around here are like, Red. You know the kind of life she's got ahead of her. There are just some things a decent man can't let happen to a woman. Libby's boys are off hauling freight or I'd talk to them. They'd make good husbands."

Muriel was right, they would be good. Something burned hot and angry inside of Red when he thought of those decent, Christian men claiming Cassie.

It was even worse when Red thought of her marrying one of the rough-and-ready men who lived in the rugged mountains and valleys around the little town of Divide, which rested up against the great peaks of the Montana Rockies. It was almost more than he could stand to imagine her with one of them.

But he also knew a sin when he saw it tempting him, and he refused to let Muriel change his mind. She badgered him awhile longer but finally gave up.

He was glad when Seth and Muriel left him alone to finish his digging. Until he looked up and saw Cassie as if he'd conjured her with his daydreams.

But this was no sweet, fragile china doll. She charged straight toward him, her hands fisted, her eyes on fire.

"Uh. . .hi, Miz Griffin." He vaulted out of the shoulder-deep hole and faced her. The look on her face was enough to make him want to turn tail and run.

She swept toward him, a low sound coming from her throat that a wildcat might make just before it pounced.

She'd heard it. All of it.

God forgive me for being part of that gossip, hurting her when she's already so badly hurt.

Whatever she wanted to say, whatever pain she wanted to inflict, he vowed to God that he'd stand here and take it as his due. Her eyes were so alive with fury and focused right on him. How many times had his unruly mind conjured up the image of Cassie focusing on him? But this wasn't the look he'd imagined in his daydreams. In fact, a tremor of fear ran up his backbone.

His grip tightened on his shovel, not to use as a weapon to defend himself but to keep her from grabbing it and taking a swing.

"Stop it." Her fists were clenched as if to beat on him. "Stop saying those awful things." Red saw more life in her eyes than he ever had before. She was always quiet and reserved and distant. "Give him back. I want him back!" She moved so fast toward him that, just as she reached his side, she tripped over her skirt and fell. A terrified shriek cut off her irate words.

"Cassie!" Red dropped the shovel and caught her just as she'd have tumbled into the open grave.

She swung and landed a fist right on his chin.

His head snapped back. She had pretty good power behind her fists for a little thing. Figuring he deserved it, he held on, stepping well away from the hole in the ground. He pulled her against him as she pummeled and emitted short, sharp, frenzied screams of rage. Punching his shoulders, chest, face. He took his beating like a man. He'd earned this by causing her more pain when she'd already been dealt—more than she could bear. Of course he'd tried to stop it. But he'd failed now, hadn't he?

"I'm sorry." He spoke low, hoping to penetrate her anger. He could barely hear himself over her shouting. "I'm so sorry about Griff, Cassie. And I'm sorry you heard us speaking ill. We were wrong. So wrong. I'm sorry. I'm sorry." His voice kept crooning as he held her, letting her wale away on him until her squeaks and her harmless blows slowed and then ceased, most likely from exhaustion, not because she'd quit hating him.

Her hands dropped suddenly. Her head fell against his chest. Her knees buckled, and Red swung her up into his arms.

He looked down at her, wondering if she'd fainted dead away.

In his arms, he held perfection.

She fit against him as if his body and his heart had been created just for her. A soul-deep ache nearly buckled his own knees as he looked at her now-closed eyes. Those lashes so long they'd tangle in a breeze rested on her ashen face, tinged with one bright spot of fury raised red on her cheeks.

"I'm so sorry I hurt you. Please forgive me." His words were both a prayer to God and a request to poor, sweet Cassie. He held her close, murmuring, apologizing.

At last her eyes fluttered open. The anger was there but not the violence. "Let me go!"

He slowly lowered her feet to the ground, keeping an arm around her waist until he was sure her legs would hold her. She stepped out of his arms as quickly as possible and gave him a look of such hatred it was more painful than the blows she'd landed. Far more painful.

"I'm so sorry for your loss, Cassie honey." Red wanted to kick himself. He shouldn't have called her such. It was improper.

She didn't seem to notice he was even alive. Instead, her gaze slid to that grave, that open rectangle waiting to receive her husband. . .or what was left of him. And the hatred faded to misery, agony, and worst of all, fear.

A suppressed cry of pain told Red, as if Cassie had spoken aloud, that she wished she could join her husband in that awful hole.

Her head hanging low, her shoulders slumped, both arms wrapped around her rounded belly, she turned and walked back the way she came. Each step seemed to take all her effort as if her feet weighed a hundred pounds each.

Wondering if he should accompany her back to Muriel's, instead he did nothing but watch. There was nothing really he could do. That worthless husband of hers was dead and he'd left his wife with one nasty mess to clean up. And Red couldn't be the one to step in and fix it. Not if he wanted to live the life God had planned for him.

She walked into the swaying stand of aspens. They were thin enough that if he moved a bit to the side, he could keep his eye on her. Stepping farther and farther sideways to look around the trees—because he was physically unable to take his eyes off her—he saw her get safely to the store.

Montana Rose

Just then his foot slipped off the edge of the grave. He caught himself before he fell headlong into the six feet of missing earth.

Red heard the door of Bates General Store close with a sharp *bang*, and Cassie went inside and left him alone in the sun and wind with a deep hole to dig and too much time to think. He grabbed his shovel and jumped down, getting back at it.

He knew he was doing the right thing by refusing to marry Cassie Griffin.

A sudden gust caught a shovelful of dirt and blew it in Red's face. Along with the dirt that now coated him, he caught a strong whiff of the stable he'd cleaned last night. Cassie would think Red and the Western men he wanted to protect her from were one and the same. And she'd be right, up to a point. The dirt and the smell, the humble clothes, and the sod house—this was who he was, and he didn't apologize for that to any man. . . or any woman.

Red knew there was only one way for him to serve God in this matter. He had to keep clear of Cassie Griffin.

The china doll wasn't for him.

CHAPTER 2

T he Lord is my shepherd; I shall not want.'" Parson Bergstrom stood in the buffeting wind.

Red filled in Cassie's precious husband's grave while the parson, with his black coat and flat-brimmed hat, stood in the fall breeze, reading from his open Bible. The parson intoned the Psalm, using it as a prayer for peace and strength.

Cassie had neither.

She looked down at Griff, and the wind whipped the blanket away, exposing Griff's forever-closed eyes. One second later, dirt landed, covering the still, white face.

Had Red done that on purpose, thrown dirt on Griff's face? Her fists clenched. She wanted Red to get away from Griff. She wanted to attack him and claw him until he bled as red as his hair. Glaring at Red, who didn't seem to notice her, she saw that he had a puffy lip and a slightly blackened eye. She'd done that to him. The satisfaction of it was shocking. She wanted to shove Muriel's arm off her shoulder. To think this woman considered herself superior to Griff. All of that raged inside Cassie's head, but outwardly she forced herself to remain calm.

Each time the shovel bit into the soil mounded beside Griff's grave, Cassie felt it cut her heart, scoop it out, and toss it in with Griff. Or it might as well have. She wouldn't have hurt anymore. The shoveling went on and on, obscuring the blanketed body of her dearly loved Griff.

" 'He maketh me to lie down in green pastures: He leadeth me beside the still waters,'" the parson continued.

She was aware, in an impassive way, of the people hovering around her: Muriel, Seth, Parson Bergstrom, Red. There were others but she didn't know them and had no interest in getting to know them.

The parson was a circuit rider, and he'd been passing through town when Griff died, or the town would have settled him underground with an awkward prayer and an off-key verse of "Amazing Grace."

" 'He restoreth my soul: He leadeth me in the paths of righteousness for His name's sake.'"

The shovel bit again, working until it was a steady beat, rhythmic, in time with the words, nearly setting Cassie's nightmare to music. The pace fixed, unstoppable, like a heartbeat. Cassie felt hers beating, and it told her she wasn't dead. But Griff was and she wondered if that might not be the same thing.

" 'Yea, though I walk through the valley of the shadow of death, I will fear no evil: for thou art with me; thy rod and thy staff they comfort me.'"

Besides Muriel, every one of the twenty or so mourners was a man. Divide, Montana, was a rugged place, tucked into the Rocky Mountains. And women didn't come here. Cassie and Muriel and a couple of others were the exceptions that proved the rule. Women were too soft, Griff said. Muriel said women were too smart.

Cassie didn't have an opinion. It wasn't a woman's place to

have an opinion. But Griff had told her often enough that time would change the lack of women, and the settlers who were here first would become barons over this vast, empty land.

Griff's dream of being a powerful cattle baron was being buried along with him.

" 'Thou preparest a table before me in the presence of mine enemies: thou anointest my head with oil; my cup runneth over.' "

The hole filled until it was running over. It happened so quickly Cassie wanted to scream at Red Dawson to stop. But she'd surely screamed enough for one day. Griff would be so ashamed of her if he could have seen the way she carried on earlier. But at least that had been with Red, in private. She would not carry on so in front of this crowd.

She stood, contained and serene, perfection in her demeanor, only marred by the tears dripping off her chin. But inside, she could still see herself striking Red, screaming at him, wanting the cruel words he'd spoken to disappear and the horrible grave to vanish. She nearly staggered back. He was dead. Griff was really dead.

" 'Surely goodness and mercy shall follow me all the days of my life: and I will dwell in the house of the Lord for ever.' "

There was no goodness without Griff. God had no mercy.

The hole mounded until Red tossed in the last shovelful of dirt. He turned and gave Cassie a compassionate look that locked their eyes together.

Cassie wanted to demand he give Griff back to her. She needed to take her rage out on someone and Red was here. He looked strong enough to take it, and she already knew he was kind enough to let her attack him without returning the pain.

"I'm so sorry for your loss, Mrs. Griffin." Red's quiet words were accompanied by eyes that seemed to speak to her, as if he understood her grief and rage. As if he cared.

The moment between them stretched too long. Red's blackened eyes dropped shut as if he had to stop looking but didn't have the will to turn his head. His chin tilted down and Cassie saw him open his eyes and stare at the grave. Then, without looking at her again, he swung his shovel up to rest on his shoulder and walked away.

She wanted to scream at him. Call him a coward. Tell him to get back here and let her rant and rave. Red's broad shoulders disappeared into the crowd of men, but even after he was gone, Cassie looked after him.

"Red's a good man, Cassie." Muriel patted Cassie's arm.

No he wasn't. Cassie wanted to shout that in Muriel's face, but of course she didn't. A good man wouldn't have left her here.

" *'Yea, though I walk through the valley of the shadow of death. . . .'* " Those were the parson's words. Surely that's where Cassie stood now, in that valley of the shadow. It came to Cassie that the parson's words would come true soon and she could walk on through and then dwell in the house of the Lord forever, because without Griff she would surely die. The truth hit her, and instead of frightening her, it gave her peace.

How simple.

Griff was dead. She'd die, too.

Of course.

Without Griff to take care of her, there was no way to go on. She clutched her hands around her stomach. Her baby. She'd never know this little one she loved so much. Would God judge her harshly because she hadn't protected her child?

Something fierce rose in Cassie that wanted to fight for her child. But how? Griff had told her so often that she was stupid and useless. And this moment proved Griff right, because she couldn't imagine how to live without her husband. So, she'd die and her precious baby would die with her. Through her grief and her overwhelming failure, she was almost relieved. Death—so simple.

"Let's get on with it, Parson." A rough voice broke through Cassie's grief and fear and roused her temper. Fine enough for her to decide to die, but no one had the right to tell her to get on with it.

Muriel stood on her right, supporting her. Now her arm tightened around Cassie's shoulder until it hurt. "This is not the time."

Time for what? Cassie wondered, slowly bringing her concentration to focus on the group around her.

The men surrounded the filled grave. Now they stepped nearer. She noticed the ones across the grave from her walked across the newly filled hole.

"The parson's here. We get it done," the same voice growled.

Cassie was watching this time. She saw an overweight man, with a full beard more gray than brown, shouldering his way to the front of the assembly. He came so close to Cassie she could see the line of tobacco that drooled from the corner of his mouth and stained his beard. She caught the hot, rancid odor of his breath and the stench of his unwashed body. She glimpsed his blackened teeth.

"Back off, Marley." The voice came from farther back in the crowd. "She hain't a gonna choose you anyhow. You're old enough to be her pa and fat enough to be let out with her cows."

The crowd broke out into loud, coarse laughter.

"Miz Griffin likes 'em old, don't ya, sweetheart?" a third man shouted.

More laughter followed.

"Well then, you're it, you old coot." Someone shoved the old man aside and others jostled forward to take his place.

Cassie couldn't keep up with who was talking. She felt

Muriel's fingers tear loose from her shoulder and turned to see Muriel being jostled aside and pushed away until Cassie couldn't see her anymore. Seth was on her left, and the parson pushed up close to stand in the spot where Muriel had been. He and Seth were knocked into her until she thought she'd be crushed between them.

"Stay back!" Seth shouted.

"Give her time." The parson sounded like he was threatening the crowd, but they showed no affect from his words.

One man's beefy arm snaked past Seth and caught hold of the sleeve of Cassie's black silk dress. "Take care of your fussy dress, darlin'—you won't be gettin' no more. No matter who ya choose."

Seth shoved the man's hand away.

Choose? What were they talking about? She shrank away from the reaching, grasping hands but backed into someone, and a frantic look over her shoulder told her the men were behind her, too. Her heart started to pound in fear.

Through the milling crowd, she looked down the slope to town and caught a glimpse of Red walking toward the stable, his shovel resting on his shoulder. She saw Muriel rush up to Red and catch his arm and start talking rapidly, waving her arms and pointing at Cassie. Red looked at Cassie and shook his head.

Cassie thought of how she'd attacked the man and felt shame. She also felt some regret that she hadn't taken another swing at him.

Another man touched her, this time on her protruding stomach. "Iffen it's a boy, you kin call it after its pa if you choose me."

The parson shouted, "Please, gentlemen, can't you see she's in no emotional state to make this choice now? She needs time to grieve. Her husband is newly dead. Maybe in a week or two."

A week or two? Cassie tried to understand that. The parson expected her to be done with her mourning in a week or two? Cassie knew she'd be mourning Griff for the rest of her life, be it short or long.

"He's cold, Parson. That's all we need to know. You're a pretty li'l thing, china doll. I'd sure like you keepin' me warm through this next winter."

Cassie gasped. She'd overheard gossips on occasion call her china doll—not least of all Seth and Muriel this morning—but no one had ever called her that to her face except Griff. And he meant it warmly.

"Pick, li'l lady." A tall, thin man pressed forward from the right. "I've got chores to get to at home."

"See here, I won't stand for this." The parson stumbled and nearly fell, knocking into Cassie.

"You're leavin', Parson. We get it done now, today, or she'll be livin' with one of us for months till you come back. Griff's young'un'll be born and she'll be broodin' with a new one by then."

"She will if she don't marry an old codger like you."

An outburst of laughter sent Cassie stumbling backward. Her stomach heaved at the sickening things they were saying.

"It took Griff years to get a babe on her. Maybe it's her."

"I'd be willin' to keep trying were you to choose me, china doll." That brought the loudest outbreak of laughter yet.

She knew what they were talking about, but she kept turning her mind away from it. Without Griff, the only choice she could see before her was to die bravely. It was inevitable so she accepted it. It had never occurred to her to save herself by choosing another husband. She looked around the crowd, and more than ever death sounded like a better option.

"A barren woman's better than no woman at all."

"Choose, Miz Griffin. I'm young. I've got a good place, well started."

"You live in a soddy, Harv. Think she wants that after what she's livin' in now?"

The men bandied their crude jokes and shoved each other, trying to get close to her.

The parson fell to the ground beside her, and arms jerked him sideways until he disappeared in the crowd. Someone slid his arm around the girth of her protruding belly and pulled her hard against him.

Her head started to spin, and her knees threatened to give out. The mob pressed closer and more hands clung to her, touching her, sometimes improperly, but there were so many that each bit of contact was as much a violation as the next, regardless of where that touch occurred. She wished she could sink beneath the dirt that sheltered her husband.

"Miz Griffin will marry me," a voice thundered from the back of the crowd. The men turned at the harsh, tyrannical voice that overwhelmed even this rough assembly.

Cassie recognized that awful voice. Mort Sawyer had arrived.

A huge black horse pranced right up through the middle of the mob. Mort seemed unconcerned if he trampled anyone under iron-shod hooves, and the men seemed to know it. They snarled and grumbled in protest, but they fell back far enough to allow the man through, like wolves giving way before the leader of the pack.

Five other horses followed the black, driving the mob back farther. Cassie recognized several of the riders, particularly Wade Sawyer, the young, hungry-eyed son of the rancher. The younger man rode one pace off the lead horse. Wade studied her with piercing green eyes that sent a shudder of fear climbing like a scurrying insect up the back of her neck.

"Miz Griffin, I'm mighty sorry to hear of your loss." Mort tipped his black Stetson. He spoke like a man paying heed to a social nicety with no emotional interest in his words. And why not? He didn't really know her. She'd taken pains to never speak to him and to stay out of his sight. And the little Mort had to do with Griff had been unpleasant. Tense meetings over the natural spring just behind Griff's house, one of the few in the area that flowed freely even in the dry season. Mort Sawyer had the bad habit of turning his cattle out during the long summer months, so they could drink from that spring.

Mort dispensed with his hollow expression of sympathy and returned to his usual imperious tone. Mort's ability to dominate with that voice made Griff's endless chiding sound like playful schoolyard banter by comparison.

Mort Sawyer, the name Griff had spoken with his dying breath.

Most of what he'd said toward the end was incoherent, so if he was cruel, she didn't hold him to blame. If in his delirium he knocked her to the floor a few times, it wasn't his fault. He'd fallen into a stupor, occasionally rousing to swallow a few drops of water or rant at her for letting him get so sick.

Then, as Griff's breathing became shallow and his eyes fell shut, he found the strength to speak one last time. "Sawyer never got the spring while I lived."

Cassie remembered the triumph in Griff's voice, like his life had been a success and now he could die happy.

"I reckon Miz Griffin's comin' with me. Parson, let's get it over and done."

A howl of protest exploded from the other men and brought Cassie back to the present. The volume of the noise forced Cassie back a step. She ran into someone and turned to face the heavy, tobacco-chewing man and be assaulted by his breath again.

Mort Sawyer's son, Wade, pushed his mount past his father and reached for Cassie. He leaned down, grabbed her under her arms, and yanked her up onto the saddle to settle her in front of him. Her legs scraped painfully on the saddle horn.

Wade turned to his father. "I want her, Pa."

"She's mine, boy. We've had it out. The spring's gotta be in my hands."

Wade lifted Cassie's chin roughly until she looked straight into his eyes. She'd looked into those eyes before. Too many times.

Wade had the habit of dropping by her home when Griff was gone. He'd done it too often for it to be chance. Now he studied her with those weird, bright green eyes, the color of envy and rot. Wade Sawyer was responsible for one of the few true acts of defiance Cassie had to her name. She'd learned to shoot. Practicing when Griff was away. And she'd kept a gun close at hand all the time.

Of course, she didn't have it now when she needed it.

Wade sank his fingers painfully into her jaw and leaned his face so close that for a second Cassie thought he meant to kiss her. She jerked her head sideways to escape his grasping fingers and pushed at the hand that shackled her waist but couldn't dislodge Wade's grip.

He was amused by her struggles. Only inches from her, Cassie saw he had a black eye and a slightly swollen lip that seemed to underscore the violence in him. She thought of Red and the black eye she'd given him and wished she'd been responsible for Wade's.

He said loudly enough for the crowd to hear, "Well then, I guess you're gonna be my new mama." Then Wade kissed her until she felt bruised. Releasing her, he looked at her with greedy eyes that didn't match the humor in his voice. Dead serious eyes that claimed her in a way no marriage could.

Mort edged his horse next to Wade's and grabbed Cassie then hefted her into his lap. His beefy arms settled around her, even before Wade's had left her body.

The touch of the two men induced shudders so violent that she lost a battle with self-control, just as she had this morning with Red. She wrenched against Mort's grip and started shrieking like a madwoman.

She caught Mort Sawyer in the belly with her elbow, and his response was a mild grunt. He wrapped his arms more tightly around her fat middle and roared, "Where's the parson?"

She struggled more wildly, kicking at Mort's leg and making his horse prance sideways. She looked around at the men. They had all fallen back and seemed content now to watch the show.

She heard the parson say, "I'll not marry a woman to someone against her will, Sawyer. I won't stand before God and conduct such a travesty. This isn't something you can dictate. You let her go right this—"

Mort's horse charged forward under his master's skillful hand. Mort reached down and grabbed the parson by the front of his black suit. He lifted the man onto his tiptoes with one hand while he controlled Cassie with his other. "You'll marry us, Parson, or I'll take her home, and when she's broken in, maybe after she's given me a son or two, she'll agree nice enough."

Wade laughed, but it was a sickening, hollow sound. "I'm gonna have a baby brother."

Mort shoved the parson back and he fell to the ground. A man who would do that to a preacher would do unspeakable things to his wife.

Darkness spun in front of her.

A quiet voice behind her cut through the noise. "I'll marry Mrs. Griffin, if she'll have me."

Cassie's head cleared, and as she twisted around to locate the owner of that kind voice, her eyes focused on Red Dawson. The man she'd hated more than any other on this earth ten minutes ago.

"Beat it, Dawson. She's mine," Mort Sawyer said.

Montana Rose

Cassie remembered Wade's eyes. Even though she had always been sheltered, she knew terrible things were in store for her if she was taken to the Sawyer ranch.

Mort marched the horse straight at Red.

Red stopped the horse by patting its nose. "Whoa, boy, easy there."

Then he looked at Cassie. With a voice as out of place as a breeze in the midst of a tornado, he asked, "Whattaya say, Cassie, will you marry me?"

"Parson, it's settled. We get it done now!" Mort roared.

Cassie heard the violence in Mort and recalled the foulness in Wade and smelled the filth in her nearest other suitors. . .and saw the decency in Red's eyes. She still hated Red Dawson, although less than she had a few minutes ago. Or more correctly, she now hated other people more.

Unless Griff's grave opened this minute and let her jump in, Cassie didn't see as she had much choice. A minute passed as the chaos went on around her and the trampled grave stayed closed, and as if someone else spoke out of her lips, she said, "Yes. . ."

She almost said, *Red*, before it occurred to her that Red must be a nickname. She didn't know the name of the man who proposed to her. It was humiliating to ask him.

Somehow it seemed less humiliating to just say, "Yes, I'll marry you."

CHAPTER 3

Cassie was a widow one day and a newlywed the next.

The wedding was held at the cemetery with a good share of the wedding guests standing on her dead husband's grave.

She didn't so much have wedding guests as she had a lynch mob. Twenty-five armed men wanted Red Dawson dead. Cassie thought that no doubt one of Red's murderers would then insist on marrying her. If the pattern continued, she'd be forty or fifty times a widow within the next few hours. At that rate, Divide would be a ghost town by the weekend.

Cassie Griffin's contribution to Montana.

Red had reached up to take Cassie off Mort's horse. Mort had spurred his horse away, but Red had caught the reins and soothed the animal while glaring at Mort.

"You will do the right thing, Mort Sawyer. Before God and all these witnesses, Cassie has refused your offer of marriage and accepted mine. Now let her down."

Cassie felt the hands on her body, not sure who all was touching her. But Red lowered her to the ground. She suspected that "all these witnesses" was a better incentive than "before

God." Considering his treatment of the parson, Mort didn't seem to be much interested in what God saw when He looked into Mort's black heart.

Red pulled Cassie to his side, looked down as if to check that she was in one piece, and then reached his hand down to assist Parson Bergstrom in standing.

"Let's get it done quick, Parson." Red slid his arm around Cassie, and Seth did some shoving to get to her side. The crowd grumbled, but even Mort Sawyer only made noise.

"Do you, Cassie Griffin, take Red Dawson to be your lawfully wedded husband?" The parson spoke the words so fast it was obvious he was scared to death.

To Cassie, that didn't speak well for the man's trust in eternal life. But maybe he believed well enough, he just didn't want to pass through those pearly gates into eternal life right now today.

Someone said, "I do." Cassie suspected it was she.

"Do you, Red Dawson. . ." The parson repeated the most abbreviated version of marriage vows Cassie had ever heard—though in truth she hadn't heard many. The parson used an economy of words, most likely planning his escape all the while.

The service took about two minutes, including the time it took for Red to get Cassie off Mort Sawyer's horse. How he managed it Cassie didn't really know. There was a relentlessness to the way Red moved. He seemed unconcerned with the hostile explosions surrounding him.

The only rational thought Cassie had about Red was if she'd blackened Griff's eye the way she'd done to Red, the punishment would have been severe and swift. She expected nothing less with her new husband. Hopefully Red would wait until they were alone to mete out her punishment.

Wade Sawyer was openly furious, but his father controlled him, maybe thinking the cold-blooded murder of an unarmed man in front of dozens of witnesses might be too much for even a Sawyer to walk away from.

Cassie was summarily married, and Red took her arm and led her away from the mob toward the stables. He stooped to pick up his shovel on the way.

Cassie remembered the argument she'd seen Muriel having with Red in the same spot where the shovel lay. "Muriel nagged you into marrying me, didn't she?" Cassie looked at Red fearfully. Now Cassie veered from grief and shock to humiliation.

"I did what I thought was right, I reckon." Red hurried her to the stable, whether because he had work to do or because he was looking for shelter from the horde, Cassie couldn't say.

Then she thought of the way Wade had looked at her and the tyrannical way Mort had taken her from the other men. Well, she'd made the best of a bad situation. She'd come up with a plan.

Death.

Marrying Red Dawson was her second choice, and it was a poor second. But, all things considered, she'd do it again.

They moved on toward the stables, her wedding guests prowling around behind them. Cassie had a moment to wonder if possibly Red lived in the stables. She really didn't know the man at all. She'd seen the red hair a time or two around town, and fortunately his nickname was easily recalled. But Red Dawson, along with almost every other person in Divide, was a stranger.

Red went into the stable and headed for a saddled buckskin that was half as tall and a quarter as pretty as the magnificent bay Cassie had ridden to town bareback when Griff died. The bay had been stabled here ever since.

Cassie looked over at the regal animal who stood eating in a stall. Seth had gone for Griff's body without taking Cassie along. He'd brought her dress and Griff's suit because she quoted

Griff's careful deathbed instructions. Seth had fed and watered the other bay, left out at the ranch. That one was a matched partner to the one she'd managed to bridle and climb onto after a long struggle. The two horses were the only livestock Griff had left when he died.

Red didn't even look at the bay. He hung the shovel on the back of his saddle, turned to stretch out his hand to her, and said, "I'll give you a leg up."

"I'll ride my own horse." She realized with a start those were not proper words for a wife to say to her husband.

His ordering her onto his horse, telling her what to do—that was something familiar. Her objecting—that was rude.

She clamped her mouth shut, determined to be as good a wife to Red as she'd been to Griff. But they really did have to take the horse.

"The horse belongs to the bank." Red held his hand out, waiting for her to come to him.

Cassie shook her head, trying to rattle the words around inside her head so they made sense. "B–Belongs to the bank? I don't understand."

"They're mortgaged, Cassie. Your place has a lien on it for the property, the livestock, and the contents of your home."

"Griff mentioned a loan. But surely the horses…we brought them west with us. They were from my parents' stable. I know they were paid for."

"They were paid for then…maybe."

Red's tone made Cassie wonder how much was known publicly about her finances. Obviously far more than Griff had ever told her. Griff had always told her a woman shouldn't concern her weak mind with money matters.

Red went on. "Now they're mortgaged. I can't afford to pay off your loans. I'd end up owning horses I don't need, a house miles away from my place, and fancy furniture that won't fit in my soddy. The bank can take 'em."

"How did you know about the loan?" Cassie struggled to keep up. Every word he spoke was news to her.

"It's a small town." Red shrugged. "And I work at the bank some, washing windows and such. I hear talk. Besides, it's no secret. Everyone knows." He reached for her, pulling back as he studied her stomach. He ran one finger over his puffy lip, glanced at her for a second, and then said, "I'll have to. . .to lift you onto Buck. Excuse my. . .my *familiar*. . .uh. . .touch." He very carefully, looking alarmed, put his hands under her arms and lifted her so she sat facing sideways on his saddle. He settled her gently.

"Uh. . .try hooking your leg over the horn."

Cassie shook her head, confused at what he was asking her to do. "I. . .I don't ride. . ."

"I don't have a sidesaddle. You'll just have to learn to ride Buck like this or straddle the horse. Except, if you do that, your skirts'll. . .um. . .they'll. . .well. . ." Red's face turned a color that matched his hair. "You'd best just figure on sittin' sideways."

With another nervous glance that met her eyes, he gingerly took hold of her right leg and swung it around the saddle horn. Again he was gentle and Cassie thought of the sharp scrape of Wade Sawyer's saddle horn when he'd slammed her onto it. She grabbed at the saddle horn through the layers of her gown.

Red untied Buck and swung himself up behind the saddle with a single graceful leap. He pressed against her back as he shifted the reins from one hand to the other. He brushed her arms and sides. He looked around her and his chin nudged her hair.

When he got so close, touching her, close enough to smell the earthy scent of dirt and sweat, Cassie realized what she'd done by marrying him. She thought of a husband's manly needs. Her stomach quivered at the humiliation that lay ahead of her. If only he wasn't as demanding as Griff had been. He'd left her alone at first, because he said she was too young. But for the last year, scarcely a season had gone by that Griff hadn't come to her bed. Griff had explained that it was her duty so she'd endured it.

Then she remembered what else Griff had said. A woman was unclean when she was with child and he wouldn't be with her until after the child was born. She barely suppressed a sigh of relief. Surely she had time before Red claimed his rights. Maybe by the time the baby was born he'd forget what his rights were.

Red shifted his weight and made a clucking sound to start his horse moving. She shifted forward so he wouldn't be so close, but he caught her. "Hold still. I can't see when you lean that way."

Cassie obeyed quickly, hoping she hadn't annoyed him.

"It might be a good idea to stop at the bank and talk this out with Norm. He'll move to claim the property, but I don't want him to think we're not willing. It'll ease his mind some if we tell him we expect it."

Red steered Buck around to the back door of the bank. Red slid off, reached up, lifted Cassie down, and led her into the bank through the back door. "It being Sunday, the bank isn't open, but that Norm always has something that can't wait until Monday."

She'd never been inside the bank. She'd always either stayed home or remained in the carriage when Griff had bank business. A door was ajar next to the safe and Red walked toward it, but Cassie hung back.

"Norm, I can always trust you to be working on the Lord's Day."

"Now, Red, don't start," a deep voice replied. "I never catch up."

"Can I talk to you a minute?" Red asked.

"Come on in my office."

Red rounded the counter then leaned back to look at her. "Come on, Cass. I'm in a hurry. I've got chores."

As always, Cassie obeyed because a woman must always obey her husband, but she couldn't imagine why she needed to hear this.

"Hey, Norm. Cassie Griffin and I just got married." Red reached across the desk and shook hands with the formally dressed older man who rose from his chair.

Red was dressed in coarse brown pants and a shirt made crudely from flour sacks. He was liberally coated with dirt from his grave digging. But he greeted Norman York like they were close friends. Griff had always called him Mr. York.

"Congratulations, Red. Congratulations, Miz Griffin, um, Miz Dawson, that is."

For the first time, Cassie realized she had a new name.

"Sit down." Mr. York gestured to the pair of heavy wooden chairs that faced his desk.

"No thanks, Norm. We're in a hurry. Stock's waiting." Red got right down to business. "Now, we've heard about the mortgage. The one bay is in the stable and the other un's out at Griff's place. Seth fed him enough for a couple of days. We're turning over ownership now. I'm not going that direction, so you'll have to bring him in yourself. Reckon the whole place is yours now, so handle things any way you want."

"Griff's furniture. . ." Cassie began to protest.

"I'm sorry, Mrs. Dawson." Norman York became very formal. His grammar improved along with his posture. "Your husband mortgaged everything—the house and its contents. I really can't allow you to take anything out of it. Of course the dress you're wearing is yours to keep. Although I think there's a bill at Seth's to settle up on it."

Montana Rose

"But, there are personal things, my great-grandmother's pearls..."

"Those are included in the mortgage, Miz Dawson."

"I...I inherited them. They have been in my family four generations. Griff wouldn't mortgage them!"

Mr. York went to a cabinet and pulled a file drawer out. He sorted through papers until he found what he was looking for. He handed it to Cassie.

She read it with ever-increasing shock. "My mother's cameo? And the...the *frames* my grandparents' portraits are in? But the portraits, surely I can have them?" Cassie looked up from Mr. York to Red, humiliated. She struggled to gain control of herself. It didn't matter. Her heirlooms were all just foolish vanity. Surely that is what Griff thought.

She glanced back at the note one last time and lost her composure. "My Bible?" She looked up at Mr. York. "No, a Bible has no monetary worth. But it's been passed down for generations in my family. It's precious to me. No one else would ever want to buy it."

Mr. York fiddled with his string tie for just a second as if it had been pulled a bit too tight. "The thing is, Miz Dawson, that Bible came from Germany a long time ago. I told your husband the same thing, that no one wants an old Bible except the folks who have their names written in it, but Griff knew that huge old book was a New Testament of something called a Gutenberg Bible. It's worth quite a bit. I will have to ship it back East to sell it, but it alone is mortgaged for over two hundred dollars."

"Two hundred dollars?" Red exclaimed. "For an old Bible?"

"I know it's crazy for any book to be so valuable." Mr. York nodded. "Your husband—uh, that is, your former husband—tried to convince me it was worth far more than the amount I agreed to. We could build a church with that. A big, beautiful church. If things settle up right, the Bible is the first thing I'll save back for you. But you can see that I can't just give it back. I will get the photographs for you but not the frames."

"My family Bible is mine. Griff had no right—"

"The fact is, Miz Dawson," Mr. York cut her off with considerable force, "a woman's possessions become her husband's on the day they marry. Now you may not understand that, but it's the law. Griff had every right to mortgage that Bible. And if you didn't want him to, you could have lived without your silk dresses."

"Norm, that's enough," Red said.

Mr. York quit glaring at her and turned to Red. A look passed between the two men, but she couldn't gather her wits enough to analyze its meaning. She was struck speechless by the venom in Mr. York's voice. He blamed her for her fancy clothes. He probably blamed her for every beautiful thing Griff had bought. Her whole world shifted at that moment as she realized that the cutting comments she'd overheard about the china doll and the rather stiff way Muriel had always treated her came down to the perception that she was the one who demanded everything be so fine. Mr. York clearly believed that. Did Red?

This was a fight she should never have started. She swallowed hard and felt doubly stupid for having argued with the man while she was so ignorant of the law and of a man's rights. Finally, she folded her hands, searched deeply for the china doll, and regained her self-control. She spoke demurely, her eyes lowered. "When you get the Bible, would it be all right for me to copy the names out onto a piece of paper? I'd like to keep a record of my ancestors."

When Mr. York spoke, his voice had none of the unkindness that it had before. "That'll be fine, Miz Dawson. I'll have the Bible here when Red comes to town next week. He can bring it out to you, and when you've finished with it, send it back."

40

Red looked at her. "It's time to go. I'll take care of the bill at Seth's now. I know there's a bill at the lumber mill and one at Harv's. Anywhere else in town?"

Mr. York said, "The doc, the stable. . .check the blacksmith."

Cassie listened to the list and felt the weight of all she owed press down on her shoulders. She swayed slightly and held herself upright by sheer force of will.

Red nodded. "I'll take care of it."

"It's not your responsibility, Red. No one expects you to stand good for her fancy. . .that is. . .for Griff's bills."

"I pay what I owe, Norm." The tone of Red's voice pulled Cassie back from the edge of a faint. There was something cold in Red's voice.

"I didn't mean to imply you don't pay your bills, Red." Mr. York pulled a kerchief out of his breast pocket and mopped his brow.

"Good, I'm glad to hear you know better'n to say different. When I married Cassie, I reckon I married her bills. I knew that going in."

Married her bills? Cassie couldn't quite make sense out of that. Married her bills?

"I know, Red." Norman York held both hands in front of him. "If I come out ahead on the mortgage, you have my word I'll put it to his other debts. But I don't think there's gonna be much."

"Mort'll take the spring," Red warned. "You'll have to be careful or he won't pay for it. Too bad there's not a second bidder."

"Maybe Linscott will come in on it." Mr. York watched Red closely as if afraid of him. "He's got adjoining land."

Cassie would do well to remember that Red was a man people feared.

"Yeah, but it's too rugged between Tom Linscott's land and

that spring. He couldn't use it."

"Probably not." Mr. York sounded thoughtful. "But he surely does hate the Sawyers. More importantly, Tom's not afraid of Mort."

"Throw in that Tom would usually rather fight than get along." Red nodded.

Cassie thought the name Tom Linscott was vaguely familiar. She had a mental image of a huge, dangerous black stallion and a fairly young man with overly long white hair who'd struggled to control the beast and nearly run Cassie down in the street one day as she'd followed a few paces behind Griff. Linscott had apologized and seemed genuinely sorry and worried at her fright. Then Griff had lit into him and all of Mr. Linscott's kind concern deserted him as the two had exchanged unpleasant words. It was one of the last times Cassie had been allowed to come to town with Griff.

"Yep, making Mort pay through the nose for that spring will suit him. I'll see him before I talk to Mort."

"Mort's probably moving his cattle in on it already. And he wanted Cass, so he's mad."

"He really wanted the spring, not me," Cassie said faintly.

Mr. York nodded. "I'll watch him."

"Wade wanted me." Shuddering, she wasn't aware of saying it out loud.

Red turned to her and laid one hand gently on her shoulder. "I know, Cassie. I saw. That's why I stepped in. No decent woman would be safe around him."

Cassie remembered the evil in Wade's green eyes and recoiled from the memory. She forced herself to focus on the banker. "If my dress is not paid for, Mr. York, perhaps I could return it."

She turned to Red. "It's not useful for every day, and if I'm to have only one dress. . ."

Montana Rose

"We can check with Seth. You're a little thing, but with the waist let out. . ." Red shrugged and shook his head. "I doubt Muriel will fit in that thing, and no woman in town wears silk anyway."

"Maybe one of the girls at the Golden Butte—" Mr. York stopped talking when Red turned toward him. Cassie couldn't see Red's expression, but Mr. York mopped his brow again.

Cassie wondered who or what the Golden Butte was.

"Let's go, Cass. We've got a few more stops."

Cassie followed behind Red. He strode out the back of the bank with Cassie trailing along.

CHAPTER 4

Wade shoved past Anthony Santoni as he emerged from the Golden Butte. Santoni was just going in. Wade sneered at the worthless man who lived off his wife and openly betrayed her in the Golden Butte.

Across the street, Wade saw Red and the china doll walk past the alley that opened between the bank and the general store. Swallowing hard, Wade's hands trembled as he wished for the guts to reach for his gun and separate the china doll from her new husband. She'd been in Wade's hands. He looked down at his shaking fingers, which flexed and burned with the memory of holding her. And having her torn away.

At least his father had failed. That was one bright spot in this mess. Red had thwarted that fat old man today, and Wade couldn't help but enjoy that. Except his father's failure had been his own because now the china doll was beyond his reach.

Wade touched the tender bruises on his face. His father's plan had been sickening, but at least she would have been at the ranch. Now she'd be with Dawson instead.

Thinking of his china doll with that dirty odd-job man,

living in his decrepit house on his poor excuse for a ranch, made Wade want to hurt someone. His hand went to his Colt revolver.

Tom Linscott chose that moment to ride that brute of a stallion down Divide's main street. Linscott rode up the street toward the doctor's office. Wade had heard one of Linscott's hired hands had broken a leg falling off a bronc. Linscott must be coming in to visit.

The tall Swede cut in front of Wade in a way that prevented him from looking down that alley. The china doll was long gone, but it was easy to switch his anger to Linscott. The man had never given Wade his respect due as son of the area's largest rancher, and that rubbed Wade wrong. Especially since Linscott wasn't that much older than Wade.

Wade strode down the street to block Linscott's way. Linscott wasn't one for the Golden Butte, neither the girls nor the whiskey. The man had a hair-trigger temper and seemed like he was born looking for a fight, but he didn't have the vices Wade enjoyed.

Linscott was heading into the doctor's office without watching where he was going, and Wade made a point to step right in Linscott's path and slam his shoulder into the man. Linscott was a couple inches taller than Wade and twenty pounds heavier, all hard muscle. A part of Wade wanted to hurt somebody and hurt him bad. Another part expected to be given a beating. It seemed like the physical pain canceled out the pain in his heart to think of the china doll married again.

Linscott stumbled back then lifted his gaze to Wade and scowled. "You looking for a fight, Sawyer? Because you'll find one with me. I don't step aside for a little man just because he's got a big old brute of a daddy."

Wade wanted to put a notch in his gun. He'd been hungry to claim he'd killed a man for a long time.

Linscott shook his head in disgust. "You're such a fool,

Sawyer. Get out of my way."

Wade's fingers itched and they flexed near his six-gun.

Laughing contemptuously, Linscott said, "You haven't got the guts to pull that gun, and if you did, I'd beat you to the draw and put you down like a rabid skunk."

Wade took a wild swing and landed a blow to Linscott's chin, mainly because the man wasn't taking any of this seriously.

Linscott staggered back, and his head knocked into a post supporting the overhang on the doctor's office. Then Linscott's famous temper ignited. He cocked his arm and hammered Wade in the face.

Wade hit the wooden sidewalk with a thud.

Two hands from the Sawyer ranch came out of the Golden Butte, and Wade landed at their feet. They both pulled their guns in the flash of an eye and aimed them at Linscott.

Wade looked with smug satisfaction at Linscott. He'd bought into a fight with the wrong man.

Linscott took two steps back, rubbing his chin, looking with cool eyes between Wade and his cowhands. Still, Wade saw no fear on Linscott's face. Wade envied the man his guts and hated him at the same time.

"I'm not fighting your whole ranch, you yellow coward. You want to come at me, you come alone." Linscott shook his head in contempt then turned as if the guns weren't of any concern to him at all. Somehow that dismissal made Wade's feelings of failure deepen.

One of the men standing over him said, "Pick a fight with someone you can beat next time, you young pup. Maybe a little girl-child." Both men laughed and holstered their guns as they stepped over Wade to head for their horses.

Burning with shame, Wade hated everyone until the fire of it nearly burned a hole in his soul. That hate reminded him of the one person he didn't hate.

The china doll.

She was only out of his reach as long as Red Dawson was alive.

He could accomplish two things at once. Kill a man and have his china doll.

Wade finally thought he could do it. He could kill. True, he'd never been able to before and he'd had his chances to draw and ducked them. But he'd never felt this kind of rage. He wanted this enough.

He pictured it.

Red dead.

The china doll his.

He'd be saving her, rescuing her. For that, Wade could kill.

Red and Cassie walked down the dirt walkway that ran behind the bank and led to the back doors of four other stores. All closed for Sunday.

Cassie stayed a step behind Red and didn't speak when he went to the back door of the first one and knocked.

One by one, they were invited into the family living quarters. Each had a bill with Lester Griffin's name on it. Red talked quietly. Cassie remained several paces behind, embarrassed by the business being conducted in front of her.

Griff had always told her a woman had no head for figures and it was not her place to buy and sell. Now Cassie felt as if she was watching something unseemly, and her cheeks warmed until she feared she blushed crimson. She got some scowling glances from the people with whom Red conducted his business, but he seemed to be ignoring her. That was a situation she hoped continued.

Before they were done, they'd been on both sides of the street and stopped in nearly every store in Divide.

They left the general store for last.

"Cassie needs a better work dress, Red." Muriel gave Cassie a sympathetic look as if the expensive black silk she wore was something to be ashamed of.

Red and Muriel debated about her dress for a while. Cassie did her best to behave herself and not listen.

Then Muriel led Cassie into the back room. "I've got one that I hope will fit. It's not cut for a woman who's expecting, but it's several sizes too big for you so I think it'll work." Muriel patted Cassie on the arm.

Cassie looked up at Muriel. "I'm sure it will be fine."

"Red told me that you overheard what we said about Griff and you, honey." Muriel didn't look like a woman given to tears. She was tough and weathered and she'd seen too much, but Cassie thought the older woman's eyes watered a bit and there was definite regret in her expression. "I apologize for that. It was gossip and it was sinful. I'm ashamed of myself. I hope you can forgive me." Muriel extended a thin blue calico dress to Cassie.

"I forgive you." Cassie didn't really see it as her place to give or withhold forgiveness. She'd come to expect criticism for her incompetence in all things and accept it. Her fury had been all to defend Griff and she'd burned that off long ago. Red had the black eye to prove it. The events of the day had left her too exhausted to hold much anger.

"Thank you. I know I talk too much. I plan to study my Bible again tonight. Red reminded me of the verse, from Luke. Part of it says, 'That which ye have spoken in the ear in closets shall be proclaimed upon the housetops.' I certainly learned that lesson today. My words were a sin and I hurt you with my sinning. I am sorry." Muriel gave Cassie an awkward hug.

"I've never heard that one before." Cassie wondered if what *she* thought in private would be proclaimed from the housetops. If that was so, God was going to be very hard on her on Judgment Day, because Cassie's thoughts were sinful beyond redemption. She usually kept them to herself, but she'd shouted at Red and hit him. Her stomach twisted when she thought of how he'd retaliate later...in private. It took a terrible effort to keep from breaking into tears.

"Do you need help changing?" Muriel looked doubtfully at Cassie's heavy silk dress, the skirts held wide with petticoats and a bustle. At least the row of tiny buttons ran up the front, or Cassie most likely couldn't have dressed alone.

"I can manage, thank you." Cassie blushed to think of Muriel or anyone being near her while she was in her under-things. Griff was always chastising her if he caught so much as a glimpse of her throat or ankles. To her knowledge, Griff had never—day or night—seen even a bit of Cassie's skin except her face and hands. He'd stressed the decency of that, and Cassie had learned to never flaunt herself.

Muriel pressed a brown paper–wrapped package into Cassie's hands. "This is a wedding present. I know the bank is takin' everything. So you'll need this. Red'll be good to you, Cassie. He's a good man. Leave the silk behind. I'll get enough for it to settle Griff's bill. This calico is better for life out here anyway."

After Muriel left, Cassie missed the motherly lady. Except for the gossiping at the grave site, Muriel had been nice to her since Griff had died. She exhibited none of the cool politeness that had always been between them. Griff said Muriel and Seth were common and beneath them, so although Griff had to do business with them, Cassie kept her distance. But Cassie had leaned on Muriel since she'd come to town for help. She'd stayed in her rooms above the store, and what bit of food she'd eaten, Muriel had prepared and served.

Remembering those shocking words out at the grave site,

Cassie realized that Muriel and Seth actually looked down on Griff. It was such a shift in Cassie's world that she turned her thoughts away from it.

Without Muriel, Cassie had a long struggle to get changed. It had taken forever to get the black silk dress on earlier today. Cassie didn't see the dark blue silk she'd worn to town. Most likely it was mortgaged, too.

Finally she donned the blue calico. It took only minutes. It was far too big, but that was a good thing or it wouldn't have fit over her stomach.

Cassie left behind her stylish black hat, the reticule, and her lace handkerchief. She had several heavy petticoats. She left them, too, keeping only her shoes and her chemise and stockings. The stockings were silk, but they were the only ones she had, and modesty required she keep them. Then Cassie remembered the solid silver pins in her hair. She removed them and left them for Muriel, letting her heavy dark hair drop into a plain braid down the center of her back.

When she emerged from the back room, pounds lighter in the simple dress, Red and Seth were debating something heatedly. Red saw her come out and fell silent for a moment as he looked at her. Then he shook his head sharply, spoke again to Seth, and turned to her. "Let's head out."

Before they could start toward the back door, the bell over the front door rang and drew their attention.

A woman walked in whom Cassie had never seen before. A strange woman, wearing a riding skirt and a flat-topped black hat with a silver band. She pulled her gloves off as her boots clunked on the wooden floors. Spurs jingled with every step. A woman wearing spurs?

"Howdy, Belle." Seth moved to stand behind the counter. "I'm mostly done with your list."

"Thanks, Seth. The wagon's out front. Sorry to bother you

on a Sunday. I appreciate you opening up for me." Belle tucked her gloves behind her belt buckle.

That action drew Cassie's gaze, and she realized that the woman was with child. Not as round as Cassie but definitely expecting.

The woman, Belle, looked up, and her gaze froze on Cassie, moved to her belly, and then their eyes met.

Muriel had been standing in the hallway to her living quarters, behind Cassie and Red. Now she squeezed past Cassie and went to Belle. "This is Cassie Dawson. She and Red got married today."

Belle's eyes slid between Red and Cassie, and Cassie had the strangest urge to throw herself into Belle's arms. She had no idea why. The woman was a bit older than she, but not that much. Still, the woman had the look of a mother, a warrior mother.

"Today?" Belle asked Muriel, but her eyes stayed on Cassie, flickering to her obviously round stomach again.

"Her husband died, just yesterday. Lester Griffin?"

Belle snorted and Cassie caught way too much meaning from that sound. Here was another person who thought ill of Griff.

Red shifted a bit closer to Cassie as if she needed protection. But there was no danger to Cassie from this woman.

Belle walked straight for Cassie then, spurs ringing.

Muriel gave way like dust in the wind, and Cassie had a shocking urge to smile.

Red held his ground, but Belle ignored him and spoke past his shoulder straight to Cassie, "Was this your choosing? This marriage?"

Cassie was speechless. Her choosing? What did that have to do with anything? "Wh–What do you mean?"

"Belle, it's done." Red leaned as if to block Belle from Cassie, but she glared at him so hard he straightened, shifting so they stood in a circle in the hallway of the store.

This woman had made a man move aside with a single look. Cassie's heart started pounding. She'd never heard of a woman who could do that.

Belle turned to Red. "Yes, it's always *done*, isn't it? Done to a woman. No one gives us a *choice*. Look at her. She doesn't even know what I mean by 'choosing.'"

Muriel came up behind Belle. "It's all right, Belle. She had to pick a man. You know that."

Belle rested her hand on her belly. "I don't know any such thing." Her jaw tightened, but kindness was there, along with anger. "You can come home with me."

Red shook his head. "She's a married woman."

"She belongs with her husband, Belle," Muriel said.

Belle ignored them both and spoke to Cassie. "You can come home with me if you want. I've got a husband who spends most of his time hiding from work and three daughters who would love a big sister. When that baby comes, I'll have one more. We'll pray it's a girl. And I'll help you; you'll help me. We'll get by. What do you say?"

Cassie almost launched herself at Belle, grabbed her, and clung to her.

Some of that must have shown in her eyes, because Red stepped close and slid his arm around her shoulders. "We were married before God and man, this very day. My wife stays with me."

Muriel's eyes snapped with satisfaction. Cassie didn't understand that.

Cassie nearly shook as she realized she'd bound herself to a man she didn't know. A man she'd have to obey. Tears burned her eyes. This was a way out. She knew if she said the word, Belle could make it happen. Just as Red was strong enough to snatch her out of Mort Sawyer's arms, Belle was strong enough to settle things her way. Cassie marveled at the woman, her strength, her confidence. Muriel had a glimmer of it, but this woman looked like she'd stand toe-to-toe with any man and come out the winner.

"Let me talk to her, Red."

So Red and Belle knew each other? Why had Cassie never seen this woman before? There weren't that many women. Surely Cassie wouldn't have forgotten one.

"You can talk to her, Belle, but she stays with me." Red's shoulders relaxed. "If it helps any, maybe you should know Cassie gave me this black eye."

Belle's head whipped around to stare for long moments at the purple bruise. "Well, maybe she will be all right."

Muriel snickered.

Red let Belle come close. Belle rested a work-roughened hand on Cassie's shoulder. Cassie felt the calluses through her dress. The hand was scarred and brown and so strong, Cassie wondered what Belle could hold on to with that hand.

"I know you took vows," Belle said quietly, "but just tell me, if there'd been a choice, would you have married again today, a day after. . ." Belle fell silent, shaking her head. "Lester Griffin, worthless excuse for a man. Dead now. No surprise. How old were you when you married him?"

"F–Fifteen."

"I was fifteen when I first married."

"First?"

"William was my first husband. I'm on my third. I tend to marry stupid and they all tend to die, although Anthony seems to be hanging around so far."

"She might have married fast, Belle, but she didn't marry stupid." Red settled his Stetson on his head and his voice sounded warm. Considering how tough Belle was, that warmth didn't make sense to Cassie. It was almost as if he. . .pitied this woman.

Belle snorted. "I've decided *married* and *stupid* are the same words. I'll bet if we had a dictionary, one would define the other."

Muriel coughed and covered her mouth.

Cassie was shocked and almost smiled at the nerve. What would she give to have the courage to speak so to a man. . .to anyone?

"What's done is done. I'll take care of her. And you should have known better than to marry Anthony anyway."

Belle jabbed her thumb over her shoulder at Muriel. "Except I had people like Muriel saying a woman has to have a man."

"Well, she does, Belle."

Belle turned around and glared at Muriel. "I didn't."

"Cassie does."

Belle, her back to Cassie now, stood solid, staring at Muriel.

Finally, Belle gave a harsh jerk of her chin as if it was decided. Belle turned back. "I reckon she's right that you needed someone to take care of you, and I live a long way out. No one would have thought to come for me." Belle's brows formed a straight line, with deep furrows between. "But I'd have taken you in, Cassie. No woman has to have a man. But I reckon you needed someone. If you ever need a place to run, come to me. I live in a mountain valley through the gap worn by Skull Creek."

Cassie realized she believed this woman. If Cassie needed a place, Belle would take her in. Tears burned her eyes as she nodded. "Thank you."

Belle turned her eyes on Red. "You treat her decent. I'll come and check, and I'd better like what I see." With a deep sigh, she shook her head. "Seth, you got my order ready?"

"I'll be at it awhile, Belle."

"I'll leave the wagon out front. I need to talk to the blacksmith, then I'll stop by Herschel's and see if they'd feed me on a Sunday." Belle turned to Red and shot him a look that could have nailed a two-by-four to a fence. "I *will* stop by. Do you hear me?"

A smile bloomed on Red's face. "I hear you."

Belle's expression softened. "You're right. I never should have married Anthony. What was I thinking?"

Red tugged on the brim of his hat. Belle turned and weaved her way around Muriel. Seth handed her a wooden box full of supplies and followed her out, carrying another one. At the door, Belle froze. Seth almost ran into her from behind.

Cassie saw Belle staring out the front window of the general store at a building at the far end of Divide's modest Main Street. Cassie saw the words Golden Butte painted over the swinging doors to the building. The banker had said something about Cassie's silk dress being worn by the ladies of the Golden Butte and then he'd looked nervous.

A dark-haired man had stepped out of that building on the arm of a woman dressed in a shocking red dress, starchy with frills and lace, cut up to nearly her knees in front.

Seth said, "I'm sorry Anthony stepped out just now."

Belle turned her head with a hard jerk as if she had to physically tear her eyes away from the sight. "He's in town more than he's home, Seth. I'm used to my husband shaming me. I don't care anymore."

But Cassie saw the downward turn of Belle's mouth and knew Belle did care. This hurt, and Cassie knew all about being hurt.

"What was I thinking?" Belle shoved the door and stepped out.

Cassie watched as the dark-haired man noticed her. The woman in red stepped out of his arms and flounced back into the building. The man—it had to be Belle's husband, Anthony—turned and walked quickly in the opposite direction.

Belle went to her wagon as if nothing had happened and set her box inside. Then she walked directly away from Anthony with the thud of boots and the clink of spurs.

Red and Muriel exchanged long glances. Cassie remembered the pity she'd sensed in Red and knew Belle's husband with another woman on his arm was a usual occurrence.

Settling his hat more firmly, Red rested his hand on Cassie's back. "Let's head out."

Confused by that rare, frightening look at a woman who would stare a man straight in the eye and say her piece and feeling awkward about witnessing Belle's shame, Cassie did as she was told and headed out, following Red. The way a woman was meant to behave.

She remembered the way Belle had looked at her, straight out along that hat brim. Eyes direct, speaking her mind, issuing orders that sounded like threats. Cassie felt like a huge world yawned at her feet. A world she might have entered if she'd had the nerve to go with Belle. But did that bold gaze and her strong words cause Belle's husband to disgrace her?

Cassie would never follow Belle's example. Instead, she obeyed. It was her place.

Muriel hurried and got the wrapped package Cassie had forgotten in the back room and handed it to Red. He walked beside Cassie to where Buck stood at the back door. He stored the gift in his saddlebag and slipped his hands under her arms and hoisted her gently onto the horse just as he had the first time. He hooked her knee around the saddle horn again, and she clung to it through the layers of calico. She had a much better grip without the silk and petticoats.

He jumped on behind, and as he did, Cassie dared a glance at his face. His jaw was set and his eyes flashed with anger.

Had it angered him that she'd listened to Belle? Was it the bills Red had paid? Was he remembering that she'd attacked him at the graveyard? It looked as if he'd wait and make her pay for misbehavior when they got home. She was grateful her humiliation would be, at least, in private.

She shuddered to think of the times Griff had been this upset with her. He hadn't done it for a long time, but she well remembered the heavy belt he'd used almost daily when they were newlyweds, before she learned a woman's place. Fear climbed inside her at what was to come until she could learn to please Red Dawson. Burning tears cut her eyes. Knowing men hated tears, she swallowed hard and stared at the horizon to keep them from falling.

They rode out of town in the opposite direction of Griff's holding. Then Red leaned forward. She braced herself for his angry words.

"Buck is strong and you weigh next to nothing. I always run him flat out the whole way home, but we won't be able to do that riding double. We'll push hard for a while, though. I asked Doc and he said a gallop wouldn't hurt the babe if you didn't take a fall. But Doc said I shouldn't trot, so we'll take off fast. It's a far piece to my land."

She was so shocked at his concern for the baby she didn't answer him. He rested one hand on her rounded waist to steady her and clucked at the horse. The short-legged horse shifted smoothly to a ground-eating gallop. No more talk was possible.

Although Cassie would have loved to enjoy the wild ride, she couldn't relax until she'd received her punishment and made amends in whatever way Red demanded. She just held on and tried to make herself as small as possible.

It was the same thing she'd been doing since the day her mother died when she was twelve. Griff had become her guardian, and he'd helped her understand how much she had to learn. And though it was a terrible burden to him, he'd been left with the chore of being her teacher and wouldn't shirk it.

CHAPTER 5

Cassie woke with a start to feel strong arms carrying her.

Still groggy with the first deep sleep she'd had in too long, she rubbed her cheek against warm, coarse cloth and used her arms to hold herself steady.

She almost went back to sleep, when she heard a deep voice say, "Are you awake, Cass? I've got to set you down. I can't do the door one-handed."

Cassie's eyes flickered open and she looked into Red Dawson's face. They stood on the ground, beside his horse, and he had her cradled in his strong arms. In a split second it all came back to her. Griff, the funeral, her wedding, all those bills, Red's anger. And here she lay with her arms wrapped around his neck. She pulled quickly away from him and he set her down. She carefully folded her hands, fixed her eyes on the ground, and waited for him to mete out the punishment she had coming.

It took her a second to realize Red was gone. He had walked on without her and was wrestling with a wooden door in the side of a hill. He got it open and said, "This is home, such as it is."

Cassie stood, transfixed, staring at the door, wondering where her punishment was.

Red waved her forward. "Let me show you what little there is to see, then I've gotta do chores."

Cassie obeyed. He waved her in and she flinched when his hand got too close, but she quickly controlled herself. Griff had hated that and punished her more severely for it.

She walked into a cave.

Red stepped briskly in behind her and brushed past where she stood frozen near the door. "The front part's a soddy." He pointed to an opening on the far wall. "I built it onto the mouth of a cave. The cave is my. . .our. . .uh. . .*your* bedroom."

"That one"—he pointed to another much smaller opening with a buffalo hide hanging over it—"is a smaller cave. It's real cool because a spring comes out of the rock right there. We don't have to haul water, and it keeps milk and butter chilled. I was real lucky to find this spot.

"The big cave has a second way out that I'll show you later. It winds through the mountain some," Red said. "What you need for food is in the cooler. That's what I call the little cave, and what you need for cooking is here." He walked across the room to a dry sink and a huge stone fireplace. He turned toward her. "You cook, don't you, Cass? I can do it. I always have for myself. But. . .well. . .that is. . ."

Cassie nodded silently while he fumbled around asking. Then she forced herself to speak. "Yes, I'll cook." She'd been good at it at one time, but Griff had very special tastes and he had never been satisfied with her efforts.

She would have to learn all Red's personal preferences in food now. If only she could feed him this once tonight without shaming him. For now he seemed to have forgotten his anger, although she knew a man never forgot for long.

Red moved to a wood box near the fireplace. "I'll get a fire started then." He hurried through the chore.

Cassie compared Red's fireplace to Griff's stove. Griff's had been a huge rectangular monster with water wells and two baking chambers. It had levers to adjust the heat and keep the food cooking at just the right speed. Griff had been disgusted with her for running it so poorly.

Cassie had cooked over an open fire on the trip out West. She'd been better over a fire than she'd ever been with that intimidating cast-iron cookstove.

Red finished lighting the fire. "I'll get a bucket of water so you can wash and have some for cooking. Then I've got chores."

Red disappeared into the little cave and returned with a large tin bucket. "I'll be late. If you're tired and want to go to bed, it's through there." He pointed to the larger door. "I'll sleep in the. . ." Red faltered. "I—I want you to know—I won't b–bother you none, Cassie. Just take the bedroom. I'll find a place out here."

"What would you like for supper?" She didn't recognize her voice. She didn't recognize anything about her life. She was still too confused by the changes of the last day.

"Anything's fine." He shrugged and plucked a battered hat off a nail by the front door, hanging his nicer Stetson on the same nail. He was very close to her, studying his broken-down hat intently.

"I know it's not what you're used to, Cass." He glanced up and away quickly. "I know it's not fancy. When you. . .when Mort was grabbing you, I knew I had no business asking a lady like you to come out here. But I. . .there was no one else to. . .I had to step in."

He was embarrassed. Cassie almost smiled when she realized it. The impulse shocked her. Griff hated frivolity. She couldn't remember the last time she'd smiled. Red was worried that she didn't like his home. Something eased inside her, and she laid her hand over his to make him stop torturing his hat.

He looked up at her and she saw the pure blue of his eyes. "It's a fine home, Red. And I know what was ahead of me with Mort." She couldn't stop herself from squeezing his hand tight. "Thank you. You don't have to sleep out here. We're married and I understand what that means."

Offering him that assurance almost made her sick, but she knew her duty. Red had his rights. Except she was unclean. But Red would know that. If he didn't, she'd be glad to remind him.

"Now tell me what to make you for supper. I'd like the first night to be something you really like, and I don't know your preferences."

Red smiled. "Anything I don't have to cook myself would be a treat, Cass. There's a ham back there if you'd like to fry a couple of slices of that. Anything, and only if you're feeling up to it. I. . .I haven't told you how sorry I am about Griff."

He had. He'd told her more nicely than anyone else. And to repay him she'd given him that black eye. But she didn't correct him.

"I know this has been hard for you. Now your man is gone and a baby is on the way. Even. . .even if I share the bedroom, I'll. . .I'll keep a respectful distance. You'll have your time to heal, Cass."

He looked at her a moment longer, and for a while Cassie forgot everything but Red and his pure blue eyes.

Then he looked abruptly down at his hat again. "Gotta go." He almost ran out the door, leaving it open to the fall breeze.

Belle slammed the bridles down on the support beam. She whipped the wall as she hung the traces on the nail, not caring that she missed and the leather and metal slid to the floor with a *clank*. She turned to the wagon full of supplies and fought the temptation to start throwing bags and cans.

"Ma, what happened?"

Belle turned to see Lindsay staring wide-eyed. Belle closed her eyes and pulled in a long, slow breath, fighting to control her temper. The only trouble with that was if she quit being mad she was afraid she might cry.

Well, she wasn't going to do that. That was weak. She'd just stay furious.

She'd always been honest with her daughters, so she saw no reason to be less than that now. She paced the length of the barn toward Lindsay. "I saw something in town today that's just got me all churned up." And no, she wasn't going to talk about Anthony. She was blunt with her girls, but they didn't need to understand this.

She got close to her thirteen-year-old and realized Lindsay was only two years younger than Cassie Griffin Dawson had been when she'd married that no-account Lester Griffin. And now at eighteen, Cassie had just been forced into another marriage. It was too much like Belle's life.

"Who, Ma? We don't hardly know no one in town."

It was Belle's life all over again, except Belle had been able to take care of herself. Cassie Griffin was helpless. Belle caught Lindsay by both shoulders. Lindsay, to her credit, didn't flinch, despite Belle's blazing temper.

"I've done my best, Lindsay, to make sure you're never helpless. You understand that it's about more than me needing hands on this ranch. You know how much I love you girls and want to protect you."

Lindsay shrugged under Belle's grip. "I know you need help. I know husbands are worthless."

Belle flinched internally. Not all men were worthless. She knew that. Her pa had worked hard and had been a good rancher. He'd treated her wrong in the end, once he'd been blessed with a son to inherit the ranch after years of grooming Belle to run it. But mostly her pa was a decent man.

Seth at the general store stood at Muriel's side and did his full share and more. Red Dawson owned a fair piece of land and ran a good, solid operation. That's the only reason she hadn't hauled Cassie out of there at gunpoint. That and knowing she'd probably end up arrested, and her worthless husband, Anthony, would have a free hand to break the unusual agreement she'd made him sign before they were married, leaving her sole owner of the Tanner Ranch. Plus the idiot would let her girls starve to death.

She didn't correct Lindsay, though. Best to believe all men were worthless and prepare yourself to manage alone. Then, if she failed her girls and let them end up married, they'd be able to fend for themselves.

"There was a woman in town. . .a girl. . .eighteen, not that much older'n you. Her name's Cassie Griffin."

"Eighteen's a lot older'n thirteen, Ma."

"But she married today for the second time. She first got hitched when she was fifteen. That's only a little over two years from your age."

"Well, I'm not ever getting married so don't worry about it. And remember you promised not to either."

Belle nodded. "I remember. Once Anthony dies, I promise. No more husbands." Belle laid her hand on her belly and spent five seconds in hard, concentrated prayer.

Please, please, a girl, Lord God. Let it be a girl.

How could she possibly raise a boy up to be anything other than worthless? Any male seemed to have a powerful inclination toward that result.

Lindsay interrupted Belle's prayer. "I've heard of Griffin's house. Big, shiny mansion of a place."

Montana Rose

Her girls had almost never been to town. Belle had to travel several hours fast and hard to get there, stock up supplies, and get home, which was slow with a loaded wagon. She only made the trip once or twice a year, and she never took the girls.

Emma rode into the barn from the corral door. She rode a green, broke filly that had lines Belle wanted in her saddle stock. The horse was behaving perfectly.

"You've got her settling in nice." Belle admired her second-born's hand with the horses. Emma had a rare knack.

"She's a little beauty, Ma. We did some cutting today and she really got onto it. She'll give us some good foals." Emma patted the bay's shoulders, already strong and broad as a two-year-old.

Her two oldest daughters were a matched pair. Flyaway white blond hair, eyelashes and brows just as white, shining blue eyes so pale they were almost gray; they were the image of their pa, William Svendson. Her third daughter, Sarah, was a redhead with a thousand freckles and emerald green eyes. Her pa, Gerald O'Rourke, used to say Sarah's eyes were as green as Ireland when the whiskey was on him...which was most of the time.

Belle, with her straight brown hair and light brown eyes, didn't seem able to pass on a single physical trait to her girls. She had no doubt the baby she carried now would have black curls and snapping black eyes like Anthony Santoni, worthless husband number three. But if they didn't carry Belle's looks, they carried her strength. She could still teach 'em what they needed to survive.

"Put your horse up and come listen while I tell Lindsay what happened."

Emma made short work of her unsaddling. The eleven-year-old was better at handling a horse than Belle or Lindsay, and that was saying something.

"What is it, Ma?" Emma pulled her leather gloves off as she walked toward Belle. No spurs. Belle had a gentle hand with

65

the stock, but she knew a spur came in handy on rare occasion. She couldn't convince Emma they were necessary.

She repeated to Emma what she'd told Lindsay about Cassie Griffin. "I just want you girls to know that you never have to get married if you don't want to."

Emma and Lindsay exchanged long looks.

Lindsay spoke first. "We don't plan on getting married, Ma. We've learned our lesson from watching you."

"Good." Belle nodded. "I should hope so. Husbands bring you children, of course." Belle rested her work-scarred hand on her round belly. "A nuisance being with child, of course. Slows me down some. But you girls, well, I reckon my life is only worth living because I've got you."

"So, you mean you've changed your mind and you think we *should* get married?" Emma asked fearfully.

"No, no. Of course not. I'm just saying some good can come out of the whole mess. I'm trying to lay the whole truth out for you is all."

Her girls nodded, their expressions grim.

"I just want you to know that you don't have to make a choice like that because people tell you a woman *has* to have a man. You can make it on your own. As long as I'm alive you'll have a home with me. We run this ranch smooth and easy."

"Well, Ma, we work from can see to can't see." Emma slapped her gloves against her hand. "We bust broncs and brand steers and dig dams and cut and stack hay. So *easy* ain't 'zactly right."

"I mean easy except for the backbreaking work. By *easy* I mean we do it right. The ranch runs easy. . .without a hitch. Don't interrupt me while I'm explaining things to you."

"Sorry, Ma." Emma tucked her gloves behind her belt buckle.

"This is an important point. That little woman today. . ."

Belle considered Cassie little more than a child. Both in age and in temperament. The woman was being led along by that meddling Muriel and Red Dawson. Truth be told, Belle wasn't yet thirty, but she felt as old as the hills that surrounded her beautiful mountain valley.

"That woman, Cassie, wasn't given a choice today. I don't know much about the man they forced on her. There's such a thing as a decent man, I've heard. Seen little sign of it, but that's not my point." Belle wondered if Sarah had supper going in the house yet. Most likely. A dependable child, her Sarah.

"What is your point, Ma? I've got chores left." Lindsay looked bored.

Belle suspected she'd told her girls all of this before. . .a thousand times or more. But seeing Cassie today, quiet, obedient, being told what to do and who to marry and most likely how to breathe, had scared Belle to death. Belle was ten times as strong as Cassie Dawson, and *she'd* fallen into the same a-woman-had-to-have-a-man trap as Cassie.

Belle had to save her girls from such a fate. "You don't have to marry some man just because you're of marrying age. A woman can get by on her own. I am raising you girls to work and work hard. The strength of your back and the sense in your head will carry you through life without having to drag some worthless husband along with you. Might as well just tie an anchor to your leg and tow that."

Belle took a couple of steps toward the barn door so she could see the house. "Has Anthony come around?"

"He's not on the roof?" Lindsay came up beside her.

"No. And I saw him in town today, but I had a lot of errands and figured he headed home before me. And riding horseback he'd've made good time. I suppose he'll come back. Free food."

Emma pointed toward the Husband Tree. "He's there."

Belle squinted. Sure enough, Anthony was sitting on his

backside. . .as usual. But instead of climbing on the roof, which he was partial to—somehow that must make him think he was beyond Belle's reach, as if Belle would ever *want* to reach him— he was sitting, his back propped up by the Husband Tree.

"Does he know he's sitting on one of the other husbands?" Lindsay asked.

Belle shrugged. "Don't know. You can't tell there are graves there anymore. I didn't waste time markin' 'em. But I'm sure that's the side your pa is on. I wanted him to face the ranch. I don't remember if I buried Gerald on the left or right side. I didn't give it much thought. And I sure didn't care if *he* could see the ranch layout. Better he should face the Golden Butte in Divide." Gerald had liked the Golden for its liquid pleasures, while Anthony was more interested in the sweeter enticements of the place. William had never gone there, she'd give him that. He'd just grumbled and griped and taken long walks.

"Well, Anthony's still alive and kicking so far." Lindsay turned to look at the chicken coop. Belle was proud of the girl for being more interested in chores than the problems of being yoked to a slug of a man.

Belle sighed. She'd been a long time in town, and then she'd had the heavy buckboard to pull home. "He could live a long time, I reckon, although he's stupid, and stupid'll get you killed in the West."

"Are you done telling us *again* we don't have to get married, Ma? 'Cuz I got chores." Emma pulled her gloves free and started tugging them on.

"I'm done for now." Belle wasn't really. She didn't think she'd said enough. "I just. . . Today, hearing about that young girl passed around like she was a box of groceries, it just hit me hard."

She looked from Lindsay to Emma and back. "I want to save you from husbands if I possibly can."

The three of them looked at Anthony. The way he sat, his head leaned back, he looked like he was catching a nap. Resting up for bedtime, no doubt. It didn't matter if he was rested or not, he had his own bed. Belle slept with her cast-iron skillet these days.

"We hear you, Ma." Emma headed for the hog pen.

"Loud and clear." Lindsay went to saddle her horse.

Belle watched them walk away. Her pride in them. . .well, she was back to holding on to her temper to keep the tears away. She laid her hand on her baby, due in early spring.

Be a girl. God, let her be a girl.

She went in to have the same heart-to-heart talk with Sarah. Even at eight, the child wasn't too young to learn her lesson. Belle ignored the pain of Anthony's betrayal. It was an old pain. Instead, she nursed her fury over the fate of that poor, sweet, helpless Cassie Griffin Dawson.

It was, quite possibly, the sweetest moment of Cassie's life, at least the sweetest in the years since her mother had died. Cassie stood, stunned at Red's kind speech about Griff and her baby and keeping his distance.

For the first time, Cassie realized that Red was very young. He carried himself with such ease, and he was treated with deference by a lot of men and as an equal by the others. For some reason she'd been thinking he was Griff's age. But the twisted hat and the stuttered speech made her think differently. Now she wondered if he wasn't about *her* age. He had to be twenty-one to file a homestead. But if he'd been here two years like Griff and her, Red could be twenty-three, a barely grown boy striking out on his own in the West. She wished she had the nerve to ask him his age. That wouldn't be too forward a question for a wife to ask. Or would it? She wished Griff was here to tell her.

She explored the cave she now lived in, and somehow the combination of realizing her husband was hardly more than a boy and finding out she lived in a cave made her feel young and adventurous. She'd gotten to thinking of herself as the same generation as Griff, but she was only eighteen.

The bedroom was large and very dark. There was a good-sized bed. Only one. Not two smaller ones like Griff said was appropriate for a married couple. In fact, at Griff's house she'd had her own room. She felt heat rush into her face as she realized what she'd been offering when she told Red he could join her in the bedroom. If he suggested staying in the front room again, she'd agree.

She found the little notch in the back of the room. The passage winding away into the heart of the mountain caught her imagination and she was sorely tempted to explore. She stepped away from it. She had to ask Red first. She didn't want to start her marriage by being disobedient.

She left the bedroom and went into the cooler. She was amazed at the drop in temperature. She followed the pleasant trickle of water, careful not to trip over anything. She was clumsy and she'd gotten worse with the baby on the way. Griff had rebuked her for it many times.

She found a brisk little spate of water pouring out of a crack in the rock. It landed in an overflowing pail on the floor and disappeared into the ground. She touched the water and shivered from the frigid temperature. Cold water. What if it stayed cold in summer? What a luxury that would be.

Her eyes had adjusted to the dim light and she saw food piled everywhere. Hams hanging over her head. Eggs! Cassie hadn't eaten an egg since she came west. It was all she could do not to grab one and take it directly to the stove to cook.

Red must have chickens and pigs. There was butter, and a

pail of milk hung on a nail on one wall. A milk cow, too? She found potatoes, carrots, onions, and beets. There was flour, salt, sugar—both brown and white—honey, and cakes of yeast. She couldn't begin to search through all of the crates and barrels packed in that room.

She had lived in a beautiful home with Griff, but food had sometimes been a problem. There was the spring near their home and he'd had good luck fishing. But they'd eaten a lot of trout. Griff wouldn't let Cassie help in the garden, although as a child she'd enjoyed working by her mother's side. Griff had helped her understand how crude her mother had been to do man's work. She wondered how long Red had been here to be so established. Then she realized how much time she'd spent dreaming over the food and hurried to work on supper.

The main room of Red's home was small. The fire blazed cheerfully now and cut the chill in the kitchen. The sink was simply a hollowed-out log split in half, with a hole in the center of the bottom and a bucket under the hole to catch draining water. A small but well-built table with two sturdy chairs sat near enough to the fireplace to make a meal cozy even on a cold night.

The floor was dirt and a handmade broom stood in one corner. Cassie wasn't sure how she'd know when she was done when she swept a dirt floor. She looked around the room and realized that except for a few pots and pans, there was nothing in the house that wasn't handmade. Red had created this strange house with nothing but his bare hands. Cassie wondered at the pride a man would have if he could care for himself like Red did.

She started a rising of bread. They would have fresh-baked bread for breakfast. She warmed the ham in a cast-iron skillet and hung it from a hook in the fireplace. She pared potatoes, careful to waste as little white flesh as possible, put them in the covered pot full of water, and tucked the pot into the corner of the fireplace. She made biscuits. The heat was uneven and she feared things would burn, so she kept a careful eye on everything. Ham, potatoes, and biscuits. If she could get a good gravy from the ham, it would be a simple but tasty meal. She wished she could figure out an excuse to fry eggs with the meal. She'd do it for breakfast, she promised herself.

The bread had risen. She'd punched it down and shaped loaves which were rising again. The table was set with one tin plate and one chipped china plate, the only plates she could find. The food was done. Even the mashed potatoes were whipped high with butter and milk and set in a pan of warm water, waiting for when Red came back.

The door swung inward and Red entered, looked at her, and smiled rather abruptly.

Cassie had the impression he'd forgotten he was married.

CHAPTER 6

Red hadn't been able to think about anything all day except that he was married.

Married!

He'd left here yesterday a single man with too many chores and too many goals and not a second to spare for anything else. Now there was a woman in his house. He looked at Cassie and saw the most beautiful woman on earth.

She turned from his fireplace in his kitchen, and he thought back to how he'd held her in his arms all the way from town. He'd loved every minute of it.

"H–Hi, Cassie. I see you're cooking." He felt like some kind of monster to marry a woman standing on the freshly dug grave of her husband. But he'd seen no way out of the marriage. The crowd wasn't even going to allow them to move out of the cemetery.

Cassie nodded and didn't speak. Which gave Red a moment to remember why he'd married her—to save her. And why he shouldn't have—because she wasn't a believer.

Marrying Cassie was a sin, the greatest sin of his life.

But he'd had to help her.

But he could have thought of *something* short of marrying her.

Except he couldn't think of *anything*.

But he should have tried *harder*.

But he'd tried *hard*!

The events had chased themselves through his head over and over while he did his chores until he'd wanted to crack his head into a rock a few times, hoping the pain and a big knot on his head would give him something else to think about.

It was just that at the time Muriel had been nagging him to save the poor little thing. That overbearing Mort Sawyer had been ignoring Cassie's pleas and demanding to the parson that they "get it done." Then Cassie'd started screaming to raise the dead, which considering they were standing on her dead husband at the time, she might have been trying to do exactly that. Throw in Wade looking on all hungry and evil and it had all forced his hand.

Except that wasn't really the whole exact truth. Yes, it was part of the truth but not all of it. Red figured the only fool bigger than a man who tried to lie to himself was a man who lied to God. Both were just a pure waste of time. Red supposed he was seven kinds of a fool, but at least he was an honest fool. And the plain honest truth was he *wanted* to marry Cassie. He wanted to marry her almost desperately. In his own way he was just as bad as all those ruffians who were fighting over her.

Red couldn't shake the idea that somewhere God had spent a lifetime preparing a perfect mate just for him, a woman who was a believer above all else, and Red had just gone and tossed God's plan back in His face by marrying the wrong woman. Cassie Griffin. Cassie Dawson. *God, forgive me,* he thought. *I do like the idea of her having my name.*

Red had done his chores thoroughly, but it was a good thing

he'd done them a thousand times before because his mind was not on his tasks. Even though Rosie was going be hurting bad by the time he milked her, he left the cow until last because he didn't want to go back to the house to leave the milk. He almost dropped everything ten times and ran back to the soddy to see if Cassie needed help finding supplies, or lifting a bucket, or squashing a bug, or crossing a mud puddle....

Oh, no doubt about it, he had it bad. He wanted that woman, that overindulged, beautiful, non-Christian woman desperately. He sat down to Rosie and she thanked him for his prolonged neglect by kicking him soundly on his backside. He figured it was just what he needed.

And now here his wife was, smiling at him, a sweet, shy smile, and he thought about how he'd finished with Rosie and grabbed the bucket of eggs and forced himself not to run to the house.

He'd been twenty feet away when he smelled the cooking. He'd assumed she wouldn't cook. He knew she was pampered. A person only had to look at her beautiful clothes to know that. And everyone said Griff was broke because of Cassie's greed. Red didn't listen to gossip, and he held that a man had free will; and no one, even a wife as pretty and perfect as a china doll— which is what everyone called her—could make a man spend money if he didn't want to. And Red had known Griff enough to know the man was stiff-necked and arrogant all on his own. No one could blame Cassie for that. But whether Cassie was spoiled by Griff's wish or her own, Red had never known. He did know he hadn't expected the cosseted china doll to cook. Yet there she stood, holding a heavy pot in her hands.

Red had seen the Griffin place and he knew Cassie didn't lift a finger outside. He'd seen Griff working in the garden and hauling water, and everyone knew she bought all her dresses ready-made, so she didn't sew. Those were all chores that most women would do, especially when there was so much work on a ranch and Griff didn't hire any hands.

But Cassie refused. Why even on trips to town, on the rare occasion that Cassie would lower herself to appear, she rarely left the carriage, sitting alone, ignoring all and sundry. Yes, there was no doubt Cassie was spoiled.

But she'd cooked. He wondered how a man could unspoil a woman. He'd better figure it out, because however Cassie Griffin was, Cassie Dawson was going to have to rough it. There'd be no more silk dresses. Yup, Cassie was going to have to learn, and if it had to be the hard way, so be it.

He felt all strict and manly standing there with the milk and eggs. He was thinking that milking cows and collecting eggs were woman's work and she'd better start carrying her weight around here with the stock, too. Then he asked God for an extra-large dose of wisdom and went inside to the wonderful smell of warm food and the even more wonderful sight of a beautiful woman.

She looked at him with that perfect china doll face. She blinked her huge brown eyes at him, and he thought maybe he could see why Griff would die trying to keep her happy.

Red stepped inside, setting the eggs down to swing the door shut without taking his eyes off his brand-new, beautiful, perfect wife.

His last thought as the door thudded shut was that he'd have to be careful, or he'd end up dying trying to keep her happy himself.

"Red Dawson, you're gonna die." Wade Sawyer lowered his rifle and rolled onto his back with a deep grunt of self-contempt. "I should've done it. I should've killed him where he stood."

He'd had Dawson in his sights. One shot and the china doll

would be his. He'd take her away and not bring her back until she had accepted Wade as her husband. Not even his pa would have a chance at her.

He rested against the cool rocks on the overhang near Dawson's poor excuse for a house. "No one would have known. And even if anyone wondered, who would challenge a Sawyer's word?"

Something quick and hard twisted in his stomach as he watched the dusk settle in through the branches of an overhanging pine. The china doll was nowhere in sight. A stray bullet could have hit her. Wade tried to convince himself that he'd held off with the shot because of that. But it wasn't true. The truth was he was a coward. He should have killed Dawson. He should have proved to himself that he was man enough to take what he wanted.

He'd never had the guts to kill a man. He'd had his chances. Drunken cowpokes looking for trouble. Rustlers. A cardsharp once who had cheated him. His father's men were always around, backing him up, like they'd done today with Tom Linscott. And some of Pa's hands were salty enough that they'd step in eagerly to do any shooting without Wade having to show his yellow streak.

"I'm a coward. I should have killed him, but I'm too yellow." Wade stared up at the sky and hated himself for being weak. Losing the china doll today was the final proof of it. He should have stood up to his pa. He should have told that old tyrant that he'd have to kill his own son in order to claim that beautiful woman.

When they'd heard about Griff, he'd told Pa he wanted her. His pa had said, "Let's share her, boy."

It made Wade sick to think it now, and to stop his head from working, he sat up and fished his pint of whiskey out of his saddlebag and took a deep pull on it, trying to drown out the sound of his father's filthy suggestion. His pa had gotten in the habit of thinking himself above the law. And that included the laws of God. Once a man started thinking that way, everything he wanted to do was right.

Surely even his father's arrogance didn't extend so far that he meant share the china doll. . . . Wade's mind veered away from the thoughts and swallowed more of the rotgut. What Pa had *meant* was he'd take the land and Wade could have the woman. But that wasn't what Pa *said*. And even if Pa intended to leave Cassie to Wade, Pa would still be her husband and Wade wouldn't be able to marry her and treat her honorably. Even the hint of something so foul happening to the china doll drove Wade into a rage.

When Pa had said those words, "Let's share her," Wade had lunged.

Mort, in his seventies and half crippled from arthritis, had backhanded Wade so hard he'd been knocked to the floor. Then he'd kicked Wade in the ribs until Wade had cried and begged him to stop.

Mort had grabbed his hair and jerked his head back and roared, "You come at me, you'd better be ready to win, you whinin' pup. You're eighteen years old but you're lyin' on your belly crying like a baby girl. Now I expect you to back me up today."

Wade should have crawled out of the room and come back with a gun. Instead he'd followed his father's orders and humiliated his china doll. He'd mocked her in front of that crowd. He'd played the fool because he always did.

He thought about how much he hated his father. How often he'd dreamed of having the strength to beat him into the dirt. How often he'd had nightmares that ended in his own death at his father's hands. But his other favorite dream ended when he killed his father. He woke up half crazy from all those nightmares, and only whiskey would quiet the torment.

Now Wade drew deep on his brown bottle, then lay on his back and nurtured his anger and fed his hatred, focusing it on Red Dawson.

The rage boiled in Wade's stomach, a killing fury stirred in him, and he rolled back over, picked up his rifle, and took a bead on Dawson's door. If Dawson stepped outside at that instant, he'd die.

Wade was ready. He was finally ready. He was finally man enough to kill.

He waited and watched and wanted and hated.

Cassie had been rehearsing what she'd say when Red returned. She was determined to talk at least a little, since she'd been mostly mute the whole time they'd been together. Griff had wanted an intelligent conversation with dinner. He'd always said she couldn't hold up her end because she was so uneducated. Which was true. She'd quit school at fifteen when she got married. And he'd pointed out that her mind was naturally childlike, as was the case with most women. She thought that was true, too, because inside her head she spent a lot of time screaming and complaining and making sharp, crude remarks—very childish.

But Griff needed to be allowed to discuss his day. He said a man couldn't relax properly without that. She had learned to smile politely and nod and make encouraging comments to keep him talking. She would try to talk enough to let Red tell her about his day but not so much as to annoy him.

"Everything's ready. If you want to wash up, we can eat right now." She hoped she wasn't being bossy.

Red smiled wide. "It smells great. To walk in and have a meal set down in front of you is a real nice thing, Cassie. It makes me feel like a king. Thank you very much for this."

Cassie was dishing the ham onto Red's plate and she almost dropped it. Making dinner was her duty. The notion that Red would thank her for that almost knocked her over. She nodded and almost smiled, but she controlled the silly impulse. "There's water warming in the fireplace. I could ladle it for you." She set the ham down and moved toward the fireplace where she'd settled a pot of water to warm.

"No, I'll get it. You've done enough." Red waved her away and hurried to scoop water into a basin. He set the basin in the sink, rolled up his sleeves, and washed his hands all the way to his elbows. Then he washed his face and ran his hands into his hair, finger-combing it. He took the bowl outside and tossed the water and came to the table.

While he washed, Cassie spooned a plateful of potatoes, gravy, ham, and biscuit for each of them and hung a coffeepot over the flames to be ready when dinner was done.

As Red pulled out his chair, Cassie sat quietly, ready to memorize any critical word he said about the potatoes she'd whipped so smooth or the gravy she'd fussed over to rid it of the tiniest lumps. She needed to confess her use of yeast on the biscuits because he would no doubt disapprove of extravagance. And she was afraid she'd made too much of everything and it would go to waste. Or too little of everything and Red would go hungry. She took small servings herself, even though the wonderful smell of ham had been torturing her for an hour. She would take more later if there was any left.

She picked up her fork and lifted the first bite of the luscious meat to her lips, when Red said, "We say the blessing first, Cass."

She almost dropped her fork. Those were words her mother had always said to her as a child. *"Before we eat, we ask God to bless the food, Cassandra."*

Griff said it was a meaningless ritual.

Cassie laid down her fork and folded her hands in her lap. She nodded at Red then bowed her head.

There was a long silence and it took all of Cassie's willpower not to peek at Red and see if he'd prayed silently and was now eating without her while she sat, eyes closed, waiting. When Red finally spoke, it wasn't like the sweet, memorized prayer her mother had always said. Red just talked to God.

"Father, Cass and I got married today. You were there, Lord, I felt You there. Bless this marriage we began today and bless the soul of Lester Griffin. And take care of the babe, Lord. It's a big responsibility. I need You to give Cass and me the wisdom to be good parents. Thank You for this wonderful meal Cassie made. Let us use the strength we get from this good food to do Your work on this earth. In Jesus' name. Amen."

Cassie lifted her head and said, "That was a nice prayer, R—uh. . .uh. . ." Cassie was struck speechless. She pressed her fingers over her lips as she realized that she didn't know her husband's name and found she couldn't call him Red.

"What, Cass? Is something wrong?" Red looked worried and she saw him take a quick glance at her stomach.

Cassie dropped her eyes to her lap and whispered, "I. . .Red isn't. . ." She glanced up at him, afraid he'd be angry at her stupid question, but she had to ask. She whispered, "Should I know your real name?"

He looked dumbfounded for about two seconds, then he grinned so widely that she lifted her fingers away from her lips and smiled back.

"I reckon a wife oughta know her husband's name," Red announced and started laughing. Cassie was amazed to hear the sound of laughter come from her own lips. It was a sound she hadn't heard for three years. She slipped her fingers back over her mouth to stop herself.

She remembered the moment, the circumstances of the last time she'd laughed. Griff had asked her to marry him and she'd yelled, "Yes!" and laughed and flung her arms around his neck. He'd pulled her arms away from him roughly and shook her so hard her head had snapped back and forth and tears had come to her eyes. He'd told her she was making a fool of herself and to please try and moderate her voice and not flaunt herself.

Griff had corrected her from the very beginning, even before her mother died when he'd cared for the family accounts. Then, when he'd been put in charge of Cassie's inheritance, he'd been even more strict. She accepted that because he was so much older and wiser. But Griff had always been kind, carefully explaining things to her and with incredible patience telling her he didn't expect much from her until she'd had the chance at proper training.

But that day, he had shaken her so violently her neck stung and she could feel the bruises forming on her arms. She'd immediately apologized, and she'd begun the hard work of growing up so she could be worthy of a man as fine as Griff. She'd never, never shouted again and she hadn't laughed out loud in three years.

Now Red was laughing, and she had laughed back. He didn't seem upset at all. Cassie decided in that moment that it wasn't what the rules were that was important. It was finding them out and obeying them. She would have to learn a whole new set of rules, but she could do it. She could be the wife that Red deserved.

"My name is Fitzgerald O'Neill Dawson. My mother was born in Ireland and she landed all her love for the Old Country right smack on my head with a single name."

"Fitzgerald O'Neill Dawson?"

"It's a mouthful." Red turned to his ham and started cutting.

"It's a fine name. Do you want me to call you Red?" She'd

always called Griff by his nickname because he had dictated that she should. Now she waited for Red to make his wishes known. Cassie carefully imitated Red's motions, picking up her fork and knife seconds after he did.

"Red's okay. I doubt if I'd know to answer if anyone called me Fitzgerald of all things. Even my ma called me Red."

"Tell me about your parents, Red," Cassie asked politely. She was suddenly excited about the wealth of questions she could ask of a man she didn't know at all. She could keep him talking for months.

"Well, let's see. My pa was a parson. Ma had hair as red as mine, and there were ten children in all."

"Ten children!" Cassie gasped.

"Yeah, I was the youngest. Six of the kids died of one thing and another, mostly before I was born. So, there are four of us grown. Let's see. . .of the six that died, we lost one in the War Between the States. Another fought and got home okay, but scarlet fever went through and killed him. Another brother, the one that was next older than me, and the two sisters next older than him died of yellow fever before I was born. And I had a sister who died having her first babe. I was old enough to remember that."

A somber expression crossed Red's face as he recited this litany of death, but he didn't dwell on it. Cassie didn't expect him to. Death was a part of living and it made no sense to rail against it.

Red continued. "I'm a straggler anyway. Then losing those three that were next older, there's a long spread of years between me and the rest of the family. Pa did his preaching on Sundays and owned a feed store besides. Ma and all us kids helped out. The whole bunch of them settled down young and started right in raising families. Last count I had five nieces and eight nephews. I guess I'm the maverick of the family, but there was always something that called me to ranching. Ma said it was the Irishman's love of the land. Pa said I was a dreamer. When they opened Montana for homesteading, I jumped at the chance. They were old when I was born, near fifty, and they've both passed on now."

"If you're a rancher, why do you dig graves?" Cassie asked.

"I turn my hand to a dozen jobs in town to make this place pay. The general store lets me work off my bill. The blacksmith keeps my horses shod. I bought a horse at the stable in town, and I'm paying that off with a pitchfork. Whatever it takes to get done what needs doing."

"And how did you decide to live in this cave?"

Red grinned and shrugged. "I've got a better home for my chickens and pigs than I do for myself."

"Oh, no! This is a wonderful home," Cassie protested.

"Do you really like it? Because I didn't want to build a house for a few more years."

"If you do build a house, whenever you do it, could we just add it on to this one?" Cassie asked. "I'd never want to give up that cold spring."

"Yeah, sure, that's what I've always had planned. It may be awhile."

Cassie heard the note of warning in his voice. She said, "I like it just the way it is. When a house gets too big, it's next to impossible to keep it warm. This is so cozy with only the fireplace burning."

Cassie went back to her meal while Red talked. Asking questions was the perfect way to pass the rest of her life.

"Now tell me about your folks, Cass. You and Griff came from New York, right?"

Cassie was struck dumb. She had a mouthful of mashed potatoes, and she had to force herself to swallow them. She hadn't been asked to offer much to a conversation in years.

Montana Rose

Suddenly words wanted to rush out. She had so many things she wanted to say, the words jammed behind each other like piled-up logs at a narrow spot on a river.

She just looked at Red and shrugged silently, acting just as stupid as Griff had always said she was.

CHAPTER 7

D o you have brothers and sisters?" Red scooped himself a big bite of potatoes.

Cass found she could answer a direct question. "No, I am an only child."

Red looked up from his plate. "That sounds lonely. Although I was so much younger than my brothers and sisters, in some ways, I was almost an only child, I reckon."

Red ate his potatoes, then casually sliced a generous piece off his ham steak and laid it on Cassie's plate. "I've got too much here."

She didn't know if handing her food counted as a criticism or not. She didn't have time to decide.

"So what does your father do for a livin'? Or has he passed on?" Red attacked his meal with relish.

Cassie realized that as long as he talked, he couldn't eat. Maybe he thought it was rude of her to question him when he was hungry. She inhaled slowly and decided she had to talk so he could finish his meal.

"My father worked for the railroad. First in an office in

New York City, but before I was born, they'd moved to Illinois, to Chicago. Mother was Spanish, but several generations ago."

Red smiled. "The pearls from the Spanish countess."

Cassie nodded and resumed talking. "She was four generations away from the Spanish countess, and our family these days is more German and English than Spanish. But my mother was still as proud of being Spanish as your mother was of being Irish."

Red was eating with relish now, and Cassie's heart lightened at his enjoyment. "Father died when I was very young. I just barely remember him. He left us quite well fixed, though. Mother and I lived alone from then on in a large house in Chicago. Mother died six years ago. I was twelve."

Red stopped eating and his forehead wrinkled. "That's really hard to lose your parents when you're still a child. Who took care of you?"

"Griff did."

"What?" Lowering his fork, Red stared at her.

He looked so shocked, Cassie hurried to explain. "There was no other family, and Griff was an assistant my mother hired to see over our affairs after Father died. He had fallen out with his father and been disinherited, so he had no start in the world. He became less of an employee over the years and more of a family friend. When my mother died, she'd left the management of my estate to him and named him my guardian. We were married when I was fifteen."

"Wow, that's young for marriage." Red slathered butter on his biscuit.

Cassie found that watching his hands and the melting butter was easier than looking him in the eye. "One day, when we'd been married about a month, I overheard some gossip between a storekeeper and our cook about Griff marrying me when he was closer to my mother's age than mine. Griff was furious at me for listening to gossip, especially because I had gone out to the shops without gaining his permission. He fired the cook at once, of course, and I was forbidden from leaving the house alone again." Cassie rubbed the side of her face, still remembering the stinging slap she'd earned for her childish defiance. It wasn't the first time Griff had punished her, but it was the first time he'd left marks where they'd be visible to others. She'd been banished to her room for two weeks, allowed to see no one but Griff until the bruises faded. She'd been so badly behaved back then.

"My pa didn't forbid my ma to do much. She wasn't one to take orders a bit good." Red took another bite of biscuit and chewed slowly, watching her so carefully she wished she could end her story.

"I convinced him to forgive me, but he was still very upset about it. To avoid the talk, Griff decided to come west. He had dreams about being a cattle baron and proving himself to the world. With my inheritance, it seemed like Griff's dreams could come true. But it takes a lot to get started in the West."

"Not if you live off the land like I do." Red had quit eating.

"Griff wanted a home for us like the one we'd left behind, and of course, things Griff wanted to make our home pleasant were so costly out here." Cassie sighed. Things Mr. York and probably others thought she'd demanded.

"Then Griff was cheated when he bought cattle. They never gained weight well and most of the calf crop was lost. The grass on our property was never as lush as we had hoped. And the property was heavily wooded and mountainous rather than grassland, not what had been represented to us at all. It was just one thing after another. We'd have made it, I'm sure, if Griff hadn't died."

Cassie noticed Red's plate was nearly cleared. "Do you want more? There are more potatoes and biscuits."

Montana Rose

Red shook his head, leaned back in his chair, and rested a hand on his stomach. "I am stuffed. I can't remember when I've enjoyed a meal more. The food was delicious, and I did like havin' a beautiful woman talk to me while I ate. I'd drink a cup of coffee, though."

Cassie stood, but Red waved her back. "Let me get it, Cass. You've had a rough day." Red moved to the fireplace and picked up the heavy coffeepot with a towel to protect his hand. He poured them each a fragrant cup of the boiled coffee and, with a *clank* of metal on metal, returned the pot to the hook.

He moved gracefully, at home in the kitchen handling women's work. Griff had never lowered himself to do anything like that, but somehow, when Red did it, it didn't seem like he was less a man. Cassie added a new rule to her collection. Man's work and woman's work wasn't the same in every family. Instead, like all rules, they were set by the man to be how he wanted.

Red slid a cup of coffee in front of Cassie. She cradled the tin coffee cup in both hands, absorbing the warmth even though it wasn't a cold night.

"When is the baby due, Cass?" Red settled back in his chair.

Shocked, she lifted her head from her contemplation of the new rules. She'd never dreamed Red would ask such personal things about the baby. Griff had avoided the whole subject, saying it was inappropriate to discuss such things. She felt her cheeks heat up as she floundered for something to say.

"I didn't mean to embarrass you." Red sat up straight in his chair, looking as uncomfortable as she felt.

That made Cassie feel even worse. The only reason he would have mentioned her embarrassment was if the heat in her cheeks meant she was blushing. She set down her cup and clapped both hands over her cheeks to cover the red. "I didn't think you'd want to talk about it."

89

"If you're uncomfortable talkin' about it with me, I understand. I just want to know when it's due. We may need to have the doctor out, and as winter comes on, that gets harder, so I was wonderin' if it's very soon." Red shrugged and lapsed into an awkward silence.

"I. . .I don't exactly know. How can a woman know such things as when it's coming?" She wanted to tell him what he needed to know.

"You mean you don't know how long you've been expectin'?"

"Um. . .I know that. Griff thought it was unseemly to discuss fe–female things. . . ." Cassie fell silent, exhausted from forcing such personal words past her lips.

"Oh." Red nodded for a second. Then Cassie was amazed to see him smile. "I don't really think of having babies as a female thing, Cass. Well, in a way it's probably the most female thing there ever was, but there's got to be a father somewhere and it looks like I'm it. So, that makes it a male thing, too. So, tell me how long."

"I. . .I knew I was. . .that is, my time. . .my lady's time. . . didn't. . .wasn't there. . .in March last. I told Griff about it a couple of months ago and he said I was most likely bearing a child, and we weren't to discuss it or be. . .be close until after, because a woman was unclean when she was bearing. . ." Cassie gave up again, humiliated. She propped her elbows on the table and rested her burning face in her hands.

Red caught one of her wrists in his hand. "Cassandra Dawson?"

Cassie looked up and saw Red smiling kindly at her. "Yes?"

"We aren't going to have things we don't talk about in this house. Having a baby does *not* make a woman unclean. I reckon I'm the head of this house, and I say that's the way it is. Now, if you need to blush over this, that's okay, but we're still gonna talk about it. If you missed your. . .um. . .time in March, that means..." Red sat silently for a few seconds and Cassie saw him ticking off his fingers. "That means you're seven months along. A woman takes nine months to grow a child inside her, so you'll be having this baby in December. We've got two months."

"Nine months...are you sure?"

"Cass, didn't anybody ever tell you these things? Didn't your ma have a talk with you, or wasn't there a woman friend?"

"Mother died when I was twelve. I can't remember her saying anything about it except what to do about my...my..."

"Your monthly lady's time?" Red asked gently.

Cassie's cheeks heated up again. She nodded, hoping they could move on from this topic. "I've got to clean up the dishes." She reached for the plate in front of Red.

Red had never released her wrist. He tightened his grip and held her still. "So you have no idea what to expect when the baby comes?"

Cassie shook her head, keeping her eyes on the table.

Red tapped her on the chin, and she looked up at him. His eyes were as warm as a Montana summer and he smiled at her even as, with his calming touch, he held her in her seat and made her look at him. "There is nothing wrong or unclean or embarrassing about having a baby, Cass. It's the most natural thing God ever created. Birth is the foundation of the world. Every plant has a seed, every animal recreates in its own kind. God put people on the earth and told them to be fruitful and multiply." Red let go of her wrist and slid his chair out from the table so he could lay one hand on her stomach. "This baby is a gift from God."

Cassie flinched away from the unfamiliar touch. Griff never touched her, never held her hand except for a moment when she would step out of a carriage perhaps, never hugged or kissed her. Except for the brief and infrequent coming together in the dark, nothing physical ever passed between them.

Red didn't let her move away from him, and after the first

shock, she found she liked his touch. It was like a part of her uncurled and grew, nurtured by the human contact. She didn't tell him all that, but she forgot herself enough to lay her hand over Red's and press it against her stomach.

"Cassie, I want you to take pleasure in this gift and understand the glorious work you are doing to bring a new life into the world. This baby will be a blessing to both of us."

Red's voice was so solemn Cassie felt as if they were exchanging wedding vows a second time.

"I'll try, with God's help, to be a good husband to you, Cassandra Dawson, and a good father to the baby. We took vows before God today, and I want you to know I intend to keep them. I don't think we know each other well enough to promise to love like a romantic love. That will take time. But for now, I love you because God calls us to love others as we love ourselves, and I can promise to keep doing that. I'll honor you. That means I want to know what will make you happy. I'm not talking about things. I can't give you nice things like Griff did, but I want to give you what you need for your heart and your soul. I'll give you all of that as part of honoring you."

Cassie nodded, unable to look away from Red's kindness.

"And I'll cherish you. That means love, too, but to me it means more than that. It means enjoying all that is special about you and making sure you know I do."

Cassie listened, wide-eyed. She'd never heard such talk from a man before.

He went on. "And the vows say a woman has to obey her husband, but I want you to know I'll never ask you to do something that sets wrong with your conscience, and I won't be issuing a bunch of orders and demanding you obey them. We'll talk things through and make decisions together. If the day comes when we just can't decide something, really disagree over what is right and wrong, I may pull out the marriage vows and try to insist you obey me, but I don't make a very good dictator. I had too many bossy older brothers and sisters.

"Getting married like we did was a crazy thing to do, I reckon, but we've done it and now we're going to build a life together, doing our best to love and honor and cherish and obey. So don't be embarrassed about anything, Cass. There shouldn't be anything a wife can't say to her husband, okay?"

Cassie nodded, and the heat of tears burned behind her eyes. She had the strange sensation of the china doll Cassie and the screaming, childish Cassie drawing together until they were nearly one. She pressed her hand more firmly over Red's, which still touched her stomach, and wanted to say something as nice to him as he had said to her. Maybe that she liked him to touch her and she'd be glad to obey him—he didn't need to worry about that.

At that moment the baby kicked. Red pulled away with a gasp, then he stared at her stomach. "It moved!" He laid his hand on her again.

After a second, Cassie pressed both of her hands over his. "Try over here." She guided him to where there was more movement. The baby kicked harder this time.

He looked up from staring at her stomach. "Does it do that all the time?"

Cassie nodded and couldn't stop herself from smiling. Until this moment she'd thought Red must know everything about babies. But she remembered that he'd started this off by asking her questions. Now, with that little kick, she realized she knew lots of things he didn't. Eagerly, she said, "The baby kicks a lot. Sometimes I can't get to sleep at night for the kicking and rolling around it does."

"Rolling?" Red asked, his eyebrows arching to near his hairline.

Cassie nodded. "It sometimes feels like she's trying to beat her way out. Sometimes the whole top of my stomach stretches back and forth and I can picture the baby's head bunting me. Or over here."

She moved Red's hands slightly to her right side, at waist level. "I'm sure that is her feet." Cassie looked up at him. "The movement is littler but harder, if that makes any sense."

"Her, huh? You think it's a girl?"

Cassie hadn't realized she'd said "her." Imagining the baby to be a little girl was something private she wouldn't have admitted to if she'd been thinking. "Men want boys, I guess," she said, feeling her cheeks heat up.

The baby kicked again and Red moved his hand to find the source of this activity. "Is it exciting to think about a little person living in there?"

Cassie had never thought about it that way because Griff didn't want her behaving like a giddy girl, so excitement was something she controlled. But now that Red put it like that, she decided it was very exciting. "It's strange isn't it, to think that he—"

"Or she," Red interrupted.

Cassie smiled. She wanted it to be a baby girl so badly. "That he or she is in there, alive and waiting to get out. Nine months—no one ever told me that. That's only two more months. I'll have a baby by Christmas."

Red had both hands on her stomach now. He moved them around, searching for more movement. He looked up at her and lifted one hand to lay it on her cheek. "*We'll* have a baby by Christmas, Cass. We're in this together from now on."

Cassie's eyes burned with tears again, and she had the strange sensation of feeling safe. She'd never been safe with Griff, because she was always waiting for him to find fault with her and punish her. Now, at the surge of safety, hot tears spilled onto her cheeks.

Red wiped them away with his thumb. "Don't cry, Cass honey. I know you miss your husband and—"

Cassie kissed him. She leaned forward, only really thinking about making him stop talking because she was so ashamed at her disloyal thoughts about her newly dead husband. Her hands were full holding Red's on her stomach, so all she had left was to bump her mouth into his.

The kiss was over before it started, but it had the desired effect. Red quit talking.

Cassie jumped to her feet when she realized what she'd done. She knocked the chair over behind her as she backed away and might have fallen if Red hadn't caught her arm.

"It's okay, Cass. I know it's. . .I understand you're still in mourning." Red pulled her close and wrapped his arms around her. She stiffened against him, but he didn't do anything but hold her and smooth her hair. It felt so wonderful that she slowly relaxed against him. But relaxing was a mistake because the minute she did, she started to cry.

Red's arms tightened. The first tears were for Griff, and those tears flowed faster when she thought of her cowardly decision this afternoon to die, denying her baby life. The tears deepened into sobs over her fear of Mort and Wade Sawyer and all the men who had touched her. She wept over her terror of Red's anger about her bills. Then her body shuddered from the relief that he hadn't punished her for them, even though she knew he and every other person in town blamed her for Griff's financial straits.

She cried until she wasn't aware enough anymore to know why she was crying.

And always Red was there. He rubbed her back and brushed her hair off her forehead and crooned sweet words into her ear, surrounding her with strength and kindness.

The storm started to wane at last, and she became aware

that she was sitting on Red's lap. Her cheek was pressed against his coarsely woven shirt and her arms were around his neck as if he was the only steady thing in a reeling universe.

She pulled her arms away from him, ashamed of the closeness between them. Slipping sideways, she tried to stand.

Red didn't let her go. "Just rest another minute, Cass. You needed to cry those tears. You've been through a terrible time. Just let me hold you." There was an extended silence while she relaxed back into his arms, ashamed of herself for using his strength when she should have her own.

At last the trembling weakness receded. "I need to clean the kitchen, R–Red." She stumbled over his name again. Odd that she was having trouble saying it.

Red tilted her chin up with one finger. "You're going to sleep, little mother. I'll clean up in here."

Cass said, "This is my job. I'll do the—"

"Do you know how to milk a cow?"

The question struck her as so strange she didn't answer.

He smiled. "Would you be willing to learn? And I'd like you to gather the eggs, too. There are a few things left in the garden, some beets to dig and a few pumpkins that I left, hoping the frost would hold off and they'd ripen. I'd be obliged to you if you'd tend to those things, and most of the time, I'll be thrilled if you clean up after meals. But I'm used to doing for myself, and when you've had a hard day, I'm willing to pitch in."

Cassie was amazed that Red had framed his offer to help so perfectly. It was as if he knew she'd want to do her part, and he was reassuring her that accepting his assistance this once didn't mean she couldn't contribute. The words could have come from her own mind. They were possibly the only words that would have made her leave the kitchen to Red.

"I'll be proud to help with the milking, Red. I've never done it. We didn't have a milk cow, but I'd try real hard to learn. I'll help wherever you need me. I want to be however you want me to be, Red. Just tell me what to do."

"Right now, I'm telling you to go to bed. We can start worrying about chores tomorrow."

Cassie nodded and eased herself off Red's lap.

"Oh, I almost forgot." Red went to the saddlebags he'd brought into the house with him when they'd first come home. "Muriel said you'd need this tonight."

Cassie looked at the brown paper package and vaguely remembered Muriel saying it was a wedding present. She unwrapped it and found a snow white nightgown. It was embroidered around the neck and made from the softest flannel Cassie had ever touched. She thought it was more beautiful than the finest silk.

She remembered it was not an appropriate piece of apparel to look at in front of Red and blushed as she folded it quickly and held it against her chest. She looked nervously at him and expected him to say something about immodesty as Griff would have. But he was smiling at her as if he were reading her mind and found her embarrassment at looking at a nightgown in front of her husband funny. Another one of those new rules she needed to learn.

"I'll go on to bed then," Cassie murmured.

Red nodded. "Good night, Cass. Sleep as late as you need to in the morning."

Cassie hung her only dress on a nail in the bedroom and donned her nightgown quickly in case Red would come in. She crawled into bed. Her muscles ached as if she had been beaten. Her eyes were as scratchy as sandpaper from all her tears. The white nightgown wrapped around her, touching her almost as warmly, not quite but almost, as Red's hands.

Her husband had been buried today. She'd been married today. Already her new husband was superseding thoughts of the old, and she supposed that made her as stupid and childish as Griff had always said she was.

The day was finally over, but she was afraid the guilt and confusion would last the rest of her life. This had to be the worst day of her life, but she had survived it. Tomorrow would have to get better. Tomorrow Red was going to let her help him. It was something she had longed for with Griff, but he'd never given her the chance to prove herself.

She fell asleep planning a wonderful new life where all her dreams would come true.

CHAPTER 8

Red's life was a nightmare. And he was never going to wake up.

"Cassie! Don't open that. . ."

Cassie started screaming and flapping at the escaping chickens.

". . .gate!"

Cassie screamed and started yelling, "Shoo, no, stop! Shoo, chickens!" and frantically waving her skirt at the escaping hens. Her noise and flapping skirts only served to make the chickens run out of the coop faster.

It bothered Buck, too. It was just pure bad luck that when Buck started crow hopping, Red was on one of the chancier spots on the steep path down to the spring where his animals watered.

Red was watching Cassie instead of minding his horse. So he was unseated—and slid over the edge of the cliff. The drop-off wasn't sheer, and there was some brush growing. He grabbed it and dangled for just a few seconds before he clawed his way back from the brink. There were lots of stunted evergreens on the slope, all the way down, so Red figured if he'd missed the first bushes, he'd have caught the later ones.

As he dragged himself back onto the trail, he saw Buck run off, kicking his heels. Once he'd landed himself on the level ground, slightly panicked at the close call, he admitted he hadn't been *that* close to death. The last drop-off, which was thirty feet straight down to jagged rocks, was still quite a ways away when he'd stopped sliding.

Cassie, as near as Red could tell, hadn't noticed him fall, because she was busy jumping and screaming and flapping her skirts to try and stop the chickens from flying the coop.

He rushed over to calm her down. "Cass, honey, calm down."

She whirled to face him, looking terrified. She didn't seem to register his dirty jeans and torn shirt or his scratched-up arms and face. Or the fact that his hat now had a horse's hoof-print stomped straight into the crown.

"Red, I'm so sorry. I—I didn't mean to let them go." Cassie turned to him with fear in her eyes.

He had scolding words pressing to get out, but he couldn't say them. How could he yell at her when she looked so scared? Instead of shouting, which had been his natural inclination, he said, "Don't worry, Cass. They get out from time to time. They used to do it to me."

That was the truth, strictly speaking. They'd gotten out just this same way when he'd gathered eggs for his mother.

He was five at the time.

He'd learned his lesson then, and he reckoned Cassie had just learned hers, so there really wasn't any point in talking about it.

"Don't worry, Cass. Just remember to always close this outer gate before you open the inner gate. Then close the inner gate while you're inside, and on your way out, make sure all the chickens are in the inner yard before you open this outer one."

Montana Rose

She'd left both of the gates wide open. "Yes, Red. I'll never leave them open again." She pressed her hands to her chest, and he could have drowned in those big, scared eyes.

"Most of them will come home to roost come nightfall." He patted her arm to get her to calm down. "I let them out to scratch most days in the spring and summer."

In the spring and summer when there were weeds to pick at and bugs to chase. In the fall they'd wander far afield looking for food, then they'd roost wherever was handy. Red didn't tell Cassie all that.

"Gather the eggs and go on back in and start breakfast. I'll milk Rosie and bring in the bucket."

Cassie still looked nervous. She said with an almost pathetic eagerness, "Didn't you say last night that you wanted me to milk the cow?"

Red's stomach sank at the thought of what Cassie might do to his precious Rosie. Rosie, a big-boned black and white Holstein, had followed him out here from Indiana, tied behind his covered wagon. He'd raised her from a calf. Rosie was one of the gifts Red's pa had given him when he'd first gone out on his own. It was one of the last things his pa had done before he died. In short, Red had known Rosie a lot longer than he'd known his wife.

"Sure, I want you to learn." Red propped both gates wide open and scattered cracked corn around the inner yard, hoping some of the chickens would come around scratching for food. "But I'll be done by the time you've hunted up all the eggs, so I'll take care of her this morning."

Cassie nodded and entered the little chicken yard. "Ugh!"

He turned from his hurried trip to the barn to get Rosie milked before Cassie could help. She had a sickened expression on her face as she scraped her foot. Red wondered what kind of person didn't know to watch her step in a chicken coop.

Turned back to the barn and his milking, Red noticed Buck loitering around the corral, still loose. The horse looked eager to enter his pen but turned contrary when Red tried to catch him.

"Get back here, you old galoot." Red hustled after the stubborn critter and finally cornered the beast.

By the time he got to Rosie, she was overdue for milking and kicked him a couple of times to remind him to keep to a better schedule.

"Do you want me to try?" Cassie had leaned down over his shoulder.

He jumped. Rosie, startled, kicked over the nearly full bucket of milk. The bucket skittered across the barn floor and slammed into the hay bale where the lantern sat. Kerosene spilled across the hay.

"Cassie, fire! Get out of the barn." Red raced toward the burning hay with a feed sack.

Cassie didn't get out. She charged the haystack with her bare hands. Her skirt caught on fire.

Red grabbed her and pulled her to the barn floor. "Roll, Cassie. That'll put the fire out." He swatted at her skirt until the flames were gone, and then he turned back to the crackling barn.

Red had dropped his burlap bag. He retrieved it and dunked it in the spilled milk and doused the flames.

Red turned to ask Cassie what in heaven's name she'd been doing with a lantern in the barn in the full daylight. She stood behind him, tears streaming down her face.

Red's anger fizzled away as surely as the fire. "Now don't cry, honey." Red went and slung an arm around her trembling shoulders. "We're fine. The fire's out."

He glanced down at her charred skirt. Her one and only dress. He shuddered to think of how badly she could have been burned. He tipped her chin up to look at him.

Montana Rose

"Everything's fine now, Cassie. I want you to stop that crying, okay? The important thing is that you weren't burned. There's no damage except to a little bit of hay, and I have plenty. It was pure clumsiness on my part to let Rosie knock that bucket of milk over. I'll be more careful next time."

Cassie pulled herself together and squared her shoulders. "It's my fault. I shouldn't have startled you. I shouldn't have brought the lantern in with me. I was trying to learn to light it and I wanted to ask you if I needed to turn the wick down. I'll never bring a lit lantern into the barn again. That hay catches fire too easily."

"That's a right good idea. I think we oughta make that a rule. I'll never bring one in here either." Red wanted to say, "Only an idiot brings a lantern into a barn full of hay and leaves it sitting close behind a cow like that." But he figured she'd learned everything his yelling would teach her. And besides, he wasn't much of a yeller.

Red smiled down at her pretty, sad face. "It was my fault and you're sweet to try and take the blame, but I won't have it. Just go on back to the house now and start breakfast."

Please, dear Lord, let her go back to cooking. She has a knack for that.

Cassie sniffled for another second and the terror faded from her eyes. She nodded and headed out of the barn.

With a sigh of relief, Red turned to untie Rosie. Just as he let Rosie out into her corral, a piglet squealed, Cassie screamed, and it was all drowned out by the bloodcurdling roar of an angry mama sow.

Red raced out of the barn, took in the situation in a glance, and dived between Cassie and the furiously protective mother. "Drop the pig, Cassie," he roared.

Harriet slammed, with slashing teeth, into Red's leg. He rolled and dodged her, kicking at her gaping fangs.

103

Cassie dropped the piglet, and it ran toward the pen. Harriet whirled away from trying to kill Red and chased after her baby.

Red scrambled to his feet and rushed to the gate Cassie had so casually left open. Apparently the woman had decided she wanted to cuddle a cute but unwilling piglet. He glanced down and saw two long slits in his pant leg. Before he could check for bites, he needed to make sure the gate was secure. When he had it tightly wired shut, he turned, his temper simmering, to brace Cassie about being so reckless. He took one step toward her, and his ankle, still sore from his fall off the horse, almost gave out on him. He caught the gate to keep from falling, then decided to turn his attention to his ankle until he quit wanting to holler at his wife.

Harriet was still woofing, but she was focused on her babies.

Red bent to look for bites. He found several deep scratches on his leg but was relieved to find Harriet hadn't drawn blood. Animal bites could turn septic, and Red had heard of many a man dying from a bite that wasn't very serious.

This time he'd have to say something. Cassie couldn't touch anything on his ranch, ever again. Red turned to look at her and saw her face had gone pure white. His heart clutched and his anger vanished. Could this much fear hurt the baby? He hurried as best he could over to her side, doing his best to hide his limp.

"Are you all right, Cass honey?" Red reached for her face, to study her pallor, then hesitated and wiped his hands on his pants, still filthy from being thrown off Buck, never cleaned after he fought the fire, and now worse from being rolled on the ground by Harriet. Red had a second to think of what could have happened to Cassie if Harriet had gotten to her instead of him.

"Red, Red, I'm sorry—" Her voice broke.

Montana Rose

Red didn't give her another second to talk. He scooped her up in his arms and carried her to the house, his leg only a distant, nagging ache. He got through the stubborn, heavy door with her still in his arms and settled her in a kitchen chair. He knelt down in front of her. "You're okay, Cassie." All he could think of was calming her down before something awful happened. He jumped up and got a dish towel and plunged it into the bucket of water he'd hauled from the cooler this morning. He wrung out the cold water, then dropped back to his knees and bathed her chalky skin.

"You're fine, Cass. No harm done. I'm sorry I didn't warn you about Harriet. She's fierce about her babies. No one would ever know a mama pig could be such a dangerous animal." He felt the worst of the tension drain out of her. Her eyes, fixed wide with horror, dropped closed, and she sagged against him until her head rested on his shoulder.

They stayed like that for long minutes. Her trembling gradually eased and he felt some strength return to her muscles. She slowly raised her head.

Red sighed with relief. Her color was better. He pressed the cool cloth on her cheeks and forehead again. "Are you all right? Do you need to lie down?"

"No, I'm better now." Cassie shook her head and straightened her spine.

He had to admire that. A mama pig could take the starch out of a mighty steely spine. "You just rest here. Let me go finish the chores. Then I'll come back and get us some breakfast."

"No, you shouldn't have to do that."

Red shuddered. Then he thought of last night's supper. Yes, she could cook. If only she'd just agree to do nothing else.

He said, with a calm that took a Herculean effort, "So what's for breakfast?"

"I'll fry some eggs if that suits you."

Red nodded. "Eggs sounds fine. Let me add some wood to the fireplace for you."

"Thank you," she said so breathlessly, he felt like he'd offered to slay a dragon.

"I won't be gone long." He patted her knee, rose from the floor, stoked the fire, and made it out the door without limping.

He didn't bother to hide his limp once he was alone. He hobbled around finishing his chores, double-checking the gate as he always did.

He checked the hay pile a dozen times for any smoldering embers. Then he got to thinking about how close she'd snuggled up to him in the night last night. They'd started the night with a solid two feet of space between them, but in the morning he woke with her arms wrapped around his waist as if she craved his warmth. He thought of how her soft hair had fallen out of its braid and spread over his arm and across his chest.

He was far gone thinking about Cassie when he tripped over the basket of eggs Cassie had left sitting by the front door. He fell down and hurt his ankle a little worse.

She rushed to the door to see what the racket was. "Oh Red, I should never have left that basket sitting there. I was almost in the house when I noticed the pigs and went to look at them."

Red could blame her for everything else that happened this morning, but this one was all his fault. He reassured her he was daydreaming. Not for one second did he consider telling her what he was daydreaming about.

She lost that look she got, like she was afraid of him. She seemed to believe him when he took responsibility for this latest mess, a trifling matter compared to what had gone on earlier. He picked up what was left of the eggs and limped inside with them.

The sun was just fully up and already she'd about ruined

him. He'd never survive the week. If he did, it wouldn't matter. All his animals would be dead, his buildings burned to the ground, and she'd probably find a way to lose all his ranch land and dry up his creek while she was at it.

He tossed split wood on the embers of the fire, determined to take charge of all fire-related chores from this moment forward.

"How did your shirt get torn, Red?"

He looked down. He was more of a wreck than even he'd realized. "I reckon they're just old and have been torn for a while." Red was an honest man, but *a while* could be weeks or it could be minutes, and the fact that one of the two outfits of clothing he owned was now halfway to rags, even though it'd been fine when he'd put it on this morning, didn't mean it hadn't been "a while."

"I'll mend your clothes if you take them off and leave them with me."

"How about I just wear 'em for the rest of the day, and you can do them tomorrow?" He thought if she had anymore hijinks in mind, maybe he'd better stick to the clothes that were already ruined.

"My clothes from yesterday are still dirty. I'll wash them up today and wear them tomorrow. You can mend these then."

She smiled timidly, as if she was out of practice. "I'll wash your clothes, Red."

"Thanks, Cass. If you have time." Red tried to think of the possible disasters involved in swishing pants around in water.

She'd smiled bigger, and he couldn't think of a thing that could go wrong.

She turned to the fireplace, her charred skirt swaying. Cracking eggs into a pan, she hummed as she worked.

She was his wife. She was the most beautiful woman Red had ever seen. She was feeding him and sewing for him and doing his laundry and she'd just asked him to take his clothes off. Red decided if she wanted to kill him, he'd just sit back and thank God for every second of his life until he died.

And just in case there was a chance he wasn't going to die, he'd make sure she forgot all about his asking her to help outside and stayed strictly in the house.

CHAPTER 9

Cassie spent every minute of every day outside helping.

She was determined to learn everything as fast as she could. When Red didn't offer to show her what to do, she struggled to figure things out herself. She'd never leave a gate open again. She stayed out of reach of the terrifying mama pig. But she watched, and she did her best to make sense of the mysterious business of ranching.

The first evening as Red came in for dinner, Cassie met him at the door and pointed to the little building built with slender saplings. "Look at how many chickens came back. You were right that they'd come home." The chickens had wandered in a few at a time all day. Cassie had been careful not to go near them while they moseyed along, scratching for food.

Red pulled his hat off the peg after supper. "I'll wander the woods some and see if I can find any roosting." Red was complimentary about the beef steak she'd cooked over the open fire and didn't complain a bit when he went out around sunset, leaving her alone.

She carefully stayed outside, on watch for his return. She

guarded the closed gate to the coop so she could open it for him. He came walking in from the wooded area behind their home with his hands full of chickens. The chickens hung down at his sides. As he drew near her, they all started flapping their wings and squawking violently. Cassie used every ounce of her courage to stay on guard.

He made a lot of trips that evening, working long after dark until he'd gathered quite a few more.

"We got a lot of them back, didn't we?" She carefully closed the inner gate before she opened the outer one.

Red passed through the gate and locked it for her with a smile. "About half."

"Already?" That seemed like a good start to her.

"A great start," he agreed.

They walked side by side into their cave house, and Cassie marveled that Red had never once let his temper loose on her.

She gathered the eggs the next morning with Red right at her side the whole time. She enjoyed his company. "I only got four, Red." She waited, afraid he'd be angry. This was all her fault.

"They laid them in the woods this once. We'll get more tomorrow. It's no great loss, just a day's gathering."

She stepped close to him, the four eggs clutched in her hands. "It'll never happen again. I promise."

Red stayed close to the house all day. He said he didn't need to check his herd of cattle too often. Cassie accepted that because Griff, explaining to her that they foraged for food and needed little handling, hadn't checked his often either. Sometimes not for weeks at a time.

When he did go out riding, he made her promise faithfully to stay inside.

Red's house was so small and easy to keep tidy, the time hung heavy on her hands if she stayed inside.

One day, when he came back from checking the herd, she was sitting at the kitchen table fidgeting.

As if he read her mind, he asked, "Would you like to explore the cave off the bedroom?"

"Oh, yes. I've wondered about it, but I didn't want to go in without permission."

Red looked at her a little oddly, and then he shrugged. "Let's go."

"There are dead ends down this way." Red held her hand as they passed through the dark opening in the back bedroom. When the ground was especially uneven, he'd stay close to her side in the narrow passage, with one hand resting on her shoulder. "This part here is really steep. If being so big with the baby makes you feel off balance at all, you'd better not cross this section alone."

"I'll never step foot in here without you. I promise." Cassie thought the tunnel was spooky but found she enjoyed the little thrill of fear she got from walking through it. The tunnel descended quite a ways over its length, and it opened into the rocks right near the creek where Red took Buck and Rosie to water.

Red showed her a deeper spot in the creek where he took baths. The water was bitterly cold and Cassie preferred to warm a basin in the kitchen. But Red promised that if she wanted to bathe, he'd walk her through the tunnel and leave her in privacy to brave the chill.

"See this crack, down low here?" Red knelt and passed his hand into the crevice. "Feel how cold it is. It must have water in the back of it, same as our cooler. We could store cold things in here if the cooler didn't have enough room."

Cassie shivered with cold and excitement to know the little

details about Red's cave. She'd have liked to explore some more but didn't want to impose on Red's time.

She wasn't much help around the farmyard, because Red politely but steadfastly refused to give her a chance with milking. She chafed with the memory of Red saying she'd have to help. She knew that's what he wanted and she was determined to abide by his wishes. He no longer urged her to help outside, but she knew he was just being kind. Whenever she did start a chore, Red would jump in and do it for her. She thought it was sweet of him, but she was determined to learn. She tried her hand at milking a few times when Red had gone off to ride herd and nearly got her head kicked off. But she could tell Rosie just kicked out of cantankerousness. There wasn't any real meanness in it. By the end of the week she still couldn't get milk out of Rosie, but she felt like the little cow liked her.

Most of the chickens were back. Red had quit hunting for them at night. The mama sow had. . .well, Harriet still wanted her dead. And Cassie decided she wanted to learn to ride Buck.

She hadn't worked up the nerve to tell Red that she'd never been on a horse. With the exception of the terrifying trip to town on her bay to tell Seth and Muriel that Griff had died, and the ride she'd slept through with Red after their wedding, she'd always ridden in carriages. Griff had said it was unseemly for a woman to ride, even sidesaddle.

She was surprised to find out Red had a nervous streak. She didn't really know him, of course, but he'd seemed like a calm man. She found out he was prone to clumsiness. He'd hurt his ankle in a fall and he'd scared Rosie that first morning. When he offered her help with some job, he'd talk a little too fast and stumble over his words, and he seemed to spend time fixing things around the farm that had seemed fine when she'd been working with them.

Montana Rose

She was serving him his noon meal on Saturday when she started to ask about riding the horse. Before she could gather her courage, Red announced they were heading for town as soon as dinner dishes were done.

"Town? Why?" Cassie's stomach fluttered with excitement. She loved going to town, although she'd gotten so she avoided it whenever possible with Griff. He made her sit quietly in the carriage while he conducted his business. She wasn't to speak to anyone or even smile or make eye contact. Griff said it was familiar and indecent behavior for a married woman, and Cassie had done her best to please him.

"I've got several jobs I do in town on a Saturday afternoon. To raise money and barter for supplies. And I've got to preach tomorrow morning at Seth's. I've considered it awhile and I've decided we'll stay in the hotel. Grant has always offered me a room. But sleeping on the ground has suited me. The nights are getting sharp, though, and I think you need a bed."

"Can I help with your jobs, Red?" Cassie began cleaning up after the noon meal, hurrying so Red wouldn't have to wait when he was ready to go.

"Most of it is heavy work. That's why they hire me." Red carried his own plate to the sink.

Cassie was still amazed when he did woman's work.

"You could spend the afternoon with Muriel if you want," Red suggested.

"Why do you do all that work, Red? You have everything you need here. You grow your own food and you seem to have a fair-sized herd of cattle. Why do you do all those chores in town?"

Red began drying the dishes Cassie washed. He was silent as he considered her question. Cassie realized that the way he talked to her, not as if she was stupid but as if the questions she asked were interesting, was the thing she liked best about

113

her new husband. She also liked that he never yelled and the way he savored every bite of the food she made. It was amazing to her that he'd complimented her on the food. She'd never thought a man would bother with such a thing. Why, she even found his nervousness endearing.

Now, he stood there helping her and thought about her question as if the answer were important. Which meant the question was important and somehow that made Cassie important. It was wonderful.

"When I first moved here, I had nothing. I got out here a year before they opened this area for settlers because I reasoned that this would be next. I scouted until I found this place, the creek, the grasslands, the mountain valleys that could feed so many cattle but would be worthless without the creek. I'd even found this cave and had the beginnings of my home built. I was working odd jobs around Divide to earn enough money to buy a few cattle. I staked out a few good water holes and bought them up nice and legal as soon as I could scrape together the money. I bought ten head of cattle from a herd passing from Montana to the rail yards in Kansas City. I had the cows and the land, but I still needed money."

Red kept wiping until the few dishes were done, then poured them both another cup of coffee and settled at the table. "I had my eye on the forty acres next to me which had never been claimed, so I worked like crazy, afraid someone would beat me to it. As soon as I got the money together, I bought it."

Cassie sat down across from him.

"Doing odd jobs in town turned into bartering my labor at nearly every store where I did business. I almost never pay cash for anything, and if I get ahead, they pay me or they keep an account open for me. Like at the general store last week, I was able to have Griff's bills taken off what I had in my account, and they traded the value of your dress. So that bill is all settled.

Quite a few of them are."

"You are paying all of Griff's bills with your labor?" Cassie sipped carefully at the burning hot brew.

"Sure. Labor is how you get money. How else do you think I could do it? If I paid cash—I do have some money in the bank these days—that money is all labor, too. It's the same."

"But. . .then why didn't Griff work for them when he owed so much?" Cassie's voice faded away. She knew why. Griff would have found working for Seth beneath him. Even now Cassie could feel a twist of embarrassment to picture Red doing all that menial labor for the town shopkeepers.

"Griff had his way. I have mine. I've managed to add another 160 acres to my holdings as other settlers gave up. Because I have good water, I control several thousand more acres. I'm buying it all up as fast as I can because I don't want there to be any question about the title.

"I worked at the lumbermill to pay for the barns and corrals. I traded work with a farmer to get the chickens. I traded one of Rosie's calves for Harriet. I'm up to nearly five hundred head of cattle now, with last spring's calf crop. There's a lot of money to be made in cattle drives back East, but I take a little less and sell my cows in Divide because I don't want to be gone from my place for the whole summer. I don't hire a lot of hands like a lot of ranchers do."

"Five hundred cattle? You built that up from ten cattle in only. . .how many years?"

"I've been out here four years now, counting the year before I homesteaded. I've spent hundreds of hours hunting the hills for cows that have gone maverick. I've bought cattle cheap that weren't ready for market from settlers who were folding up. I've sold off the steers only once. I had a few three-year-olds ready to sell last spring, but I've held on to all the mama cows so they could build the herd. It's a lot of work to build something from nothing, but God gave us a bountiful world. He put gold under the ground in California and He put gold in the ground here in the form of rich soil and plentiful grass and water."

"I'd be proud to help you in town if you needed me to, Red. I'd like to be part of what you're building."

"We'll see. Like I said, a lot of it's hard labor and heavy lifting. But I'll think on it."

"Didn't you say you haul groceries from Seth's to Libby's Diner? I could carry that back and forth, just take a lot less each trip than you do. Please, Red, you've been so good about letting me help. Oh, I want to say again how sorry I am about knocking you out of the hayloft in the barn earlier. I was trying to lift the bucket of corn up there so I could pour Harriet's food into her trough from overhead. She gets so upset whenever she sees me. And now that the colder weather has forced you to move the feeder away from the fence to keep it out of the wind, I can't reach it to pour in her ears of corn. I thought you saw me raising that bucket up to the loft."

"I did see you, Cass. I just thought you looked like you didn't have a very good foothold. I shouldn't have grabbed you like that. It's all my fault. I was just afraid if I said your name to warn you I was there, you might be startled and fall. That straw can be slippery. I guess I proved that by slipping on it." Red smiled.

"Thank heavens you landed on the haystack. You could have really been hurt."

Red's cheeks got pink and his jaw tightened, and she thought it was sweet he was embarrassed at his clumsiness. His sweetness reminded her of the way he snuggled up to her every night, even though they were careful to fall asleep with a respectable space between them. This morning she felt him rubbing his chin on top of her head when he was still asleep. It had almost felt like his mouth instead of his chin, but despite his assurances that a woman expecting a baby wasn't unclean, she could tell he didn't want to kiss her.

She remembered that awkward kiss the first night they'd been together. She was the one who had kissed him. He'd never followed with a kiss of his own, so she knew he didn't like kissing. But she liked to pretend he kissed her while she slept.

"The haystack was lucky all right." Red finished his coffee in one last, long gulp. "Let's not feed Harriet that way again. I'd be glad to do that chore. She's a cantankerous old monster."

"I suppose the haymow wasn't a good idea. But I'm sure to find a way I can keep feeding her."

"Yes, well, yes...you're sure to find a way. Let me wash these two last cups."

"No, you must have chores to do if we're staying away overnight. I'll get things straightened in here and come help you as soon as I can."

Red nodded. "I'd better get going then." He practically ran out of the house.

"He's always in a hurry," Cassie murmured to herself. "I wish I could help him more." She cleared the last bit of the kitchen quickly so she could get to her outside chores.

CHAPTER 10

I'll get a horse saddled for you, Cass honey." Red tried to saddle Buck for her, planning to ride another horse himself, but she'd approached Buck then backed away with one excuse or another until she'd practically been dancing around the horse. Then Buck had started acting spooky.

"Uh. . .would it b–be all right if I just rode with you, like we did last week?" Cassie gave him a look of such longing, like the idea of sitting so near him really appealed to her. Buck had held up well being ridden double home from town last week. But Red was worried about working the horse too hard.

If Red didn't share with her, she'd have to ride Buck, because he was the best-trained horse Red owned, but truth was, Buck hadn't ever calmed down much after Cassie and the chickens had scared him. Red was afraid he was permanently spooked now and would never be as good a mount. Red had a remuda with a dozen horses, but they were green broke—rough horses born on Red's ranch or rounded up from the wild, well suited to cutting cattle when guided by a firm hand but not saddle ponies for an unskilled woman. The buckskin had come with him from Indiana, just like Rosie, and was almost as much a pet as Rosie. But he'd taken a skittish turn since he'd met Cassie, and Red was worried about Cassie riding him alone. Riding double solved that problem.

It took him a full hour to figure out Cassie had never ridden a horse before, or at least not much. She was terrified but doing her best not to let him see that.

He thought about hitching Buck up to the wagon. It was slower but it would have been okay. Unfortunately, he figured out about Cassie's fear when they were a long way down the road to Divide. It was too late to go back.

Cassie had started out sitting sideways on the saddle while Red rode behind the cantle. But that proved to be not only uncomfortable for them both, but Buck didn't like Red sitting back so far and proved it by bucking every few feet. Cassie had nearly fallen off a few times. Red fixed that by moving into the saddle and holding her firmly on his lap just as she had been after their wedding. Red found this arrangement to be no hardship.

Even after Red moved, Buck was fractious.

"Is this how it usually is to ride a horse, Red?" Cassie tried to sound calm, but Buck wasn't cooperating. Now Cassie's flapping skirts and her constant squirming around on Red's lap weren't making his horse a bit happy.

Red was happy. . .just not his horse.

"Buck's a little jumpier than usual, I reckon. He'll calm down once we've ridden a ways." Red hoped.

Cassie's constant nervous fluttering wasn't bothering Red at all. He liked the feel of her against him, and every time she moved, he realized that being married was a wonderful thing. But Buck wasn't married to Cassie, and he probably didn't think she was heart-stoppingly beautiful, what with Buck having his own standards of beauty that included four legs and gigantic teeth. So Buck didn't like her one bit.

119

They'd been on the trail a far piece when Cassie said, "I'd like to learn to ride a horse, Red."

"Learn to ride? What's to learn? You're doin' it."

"This is only the third time I've been on a horse in my life. I should know how to do it if I'm going to be a rancher's wife, shouldn't I?"

Red's stomach sank at the thought of what lay in store for him if Cassie got her mind set on the death-defying task of riding a horse. Then under the fear, he registered what she'd said. "Only the third time? How did you live in Montana for two years and come across the prairie in a covered wagon without riding a horse?"

"We had the carriage and Griff said riding was not ladylike. So I never. . ."

Red felt a little stir of his temper. It usually wasn't too much trouble, but sometimes he had a little problem with it. "Cassie, Griff told you not to ride. Griff told you not to talk about the baby to the point you don't know a thing about what's to come. Griff told you a woman was unclean when she was carryin' a child. Griff mortgaged all your family heirlooms without telling you so you could have a useless new silk dress every year. Excuse me for speakin' ill of the dead, Cass, but your husband wasn't very smart, was he?"

All Cassie's fluttering and squirming stopped. She sat frozen in his arms.

Red tensed up when he realized he'd gravely insulted his new wife's dead husband. It wasn't a good way to endear himself in her eyes. He started to apologize, but he wanted to see her face first to judge just how hurt and angry she was.

Before he could get a peek at her she said, "Do you really think Griff was wrong about all those things?"

"Now, Cass honey, I shouldn't have said that. I know you loved him and you. . ."

"Answer me!" All the softness was gone. She sounded almost frantic.

"Well, don't you?"

Another silence, longer than the first, stretched between them. "You mean I get to decide if I think he was smart or not? Surely that's not a woman's place."

"I don't rightly know if Griff was *smart* or not. I just said he did some things and told you some things that weren't smart. No one can know everything. I'm sure Griff was real smart about lots of things, but he was wrong about some things, too. He shouldn't have said you were unclean. But maybe that's somethin' he was raised with. Some people have funny notions. And he should never have mortgaged your things. I know all about the law and how it treats property between a husband and wife, so legally those things were his. But there's right and wrong, too, Cass. Morally those things were yours. Maybe you would have agreed to mortgage them, but I'm bettin' you'd have said, 'I want my family Bible more than I want a new dress.' Now isn't that right? Isn't that what you'd've said?"

It took a long time, with Cassie staring at her hands, before she answered. "I'd have parted with the Bible for food, for something we really needed. Well, maybe not. No, not the Bible. I wouldn't have parted with that ever. That book was something my mother treasured. I'd have gone hungry before I parted with that big old book. . . ."

Her voice faded and Red was afraid he'd made her cry. He felt like a brute to have reminded her of her precious belongings. He'd hurt her with his words when she was the most precious thing in the world to him.

"But the pearls and the portrait frames, I would have held on to them if I could, but I would have let him have those if it was for something that was important to the ranch. But I'd have never mortgaged them for a dress. I had two other black silk dresses. Griff wanted me to always have new things. He said we needed to keep up the right appearance."

Red tried to distract her from her keepsakes. "And as far as not thinkin' a lady should ride a horse, why honey, I've never known a lady in Montana who *didn't* ride a horse. Even in Indiana most ladies rode. Surely Illinois isn't much different. Griff was just plain wrong about that."

"When he was dying, Griff kept insisting I not go for help." Cassie looked up at Red, her eyes brimming with tears. "I didn't know how to catch the horse, so it was easy for me to mind him. Then I waited too long. When I finally did catch one, I couldn't make the horse obey me. It went back to the house at least six times before I got it going toward town. But it didn't matter by then anyway; Griff was dead. I stood by and let my husband die rather than ride for help. I didn't do a thing to save him because I was a coward. A stupid, cowardly child. That was one thing Griff was right about." The tears overflowed and Cassie looked as if she hated herself for failing that idiot Lester Griffin. Like she still wished he was alive so she could be married to him.

Red knew all the stories about redheads having fiery tempers. And he knew, in his own life, that there was some truth in that. He didn't get angry very often, but on occasion he really blew up. Listening to Cassie say Griff called her a stupid, cowardly child set him off like dynamite detonated inside him. He clamped his jaw tightly shut and didn't let the words escape that were roaring around inside him. He'd already insulted her husband once today. He knew he didn't dare do it again. He'd remember her tears of grief for Lester Griffin if he lived to be a thousand.

Red prayed for restraint. He'd wrestled with his temper all his life, and the grace of God had helped him gain pretty good control of it. He froze his jaw solid and prayed and tried not to let his fury spread to his body for fear he'd squeeze Cassie so tight she'd squeak. And he asked God to forgive him because he was sorely afraid that if Lester Griffin had been standing in front of him right now, he'd have beaten him to within an inch of his worthless life.

Cassie seemed to be lost in her guilt about letting that no-account husband of hers die, so Red was free to struggle with his temper. He finally felt controlled enough to say through clenched teeth, "You're not stupid, and you're not a coward, and no woman who's gonna have a child any minute counts as a child herself. So Griff was wrong about that, too. Now, hold on 'cuz Buck is rested and we're gonna gallop."

He kicked Buck in the sides before she could respond to him, because he was very much afraid that if she called herself stupid and Griff smart again he was going to say something he'd regret. Buck broke into a ground-eating gallop. Red felt his horse's enjoyment of the hard run in the way Buck relaxed between Red's legs. Buck forgot about the fidgety woman who had been annoying him for the last week.

Red wasn't so lucky.

He had the jolting realization that he'd just fallen completely in love with his wife. His wife, who was still in love with the village idiot.

With murder in his heart, Wade watched Dawson and the china doll ride away.

He'd learned the woodlands around the Dawson place so well he could come within a hundred feet of the house without being seen. He didn't have his rifle today. Today he had other plans.

He saw the way Dawson held Cassie. Wade pulled the flask out of his hip pocket and tried to soothe the inferno of jealousy with the bitter whiskey. He touched the pearl handle of his six gun. He wasn't after Dawson today. He walked up to the front door of Dawson's decrepit shack and went inside.

He'd loved walking around inside the Griffin place. He'd loved to run his hands through the china doll's silks. He'd touched her combs and jewelry and kept strands of her hair until he'd gathered enough to make a little braid of it to keep in his pocket.

Now he needed more of her. It had been too long since he'd had her alone, as he sometimes did at Griffin's when her foolish husband went to town. Wade knew the fear he sensed in her was fear of her attraction to him. Any decent, married woman would be afraid of such stirrings. If he had just had his chance and the china doll wasn't bound to someone else, she would have turned to him.

He wandered through the house looking for signs of her. He didn't find a single dress. There was no silk or satin any-where. She had no mirror or hair combs that he could find. He gathered several strands of hair from her pillow, but there was nothing else.

"You've come down in the world, china doll. First you were married to a man who hurt you. Now you're married to a man who can't give you nice things." Wade took a long pull on his flask and savored how eager she would be to come to him.

"And maybe Red Dawson hurts you, too." Wade thought of Red putting his hands on the china doll and fury burned in his gut. "I want to rescue you from this."

He reached into his pocket and pulled a handkerchief out. It was so delicate that his calloused fingers snagged it when he rubbed it between them. He thought of leaving it for her. But he knew better than to let Dawson know he was around. And besides, he didn't want to give up this latest memento he'd claimed from the Griffin house. Most of the things had been taken out and sold to pay off the bills that no-account Lester

Montana Rose

Griffin had run up. There wouldn't be any more pieces of Cassie to collect. Wade rubbed the handkerchief and smelled the beautiful scent on it and pitied her.

Drinking deep of the whiskey fueled his anger, and he wanted to lash out and destroy this ugly home she'd been imprisoned in against her will. He raised his fist to smash the lantern, shouting, "Red Dawson stands in our way!"

Something almost echoed in the decrepit excuse for a house and Wade paused without wrecking the lantern. He listened again. The echo he'd heard wasn't his own voice. It was something else, something far away and quiet and small, but it seemed to burrow into him deeply. It was all wrong. He knew the way he was acting wasn't reasonable. But he couldn't stop thinking about the china doll. It ate at his gut to think of her trapped here, like Wade was trapped with his father. Wade wanted to run off, start a new life without Pa telling him every breath to take. But he couldn't leave the china doll. He had to save her. Then they'd run together.

Whatever that echo, it calmed him enough that he didn't smash the house to pieces and burn it to the ground. But he didn't stay and listen for it again either.

Instead he took a long pull from his whiskey bottle and stormed out before he did something stupid.

He needed to plan.

He needed to set her free.

CHAPTER 11

W here's Anthony, Ma?"

Lindsay lightly touched her roan's neck with the reins and used her knees to steer the horse close with its travois on the back, then swung down to help with the harvesting. Blond and pencil slim, thirteen-year-old Lindsay was as tough and competent as a seasoned cowhand.

Breathing a prayer of thanksgiving that none of her girls took after their pas, except in looks, Belle looked up from where she plucked a pumpkin off the vine. "I haven't seen him since the noon meal."

She set the pumpkin on the growing pile. The last of her fall garden was nearly stripped clean. She straightened and rested one hand on her back. Good thing the baby would come by spring. She didn't want to do branding while she was expecting. Her belly got in her way.

"What do you need him for?"

"These pumpkins are heavy, but it's not like it's really *hard* work. I thought maybe he'd pitch in." Lindsay pulled her pumpkin free with a *snap* of the crisp, dead vine.

Belle chuckled. "Well, you are a dreamer, youngster. I suppose you can hope, but it's not likely to happen."

"I saw him." Sarah came walking up from the derelict cabin they lived in. "He was sitting under the Husband Tree again. Did you ever tell him he was sitting on one of the husbands' graves?"

Belle straightened and looked up the long slope to the bluff that towered over her house. A lone oak where she'd buried William and Gerald. "Too bad he doesn't die up there and save me the work of hauling him up."

"He might live, Ma. Just because you've chosen men who proved to be rickety in the past doesn't mean Anthony won't last."

Belle knew that to be the absolute truth, but she could hope. The only good thing about being married to Anthony was it kept other men from coming around the place.

She settled her eyes on the oak tree, its branches swaying in the brisk fall breeze. Winter came early up this high. The first snow could come any time.

"And he doesn't get drunk near as often as my pa did." Sarah was too young to remember her pa, but Belle made sure Sarah heard all about him.

"And Anthony's never come after you with his fists." Lindsay picked up another pumpkin and set it in the heavily laden travois.

The horse snorted and shook its head, jangling the traces. But the animal stood still, trained well by Belle and Lindsay and Emma.

"I think he's just too plumb lazy to get after anyone." Belle grabbed the heavy orange pumpkin, remembering how heavy Gerald's fists could be. But he hadn't landed many blows. A well-placed frying pan had proven to calm him considerably. And once he knew she'd use it, he'd quit with the fists anyway, unless he was powerful drunk. And then he was easy to best.

"I like him up there better than on the roof." Lindsay stared at the man barely visible, leaning back against the tree trunk. "It gives me the creeps the way he sits up there like a turkey buzzard."

"Where's Emma?" Belle looked around, not alarmed, just curious. Her girls were completely competent around the ranch. She didn't spend too much time fussing after them.

"She's dragging windfall limbs out of the spreader dam. She wants to clear the water paths before they freeze."

"I've a mind to ride over to see the Dawson place one of these days."

"You're still worried about that woman they forced into marriage." Sarah straightened with a pumpkin nearly her own weight in her arms.

Belle smiled. Her girls knew how to *work*! "I just. . .well, honestly it's bothering me day and night. That little girl looked so trapped and scared." Belle shook her head, wishing she could dislodge the image. But even her dreams were haunted by Cassie. What if Red Dawson used his fists? Belle could protect herself, but Cassie wouldn't know how.

"You can get away once the fall garden is cleared."

"No, I've got three herds left to bring down from the high pasture. And the snow will close us in before you know it. What if I rode out and the snow came before I got back? I could be shut out until spring." The thought terrified Belle. Her girls stuck in here alone all winter. Oh, they'd survive. They were tough as all get-out. But it would be a hard, cold winter for them.

"How far is it? You could watch the weather. And the cattle, well, just because a snow closes the pass doesn't mean you can't still bring in cattle. It stays nicer in the valley than it does up on the gap."

"I think I'll do it." Belle rested her hand on her stomach

and thought of the long, hard ride up to her high pasture. She wished she'd dared to skip it this year. She'd have to be out overnight, and the ground seemed to be harder than when she was younger. Smiling at herself, she decided maybe she would wait until spring to ride up. If the cattle up there got hungry, they'd come down closer to the ranch. They knew where the hay was stacked.

"Maybe I'll ride over there in the next few days. There's one pasture that closes up early, and if I don't bring those cattle down, they'll have to spend months up there and the grass might not hold out. But most likely the cows will be all right. I don't think many cattle went up that high. And it'll bother me all winter if I don't go check on Cassie." Belle straightened and rested both hands on her back. Carrying pumpkins when she was round as a pumpkin herself was hard work. "And girls, I'll warn you right now. If I don't like what I see, I might just grab that girl and bring her back with me."

Lindsay brightened. "That'd be great, Ma. I'd like another sister."

Belle smiled. She'd seen the possessive look on Red's face. He wouldn't give up his property without a fight. But maybe she could check on the girl, and if she didn't like what she saw, she could pretend to leave, then watch the ranch, and when Red left, snatch Cassie and bring her home. The mountain gap would snow shut, and by spring maybe Belle could teach the girl how to handle herself. Give her a frying pan of her own. Belle had a spare.

Satisfied with her plan, she said, "I think I'll do it. We most likely have a few weeks before the first big snow, so I'll put off fetching down that one herd...maybe until spring. I'll make sure it's a fine day then just run over to the Dawson place and back."

"You rescue her if you've a mind to, Ma. It'd be fun to not be the oldest for a change."

Belle felt as righteous as a fire-and-brimstone preacher as she bent to pick up another bright orange pumpkin, thinking of the misery she could spare that poor little Cassie Dawson.

Cassie had never had so much fun in her life.

She laughed as the buckskin ran full out into the cool fall afternoon. What a wonder. Her husband *liked* her to laugh.

Red held on to her so tightly that she didn't think the baby had been bounced around much at all. He'd ridden straight to the general store, which surprised her. She expected him to go to the stable first and see to Buck. He'd jumped off the horse and lifted her down without a word. Then he'd caught her by the hand and dragged her into the store and found Muriel.

"Cassie needs somewhere to spend the afternoon," he snapped at Muriel.

Cassie turned to look at him, wondering where that angry voice had come from.

"She doesn't know the first thing about having a baby either. Could you talk to her?"

Cassie felt her cheeks grow so hot with embarrassment she half expected her head to ignite. She dipped her chin down so no one could see her red face.

"Hmm..." Muriel said no words, but the sound, well, Cassie glanced up at the woman and saw some strange kind of satisfaction on Muriel's face as she looked between her and Red.

A smile lurked behind Muriel's understanding nod. Cassie didn't have time to beg Red not to leave her because he must have taken that noise to be agreement on Muriel's part. After his abrupt request, he took off like the building was afire.

Cassie looked after him, worried that it was something she'd said. "Maybe I should—"

"He's a man. Ignore him." Muriel caught Cassie's hand and

pulled her toward a table full of gingham. "We'll just have a nice chat. I don't get to visit with womenfolk much."

"He's a man. Ignore him"? Cassie thought those words might well qualify as blasphemy before God. Griff would have certainly said they did.

"I just got a shipment of dress goods in on the noon freight wagon. Can you help me stack them on this shelf over here, Cassie?"

Cassie was relieved to be asked to help rather than be given a lecture on the details of something so personal as childbirth. "I'd be glad to help."

Long before Red came back, Cassie and Muriel were fast friends. Cassie couldn't believe this nice lady had lived so close to her for two years and they'd never spoken beyond polite niceties.

Libby Jeffreys came over to put in her usual weekly order and pick up a few necessities that couldn't wait until Red delivered the supplies. Seth came in and out of the store, filling Libby's order, and left the women alone.

Muriel poured coffee, and Libby stayed for over an hour, drinking coffee and laughing over the comings and goings of Divide. Leota Pickett came just as Libby was leaving, and Libby settled back into the rocking chair, one of four Muriel had by her potbellied stove, and accepted another cup of coffee.

Cassie realized all of them were hungry for talk with another woman. She'd never known it before today, but she was hungry for it, too.

They all gave her polite words of sympathy for Griff and asked avidly how life was with Red. Somehow, without her noticing, they started talking about babies. Libby had two sons, grown and on their own, both bachelors living nearby. Leota Pickett had five young'uns at home, the littlest still in diapers. Muriel surprised Cassie when she talked about two children she'd lost in a diphtheria outbreak just before they moved west. There were never any more children for her and Seth. Muriel's grief was old, and Cassie had the impression it was almost a comfort to her because it was all she had left of the two toddlers she'd lost.

The ladies started talking about how they brought the children into the world, giving shockingly specific details, then laughing wildly over things they'd said and done during their laboring. Cassie was only vaguely aware that she was learning dozens of things she needed to know about delivering a baby. And Muriel promised she'd come and help bring the baby, saying she'd done it many times, including for Leota's youngest. All Cassie had to do was send word. Cassie wasn't sure how she'd do that, but Muriel mentioned that there was a ranch owned by a family of bachelors only a thirty-minute ride from Red's holding. Red would have plenty of time to ride to the Jessups' and one of the Jessup hands could come to town.

They had everything settled, and Muriel had even come up with a swatch of cloth that matched Cassie's singed dress. After Libby left, Muriel and Leota sewed on a patch while Cassie was still in the dress. She sat and watched them.

The two older ladies had dozens of suggestions for house-keeping that were a revelation to Cassie. And with a little en-couragement, she told them about her week, including the array of mishaps that had befallen Red.

The ladies laughed hysterically until they couldn't keep stitching. Cassie didn't understand their wild laughter at Red's expense, but they wouldn't let her feelings remain wounded. They teased her until she was laughing with them and told her little ideas for handling livestock and gardens and lanterns. Cassie absorbed every word.

Leota overstayed the time she should be away from her children. She explained to Cassie about Red taking over some of the stable chores so Maynard could come in from work early on Saturday, and how Leota cherished her few minutes at the general store with Muriel and her long evening with her husband at hand for a change. Then Leota hurried off.

Muriel propped a sign on the counter that said customers should holler for help. She took Cassie into the back to start supper. Cassie was able to help Muriel, but Muriel had lots of little tips for preparing dishes. Cassie remembered working beside her mother in the kitchen occasionally when she was a child, but her mother had employed a cook, so preparing meals was a special event. Her mother's advice returned to her some because Muriel had the same patient way of talking.

The general store had a busy time later in the afternoon, and Muriel couldn't visit with her anymore.

"I think I'll start delivering Libby's supplies to the diner," Cassie said.

Muriel shook her head as she filled an order. "You just leave that for Red, now, Cassie. I'm not allowing you to tote bags and boxes."

"But I want to help," Cassie insisted. "I feel guilty letting Red pay all our bills. Red told me work and money are the same thing, so it'll be like I'm paying for my dresses myself."

"You're a sweet girl to want to help, but—" The bell rang and another customer came in. Muriel didn't have time to talk. "Go ahead then. Libby's things are stacked by the back door. But just take small things, and promise me the minute you get tired, you'll stop. Any little thing you take will lighten the load for Red later."

"I'll be sure to quit when I get tired." Cassie hurried to the back door, feeling like she was really contributing to the ranch at last. Then she saw the mountain of food Seth had set aside for Libby. Cassie's inclination was to forget about helping, but she'd made too big a deal about it, and remembering Muriel's words that even a little bit would help, Cassie decided she'd just carry one thing at a time.

Cassie appeared in Libby's Diner with a fifty-pound bag of flour in her arms. "Where do you want this?"

"What in the world are you doing carrying that heavy thing?" Libby rushed to lift it out of her arms. "You're in a delicate condition. Red would have my head if I let you deliver my groceries."

Cassie didn't want Libby to get in trouble. "I'll just carry lighter things from now on. I'll leave the big loads for Red. I promise."

She hurried away before Libby could forbid her to help. She crossed Main Street, went through the alley to the back of the general store, and went in. The door didn't close behind her, and she turned to see a crowd of men. Each of them scraped their feet a bit and apologized for following her and picked up a case of this or a crate of that. They delivered Libby's groceries in one trip.

Cassie followed them back, carrying a small basket of eggs. She sheepishly offered them to Libby. "Does this ruin Red's job? Neither of us did the work. We shouldn't get paid for it."

Libby just laughed. "You are a natural, honey."

"A natural what?" Cassie didn't know what she meant.

Libby laughed harder.

All the men had quietly returned to their seats and were eating at the meals they'd deserted.

Cassie gathered every ounce of courage she had, plus manufactured a little from out of thin air, and said, "Thank you all so much for your help. I appreciate it more than you can ever know." ·

Every man stared at her as if she'd spoken some foreign tongue. Then all jumbled together they said, "You're welcome, Miz Dawson," or, "Glad to help, ma'am," or something like that.

Cassie thought she heard someone say, "Red's a lucky man." It occurred to her that any of these men might have asked her to marry him a week ago.

Cassie went back to Muriel's.

Muriel was bustling back and forth, filling one order after another. Finally Cassie, who was sitting in rather nervous silence at the heating stove, gathered her wits about her enough to start helping. She really thought she did help this time. The crowd dispersed quickly after her efforts doubled the speed with which the customers, all men, were waited on. She acknowledged all their kind remarks and asked their names. Griff's words about them being riffraff echoed in her ears.

Muriel heaved a sigh of relief when the store finally emptied. She turned to Cassie and said, "If Red is going to keep coming in here and doing his odd jobs every Saturday, why don't I hire you to work with me here. Saturday afternoon is my busiest time. I'd love the help as well as the company. Once the baby comes, we'll set up a cradle, and any time the baby needs you to nurse him or change his diapers, you'll be able to take a break in the back room."

"It sounds just fine, Muriel. I'd be glad to help. Would you let me work off Griff's bill and then use what I earn toward the supplies Red and I need?"

Muriel said, "Griff's bill is taken care of, but you can swap for supplies."

"I'd need to ask Red first. But if it's okay with him, I'd be most grateful for the chance. Do you think I dare to make all the men in town deliver Libby's groceries every week?"

"What?"

Cassie told her how she'd managed to deliver that mountain of supplies.

Muriel laughed until she had to wipe her eyes on her calico dress.

So Cassie, who'd become the china doll for her last husband, became an odd-job girl for her next one. She thought it was an improvement.

CHAPTER 12

"Cass, wake up."

She had the odd sensation of being a baby back in her mother's arms. Being rocked gently back and forth. She fell back asleep. The rocking continued.

"Cass honey, wake up. We gotta go."

The gentle voice kept pestering her. She was disoriented for a few seconds.

Red crouched in front of her; his hand rocked her shoulder and he spoke in hushed tones. "I'm sorry it got so late. I had more to do than usual. And thanks for delivering the groceries. Libby told me all about it."

Cassie realized she was asleep on Muriel's couch in the dim light of early evening.

The first thing she thought of was how she'd ruined his job at the diner. She whispered because he was whispering. "I'm sorry, did Libby still pay you? I didn't mean—" She stopped her mumbled apology when Red smiled at her.

"Don't worry about it. Libby said if they volunteer to help you when you're doing my work and the job gets done, it's all the same to her."

Cassie pushed against the couch, her stomach a bit unwieldy in her groggy state. Red slipped his arms under her shoulders and knees and lifted her into his arms. She was fat with the baby, but he lifted her as if he didn't notice her weight.

He continued speaking softly. "Muriel said you'd eaten with her and Seth. Then we decided to let you sleep while she fed me and told me about the job she offered you."

"Is that okay with you, Red? She was really busy. I just pitched in to help her. It was only after we were done that she suggested paying me."

"It's fine for now, but I told her when the baby got closer it might be too much for you. We don't want you to be exhausted now, do we?" He hefted her up and down a few times in his arms as if to remind her that she was indeed very tired or she wouldn't be cradled in his arms this way.

"I'll be careful, Red. Muriel will know what I can and can't do." Cassie leaned closer to him to share her wonderful discovery. "Muriel knows everything about babies. She and Libby and Leota told me so much today. I feel smarter already. Except then later I thought of a lot of questions, so I want to talk to them again. And the way they just talked and talked about having babies and caring for them, like it was the most natural thing in the world to do, it made me feel better about everything. And, I. . .I shouldn't have done it because it was disloyal to Griff, but I said about an expectant mother being unclean and. . .oh, Red, the things they said about Griff. It wasn't right at all and I made them stop, but maybe there are more ways than just his of seeing things." Cassie laid her heavy head on his shoulder, exhausted and a little shocked at the way she was chattering and saying such a horrible thing about Griff. She'd have never admitted that if she wasn't still half asleep.

"I got us a room at Grant's. 'Bye, Seth, Muriel, and thanks."

Montana Rose

Only then, as Red carried her out of the room, did Cassie realize Seth and Muriel had been standing just behind him the whole time. She felt her cheeks heat up at the thought that they'd seen Red hold her so close. She thought about the whispered conversation she and Red just had and realized she'd been unconsciously keeping quiet because she'd thought everyone else in the house was asleep. Next she wasn't sure if she'd said critical words to Red about the ladies for being upset at Griff. She peeked around Red and said, "Good-bye."

Seth waved and Muriel had a satisfied smile similar to the one she'd had this afternoon when Red had left Cassie in her care.

Cassie worried the whole way to Grant's Hotel. Then she realized Red had carried her the entire distance, right down Main Street, and she worried about that. It was quiet and all the businesses were closed. The only thing lit up was the Golden Butte, and tinny music came out of the swinging saloon doors.

She was still consumed with her doubts when Red set her down in their room. Letting him carry her the whole way was so rude. "Is it very late, Red? It gets dark early this time of year, but it's not full dark. We don't have to go to bed yet if you don't want to."

"I have preachin' tomorrow 'cuz Parson Bergstrom is out of town. I've already thought of what I want to say, but I want to spend a little time studyin' on it, so if it's all right with you, I'll sit up for a while with the lantern on. If it doesn't disturb you, that is. I think you should sleep, Cass. You've had a big day. If my reading bothers you, Lars will let me use his dining room."

"I'm sure you won't bother me," Cassie said politely. She felt anxious at the idea of his leaving her alone in this unfamiliar room.

"Okay then, I'll read in here. I'll give you a few minutes of privacy to get ready for bed." Red politely left the room while she hurried around to find her nightgown.

She changed, and when she was ready, she cracked the door open an inch and peeked out. He was leaning patiently against the wall straight across from her door, reading a Bible.

"I'm ready now," she said shyly. "You can come back."

She ducked behind the door and crawled into bed quickly before Red came in.

Red sat in a rocker, reading his big black Bible by lantern light.

She thought it was the most comforting sight in the world. "What are you reading?"

"I'm going to talk about marriage tomorrow morning. That's all I ever do, talk about what I've done during the week and how God has been with me. I don't exactly preach a regular sermon. I'm studying with the parson to be a licensed minister. He's helping me get approved through his mission society so I can take over in Divide and he can serve other towns."

"Is that hard, to get licensed?"

Red shrugged and she saw his strong shoulders rise. He carried a lot of weight on them, with no complaint. "It's a lot of Bible study, but I like doing that anyway, so no, I wouldn't call it hard."

She compared Red's tattered Bible with the massive elegant book her family had handed down. No one had ever read it because it was printed in German. It was only for recording family history and for show. Her mother had often told her it was a gift to royalty, given to Cassie's countess great-grandmother back in Spain. She ached to think of giving it up, but it couldn't be helped now.

On a soft sigh, she relaxed as she watched Red's competent hands silently turn the tissue-thin page. She decided she liked Red's Bible better.

She fell asleep almost instantly.

Montana Rose

Red always got to sleep late on Sunday.

It was something he'd been doing ever since he'd taken over the preaching at Divide, as if his body had a clock of its own and it knew he was miles from his stock and his morning chores. Usually he was outside on the hard ground, something he enjoyed. Although in the winter, it got a little rugged. Muriel had been known to let him sleep on the floor inside, since they held the church services in the general store. But this morning he woke in a soft feather bed. One he'd turned and beaten himself just yesterday. He could still smell the fresh outdoors on it from when he'd let it lie in the sunlight for a while.

He didn't think much about the smell and the fluffed-up feathers. They were just a little slice of pleasure added to how Cassie felt in his arms. She was hanging on him just like every morning. Red took a long time praying his thanks to God for how nice she felt. He marveled at how wonderful heaven must be if it was better than how he was feeling right now.

He had plenty of time before he needed to get up for services. They didn't hold them until real late, nine o'clock, so people could get their morning chores done and get in from out of town.

The time at church was Red's favorite time of the week. He wasn't a man who believed you had to go to church to talk to God. He carried God with him in his heart all the time, but he loved the joy that rose up in his soul when he talked and sang with other believers. Sharing his faith as a preacher inspired him to study his Bible and pray to God a dozen times a day. He found something exciting every time he read, and God touched his life in a hundred ways during the week that he wanted to tell people about.

He didn't run a church service in a very normal way. He

didn't exactly preach a sermon like Parson Bergstrom did. He'd just start talking about something he'd read and how he'd reacted to it. He'd ask the people who were there what they thought about his impressions, and they'd all end up talking long and hard about the Bible verse he'd selected that week.

He was especially looking forward to this Sunday morning. Being married had given him a new angle on a lot of the Bible. He was viewing love from a husband's perspective now, and that had given a depth to several Bible stories that he'd never thought of in quite the same way.

He kept coming back to Ephesians and the directive from Paul for wives to submit themselves to their husbands. There were three verses that talked about wives, and Red figured that was where the wedding vows got the word *obey* for wives but not for husbands. Then for the next ten or so verses it told husbands all they had to do for their wives. Care for her as he would his own body. Love her as Christ loved the church. Die for her if need be just as Christ died for everyone. The Bible made far more demands on the husband than it did on the wife. And Red reckoned that if a man held up his end of the bargain, no wife in the world would have trouble obeying a man that decent.

He hugged Cassie a little tighter and smiled to himself. Cassie didn't obey worth a hoot. But then Red didn't exactly order her around either. It just wasn't in his nature to be bossy. His main goal in life was to protect her from one brush with death after another without hurting her feelings any.

He kissed the top of her head as he did every morning and admitted she was getting a little better. She never made the same mistake twice. It was just that she kept coming up with new ways to kill herself and him with her. He thought if they could just live out the next couple of weeks, she might turn into about the best little wife a man ever had.

He got kicked in the side, and Red almost trembled from

the stunning sensation of a little life growing inside Cassie. The tiny assault drew him from his satisfying musing about marriage to a more personal inspection of his lawfully wedded wife.

Cassie's head nestled on his left shoulder. Her black hair had been braided when she went to bed, but as it did most nights, it escaped her ribbons. It was spread across his chest and her back all the way to her waist. Her left leg was hooked over his. Her warm belly rested between their bodies, and maybe the little feller was saying it was too tight a squeeze because he seemed to be trying to knock himself a little more space.

Red's arm rested across the top of Cassie's stomach, and he didn't resist the temptation to brush her hair aside, smoothing it over and over. Once in a while the babe moved so vigorously that Red thought he must be doing a somersault. He laughed silently at the energetic tyke and longed for the day he'd come on out and join the family.

Red knew he ought to just slip out of bed as he did most mornings at home, but this was Sunday and they had a good hour to dress and eat breakfast before services. He had no excuse to tear himself away. So he smoothed her hair and held her close and decided Sunday, already his favorite day, had just become about a hundredfold better.

Cassie's breathing became slightly less regular, and he knew she was waking up. He watched her face closely, eager to memorize every nuance of her expression when she realized how she was clinging to him. Like the mornings when he hadn't slipped away quickly enough, he expected her to pull back in alarm and put about a foot of space between them. He didn't mind, not too much. He thought her trust in him and her desire to be close to him when she was sleeping was a good sign because her actions weren't all clouded up with grief and embarrassment. She honestly liked to be held in her sleep, and he thought with time that would spread into the daytime. And he'd be glad to be the one to hold her for the rest of her life.

She rubbed her cheek against the bristly hair that peeked through the top of his nightshirt, even turning a bit to lightly scratch her nose. She muttered a bit and the babe kicked again. Cassie's hand glided slowly across Red's waist to rest on her stomach. Her eyes fluttered open and she stared straight at Red.

Quickly before she could pull away, Red ran one finger down the curve of her cheek and said, "I like feelin' the babe move this way. Thank you for lying close to me like this."

Red felt her control that little jump of embarrassment that accompanied waking every morning. Instead, she let her hand rest on the baby, and Red's hand joined hers and they stared at the visibly moving white flannel on her belly and just incidentally went on holding each other.

After her muscles had relaxed against him, Red said, "Tell me what all Muriel and Libby and Leota said about babies yesterday."

Cassie surprised him by laughing. He thought that meant she was comfortable hugged up against him and that made him happy.

"Oh Red, the things they said right out loud. Private things I'd never before heard anyone say."

Red tilted her chin up. "Now Cass, just because you've never heard it before doesn't mean no one else has. You've been mighty sheltered, with your mama dying when you were so young and Griff being uncomfortable talking about such things. I want you to talk to me about this. I'm telling you right now, nothing is too personal for a wife to say to her husband."

Cassie nodded. "You're right. It just seemed so. . .sort of wicked, I guess. But they aren't wicked ladies. I know that. So I decided to listen and learn and we ended up laughing at the whole business of delivering a baby into the world. Muriel asked me terribly personal questions and I answered all I could. She. . . she wanted to know how evenly my l–lady's time was spaced. When I told her sometimes months apart, she wanted to know how long before I missed my. . .time had I been. . .been. . ." Cassie stopped talking.

Red rubbed one finger down the length of her nose. "Say it, Cass."

"She wanted to know when Griff and I had. . .had seen to his. . ." Cassie had buried her face more and more in his chest. "His husbandly. . .prerogatives." She glanced at him when she was finished and her face was blazing red.

Red wanted to blush, too. When he'd said they could talk about anything, he hadn't expected this. He wanted to yell at her that he didn't want to hear about her and Griff, but he stayed calm because he'd be taking back all he'd said about them talking about anything. "And what did you say?"

"I said I wasn't sure exactly but it was the one in the winter."

"The one in the. . ." Red choked his startled question.

Cassie looked at him uncertainly and he struggled valiantly to keep a straight face.

She looked back at his chest. "Yes, and very often the one in the winter was toward the end, so early to mid-March. Then, when I said that, for some reason they all three started laughing like crazy and they wouldn't tell me why. I guess it's because I don't know anything and that struck them funny, but they didn't want to hurt my feelings by saying so. Then Muriel said the baby would come in mid-December. That's six weeks. And she told me how to know the laboring had started and that you're to send word to the neighbors and one of the Jessup hands would come for her. Is that all right?"

Red heaved a sigh of relief at the suggestion. He'd been terrified that he'd have to deliver the baby on his own. He'd seen a lot of baby animals born and even aided a few cattle that were having trouble, but he'd been having nightmares about being alone and letting Cassie and the baby die because of some stupid mistake. "Yes, that's a good idea. The Jessups will be perfect. They're good friends of mine."

Cassie revealed details about having babies that Red found extremely embarrassing. He realized she'd taken his order to talk about everything to heart. For a while he wondered if he'd started something he was going to regret because he didn't want to know some of this stuff, but he'd made the rule. He couldn't quite believe Cassie was telling him all of these amazingly indelicate things.

Then with dawning delight, it occurred to him that Cassie had obeyed him. The more he thought about it, the more he remembered dozens of times when she'd quietly obeyed him in the last week. He'd just been lying here thinking that she didn't obey worth a hoot, but that wasn't true.

She wasn't disobedient. She was incompetent.

Her attempts to help around the ranch were well-meant efforts to obey his pronouncement the first day that he'd like her to milk and garden and gather eggs. He hugged her a little closer and controlled a shudder at the graphic things she was saying to him. He wondered if women talked like this all the time or had Muriel taken his gruff edict that Cassie didn't know anything about having a baby seriously and swallowed her own embarrassment.

He did his best to ignore what Cassie was saying and decided the next week was going to be different. He wasn't going to resist her attempts to help anymore. He was going to teach her, just like Muriel had done.

Cassie took a break from her gory tales of blood and screaming women, tales that didn't seem to be upsetting her at all, and Red said, "We have to get up and go to church now."

"Yes, Red." She rolled away from him, got up, and began collecting her clothes.

Red's heart expanded at how instantly she'd submitted to him. It made him feel like a king. He wasn't sure it was Christian to feel like a king, so he tried not to enjoy it too much.

CHAPTER 13

Cassie was surprised when Red went to the back door of Bates General Store and went in without bothering to knock.

He went through the hallway that passed the living quarters without making his presence known to anyone and started moving things around in the store, clearing a space for people to gather around the stove.

Cassie started to help, but Red said, "Not the pickle barrel, Cass. I'll get that. It's too heavy for you and it spills easy. If you want to help, pull the lighter barrels to one side, the crackers, and those crates of apples."

Cassie did as he directed but wished she was more sure of what all needed to be moved. Red never was one to give very good orders, leaving it to her to figure it out alone. She much preferred being told specifically what to do.

She took everything light, which was a goodly share of the stacks of supplies in the store, and he took everything heavy. After just a few minutes, Red called a halt, saying there was room enough for everyone to gather.

Muriel came in about then and stopped short. "I would

have lent a hand, Red. I was poky this morning."

"Nah, we were fast. Cass did most of it." Red smiled over at her and her heated cheeks told her she was blushing.

Muriel went to the front door, picking her way carefully through the jumbled merchandise. She unlocked the door. "Cassie's a worker, all right. She saved the day yesterday. I declare I would still be here filling orders if she hadn't taken a hand."

Cassie thought her head would explode from the effort to contain her pride. *"Cassie's a worker."* She'd never heard it said about her before.

Libby came in just in time to hear the last of Muriel's comment. Her husband was just behind her and several more people were with them. "You should have seen her bring my supplies, Red. She carried a fifty-pound bag of flour in her arms like a baby and asked as sweet as you please where she should set it and that she'd be back with the rest. Every man in the place stood up from his chair as if they had springs in their backsides and just followed her back to Muriel 'n Seth's."

Libby's husband, Ralph Jeffreys, laughed, and Cassie looked at Red again, uncertain if she robbed him of his honest pay.

Ralph said, "I was there when she came back, carrying, what was it, Cassie, a can of peaches or a. . ."

"It was eggs," a man just entering the store said. "We weren't about to let this pretty li'l lady, with a baby on the way to boot, carry five hundred pounds of groceries for you. I'm right ashamed of you for asking her to, Libby Jeffreys."

Libby turned in outrage. "I never asked her to carry five hundred. . ." Libby saw who was talking, gasped out loud, and chuckled. "Sam, you scalawag! I didn't know you were back from hauling."

The newcomer came and lifted Libby into a bear hug, laughing. "Howdy, Ma. Just teasin'."

He tipped his hat to Cassie, who had backed a little away

from the growing crowd until she was standing pressed against Red. Red rested his hand on her waist and anchored her to his side.

In the next ten minutes, the general store became crowded with people, friendly and happy to see each other. Red greeted each of them by name and shook hands. He introduced Cassie to them and she said, "Hello," trying to put names and faces together. She recognized quite a few of them from yesterday in the store, and although she continued to greet them by name once they'd been introduced, she soon gave up any hope of remembering all these men, overwhelmed by the sea of strangers.

She did know Norman York, and she tried to remember Leota Pickett's husband and the little Pickett children. Children were a rarity in Divide and they were enchanting to her. She was sure she'd never forget their names.

Then as quickly as the people began crowding in, everyone settled into silence, and Red left her side and stood close to the heating stove. He said, "Let's start with a prayer."

Cassie found herself startled to have her husband in charge. Of course she'd known he was leading the service. He'd said so often enough. But somehow she hadn't really thought what that meant. It had just seemed like another of his many jobs. Now a strong surge of pride in her handsome husband swelled in her chest as he took charge of this large group.

She remembered the fire-and-brimstone preaching she'd grown up with in Illinois, and she waited for that kind of intensity to come out of Red. But Red just stayed his sweet, quiet self. He prayed in front of all these people with the same casual, loving manner he'd used before their meals.

Halfway through his prayer—Cassie expected it was only halfway because she'd heard a lot of praying as a child and knew it was a lengthy proceeding—Red said, "Many petitions in prayer are pleasing to the Lord. Would anyone like some concern of his heart lifted up to God?" A deep voice behind her spoke to God about his brother's broken leg healing straight and strong. Another asked for his ailing mother in St. Louis to be remembered. And so it went. There were many needs in the West and many worries.

She could sense burdens lifting as they all put their worries before God and prayed together. She didn't speak out loud, but for the first time in a long time, she prayed, too. She prayed for her baby's health and for Red's safety and for more of the chickens to come back. Then Red surprised her by resting his hand on her shoulder. He'd moved away from her when he'd started talking, but he had moved closer to her during the prayer. He prayed for Griff, for God to shelter his immortal soul. Then Red thanked God for her.

Cassie couldn't contain a tiny gasp of pleasure. Red didn't ask God to make her less clumsy and stupid. He didn't pray for childlike Cassie Griffin Dawson to quit shaming him and grow up. He thanked God so kindly for making her his wife that she couldn't help but believe he meant it. And he prayed for the baby and prayed quite fervently for Muriel to get there in plenty of time to help deliver it. That made everyone laugh, which Cassie didn't understand, but the laughter, laced with the sweet prayer and Red's kindhearted thanks for her, had lifted her spirits so that she laughed a little herself with the pure pleasure of the day.

Then Red said his, "Amen," and moved back to where he'd stood in front of everyone and started talking about marriage. He didn't preach a sermon like any she'd heard before, and the congregation seemed to feel free to interrupt him as often as they liked. One man said marriage was a bad subject since so few of them were married.

Red said, "Leave your cattle to the wolves and go find a wife. It's worth it."

Everyone laughed and Cassie was so pleased with Red she was sorely tempted to cry.

He talked about a wife obeying her husband and how all the burden lay with the husband, because he is called to love her more than his own body and to never do anything to harm her soul, so a man must never ask a woman to obey anything that is against her own ideas of right and wrong.

Seth told him to change the subject before Muriel got the bit in her teeth.

Muriel said, "When have I ever obeyed you anyway, old man?"

All in all it was the oddest and most wonderful church service Cassie had ever attended. It didn't escape Cassie's notice that Red very quietly kept things from straying from the basic subject of his selected Bible verse.

A spirited debate bounced back and forth between people of goodwill with lots of laughter and a warm display of genuine love between the three married couples: the Bates, the Jeffreys, and the Picketts. It dawned on Cassie after a bit that she hadn't included the Dawsons in that count of married people.

And as she thought of the questions Red had asked and how they applied to her, she thought, *I'll be proud to obey you, Red.*

The whole room turned to face her and it took her a second to realize she must have spoken her thoughts aloud. She wasn't sure if she blushed or not. She'd done so much of it lately it was getting harder and harder to humiliate herself. It didn't matter. They wouldn't have stared at her any harder if she'd grown a second head.

Red moved from his spot at the front of the group and stood beside her.

Cassie wasn't sure if her outspoken comment had shamed him or not, and despite everything she'd learned about Red this week, she couldn't control the surge of fear that he would punish her for talking out loud in public like that.

"Cass, I am a lucky man. I reckon you will obey me, 'cuz you're such a sweet thing, you'd just naturally do your best to make me happy. But I want you to know I won't ask you to go against your conscience, and I'll listen if you disagree with me. And if you are ever upset with me, it'll be as much my doing as yours, so you can speak right out and never be afraid of me."

Cassie remembered her first wedding to Griff, with her wild desire to die along with him and her terror of the Sawyers and the surly mob keeping her ears deaf to what was being said. Now they stood before believers and Cassie looked into Red's eyes. "I'm lucky, too. Thank you for marrying me. I know you didn't want to."

Red smiled. "I didn't think I should, but that's a long way from not wanting to. I wanted to marry you something fierce, Cass honey."

He leaned down, and Cassie thought he was going to kiss her. They hadn't kissed since their wedding night, and that had been her doing. Although she'd dreamed that he'd kissed her hair several times while she'd slept beside him and the dreams had been nice. Now maybe he was going to do it for real.

Wade Sawyer chose that minute to slam the door open. "I got an order here, Seth. I need it right now!"

Wade's belligerence broke into the pleasant church service and garnered everybody's attention.

Muriel slammed her fists on her hips and stepped in front of Wade. "See here, Wade. We're closed on the Lord's Day and well you know it."

Wade swaggered up to Seth, who had stepped to Muriel's side. He ignored Muriel as if she were nothing more than a buzzing mosquito to be brushed aside as a nuisance. "I've ridden all the way into town and you're here doin' nothin'. I'm not goin' back without my order. You've done enough Bible thumpin' for the week."

Seth said quietly, "We've been over this before, Wade. There's someone in from the Sawyer outfit nearly every day of the week. I know for a fact you were in town yesterday."

"Don't tell me you won't fill my order." Wade stepped forward, looking hard into Seth's eyes. "I saw Belle Tanner loading a wagon just last week. If you'll do it for that woman, you'll do it for me and like it."

"Belle had to make a special trip and she almost never comes to town from clear out where she lives. Of course I was willing to help her out. The Sawyer place is right outside of town. Leave the order. We'll have it ready first thing tomorrow, and when someone from your ranch is in town, he can pick it up."

Wade's eyes narrowed, then they shifted past the Bates and found Cassie.

Dread twisted in her gut like it always did when Wade was too near. She saw in his greedy green eyes that awful hunger, that fixated look that was only for her. He hadn't come in here to get supplies. He'd come in because he'd known she was here.

That sounded like her pride talking, thinking Wade was interested in her. But for whatever reason, it was true. She knew it. Wade's eyes reminded her that she knew how to shoot a gun—she was quick and accurate, and just maybe, with those mean eyes on her, she could even find the courage to pull the trigger. Of course this was the second time in a week that she'd come face-to-face with Wade and didn't have her gun handy.

She took a step back and bumped into Red. He put his arm around her waist. Red's hand was an anchor in a sea of fear. She grabbed his hand with both of hers and held it firmly around her.

"Miz Griffin." Wade tipped his hat.

"It's Dawson now," Red corrected him in a mild tone.

"Oh, yeah. The widow lady remarried. I seem to remember she was so anxious for a man that she stood plumb on the fresh-turned dirt of her dead husband to take her vows."

Several people in the crowd gasped. Cassie didn't know if it was because of her and the location of her marriage or Wade's callous words.

"Wherever she took her vows, Wade, she took 'em." Red sounded so quiet, but Cassie heard the strength behind his words and hung on to him even harder.

Wade reached one hand into his pocket and several men tensed as his hand moved near the gun that hung low on his hip.

Cassie remembered again that she'd learned to shoot, but now she didn't even have a gun anymore. It had been lost when her home had been taken for the mortgage.

Wade pulled something from his pocket. "Me and Pa are runnin' your old place, china doll. The bank took everything you and your worthless husband had left. We found some things left behind. It's trash but you might want it." Wade unfolded what he was holding and very deliberately pulled his knife and slashed it in half, then slashed it again. He wadded up the pieces into a tight ball and tossed them at Cassie.

Cassie flinched away, but Red's hand came up and deftly caught them. Cassie reached for them, but Red whispered, "Later, Cass. Not in front of Wade."

Wade said, "We'll use your house for a line shack. It's a fool's house. Too big to heat and too far from our ranch for any use. Maybe we can store hay in it."

Cassie was surprised that his insults toward her house didn't upset her. The fact that she didn't care about the house gave her the strength to face Wade straight on and wave her hand carelessly. "If the house is yours, then do with it what you will. It's nothing to me."

"Even after the floors rot and the rats move in it'll be better than the hole you're livin' in now with Dawson."

Cassie gasped indignantly. Odd how the slur against Griff's house left her unmoved but his insults to Red's house were fighting words. She met Wade's eyes but she couldn't hold the look. Wade's eyes burned with something that had always scared her. She still had the china doll inside her, and she said placidly, "Red's got a wonderful home. We have everything we need."

Wade's face contorted into rage. "So then you must have Dawson bowin' and scrapin' for you just like you had Griffin."

Cassie saw Wade's weasel eyes shift to Red. "I often wondered what she did for Griff that he'd let her walk all over him like that. Tell me, Dawson. Does she earn your favors like a real flesh-and-blood woman? Or is she as cold as the china doll she seems to be?"

Red suddenly moved, and Cassie felt his anger at Wade's crudity. She caught him with a quick backward move of her hands.

She said clearly, so clearly that it was possible Mort Sawyer could have heard her out at the ranch, "Remember we're in church, Red. And remember the man who won has to be big enough to stand a few temper tantrums from the loser." She looked over her shoulder and smiled sweetly at Red.

He glared down at her for a second, obviously frustrated, then he relaxed. "Only 'cuz we're in church, Cass. The 'temper tantrum' comment from you wouldn't have saved him any other time."

"Saved me?" Wade blustered. "The day a man can hide behind a woman's skirts and that'll stop. . ."

"Enough, Sawyer. We're in the middle of church." This was from Norm York. "Your pa wanted Cassie's spring and he paid a fair price for it. You Sawyers got what you wanted. You've no call to come in here insulting a fine woman and threatening Red. You're standing in front of dozens of witnesses to your actions, and you can't get away with starting anything. And if something happens to them any other time, you're the first one we'll come looking for. So you'd better pray they don't even accidentally get hurt. If you want to stay and hear the preaching, we welcome you."

Suddenly Mr. York's voice became very sincere. "We do, Wade. Forget all this anger and stay. We have God here with us, and you need to hear about Him. There is always room for anyone who wants to worship the Lord. But the store is closed on Sunday and always has been, as you well know. We need to get back to services."

Cassie noticed that every man in the place squared off against Wade, some moving to place themselves between Wade and her until she couldn't see him anymore. Even though anyone from out of town would have a rifle on his horse because of the dangers along the trail, none of them brought a gun into church. Wade was the only one armed.

Seconds stretched to a minute.

Cassie leaned sideways to see Wade. His eyes, burning with anger, shifted from one man to another. He flexed his fingers as if fighting the urge to destroy anyone who thwarted him. His eyes connected with Cassie and they held. Under the anger and hunger, Cassie saw something else. Some deep longing that told her Wade wasn't just fighting because he was a troublemaker. Wade's desperate yearning aimed straight at her made her shudder deep inside.

With a sneer, Wade's hand dropped away from his gun. "This isn't over, Dawson. You got what's mine and I aim to get it back."

She couldn't see him anymore, and she stayed behind Red, not wanting Wade's eyes on her. But she heard the obsession in his voice, and icy fingers of fear crawled up her spine and grabbed at her throat.

She saw him again as he turned and wrenched the door open, slamming it behind him so hard the glass rattled.

The congregation stood silently for a moment. Cassie saw

fear on many of the men's faces. She knew the ruthless Sawyer bunch had made dreadful enemies.

Finally Red broke the silence. "Let's bow our heads and pray for Wade and his father."

Several people turned sharply to face Red, their faces revealing they were not ready to let go of their anger or fear. Most nodded soberly.

"He's so lost," Muriel said.

Cassie couldn't believe the gentle murmur of agreement. Not a minute ago a fight brewed that might end in the deaths of some of the people in this room. Now they were praying for a man they so obviously feared.

She thought of her practice with Griff's gun and her own desperate plans to protect herself. Never for a second had she considered praying for Wade. This was a kind of Christianity that Cassie didn't understand.

A peace settled over her as Red's comforting voice started talking to God in a way that made it seem God was a personal friend.

Cassie prayed that God would be her friend, too.

CHAPTER 14

Cassie wondered about the papers in Red's pocket as the church service wound down, the general store was put back to rights, and she and Red prepared to head for home.

He lifted her onto his horse, and she decided to get settled into Buck's gallop before she asked.

She awoke when he swung off the horse in front of their house. He was still holding her.

She insisted she could walk.

He just nodded. "I know you can, Cass honey." He carried her inside and set her on a chair.

"Thank you, Red." She didn't admit it, because it made her feel like a burden, but she was secretly glad she hadn't needed to use her shaky legs.

She sat on the chair, letting her head clear for a few seconds. And then she remembered Wade. "What was it Wade tore up?"

"Let's see." Red pulled the wad of paper out of his pocket and smoothed it.

Cassie recognized it. "My family portraits and the painting of the countess."

Tears burned sharply across her eyes. She forced herself to say what Griff would have wanted to hear. "It's. . .it's only portraits. It's all frivolity."

Red lay the mangled pieces of paper and canvas side by side on the table. "They're not frivolous. We'll fix 'em. They won't be nice like before, but we'll remember what your family looked like, and that's the real point of portraits, right?"

Cassie thought of how lovingly she'd cared for those paintings all of her life and her mother before her, so there was never any damage to the canvas and no sun faded the color. But what Red said about remembering lifted the dark sorrow from her heart. Griff's voice, accusing her of childish longing for unimportant things, faded.

"You're exactly right. The portraits are important." She smiled up at him as he bent near her shoulder, arranging the portraits. Red knew *why* they were important, and that reason wasn't lost because of wrinkled paper, nor was it frivolous. She felt immensely better and began helping him put the pieces together like a jigsaw puzzle.

Red produced another paper from his pocket and bent over her shoulder to smooth it out on the table. They had copied all her ancestors' names out of her old family Bible. As they worked on the torn portraits, Red asked, "Did you mean it about the Bible, Cass? You weren't just being brave? It's a beautiful old book. I've never seen one so big and grand. If you want to keep it, we can think of something."

"It's not even in a language we can read." Cassie shook her head. "Of all the things we might save from my past, I think the Bible is the least important. And Mr. York seems to think he might get more from it than even the mortgage price. I like your Bible better. Maybe there's a place in it for my family's names."

Red glanced sideways at her and smiled. "There is. I got

this Bible new so I've never written in the pages set aside for that kind of thing."

The smile warmed Cassie's heart as their gazes held for a long moment. Then Red turned back to the tabletop. The portraits began to take shape in front of them. "These folks are your mother's grandparents, right, Cass? And the oil painting is the countess?"

"Yes, my grandfather was one of the original executives who began building the railroad." Cassie pointed to a stern-looking man with a slight twinkle in his eye. "My grandmother was one of the finest hostesses in New York. Mother always said I looked just like her and she looked like the countess. I just barely remember them. They came to visit us in Illinois several times, but Grandfather died the year after my father, and Grandmother just a few years after that."

"Do you know stories of your ancestors, Cass?"

Cass looked up from her scraps. She'd been enjoying making her grandparents emerge from the mess. "Oh, yes. Mother talked about them all the time."

"I can see our children putting these portraits together just like this and you telling them about their heritage. We'll do it as often as we can. We can tell them about my ma and pa and my brothers and sisters, and your great-grandma, the countess, too. We'll hand down more than portraits to them, Cass. We'll make sure they know where they came from."

"They?" Cass said, her voice faint.

"Sure. I want to have a big family. Don't. . ." Red's voice faltered as he looked away from the work he was doing. "D–Don't you?"

They looked at each other before Red straightened away from her, his cheeks turning as red as his hair.

Cassie knew what a big family meant. It meant she was going to have to really be married to Red. Her first reaction was dismay, but after she had a second to think about it, she knew she'd agreed to a real marriage when she took her vows. And she remembered how he'd almost kissed her just before Wade barged into the church service, and how much she'd wanted him to. Yes, she'd be willing to have a big family if it would make Red happy.

All she said was, "I hope they all have red hair."

Red smiled and rested one hand on her shoulder. "That's fine for the boys, but I hope the girls are all as beautiful as you. I'd like to stay and help you get the portraits finished, but I've got chores waiting."

"Oh, let me help, Red. I want to share the work with you."

Red hesitated, and Cassie guessed he was thinking how tired she was. It made her feel like such a burden to him. He was always making excuses why she didn't have to help.

"I've been thinking, Cass. I want you to help, but I haven't been taking the time to teach you. Now I want you to milk Rosie today and feed the chickens and Harriet, but I don't want you to start without me. I know you've been trying to do these things to save me time, but at first it's gonna take *more* time because learning always does. Now, I've got to water Buck and Rosie before anything else. Don't start without me." He shook his finger in her face. "Promise me. Not even with the chickens. There're a couple of things I want to show you about them I didn't get to before."

"I'll wait, Red." She thought taking direct orders was the safest thing in the world. She longed for Red to tell her just what to do.

"And don't start a fire in here yet. I don't have time to do it, but it's tricky. I'll teach you how to do that, too. It'll be chilly for a while, but we'll just have to wait for a fire even if that makes dinner late."

She nodded, elated to be obedient. "I promise I'll sit and

work on these portraits until you're ready for me."

"Good, yes, that's a good idea." Red bent quickly down to his Bible and opened it to a paged lined but with no writing. "And put your family names in here while you're waiting. I'll hurry. I should be ready to milk Rosie in fifteen minutes. I'll call out when I'm back from the stream."

Cassie smiled at him, her heart soaring.

Red grabbed his hat from a nail beside the door. He glanced back to see her still smiling at him. His hand faltered as it reached for the wooden peg that latched the door shut. Something passed over Red's face that transfixed Cassie. He stood there frozen for a long minute.

Suddenly, he jammed his hat crookedly on his head, took two broad paces toward her, and lifted her out of her chair by her shoulders. He kissed her hard and quick, then set her back in the chair and left without looking back.

Cassie sat dazed, feeling his strong hands on her shoulders and his warm mouth on hers. It was over so fast that she hadn't really felt anything while he was kissing her. But after he left, she started tingling until her whole body was buzzing with the pleasure of Red's abrupt kiss. She forgot all about her grandparents' portraits and her ancestors' names and sat daydreaming. She wanted him to do it again. They'd have a lot of children, because Muriel had explained what caused babies, and she knew kissing led to that cause, and she'd liked his kissing very much.

Cassie almost hummed she was so happy thinking of the future and all the kissing she and Red were going to do.

He was wrong to kiss her like that, and it wasn't going to happen again! Not until he was sure Cassie wasn't doing it out of a need to be submissive.

Red rode the buckskin to the spring, berating himself for his rough treatment of his sweet, kindhearted Cassie. He pegged Buck there and went back for Rosie, who was her usual cranky "you're-late-milking-me" self. Rosie didn't like not being milked until the afternoon on Sundays.

He tied Rosie so she could drink, led Buck home, and went back for Rosie.

Rosie was cranky about being dragged home. "I know I'm hurryin' you, girl, but I'm afraid Cassie will forget her promise and start helping in some dangerous way or other."

Rosie jerked her head and almost pulled Red over backward. He turned and thought he saw skepticism on her long face. "Okay, the truth is I just want to get back to her. I want to hold her again, gently this time, not like the ham-handed ox I was earlier."

Rosie mooed loudly and Red realized what he'd said. "Well, I didn't mean any offense to oxen, of course. That's your family, I know. But I'm not supposed to act like one. And anyway, I can't kiss her again."

Red glanced back as if maybe Rosie could give him some advice. "I can't. It's too soon for her."

He wanted a real marriage in every way with Cassie. Almost like watching a flower unfold from its bud, he could see Cassie blooming. It was as if she'd hidden her real self to be a perfect wife for Griff.

Cassie didn't even realize how Griff had used her. Griff had abused his position of trust to marry her. Then he'd squandered her wealth and left her at the not-so-tender mercies of the men in Divide. The things she'd said about Griff calling her unclean and the money Griff had spent on foolishness made Red so mad he wished Lester Griffin were here so he could beat some sense into him.

But if Griff were here, then Red wouldn't be married to Cassie. His breath caught on the delight of having her waiting for him in the house.

Red had even put aside his worry about Cassie's faith. She bowed her head with him at every meal and she'd seemed content to attend services with him. Red had the sudden unsettling thought that maybe Cassie was trying to turn herself into a perfect wife for Red Dawson, just like she'd turned herself into a perfect china doll for Lester Griffin.

Red's heart panged at the thought and he froze in mid-step. Rosie plowed into him and shoved him along until he was walking again.

Cassie had agreed so sweetly to wait for him to do the chores. Red had told her to sit in that chair, and suddenly he was sure that she wouldn't even stand up the whole time he was gone. She'd said, "I'll be proud to obey you, Red," right out loud at the church service. He didn't want Cassie to twist and turn herself around trying to become whatever Red wanted her to be. That made him no better than Lester Griffin. He wanted Cassie to feel safe enough to be herself.

She'd been living by someone else's wishes since she was fifteen. No, since she was twelve, because that's when Griff had first gotten charge over her.

Red remembered seeing Cassie sitting perfectly still in the carriage waiting for Griff. He thought of the times he'd seen her, her hands folded in her lap, the unnatural look of composure on her face. She had been out there because Griff had insisted she stay, like a trained dog, confined to that carriage as surely as the horses had been tied to the hitching post.

With a flash of insight, Red knew no one learned to be so submissive without a harsh taskmaster administering the lesson. He thought of the fear that flashed in Cassie's eyes every time she thought she might have displeased him. Once she'd even flinched away from him.

Sickened by the direction of his thoughts, Red knew that

there'd been more than scolding and insults involved in Griff's discipline. It took a hard hand to wring that kind of fearful obedience out of anyone—man, woman, or child.

At that moment Lester Griffin was fortunate to be dead and beyond Red's reach.

Red contrasted Cassie's detached serenity in her Mrs. Griffin days with the girl who had pitched in and helped Muriel yesterday. Was that what Cassie wanted to do, or was she just following Red's example?

Red knew then that teaching her all of the ranch chores would be easy, and he knew he could have the perfect little ranch wife, hurrying to do his bidding. And he could kiss her as often as he liked and have a dozen children if he wished. And he'd never know if any of it was what Cassie wanted.

He also realized he couldn't know if Cassie's faith was real. Red the husband could fumble around and do his best with Cassie, but Red the preacher couldn't settle for letting Cassie's soul be neglected.

Red decided to start out teaching her because she really did need to learn, but what he wanted was for her to defy him. He wanted Cassie to look him in the eye and say, "I'm doing enough around here. Do it yourself."

He tied Rosie up in her stall and started for the house. He thought ruefully that at least he no longer wanted to grab her and kiss her senseless. She'd just go along with that, too.

As he reached his soddy, he realized that his mind had led him in a big circle that took him right back to where he started.

Until he was sure what her wishes were, he was never going to kiss her again.

Wade scuffed his foot against the bedding of pine needles as he waited impatiently for Dawson to go into the house. He was learning their schedule.

Morning chores. Ride out to check the cattle. Noon break. Ride out for slightly longer to check the cattle. Evening chores. Supper. Dawson always stayed inside after supper. Always hurrying, always working.

Wade knew better than to leave much sign of his passing. Although Dawson never scouted around the highlands behind his cave, he did move like a man who had lived in wild country. He would study the landscape. Take time to look at the sky. Pay attention to any ruckus set up by his horse or his stock. Wade wondered if that was how Dawson always acted or if he was suspicious for some reason.

Wade knew his pa was suspicious. Pa had never paid much attention to what Wade did. There were plenty of hands to take care of things. But Wade had taken to leaving before first light almost every day and riding for over an hour to set up his lookout of the Dawson ranch, and Pa had noticed. So far Wade had defied his father's curt questions about Wade's comings and goings. The defiance felt good and added to the visceral pleasure he got from watching the china doll.

Wade waited hungrily for a sight of her. She came out and helped with chores a lot, and Wade could hardly keep himself from charging down to that pitiful ranch and grabbing her. Oh, she'd fight him. She was a respectable woman, after all, and she was married. But inside she'd be glad he took her. She'd even be glad if her husband was dead so she'd no longer be bound to him.

Wade remembered how he used to watch the Griffin place until her fool husband rode off to town. As soon as Griffin was gone, he'd ride up to the house. He'd come up on the porch and hammer on the door until she opened it. Then he'd deliberately stand too close to her. He thought of her fear. Because his love for her was hopeless, he'd been furious. He'd wanted her to be afraid. But now he understood. She wasn't afraid of Wade. She was afraid of what he made her feel.

The anger surged upward again, and he grabbed for his whiskey flask to wash the anger back down before it choked him. He thought about Dawson inside that house with the china doll for the night, and suddenly something snapped inside him. He wanted to kill Dawson, then drag the china doll off and marry her before his father knew anything about it. And if his father objected, Wade would kill him, too. Wade's hand itched to pull his revolver and go down to that house and have it out once and for all.

Wade's eyes traveled over the Dawson place, and he noticed the cattle moving slowly toward a water hole Dawson had dammed up across his creek. Wade's eyes narrowed as he thought of how he'd always pulled back from killing. He took a long pull on his whiskey, let the burn stoke the fire of his rage, and thought of a way to strike a blow against Dawson.

This he did have the guts to do, and maybe it would make the next time, the time Dawson died, easier. Wade drank until his conscience was silenced then he planned. Soon he left his lookout and rode home to get what he needed to strike before morning.

CHAPTER 15

Belle rode out before first light.

She'd told the girls she was going, and they were already hard at work before dawn anyway. The three of them would stay outside until breakfast time. Anthony would be awake by then. . .maybe.

The weather looked fair, and she pushed her mount hard to eat up the ground.

Still, it was midmorning before the Dawson place came into sight. She'd never been here before and she noticed the way the soddy was built up against the canyon wall. Smart. She wished she'd have thought of that. She had a lot of skills but she'd never had the knack for building a sound structure, and there was no one to teach her. Her house and barn showed it.

She rode straight up to the soddy, noting the solid barn and the tight corrals. Even the sod house was square and solid looking. She tied her horse to the hitching post and strode to the front door, pounding on it.

It took a long time, but finally the heavy door, hinged with leather straps, scraped open and Cassie looked outside.

Belle thought she looked about the same age as Lindsay, and it made her mother's heart turn over to think of this woman on her second marriage, having a baby she had probably never asked for. It made Belle want to go to war to protect her.

"Uh. . .you're. . .Belle? Right? Belle Santoni?"

"Most folks call me Belle Tanner. They can't keep up with the different husbands." Belle nodded. "Just stopping in to visit if that's okay."

Cassie nodded and swung the door wide. "I've got coffee on. Red usually comes in for a cup about now. There's plenty and I've fried some doughnuts."

Belle could smell the grease and sugar and the savory hot coffee. The house smelled wonderful and Cassie smiled as she let Belle pass.

Belle felt awkward. She'd expected to find the girl in terrible straits. And perhaps she was. But it was hard to tell from the smile on her face.

Looking around, Belle noticed the cave entrance. "He built this in front of a cave?"

"Come and look. The cave is our bedroom, and over there"—Cassie pointed to a circle of buffalo hide hanging on the wall—"is a cave with a cold spring running through it we call the cooler."

Instead of rescuing the girl, Belle was struck dumb with envy. She got a full tour then settled in at the table with coffee and sweets.

"When's your baby due?" Cassie laid her hand on her stomach.

"Spring or thereabouts."

Cassie's eyes grew round. "Don't you know for sure either?"

Either? Feeling her brow furrow, Belle tried to answer in a way that would keep Cassie talking. Didn't the woman know when her child was coming? "Well, it's never exact. But I can guess pretty close. When is yours?"

Cassie began talking like a woman who was starved for another woman. Belle knew she'd be half mad with loneliness if her girls weren't always at hand.

"Muriel told you what?" Belle gasped at the amazing amount of detail Muriel had dumped on Cassie. Belle considered setting the poor thing straight but worried she'd just upset Cassie more with conflicting information.

"And then her mother-in-law had her bite on a stick so. . ."

Belle had never considered biting on a stick. The idea had merit. Belle listened more closely. When the girl ran down, Belle said, "I've had my young'uns pretty much by myself, without knowing overly much about what to expect. They just go ahead and be born no matter what you do. Not much sense learning a bunch of rules about 'em 'cuz my three were all different."

Cassie's eyes grew wide. "They're different? What do you mean?"

"Well, different lengths of time that the laboring goes on. Different feeling to each time, one'll be harder, the next easier. Not much rhyme or reason to it."

"Leota Pickett has five, and she said hers were all mostly the very same."

Shrugging, Belle changed the subject. "So, how do you like married life?"

"It's wonderful but kind of sad, too."

"What's sad about it?" Belle knew good and well what was sad about married life. The list was so long. . .well, there wasn't enough paper and ink in the world.

Blushing, Cassie leaned close and whispered, "Red won't kiss me."

Belle jerked upright in her chair. "He won't?" Belle never had that problem.

Cassie shook her head, her cheeks blazing pink. "You've been married three times. Could you get any of them to kiss you?"

Because she couldn't collect an intelligent thought in her head, Belle poured her coffee down her throat even though it was still nearly burning hot and held out her cup. "Can I have some more?"

Cassie hurried to get the pot and pour while Belle tried to gather her thoughts.

By the time Cassie settled in, Belle said, "So you must like having a husband, then?"

Cassie nodded.

"Did you like your other one?"

Cassie froze, her eyes wide as a startled deer. "Of. . .of course."

Belle shook her head. "I didn't figure you did. Worthless man. My husbands have all been pretty much worthless. Made more work for me."

"Well, I'm trying to work, but Red won't let me do much, and he hovers. Can I ask you a question?" Cassie had a look like she was scared to death of the next words she planned to say.

"Sure." Belle braced herself. This was going to be more overly personal details about having a baby. The girl was just full of questions and strange information.

"The way you talked to Red, and Muriel and Seth for that matter, how. . .how did you work. . .work up the courage to speak so boldly? I've never known a woman to be so. . .so. . ."

"Cranky?" Belle fought a smile.

"No, well, yes, a little I guess, but I wish. . .I mean, do your husbands like it? Did they tell you to act that way?"

Belle set her tin coffee cup down with a *click* and rested her arms on the table. She bent closer to Cassie. "No man tells me how to act. I act as I like, and he can put up with it and keep his mouth shut or get out."

Cassie's eyes got wide, and Belle wondered if the girl was

going to tell Belle to get out. But those eyes studied her. Quiet, watchful.

"What are you thinking?" Belle had spent most of the last fourteen years shut up in her mountain valley. Truth be told, she hadn't been around women much. . .nor men. . .save her children and the husbands.

"I'm just trying to remember the way you look straight into my eyes. The way you speak as if you don't give one tiny fig if I like it or not. That's. . .that's. . ."

"Arrogant? Rude? Stupid?" Belle arched one brow.

"Wonderful." The word was breathed quietly. "Did your mother act like this or did one of your husbands ask it of you?"

Belle was torn between snarling and smiling. The thought that one of her husbands would order her to be so contemptuous of him was really pretty funny. "My mother was a perfect Southern lady. My husbands have been content to let me be however I want to be as long there's plenty of hot food and I let them slink off and hide come chore time."

"Griff said a woman's place was in the home and it was shameful to do men's work."

Belle didn't respond but just stared straight into Cassie's eyes, wondering if the girl would realize that she'd just insulted Belle mightily.

"But I think it's wonderful. I wish I was more like you."

And just like that, Belle had a sister. Not a child like her girls, but a woman who didn't look down on her. Even admired her. Belle wanted to take Cassie home now more than ever.

The door opened fast and Red came in, breathing hard.

Belle suspected he'd recognized her horse and figured she was here to kidnap his wife. Well, Belle knew for a fact Cassie wouldn't want to be kidnapped, and it made Belle so curious it was killing her. How could Cassie be *happy*? Was Red an actual *good man* or was Cassie just that gullible?

Belle had to admit the ways of God were a pure mystery.

The little pang of jealousy surprised Belle as she studied Red. His eyes were sharp. His chest heaving as if he'd sprinted. But he didn't say a word except to greet her.

"Belle, you've come for a visit. Good to see you. You should have brought the girls."

Belle had tried to be casual with Cassie, but because she didn't know how to be much else than blunt on the normal course of things, she said, "I came to check if she was all right."

"I'm glad you did. And you can see, she's fine."

Belle turned back to Cassie, who was busy staring at Red as if she were trying to think of a way to trick him into kissing her.

"It defies reason, but she does seem to be fine."

Red laughed as he poured himself coffee then settled onto the floor by the fireplace before Belle even realized there were only two chairs in the house. "I spent the morning trying to help a critter bent on killing me even though I was trying to save his life." Red was off telling them both about a rambunctious steer that had gotten its horns hung up when it was trying to climb into a really tight clump of aspen trees. When Red tried to get him, the steer had fought as if Red were planning on turning him into a steak dinner.

Red was obviously here to watch out for his wife. But he wasn't rude about it. In fact, he was so kind and friendly, and had so obviously been working hard all morning, that Belle was nearly unable to believe Red's story.

A sudden flash of insight told Belle that *all* men weren't worthless. And didn't that mean that the problem was really with *her* because she picked such a poor lot? It was a sad thing to admit.

Belle stared into her cup of coffee while Red told his story, Cassie hanging on every word, laughing given half a chance.

Red made the story alive and funny with his arm movements

Montana Rose

and exaggerated tones. Belle realized she'd never had this long a conversation with one of her husbands. Oh, she'd talked at them and they'd talked at her, but they didn't interact. She expected nothing of them and they gave her exactly that. Would Anthony be different if *she* were different? Maybe. Belle had never considered it before.

When Red finished his tale, Belle decided since she had a chance at talking to a man who might have some sense, she'd see if she could learn anything. "How'd you build this sod house? How do you make it weathertight?"

Red leaned forward. "Is your house giving you trouble? Maybe Cassie and I could come up for a day and give you a hand. I don't suppose Anthony—"

"Anthony is nothing." Belle wondered now if that was completely fair. "And you can't come because the pass is getting ready to blow shut. You might find yourself trapped in there for the winter."

"So why are you out here? Aren't you afraid of getting snowed out?" Red looked straight into her eyes.

Belle had dealt with too many weasel men in her life. She wasn't used to this kind of straight talk and respect. She could give Red nothing less than the truth. "I just needed to make sure about Cassie."

"I'm all right, but thank you for worrying."

Belle turned to Cassie. "I—I haven't been able to stop worrying about you. You remind me of myself when I was younger. Married to a man who wasn't much use. Then alone and forced to marry again. It was hard. I felt like I could protect you from that life."

"I don't need protection from Red." Cassie's cheeks pinked up again.

Belle realized that what Cassie needed was a husband who would kiss her. Well, Belle could give her no advice or guidance

175

that didn't include a skillet. She saw the way the man looked at Cassie and the way Cassie looked back and suspected Red would figure everything out on his own and soon enough. She'd be switched if she'd give advice on that. And anyway, she'd never tried to get a man to do such a thing in her life. Avoiding a husband was the trick she'd perfected. She laid her hand on her belly. Nearly perfected.

"You're going through the winter with a house that isn't tight?" Red sounded worried, as if he were considering following her home and helping out.

"We'll be fine."

"Do you know how to drive straw into the chinks to stop the wind?"

Belle shook her head.

"Come on outside and I'll show you what I do. It makes a big difference. And I use mud to plug up holes, too." Red stood without a single grunt or groan, no whining that Belle was making work for him or nagging him.

"Can I come, too?" Cassie asked.

Red smiled at her, a private kind of smile that made Belle's heart ache in a way it never had before. She didn't even know why it hurt.

"Sure. Come along, Cass honey. Get your coat, though. It's sharp out today." He even helped Cassie on with her coat.

Red insisted on telling her about how to chink the cracks in her house.

Belle had never had a man. . .outside of someone from the Bates' store, do anything to help her. Belle went home alone, no kidnapping necessary, riding hard in case of a sudden storm, confused by Red's kindness and Cassie's longing for her husband to kiss her.

The gap hadn't closed, but a storm was brewing in the west, and Belle's heart pounded to think she'd have been trapped away

176

from her children all winter. She did a ragged job of tarring the house and chinked the holes with hands full of straw, showing her girls how to help her.

Anthony had gone back to sitting on the roof, but their activity so close seemed to disturb him, and he climbed down and walked up to the Husband Tree to find peace. She watched him go, trying to imagine wanting him to kiss her. She put up with what she had to because a man had his rights, but she avoided it whenever she could. As he strode away, Belle considered all she'd learned today. Mainly, if all husbands weren't no-account, then she'd either picked in ignorance or deliberately married bums. And either way it added up to her being an idiot.

And a tiny, guilty part of herself wondered if she hadn't been so bossy and rude, if maybe William or Gerald or Anthony might have stepped up.

Looking up, she saw Anthony planting his backside down to sit and lean against the Husband Tree. She decided she'd give the man a chance to be a man.

"You like me, don't you, girl?" Cassie leaned her head into Rosie's flank.

The ornery cow slowed her kicking if Cassie wedged her head in the exact spot Red had shown her. Rosie kept chewing on her manger full of hay, but her tail quit twitching for an instant and Cassie took that for a yes.

Rosie liked her. And miracle of miracles, Harriet seemed to be beginning to like her. It wasn't that the sow wasn't fully prepared to kill Cassie at the drop of the hat. That was a given considering a mama sow's temperament. But Cassie was slopping Harriet every day and staying well away from the little pink piglets, and as her part of keeping the peace, Harriet had quit rushing the fence, woofing and snarling with her jaws gaping.

It was a start.

The chickens didn't seem to care about her one way or the other, but Cassie had learned chickens were close to the dumbest creatures God had ever put forth upon the earth. Red said they were only close to the dumbest because he'd worked with sheep before. He said sheep were just waiting, watching for any possible opportunity to kill themselves with their stupidity, which was the reason he didn't have any—they'd all died.

Even Buck was starting to like her. Sort of.

Red had given her riding lessons every morning that week, and she was learning that there was no great trick to riding a calm, well-broken horse. A horse was a living creature, though, with a mind of its own, and Buck had boosted Cassie out of the saddle once. When she'd fallen, Red had almost had a heart attack, and he'd declared no more riding until after the baby was born. But Cassie had wanted to continue, and in the end he let her ride, but he insisted on leading Buck every step of the way. She was now riding him twice a day down to the creek when Red took him for water.

She was also leading Rosie down, which Red let her do completely alone, and she had taken over the milking and most of the barnyard chores so Red was free to ride herd on his cattle. Red acted like Cassie was his dream come true because she was helping him so much.

Cassie had also found a barn cat that had the temperament of a rat rather than a pet. The cat slinked around the edges of the farm, only showing itself by accident. Cassie started putting out milk for it, but Red said not to bother. It lived on mice and that was how it should be. Cassie sneaked and put milk out anyway. The tiny defiance made her almost giddy. The milk was now gone every morning, but the cat still wasn't a lick friendlier.

Montana Rose

Rosie chose that moment to kick the bucket of milk right into Cassie's face. Dodging the hooves, Cassie fell backward onto her seat.

Red was just entering the barn. He rushed over to her side and stepped between her and Rosie. "Maybe it's time for you to give up some of your outside chores, Cass. Now that the babe's getting closer, you oughta be more careful. I think—"

Covered with milk, Cassie wailed, "You think I'm too stupid to learn anything."

Cassie clamped her mouth shut on the criticism of her husband. How had she dared to speak to him like that? She thought of Belle and her straight talk. Belle would certainly criticize if she thought it was deserved. But she certainly wouldn't whine.

"Now, Cass honey." Red slid his hands under her arms and lifted her to her feet. "Stupid's got nothing to do with it. Think how long it'd take me to teach the chickens to milk Rosie."

Cassie was on the verge of tears, but the image Red drew made her giggle instead.

"You're much better at this than our hens would be." He pulled a handkerchief out of his back pocket and swiped at the milk dripping off her head. "It's all in who you compare yourself to. From now on, if you're feeling like you're bad at something, pick the chickens to compare yourself to, 'cuz you'll come out of that contest feeling brilliant."

"So you'll let me keep doing it?"

Red hesitated. "For a fact, my ma milked the cows up to the day I was born, or so I've been told."

"Then it must be all right."

Red shrugged. "I s'pect. I just don't want you to get hurt."

Red's eyes got an intent look that made Cassie think back to the day he'd kissed her. His gaze went to her lips for an instant and Cassie wondered if there was still milk on her face. But if her face was dirty, she didn't want him noticing. Besides, she had to focus on her real goal—protecting one of her beloved chores.

Turning quickly back to Rosie before Red changed his mind, she crouched down and wedged her head into Rosie's flank. Locking her knees tight around the bucket, Cassie went back to work and got a few more cups of milk out of the little cow.

Red stayed nearby. Then, when Cassie was done, he went to let Rosie out in the pasture and Cassie went back to the house.

Yes, Rosie and Buck and Harriet liked her. But none of that mattered a bit because Red didn't like her. Oh, he was nice as could be to her. But he'd never come close to grabbing her and kissing her again like he had last Sunday.

Cassie didn't know what she'd done.

Saturday at noon, Red prayed with an unusual fervency over the dinner, asking for God's leading about whether they should go to town or not.

Cassie decided he must have gotten an answer because he got up from the table as soon as he was done eating. "I want to check the cattle. Then I'll do evening chores early while you clean up in here."

"Let me see to Rosie and the other livestock, Red. I did it fine for the last two days, didn't I?"

She could see Red waffling. He was so sweet to her, always wanting to be right on hand in case she needed help. He was letting her do nearly every chore she considered hers now, but the man did like to hover. She was surprised when he gave a quick jerk of his head in agreement.

"Milk Rosie, feed Harriet and the chickens. There might be a few eggs by now. Don't water anything. I don't want you lifting those heavy pails. And you can't go to the stream yet with Rosie. Leave that for me."

"I'll handle it."

"C–a–s–s?" Red drew her name out until it was nearly three full syllables. "Promise me."

Cass almost smiled even though she was pretty frustrated. He was getting to know she had a knack for not lying while she let him believe something that wasn't quite true. That had worked well on Griff. "All right. I promise."

"I'll be back before you're done with everything anyway. And Cass. . ." He waited until he had her full attention.

"Yes, Red?"

"Be careful of Harriet."

"Yes, Red."

He headed for the door then stopped and turned around. "And don't let Rosie kick you. Remember if you push hard. . ."

"With my head against her flank," Cassie talked over the top of his familiar instructions, "she can't get any force behind her kick." Cassie nodded. "Yes, Red. I'll remember."

Red gave one approving jerk of his head, reached for his hat, and put it on his head. "And don't leave any gates open. None. Remember the inner and outer gate for the chickens, and for heaven's sake, don't open Harriet's—"

"No gates," Cassie interrupted, then realized how rude she'd been to cut him off like that. "I won't forget, Red."

Red hesitated.

Cassie knew he was thinking up something new to be worried about.

He reached for the door latch then dropped his hand away. "And if anything goes wrong, or something comes up that we haven't talked about, don't try and figure out what you should do. Just wait. . ."

Cassie stood beside the table with her hands folded in front of her and tried to reassure him. "I'll just quit. I'll leave anything I'm not sure about to you."

This time Red got the door open, but he turned back and his face was really grim.

Cassie had a feeling this warning was more important than the others and maybe it was the cause of all the others.

"If anyone should ride up. . .well, it's always a good idea to be careful."

"Anyone? You mean like Belle might come over again?" Cassie had enjoyed her visit with the strange woman.

"I was thinking. . .Wade. . ." Red's voice died away.

Cassie could tell he'd been recollecting Wade and his threats and wasn't sure if he should worry her about it. She'd been thinking about Wade, too, and not wanting to worry Red about it. "Wade? You think he'll come?"

"I don't know, Cass." Then Red said gravely, "I think he might. Sometime."

She hadn't wanted to tell Red this because he already watched over her so, but almost against her will she said, "He used to show up at Griff's house when Griff went to town. I—he never did anything but talk, but I knew it was deliberate, him coming out when I was alone the way he did. He must have been watching. Except Griff had a routine, so maybe Wade just knew Griff went to town every Wednesday."

Red's brow furrowed and he dragged his hat off his head and clutched the brim.

Cassie didn't like to be the one to start putting worry lines in Red's face.

She liked his face very much just the way it was.

CHAPTER 16

Red knew that dead coyote hadn't been an accident. "If he ever shows up here, I want you to go into our bedroom and go into the tunnel."

If a man would poison an animal, he'd hurt a woman. He tossed his hat at the peg, not even bothering to check if he'd hung it up, and grabbed her by the wrist. "Let's find a good hiding place for you."

Red didn't tell Cassie somebody had poisoned his water hole. But maybe he should.

He hated to scare her. But if Wade had bothered her when she was married to Griff, then she was scared already and rightly so.

He'd found two dead coyotes and a dead grouse in one of the water holes he'd built. And there were no buts about that. Those animals had been poisoned and Red could read signs. Wade's horse's hooves were around that pond.

He started dragging her into the tunnel, but she pulled hard enough to stop him. "Red," Cassie interrupted his musing, "let's think it over while we're in town. Wade won't come if you're close by. At least he never did at Griff's. And if he does, well, I'll find a spot to hide." Cassie looked over her shoulder at the crevice in the back of the bedroom. "I've explored it and I could duck into a couple of little nooks. He'd never find me. We'll pick out a good spot together when we're back from town."

Red looked from the door to Cassie to the dark slit in their wall that led into the bowels of the earth. Cassie's plan was full of holes. Wade could find her if he took a lantern from the kitchen or if Cassie made a noise at the wrong time.

She walked over to Red and laid her hand on his chest. "You take good care of me, Red. The tunnel will work if need be. And anyway, you never go off and leave me, not for long. It's not like it was at Griff's."

"You always call it Griff's."

"What?"

"Your old home. You call it Griff's. You call everything Griff's. Doesn't it strike you as odd that you say Griff's carriage, Griff's horses, Griff's house?"

"Well, it was all Griff's. It doesn't seem so unusual to say that." Cassie kept looking at the tunnel.

Red wanted her to hear what he was saying. In frustration he took hold of her elbow and turned her to face him.

Her forehead furrowed and she tried to answer him again. "It doesn't mean anything. They were Griff's, mine, both of ours. What difference does it make what word I use?"

"I think it does make a difference. This is your home, Cass. I don't want you to say, 'Red's house' or 'Red's cow.' It's all *ours*. I want you to think of it that way. I wonder if you really thought of the house you shared with Griff as yours."

Red could see the protest forming on Cassie's tongue. Before she could speak, he said, "In a way, since it was all your money, inherited from your ma and pa, that house and everything in it was more yours than his. But you never thought of it that way.

Montana Rose

Why do you suppose that is?"

"I guess it was because Griff knew just what he wanted, and I didn't care that much. He had such a clear idea of how our home should be built, how our furniture should be, how we should dress and conduct ourselves. He was a fine man to step in and take care of me like he did. And I. . .well, I was so grateful to him, taking me. . .all young and stupid and clumsy, and helping me grow into a woman who was worthy of him."

"Worthy of. . ." Red almost shouted the words, then he cut them off.

"What is it, Red? I'm grateful to you, too. I didn't mean I still want to be how Griff wanted. I want to be just how you want now. I'm trying to learn your ways."

Red grabbed her by her shoulders and pulled her up to within an inch of his face. A chill of fear flash across Cassie's face and it made him sick to think of how she'd learned to fear a man's anger.

"Red, I'm sorry. I didn't mean to. . ."

She quit talking. Red watched the huge internal effort she made to keep her feelings from showing on her face. She battled with herself until a deep serene expression emerged from the turmoil. Griff had trained her well. He'd taught her that she could only be loved when she'd achieved that appearance of tranquility that made her look as perfect as a china doll.

She had hold of her composure now. "I will remember what you said and refer to this house as ours, Red. I can see why you wish it that way. I'll try to call Griff's. . .um, I mean my old house mine from now on. It was just a bad habit to say it the way I did. It won't happen again."

"Cass. . ." Red pulled her roughly into his arms and held her very close.

She began to apologize again. Then she slipped her hand between them and rested her fingers over her mouth.

185

Red looked at her hand then back at her eyes. He could see that she was fully prepared to stand here until he'd said his piece. He glanced back at her fingers, and some of his irritation faded as he watched those fingers touch her pink lips. For just a few seconds he forgot what they were talking about. At last he tore his eyes away from her mouth. "If you disagree with me, you can say so. I want you to speak your mind."

"Yes, Red," she said from behind her fingertips.

"And you don't always have to say, 'Yes, Red.'"

"Yes, Red. . .I mean, I'm glad to mind you. It's a woman's place, after all."

Red clenched his jaw tight until he saw a shiver of fear pass through her. Red relaxed his hold on her shoulders and rubbed her arms, trying to reassure her that she was safe with him. No matter what he said, she just agreed so pleasantly, it could turn a man's head if he wasn't careful. But he didn't want an obedient, frightened china doll. He wanted a flesh-and-blood woman. "Ah, Cass, can't you hear me?"

"I hear you fine. You just said—"

"Don't you get my meaning, though? I don't want you to ever be afraid to speak up. I—I wouldn't ever hurt you, Cass. I mean. . .I'd never raise my hand to you."

"If you wanted to do that, if I'd done wrong, well, a man has a right—"

"No man has a right to hit a woman," Red roared.

She stepped back a pace before she found that blasted composure and stood her ground, obviously awaiting whatever resulted from Red's anger.

"Stop doing that." Red grabbed her and shook her again, but not hard, considering how furious he was.

"Doing what, Red? Just tell me what I'm doing wrong and I'll stop."

"Stop that. Stop agreeing with me all the time. If I yell

at you, it's because I lose my temper. That's *my* sin, *not* yours. I would never strike you, and if Griff did, then he was *wrong*. There's no excuse for a man treating a woman like that."

Cassie clung to the appearance of serenity.

Red inhaled and took a step back from her. He rubbed his hand across the back of his neck several times and stared at the floor. Finally he looked up at her. "Okay, you want to obey me? Then here's the rule. I order you to tell me what you're thinking. Every time I say something, I want the truth from you, even if the truth is, 'Red, I think you're as dumb as a post and as smelly as a polecat.' I want you to start telling me what you want. I want you to say at least once a day, 'Do it yourself,' or, 'Quit bossing me around,' or, 'Eat it or throw it out to Harriet, but I'm not making you something else.'"

Cassie's eyes widened at the horrible things Red was ordering her to say. "I could never do that."

"Oh, so you're disobeying me then?" Red crossed his arms and glared at her. "I thought it was a wife's place to *obey*. And I like a *mouthy, rude* woman with her own ideas and her own emotions. I want you to have a coat as prickly as a porcupine and a hide as thick as a buffalo and a spine as solid as the Rocky Mountains. I don't want you doing a single thing you don't want to do. I can't be happily married to a woman who doesn't nag me a little. All this polite, 'Yes, Red,' and 'Whatever you say, Red,' is making me *crazy*. You work on it and I'll tell you when you're finally doing it enough."

She clamped her hand harder over her mouth.

Red grabbed her hand and pulled it away. "You can't sass me when you're holding your mouth closed."

"I. . .I. . ." A tiny giggle escaped Cassie's lips.

The sound eased some of Red's frustrated anger, but he continued in the same domineering tone. "And I like laughing, too. Big, loud belly laughs. I'm an unhappily married man if you don't laugh every time you take a notion to."

"You want me to call you a polecat?" Cassie giggled a little louder.

"It's an order." Red said it sternly, but he didn't try to keep the pleasure from shining out of his eyes when he heard her laugh.

"I don't think I can do it right now. Um. . .call you a. . .a polecat. I'll have to work up to it." Cassie giggled again.

Red smiled at her then sobered. "I don't know what things were like between you and Griff, but I'm not like him. I want a woman to stand beside me, not trail along behind. That was Griff's way, but it was wrong. I don't want you to be afraid of me. And maybe if you sass me a little, even if I get mad, you'll see that you can trust me to never hurt you. I promise it before you and before God. I want you to believe me."

The fear returned to Cassie's expression, but this time Red didn't think she was afraid of him. He thought she was afraid of the whole idea that Griff was wrong to control her so completely.

"Red, if you don't want to step in and tell me what to do, now that Griff's gone. . ." Cassie's voice grew so weak he could barely hear her. "Then who is going to?"

The last of Red's anger died away, replaced with a deep compassion unlike any he'd ever known. "I reckon you're a woman grown." He laid his hand on her belly. "You've got a babe on the way who's gonna need a ma correcting him and teaching him right from wrong. I saw you reading Norm's mortgage note at the bank. Do you know how few of the men out here can read? You're smart, Cass. And God gave you a conscience like anyone else. You can just take over the job and tell yourself what to do."

"I don't have much practice at that," she whispered.

"Well, it's time to start getting some, Cass honey. Now I have to go do chores and check the herd. We're gonna be late to town as it is. We can talk on the way, unless you fall over asleep again."

Red saw a war taking place within her. He saw the fear and excitement battle for control. He didn't think it was a battle he could fight for her.

Finally, fear overcame the first meager surge of self-rule. She went back to the meek little Cassie he'd wanted to banish. "I've been getting better with Buck. Do—do you want me to ride him by myself this time, or will we still ride double?"

Red hesitated, dissatisfied with the results of their talk. But he didn't know what to say and he didn't have time to say it if he did. And he was afraid if he opened his mouth again he might just blurt out something like, "I'm completely in love with you."

Finally he plunked his hat on his head and said, "One hour. And don't forget what I said about Wade." He ran like a yellow-bellied coward out the door.

Cassie watched him go, thinking how different he was from Griff.

She'd controlled herself because Griff had never spared her a punishment because of apologies or tears or pleading. In fact, his rebukes were more stinging if she carried on. But in the last year especially, if she could become the china doll, if she could face him calmly and let him do his scolding until he was finished speaking his mind, he'd often "spare the rod" as he put it. She'd forgotten for a bit those hard-taught lessons of Griff's. She knew if she'd only be a good enough wife, Red would call her sweet names again. She vowed in her heart to try harder to please him, to learn faster, to take more of the burden from his shoulders.

Cassie thought she had him figured out now. She might even

try just a little to sass him once in a while, because although she could tell he'd been joking, Red was a man who liked to laugh, and if she did it just right, she thought he'd like a little more show of just the right kind of spirit from her.

And Red respected work. She had to work harder. It was all going to be fine. She was sure of it. She'd keep listening and learning and working hard, and after a time, maybe she could work her way straight into Red's heart.

CHAPTER 17

This time Libby and Leota and Muriel were ready for her.

Cassie woke as Red lowered her to the ground. Leota came hurrying up to the front door of Bates General Store before Red had completed his brief hellos to Muriel and Libby and rushed off to work.

Cassie said, still half asleep, "I can stock shelves if there aren't any customers."

Muriel laughed. "I'll work you like a mule later, Cassie. I've got a pot of coffee on the stove and I've pulled up four chairs. Sit."

She waved all the ladies toward her heating stove, and Cassie welcomed the warmth. The fall weather had lingered more than usual this year but the wind bit as if to warn them winter was coming. The cold didn't keep Cassie from sleeping. In fact, she seemed to need a nap most afternoons. It was one of the things she'd wanted to ask the ladies about. It was actually one of the few questions that she had the nerve to ask outright. She hoped to slip the other, more embarrassing questions in later. She held her hands out to the stove until some of the chill left then headed for the rocking chair the other ladies had left vacant.

Libby pulled yarn out of a cloth bag she was carrying, and Leota began stitching on quilt blocks, each only an inch square. Muriel had a basket sitting beside her chair and lifted a half-darned sock out of it. "I should have some handwork to do, too," Cassie said awkwardly.

Muriel smiled up at her. "You just sit there, young lady. You're growing a baby. That's work enough."

Cassie sighed as she sat, still slightly groggy and bemused from her long rest in Red's arms. "I declare, I take an afternoon nap just like a child. It doesn't mean I'm sick, does it? Or could something be wrong with the baby?"

Muriel laughed. It was such a pleasant sound. Cassie hadn't heard much laughter in her life. At least not for a long time.

"Seth's mother was such a sweet lady." Muriel sighed, and her eyes were looking at far-off memories that no one else could see. "I remember once, before I knew my eldest was coming, I was at her house helping her with threshers. Ten starving men and they ate like mules as much and with as many manners. It was right after the noon meal. The men were gone back out and we'd cleaned the kitchen. I sat down at the table to visit with her and I fell asleep. I didn't even know it."

"Four hours later, Seth was there, waking me up to take me home. I'd spent the entire afternoon with my head lying on my arms at the table. My mother-in-law must have tiptoed around that whole time but she let me sleep. I tried to apologize for it and she smiled so kindly at me and said, 'A baby takes a lot out of a woman.' And I said, 'What baby?'"

Leota and Libby laughed and Muriel joined in. Cassie's heart eased some when she realized she wasn't the only woman who'd had to be told she was with child. "I didn't know there was a baby coming until July."

"That's four months. You must have been feeling some movement." Leota laid two little squares together and began a row of tiny, neat stitches.

Cassie said, "I remember some now that I'm feeling it a lot, but back then I didn't recognize it as anything but muscles twitching."

Libby's needles clicked efficiently. "That's just what it feels like at first."

"I only found out in July when I mentioned it to Griff because I was worried about my. . .my time not coming for several months. I might not have said anything then except he was. . .he wanted to. . ." Cassie didn't know how she ended up going down such personal paths. Muriel had told everyone about finding out she was expecting without having to refer to marital intimacy.

"It was time for the one in the summer?" Libby asked lightly without looking up from the dark red yarn in her hands.

Cassie nodded.

All three women started laughing.

Cassie felt she had to explain. "It's just that, at first Griff said I was too young."

"Too young for what?" Leota asked blankly.

"Hush, Leota," Muriel said with her lips quivering suspiciously. "Too young to be. . .umm. . .together as man and wife, right, Cassie?"

Leota looked at Muriel then quickly returned to her sewing.

Cassie said so softly her voice almost squeaked, "That's right. I was fifteen when we married. Griff said that was too young. So, it's only been the last year he's. . ."

Muriel said, "Decided you were old enough?"

"Yes," Cassie said with a sigh of relief. "And then he wasn't. . . that is, I wasn't. . ." Cassie was suddenly exhausted and wanted the whole conversation to end.

Muriel set aside her darning and got to her feet to pour coffee. "You weren't old enough very often?"

Cassie nodded and the ladies started laughing again. Muriel had to lean on her chair until she got control of herself.

Cassie's cheeks warmed. She'd embarrassed herself again but she wasn't sure how. Just the reference to such a personal topic, she imagined. "I thought he should know before. . .before. . . lest there be anything wrong with me. And it was a good thing, because a man isn't to. . ."

Leota lowered her quilt blocks and exchanged a quick glance with Muriel and Libby that somehow left Cassie out. "He said you were unclean." The ladies all sobered.

Cassie remembered their reaction to that last Saturday and hurried to change the subject before they began to once again berate Griff.

"Red taught me how to milk his cow this week, and I'm caring for the chickens and our sow and her piglets."

"A mama pig is a fierce critter," Muriel said. "Take care around her."

"She attacked Red once." At the ladies' urging, she told about Harriet and Red's accident, and the struggles she'd had trying to feed the grouchy mother pig. They seemed delighted with her stories of life with Red, so she talked more than she could ever remember talking in her life.

On occasion, Muriel would have to get up and help a customer, but she hurried them through ruthlessly and came back to the stove.

Leota finally slipped her needle securely into her growing quilt and got to her feet. "My husband will be hauling the children on his back through town, screaming my name, if I don't get home."

Libby rolled the scarf around the ball of yarn and pinned the whole thing together with the two long knitting needles.

Montana Rose

"I have baking to see to before suppertime."

"I don't think I'd better carry anything over to your diner, Libby. I don't feel right about the help I got last week."

Libby said, "Carryin' for you last Saturday and hearin' your sweet thank you was the highlight of those men's lives. You shouldn't deprive them of the pleasure."

Cassie laughed and she wished she could do this job for Red, but she didn't haul the groceries.

The general store got busy as the afternoon wore on. Muriel said menfolk didn't buy anything ahead. They just noticed they needed something when they ran out, so right before suppertime every night she had a crowd.

Red appeared briefly out of the back room and said, "Hi." He hurried away with a wooden box of supplies for Libby.

After that, Cassie was aware of every movement from the back of the store, but Red never came up front again.

Mort Sawyer came in with an order and seemed surprised to see Cassie folding a bolt of cloth in front of the counter. He said hello gruffly.

Cassie inhaled slowly and said, "I heard you bought the spring, Mr. Sawyer. I know you wanted it. I'm glad it worked out."

Mort studied her with narrow eyes, and she knew somehow he'd taken her comment as offensive. She opened her mouth to apologize for she knew not what, but Red came from the back at that moment. He'd come to lend support. She smiled gratefully at him.

"Afternoon, Mort." Red stood beside Cassie, with one hand resting on her lower back.

Mort had been annoyed with her, but surrounded with people like she was, Cassie hadn't really been afraid of him. When Red showed up, Mort seemed content to refocus his temper on Red.

195

"Your interference cost me over a thousand dollars. There were two other bidders on that worthless spring, and it should have been mine along with her." Mort tipped his head at Cassie like she was nothing except a part of the bargain.

"You know that's not true, Mort," Red answered mildly. "Cassie no more belonged to you than that spring. And a thousand dollars is a fair price for a good water source like that. And you can afford it. Plus you got the house—"

"That house is worthless and you know it! No one can live in it back in there!" Mort said gruffly.

"Rip it apart for the wood then." Red shrugged casually. He tightened his hold on Cassie's back just a little as if to apologize for Mort's dismissal of her beautiful house. Cassie stood calmly beside Red, determined to make him proud of her. She didn't even flinch when he suggested tearing down Griff's house.

Wade stepped into the store at that second and came to stand beside his father. Standing side by side like that, Cassie thought Mort had the look of an aging wolf. Some of his strength was gone, but he'd replaced it with a lifetime of brutal lessons. Wade looked like a fox, with shifting eyes and a mind that turned to slyness. He had none of his father's strength of character. Even though Mort used his iron will to solidify power at the expense of others, no one could deny that Mort had what it took to conquer this unforgiving land. Wade would have never made it out West without his father's wealth and power to ease the way.

In a moment of insight, Cassie knew that Mort was the cattle baron Griff had always wanted to be. She had an urge to smile as she thought how far from Mort's vicious ruthlessness Griff had been. Griff had been more fox than wolf, too, but without Wade's sadistic streak. Then Cassie thought of the times Griff had raised his hand harshly against her and wondered if Griff didn't have more in common with Wade than she wanted to admit.

Then she wondered about Red. He'd said he had five hundred head of cattle. Did that make him a cattle baron, too? "How many head of cattle do you have, Mort?" Every person in the place turned to look at her before she realized she'd spoken aloud.

Mort wouldn't probably have deigned to answer her question except it gave him a moment to boast in front of all Muriel's customers. "Over ten thousand head."

"And how much land?"

Mort said, "With my water claims, I control forty thousand acres. It's the biggest spread in western Montana."

Cassie shook her head from side to side. Mort and Wade watched her, curious about her question. She even thought she saw a gleam in Wade's eye like maybe he thought she was considering whether she'd chosen right to marry Red when she could have had a Sawyer. "If you're so well-to-do, then surely a thousand dollars isn't that much to you. Why are you so upset about spending it?"

"I can afford twenty times that amount if I want to!" Mort roared at her.

Two weeks ago, Cassie would have fainted dead away in the face of all that male anger, but Red was beside her, and he'd even been angry with her before and it hadn't been so bad. Somehow Mort had lost a lot of his power to intimidate, and it was easy for her to stand face-to-face with the two of them. "And why do you need me for a wife?"

She turned to Wade. "Or you? With all your land and cattle and the nice place you live, can't you go find a wife somewhere who *wants* to marry you? I know women are in short supply, but get away from here for a few months. Denver is a big city. Go spend the winter in Denver and bring yourself a wife back. Chasing after me the way you've been isn't necessary for a rich man like you."

Cassie didn't think she was being rude. It just seemed like common sense. Of course a man ranching alone couldn't abandon his place and go wife hunting. But with all the hands on the Sawyer place, Wade didn't have to be alone if he didn't choose to be.

She didn't expect Wade to lash out at her like a striking snake. He grabbed her arm and yanked her forward until she was so close to him their noses touched. "No little snip of a woman is gonna tell me..." Wade's eyes flickered with a stunned look and he loosened his hold on Cassie. He sank to his knees in front of her.

As his face left her vision, she saw Red's arm around Wade's neck, choking him so tight that Wade lost consciousness within seconds of Red's getting ahold of him. Red grabbed Wade by the collar to stop him from falling on his face.

Muriel stepped to Cassie's side and pulled her back as Cassie babbled, "I didn't mean to be insulting. I—I just thought— It's just common sense that he'd—"

"Let up on him, Red," Mort said quietly.

Red stepped back, grim lines etched around his mouth. He still spoke calmly, but there was iron in his voice. "He's not gonna lay his hands on Cassie. Get him under control, Mort, before he comes to a bad end. You've raised yourself a poor excuse for a man. He's been prowling around my place, and he poisoned my water hole this week. I'm letting it pass because none of my stock died, but I'm watching for him now. He won't get off so easy next time."

"You can't prove nothin', Dawson." Wade dragged in a deep breath of air. His voice was hoarse.

"I can read signs, and every man here knows it. Your horse steps high and takes a long pace, and your boots leave a mark as good as a signature. There's law out here, Wade, even for a Sawyer. And if you ever touch Cassie again, you'd better hope

I remember I'm a Christian man, because that's the only thing that will protect you."

Cassie was standing well back from Wade. Red was right behind him. She was watching Wade struggle to his feet until she glanced at Red. He wasn't looking at Wade. He was focused on Mort.

Right before Cassie's eyes, that hard, old tyrant shrank to something far more human, and Cassie could see that Red was Mort's equal. Red was as tall. He wasn't as broad, but that was because Mort had gone more and more to fat over the years. Red had broad shoulders and corded muscles in his arms. But the thing that really made Red a man to respect was the force of his will. He held Mort's eyes and spoke with a confidence that no one could deny. There was no threat in Red's voice, only promise.

Wade staggered sideways as he stood and knocked into his father, breaking the stare down between Red and Mort. Mort looked at his son and disgust crossed his face.

For a second Cassie felt sorry for Wade. Wade had grown up weak because his will had been broken by his father.

Cassie knew in that instant that Mort might respect Red and leave him alone, because Mort was the kind of man who would face anyone head-on. But Wade would turn to deviousness—like poisoning a water hole or manhandling a woman or shooting someone in the back. Mort couldn't promise anything for Wade and Cassie knew it. She hoped Red did, too.

"It's over, Red." Mort turned to Wade. "You hear that, boy? There'll be no feudin' with the Dawsons. You stay off his land and keep away from the china doll. She ain't for you. Not anymore."

"I hear you, old man." Wade sneered and started for the door. "I hear you bawlin' 'cuz you're afraid of the preacher here."

Mort snapped at his son. "Remember what I said, Wade. It's over."

Wade jerked the door open and left the store, slamming the door much as he had the Sunday before.

Mort turned to the gathering of people around him, and stepping past them like they were stray dogs beneath his notice, he went up to Seth. "I'll be back for my order in an hour, Bates. Have it ready." Mort thrust a piece of paper at Seth and left the building.

The second he left, Cassie rushed to Red's side. "I'm sorry, I didn't mean to start all that. I didn't mean to be so bad-mannered. I'm the cause of—"

Red leaned down and kissed her. He didn't kiss her for long, but she quit talking to try and catch up with the kissing. He pulled away and said flatly, "Don't go anywhere alone, Cassie." He looked up and said to Seth, "You see she minds me, Seth. You have to watch her every second. She's a wily little thing."

Several people laughed, and some of the tension in the room fell away.

Red looked back at her. "And don't you dare take the blame for Mort and Wade Sawyer. There's not another man in this place, maybe in the whole *territory*, who would grab you like that even if you spit on him and told him his lacy pantaloons were showing under his skirts. Why, most of us would thank you for the insult and keep the spit for a memento of having a moment of your attention."

Several men surrounded them and they all added their agreement to Red's statement.

One of them said, "I'd be much obliged for you to spit on me, ma'am," and the crowd laughed.

"No decent man hurts a woman, Cass." The way Red was looking at her, she knew he was talking about Wade, but he was thinking of Griff, too. And these crude, uncivilized men who had always been beneath Griff's notice felt the same way.

There was silence between her and Red for a second until she nodded slightly.

Red rubbed her arms as he did sometimes, as if she were chilled and he wanted to warm her. "The Sawyers were pestering the people around here long before you or I came, and a sweet little thing like you can't make 'em better and you can't make 'em worse, so don't bother to try."

Red's tone lightened and his smile took on a teasing quality. "Anyway, even if it's all your fault, it doesn't make any difference."

"Why not?" Cassie asked suspiciously.

Red leaned so close his lips brushed against her ear. " 'Cuz, I knew when I married you, you were gonna be trouble."

Cassie pulled away slightly, trying to conceal her hurt.

Red caught her chin with two fingers and leaned in close and spoke so nobody could hear. "Now's when you're supposed to say, 'Red, you low-down, worthless excuse for a man, I'm not trouble. You are. And if I am any trouble, I'm worth every minute of it.'"

Cassie could feel her cheeks turning pink at the very thought of speaking so to her husband. She whispered something completely different than what he'd ordered her to say. "Red, I think you're about the finest excuse for a man I've ever known."

Red's eyes looked deep into hers. For a long moment Cassie felt joined to another human being in a way she never before had. Then he seemed to remember himself because he shook his head a little. "You are one disobedient woman. All this niceness is a big disappointment to a man who likes sass."

"I promise I'll try to be meaner," Cassie said demurely.

Red laughed and tapped her on the tip of her nose. "You do that."

Cassie had a sobering thought. "Mort can't control him, Red," she warned softly.

"I know. But I had to give him a chance to try. I've never killed a man, and I never want to. I don't want it to come to that. It's about more than wanting something like that on my conscience. I don't think it's too judgmental of me to suspect that if Wade died now, he'd never make it to the Pearly gates. In some ways it would be better for *me* to die than him because of what he's facing in the afterlife. I don't know if I'd have the courage to die to save the life of a man like Wade Sawyer, but it would be the right thing to do, I reckon. But I have you and the babe to consider. I have to protect the two of you. Maybe Mort can do something. Maybe he'll send him to Denver like you said."

"Oh, but the poor woman who'll end up married to him."

Red smiled. "Maybe he'll marry someone like Belle Tanner. She could handle him."

Cassie arched both brows. Belle *could* handle Wade. "But Belle's already married."

"True, but her husbands don't seem to be permanent, exactly." Red looked out the door as if seriously considering introducing Wade to Belle. Then he shrugged. "Let's don't worry about the imaginary woman he marries now. I've got food to deliver and the windows to wash at Grant's and a few more things to do before I can quit for the day."

"I wish I could help you with the food, Red."

Muriel interrupted. "I can't spare you, Cassie. Red's gonna have to do it alone."

A look passed between Muriel and Red, and Cassie knew Muriel had special instructions to not let Cassie overdo. Cassie's heart warmed to think people were taking care of her.

Red headed to the back of the store, and, to Cassie's surprise, a dozen men who had gathered to get supplies while Mort and Wade made their fuss filed past her, each tipping his hat. They followed Red back and each hefted an armload of the goods that were sitting there, gathered to fill Libby's order. Cassie hurried to the hallway to watch and saw the men follow Red across the street.

Red was ahead and didn't notice them until he was opening Libby's door. He turned enough to see he was leading a parade, and he started laughing. Cassie smiled to see Red's shining white teeth and generous smile. Then, although he had two fifty-pound bags of flour on his shoulder, he held the door for the whole long line of men.

The men filed straight back out and came to be waited on at the store. Cassie made sure to thank each of them personally and did her best to call each by name.

CHAPTER 18

Mort knocked Wade into the wall. His head cracked against the rough native stones of the fireplace in the huge Sawyer dining room and he sank, stunned, to his knees.

His father drew back his fist. "I'm not telling you again, boy!"

That huge club of a hand hammered Wade's jaw. Wade flew sideways, landing with a *thud*, stretched out flat on his belly. His head reeled.

"You leave that woman alone!" Mort's boot slugged Wade's chest, flipping Wade to his back. "I'm sick of you sniffing around her!"

Another kick made the room go dark. Wade struggled to remain conscious. Through blurred eyes he saw a smear on the floor where blood dripped from his nose.

He was a man. Eighteen just last summer. Wade lay there and wished his father dead. He hated himself for not having the guts to kill him.

He struggled for air. In his muddled brain he heard the china doll cry for help. She'd been done wrong, too. Wade had seen the marks Griff left on her porcelain white skin. Now Dawson had her. Wade's head spun and he clearly saw Dawson raising his fist to poor Cassie. She'd told Wade to go to Denver. Now he heard the real meaning.

Go to Denver and take me with you.

"Get up! Stand up here and take it like a man!" Mort taunted.

Wade didn't move. He knew his father in a mood like this, and only abject submission would make him stop.

Wade swore it was the last time.

"You're a little coward. How'd a man like me raise such a weakling?" Mort leaned down and grabbed the front of Wade's shirt and lifted him until his feet dangled above the ground. "The hands laugh at you to your face."

Mort threw Wade against a table. He crashed to the floor. A broken pitcher slashed his skin.

"They sneer at you right in front of me and I can't even call them on it because they're right." Mort kicked him in the stomach. "I'm ashamed to call you my son."

Wade coughed and spit up blood. He didn't move. His vision blurred and the blood seemed to be doubled and tripled. He lay there, trampled into the floor like dirt and knew every word his father said was the sheer truth.

He was weak. He didn't have the nerve to pull his gun. If he could kill a man, his father would respect him. Maybe even fear him. And maybe, if Wade ever found the backbone to use his weapon, his father *should* fear him.

Mort finished his tirade and stormed out, slamming doors. Wade laid there, a whipped pup.

The cowhands, when Wade had been knocked down by Tom Linscott, had called him a pup.

Gertie, their housekeeper from the time Wade's mother had died, came in as soon as the door slammed and sank to her knees beside Wade. She already had a wet towel to wipe away the blood. "I'm so sorry, Wade. Poor baby," Gertie crooned as she bathed his face, bathed his face like an infant that had made a mess eating his food.

"Poor baby," Gertie called him.

"Ashamed to call you my son," his father said.

"A poor excuse for a man." That's what Red had said in front of nearly the whole town.

He couldn't fight his father or the cowhands, and Gertie meant no harm. And anyway, all he wanted was to get away from them. They had nothing he wanted.

But that wasn't true of Red Dawson. Red Dawson had Wade's woman. His china doll. Wade needed to save her from a life like the one Wade lived. She'd asked him today to take her with him and go to Denver.

And there was only one way the china doll would be free to go with Wade.

Red Dawson needed to die.

Cassie kept getting better at the chores, and Red was less afraid she was going to kill herself. Or him.

He let her do more without supervision. As winter closed in around them, Red brought all the cattle down from the rugged high pastures to the grasslands that opened up in front of his home. He'd saved back the lush prairie hay that grew there and let it cure on the stem. It simplified his chores in the bitter cold and kept the cattle fat and contented through the winter.

Red scouted more carefully around his holding than usual and found a dozen spots where Wade had stood for long stretches of time and watched the house. He never caught Wade lurking around and he didn't see any new tracks—which would have been impossible to hide in the almost daily dusting of snow. Red stayed as close as possible to the cabin, but he made a quick check of his cattle every day and no more water was poisoned.

He kept up his guard until the next Sunday, when on their ride home from the church service, Cassie said, "Muriel saw Wade get on the stage for Denver. He's gone for the winter, the Sawyer hands all said. Maybe for good."

Cassie turned to look at Red, holding her on his lap like always. Red had offered to take the buckboard, but it doubled the time it took to reach Divide, and Cassie found it no hardship to be held in Red's arms. "Muriel said he was so battered she could barely recognize him. He'd taken a terrible beating."

Red closed his eyes and breathed in slowly. "Mort. I know Mort raises his hand to Wade. I've heard talk." Red's eyes flickered open. "Can we say a prayer for him, Cass honey? I know he's a bad man, Wade, but I—I shouldn't have turned Mort against him that way. That's my fault. What is wrong with a man that he could do that to his son?"

"Mort's a strong man, Red." Cassie rested a hand on her husband's cheek. She'd made herself some bright red mittens, taught by Muriel, and the yarn earned with her own work. She loved them, but the joy went out of her when she thought of Mort turning those huge hands on his son.

"Everyone thinks of Mort as strong, but he's not. He's a weakling." Red looked angry and troubled.

"No he's not. How can you say someone with his wealth and power is weak?"

Red leaned down and kissed Cassie on the forehead. "It's pure weakness to hurt someone smaller than you. It's a weakness of the mind and the soul. It has no bearing on how strong his back is."

They rode silently for a moment, then Red looked down at her. "Let's pray. I know we're scared of Wade, and I'm glad he's gone, but it's right to pray for your enemy. It's right to bless those who curse you."

Cassie lifted her shoulders a bit. "Sometimes the Bible doesn't make much sense."

Red's grim expression lifted and he managed a small smile. "That's when I like it best, honey. When it makes no sense, that's when it's telling us something really important."

Cassie frowned. "Well, that makes no sense either. But I'll be glad to pray along with you." It was the least an obedient wife could do.

Despite his compassion for Wade, knowing the man had left the back country was a relief. Red finally began to relax.

Wade had taken Cassie's hint and left for Denver, or that's what he told everyone. Truth was, he'd climbed off the stage at the first stop, untied his horse from the back of the stage, bought a pack horse and a winter's worth of supplies with the money he'd saved up, and rode back to Divide.

He settled in with a spyglass high above the Dawsons' place. Dawson had increased his vigilance for a while, and Wade had stayed far into the back country. He'd even found a line shack not too many miles from the china doll and set himself up for the winter.

Wade watched carefully and he could tell when Dawson finally relaxed and began staying away from the ranch for longer stretches of time.

The occasional glimpses of the china doll were like drips of water to a man dying of thirst, and the day came when Wade couldn't stand it anymore. He took a long draw on his whiskey to try and quench that thirst and reached into his pocket to stroke the handkerchief he'd stolen from the Griffin place. He longed for it to be her he touched.

Wade had gotten his hands on the china doll in town for just a few seconds before Dawson had humiliated him. His fingers still burned from that touch. The need to feel her again was a fever in his blood.

She'd never agree to come away with him. The enormity of leaving her husband would stop any respectable woman. He would make the decision for both of them. After awhile she'd thank him.

Often enough he'd watched from a hill near the Griffin place. He knew plenty about how the china doll had suffered under Lester Griffin. Just as Wade had suffered under his father's brutal hands.

Wade had found a way out. He'd get her out, too. She'd thank him when Dawson was dead.

Wade emptied the flask down his burning throat then switched to drinking straight from the bottle as he waited for Dawson to ride away after the noon meal. He'd be gone for at least an hour. Wade watched the china doll stand at her door, then she turned and seemed to stare right at him. Wade gasped, jerked the spyglass away from his eye, and dropped behind a rock, breathing hard. But then he realized she'd known he was here. She was saying, "Come for me."

He lifted himself up, looked through his spyglass, and saw she'd gone inside. But he knew it was time.

Wade didn't hesitate.

"Can I speak with you, Anthony?" Belle had been working up the courage to talk with her husband for quite a while.

It went contrary to everything she knew about husbands to try and speak honestly with the man. But she felt goaded into trying by what she'd seen between Cassie and Red Dawson.

Anthony looked up from where he sat, morose and sulking,

under the Husband Tree. "My back hurts, Belle. Don't start in nagging about chores. That's all I ever hear—"

"I'm sorry you've got a bad back." Belle swung down from her horse and tied the animal to a low branch of the Husband Tree.

She was pretty sure her bay was standing on top of Gerald.

She sank down onto the cold ground, wondering how Anthony could endure it up here for hours. Surely working would keep him warm.

"I didn't come up here to nag you."

Anthony arched his brows in surprise.

Belle didn't blame him. She'd never gotten this close to him before by choice. Even now she didn't touch him. She didn't even consider wanting him to kiss her like that strange Cassie had spoken of.

"Well, what else would you ever have to say to me, Belle?"

Belle looked sideways at him. He was a beautiful man. The curls were out of control on his head and shining black in the cold sunlight. His eyes were a gleaming blackish brown, his nose strong and straight. Belle had seen a picture of a statue chiseled by some ancient Italian artist once, and Anthony, true to his Italian heritage, looked like that carved stone. *David*, that had been the name of the statue. King David from the Bible.

God, why did I marry him? Not because he's so handsome. Please, dear heavenly Father, don't let it have been for something so shallow.

After Gerald died and the men had come a-courtin', she'd balked and said no and done her level best to discourage the stream of suitors. Then one day she'd been tired of it all, worn out from running the men off. And Anthony, who'd been persistent, had come along, and she'd said yes just to make them all stay away. She'd married Anthony because he'd been the first to come along that day.

Montana Rose

She rested her hand on her growing baby and knew this child—*please, God, let it be a girl*—would be beautiful. "I came up here because I want us to try and figure out a way to get along."

Anthony wrinkled his perfect brow. "Since when?"

Belle shrugged. "I've never given you much of a chance. I know that. But I quit even pretending to care when I caught you coming out of the Golden Butte stinking of perfume."

Anthony picked up a stick and began poking at the hard ground. He sat with his knees pulled up to his chest, scowling, refusing to look at her. The very picture of a sulking child. "I told you that was your fault."

"Yes, you did. And I told you we were done. I meant it. I won't be with a man if he's not faithful to me. So we live here, and I do as I please, and I don't care what you do."

"So why are you up here?"

Belle sighed. Why indeed? Because of Cassie Dawson wanting advice on how to get her husband to kiss her. Because Red Dawson acted so worried that Belle's house might be cold in the winter. That visit left Belle with the terrible knowledge she was missing out. She couldn't be a true wife to Anthony, not when he'd betrayed their vows. But was Anthony right that it had been her fault? She'd only met his manly needs grudgingly and infrequently, she knew that. She didn't like that part of marriage. Had she driven him to unfaithfulness?

Ultimately it didn't matter. She'd done what she'd done and Anthony had done what he'd done, and now they were left with the third wreck of a marriage in Belle's life.

She didn't trust him for good reason, and she had no intention of starting. But they could be civil. She could try to make their marriage some tiny bit normal. Having him lurk up on the roof or on that hill like a huge bird of prey was unsettling.

"Come on down and join the family. We won't make you do anything that'll hurt your back." Belle had to fight to keep

211

her voice sounding sincere. Anthony's back had started hurting the day after their wedding and he'd never done a lick of work since. "Maybe you could just talk with us, even ride out with the herd with us."

"Riding hurts."

Belle didn't mention that the man managed to ride hours to the Golden Butte at least once a week. She also knew they were snowed in now. He wouldn't get out again all winter. She wished fervently he'd have been snowed on the wrong side of the gap.

"Fine, no riding. But Anthony, I'd like a chance to make our marriage better."

He finally looked up. Something flared in his eyes and he reached for her hand. She flinched away.

Anthony's hand clenched into a fist. "I thought you said you wanted to make things better."

"There are other ways things can be better. As far as. . ." Belle rested her hand on her baby and held his gaze. She was used to looking a man in the eye, and it didn't come natural to be submissive or act demurely. She only knew how to take charge and speak her mind. And those skills weren't of interest to most husbands.

"I get it." Anthony's hand lifted to rub his head. "The skillet stays beside you."

Belle nodded. "But come on down anyway. Let's try and do something to make this marriage a happier one."

Anthony picked up his stick again and poked the hard ground. "I'll be down in a little while."

Which Belle knew meant. . .in time for dinner. She nodded and stood awkwardly, her growing stomach making everything harder.

She swung onto her horse and rode down the long, long hill from the Husband Tree, wondering what in the world could possess Cassie Dawson to *want* her husband to kiss her.

212

CHAPTER 19

C assie sighed as Red left the house without kissing her again.

She knew better than to hope he would. But knowing better didn't stop her.

She stood in the doorway and watched him ride away, and she smiled to think of how totally he'd come to trust her with the chores. He let her do everything now but ride herd with him, and considering her advanced pregnancy, she didn't even ask about it. Someday, though.

She turned back to go inside and tidy her kitchen, but as she moved, something bright glittered in the corner of her vision. She stopped and looked up at the nearby mountain peak, but she didn't see the flash of light again. A shudder of fear shook her and she didn't question it. She had stood here many times over the last few weeks. She had never seen a reflection before.

She grabbed the rifle off the rack above the front door and headed for the tunnel. She dashed into the opening and knew exactly where she was going to hide. She entered the narrow passage, using one hand braced against the stone wall to balance.

She didn't go far. In the pitch darkness, she found the first side tunnel. She had to get down on her hands and knees to crawl in, and with her girth from the baby and her long dress and the rifle, she barely slipped inside. She struggled through the narrow entrance for only a yard before it narrowed to only a foot high beside a trickle of water.

Cassie had pictured the spring that ran through their cooler, dripping into this little cavern for as long as there had been mountains. It had eaten away at the rock until it had dropped low enough to change directions and began running into the cooler.

Or maybe God had put it here for Cassie. For this moment.

There was no place that was completely dry. The ceiling was so low she had to rest on her side in the dank, cold crevice. The frigid water seeped through her dress. She shivered against the cold stone and called herself a coward to hide like this. She almost climbed out, but she couldn't shake off the fear that clutched at her heart. She was a coward, scurrying into a hole in the ground like a scared rabbit.

Time stretched and Cassie prayed for warmth and safety and Red. The cold chewed at her skin like a hungry rat until she shuddered with it, and the black mountain pressed down on her soul. She railed against her cowardice and almost crawled out a dozen times, but there was an almost supernatural strength to her fear and she couldn't overcome it.

Then she heard something that chilled her more deeply than the water ever could.

"China doll?"

Wade.

He spoke softly, coaxing as if she were a timid animal in need of taming. "Where are you, girl? I've come for you." His voice got stronger then faded as he moved around their cabin.

"Where are you, doll?"

There was a long silence.

She curled her body around the baby to try and keep her little one warm. As she lay there, she prayed for Red. If God could give Cassie a feeling of fear, then He could give one to Red, too. Then she thought of Wade's guns and feared Red *would* come. If only Wade wouldn't find her. If only he'd give up and go away.

"Are you in here, china doll?" Cassie jumped and scraped the gun against the cave floor. Wade had found the tunnel. He was close. Close enough to hear the slightest sound. She was cornered if Wade found her hiding place. The weight of the mountain surrounded her. She was trapped, and fear sucked the air out of the cave.

The wheedling left Wade's voice. "My woman doesn't hide from me!" He was standing directly in front of the opening now. He had a lantern and wouldn't have to lean down much to light up the fissure and see her.

Cassie felt the panic rising. She forced herself to remain still and hoped the frantic pounding of her heart wasn't audible.

"Where are you?" Cassie heard Wade's fists slam against the cave. He stepped farther into the cave, past the fissure where she hid, and called out again, more furiously. "I've come to save you. I'll take you away from here. Where are you?"

He moved on, ranting as he went. "I'll never stop hunting for you. Never!"

Cassie didn't dare move. Between the frigid water and her fear, she shivered violently. She buried her face in her drawn-up knees to cover the sound of her teeth chattering.

Wade's voice faded away, but she remained in hiding. She could feel him, crouching in the dark, waiting for her to move so he could pounce.

She moved beyond cold to pain, and only sheer terror kept her from leaving her hiding place. Then the shivering stopped and the cold didn't bother her so much. She began to feel drowsy and relaxed.

She hugged her baby close and laid her head on her drawn-up knees, against her soaked, frigid skirt and prayed.

Lord, keep Red safe. Protect my baby.

She remembered the compassion of the church members and Red's worry about Wade being hurt by his father and managed to send up a prayer for Wade. Then she remembered the lesson Red had taught last week. She couldn't think of all of it. The only words that she knew were, *"The Lord is my light and my salvation; whom shall I fear?"*

She understood that verse so clearly now.

"Whom shall I fear?"

No one.

In her soul—the only place that really counted—Cassie was safe.

"Whom shall I fear?"

The safety that verse gave her was almost like a voice telling her it was all right to come out now. She believed it. Wade was gone, and if he wasn't, he couldn't really hurt her. God was with her in life and death.

Again that voice inside her said, *"Come out. It's safe to come out now."*

She tried, but it was so much effort to move. She'd rest just a few seconds more.

In perfect peace, with no fear in her heart, she fell asleep.

The cabin door was wide open to the cold winter wind.

"Cassie!" Red dug his heels into Buck's side. He started praying before Buck took his first galloping stride.

"Cassie!" He saw hoofprints that had trampled down the new snow around the door.

Wade.

And he'd been here a long time and been gone a long time. Red charged into the cabin yelling, "Cassie! Cassie, are you here?"

He was greeted with dead silence. He saw the overturned table and the pans knocked onto the floor and felt Wade's fury.

Red ran toward the tunnel. He stepped inside. "Cassie!"

His voice echoed off the stone walls, mocking him. She wasn't here. Wade had taken her. Red ran for the door and leaped onto Buck's back.

He stopped after just a few dozen yards. There was something wrong with the tracks. Red swung down off Buck and tried to push his panic aside long enough to think.

God, where is she? Help me find her. Keep her safe.

Red crouched beside Wade's tracks and knew immediately what the problem was. The tracks were the same depth as when Wade rode in. The horse wasn't carrying two riders.

Red rushed back to the cabin. Could she be inside that tunnel, hurt too badly to answer? Or dead?

He stepped into the blackness of the tunnel then turned back to go for the bedroom lantern. It was gone. Wade must have found the tunnel and hunted through it, using the bedroom lantern. The one in the kitchen lay smashed on the floor, useless.

Red didn't have time to rig up a torch. He stepped into the tunnel, thinking of all the nooks and crannies where a scared little woman might hide. He felt his way along in the pitch-black corridor, calling for her, his hope faltering with every step.

Then he tripped. He fell heavily to the ground, which was strange, because he had been moving slowly and hanging on to the wall. And when he fell, his hand slid on the wet stone and he felt fabric.

Cassie's skirt. He remembered this cold little crevice.

"Cassie!" His voice wavered and cracked.

She didn't respond. Didn't move. He followed the wet fabric and found a leg. She was wedged into a fissure in the rocks so small Red had never gone into it.

He eased her out of the icy little hole, his heart clutching at her stillness. When he had her all the way out, he laid his ear against her chest and heard a heartbeat, weak but steady. She was so cold, so utterly still.

Red lifted her carefully in his arms, cradling her against his chest. He carried her out into the dim light of the bedroom. Her dress was so wet it dripped. He stripped her out of her soaked clothing, pulled her nightgown over her head, and laid her on the bed.

He saw no bleeding. He lifted her eyelids and her eyes flickered back and forth, and she moved slightly as if in protest.

He ran his hands over her body looking for bumps or broken bones and found only cold. Her lips were pinched and blue. Her fingernails were pure white. He had lived in Montana long enough to know what cold could do. And he knew how to combat it.

He kicked his boots off and shucked his pants and shirt, and wearing only his union suit, climbed into bed beside her, pulling the blankets over both of them. He held her close in his arms, cocooning the babe between them. He massaged her back and legs, wiped his tears on his sleeve, and asked God for a miracle.

For long moments he rubbed her arms, trying to warm her chilled skin. There was no response, no movement, her breathing shallow, her heartbeat faint.

Red's prayers were broken by fear as he held her and tried to share his heat. "Please, God, don't take my Cassie away from me. Protect her, Lord. Please." Red sent his petitions to God with such fervency that they generated their own heat.

Montana Rose

Moments passed. Red could feel Cassie slipping away from him as if she were being drawn back into the mean, hard cold of the stones. The door to the outside was still open. He'd been running when he came in and let it swing wide. He needed to go out there, close the door, and stoke the fire to warm the cabin up, but he was afraid to leave her, even for those few minutes.

"Please, God, please. Protect her, Lord. I love her." Red kissed her cold, blue lips and rested his face against hers, shuddering from the lifeless, waxy cold.

Then her teeth chattered.

Red pulled back when he heard that bit of sound. She lay motionless, but he knew she'd responded. He continued caressing her, praying for her, calling her back to him.

The shivering started small and lasted only a minute before it stopped and she lay quiet for a while. Then it came again. This time it hit her hard, shaking her violently.

Red held her through it, rubbing her arms and back, moving his legs against hers and tucking her icy feet on top of his. Her teeth rattled until he was afraid they might break. Her body vibrated wildly. He massaged her and called softly. After turbulent minutes that seemed to stretch out for hours, the shivering eased. Red looked down at his precious wife and saw her brown eyes flicker open. He wasn't sure if she was awake or not. Her eyelids closed heavily.

"Wake up, honey," Red crooned. "C'mon, Cass. Come all the way back to me."

She shifted against him and her arms went around his waist. Her fingers were like icicles on his back and he pulled her hands around and tucked them between their bodies. He pressed her head into the crook of his shoulder, and her nose was so cold he couldn't control a little jump. He prayed aloud, hoping she could hear and draw comfort from his words.

The shivering started again. It lasted longer this time. The wracking seemed like it would tear her apart. How much could Cassie or the baby take? When this bout passed, Red looked down, hoping for another glimpse of her eyes. She was awake and staring at him.

"I'm here, Cass. I'm so sorry I wasn't here sooner. But I'm here now. You're going to be okay." Red prayed it was true.

"Wade came. I hid from him."

"You did good." Red hugged her close. "He didn't find you."

Cassie slid her hands down to lie on her stomach. "I tried to take care of her." Her voice broke and tears filled her eyes. "I tried."

"Did he hurt you, Cass honey?" Red didn't think Wade had gotten his hands on Cassie. If he had, she wouldn't be here.

Cassie shook her head. "No. No, he never found me. I was so afraid. But then. . .I wasn't afraid anymore, just tired. 'The Lord is my light and my salvation; whom shall I fear?'"

The shivering resumed. This time it wasn't as hard or long.

Red cradled her and praised her and stroked her cold body back to warmth. She tried to fall asleep, but Red didn't let up on her until he was sure she was warm again.

When the shivers receded for good, he finally let her sleep. He left her to warm the cabin up then lay back down beside her, pulled her into his arms, and held her, so relieved he couldn't stop the tears. So in love with her he was afraid to feel the force of it.

Then he thought of Wade, and the anger slammed into him like a freight train.

Red recognized that temper that went with his red hair. He controlled it pretty well, but at that moment he was overcome. He held his wife and his babe and he wanted to stay this close to both of them forever. But, almost as much, he wanted to get his hands on Wade Sawyer and tear him apart.

Montana Rose

The fury consumed him as he lay beside Cassie's limp, sleeping body. He imagined himself hunting Wade down and thrashing him to within an inch of his life. He savored the vision. He reveled in the power of his hate. Ideas for Wade's slow, lingering death paraded across his mind, and carefully avoiding thoughts of God, he planned how he'd make Wade pay.

Just as he was mentally meting out Wade's final punishment with his bare hands, Red got a message from God he couldn't ignore. He got kicked in the stomach.

With a jolt, Red realized it was the first time he'd felt the babe move since he'd found Cassie in that icy little cave. He'd been so worried about both of them, but Cassie had taken precedence. The little kick told him his child was all right, too. It was as if his rational mind returned to him.

Red had a sense then of Satan sitting on his shoulder, suggesting ways to hurt Wade. Urging vengeance. Calling it justice when it really was hate. Red knew the devil well enough. He'd had temptations before. One of them was lying asleep in his arms right now. Red also knew his Master's voice, even when it came in the form of a swift kick.

He banished Satan by replacing him with love. Pulling back from Cassie just a bit, he laid one big hand over the little tyke and got kicked again. Red smiled down at Cassie's oversized belly. The babe was stirring so vigorously Red could see Cassie's flannel nightgown move. Red got the message.

He whispered, "I'm sorry, little one. You don't need a pa with a mean temper, do you?"

The babe kicked him squarely in the middle of his hand, and Red took that for a no.

"But what are we going to do? How am I going to protect you and your ma from him?" Red asked it of the babe, but the answer came from God.

"The Lord is my light and my salvation; whom shall I fear?"

Who indeed. Not Wade Sawyer.

Easy to say.

"Greater is he that is in you, than he that is in the world."

Wade was in the world, and today, although it had been a close thing, God had protected Cassie. They were safe.

"If God be for us, who can be against us?"

Well, Wade was definitely against them. But who was Wade compared to God? Red almost sat up in bed when he remembered falling practically on top of Cassie. Thinking about it now, he wasn't sure why he'd stumbled. He'd been walking carefully, holding on to the wall. Yet he'd fallen and his hand had landed on the tiny bit of Cassie's skirt sticking out of the hole.

Red smiled. God was definitely for them.

Then he thought, *"Love thy neighbour as thyself."*

That one stuck in Red's throat and his smile faded.

The babe kicked him.

Red hesitated and Satan whispered about justice and hate.

The babe kicked him again.

"Okay, little one," Red whispered so Cassie wouldn't be disturbed. "But Wade doesn't make it easy."

The babe booted him hard.

Red had to forgive Wade. It grated on him something fierce, but he knew he had to. He pulled Cassie back into his arms, and the babe seemed to do a somersault of approval. Red grinned, and Cassie shifted against him and moaned sweetly in her sleep.

Forgiving didn't mean trusting someone who wasn't repentant. But Wade was in worse trouble than the Dawsons. Red closed his eyes.

Thank You, God, for the miracle of life I'm holding in my arms. The miracle of two lives. Bless Wade. Bring light to the darkness that surrounds him. I love him, Lord. I do. He is Your creation. And I forgive him. But I hope You'll forgive me, Lord, if it's a sin that I'm not going to trust him.

Montana Rose

He caught himself just as he dozed off. He had left Buck bridled and saddled, running loose. His home had been trashed and he still had evening chores to do.

With a quick check of Cassie's fingers and toes, which looked pink and plump now, Red got up and did his chores at a run. Then he quickly straightened the house, built up the fire, and hung Cassie's wet things to dry. When he got back to Cassie, she had rolled all the way to his side of the bed as if she were hunting for him to snuggle up against. He shucked his clothes again and crawled right back into bed with her.

Cassie had said, "The Lord is my light and my salvation." Did she mean it? Had Cassie really made her own commitment to the Lord?

Red prayed she'd moved beyond just saying what he wanted to hear. He prayed for her and thanked God for her every second he had. . .until he fell asleep.

Chapter 20

Cassie's eyes fluttered open and she rubbed her hand over Red's chest and savored the warmth.

Warmth!

She jerked to a sitting position in bed with a cry of fear and fell back because she was anchored by Red's arm.

"Don't be afraid, Cass. You're okay." Red untangled her hair from around his arm and behind his head.

Cassie looked at Red and started to remember what had happened after she'd gone into that dark little hole to hide from Wade. She looked into his kind, worried eyes, and with a little cry of anguish, she threw herself back into his arms.

He cradled her and crooned and stroked her arms.

She remembered this from last night. It was so fuzzy she wasn't sure what had happened and what she had dreamed. "You came for me. You saved me." She clung to him and shuddered from fear.

"You're okay," he murmured. "We got through it."

Red brushed her hair back off her forehead and chucked her under the chin so she'd lift her head from where it was burrowed against his chest. "You were so smart, Cass honey. So brave and strong. You saved yourself. I'm so proud of you."

Confusion warred with doubt. She shook her head slightly. "No. I was so afraid. I was such a coward. Running and hiding like a stupid—"

"Cass honey," Red interrupted softly.

"Yes, Red?" Her eyes flickered to his lips and back to his eyes.

"Shut up." Red kissed her.

It worked. She shut up.

Then he pulled away from her. His lips were moist from her kisses. She knew because she couldn't quit glancing at them to see if he might be going to kiss her again.

He rested his hands on her shoulders and firmly moved her back from him. He had to unwind her arms from around his neck, and while he did, Cassie sneaked in another kiss and he put up with it for a while. Quite a while. Then after a minute or two...or three, he went back to holding her away.

"Now, listen, young lady..."

He sounded like a scolding father, and because that was so unlike Red, whom she didn't think of as a father at all, she smiled. He tapped her under her chin again, and she realized she was looking at his lips. He seemed to want her to stop that. She really tried.

"I'm listening," she said demurely, trying to follow whatever order he was obviously getting ready to give.

"You were *not* stupid and you were *not* a coward," he said sternly.

"But I was, Red. You don't know. I was so afraid."

"Being afraid doesn't make you a coward, Cass. In this case, being afraid is just plain good sense."

"But I ran. I hid like some wild animal in a hole in the ground. I should have...have shot him or something."

"Well, the only trouble with shooting someone is that once you've done it. . ." Red hesitated.

"What?" Cassie asked.

"Once you've shot someone, then. . .well, the thing is. . .then you've. . .you've *shot* someone, if you get what I mean."

Cassie shook her head, feeling stupid again.

"It's not something you can take back."

Cassie stared at him and slowly nodded her head. She was glad she wasn't living with that on her conscience. But she'd still been so helpless. She'd been alone in that black hole with her terror, so completely at Wade's mercy. She'd felt so weak and pathetic.

There'd been so many times in her life she'd wanted to fight back, not just against Wade, and she always was left cowering in fear. Red had said she was smart and strong and brave. She was none of those things. But a husband's word was law, so she let herself enjoy the thought.

"What are we going to do, Red?"

"I don't know, Cass honey. I've been thinking about it ever since I found you. I can't ride off and leave you here alone again, not for even a minute."

"Could I ride with you to check the cattle?"

Red was silent for a moment.

Cassie hastened to embroider details on her plan. "I could ride with you on Buck. When you find a herd you need to work with, you could set me down somewhere out of the way but where we could see each other."

"It's so cold," Red said doubtfully.

"It's cold for you, too."

"I'm not carrying a growing babe."

"I've got a good coat."

"It could work. It's better than the plan I came up with."

"What was that?" Cassie was prepared to do whatever he said.

226

"Well, I had this picture in my head of building a corral around the cabin and turning Harriet loose in it."

"A guard pig?"

Cassie looked at him for a long moment, and then he grinned at her and she started to giggle. She buried her head against his chest and he held her close, and they laughed until the baby kicked them into getting up.

"You can come with me for today. We'll try it a day at a time," Red said as he grabbed Cassie's dry clothes for her then proceeded to get dressed.

"Yes, Red." Red had his back politely turned, so Cassie quickly slipped out of her nightgown and into her chemise, then grabbed for her dress.

"And I'll show you a better cranny to hide in that's not so cold, and we'll put the buffalo robe in it if I ever go off even for a second."

"Yes, Red."

He glanced over his shoulder to give her a disgruntled look, and she wondered what she'd done. She thought with the tiniest spark of annoyance that she really could hardly be any more obedient.

Red's expression cleared. "How did you sneak into the passage without Wade catching you?"

"I saw a flash of light high up on the hill. It scared me. I just grabbed the rifle and went straight in. I'd been in there quite a while before he came."

Red was silent for a long while. "I think you were scared because God was warning you."

"You do?" Cassie asked in wonder. If God had talked to her, it was her very own miracle.

"I came in early from checking the cattle because I couldn't shake off worrying about you. I think God was speaking to me, too," Red said with calm assurance.

"He took care of us," Cassie whispered. She knew it was true, because the fear she'd felt at that little flash of light went beyond a normal reaction.

Red said quietly, "Let's remember to always trust our instincts. God is watching over us, and if we're open to His leading, I think we'll be safe."

"Yes, Red. I will, Red," she said fervently.

Red looked annoyed again and she stood quietly waiting for him to reprimand her, but he never did.

Red shook his head as if to clear it. "I think the babe talked to me last night."

"The baby and God? All in one day?" Cassie said with what she hoped was well-concealed teasing.

"Yep." Red slung his arm around her and led her out to the kitchen. "It was quite a day."

"So what did she say?" Cassie noticed they'd gotten dressed in the same room at the same time. They'd never done that before.

"Well, first off, she said she's a he."

"She did not!" Cassie protested.

Red told her a silly story about being scolded with a series of kicks and twists while they made breakfast and did the morning chores together.

"Instead of checking the herd this afternoon, I want to ride to town and tell the sheriff about this." Red ate his steak at noon, but his stomach did back flips when he thought about Cassie so cold, so near death.

"Yes, Red. That's a good idea."

Red hated that obedient tone. But they were going to town regardless of her tone, so it would be stupid to growl about it.

"I doubt the law will step in, but I want a formal complaint so if Wade comes around again, we'll have some proof that he's been a problem before."

Cassie began cleaning as if he'd shouted at her to hurry.

Red shook his head at his submissive little wife then hurried to do a few chores. They rode to town, and though the town marshal didn't sound like he planned to pursue the matter, Red insisted on going through the motions.

Since it wasn't a Saturday, they went to pick up a few things at the general store, planning to rush home.

Muriel insisted on hearing the whole story of Cassie's plight. "Humph. That marshal is bought and paid for by the Sawyers. He won't do a thing."

"Well, there's not much he can do, really. All Wade did was walk around in our house a might clumsily, broke a few things. And no one saw his face, though Cassie identified his voice. If Wade could be found and forced to admit he was there, he'd just say Cassie should have come on out. He had no idea of harming her." Red's chest hurt when he thought of the way his cabin had looked. The violence in the damage. The strength of the fear God had placed on Cassie's heart.

Muriel snorted.

A group of Sawyer hands came into the store just then.

"You know Wade was out at the Dawson place today?" Muriel asked.

The closest man, Red knew he was the Sawyer foreman, shook his head. "He's quit the country. I saw him get on the stage to Denver myself."

"He's not in Denver." Red stepped in front of Muriel, not wanting the feisty woman to draw down the ire of the Sawyer bunch on her. "I recognized his tracks and Cassie heard him. She hid because she knew he was up to no good. Where is he?"

The burly cowhand scratched his grizzled chin. "We haven't seen him for a while or more. Him and his pa had it out, and Wade took off. The boy had a pair of black eyes and a split lip when he left. His pa don't put up with mouth offa his kid, and Wade had used up all his chances."

Red inhaled slowly as he thought of a father who'd hurt his son like that. He stared at the man, looking for shifty eyes. But the man seemed to believe what he'd said about Wade being gone. All that meant was Wade had lied to them, too.

"As far as we know, Wade is still in Denver."

Red and Cassie headed for home in the fading light of Montana's early evening. This time Red knew he'd never relax his guard.

CHAPTER 21

I need to warn you girls what I've done." Belle waved her girls closer.

It wasn't hard to catch them without Anthony around. Being not around was the usual state of things.

Lindsay, Emma, and Sarah drew close, the whispered words drawing them in. They were in the barn shortly before it was time to eat dinner.

"I've decided it's a sin the way I treat Anthony."

Emma's brow puckered. "You mean feeding him and washing his clothes and picking up after him and giving him money to go to town twice a week? That's a sin?"

What Anthony did in town was most definitely a sin. But Belle had caught him stealing a few times, and when he was cornered, the man had a dangerous look in his eyes that made Belle want her skillet handy. Even though it sickened her to think what Anthony did with that dollar, she'd taken to giving him a dollar about twice a week, which seemed to be enough to keep him calm. Besides, she liked having him gone from the ranch, so it was like she was paying to have a couple of days without his brooding presence. Money well spent.

"No, it's a sin that I've treated him badly."

"How, Ma?" Sarah asked, her face worried as if her mother's confessing to sin scared her.

"Well, I've. . .I've been bossy and unkind and hostile. He says his back hurts, and instead of feeling bad for him, I've treated him like a liar, and a lazy one at that."

"He is a liar, Ma." Lindsay scowled.

Belle knew they'd all seen Anthony ride away on his horse, as fit as could be. His back only hurt where there were chores. The man *was* a liar, and no Christian charity could change that simple fact.

"Yes, I agree." Except that wasn't what Belle wanted to do. She needed to encourage her children to give the man the benefit of the doubt. "I mean, it's not for us to judge him." Belle pulled her flat-crowned hat off her head in frustration. "What I really mean is Anthony's sin is between him and God. We are still called to treat him with kindness and"—she wasn't sure she could choke out the word—"l–love."

All three girls inhaled sharply and straightened away from the little circle they'd formed.

"You're saying you're in love with him, Ma?" Lindsay shook her head. "I think that's a bad idea."

"No, for the love of heaven, I'm not saying that!" Belle felt sickened by the very thought. "I'm saying God called us to love our neighbor as ourselves. I'm saying I learned something when I went and visited Cassie Dawson."

"Who?" Sarah twisted her mouth as if the conversation was a nuisance, which it was. Sarah had supper to get and Belle knew it.

"She used to be Cassie Griffin. I told you how they forced her into a marriage. You remember that, right, girls?"

"So you're saying it's okay to let someone force us into

marriage?" Emma started wringing her hands.

"No! Now listen to me. Don't you *ever* let someone force you into marriage." Belle whipped her hat against her leg, wondering why she'd ever started this. "I'm saying I'm going to try and love Anthony as a neighbor. As a child of God. No, good heavens to Betsy, I don't love the wretched man."

That probably wasn't the thing to say if she was going to try and be a better Christian when it came to Anthony. "What I mean is, Anthony's lies, Anthony's laziness, those are between him and his Maker. And our behavior is between us and God. That's all we can control. I've been sinning by being unpleasant to the man, and I'm going to try and change. You know, I worry for Anthony's soul, though it's wrong to judge."

Belle had judged him as belonging to the netherworld before she'd been married to the man for two weeks, but that was her own sin. No sense spreading that to her children. Although she had to admit that realization had come a bit late.

God forgive me.

"I'm saying maybe we can. . .reform him. Show him how Christians are supposed to act. That's part of being a good Christian. Being a good example and behaving in a way that draws others to our faith. And I've been less than a good Christian to Anthony, and worse, I've been a poor example to you girls. I don't know if he'll come, but I told Anthony I wanted him to join the family. Even if he doesn't work, he can be with us, talk to us, join in with things besides meals. And I just wanted to warn you girls because I'll no doubt be saying things to him you don't understand. You might even find them shocking."

"What kind of things, Ma?" Sarah shifted her weight.

"My plan is to be. . .to be. . ." Belle shuddered and she knew the girls could see it, but she soldiered on. "Nice to the lazy coot."

All three girls gasped in shock.

Belle nodded. "I knew you wouldn't understand. That's why I had to warn you. And if you can possibly do it, try and be nice, too."

Lindsay shook her head, not in disobedience but rather as if she couldn't imagine a single nice thing she could say to her stepfather.

Belle patted her on the shoulder. "Just try. I know it goes against the grain."

All three girls nodded as if Belle had just ordered them into a war zone. . .unarmed.

She decided to arm them somewhat. "There's a Bible verse I heard once that said being kind to people who are bad to you is like heaping hot coals on their heads. So maybe it'll help to imagine you're doing that while you be nice."

Emma shrugged. "That might work."

"It's worth a try." Lindsay started pulling her gloves on.

"I'll do it." Sarah squared her shoulders and stuck out her chin. "But they're gonna be red-hot coals."

"Whatever it takes. Now go get supper on while we finish the chores."

"Will Anthony be coming in to help us with the chores?" Lindsay was being sarcastic.

Belle recognized the attitude. It came straight from her. "I doubt it. I saw him coming down from the Husband Tree and climbing up on the roof." Belle shook her head in disgust and tugged her hat back onto her head, pulling the flat black brim low over her eyes. "I'm going to go see if I can talk the idiot into coming down so I can get started being nice."

"She's turning somersaults again." Cassie rested her hand on her stomach as she settled into bed.

Montana Rose

Red grinned and laid his hands beside hers. "He's still talking to me, just like that day you got cold."

"*She* can't talk yet." Cassie shoved at his hands, but Red held on.

"Be still, woman, so my *son* can tell me how he's doing." Red loved feeling the baby move and telling Cassie there was a little boy growing in her. It was closest she'd come to sassing him.

He quit letting her lie apart from him when she came to bed. He'd always pulled her close after she'd fallen asleep, but now he pulled her into his arms the minute she lay down. Better still, she came without protest.

Checking the cattle together worked better than Red had hoped. Occasionally there was an injured longhorn that needed doctoring, and after scouting around to make sure Wade wasn't in the vicinity, Red would find a sheltered spot and set Cassie down to watch from a safe distance while he roped and hogtied the beast and tended it. Every day there were a few head of cattle that needed something special. If possible, Red drove them back to the ranch and worked with them while Cassie did her outside chores.

That worked until the day Red came into the house and Cassie wouldn't face him. She always turned around from where she was working on supper to smile hello. Red hadn't thought much about it until she didn't do it. She stayed hovering over the fire with her back turned to him. He surely did miss her cheerful greetings.

"Hi, Cass. Supper ready?" He waited expectantly for her to warm his life with her hello.

She said, without turning around, "Hi. Meal's almost ready. Go ahead and sit down."

Red couldn't say a thing was wrong with the way she was stirring at the pot of stew she'd made, but he kept a sharp eye on her. She had the plates beside her on the sink, and she reached

235

over for one with her back still turned. She started scooping up a plate of stew, and when he went beside her to wash from the basin of hot water on the sink, she turned away from him and set the plate on the table. He washed as she fussed with setting the plate just so. Then he went to the table and she turned back to the fire and got the other plate.

He waited for her to sit down until she said in an overly casual voice, "I think I'd better just tend this stew a bit more. Go ahead and eat without me."

Red surged up out of his chair and grabbed her arm. She cried out in pain and he let go immediately. "I'm sorry. I didn't mean to be so rough." Then Red thought about what he was saying. He hadn't been rough!

He said sternly, "What's going on here, Cassie Dawson?"

There was a long silence as he stood behind her and she faced the fire. Finally, with tortuous slowness, she turned around.

"What happened to your face?" Red reached to touch her then pulled back. She had a scrape across the whole side of her cheek and down her neck. He thought about the pain he'd caused her when he took her arm. "Let me see the rest of it."

Cassie started shaking her head. "Red, it's not as bad as it looks. It's just a scrape!"

"I want to see your arm. Right now!" Red stepped so he was behind her and started unbuttoning her dress. As he did he noticed a dozen slits in her sleeve that had been carefully mended.

"Red, please! You're overreacting!" Cassie turned to look over her shoulder at him in alarm as he clumsily undid the buttons down the back of her dress.

"What happened to you? How did you. . ." Red quit talking and gasped as he pulled her sleeve down. The scrape went down her neck, over her shoulder, and the length of her arm.

"Cassie," Red whispered in dismay. "Was it Wade? Did he hurt you?"

Cassie clutched the dress to her front. "No, I haven't seen Wade at all. I. . .I just fell."

"Fell where?" Red said in alarm. "I was around the place all afternoon. I never saw you fall."

Cassie didn't answer.

Red, unaccustomed to anything but complete obedience from his little wife, looked away from the nasty damage to her arm and neck and saw a stubborn expression on her face. "Ca–a–assie," he said gravely. "Tell me."

"You'll be upset." Cassie turned to face him, pulling her dress back into place. "It was my fault. I don't want you to. . ."

"*Now, Cassandra Dawson.* Tell me *exactly* what happened and *do it right now!*" Red thought he sounded just like his father used to when Red was naughty. But Red didn't want to treat his wife like a naughty child.

That stubborn look settled more deeply on her face. Red had the feeling that Cassie was saying some unpleasant things to him inside her head. He almost smiled. He'd wanted her to stand up to him. The trouble was, now that she was thinking about doing it, he didn't want it at all. What if Wade *had* come and somehow scared Cassie into keeping it a secret? What if he'd snuck up on the house somehow and gotten to her when Red was—

"I fell watering Buck!" Cassie said with a scowl after she'd finished fastening her buttons. "I just slipped is all, and I don't want you saying I can't. . ."

"I saw you take him down to the creek. He was walking ahead of you like always." Red let go of his worst fears as he thought about his cantankerous horse.

"He's getting better, Red. I'll be more careful."

Buck had never forgiven Cassie for flapping her skirts the

first morning she'd lived here. And he *wasn't* getting better. If anything, he had learned he could bully Cassie and was worse than ever.

"That horse has taken to dragging you along behind him," Red said. "You're too long on belly and too short on legs to make him mind."

"It's not Buck's fault I fell." Cassie crossed her arms and glowered.

"Yes it is. You shouldn't be watering him." Red felt a cold sweat break out on his forehead, picturing Cassie falling on that steep slope to the creek.

"Now, Red, don't say that." Cassie raised her hands in front of her as if asking Red to stop. "Please don't say I can't do it. It's not his fault. My hand just got twisted in the lead rope and I ended up sliding a ways. He didn't—"

"How far?" Red interrupted.

"How far what?" Cassie said, twisting her hands together.

Red knew she was ducking the question. He said through clenched teeth, "How far did he drag you after you fell?"

Cassie's jaw firmed and her lips clamped together. Red thought she was going to tell him to go soak his head. He had another quiver of humor go through him, but then he thought about Buck dragging her.

"*You tell me right now, wife, and that's an order!* When did you fall? And how far did he. . ."

"I fell right over the crest," she almost shouted.

"How far?" Red stormed at her.

"The rest of the way to the creek," she snapped back.

Dead silence reigned for just a second while Red contemplated his beloved Cassie being dragged down that treacherous path.

Speaking barely above a whisper through a throat nearly swollen shut with fear, Red asked, "And you thought you could hide this from me because you're worried about losing one of your precious chores. Right?"

Cassie's stubborn expression faded, and she looked like the worried, obedient little wife he was used to. She nodded.

Red leaned down so his nose almost touched hers and bellowed, "*You should be worried! You're losing all of them! You are going to mind me, woman!*"

He watched her fight to keep her temper from overflowing. She opened her mouth to speak a dozen times, but each time she stopped.

He wanted to goad her into fighting because it would do her good to stand up for herself. But this wasn't the time. He wasn't going to give on this. And maybe she was just too submissive to argue, or maybe she could see the stubbornness on his face just like he could see it on hers.

In the end she just said through clenched teeth, "Yes, Red."

CHAPTER 22

Wade heard the shouting.

He normally didn't come this close, but the raised voice carried up the draw to the hilltop where he watched, and he'd come down a long way toward the house, afraid Dawson was hurting his china doll right now. If only Dawson would go away, leave poor china doll for just a few minutes.

There was no window in that nasty little dirt structure, but the snow was trampled enough around the place that Wade dared to approach close enough to listen through the door. Wade had abandoned the line shack he'd found and moved into a cave a bit farther from the Dawson place. He was now a long way up the mountain, barely able to see the goings-on with his spyglass. But today for the first time, voices carried and Wade had set out at a run to save Cassie.

Dawson seemed like an easygoing dolt with his odd jobs and his work as a preacher. But Wade had learned that Dawson's eyes were sharp and he could read signs like an Indian scout. Wade had moved his campsite farther back four times now as Dawson's snooping had brought the man close to Wade's hideout.

Montana Rose

Wade rested his hand on the butt of his holstered gun, longing to rush in, finish Dawson, and clear out with the china doll in tow. But he couldn't charge in with guns blazing. He couldn't risk hitting the china doll with a stray bullet.

And there was more to it than that. Wade rested against the sod wall abutting the door. He tilted his head back and stared at the sky, sparkling with a thousand pinpoints of light. What if he went in and couldn't pull the trigger?

Please give me the courage to save her.

Wade closed his eyes and came the closest to praying he'd ever done in his life. . .at least for a long time. He needed the courage to save his china doll.

Wade waited and hoped, but that courage didn't come. He was a coward. His father was ashamed to call Wade his son. He was a poor excuse for a man.

His mother had put herself between Wade and his father many times. His mother had taken the same kind of cruelty as the china doll. Except Wade's mother had died bringing a second baby. She'd called Wade in, knowing she was dying. Now, as Wade stood in the frigid cold, shut out of the love he knew the china doll held for him, he was transported to that horrible room, six years old, listening again to his mother's sobbing apologies for dying, for leaving him alone.

And she'd been right to apologize, because Wade had soon learned just how much his mother had sheltered him. With that shelter gone, Wade had taken the full brunt of his father's anger.

Now Wade wished he could be that shelter for the china doll. He could protect her, save her.

Red's voice came though the wall again.

Was he hitting her even now? With a coward nearby who was too weak to protect her. The china doll was taking that same treatment from her second husband.

Red yelled, *"You are going to mind me, woman!"*

And the china doll answered in a sweet, scared voice, "Yes, Red."

Words Wade had learned to say to his father, quickly, with just that same obedient tone. And yet, even knowing that, Wade stayed outside. A coward.

Had Red beaten that tone out of the china doll?

"Yes, Red."

The words echoed in Wade's mind as if they were repeated over and over. And still Wade-the-Coward stayed outside.

Wade sank to his knees in the bitter Montana November and hated Red Dawson.

Hated his father.

Hated himself.

All the outside chores were strictly Red's now.

November gave way to December, and winter came down around them so hard that Red didn't attempt the trip to Divide anymore.

Red held a simple church service for the two of them those days and gained some confidence in Cassie's faith, although he always wondered if it was real or if she was just following his dictate. In the end, he couldn't even decide if it mattered.

If she believed, for whatever reason, it was good enough. Except he worried that if something happened to him and she got a new husband, her new husband might not share her faith, and it would die as easily as it had been born. That in turn meant the only way to make sure Cassie got into heaven was to outlive her. Red couldn't exactly fit that notion with any scripture he'd ever read.

Because he couldn't rightly decide what to believe, he also called a halt to the kissing after that one sweet night. He just couldn't stand the thought of her accepting his touch without thinking she had a choice. She'd tried to kiss him a couple of times and Red said no. It was the closest she came to being annoyed with him. Well, fine. It would do his obedient little wife some good to get mad.

The baby was due anytime, so Red took to staying even closer to the house. He'd found definite signs that Wade was in the area until the last few weeks. No footprints or horse tracks had shown up lately. Red reluctantly left her alone in the cabin if the weather was too bad, but he was never gone for long.

He went out to ride herd on his cattle one particularly bitterly cold day with snow sleeting down, turning the whole world into an icy, slippery nightmare. He stayed away from Cassie as long as he thought he dared. Then in a wind that had picked up to near-blizzard strength, he made his way back to the house. He found Cassie coming out of the chicken coop.

While he was still at a distance, he saw her walk slowly over the glaze, carrying a bucket of eggs. She was in the house before he could get to her, so he put Buck away with a fine fury riding him and marched into the house to have it out with his contrary wife.

He shut the door with an unnecessarily loud *crack*.

Cassie whirled to face him with her usual welcoming smile.

"You're supposed to stay inside. You know Wade could be around, and even if he isn't, it's a sheet of ice out there. You could have *broken your fool neck!*"

Cassie's smile quickly faded to fear.

Red stormed up to her.

"B–But, Red, Wade wouldn't be out in this weather. And you're working so hard. I thought just this once it would really save you—"

"You," Red cut her off, "don't save me *ten minutes* with your blasted help. But I'd spend the rest of the winter working double-time if you broke your leg. If you don't have the sense to be afraid of Wade, you could at least have a little consideration for me!"

Cassie flinched away from him.

That made Red madder. She had a lot of nerve being scared of him when he'd been so patient. . .except maybe for right now.

"But Red, I can at least feed the chickens and gather the eggs. It's not like the chickens can drag me along on the ground."

"Don't argue with me." Red felt his temper flare white hot when she referred to the way Buck had bullied her. Her scrapes had barely healed from that episode. "It's icy outside. You could fall on your way to the chicken coop."

Cassie nodded, and her meek obedience blew the top off what little restraint was left on Red's temper. He bent over her so she had to lean back to look him in the eye. "Say it," Red demanded.

"Say what?"

"You know."

"No, I don't know what you're talking about, Red." Cassie furrowed her brow. He knew she was trying desperately to think what he wanted from her. Trying to be the obedient wife. Trying to be everything he wanted before he had to ask. But he didn't want that. He wanted her mad. "Say that nasty, awful thing you're thinking. Mind me, wife."

Cassie's eyes widened, and Red knew she really had been thinking something awful. He almost smiled.

"Why Red, I wasn't thinking anything nasty about you," she said sweetly.

"And I say you're a liar," Red announced with soft menace.

Cassie's eyes flashed.

Somewhere buried inside his meek little wife was a volcano under intense pressure and threatening to erupt. He couldn't stop himself from goading her. "A liar, and a poor one at that.

And a coward who won't speak her mind."

"Red Dawson, I am not. . ." Cassie's fingers flew to her mouth.

Red pulled her hand away. "What did you just say to me? Did you contradict me, woman? No wife of mine is gonna say anything to me but—" Red spoke in a wavery falsetto, a terrible mockery of a woman's voice, " 'Yes, Red. Yes, sir. I'll do whatever you say, and I'll do it right quick.' "

Cassie made the same instinctive movement she always made with her fingers, but this time she pressed her fingers against Red's mouth. He fell silent. Then from behind her fingers, he said softly, "Say it, Cass."

Her cheeks turned the most amazing shade of pink, and she sucked in a deep breath but didn't speak.

Red caught her hand and lifted it from his mouth and held it gently. "Say, 'You're a polecat, Red Dawson.' Tell me I'm a mangy, growly old bear. Tell me I'm a sneakin', low-down coyote. Tell me I'm as mean as a rattler and as cantankerous as Buck and as stubborn as an ox. Say it or admit you're a liar and a coward, Mrs. Dawson. Tell me I'm a—"

"All those animals," Cassie interrupted, "are put here by God for the exact purpose they serve." Rather sharply she added, "*You're* the problem."

Cassie seemed to realize what she'd said, and she pulled back a step. She'd have covered her mouth again if Red hadn't held tight to her hand.

Red grinned for a second. Then he tipped his head back and laughed out loud. It was a full belly laugh, and when he looked back at her, his eyes were damp from laughing and he had to wipe them. "Why, Cassandra Dawson, I do believe you just insulted me."

"Oh, Red, I'm sorry."

Red pulled her into his arms and kissed her. He kissed her

until he felt the starch go out of her knees. Then he swept her, big belly and all, into his arms, strode to a chair, and settled her on his lap so he could surround her completely.

Cassie pulled back, bewildered. "Red, does this mean you'll kiss me when I'm rude to you?"

"I reckon it does, Cass honey."

"I. . .I've been wanting you to kiss me, Red. I just never dreamed the way to get you to was to—"

Red kissed her again just for saying she wanted him to.

Cassie wrapped her arms around his neck, then slid her hands to his face and lifted herself away from him. "If you wanted me to be sassy, you should have told me you'd do this."

Red laughed again but not for long. He started kissing her again, exploring her face with his lips. He had been tormented by how sweet she smelled when she lay next to him and the tiny sounds she made as she slept. He'd dreamed of tracing the outline of her perfect, silken cheekbones with his lips.

He was so busy satisfying his curiosity that it took him awhile to notice Cassie wasn't being a shy little creature now. She had her arms tight around his neck, and she made little gasps and sighs of pleasure that were driving him crazy even before he was conscious of them.

Then suddenly she let out a gasp that was different from the others. She went rigid in his arms, so tense and distressed he pulled back, ashamed at his lack of restraint. He didn't get a chance to apologize.

Cassie snatched her arms away from his neck and grabbed at her stomach. "Something's wrong."

Red looked from her belly to her face to her belly to her face about fifteen times before he got his eyes under control. "Is it the babe? Do you think the babe's coming?"

Cassie's attention had been riveted on her stomach. When Red asked about the baby, she looked up at him frantically. "I can't have the baby yet!"

"But I thought you said it was due the middle of December. That's now, Cass. Why can't you have it yet?" Red tried to think of every possible thing that could be going wrong that made it dangerous for Cassie to have the baby right now.

Tears filled Cassie's eyes as she looked to him to fix whatever was wrong. She wailed, "Because I'm too young to be a mother!"

Red had seen her cry a few times, silent tears with an occasional genteel sob. Her mouth hadn't twisted, her skin had been pure, flawless white. She had cried more beautifully than any woman Red had ever seen. And with a bunch of big sisters, he'd seen a few.

This was nothing like that. Cassie opened her mouth and made a terrible ruckus with her sobs. Her skin got all blotchy, tears turned her eyes red, her nose ran, and her hair started sticking to her face wherever she was soggy.

Red rubbed her back. "There, there." It was all he knew about birthing babies. Although he'd made Muriel tell him a few things.

Birthing babies? Muriel! Red thought of the vicious sleet pounding down more fiercely every minute. No one was going to make it out here to help bring this babe.

"Ouch!" Cassie shouted through her tears.

"What? What's happening?" Red asked desperately.

"You're crushing me!"

Red was sitting, thinking about what was in store for them, and he'd been strangling her. He relaxed his hold.

"Go for help, Red," Cassie whispered. Her voice caught. She gasped raggedly for a second, then she choked out, "Go to Jessups' and send for Muriel."

Red was struck speechless. He wasn't going ten feet in this weather. He was going to have to do it alone. Cassie was too young to have a babe, and Red realized with a sickening twist of his gut that he was, too.

An urgent desire to do something, anything, made Red stand with Cassie still in his arms. "Let's get you to bed." He carried her into the bedroom.

By the time Red had her in the back room, she started pushing at his shoulders. "Let me down. I'm not going to bed."

Then she glared at him. "Muriel can't come out in this weather. Don't you dare go for her!" Cassie sounded calm and confident, not the frightened little girl she'd been two minutes ago and not the shy, submissive wife she was the rest of the time.

Red was having a little trouble adjusting. "No, I mean, yes, I mean, what do you want me to do?"

"Let me down this instant!" Cassie shoved at his shoulders again.

He lowered her to the floor, never letting go of her in case she sank into a heap on the ground or started moaning again or burst into flames. . .or whatever women in labor did.

"That took me by surprise, but now that I'm ready for it, it won't be so bad next time." Cassie looked around the bedroom ceiling as if she were searching for cobwebs and considering knocking them down. She gave a nod of her head and dusted her hands together and left the room.

Red trailed behind her.

Cassie headed for the cooler and ducked inside.

"What are you doing? What do you need in there?" Red joined her in the cramped room. She was slicing the ham.

Red grabbed the knife from her. "We don't need to eat now."

Cassie turned to him. "I don't believe I'll eat, no. But it's near your noon mealtime. You'll be wanting something."

The mere thought of food made Red want to choke. "Don't you think you should lie down?" Red asked, hacking at the ham just for something to do.

"Muriel says I should stay up for as long as possible. She said I'll be so sick of lying in bed by the end that I'll want these first few hours back."

"Hours?" Red stopped slicing and looked sideways at her. "How many hours?"

"Muriel said her first child made his appearance about twenty-four hours after the first pains."

"Twenty-four hours!" Red yelled.

Cassie patted him on the arms as if he were the one facing a full day of pains.

"Yes, but Libby said her first was only four hours and Leota said ten, so I guess we can't know for sure." Cassie took the slice of ham and didn't mention the fact the Red had hacked it into four pieces. She left the cooler.

Red hurried to catch up.

Cassie turned into a woman Red had never met before. She was utterly calm, totally competent, and almost maniacally busy.

She cooked him a noon meal even though it was only about half past ten. He didn't mention that fact, and she didn't seem to care. She peeled potatoes and mixed a batch of biscuits. She started a new rising of bread for tomorrow and wiped every inch of the kitchen.

And she talked. She talked more words in the following half hour than Red had heard her say since they'd gotten married.

"I never gave eggs much thought back East. Then when we got out here and there were no chickens, Griff had some sent from St. Louis. The cost of those chickens! And none of them lived out the first week we had them. We had a pig that died, and a milk cow that never gave us so much as a swallow of milk. Griff told me coyotes got the chickens and. . ."

Cassie bustled around the kitchen at about twice her

normal speed, chattering about chickens and how much she liked eggs. She occasionally asked his opinion about something, and it took Red about five minutes to catch on that he'd better have an answer right quick, but it'd better be a short one. Her eyebrows would furrow, and she'd look nervously at him if he didn't hold up his end of the conversation. But if he answered more than, "Yes," or, "No," or, "Whatever you say," she'd start talking right over top of him. She was listening to him for the sound but she wasn't really *hearing* anything he said. He just humored her because he didn't have any idea what else to do.

He took anything the least bit heavy out of her hands and moved it to wherever she had in mind. He stayed out of her way as best he could, while she whirled from the table to the sink to the fireplace, preparing him a dinner he didn't think he could begin to eat.

Red had been hovering nearby for nearly half an hour, watching her for the first sign of impending disaster—which Red assumed was inevitable—when she stopped in her monologue to stiffen and hold her stomach.

The exact moment she started breathing hard, he stepped away from her because she'd been heading for the cooler with a bucket. He'd taken it from her, almost resulting in a tug-of-war before she let it go. He headed to the cooler to refill it. He glanced back at her and saw her gripping the back of a chair with whitened knuckles and staring blankly into space. He dropped the bucket and dashed to her side and held her.

"Don't touch me," Cassie snarled.

Red jumped back as surely as if a rattler had attacked him.

Then her voice deepened almost to a growl. "Get your filthy hands off me."

It was a voice he'd never heard come out of his submissive little wife before.

Montana Rose

The minute he backed away, Cassie turned to him and grabbed him around the waist. She buried her face against his chest. "Hold me, please, Red."

His head spinning, he cautiously wrapped his arms around her. He kissed her silken hair softly, like he did when they slept side by side. He rubbed her rigid shoulders. She moaned as if the touch were comforting. He felt her stomach grow hard between them, and his heart ached as Cassie whimpered with distress and burrowed closer to him. Since she seemed to like her shoulders rubbed, he slid one hand down her back and around to massage her taut belly.

"What are you doing?" She shrieked like he'd tried to push her off a cliff. "Get your hands off me." She shoved hard at his arm.

Pulling away from her, he stammered, "I'm. . .I'm sorry. I won't touch you if you. . ."

A loud wail broke off his wretched apology. "You think I'm fat and ugly." Cassie buried her face in both hands and sobbed as if she'd lost her best friend in the world.

"Cassie, no." He stepped away from her. "I think you're—"

"Red!" She hurled herself back into his arms. "Don't let me go. No matter what, never let me go."

Red held his hands carefully out at his sides, afraid to touch her as she snuggled up against him. He slowly lowered his hands, ready to snatch them back at the first sign of trouble. When his hands settled lightly around her waist, she whispered, "Thank you. Thank you so much."

He held her closer, careful to avoid her stomach, thinking that might have been the problem. Gingerly he moved with her to a chair and sat in it with her, as he had during her first pain. He rubbed her back and made meaningless noises of comfort to her, and thought, *Thirty minutes down, twenty-three and a half hours to go.*

The worst-case example was Muriel's daylong laboring. Red didn't see any reason to hope for the best. He held her and rocked back and forth and prayed for divine intervention.

Suddenly, she shoved his arms away from her and stood briskly. "What are you thinking? I've got dinner to get on." She hurried back to the fireplace.

He wondered whether his twisting stomach could hold down a single swallow. And would he make her angry if he refused to eat? Worse yet, would she start crying again?

She started humming softly while she worked.

It occurred to Red that she had been yelling at him and demanding that he do her bidding and do it right now. With a sudden melting in his heart he thought, *I'm finally meeting the real Cassie. . .except insane.*

He knew it was true. This was Cassie with all of her conditioned behavior stripped away. Sassy and demanding and efficient and filling his home with music. He'd been half in love with her since the first time he'd laid eyes on her, and his heart had softened to her right from the beginning of their marriage, but now he knew that hadn't been love because now he knew what the real thing was.

Love, fierce like a lion defending its cubs, roared through him. This Cassie was who he wanted, and he wasn't going to settle for anyone else. He wished fervently that after the babe was born she'd stay like she was right now, but he knew there was little chance. It would take time, but they had all the time in the world. He'd dig this woman out of her shell if it took him the rest of his life.

Cassie grabbed at the heavy skillet she had hanging on a peg on the wall, and Red rushed to lift it for her. She whacked at his hands with a wooden spoon. "Don't you have any chores to do outside?"

"I'm carrying this frying pan for you." Red pried her fingers off it. "Now tell me where you want it."

She fussed and scolded at him as she shooed him toward the fireplace.

Red thought, *Maybe we don't have all the time in the world. A man can die a hundred times, in a hundred different ways, in twenty-four hours.*

CHAPTER 23

She had to finish dinner.

She had to clean up the kitchen afterward, not just tidy but clean down to the bone.

She had to scrub the floor, but she couldn't scrub a dirt floor. But she had to!

She had to scald all the cook pots and search out the last particle of dust. Cobwebs! There might be cobwebs!

What about the slit that opened off her bedroom? What kind of filth lurked in that dark passageway? She had to ferret out every threatening speck so nothing dirty would touch— Her mind veered away from the why. She didn't dare think about the baby on the way.

She became aware that under the urgent need to hurry, she was hearing two different voices guiding her. For the first time in a long time she was separated from herself. The china doll, trying to be perfect, but with a twist because the china doll had been trying to be perfect for Griff. Now, her only standard was for herself, because Red never asked her to be perfect. But in some disjointed way, she knew the drive to have everything sparkling clean and in order was linked to the china doll.

And the other Cassie, the furious, childish Cassie, wanted everything just right, too. But she wanted to holler. She wanted to hit something. She wanted to make Red clean the stupid house himself, for heaven's sake. She shouldn't have to clean in her condition.

Which led her to think of the baby coming, and her mind careened off again. Having a baby was too huge. She was too young. She wasn't ready to give birth to a child, let alone raise one.

Panic roiled in her stomach, blared in her head. The childish Cassie wanted to release all of the tension with violence. . .or at least with a temper tantrum to end all temper tantrums. She yanked tight on the reins of her emotions and kept the angry, terrified Cassie silent.

To cover her turmoil, she forced the china doll to the forefront of her mind and worked. She had to wash and iron her nightgown. It had to be immaculate. She grabbed a bucket and hurried toward the cooler.

Red took it from her.

She nearly jumped out of her skin. "What are you doing in here?"

"I've been here right along, Cass." Red gave her a worried look as he rested his hand on her arm. "I'll get water. You shouldn't be doing heavy lifting."

"Everything has to be clean. Everything has to be absolutely clean." Her ears hurt a little, as though she'd shouted the words, but it hadn't sounded loud, so that couldn't be the source of the pain. Somehow her ears hurting must be Red's fault. She wanted the nightgown washed in boiling water, and he was holding on to the bucket. Everything in the room had to be spotless.

He glanced around the room. "It's fine. You won't even be in the room anyway."

Not be in the room? A vision of her baby being born without her being in the same room with it ricocheted around in her head. What kind of stupid thing was that to say?

He stared at her funny for a few seconds, and Cassie had the sudden sick feeling that maybe she'd spoken her thoughts out loud. She shook her head. Impossible. She'd never call Red stupid, no matter what kind of idiot he acted like.

His eyes widened and he glanced nervously from her, to the bucket, to the cooler, and back to her again. She got the impression he was afraid to leave the room.

She had to wash her nightgown. The baby might take twenty-four hours, but she didn't want to rely on that. She reached for the pail, determined to take care of fetching water if he was too lazy and useless to help her.

His eyebrows shot up all the way to his red hair. He held the pail away from her and practically ran into the cooler.

She wondered what had him acting so weird.

He came back out with a full bucket. They always left one sitting under the trickling spring to fill. Speaking softly, using the same voice she'd heard him use on a spooky, green-broke horse, he said, "I'm not acting weird."

She thought that was an odd comment to make. It was as if he'd read her mind. She shook her head to clear it of such a distracting possibility.

"My nightgown." She raced into her room and came back with the white gown Muriel had given her.

She tried to take the pail from Red.

"Where do you want it?" he asked.

"Fill a basin and hang it over the fire."

He did as she asked with alacrity.

She threw her nightgown in the still-cold water to soak. While she was there, she checked the cook pot, fiercely determined that today of all days the potatoes wouldn't be scorched. She leaned into the fireplace, and using a towel to protect her hand, she lifted the lid on the pot that hung side by side with the stewing nightgown and stirred.

Red took the lid out of her hand and pulled her away from the fire and dealt with the potatoes himself.

Then she elbowed him aside and checked the ham in the cast-iron skillet that sat nestled off to the side of the flames.

"Watch out for the fire." Red pulled her back.

She was just straightening from her task to slug him in the shoulder when the baby made itself known again. She looked down at her stomach in disgust. How was she supposed to get her work done and forget about the coming difficult hours if the child kept pestering her?

"You'll do fine, Cassie. We'll get everything done that needs doin'."

He was reading her mind again and that made her angry, and she had to clamp down on the irate Cassie inside of her all the more. She was aware of Red uncurling her hand, one finger at a time, from his shirt. But she didn't remember how her hand had gotten there to begin with. Then the pain got strong enough that all she was conscious of was Red holding her and sharing his vast strength with her. When it eased, she was sitting in his lap again, and that struck her as completely ridiculous when she had dinner cooking and a house to clean. She leaped off his lap and went back to work.

The noon meal was fine except she didn't eat it and Red ate his so fast she didn't remember his sitting down to the table. And it was all burned because she was forever finding herself hugged up tight against Red. One time she stood up to find the potatoes boiled dry and scorched until they were ruined. Red said he liked them that way and set the pot aside.

The next time the pain eased, the ham had dried out. Cassie didn't mean to cry over something so insignificant as a burned piece of meat, but she heard Red telling her not to cry and so she supposed she had. Red didn't seem to mind the blackened ham. He said he loved ham and potatoes just that way. And when the biscuits burned, Red was the one who pulled them out of the fire, and he blamed himself for not getting them sooner, so that was his own fault.

She thought, *Why does he keep distracting me and holding me when he knows I have work to do?*

"I'm sorry," he said. "I'll never distract you again. I promise."

Which was stupid of him since she hadn't told him what she was thinking.

Then he said, "I agree completely. It *was* stupid of me."

Which confused her all the more, especially since a few minutes later she found herself in his arms again, and after his promise!

He dished himself up a full meal, then she was being held close and the meal was gone. She wondered if he'd enjoyed it.

He said, "It was delicious."

At that point she resigned herself to having a husband who could read her mind and released that worry from her over-crowded collection of worries.

Somewhere the acceptance of Red's mind reading reached through the strange panic that had seized her from the moment of her first pain. She started to feel almost entranced by him. His voice seemed to be the only solid ground as her body acted on its own, hurting her for no reason.

Red crooned to her and stayed by her side while she fussed over her kitchen and the bedroom. He took orders, stirring her gown in the boiling water and rinsing it and wringing it out. Then he even heated the flat iron and pressed the nightgown until it was dry and left it draped over a chair near the fireplace to rid it of its last bit of dampness while he helped her hunt down cobwebs in the cave passageway.

Montana Rose

At some point, she quit working altogether and just sat in a chair Red always had at hand and barked orders at him. Then her stomach would begin to tense up and she'd freeze up from her chores, and Red would be right there, a port in the storm that raged around her. He'd hold her and whisper gentle petitions to the Lord for courage and wisdom. The time came when the pains became too persistent, and she had to give up on cleaning the house, although she demanded he mop the kitchen floor.

"It's a dirt floor, Cass. It'll turn to mud."

Then he was wiping tears from her eyes and promising he'd scrub the floor until he was down to bedrock. He held her then and kissed her hair and talked in the casual way he always did to God, bringing a holy presence into the room with them.

He asked her about preparing the bed for the time the baby would come.

She told him of Muriel's instructions on how to boil water and lay out the baby's clothes and sterilize a knife to cut the cord and lay thick sheets on the bed to protect the mattress. Cassie didn't know what the mattress was being protected from, but she was determined to follow Muriel's orders to the letter.

The lantern was lit, which seemed odd to Cassie, because it wasn't noon yet, and Cassie found herself with bare moments between the pains to try and bring order to her thoughts. She thought about demanding time and privacy to put on her nightgown, but then her stomach was grabbed as though a mountain lion sank its teeth into her belly, and somehow she was in bed, wearing her nightgown.

The next clear thought she had was that she must have put her nightgown on very swiftly and gone to bed, because somehow she was in bed but she didn't know how she'd found the strength. Unless she'd found it from Red. He was always there. Always within reach.

The petulant Cassie began to rear her head more fiercely.

She wanted to hurt Red because she was hurting, and it didn't seem fair that she had to hurt alone. She wanted to scream at him and loathe all men through him, because he could never have a child, but he could make a child grow inside a woman and then leave her to die alone.

She even daydreamed of taking a swing at him several times. The china doll controlled all those ugly impulses though, kept them tucked inside, free to rage in her imagination without harming the man who was her only grasp on life.

Suddenly the pains changed. She felt as if she were caught up in the center of a tornado. She saw all the whipping winds whirling around her, but she herself was spared their violence for an instant. Then weight, like the entire mountain over her head, pressed down on her belly, crushing her, crushing her baby. She wanted to cry out because of the unfairness of their home caving in on her after she'd been through so much. Red's voice reached her, warring with the terror in her mind, offering words of calm assurance.

Red sat beside her on the bed. She heard him pray over her as he wiped sweat from her brow. He calmed her as the mountain receded and her bedroom took shape. He moved away from her and she wanted to cling to him.

"It's coming, Cass honey. The baby's coming. I see the head. It's almost time. It's almost over." He kept talking, kept calling on God to be with them, to give them strength sufficient to the task they faced. The words eased the rest of the weight from her, even as she felt the agonizing pressure again. But the mountain didn't cave in again. Red's words kept the roof from falling.

Strength sufficient for the task. That's all she needed. She asked for that herself, speaking the words out loud. She didn't need to take on the whole world…or even face the next twenty-four hours that it would take for the baby to be born. She only needed to survive the very instant she was living in. She asked for the baby to live even if she gave up her own life, as seemed inevitable now. The pressure intensified, then relented enough for her to take a breath, then came surging back.

Red shouted just as the strain on her body became un-endurable. And in an instant she went from agony to relief. And Red laughed out loud, and something dark lifted away from Cassie's mind, far enough that she heard a quavering noise. The noise, that tiny cry gripped at her heart and held on so tightly she knew it would never let her go, and she knew she would never want it to.

Her eyes darted toward the noise to see Red standing with a writhing, noisy, messy creature in his hands. She was so exhausted that she couldn't make sense of what she was seeing. Reality tried to force its way past her confused, exhausted mind as a tigress awoke in her at the sound of her unhappy child, but for a long minute she couldn't make that squalling, white and red bundle in Red's arms be the baby she knew she'd just borne.

Then Red pulled a soft blanket around what he held. He sat on the bed beside her on her left and held the baby in the crook of his left arm. He leaned close to her until the noisy baby would have rested across her chest if he'd put it down. He tilted the baby so she could see its face, and the wild confusion that was fogging her mind cleared and the baby was real to her at last.

Red laughed and drew her attention briefly away from the child, the extension of herself. Red was a mess. A joyful mess. His hair was wild as if he'd run his hands through it a thousand times in the few minutes since her pains had started. His brown shirt was wet and tinged pink all across the front. His sleeves were rolled up to his elbows as he liked to wear them when he did his woodwork in the evening.

She forgot about his being a mess when she looked in his eyes. He was looking at the baby, and for a moment, Cassie saw the eyes of a man who had witnessed a miracle. She drank in the wisdom and purity of what she saw in Red and absorbed his joy into her soul.

After a bare second studying him, she looked back at her baby with a renewed strength of her own. All she could see was a tiny, wrinkled face. Red had the blanket she'd knitted wrapped snugly around the squirming infant, even over its hair.

The baby howled with its eyes shut tight and its mouth wide open. The baby's whole body shook from the force of the cries. Suddenly, five tiny fingers poked up from the blanket. Cassie was awestruck by the miniature perfection of her baby. One of Red's big work-callused hands reached between Cassie and the baby, and he touched the wee baby fingers with one of his own, lifting and caressing gently.

The baby's hand suddenly grasped hold of Red's index finger. The tiny hand didn't reach all the way around, but the grip was tight. Each finger bent, grasping firmly. There were nails, so little they were barely visible, tipping each finger.

Everything a human being ever had, the baby brought with it into the world in a package so small it would fit inside a mother's belly, and Cassie knew why Red looked as though he'd seen a miracle. She was witnessing one, too.

She looked away from the baby to Red. He was still smiling; his eyes still blazed with joy. But now a tear streaked its way down his face. Cassie felt her whole world tilt dangerously at the sight of the single tear. She wasn't aware of moving, but she saw her hand touch Red's face and wipe the tear away.

When she touched him, he looked away from the baby. Something solid stretched between them as their eyes locked. More than an emotion, more than a shared memory, it was a connection so tangible that it could have been built from stone.

Montana Rose

Cassie believed she could hold it in her hands if she wished. Cassie felt it, whatever it was, wrap around her just as the baby's cry had, entwining with her heart so deeply that it could never be undone.

CHAPTER 24

Red's hand came to rest on Cassie's where it lay on his cheek. He pressed her palm against his skin. The baby screamed louder, and the wriggling presence between them deepened the closeness Red felt between them, if that was possible.

Red's heart turned over to see dark circles under Cassie's heavy-lidded eyes. He knew how tired he was after staying by her side during the endless day and night of her laboring. He couldn't imagine her fatigue. He knew he should insist she rest, but the love that glowed out of her for the baby was too precious to interrupt with something as earthbound as sleep.

Her feather-light touch on his trailing tears moved him so profoundly that he knew he would never be the same. He leaned down to Cassie until their bodies cocooned the baby gently between them, and still holding her hand, he kissed her. He pulled his lips away a scant inch. Her eyes had drifted shut. "Open your eyes, Cass."

She did, but he could see the struggle she put up to keep her heavy lids raised.

He looked at her, but his gaze reached inside and joined

with the ties that were binding them together, until he was part of her and she was part of him. "I love you, Cassie Dawson. I love you and I love our little. . ."

With a sudden start, Red remembered something vital.

A tiny spurt of fear flashed in Cassie's eyes. "What is it?"

Red said, chagrined, "I just realized I don't know if the baby is a boy or a girl."

They looked at each other again, and suddenly they were laughing. All the fear and hard work and wonder erupted from them. Red's deep, warm chuckle and Cassie's gentler laughter mingled, as surely as their hearts had mingled moments ago.

They didn't laugh for long, because the baby gave a particularly furious roar of anger and drew their attention. Red held the infant while Cassie, with hands trembling from exhaustion, unwrapped the blanket.

"A girl," Red whispered. "She'll be as beautiful and ornery as her mama."

Cassie said, "I'm not ornery." Then she said, "Look at her toes." They were as perfect as the rest of her.

Red said, "Check her over good. Then we'd better wrap her back up."

Cassie nodded. "She needs a bath. . .but out by the fireplace where it's warm."

"Should you feed her first?" Red asked.

Cassie looked up at him when he asked. He could see he'd startled her. Then, inexplicably, she was crying. Through her tears she said, "I'm the worst mother who ever lived!"

"I'm sorry, Cass. I didn't mean. . ." He knew she couldn't hear him over her tears, so he quit talking. Her body was battered with the force of her sobs. Red hugged her awkwardly as she lay on her back with the baby still between them in his arms.

The crying eased a bit, and he said, "You don't have to feed her yet if you don't want to."

She snarled at him so savagely he was reminded of a mountain lion he'd come face-to-face with his first year in Montana. "I will, too, feed her. And I'll do it right now!"

The baby jumped wildly when Cassie yelled. She still lay half on Cassie's chest, half in Red's arms. Both arms and legs flew out, her whole, tiny body jerked, and she howled as if someone had stuck her with a pin.

"I scared her." Cassie started crying all the harder.

Wade heard the baby cry.

The child had been born. Something cracked into pieces in his heart to know that the little one had come. Wade didn't know much about birthing a child, but he knew it was a long, hard business for a woman, and he hadn't been there to help or protect his fragile china doll.

He'd crept up to the cabin in the vicious weather early this morning when Red didn't emerge to do his usual chores. He had to know what was going on inside.

He might get caught, coming this close in the daytime, but if he was careful, the storm would cover his tracks and he could have a moment to be close to the china doll.

He crouched by the door to the soddy and ached from the awful cold.

He'd traveled into the high country to keep Red from discovering him. He rarely came down close enough to even spy on his china doll from the high hills. But yesterday the storm had given him enough cover to risk getting close enough to where his spyglass worked. And he'd seen no sign of anyone all afternoon and evening yesterday, nor anyone this morning. With the security of the storm to shield him, and starving for a tiny bit of his woman, he'd crept down close.

The only shelter Wade found big enough for himself and

his horse was a miserable cave that seemed to catch the wind. The gale whipped around inside and moaned until Wade heard voices in the howling current. Sometimes his father's, sometimes the china doll crying for help, sometimes. . .maybe. . .God's.

Wade had taken money from his account in Divide before he'd laid the false trail out of town, but he'd spent almost none of it. He could afford to live better, but he'd have to go to town to spend it. There was warm food and light at his father's ranch. But Wade refused to take another beating in exchange for shelter.

He listened to that baby cry and felt himself transported to another time, another baby born in a lowly place. He remembered the prayers and lessons of his mother and wondered how he'd been brought so low as to crouch in this cold, hurting all the way to his soul for a woman who'd been stolen from him.

He sank to the ground, his head bowed, and he tried to clear the traces of whiskey and hate from his thoughts. Behind that he found fear and hopelessness and terrible, aching loneliness. It was too much to bear, and he pulled his bottle from the pocket of his coat to drown the pain.

One thing did become clear. He loved that new baby as much as he loved his china doll, and he couldn't take them away in this cold. He hated to do it, but there was no way now to rescue them until the cold eased.

The strange, tinny crying stopped, and all that was left was the wind, biting into Wade's coat, laughing in his ear, telling him he'd sunk as low as a man could sink.

Thinking of that badger hole of a cave he slept in, Wade tried to figure out how that was any better than taking his father's fist. His father would laugh to know Wade had been reduced to such lowly straits.

He couldn't be close enough to protect his china doll.

He couldn't work up the guts to kill Red Dawson.

He was worthless.

A poor excuse for a man.

Finally, in desperation, he lurched to his feet and staggered into the woods and up the treacherous slope to where he'd concealed his horse. He'd leave.

His horse seemed eager when Wade swung up onto his back.

"We're gonna find a warm place for a couple of months, boy. But then we'll be back. We'll get the china doll and hightail it to Denver. Live there till the winter weather breaks."

The horse snorted and shook his head, the metal in his bridle clinking. White breath whooshed from the impatient animal.

Wade clapped the horse on the neck. He'd taught the bay to lie down in the cave, and Wade had learned to use the big animal's body for warmth. It had been awhile since Wade had met anyone whom he cared for more than this big, gentle horse.

How had Red managed to turn that cave he lived in into a place so welcoming?

Wade rode his horse down the mountain, far from Red's cave. While he rode, Wade planned. He'd go somewhere and find his backbone. He'd catch a man drunk and he'd learn how to kill.

The thought made him shudder, and Wade believed he heard the soft whisper of his mother's voice, full of gentleness and love. Or maybe it was someone else. Someone who might be near, watching, caring. Wade's mother had taught him about God, but Wade's father had taught him it was foolish to put hope in some fancy.

Wade drank deeply to silence that voice and the pain that came with hearing it. The whiskey separated him from the hurt inside and gave him liquid courage. He'd go to Denver and face down a man who wasn't a danger to him. Once he won a shootout, pulled that trigger for the first time, the next killing would be easier.

The wild air howled at him that he was a coward and a failure.

A poor excuse for a man.

CHAPTER 25

Cassie sobbed as she fumbled with the tiny buttons that ran in a row down the front of her nightgown most of the way to her waist.

Red caught both of her hands in one of his. "Stop, Cassie. Don't cry. Don't be upset. Please, I didn't mean to make you cry, Cass honey. Please."

Red's crooning comfort took awhile to penetrate the maelstrom raging out of her. He prayed silently for patience, afraid praying aloud would make her cry again. Then he said softly, "You're just tired. You didn't hurt the baby. You're fine. The baby's fine."

Slowly the latest outburst of tears eased, and Red, thinking feeding the baby was what had started all of this, propped a folded blanket behind Cassie's shoulders and adjusted it until she was nearly sitting upright. He'd shared such total intimacy with Cassie today that he hoped she wouldn't demand modesty between them. But Cassie wasn't exactly reasonable right now. He hesitated for a split second before he slipped the buttons of her gown free and pushed the fabric aside. Then he laid the still-uncovered baby against Cassie's bare skin until the little girl's face pressed against Cassie's breast.

Cassie didn't protest, but she was still so upset, he wasn't sure her acceptance of his touch meant anything.

He moved Cassie's arms until she held the baby in her own arms. The first time she'd completely supported their little girl. The baby was cuddled securely against her. With a move so sure it was startling, the baby turned its head toward the warmth, latched on, and began nursing vigorously. Cassie jumped and Red noticed with relief she had quit crying.

"Look at the little sweetheart go," Red said with awe. "She knows exactly what to do."

Cassie nodded, but she didn't take her eyes off her baby girl. "She knows how to feed herself. It's impossible. And she knew how to grab your finger."

Red watched as, with aching care, Cassie touched her baby's hand, and the petite hand grabbed hold just as it had with Red. Cassie started crying again.

Red groaned softly, then kissed Cassie's tear-streaked cheeks and held her face cradled in his hands. He lifted Cassie's hand with the baby still clinging to her index finger and kissed both hands together.

Red murmured a prayer against their interwoven fingers. Red asked God to make him good enough to be a father and husband. He asked for patience and wisdom and unshakable faith, and he added silently a request for God to make Cassie stop crying because it was breaking his heart. He also thanked God Seth had warned him about the emotional upheaval a woman goes through during and after the birth of a baby.

Cassie spent the next hour focused totally on her perfect little girl while Red straightened the room, and, lifting Cassie and the baby from one side of the bed to the other, put on clean sheets.

Montana Rose

Red brought in warm water and a soft cloth and gave the baby a bath as it lay in Cassie's warm arms. Cassie protested that the room was too cold, but Red told her to keep the baby close to her and she'd stay warm enough. Red carefully exposed one small part of the baby at a time, cleaned it gently, and then covered her again. He even bathed the baby's head while she was still nursing and fumbled around until he'd put on his first diaper.

It was Red's idea to switch the baby to the other breast. He said it was so he could more easily wash her other side, but Cassie said something about feeding her baby on only one side and not thinking to change to the other, and she started crying again.

Red kept up a sweet, meaningless one-sided conversation as he saw to it that Cassie was adequately bathed. She squirmed with embarrassment, but considering the details of birthing a baby, she allowed it. Red even scooted her forward a bit and slid in behind her, unbraiding her hair and combing it. He spent long minutes coaxing the snarls out, intent on sparing her one more instant of pain.

When it was finally a smooth, silken mass in his hands, he tried to braid it, but he made a botched job of it, so he draped it over Cassie's shoulder and said, "I'll hold the little tyke. You braid." Cassie's hair hung down until it was a curtain around the feasting baby. Red circled his arms around Cassie and held the baby to nurse while she did her hair with trembling hands.

Finally, the room was neat. The baby and Cassie were tidy and tucked in warm. The baby fell asleep in the midst of her energetic suckling.

Red eased the baby out of Cassie's grasp, smiling at her reluctance to let go. He had pulled the cradle up to the side of the bed, but before he could lay her down, Cassie said, "Muriel said to hold her against your shoulder and burp her before you lay her down."

Red shifted the baby around, carefully asking just how to

do it. The babe slept limply against his shoulder as he patted her back, and finally she burped to suit Cassie. Then Red laid the baby on her stomach in the crib. The baby curled her knees under her belly until her bottom stuck up in the air. Red covered her with Cassie's thickly knitted coverlet. Cassie groaned as she rolled onto her side to stare at the baby as it slept.

Red sat on the bed beside her. He rested one hand on her shoulder. "Are you all right, Cass honey?"

Cassie glanced at him. "I'm fine, Red. Wonderful. Just tired. Can you believe how beautiful she is?"

The two of them looked at the little miracle that had been added to their lives that day. Red reached through the wooden slats to rub the back of a fist that was curled up near the baby's face. "What are we going to name her?"

Cassie seemed sure about one thing. "I want her name to be Dawson. We haven't talked about it, and I suppose she could be named Griffin, but I want her to be ours, Red. Both of ours. You don't mind, do you?"

Red had thought about it, and he wanted the babe to carry his name so badly that he hurt. But he thought Cassie would want to give this honor to Griff. Now, at her simple request, he felt tears burn in the back of his eyes. "I would be proud for her to carry my name, and it would be good for her to share the name we have."

He looked away from the baby, and the two of them nodded, in complete accord. "What about a first name? Do you want her called for your ma? Or if there was someone in Griff's family who—"

Cassie interrupted him. "I've pictured this baby being a girl from the first. Of course I couldn't really know, but it was just a fancy that took me. I've imagined a girl and I've always thought of her as part of these mountains. This new land. I want her to have a name as strong as the land. I want her to be strong, Red. Stronger than I am."

Red looked at his little daughter, enchanted by the little rosebud mouth that even now suckled as if she dreamed of nourishment.

He smiled at Cassie. "It's hard to see her, so delicate and pretty, and think of a strong name for her."

"I've heard Susannah means 'courage.' My mother told me about an ancient story where Susannah was a woman who defended herself courageously. I'd like a daughter who had courage, Red."

"Susannah is beautiful. We'll call her Susannah Cassandra Dawson," Red said firmly.

"Not Cassandra," Cassie protested. "The poor thing will have a whole alphabet to learn with a name that long."

But Red thought he saw a pink tinge in her cheeks that looked like pleasure, and he brushed aside her objection. "You get Susannah. I should get to pick the middle name."

"You get Dawson," Cassie said pertly.

"I think this little one is goin' to be as beautiful as her mama, which doesn't seem possible. She's goin' to be smart as a whip, so she can learn all the letters there are with no trouble, and she'll be as sweet as my Cass honey ever can be. I'd like her to share your name."

"Red," Cassie breathed his name on a sigh, "I'm not sweet."

Tears began to trickle from Cassie's eyes. She was lying on her side with both hands tucked under her head, watching the baby, so tears pooled in the corner of her right eye and streaked out of the corner of her left eye to drip on the bed.

Red wanted to sigh, but he contained it because he didn't want to sound impatient. He said, "Cassie, you're about the sweetest li'l thing I've ever seen. I tell you all the time to holler at me and call me a polecat, but you just don't have an ounce of mean in you anywhere."

"Oh yes, I do, Red. I. . .I don't think it's fair of you to go on thinking I'm a nice person when I'm not. I have so much anger churning around inside me sometimes that, even if I don't say so out loud, I know God judges me for a sinner. The things I want to say sometimes. . ." Cassie shook her head and swiped at her tears. "The stupid, childish tantrums I want to throw. No, I think we can do better than to hang my name on the innocent baby."

Red thoughtfully rubbed the side of his jaw where Cassie had given him a stiff right cross during one labor pain. She'd have nailed him several times if he hadn't gotten on to ducking. He'd bet his whole ranch she didn't remember doing it, and he had a good idea about exactly what boiled inside her, because he thought he'd heard every word of it the last twenty hours while she delivered the baby. "If you think you're confessing a sin to me, you're wrong. I couldn't be happier to hear you've got strong feelings about things. I've told you before I want to know what you're thinking."

"No, you don't." She shook her head frantically. "Trust me, Red. You wouldn't like the person I am inside."

She was so tired that Red felt guilty about talking with her about this right now. But maybe, while she was so exhausted she barely knew what she was saying and so twisted up inside with her confession, she'd be more open than ever before. Red decided he had to try. "Didn't Griff like the person you were inside?"

"Oh, no. Nobody would," Cassie said vehemently.

"And did he. . .hurt you when he was displeased with you?"

"Only when I was bad."

Red had to control himself from flinching at the calm acceptance in her tone. How could he make her understand that no man had the right to hurt a woman, especially when she claimed all the fault for herself?

Cassie continued, "He had to teach me how to be a woman. I was such a child when he married me, not near good enough to be his wife."

"Griff's way isn't my way. I believe it's wrong to hurt another human being. I'd *never* hit you. I'd *never* treat you like I had to teach you to be good enough for me."

"I want you to." Cassie looked away from Susannah and blinked guilty eyes at Red. "You're already teaching me so many things. I'm not fit, not yet, to be your wife, but I'm trying hard to learn about the cattle and the hogs and Buck. There's so much I have to learn."

Red did teach her all the time. How was that different from Griff? He knew it was, but how did he explain the difference? Then he had an inspiration. "What about all you teach me, Cassie? You know all sorts of things I don't know. That's what makes a marriage. You knew things about having a baby I didn't, and you run the house so much better than I ever did. And you're educated. You read and write."

Red brushed a wispy strand of dark hair off Cassie's forehead. "And you're kind. Griff was never kind. Did Griff ever ask you to teach *him* how to treat people with kindness and respect? He should have, because he was terrible at that, and you are so good at it. All the ladies in town love you, and all the men would die for you. Griff never inspired anyone the way you do. You could have taught him a lot."

"Me teach Griff?" Cassie asked in a bemused voice. "But he knew everything already."

Red reached both hands down to Cassie and gently turned her onto her back.

She looked up at him curiously.

"He didn't know that it was a sin to hit you. He liked the part of the Bible that said a wife should submit to her husband, but he didn't know about the next verse that said a man should care for his wife and love her as Christ loved the church. We talked about this at a Sunday service once. You know how Jesus treated people, don't you? We've been reading the Bible together long enough. He was always kind. He always acted out of love. In the end He died. He sacrificed His own life as a way to save your soul, Cass. Yours and mine. Jesus would have never looked favorably on a man hitting his wife. He'd have told Griff that the way he treated you was a powerful sin."

"A sin? But you only think that because you don't know the real me. You said I'm beautiful but I'm not, not inside where it really counts. I'm full of ugliness. And I'm *not* sweet. My heart is *black* with the anger I feel. And I'm not smart. I can be so stupid. I had to have Griff tell me what to do all the time. And now I need you to tell me."

Red didn't know what to say. He prayed silently for wisdom and listened for a still, small voice telling him where to go next. All he could think of was, "I need you, too. All of us have sin inside us. I know I do."

"Oh no, Red. Not you. You're wonderful."

"Of course I think of bad things and I try to keep my mouth from wrapping around some of the angry thoughts that want to escape from me. But I think what you're worrying about is different. I think so much of what churns around inside of you *should* be said out loud. There's nothing wrong with having an opinion, Cassie. God gave you a fine mind. Not knowing how to milk a cow is not the same as being stupid. Remember the chickens? You're way smarter'n them."

Cassie smiled mildly. "Yes, the chickens. That's right."

"I need you to tell me what you're thinking. You help me so much with the strength of your back, but I need your mind, too. I need two people thinking of all the possibilities to live the best way we know how. Can't you see that holding all of your opinions and ideas inside is a type of selfishness? I know you do it because Griff never wanted your help, but Griff was a failure as a rancher and that's the plain truth. He lost everything he had and he had a lot to begin with. I started with next to nothing and

I managed to build a nice spread. Griff didn't know everything, and he'd have benefited from your help. It sure couldn't have hurt. If anything, I'd say Griff was the stupid one."

Cassie's eyes narrowed as she listened to him. For a second, Red was afraid he'd made her mad saying such harsh things about Griff.

Then Cassie said, "Griff *was* a bad rancher, wasn't he? He didn't check the cattle hardly ever. He said they'd forage on their own, but you check them once or twice a day."

"Well, yeah. You have to check 'em or they wander off or die. Every rancher knows that."

"Griff didn't know it. We had chickens, but they all ran off or got eaten by varmints. He blamed everything on bad luck or dishonest people, but our land was as good as yours. He wouldn't listen to advice from anybody, most especially me. And he couldn't do everything himself, but he wouldn't let me help, so lots of things went undone. Even the fence that he cut himself on was badly repaired because he had done a sloppy job of mending it."

Cassie sat halfway up in bed. Red saw lines of distress deepen around her mouth and eyes, but when he reached out to her to urge her to lie back, she resisted him. He decided her opposition to his wishes was something to be encouraged at the moment.

"I'm not stupid, Red. I was always a good student in school. You're right about that. Why did I let him convince me I was?"

"He was a violent, domineering man, and you were so young that you couldn't stand up to him. Your mother trusted him to care for you, but he betrayed that trust and only cared for himself. He took all of your money by marrying you and squandered it." It made Red furious to think of the way Cassie had been robbed and cheated. "Then he died and left you with a baby on the way, all his bills for a high life he couldn't afford, and no way to care for yourself."

Cassie's eyes had dropped to the middle of Red's chest

while he talked. Red tilted her chin up to see how she was handling his blunt truths. Her eyes blazed into his. She opened her mouth then stopped whatever words were working their way out.

"Say it. Even if you think I won't like it. Even if you think it's a stupid, mean thing to say. I'd love to know what's going on in your head."

She closed her mouth and opened it again as if the words just wouldn't emerge.

Red waited, afraid to push her any further.

Finally the worst of the fiery anger faded from her eyes and she looked over at her sleeping child. "I'm thinking a lot of things, Red. They're all so jumbled I can't seem to get any of them to come out, but the main one is"—she looked back at him—"I'm glad I'm your wife. I'm glad you're Susannah's father. I think. . .I think God knew just what He was doing that day in the cemetery, and I'll thank Him every day of my life for letting me be with you." She launched herself the few inches that separated them and wrapped her arms around his neck.

Red didn't have to think a second before he was holding her snug against him.

Cassie pulled away for just a second. "I'm going to try and say what's on my mind, Red. And God help you when I do because you may not like some of it. But be patient with me, and we'll see if I can. . .start to believe I'm smart and that what I think matters. Maybe the Cassie who's been hiding inside of me all these years isn't such a bad person."

"I like everything about you, Cass honey. I only want to know more."

"Well then, the first thing that's on my mind, now that I've turned over a new leaf is. . .go away and let me get some sleep. I'm exhausted." Cassie leaned back against her pillow with her chin lifted ever so slightly in the air as if she were daring him to tell her to stay awake. She tugged at her covers, and since he was sitting on them, she gave him a disgruntled look.

He stood and helped her smooth them.

"When I wake up, I might demand you make me something to eat. How would you like that, sir?" She sounded very bossy, but a smile escaped her prim lips.

Red smiled right back. "It would be my pleasure to serve you, ma'am. You tell me how your want your eggs, and they'll come out scrambled like they always do."

Cassie nestled herself amid her blankets. "That sounds just fine." She was asleep the instant her eyes closed.

Red looked back as he left the room. He stood for a minute and reveled in the beautiful sight of his family. His two beautiful women, Cassie and Susannah. Sleeping. Trusting him for their care.

It was a moment of crystal-clear clarity. A moment with a value beyond price. They were all bound together with a generous supply of love. And, with God's help, that love would overflow into every corner of their lives. He couldn't bring himself to leave immediately and he almost climbed into bed with Cassie just to hold her close. He would soon.

Fatigue tugged at his sleep-deprived brain, but he had something to do first. He stepped out of the room, a room he'd barely left in the last day, to spend a few moments in communion with God.

He knelt by the fire, his Bible clutched against his chest, and prayed the most sincere prayer of his life.

Thank You. Thank You, heavenly Father, for the gift You've given me. And thank You, thank You, thank You for my life with Cassie, and this joy and perfect peace.

Chapter 26

Cassie declared war.

She spent the next three days ranting and raving at him as if he were a slave, and a slow, ignorant slave at that.

He served her perfectly good scrambled eggs and ham for every meal. She told him it was burned, and he was pretty sure, if he hadn't moved quickly, she'd have thrown it at him.

She barked at him when he was slow. She snarled at him if things weren't done to her specification. And if he ever dared to disagree with her, she cried.

Red thought he was losing his mind. Cassie had given birth to more than a baby. She'd given birth to a shrewish temper.

The only time she was cheerful was when she held the baby in her arms, and the little one wasn't cooperating there. Susannah slept all the time, just waking up to demand food or when her diaper needed changing. Red wished fervently she'd keep Cassie a little busier. Red was a little surprised to find out changing diapers was his job. But since it was the only time Cassie would let him touch his babe, he got to liking it.

He also gave Susannah her first real bath. He sneaked her

out of the bedroom late one afternoon when Cassie was napping and spent a cheerful hour washing Susannah in carefully warmed water by the fire and telling her all about the ranch. Susannah went so far as to open her eyes just a slit on one occasion, and Red saw that they were a light blue just like his. He enjoyed that for a moment because Cassie's eyes were a dark, shining brown, before he remembered that none of his blood flowed in little Susannah's veins. Then he decided if he wanted to think she looked one tiny bit like him, he'd just do it and that was that.

He had Susannah back in her bed before Cassie woke up. Red was relieved he hadn't gotten caught. "I've created a monster."

Cassie kept nagging him and finding fault with everything he did for her. When Red confessed about the bath, she had some choice comments about his handling of the situation, even though the little'un had obviously survived and was clean and sweet-smelling in Cassie's arms.

Red kept telling himself that this might be part of those riotous emotions Seth had warned him about. He wanted to talk to Seth about it. He wanted to talk to someone about it before the walls closed in around him. He thought at this very moment he heard the roof creaking under the weight of Cassie's constant emotional turmoil.

Red willed the weather to clear. The sleet that had locked him and Cassie inside together while Susannah was born had changed over to snow. There was no snow like a Montana mountain snow, and this looked like a prime example of nature's worst.

Red struggled out to check his cattle every day. He'd found most of them placidly waiting out the storm in a sheltered canyon just as he'd expected, but there were always a few idiots who wallowed their way into trouble, broke through the frozen creek, or hurt themselves slipping on ice.

He'd found one steer with a broken leg and found one calf born out of season. He was able to rescue the calf and reunite it with its frantic mother. The steer couldn't be saved, so Red shot it and dragged its carcass back to the house, wearing all the ginger out of old Buck in the process. Then he'd had the steer to skin and butcher and the brown and white spotted hide to tan.

That, plus the barnyard chores, kept him busy because he was battling five-foot drifts and whipping winds every step of the way. Then he'd get inside as quickly as he could, even though he wanted to drag his heels, and there would be Cassie, ranting at him for abandoning her.

The blizzard lasted three days. When the snow stopped, the storm seemed to ease inside Cassie, too. Red came inside from watering Rosie one afternoon about sunset and found Cassie dressed and at the fireplace cooking.

He shut the door quickly to keep the heat inside, and she whirled around to greet him with a big smile on her face. Red was struck by the smile. It wasn't the beautiful, serene smile he'd come to expect from his demure little wife, and it sure as certain wasn't the perpetual scowl that he'd learned she was capable of in the last three days. It was a smile full of joy and sass.

Cassie's eyes snapped with pleasure at seeing him. She hurried over to him and started unwrapping the strips of leather that held on his cowhide robe. "You'd better plan on building some kind of entryway so the winter wind doesn't come straight into the house. It gets twenty degrees colder every time that door opens."

"Good idea." Red was struck by how much that would help. Why hadn't he thought of it? "Should you be out of bed? I don't want you to overdo it."

She fussed at him, tugged at the frozen leather, and shooed him toward a chair facing the fire. "Sit down and let me help you with your boots. Your fingers are near frozen. Poor man to be out in such weather. The least I can do is help you warm up."

She had his outer clothes off in a minute, then she studied his face for a long second. "You're going to frostbite your nose if you're not careful. Here, let me warm your face." She laid her open hands over his cheeks, and the warmth of her touch made his skin sting.

Red stirred under her touch. "No sense both of us being cold, Cass. Let me sit by the fire. I'll be fine in a few minutes."

She ignored his protests and touched her thumbs to his nose. "Just sit still and let me help you."

Red almost reached for her hands and pushed her aside, so alarmed was he at the chill she might be catching, but he thought of the change in her from the china doll to the shrew to whoever she was now and decided he'd just mind her for a bit.

It really did make Red's face feel better to have Cassie's hands on him, and on a sudden impulse, he pulled her onto his lap. "There, warm my face from there, darlin'."

Cassie squeaked with surprise, but after a second of forgetting where her hands were as she flapped them at him, she returned them to his cheeks.

"This feels great, Cassie. Thank you. Are you sure it's okay for you to be up?"

Cassie shrugged. "I woke up from my afternoon nap feeling restless, so I took it a step at a time and got up. I'll quit if I get tired and dump everything right back on you." She gave him an impudent grin and raised one hand to lay it on his forehead.

"I'm fine now. I've been thawing out single-handedly for years, you know."

Cassie nodded. "I know." She left her hands right where they were. "But you've got white spots on your cheeks. I noticed them yesterday, too. I've never seen them before. It's a terrible cold day, isn't it?"

"As bad as it gets, I reckon."

"And you've been out with the cattle even in this blizzard."

"The worst is over. And all this snow will fill the creeks and ponds in the spring."

Cassie bobbed her chin silently as she studied his face. She lifted her hands away. "It's better, just red now. I've seen frostbite, Red. It's nothing to fool around with."

"It's worst on fingers and toes, and I'm careful with them."

Cassie smiled. "Good for you. Now let me up so I can get your supper finished." She pressed her hands on his shoulders.

His hands, which had been resting lightly around her waist, tightened. He could have sworn they did it of their own accord because he didn't remember thinking it through. And he definitely didn't plan in advance to kiss her.

Red hadn't done much kissing in his life. But somehow, with Cassie, he found a surprising talent for the activity. At least he thought so if Cassie's response was any indication. Her arms wrapped around his neck and her head tilted just enough so their noses didn't bump, and she settled herself firmly against him, or at least she didn't object when he urged her close. He wasn't sure who was moving first because they were both going exactly the same way. He thought maybe, just maybe, they were both the most talented smoochers who ever lived. He'd have liked to study the question more thoroughly, but Susannah picked that moment to start hollering from in the bedroom.

Cassie leaped off his lap as if a lightning bolt had struck her. She hustled from the room without a backward glance and went to fetch the baby. She came out with the squirming bundle in her arms and a smile big enough to light up a long Montana winter night on her face.

She didn't look at him and he experienced a pang of jealousy, until he decided that she was *not* looking at him too thoroughly and just maybe she was disconcerted by what had passed between them.

"Take this chair." He stood. "I want you and Susannah to be warm while she eats. I'll get supper, and tomorrow I'm gonna build you a rocking chair."

"Oh, Red." Cassie looked up at him, and the pink flush on her cheeks told him he was right about her embarrassment. She seemed to forget it now that he'd turned her attention. "You're so busy. You don't need to do another thing for me. I'll get supper."

"Sit, woman." Red lifted the chair and set it back down with a firm *crack*.

Cassie reacted by smiling at him. "Yes, sir. If you insist. I was going to make one of the steaks you brought in from the steer."

"I can do steaks," Red said. "Were you going to use the spit in the fireplace?"

Cassie shook her head. "I'd planned to fry them."

"Let me show you how we eat 'em on a cattle drive. It's primitive but it's good. Cattle drive cookin' is about all I know besides eggs and ham."

Cassie sat, dividing her attention between the baby and Red's cooking efforts. He had the sizzling steaks ready by the time Susannah was done and well burped. Cassie changed the baby's diaper while Red moved the crib out near the fire and debated with Cassie about how close it should be. Then the two of them sat and ate with the baby lying nearby, kicking and making an occasional little noise.

Susannah got bored and fell asleep. Red noticed Cassie's eyes growing heavy. He insisted she go back to bed, and although she protested, he won the round and settled her and the baby in the back room.

He cleaned up the kitchen without paying attention to his work. He was busy reliving Cassie warming his face with her hands. And with her lips.

He realized that, with Cassie at his side, he could learn to love the bitter Montana winter.

Belle struggled to her feet after milking the cow. The animal was as round as Belle and would have her calf around the same spring date as Belle got herself her last child. She swore to herself it would be the last.

God, please let it be a girl.

Anthony chose that moment to stroll into the barn from the bitter outside. The man was a living, breathing, walking, talking testament to the general worthlessness of men—Red Dawson notwithstanding. Coming close enough to see how awkward she was, fat with their child, Anthony never so much as offered her a hand, and he certainly didn't say he'd do the milking. The rat didn't even offer to carry the bucket of milk.

Belle didn't snap at him as she would have at one time. Making a serious effort, she kept the scowl off her face. Instead, she smiled. "Let's walk back to the house and talk about what we're going to name the baby. There should be hot coffee and I. . .uh. . .*we* could use a cup." She could use the coffee, because she'd been freezing in the bitter cold of the barn and had been outside working all morning. Two hours before breakfast, and now two hours since. She had three more hours to go before time for the noon meal.

Anthony, on the other hand, had gotten out of bed to eat then had gone back to sleep for a while. He claimed his back would fail him completely if he got up and moving around too early in that cold little cabin. And it was too cold to sit under the Husband Tree or atop the house.

She mentioned none of that. She was a changed woman. A woman trying to do her best to be a good wife. As if doing all the work didn't make her good enough.

Montana Rose

Sorry, Lord. I didn't mean to let slip with evil, unwifely thoughts.

At least, with the gap snowed shut, Anthony hadn't been able to go to town. Which saved him wheedling a dollar out of her. Of course that meant he was underfoot all the time. His absence was well worth the dollar she gave him twice a week.

She didn't say that either. But oh, how she wanted to. Inhaling slowly to regain her self control, she smiled at Anthony. "Now then, about the baby. . ."

"Her name will be Caterina. It was my ma's name and it'll be my child's if it's a girl. It's likely a useless hope that you can birth a son. I'd prefer it but I hold out little hope. If it's a boy, it will be named after me—Antonio."

"Antonio is your real name?" This was beyond bad that she'd never known. She'd always thought it was Anthony.

"Yes, I adopted an American form of it and my son can, too, but I am named for my father and now my son will be named for me."

God, please let it be a girl. Please, Lord. Please, please, please.

"Those names will be fine." Caterina was no decent name for a child. And if, God forbid, she had a son—*God, please let it be a girl*—she would do her best to train him up to be less useless than the average man and she'd call him Tony. She realized she was assuming Anthony would be dead and would have no say in the child's name. There were, of course, no guarantees. It was most certainly a sin for her to hope against hope.

They reached the house and entered.

Sarah was hard at work on dinner. She had a stew cooking, savory and warm.

Belle smiled at her daughter and handed over the milk.

"Thanks, Ma. Coffee's hot." Sarah poured a cup, giving Anthony a doubtful smile. The child had to work on her false politeness.

287

Belle hoped her own attempts at being nice were more successful.

"We've just been talking about the baby. Anthony wants the name Caterina if it's a girl and Antonio if it's a boy."

"You think you might have a boy?" Sarah frowned little furrows into her forehead. She pulled the cloth out they used to strain the milk and worked as she talked.

"Most likely not," Anthony sneered. "Your mother doesn't seem able to produce a proper male child."

Sarah's eyes narrowed. "Those are weird names. Can't we call her something normal, like Elizabeth or Ann?"

"It's settled." Anthony took the cup from Sarah as she extended it toward Belle.

Sarah rolled her eyes behind Anthony's back and poured another cup.

It was moments like this that Belle remembered clearly why she'd never wasted much time talking with her husband. It was a useless pastime.

"Thanks." Belle accepted her cup of coffee. "The dinner smells great. You've got it on early enough that it can simmer a long while. It will taste perfect this cold day."

"Sarah, go outside. I need to have a long talk with your ma." Anthony looked at Belle and she shuddered, though she tried to hide it. She knew that look. Where was her skillet?

Sarah glanced at Belle.

"Go on, honey. We just need to. . .talk. . .a bit more." Belle spotted the cast iron, within easy grasp. Anthony was no match for her. They'd been through this before when he was snowed in overly long. Sure she was his wife, but being polite only went so far. Maybe instead of swinging it at his head, she'd aim for his back. As long as he used it for an excuse to avoid chores, he might as well really be hurt there.

Most likely she wouldn't need it at all. Anthony could usually be cowed with a dark look and a cutting remark or two.

As soon as she calmed him down, be it with or without the use of cast iron, she'd go back to being the very soul of kindness.

Anthony smiled and took a step toward her.

Belle decided then and there that she hated winter.

Town didn't hold much attraction for her, but she hated being trapped away from it because it kept Anthony far too close at hand. Two dollars a week was money well spent.

Anthony was soon sitting, disgruntled, in the house by himself. But after she'd properly discouraged the idiot, she'd said good-bye on her way out to work, real friendlylike.

CHAPTER 27

Red loved being forced to stay near Cassie and the baby. He could become a real layabout given time, because he was drawn to the house constantly by an eager wish to check on his girls.

Cassie occasionally wished aloud that she could tell Muriel about the baby. Then she'd burst into tears. But mostly she seemed delighted to be alone with their little family.

The three of them shared a simple Christmas together.

Red got Cassie's rocking chair done in time for it to be her gift.

She knitted him a thick scarf to cover his face and he teased her about liking her warming him better. She told him impertinently that she had enough to do without that troublesome chore, and he chased her around the room. Cassie laughed out loud as they played.

"Your sassy mouth makes me want to kiss you." He caught her by the waist. "You know that, Cass. So you must want a kiss."

"I most certainly do." She giggled as he kissed her soundly.

Susannah's eyes were wide open now, and the sparkling blue

that Red had loved started to turn darker. Red lamented that she didn't have his eyes.

Cassie snorted. "I hope not. Griff would roll over in his grave."

He kissed her every time she teased him, and like any wise wife, she teased him often.

Red shivered as he came inside from evening chores. He saw the flames jump in their fireplace, and Cassie, setting the table for supper while she held Susannah in her arms, turned away from him to shelter the baby from the blast of cold. He knew he had to face the cold, hard job of building on.

"I'm going to start on that entry room tomorrow morning, Cass honey. I've been putting it off because it's so slick, with that layer of ice under everything—figured I'd break a leg trying to chop down trees. But this last snow has covered it deep and I've got some traction. I can get into the woods safely now. What do you think? How big should it be?"

Once the icy wind was blocked away, Cassie turned back with her generous flashing smile. "I'm sure you know best, Red." She held Susannah against her chest, wrapped in a warm blanket. Red could just see his precious daughter's dark hair peeking out of the top of the blanket.

"You're not being submissive again, are you?" Red narrowed his eyes, fighting to keep the grin off his face.

"Most certainly not." Cassie sniffed at him, as if obedience was the furthest thing from her mind. But truth be told, she was a sweet little thing and minded him almost too much of the time. These days though, Red decided being easygoing was just her nature. Since she could be pretty sassy in fun, Red decided he liked her obedience well enough.

They ate a thick stew Cassie had made. She'd been a really

good cook from the first. And now, with Susannah so small, Cassie didn't clamor for her outside chores so much. Red went to the fireplace and thawed while he considered his pretty much perfect life.

Cassie settled the sleeping baby in the crib then moved back and forth between the bedroom and kitchen. She pushed a chair up close to the fire for Red. She grinned down at him. "You need my help warming up."

Smiling, Red let her lay her pretty hands on his cold cheeks without a second of hesitation. As they stood there, so connected, so warm, Red remembered his surety that when he married Cassie he'd been committing a sin.

"You know God put us together, don't you, Cass honey?"

She'd been focusing on resting her hands on his cold skin. Now she raised her eyes to meet his. "He did, didn't He? Who could have figured such a thing in the middle of all that madness at the funeral?" Then Cassie wrinkled her nose. "You did your best to escape your fate, as I remember. Muriel had to practically drag you back to me."

Laying his hands gently over hers, he pulled them away from his face and entwined their fingers, urging her down onto his lap. "I couldn't see God in the choice I made that day."

Cassie's forehead crinkled just a bit, and Red knew that pinched her feelings.

"You want to know the main reason why?"

Doubtful, Cassie said, "Yes. Tell me why. What made you want to run for the hills when every other man in Divide was trying to run off with me?"

"It was because I wanted to marry you so badly." He slid his arms around her waist.

Jumping but not able to escape, Cassie said, "What? Why would that make you run?"

"I told you once I didn't think I should marry you, but I

wanted to something fierce, remember?"

Cassie nodded.

"I'd noticed you from the first time I saw you in town. Which was probably the first day you and Griff moved here." Red slid his hand up Cassie's arm and to her face until he cradled her smooth, pink cheek in one of his rough, calloused hands.

"You did?" Cassie seemed pleased with that, judging from the way she kissed him.

"I set out to avoid you as much as possible because you were so beautiful and you seemed so sweet. I wanted to talk to you and spend time with you and I knew that my feelings were all wrong for a married woman."

"I never knew. You spoke to me a few times."

Smiling, Red said, "That's 'cuz I couldn't resist a few times." He pulled her closer and kissed her more soundly, almost dazed with the full realization that he'd ended up with this almost impossibly beautiful woman in his life.

"Griff wouldn't let me talk to people. He said it was too familiar and not ladylike."

No surprise there that Griff had found a way to hurt her. But Red was in no mood to talk about Lester Griffin right now. "I believe that God has prepared a woman for me from birth to be my life partner. I settled that in my heart that God would provide that woman for me or I'd live my life alone."

"And you didn't think that could be me?" Cassie jabbed him in the chest with a pointy finger and sniffed at him.

That made him happy, that she wasn't going to pout or be hurt. "You know just as well as I do that it was a crazy way to pick a wife. Being the wife in the middle of the picking, you were none too happy about it either, as I recall."

"I'd fully decided that if God really loved me, He'd open up Griff's grave and let me join him." Cassie leaned in and kissed him a quick peck on the lips. "But God had a much better idea."

Red pulled her back and deepened the kiss. "He did indeed." Then he kissed her again, and she melted against him as surely as the spring sun melts the winter snow.

When the kiss ended, he pulled away enough to see her flushed cheeks and shining, slightly swollen lips. Their eyes met and held. "Marry me, Cass honey. I believe God chose you for me and prepared the two of us, from birth, to be together. I love you so much. Will you marry me and be my wife?"

This question wasn't about a promise made to God. Red had made that promise months ago and had from that moment fully honored those vows and intended to for the rest of his life. But right now he was asking for more. He saw Cassie's expression and knew she understood. He knew she'd say the words. He knew from the very beginning she'd have submitted to him. But finally Red knew that she'd be eager, not just obedient. His heart sped up as he waited.

She didn't make him wait long. "I love you, too, Fitzgerald O'Neill Dawson." Wrapping her arms around his neck, she said against his lips, "Yes, I want to marry you with all my heart."

The stew was set aside so it didn't scorch.

Susannah slept peacefully as if she knew her parents were hoping for some time alone.

On that cold winter night, in a dark but warm cave, Red and Cassie Dawson became, at last, fully and beautifully married.

Red built a neat little log shanty to block the wind around their front door.

Cassie stayed inside like a fragile houseplant, when she wanted to be outside helping him. But Susannah demanded her time, and the weather wasn't fit for a baby. Cassie worried that Red was exposing himself to the harsh winter. He held her and reassured her and distracted her from her worry.

She knew he wasn't really being hurt by the bitter temperature, but her heart was so full of love for her husband and her baby and her life that the happiness seemed to overflow in wild emotions with little provocation.

Cassie vowed to him that she'd never ask for anything again.

Red thanked her profusely for giving him a suggestion and told her she was the smartest woman in the state of Montana.

She reminded him with some sass that there weren't that many women in Montana so that wasn't so very much of a compliment. When she talked like that to him, he tended to laugh and chase her around the room and pull her into his arms, so she did her best to talk like that often.

When the tiny new room proved to keep the soddy warmer, Cassie made a point of reminding Red, with a snippy tone, that it had been her idea from the start.

The flashing precious newness of their young love deepened, and they expressed it in all the ways there were.

By the time winter stretched into spring, Red and Cassie had reason to hope that their family might grow larger. When that time came, Red teased her, the baby had every right to resemble him.

When the weather was finally decent for them to go to town, Red had his hands full battling heavy spring rains and a thaw that flooded all the creeks. He spent hours every day checking his spring calf crop. He and Cassie sowed a garden, although Cassie protested that it should be her job alone. He promised she'd do her share when it was warm enough that Susannah could lie on a blanket outside. Now she had to snatch free moments during Susannah's nap time and run inside frequently to check on the growing baby.

It was the end of May when the water finally subsided and they made the time for a trip to town one Sunday morning. Red didn't want to be away from the farm for two days, so they left very early, planning a one-day trip. Cassie fashioned a sling across her chest and she carried Susannah in it while Red carried her. They even galloped, because Buck was feeling his oats after a long, idle winter. The baby slept through the whole trip.

When they arrived in town, the folks were overjoyed to have their preacher back.

Muriel wept over Susannah and presented Cassie and Red with a small mountain of baby clothes she'd sewn over the winter. The Jessups, the Dawsons' neighbors, had ridden to their place and seen that the baby had come safely. Then the bachelors braved the weather and gotten to town and told everyone there was a baby girl at the Dawson place, so the clothes were adorned with lace and ribbon. Muriel declared herself to be Susannah's grandmother so fervently that no one considered for a moment objecting.

The baby was passed from hand to hand among the women. Even the men hovered near to look at her. Red realized that a baby was even more of a rarity than a woman, and he noticed with pride that Cassie generously let the people enjoy Susannah to their hearts' content.

He thought of all the questions he'd had for Seth four months ago and laughed at himself for surviving a childbirth and a baby and a new mother with that minimal advice.

The church service went well, and the whole group made plans to baptize Susannah as soon as Parson Bergstrom rode through town.

Norman York pulled Red and Cassie aside after services. "I have been waiting all winter to tell you that I sold your Bible for a shocking amount of money. Now, I know I told you I'd save it if I could, but you weren't here and I had to make a decision. I was offered enough for it that it covered everything and left money besides."

Norm told them how much cash they had in the bank, and Cassie's knees gave out. Only Red's quick thinking kept her from sinking all the way to the ground.

"I had already sent a lot of things back East on the same wagon that took the Bible. They sold first because my brother spent a long time finding the best buyer for the Bible. It's extremely rare and it will end up in a museum. So most of your things are gone, Cassie. I'd have saved them back for you if I'd had any idea of the money I could make."

Red's ears were ringing from the windfall of money. He hadn't gathered his thoughts enough to say anything, when Cassie whispered in his ear. All the confusion lifted as he turned to the wonderful woman he'd gotten railroaded into marrying. "Are you sure?"

Cassie nodded. "There'll be enough left to buy the title to the mountain valley you've been grazing."

"More than enough." Red turned to face the milling people in the general store and said loudly, "I think it's time this town had a church."

A flurry of excitement swept through the God-fearing people of Divide. The sedate good-byes turned into a time of praise and worship as they all made plans for Divide's first church.

There was also a letter from Parson Bergstrom that said he was making arrangements for Red to be named to their mission society. It would take awhile to be approved, but soon he'd be allowed to officiate at weddings. If Divide kept growing, there just might be a few of those in the future.

After church, Red arranged for some of his neighbors

to trade work with him to drive his steers into town to sell, and Muriel relaxed her rules about Sunday work to allow the Dawsons and several others from out of town to fill orders for supplies. Red also sold all of Harriet's grown piglets and, by doing that, ensured that they'd be having some company in the next few weeks when people came to pick up their hogs.

All in all, they did a winter's worth of worshipping and settled all their affairs in the few hours they were in town.

Or at least they'd settled everything until Wade Sawyer came strutting into the general store.

CHAPTER 28

Y ou're sure pretty now that your belly isn't big with Griff's whelp."

Cassie nearly jumped out of her skin when she heard the familiar voice.

Wade's voice slurred. "I should have had you when you were between men."

He staggered a little as he leaned over Cassie, and she smelled the sharp, stale odor of whiskey on his breath. She stepped away from him, but he snaked out his arm and pulled her hard against him. "I've yet to have my turn with you, china doll. I reckon I'll have at you before we're finished."

Red was there before Cassie could even look around for help. He pulled Wade's arm away from her and tucked her behind his back. "You're drunk, Sawyer. And you're insulting my wife. Go somewhere and sleep it off."

Peeking around Red's stalwart body, Cassie saw the winter hadn't been kind to Wade. Her winter had been so splendid that she'd gone long stretches without even thinking of the horror of Wade's visit to the ranch. Now it all came rushing back.

His eyes were streaked with veins and red-rimmed from too much drink. A beard grizzled his sunken cheeks, and behind the beard, his teeth were yellowed and stained. She saw in his soulless eyes the knowledge a man gained from long nights spent in debauchery. Cassie shuddered when she thought of what her life might have become if Red hadn't claimed her that day.

She leaned fully against the strength of Red's back and whispered so softly only he could hear her, "I love you."

Red's hand came around her back and rested on her waist for a brief moment, telling her that he'd heard. Then his full attention was back on Wade.

Cassie was taken by surprise by her beloved husband's voice. She'd expected anger. Instead she heard only kindness.

"Wade, you've got to get yourself straightened out. Talk to me. Let's just sit and talk. You're wasting your life. You don't really want Cassie. She's my wife and we love each other. No man wants a woman who doesn't want him. What you think is longing for her is just part of the emptiness that's inside you. God can fill that emptiness. Forget about Cassie and start worrying about your soul."

Red took a step closer to Wade. "You're still a young man. You've got plenty of years to find a wife and have a family. You've got a ranch. You need sons to pass that ranch on to. You need daughters to soften your heart with their smiles. Don't throw your best years away on drink and the Golden Butte women and hate. Please talk to me. I can tell you about how faith in Jesus can help you find your way down the right path."

Red laid his hand on Wade's shoulder.

What she saw in Wade astounded her. Longing. Wade's eyes were riveted on Red's, and in his expression, she saw a longing that ran so deep it bordered on desperation. For the first time she felt something other than fear and revulsion when she looked at Wade Sawyer. She felt love. She understood what the Bible meant when it said, "Love your enemies. . .pray for them which. . .persecute you." She found the compassion to pray for Wade.

"Please," Red said, "you've got intelligence and strength and a good life waiting for you. And if that life isn't on your father's ranch, I'll help you find a life somewhere else." Red's voice dropped so low Cassie could barely hear it. "I know how cruel your father is. You need to get away from him for good. Let's just talk and decide where you can find a new home. I'll do everything I can to help you find a new path."

Wade's eyes shifted from Red to the floor and back to Red, and for a second Cassie could see in Wade's eyes the willingness to search for a better life.

There were still people in the store. The worship had ended but the fellowship had stretched into the early afternoon. No one had wanted it to end.

Wade took an uncertain step forward toward Red. Then suddenly something visceral and cruel slammed down between Wade and all the people who stood before him. Cassie believed she'd seen with her own eyes a battle between the Lord and Satan fought within Wade's soul.

He slapped Red's hand aside. "Save your preachin' for someone who wants it, Dawson. And enjoy your wife for as long as you can keep her. She's a woman who needs pretty things around her and I can give 'em to her. She's for sale and I can outbid you any time I choose."

Wade wheeled drunkenly away from them and left the store.

Cassie was so close behind Red, she heard him whisper, "He needs You so desperately, Lord. Help me to never give up on him."

She wrapped her arms around Red's back and hugged up close against him. "Amen."

Red held her arms tight around his waist and they stood silently as the tension eased from the room.

Finally a squall from Susannah broke the silence. Red retrieved his baby from Leota Pickett.

As Red hoisted Susannah high in the air to make her squeal with pleasure, Cassie heard Maynard Pickett, Leota's husband, say, "He's dangerous, Red. He was gone all winter. After you swore out that complaint against him, no one saw him again till just a few weeks ago. Since he's been back, he's gone pure crazy. He isn't staying at the ranch and I haven't seen him sober. You watch your back and keep close to Cassie."

Red nodded and glanced her way.

She held his eyes to make sure he knew she had heard. She wanted his protection but she didn't want him to keep the truth from her.

Red sighed.

Then Susannah distracted him by kicking him in the stomach a few times and yanking on his hair.

Red settled her on his shoulder and came back across the room. "I'm sorry you had to hear such vile talk from a man, Cassie. No lady should be subjected to that."

"I'll not accept your apology. Wade Sawyer is the only one who can apologize for the way he just acted." Cassie laid her hand on Red's arm. "I thought for just a moment that he was listening to you. I thought maybe you could reach him."

Red nodded. "Muriel asked us to lunch. Then I want to get started back." He looped his arm around her waist and, with his other arm hugging Susannah, moved around the room saying good-bye to his friends.

"They had a girl?" Belle smiled at Muriel. She visited while Seth filled their order.

Montana Rose

Belle knew she shouldn't have ridden to town. She was due to give birth any day. But that was also the reason she *had* to come in. The gap had just now melted open and she needed her larders full before the baby came. Getting to town afterward was hard.

"The most beautiful little girl." Muriel's voice softened and her expression made her look twenty years younger.

Belle wondered why Muriel and Seth never had children, but it was too personal of a question to ask.

Seth came back into the store and hoisted another crate. "This is the last of your supplies, Belle."

Normally, Belle would have worked alongside the storekeeper, but Seth had flatly refused to let Belle lift the heavy boxes. Truth be told, when Sarah was born, Belle wouldn't have taken Seth's orders. But she was older now, nearly thirty. Picking up those boxes would have been a strain.

Belle knew she'd started leaving more and more for the girls, too. It wasn't fair to burden them. No more babies, ever. Never ever. *Please, God, let this be a girl.*

She thanked Muriel for the coffee, paid for her supplies, and went out after Seth.

Seth took the two steps down from the board sidewalk that lined Divide's Main Street. Belle stepped out and nearly fell when she saw Anthony. . .coming out of the Golden Butte.

He looked across the hundred or so feet separating them.

The woman on his arm giggled and dashed back inside.

Last fall, Anthony would have slunk away in sullen silence. Now, after a winter of Belle trying to be kinder to him and bringing him into the family, he tipped his hat with narrow, defiant eyes, then turned and followed the woman back inside.

"Belle, why don't you just kick him out?" Seth set the last crate in her wagon bed and fastened the back end with the rattle of metal on wood.

Belle's mind had been a thousand miles away—well, in all honestly, more like a hundred or so feet away—awash in fury and humiliation and contempt. "I spent the winter trying to figure out how to be a better wife to him." She'd never normally have discussed such a thing with anyone, let alone Seth Bates. But what difference did it make? Anthony's cheating was going on with no effort to hide it. "I've been *nice* to that polecat."

"There's divorce." Seth's grim voice with its shocking suggestion drew Belle's gaze away from the still-swinging doorway to the Golden Butte. "You don't have to let him live on your ranch. You don't have to put up with his low-down ways."

"Divorce? How am I supposed to manage that?" Belle thought of the lawyer she'd spoken to before she married Anthony. It had required a grueling trip to Helena because no lawyers were closer. It gave ownership of her ranch to her pa if she died, and her pa had promised to leave it as an inheritance to her daughters. It had been a strange thing to arrange, but a few run-ins with Gerald had scared her enough that she'd decided she needed to protect her children in the event of her death. The lawyer had written up the will and she'd forced Anthony to sign before she'd agreed to marry him.

"I don't know how it works. But I've heard of such a thing."

She knew such things as divorce occurred, but it was a disgrace. Vows were taken before God, and to break those vows was a terrible sin. Plus, Belle knew enough about it that she knew Anthony would have to cooperate, and he'd never give up his two dollars a week. No, divorce wasn't possible.

Her face burning with anger and embarrassment, she swung up onto the buckboard, her stomach making her awkward, and slapped the reins against her horses' backs. She left town far behind before she let herself cry. She could hate Anthony. She could hate Seth even for daring to comment on this shame in front of her. But that was all a waste of time when the real reason she'd ended up like this was because she was a fool.

God, what's missing in me that I keep marrying weaklings? Am I so awful no man with a backbone will have me?

Worse yet, had strong, decent men wanted her, but the missing part of her *needed* a weak man who could be bullied?

Her horses knew the way home, and it was a good thing. The loaded wagon rattled along as tears blinded her. Her head ached with the shame. Her whole body ached as the tears flowed and sobs wracked her.

She'd have never cried like this in front of her girls. And she'd have never let Anthony see her. Pride wouldn't allow it. But she wasn't crying over him. He was lower than a snake's belly, and he had no power to hurt her feelings. She cried over her own stupidity. She cried over what was broken in her to have married so poorly over and over again.

She'd been on the trail nearly two hours, wallowing in her grief, when she realized the ache that seemed to be twisting her body wasn't coming from disappointment in herself.

It was the baby.

The shock of realizing her laboring had started brought Belle out of the self-pity. She rested her hand on her stomach. It was early yet. She'd have time to get home.

What would become of her if she gave birth alone in the wild country? It was a three-hour ride home on a fast horse. She'd be more like six hours driving the wagon. She'd left long before first light to get this trip done in one day. It was closer to ride back to Divide, but not by much. She had to go home. Her girls needed her.

And she needed her girls. Lindsay had helped bring Sarah when Lindsay was only five years old.

Panic nearly took hold. She considered unhitching the wagon and riding one of the horses, but that suited no purpose. She had about three hours to get home, and that was long enough. Why, the baby wouldn't come much before morning if things went as usual. She slapped the reins and made the team step up their pace. With the heavily laden wagon, they couldn't do much better than they were now.

It was a long time before the pangs came again. But they came. Belle prayed for her little unborn daughter, whispered that God would keep them both safe.

The cool spring air gusted around her and the horses kept up their fast walk, the clomp of hoofbeats echoing in the sunset.

The three hours she had estimated shrunk to two. The contractions kept coming, a bit closer each time. Belle saw the rise ahead, the long, treacherous curve of the trail climbing up into the gap that led home. In another hour she'd make it. Not home, but through that gap, on her own land. That was home enough for her. She just might unhitch the wagon at that point, if the pangs hadn't gotten too hard.

As she struggled to move her horses along, she heard something behind her. A rider. She turned back to see Anthony coming at a fast lope. Belle's spirits lifted to know she wouldn't be out here alone any longer. Even Anthony would be better than being alone.

As he drew near, she turned. "Anthony. The baby's coming. Thank goodness you've come. I need help."

Anthony pulled his horse to a walk as he came up beside her. "What can I do?"

"You can just be with me. I'm a long way from home. I'm scared."

"Belle Tanner Svendson O'Rourke Santoni scared of something? I doubt it." He kicked his horse and picked up speed.

"Wait!"

Anthony turned to glare at her, as if she'd asked him to help with chores.

"I need you to stay with me. What if the baby comes before—"

Montana Rose

A pain hit, cutting off her speech. This one was stronger than the others. She knew her body. She knew how it felt as the birth came. She still had time, but what if she couldn't drive the team any longer? It would be hard to keep going when the time drew near. She'd need to ride the brake hard all the way down the other side of the gap.

"You've never needed me, Belle. Why should you start now?"

Belle couldn't answer until the pains faded. "Anthony, I have *always* needed you. You're the one who refused to be part of this family. I could use your help every day." She thought of how much he could help. She saw him, sitting straight and strong on his horse. His *back* was fine. But they'd been all through that a hundred times. Repeating it wasn't of any use.

"Oh, you've maybe wanted to make me help on *your* ranch. You've maybe wished for another cowhand you could work like your daughters. But that's not *need*. You don't *need* a husband, Belle. You need a *slave*. I've got too much pride to work as your slave." His voice went beyond contempt and anger. He sounded as if he hated her. His eyes told her that he definitely did. He kicked his horse and tore off at a gallop.

Yes, he'd always been lazy.

Yes, he'd always been a cheat.

But why would he hate her? Would he really be so cruel as to abandon her in pain on the trail?

"At least send one of the girls!"

Anthony laughed, his voice carrying back to her on the wind. "If I see one of your little slaves, I'll send her."

Would he possibly refuse to send help? She'd kept him fed and in spending money for a year now. Belle's spirit felt crushed as if the pains were at work on her soul. She felt the tears come again, the tears that had tormented her on this long ride home. But she didn't let them fall. She had no energy for them.

She clicked to the horses and pushed them on.

God, please have him send the girls.

Her girls would help her.

Did she really work them too hard? Did she treat them like slaves?

She began slow, constant prayer, stopping only when the agony cut her off from her thoughts. When she ran out of prayers, she began reciting all of the Bible verses she knew, and they were many. The Bible was the only book the Tanner family owned. Why, she'd taught her girls to read using it. They took turns memorizing verses during their Sunday services.

The pains came faster. She began the slow uphill climb toward the mountain gap. She remembered Seth's words about divorce. No, never. Surely Anthony would die soon and save her the shame.

Nearly another hour passed as she made the twisting trip to the crest of the hill. The trip back down would be much faster.

The pains came harder. They hadn't yet entered that horrible constant stage she knew to expect near the end. She could make it. She could get home.

She thought of the tortuous trail that descended into her valley. She had to ride the wagon brake hard all the way down to keep from overturning on the sharply winding trail. She wasn't sure she had the strength.

The wagon descended. Belle pulled hard on the wooden brake handle to keep it from running away and harming the horses. Her hands threatened to slip off the brake when a pain was upon her. She went down and down, the trail narrow, snaking. Her hand clutched the brake. She threw her body across it, hoping her weight would do what her normally strong hand couldn't. She made the first turn only a bit too fast. The wagon clattered. The horses snorted, complaining about the dangerous wagon forcing them forward at a pace that scared them.

She passed several more treacherous turns without incident,

but it took all of her strength to keep the buckboard under control. Nearly a third of the way down, a spasm hit so hard she nearly collapsed. She slipped forward. If she fell between the horses and the wagon, the wagon would roll over her and kill her.

She clung to the brake as her body seemed intent on tearing her in half.

Picking up speed as her strength waned, the horses whinnied in fear at the clattering wagon now shoving them at a dangerous pace.

A shout pulled her head up.

Someone came around the sharp curve ahead toward her. Lindsay.

Anthony had sent help.

Belle didn't have the strength to pull the horses to a stop. They rolled on past Lindsay. Too fast.

Lindsay drew off to the trailside as the wagon passed her. "Ma, what's wrong?"

Though she asked, Lindsay didn't pause for an answer. She quickly dismounted, lashed her horse's reins to the back of the moving wagon, and sprinted to jump up on the seat. She grabbed the brake, gently moving Belle aside. With Lindsay's strong hand on the controls, the wagon slowed, but it still moved too fast for safety.

"It's the baby. Didn't Anthony tell you?" The wagon seat had no back. Belle struggled to sit upright.

"No." Lindsay bore down on the brake. The last turn was dead ahead, and it was as tight as a hairpin. The wagon couldn't get around it at this speed.

The horses whinnied in fear. Lindsay fought a quiet desperate fight between herself and the mountain and that brake. The wagon slowed a bit. The tight curve ahead came nearer.

Belle's stomach contracted again. There was hardly time to

breathe between the pains now.

The brakes squealed in protest. The horses began throwing their weight on their back feet under Lindsay's skillful handling on the reins. Lindsay's shout even galvanized her own horse to pull against the wagon from behind.

They turned into the curve, still going too fast.

"Lean up the hill, Ma. We can make this, but I need your help."

Belle obeyed. Years of taking charge, doing what had to be done despite the difficulty, were too ingrained to ignore. Belle leaned away from Lindsay.

The wagon tilted. Two wheels came off the ground.

Lindsay yelled at the nervous horses and threw even more weight against the brake.

They rounded the corner and the trail straightened. The wagon banged down onto four wheels.

Still going too fast, Lindsay now could at least make the horses move a bit more briskly and stay ahead of the wagon. She began winning her fight one second at a time.

Finally, the brake caught firmly ahold of the heavily laden wagon. Seconds later they reached the bottom of the mountain trail.

Belle suspected Lindsay normally would have pulled over and given herself and the lathered horses a chance to calm down, but she was a canny girl and she'd already figured out Belle needed to get home. "What did you mean about Anthony telling me?" Lindsay asked.

Belle gasped as the pain let up. "He came past me on the trail. He wouldn't stay. I asked him to send help. When I saw you—" Belle lost her ability to speak again as another storm swept over her beleaguered body.

"He came in the cabin. He served himself supper in front of all of us without saying a word." Lindsay threw Belle a look of such fury that Belle regretted saying anything about Anthony's part in this. "I just knew it was time for you to be coming, so I rode out to keep you company."

Belle's heart broke at Anthony's cruelty. But she set that aside as another pain threatened to tear her apart. A sudden spate of moisture told her the baby had broken through. It wouldn't be long now.

"What can I do to help you, Ma? Can you ride my horse to get yourself home faster?"

"No, it's too late. I wouldn't be able to sit on the horse."

Lindsay slapped the horses with the reins and yelled. They picked up the pace to a trot.

Belle knew they still had a long way to go. The gap was miles away from the cabin. She didn't think she'd make it, but she held on, her fingers white against the buckboard seat.

Lindsay reached her left arm to support Belle's back, holding the reins in her right hand, now that the brake was no longer needed.

"The horses can't keep up this pace all the way home." Belle wouldn't harm her team to save herself. She'd give birth along the trail first. "Not with the wagon loaded."

"We'll go as long as we can. I'm watching 'em. I won't let them overdo. We'll deliver the baby out here if we have to."

Belle focused on the team, trying to keep her weight off Lindsay, trying not to be any more of a burden to her daughter than necessary.

Slave labor. Was it true?

The pains were nearly constant when the cabin finally came in sight.

"Emma!" Lindsay's shout brought Emma and Sarah out of the cabin at a run. Lindsay pulled within inches of the door.

"What's the matter?" Emma came around the back of the wagon, her eyes on Belle.

"Ma's having the baby. Help me get her down." Lindsay wrapped the reins around the brake with lightning movements. Emma threw herself up beside Belle. Lindsay and Emma eased Belle sideways.

Belle did her best to help. The baby pressed to be born.

The girls, including Sarah, nearly carried her into the house.

The commotion brought Anthony's head up from where he lay on his narrow bed. He smirked at Belle then sauntered outside.

The girls lowered her to her bed, and they were in time. Barely. The baby slipped into the world, into the gentle hands of her big sister. It was a girl.

Belle was home. She'd made it home.

But her marriage made it a sad, pathetic excuse for a home.

CHAPTER 29

For the first time since Susannah's birth, Cassie kept something from Red.

She'd been going whole hog, spouting off her ideas and feelings, and it had seemed to suit Red fine. She surely loved doing it. But now she couldn't forget the threat she'd seen in Wade Sawyer's eyes and the cowardly way she'd acted the last time he'd threatened her. She still had nightmares about that cold, wet crevice where she'd cowered. Cassie was determined to never be so helpless again.

Cassie started practicing with her gun.

Red always left the rifle, loaded and ready, hanging over the door. She didn't fire any bullets. Red never left the ranch yard long enough or went far enough for her to believe she could practice without his notice. And he would have missed the bullets. Griff had always been careless about details like that.

But she'd gotten good before. Now she just practiced grabbing it and aiming quick. The gun started to feel comfortable in her hands. She loaded it while she walked, while she ran, while she lay on her belly in the dirt. She studied the yard for shelter should she be caught out, away from the house.

She knew she should tell Red what she was doing, but she didn't want him to make her quit. And she didn't want to listen to him talk about the right and wrong of shooting a man who hadn't made peace with the Lord. . .because she was ashamed of the cowardice driving her.

She was prepared for trouble when she was alone, but as she scratched in the dirt planting a garden, she knew Red was close by and felt perfectly safe.

Safe turned out to be a luxury she couldn't afford, any more than she could afford black silk dresses.

"Cassie honey, stand up slow," Red said stiffly.

Cassie turned to see what had caused the harsh tone, expecting to find him hurt and bleeding. She froze so solid her heart had to struggle to beat.

Red stood in front of Wade Sawyer. Blood trickled down Red's forehead, and his knees wavered slightly as he walked. Cassie saw a noose snared around Red's neck.

Wade held the end of the rope in one hand and his revolver in the other. He sneered. "It's movin' day, china doll. Go fetch your things and come along with old Wade."

Cassie didn't take her eyes off Red's battered face. She slowly got to her feet. Cassie glanced at the house, and Red blinked his eyes and made a nearly invisible move with his head. He seemed to be asking her for time. Maybe time for his head to clear or time to come up with a plan to get them out of this.

Cassie sent a thousand silent prayers for help in the space of a single breath. Then she spoke with quiet authority. "Wade, untie him and quit this nonsense."

Wade didn't react. He seemed to be processing her words, and Cassie decided he was drunk again. Surely if they could bide their time, he'd sober up enough to know what he was doing was madness. Then Wade jerked on the rope he held, nearly knocking Red off balance.

Red staggered slightly to remain standing.

Wade yanked it again.

Red fumbled for the rope tight around his neck and held it in both hands. Cassie noticed him discreetly try to loosen the rope.

Wade was focused on her and seemed oblivious to Red's efforts. Wade cocked his pistol with a sharp *crack*. "Do it, china doll, or Red dies right now." Wade rested the muzzle of his six gun on Red's temple. "How about it? You in the mood to bury another husband?"

Cassie realized she had a choice. She could go into the house as if to pack her things. Once in there, she could get her hands on her gun. Wade was drunk enough that he wouldn't notice her rifle if she came back out with it hidden behind her coat. She had a better than even chance of beating Wade.

She looked at Wade's cruel, lustful face and at the blood streaming from the cut on her precious husband's head and thought, *"The Lord is my light and my salvation; whom shall I fear?"* In that instant Cassie finally knew the difference between cowardice and courage. She was terrified but she didn't go for the gun. *"Whom shall I fear?"*

She trusted her instincts, believing they were directions coming from God. "The last time we talked, Red told you to let go of your hate, Wade. Think about what you're doing. What brought you to this? When I first came to Montana, you were the rich, powerful son of a cattle baron. You were going to inherit a dynasty. You flirted with me but you never threatened to kill Griff or kidnap me. What has happened? What is eating you up inside that changed you into a man who would threaten murder?"

Wade opened his mouth and closed it again.

She remembered the last time she'd given him time to

respond to her and the vicious tightening of the stranglehold he had on Red. She didn't wait. "Have you ever heard that hate destroys the hater? Who do you hate so much, Wade? It can't be Red. He's never done anything to you. And how can it be me? You've aimed your hate at us like a loaded gun, but this can't be about us. Is it your father?"

"No!" Wade exclaimed loudly. "You leave my pa out of this."

He said it so furiously that Cassie thought she'd found the right direction to proceed.

"What did he do to you, Wade? He's a hard man. I'll bet it's difficult to have such a tyrant for a father. Has he ever let you walk your own path? Has he ever shown you any gentleness or affection?"

Wade laughed bitterly. There was a slightly hysterical note to the laughter. "Gentleness is for women. No one but a fool expects mush and petting from his pa."

Cassie saw Wade's hand tighten on the rope. Red had both hands under the noose now and Cassie could see him hold it so it felt tight to Wade but without it cutting off his breathing. Cassie had the distinct impression that Red's wobbly knees were at least partly an act, too. He just needed a little more time.

"Red fusses over Susannah all the time, Wade. A father should hug his child. He should speak of love. Your father may have treated you harshly because he wanted you to be strong, but instead it broke your spirit. You bully people and they back down because of who your *father* is, not because you're a strong man yourself. Bullies think they're strong, but they're very careful to pick on people who are weaker or sneak up behind rather than face them. But Wade, you've gone too far this time. You've faced a man who is stronger than you in the ways that really count. Red has the strength of God on his side, and so do I. We want to live because God has been so good to us in this life and we love serving Him, but we aren't afraid to die."

Montana Rose

Cassie gentled her voice. "I will not go with you. We will not submit ourselves to you. But we will be your friends. We will love you."

"You *do not love me*." Wade was listening. His shocked reaction to her words was evidence.

"Let go of Red and put down the gun. Come inside and talk to us. We *do* love you, Wade. And God loves you. If you could understand how much God loves you and how it makes His heart break to see one of His beloved children turn away from Him, you'd put down that gun and listen to us. You've tried doing it without God, and look where it's brought you. Let us tell you how to put God in charge of your life. If you do, you'll find out what true strength really is."

"You. . .you. . ." Wade shook his head as if to clear it.

Cassie looked at Red. He was ready. He could have pulled himself free of the noose and grabbed the gun from Wade's unsteady hand, but Red had known the difference between cowardice and courage for a long time. He left the rope where it was and gave Wade the chance to choose God.

The love Cassie felt for Red at that moment was almost violent. She prayed and saw Red's lips move. He was praying, too. They both asked for Wade to open his heart and take the first step back from the terrible path he'd traveled for so long.

"You love me?" Wade said it like it was unfathomable. His throat worked, and Cassie thought she saw a sheen of tears in his eyes. She remembered his longing in the Bates' store when Red had talked to him. She knew Wade wanted help. He wanted something better in his life.

He opened his mouth. Then as if no words could come, he closed it again and threw the rope aside and dropped his gun in the dirt. One hand came up to cover his face and he turned away. He began walking, almost stumbling, his shoulders slumped and shaking.

317

Red glanced at Cassie and she gave him an encouraging nod. He took the noose off his neck and ran after Wade. "She wasn't just saying that to get you to leave." Red lay his hand across the back of Wade's shoulders, and Wade stopped immediately, as if every step was a huge burden he could hardly bear. "Come into the house with us. We'll make you some coffee and a good meal, and we'll talk about how you can find your way back."

"Find my way back. . ." Wade turned to Red and spoke so softly, Cassie could barely hear it. "Back to where?"

She walked over to Wade and rested her arm on his back so she and Red were surrounding him. He was no danger now. "Back to yourself. You've lost the very best of yourself, Wade. Just like I had. And back to God, because He's the one who created you and loves you just the way you are."

"No, not like I am. Maybe once I was someone God could love." Wade shook his head and a single tear trickled down from the corner of his eye.

"Talk with us, Wade. Come meet our daughter and spend the day with us." Cassie urged him to turn and realized she and Red were nearly holding him up. He'd been drinking, but this was about more than the liquor. It was as if Wade had been knocked almost to his knees by words of love.

For the first time, Wade looked at her in a way that didn't frighten her. She smiled, and Red rested his hand on hers, where they met on Wade's trembling shoulders.

Cassie said, "Every one of us has to choose. I had started down the wrong path with my life just like you have."

"You, china doll? You've always been perfect. A man's dream set down in the middle of the wilderness."

"It may have seemed like that because I always acted the part. But the truth is I had no faith in God. I had no courage. I didn't believe in myself any more than you do. Red helped me see I was worthy of God's love. I didn't believe that when

I came to live here. But now I know my willingness to act like the perfect, obedient wife was just me taking the easy way out and letting someone else make all my decisions for me. You and I have a lot in common. Does your father trust you with any part of the ranch?"

"No, he never has. But who can blame him?"

"And does he make you feel stupid when the truth is you've just never been trained?"

"I am stupid. I never do anything the way it's supposed to be done," Wade said humbly.

"That's exactly how Griff treated me. And I think that you saw that, even though you want to believe I'm perfect. You saw a kindred soul who was going through the same thing and you wanted to save me. That's noble, Wade. That's something I respect and admire in you. We reacted differently to being dominated. I became a submissive little coward and you rebelled, defying your father by leaving the ranch and getting mixed up in every evil vice you could think of just to spite him."

"We're nothing the same," Wade said firmly. "You can't compare yourself to someone like me. I've done so many things, it's impossible for me to ever undo them."

"You're right that you can't undo them, but you can start today living your life differently. Come in with us." She knew Wade still had scars on his heart and he'd still have trouble believing in himself. Look how long it had taken her to trust herself and believe in her own worth. But Wade had taken the first step today. He'd stopped sinking deeper in sin and reached up for God. And God could reach all the way down to meet him and help him the rest of the way.

"China doll. . .I. . .I can't go near your baby." Wade looked her in the eye, and for the first time she realized those green eyes that had frightened her could be vulnerable and soft and even kind. "And you can't want me in your home."

"My name is Cassie. Please call me that. And I *welcome* you to our home." She urged him forward. "I have coffee still warm from this morning, and it's only a little early for lunch."

At her urging, Wade started toward the house. Cassie looked over at Red and she saw him nod at her with deep approval. Some of what she'd said had only really become clear to her as she'd talked. She knew God had guided her words, and she'd spoken them for her own benefit as well as Wade's.

They headed for the tiny soddy with the cave bedroom. A giant step down from the lovely home she'd lived in less than a year ago. She could see now that God could use what she'd been through. He could use her to help someone else. The honor of it made her tremble deep inside.

And as she walked, she felt the china doll shatter inside her. Gone forever. And out of the rubble a new woman emerged. Not perfect. Not even close. She was a sinner who struggled and failed and tried anew each day.

But she was also a new woman in Christ. A woman God loved, but even more, a woman worthy of being loved by God.

What had started as a nightmare on that day of Griff's death had become the fulfillment of all her dreams.

Red's hand, resting on top of hers, moved so their fingers entwined. Together they supported Wade and each other. She smiled at her husband, and they helped bear the burden of their new friend. And as she walked, she realized that her whole life had led her to a plan God had all along.

She'd been following a twisting, turning, sometimes treacherous path that had led her straight home.

DISCUSSION QUESTIONS

1. Discuss the difference being submissive and being dominated.

2. Do you think the world has warped the concept of a submissive wife? How?

3. Is Red too sweet? Do you like a hero who is a little more flawed?

4. Cassie's emotions follow the stages of grief, but they are also wildly fluctuating because she has been dominated by her husband for so long, she simply doesn't know how to think for herself. Was that entertaining or was she too scattered?

5. Do you think a person, newly freed from domination would behave this way? Have you ever known anyone who had become a doormat in their marriage?

6. Wade is the bad guy, but do you have any sympathy for him?

7. Though Wade's father, Mort, was cruel to Wade, he was a strong man in a hard land. Is he to be respected as well as despised?

8. Cassie notices similarities between Red and Mort. Discuss those similarities and how they were used for good by one man and evil by another.

9. Is the discussion of childbearing too graphic?

10. Is the scene with Suzannah being born fun or nonsense?

11. If you've had a baby, discuss your own experiences with childbirth and how skewed some of your perceptions were. How did your husband act during the birth, and how might he have acted if he'd been called upon to deliver the baby alone?

12. Could you live in a cave? Why or why not?

13. If you were transported to 1880 Montana, could you survive? Do you have the skills to feed and clothe your family without all the modern conveniences?

14. What is the fundamental lesson of this book? Self-confidence? How to find a balance in marriage? Self-respect? Courage in the face of abuse? What do you think it is?

MONTANA
MARRIAGES

2

The
Husband
Tree

CHAPTER 1

Montana Territory, 1876

Belle Tanner pitched dirt right on Anthony's handsome, worthless face.

It was spitefulness that made her enjoy doing that. But she was sorely afraid Anthony Santoni's square jaw and curly, dark hair had tricked her into agreeing to marry him.

Which made her as big an idiot as Anthony.

Now he was dead and she was left to dig the grave. Why, oh why didn't she just skip marrying him and save herself all this shoveling?

She probably should have wrapped him in a blanket, but blankets were hard to come by in Montana. . .unlike husbands.

She labored on with her filling, not bothering to look down again at the man who had shared her cabin and her bed for the last two years. She only hoped when she finished that she didn't forget where she'd buried Anthony's no-account hide. She regretted not marking William's and Gerald's graves now for fear she'd dig in the same spot and uncover their bones. As she recalled, she'd planted William on the side nearest the house, thinking it had a nice view down the hill over their property. She wasn't so sure about Gerald, but she'd most likely picked right, for she'd dug the hole and hadn't hit bones. Unless critters had dug Gerald up and dragged him away.

Belle had to admit she didn't dig one inch deeper than was absolutely necessary. Maybe a little *less* than was necessary. This was rocky ground. It was quite a chore. Her husbands had made too many chores for her over the years. Digging their graves was the least of it.

She'd risked her own life to drag her first husband, William, out of the cattle pen. The pen any fool would know was too dangerous to go into—which Belle always did, not being a fool. Rudolph, their longhorn bull, was a mite cantankerous and given to using his eight-foot spread of horns to prove himself in charge of any situation.

Then Gerald had gotten himself thrown from his horse. His boot had slipped through the stirrup, and judging by his condition, Belle figured he'd been dragged for the better part of the three-hour ride home from the Golden Butte Saloon in Divide by a horse whose instincts told him to head for the barn.

Anthony's only good quality was he'd managed to get himself killed quick. They'd been married less than two years. For a while there, Belle feared he'd last through pure luck. But stupid outweighed luck. Stupid'll kill a man in the West. It wasn't a forgiving place. And Anthony was purely stupid, so he didn't last all that long.

Between William and Gerald—that is between being married to 'em—Belle had changed the brand to the T Bar. Known as the Tanner Ranch from then on, it never changed, regardless of whatever Belle's last name happened to be at the time. She'd also had a real smart lawyer in Helena draw up papers for Anthony to sign so the ranch would always belong to Belle, and if something happened to her instead of a worthless husband, Belle's wishes would be carried out.

The Husband Tree

She tamped the dirt down good and solid. About the fifth tamp, she admitted she was using more energy than was strictly necessary. She'd whacked it down especially tight over Anthony's pretty-boy face.

Three sides of the Husband Tree used up. She wasn't up to puttin' up with a live one or buryin' another dead one. The tree roots wouldn't appreciate it.

And neither would the children.

She said a quick prayer for Anthony, reflecting silently as she spoke, that knowing Anthony as she did, it was doubtful there were enough prayers in the world to save his warped soul. Never had it been necessary for God to perform a greater miracle, and Belle asked for just that, though she didn't hold out much hope.

She finished the service in one minute flat, not counting the digging and filling, which had taken considerably longer. It had been early in the day when she'd found Anthony dead beside the house. Planting him had interrupted chores, but there was no help for it. She couldn't leave him lying there. He was blocking the front door.

She nodded to the children, four of 'em, one from each husband, and a spare thanks to William. "We got chores."

"Why'd you marry him anyway, Ma?" Lindsay bounced the baby on her hip. They were a study, those two. Lindsay so blond, the baby so dark.

"Not a lick of sense, that's all." Belle had no desire to fancy this up. She'd been pure stupid to get married, and her girls needed to know that.

"Well, have you learnt your lesson?" Sarah plunked her little fists on her hips and arched her bright red eyebrows at Belle.

"It's a humbling thing just how well I've learned it, Sarah. There will never be another husband on this ranch. You have my word."

"The folks in town'll be out here tryin' to push themselves off

327

onto you." Lindsay probably had a few faint memories of how Belle had ended up hitched to Gerald. The girl had made it clear long before Anthony died that when this one croaked, there'd better not be any more of 'em.

"I'll take the shovel, Ma. I need it to clear out the dam. Dirt's backed up on the canal you built to water the garden." Twelve-year-old Emma pulled her Stetson low over her eyes. She'd removed it for the funeral prayer, though Belle hadn't thought to require it.

Handing over the shovel, Emma grabbed it and headed downhill. The other girls turned from the grave and headed for the house. Fifteen-year-old Lindsay carried the baby, Elizabeth, born this spring not long after branding and not old enough yet to walk.

Thank You, dear Lord God, for letting Betsy be a girl. Thank You for all my girls. What would I have done with a boy child?

Eight-year-old Sarah fell in line next.

Belle watched them walk ahead of her. Each of them the image of her pa.

Lindsay and Emma had wispy, white blond hair, bright blue eyes, and skin that burned to a reddish tan from their long hours in the sun. Lindsay'd grown taller than Belle these days, and Emma now looked Belle straight in the eye. William had been a tall one, and as blond as most Swedes.

Sarah had a shock of unruly red curls, eyes as green as grass, and a sprinkling of freckles across her nose from her Irish pa, Gerald O'Rourke.

The baby, Elizabeth, whom they called Betsy, was a beautiful little girl. Belle almost had a moment of affection for Anthony Santoni. Betsy's cap of midnight black hair fell into soft, natural ringlet curls. The dark brown eyes were rimmed with abundant lashes, and her skin had seemed tanned from birth. The little girl was the image of Anthony.

The Husband Tree

Belle lifted her own straight brown hair, "the color of chocolate" her pa used to say, and thought of her odd light brown eyes—like it would have killed one of the little tykes to take after her just a smidgen. And she had no nationality to speak of either. Her family had been in the country a hundred years before the Revolution, and they'd all been busy for generations being Americans. Who had the time to study ancestors?

"We've been over this now, Ma!" Lindsay hollered to make sure Belle heard. "No more husbands, never."

"Don't waste time fussing at me, Linds. Those men have caused me a sight more trouble than they've caused you. I'm not gonna tell anyone in town Anthony is dead." They'd notice when he didn't show up at the Golden Butte to visit one of the girls. But missing him didn't mean they knew anything. Maybe they'd think he'd quit being a lying, cheating, lazy, no-account man and he was busy. Running the ranch.

It took all she had not to snort out loud at the very idea.

Belle didn't mention the Golden Butte to the girls. She never took them to town, and she didn't think they knew exactly what Betsy's low-down pa did while he was away from the ranch. Probably figured him for a drinker like Gerald.

The four girls were strung out before her, heading downhill. What a pretty bunch they were. Belle dreaded the trouble that could come to a pretty girl.

Pretty didn't matter anyway. Heaven knew that with her weathered skin and calloused hands and straight-as-a-string hair, she was nothing great to look at. The men who came a-runnin' every time she was widowed said pretty words about her appearance. But women were scarce in Montana. And a fertile mountain valley like the Tanner spread was even scarcer. The two-legged varmints would have been out here trying to turn her head with flattery if she looked like the north end of a southbound mule.

Growing up pretty—and who could judge a thing like that as

there wasn't a mirror for a thousand miles—was only a nuisance in her way of thinking. With all the water rights sewed up for over twenty thousand acres, Belle didn't kid herself that her looks brought the men sniffin' around.

Lindsay reached the bottom of the hill.

Sarah sped up to catch her and snagged Betsy out of Lindsay's arms, then angled toward the house. "I'll watch the baby and get the noon meal on, Ma." Just as she went in the door, Sarah glanced back at Belle and said matter-of-factly, "Now that Anthony fell off the roof, can I toss a couple less taters into the pot?"

Belle nodded. "He ate about three."

"We gonna save money on food now that he's dead." Emma tucked the shovel under one arm while she walked, snagged her buckskin gloves from where she'd tucked them behind her belt buckle, and began tugging them on.

Sarah went into the house.

Without comment, Lindsay and Emma headed for the barn.

Belle smiled with pride at her girls. They did take after her in one important way. The girls knew how to work. Belle hadn't been able to marry any help, but she'd sure as shootin' given birth to it.

By the time Belle quit standing around feeling proud over her girls and relieved over Anthony, Emma already had her horse caught. She rode out to work the dam, the shovel they'd used to plant Anthony strapped onto her saddle. Lindsay had disappeared into the chicken coop to fetch eggs.

Belle went into the barn, snagged her flat-topped black Stetson from a peg, and settled it onto her head. She shrugged into the fringed buckskin jacket she'd made from a mule-deer hide. Then she strapped on a six-gun in case she met any varmints on the trail, or worse yet, men come a-courtin'—those two being equal in her mind.

Rounding up one of her green-broke horses, Belle thought with pride of the well-trained cow ponies she'd been selling for good money the last few years. She let the young horse crow hop the kinks out with its usual good spirits, snagged her shotgun leaning on the fence, and shoved it into the sling on her saddle. Then she set out on the long ride to check her cattle. She had herds scattered near and far in her rugged mountain valley.

Lindsay headed into the barn to do the milking, carrying a bucket of eggs, just as Belle rode out of the corral. "I'm not forgettin' this time, Ma. And neither are you. You promised—no more husbands."

"A promise I intend to keep, daughter. Now quit with your scolding and get to work." Belle had known for some time now that both of her older daughters talked to her almost as if they were equals. She could still make them mind if it came right down to it. But mostly, she valued their opinions and listened when they talked, just as they listened to her. They made a good team, and it was possible her older girls already knew as much about ranching as Belle.

Lindsay held Belle's eyes for a long second. "I reckon you learned your lesson, all right. Anthony Santoni, worthless excuse for a man. What were you thinking to marry him?"

Belle shook her head. "He wasn't a worthless excuse for a man, Lindsay."

Lindsay's white blond brows arched. "He wasn't?"

"Nope, he was just a *man*. Same as any other man, leastways any I've known." Not strictly true. Seth worked hard at the general store. Red Dawson was a decent sort, what little she knew of him. Her pa hadn't been so bad; he was a hard worker, no denying it. But he'd done Belle wrong, and she lumped him in with the other men. "I thought I had to. It was never *shall* I get married. It was *who* shall I marry. Not anymore though. We all know well and good that a man just slows a woman down."

Lindsay gave Belle a firm nod and went on into the barn.

Smiling, enjoying being free of a husband—this time forever—

Belle spurred her horse and smiled as the wind blew the pesky wisps that always escaped from her tightly braided hair.

Thank You, Lord, for making me a widow.

Belle hesitated briefly, pretty sure that God wouldn't exactly welcome such a prayer. But the Lord giveth and the Lord taketh away. And he'd takethed Anthony, praise be. Who was she to complain?

It was great to be a widow.

Now if she could just stay one!

New Mexico Territory

"Silas!" Lulamae Tool came to the door of the livery stable, caterwaulin' and waving her arms like she was being stung to death by bees. "Help me!" Her fearful eyes met his. "Help me please, Silas."

Silas Harden dropped his hand from the saddle horn of the buckskin he was about to mount and turned to the pretty girl with the scared eyes. "What's the matter?" He strode toward her. He'd talked with her a few times, and she was a dim critter. Who knew what little thing had made her kick up this ruckus?

She whirled and nearly ran back toward the livery. "My horse!" She glanced over her shoulder, oozing with gratitude. "Something's wrong with him, and Dutch isn't here."

With Dutch the hostler gone, it was up to Silas to save the day. He felt big and strong and in charge as he picked up his pace. He caught up with Lulamae as she dashed inside.

She grabbed his arm as if she were so upset she needed him to lean on, sweet little thing.

They rounded the row of stalls, and Lulamae skidded to a stop and jumped in front of him. She launched herself into his arms and kissed him.

The Husband Tree

Silas wasn't thinking straight, or he was caught up in his notion of a damsel in distress maybe, but all he did was enjoy the moment. The woman could kiss like a house afire. In fact, he threw in with the idea and kissed her back with plenty of enthusiasm.

A shotgun blasted.

"You've ruined my daughter!"

Silas turned toward the noise. Lulamae clung like a burr, and he dragged her with him as he whirled to face the gunfire.

Hank Tool charged inside. Lulamae's father'd been yelling before he'd even seen them. Behind him came the banker along with Dutch, who owned this livery.

Hank snapped more shells into his shotgun and aimed straight at Silas's heart.

Shrieking and crying, Lulamae said, "But you promised to marry me, Silas!" Lulamae dropped to the ground, crying and clinging to his ankles.

It didn't escape Silas's notice that now Hank had a clear shot right at his heart. Silas raised his hands skyward; his head was spinning too hard for any clear thought, with the crying and primed gun and Hank's steady, deadly threats.

Things came clear when he heard Hank Tool say, "March yourself right on over to the preacher. You're doing right by my girl."

Silas figured it out then. "Hank, I just walked in here to help Lulamae with her horse. She grabbed me. We've been in here less than a minute. Nothing happened."

"You're not gonna shame Lulamae and my family and live."

Then Silas figured out two more things: Hank knew exactly what Lulamae had done, and the look on Hank's face was determined and killing mean.

Well, Silas knew he was stupid, and no mistake. He'd gotten himself good and trapped, and now he could marry Lulamae or die, because whatever kind of lying, sneaking polecat Hank Tool was, his hand was steady on that trigger and his eyes meant business.

Silas shook his head.

Hank leveled his shotgun. Dutch and the banker bought into the game with their sidearms.

"Looks like we're having ourselves a wedding." Silas marched forward.

Lulamae sprang to her feet and latched onto Silas's arm and gave him such a smug, satisfied smile, it was all Silas could do not to shake her off. Not such a sweet little thing after all. And Silas would be switched if he'd marry the little sneak. But right now he didn't have a notion of a way out as they headed for the church.

"Put your hands down, you coyote. You're only adding to the shame you've caused my daughter by walking through town, letting all and sundry know you aren't marrying her willingly."

"I think the shotgun is enough of a clue, Hank." But Silas lowered his hands even as he knew that was the *last* order he planned to obey from Hank Tool.

Dutch ran for the preacher, and by the time they got to the church, both men were standing out front, frowning at Silas. The version of the story Dutch had told had put the holy man firmly on the Tools' side.

The gun nearly jabbed through Silas's buckskin coat as they went inside and up to the front of the church. He expected to look later and find a hole worn into the leather and on past his shirt from the prodding of Hank Tool's fire iron.

"Dearly beloved. . ."

Silas ignored the preacher and looked sideways at Lulamae and knew, even if he ended up with his backside full of buckshot, he'd be glad for the scars to remind him of what a fool a man can be over a pretty gal. Outwardly, Lulamae was everything a man could want—pretty as a rising sun on a cool spring morning, sweet-talking as a meadowlark perched in a willow tree, fair-smelling as the first rose of summer.

The Husband Tree

"We're gonna be so happy, Silas." Lulamae smiled. "Aren't we?" Silas's skin crawled. He didn't answer.

Hank jabbed Silas with the gun and answered for him. "Sure you will be, honey."

The preacher arched an eyebrow at the interruption and looked back at his prayer book.

Silas was glad the preacher glared them into silence, because "Yes sirree, we sure are gonna be happy" weren't words that were capable of escaping from Silas's lips.

Because, besides being a pretty little thing, the woman was also a sneak and a liar. Add to that, Silas had talked to her once or twice on a rare trip to town, and he'd been struck by the woman's pure stupidity. She was dumb as a post, no offense to posts, which at least did what they were put on this earth to do without any surprises.

Silas thought it over a second and reconsidered the dumb part. After all, who was standing here in front of the preacher with posies in her hand, smiling and eager to say, "I do," to one of the area's up-and-coming ranchers, and who was standing here with an angry pa poking him with his shotgun muzzle until he said, "I do," or died saying, "I don't"?

"We are gathered here today. . ."

Silas decided to pick dying over marrying Lulamae. He was going to die before he married *any* woman, no matter how fetching her sweet little hide was. He'd learned that from his ma and all her man troubles well enough. Then, when he'd decided there was a woman who would suit him and he'd proposed, she hadn't stuck when times got tough.

But he was hoping to come up with a third choice. Some middle ground between "get married or die." Which, as far as Silas was concerned, were the same thing.

"To join this man and woman in holy matrimony." The preacher closed his prayer book, and Silas's stomach took a dive.

They hadn't been married while he'd been daydreaming, had they? He was more than sure he'd never said the words, "I do," but the way this day was going, maybe Hank had said them for him.

To Silas's relief, the parson droned on. An unlikely time for a sermon, but it appeared that the man dearly loved the sound of his own voice.

Lulamae smiled and batted her eyes and clung to her posies and Silas's arm. And her pa jabbed him with the long gun from time to time so Silas wouldn't forget he'd been found in a compromising position with a decent girl.

Silas much preferred the attitudes of dance-hall girls, who'd pull guns *after* they'd collected their money to make men go away.

Not that Silas had any kind of woman he was particularly fond of, and he avoided dance-hall girls out of respect for his faith. But any kind of woman was pure trouble when getting right down to it and best to be avoided. But they smelled good, and a man lost his head from time to time, as Silas had in the livery.

Silas thought of the way Lulamae had smiled and made him feel like she needed rescuing. Now Silas wasn't a man to dodge the truth when he'd made a mistake, and when Lulamae had gotten so generous with her affections, Silas hadn't gone running, screaming for the hills like he'd oughta. So everything that was happening to him right now was his own fault.

"Do you Lulamae Tool, take this man. . ."

The preacher quit with his preachifying and started asking for promises, and Silas knew the time had come to root hog or die. Honestly, he deserved this. He knew better than to let some calf-eyed woman near him. Silas had a normal man's weaknesses when sweet-talking women were involved.

Hank jabbed him again, and this time Silas wondered if his coat had been torn away and Hank had broken Silas's hide.

"Will you quit stabbing me? You might as well have a bayonet on that fire iron."

"Shut up and pay attention, Harden."

The preacher cleared his throat, glared at them both as if threatening them with eternal fire, turned aside from his vows, and did a bit more scolding, all aimed at Silas, which stung. But Silas wasn't in any position to clear things up.

"I do." Lulamae fluttered her lashes, and Silas's stomach fluttered even faster.

"Do you, Silas Harden, take this woman to be your lawfully wedded wife. . ."

Letting her kiss him like that was such a stupid thing to do, he almost deserved to end up hitched to the empty-headed little sneak.

"In sickness and in health. . ."

But no amount of guilt or prodding was going to shake "I do" loose from Silas. If he belted Hank and jilted Lulamae, he'd have to quit the country, and that rankled something fierce, because he'd just started up a nice little herd on some rugged desert grazing land that he bought for next to nothing because no one could grow a cow on that wasteland.

"For richer or poorer. . ."

He was going to be a sight poorer all right, because what Silas knew that no one else did was that back up-country, just a couple long, rugged miles on the higher slopes of the San Juan Mountains, was a beautiful valley, lush with belly-high grass and year-round water. This would be the second ranch he'd lost, and leaving it burned him bad.

"As long as you both shall live?"

He might not live all that long, considering his plans for the next few seconds.

Hank jabbed him, which Silas figured was a hint that it was time for him to say his vows.

"If so, say, 'I do.'"

The honorable thing to do would be to marry Lulamae. He'd

had the first few steps of his hoedown, and now the fiddler wanted to be paid. Except Silas'd been set up. His jaw got all tight like it did when someone pushed him hard—like Hank and Lulamae were doing.

Silas looked at the nice glass window straight ahead of him and knew he was going through with it. Or, if he wasn't as quick as he hoped, he might be leaving feet first out the main door. But before either of those things happened, he'd feed that shotgun to Hank Tool.

Silas turned to face Lulamae. He got nudged right sharp as he moved, but Hank thought he'd bagged himself a son-in-law, so he didn't pull the trigger when he should've.

Silas grabbed the shotgun and shoved the muzzle up. It went off, proving Hank was serious. Silas jerked it out of Hank's hand and dropped him with a butt stroke to his skull. Silas took two long running steps and dived through that window, knowing Hank had friends in that church and he had none.

Lulamae screamed, a sound so high-pitched it might have broken the window for him if he hadn't gotten a head start. It liked to have made his ears bleed, but mostly it just made him proud to have done the right thing.

He ran straight for the livery where his horse stood saddled and bridled outside—he'd been on his way home when Lulamae struck.

He tore the reins loose of the hitching post, grabbed the mane of his horse, vaulted onboard, and lit out, ignoring the shouts and whizzing bullets from behind, because his horse was the fastest critter in the area.

Shaking shards of glass off his shirt and trying to stop some stubborn bleeding—all at a full gallop—he hit the high country north of town and decided he'd had enough of New Mexico anyway. He left like he'd come into this miserable state fifteen years ago—with nothing.

The Husband Tree

Except he did have something. He had the sense to never get near a woman again.

He kicked his buckskin, and he got the feeling that the horse felt the same way about Lulamae that Silas did, because that horse settled into a ground-eating gallop and didn't stop until they were swallowed up into the sky-high belly of the San Juans.

Chapter 2

Anthony being dead changed his body temperature, but otherwise, as far as how it affected Belle, he hadn't changed much. Her summer had been the same as usual.

Until now.

She swung down off her horse, just back from a brutal two-day ride into a valley at the far end of her property that had led her to a disaster.

Betsy pulled on Belle's hair and kicked her legs, obviously happy to be home.

Striding to the house, knowing supper would be about ready to hit the table, Belle studied her tally book. Looking at it again didn't change those numbers one bit.

She had to thin the herd. And she had to do it now.

Snapping the book shut with as much violence as a woman could inflict on a pad of paper, she slid it into the breast pocket of her gingham blouse that was only slightly still tucked into her riding skirt. She'd pushed hard all day to get home.

The news she had couldn't wait. She fretted as she went to talk to the girls.

The Husband Tree

The weather was still nice, though the nights were getting sharp. Winter came early up here, but they still had time. Barely.

That part didn't worry her so much. The disaster wasn't about running out of time.

Pushing open her sagging door, she didn't waste time prettying up the bad news. "I've got trouble."

Emma and Lindsay were inside setting the table. Sarah usually kept Betsy in the house and cared for her and did all the cooking while the older girls did chores. But this time Belle had taken Betsy with her. The baby was still nursing, and Belle knew she'd be gone two full days. So Sarah'd planned to work outside more, and she must have, because her big sisters were helping inside.

All three girls turned, giving her their full attention. From their grim expressions, she knew they recognized her tone. Something bad.

"I found a whole herd of cattle I didn't know I had in that high valley."

"You knew there were some up there, Ma," Emma said.

"I thought maybe a hundred head, two hundred, three even. But I must have had cattle sneaking up there all last year. You know I didn't get up there to check in the spring or the fall before that."

"Because you were fat with Betsy last fall and feeling poorly. Then she was so little this spring you decided to skip that long trip." Lindsay's hands fisted. "I should have made the trip. I should never have let you talk me out of it."

"A young girl's got no business out on a long trail like that alone."

"Emma and I could have gone together. The two of us together are as tough as you, Ma."

Probably tougher, but Belle hadn't wanted them in danger. That valley was too close to the low pass toward Divide. If intruders came, they'd come from that direction.

341

"I'd say now that I should have let you go. I'd have had the whole summer to get this drive arranged. It's gonna be hard to find hands this late in the year."

"How many are up there?" Emma lived and breathed cattle and horses even more than Belle. The girl was already figuring.

"There were over six hundred head."

Lindsay's blond brows arched.

A hard breath escaped from Emma. "Our grass is stretched thin with the herd we've got. We were pushing our luck to make do until spring. . .and we were hoping we could use that high range."

"Well, there's no grass up there. They've eaten it to the nub and started heading down closer to the ranch. There's a healthy crop of calves that I've never branded—good, sturdy, fat stock that are over a year old, plus a nice bunch of spring calves. But they won't be fat for long."

"We don't have enough hay to fill in." Lindsay frowned. "We can't begin to sell that many head in Divide."

"We're going to have to take 'em to Helena." Belle jerked off her buckskin gloves and gripped them to keep from strangling herself. They'd lose the whole herd by spring if they didn't thin it. She'd been lazy, and now her daughters were in danger because they could lose everything. She'd let having a baby slow her down. She deserved *all* of this mess. But her girls didn't deserve it.

"Helena's the closest place with cattle buyers looking for a whole herd." Belle still hadn't told them the really awful part.

Sarah's green eyes formed perfect circles. "I've been with you up and down that trail, Ma. Can we punch five hundred head of cattle over those narrow passes?"

Up and down was right. And side to side and over rock slides and alongside cliffs. A more treacherous trail hardly existed in the whole country.

"More like a thousand, Sarah. We've got to thin this herd down here, too, because we don't have the grass we thought we had. I've got three thousand head of cattle, and we need to run a third of them to market."

Lindsay squared her shoulders. "We can manage that, Ma."

"We've got a hard week of work to do to cut out the cattle we want to drive and brand them. Some of those year-old animals in the highlands are thousand-pound longhorn bulls," Belle warned. "We'll take as many as possible from down here, just to skip as much branding as we can."

Emma gave a shrug. "We've had hard weeks before."

Belle liked the calm way her girls were reacting. She'd have done the same, except for the worst of it. That was making her edgy. "We need to get the cattle we want to sell penned into that canyon with the low pass toward Helena."

Slapping her gloves in one hand, Belle thought of that long stretch that needed fencing. Hours of backbreaking work, and Belle was no carpenter. She'd be lucky to build a fence that would hold cows. But the grass was still good in that canyon and the water plentiful. She'd kept the cattle out of there so she could move them in come winter. The cattle wouldn't take much persuading to stay put in there.

Sarah turned back to her stew. "We cleared the rocks off the pass a few years back. That's not so hard to drive the cattle that way."

It was a razor-sharp climb and twisted as a Rocky Mountain rattlesnake. But yes, they could do that.

"It's a big job, Ma." Lindsay started setting the tin plates around the table. "And the drive will be tough, but there's nothing you've told us to get worked up about. You seem pretty upset."

"I've waited till last to give you the worst of it."

All three girls turned back to face her. Even Betsy, still strapped on Belle's back, seemed to tense.

"We can't handle this drive alone, girls."

"We can do anything, Ma," Emma said defensively.

Belle shook her head. "Not this time."

"So we just give up? We let our cattle starve?"

"Nope. Worse that that."

"Worse than starving our herd, Ma? What could be worse than that? Unless. . .you think *we're* gonna starve?" Sarah's lip trembled.

"No, we'll live. But there is something worse than all of that."

"What is it, Ma?" Lindsay asked, her eyes frightened.

Well, good. She should be afraid. Very afraid. "I'm going to have to bring home. . ." Belle shuddered, but she forced herself to go on. "Men."

The rest of the dinner was sadder than the day they'd buried Anthony.

By a Rocky Mountain mile.

"Before I fetch them, I want to tell you one more time what low-down, worthless skunks men are. You can't trust nothin' a man makes you feel, especially if the men are good-lookin' and too ready with a smile."

Her girls listened closely while they ate.

Belle had said it all before. But she'd never say it enough.

She wished she knew a way to thin the herd of men.

Silas was so hungry for a meal not fixed by his own hand that he couldn't think of much else.

When he saw Libby's Diner scrawled on the side of a clapboard building in Divide, Montana, he practically ran in, following his nose. He sank down on a bench at one of only two long, roughly built tables.

A bustling woman with a pleasant smile brought him coffee and a plate of stew without asking him what he wanted.

That was exactly what he wanted. Besides, it was most likely all Libby had. So a lot of time was spared.

The Husband Tree

Libby laid down the food, and Silas waved at the bench across from him. "I haven't heard another voice in an age. I'd be right pleased if you'd set a spell and talk to me while I eat."

Libby was agreeable and fetched her own cup of coffee and settled in on the bench across from Silas. They'd only covered half the town when a woman walked in, ringing the bell that hung over the door.

Now, Silas knew two kinds of women. In fact, to his knowledge until this moment, he'd've told anyone that there were only two kinds.

There were the dance-hall girls, all frilled up and doused with cheap perfume, with come-hither smiles that didn't cover the hardness behind their eyes. Their conversations were heated and direct, and their hands were always reaching for men's wallets.

And there were good girls, sorta like Libby here, though Libby was old enough to be Silas's mother, so she hardly qualified as a girl. Good girls wore calico and bonnets. They kept their eyes down—only glancing up once in a blue moon with their own version of come-hither—versions that were just as potent if a man wasn't careful. Their dresses were carefully loose to conceal their curves, although that didn't work well, a man's imagination being a powerful thing. Their conversations were discreet and shy. The funny thing about good girls was, just like the dance-hall girls, the good girls were also reaching for men's wallets. It was a longer reach, though, because a good girl got to a man's wallet with a side trip past a preacher.

The woman who strode into Libby's Diner was neither kind.

Her skin was tanned until she almost looked part Indian, but her light brown eyes made Silas believe she wasn't. She wore a fringed buckskin jacket with some of the fringe missing, the way a working-man's jacket was, because one of the points of having the fringe was to have a piggin' string available at all times. She had on a split riding skirt made of softly tanned doeskin that hugged her hips and flared loose around her ankles, and chaps over the skirt. None of it concealed her curves, even though every inch of her was covered.

She had on worn-out boots with spurs that jingled when she walked. A faded blue calico blouse showed under her jacket, with several buttons open that kept it from covering her throat as a decent dress ought. It looked like it was done for comfort, not for come-hither. A kerchief was tied at her neck the way a cowboy wore one, so it could be jerked up to filter dirt on a cattle drive. She wore leather gloves and a wide-brimmed, flat-topped black hat, and a six-gun in a holster on her neat little hip.

More unusual than that, she walked with a strong stride and looked Libby directly in the eye, even as she sat herself down next to Silas on the bench. She glanced at him with eyes that were neither hard nor demure, and no come-hither to be seen anywhere.

Even more interesting, Libby looked at her and spoke as she had to Silas, no giggles and hugs, none of the frilly manners one woman had with another. "Howdy, Belle. Eatin' today?"

"Anything you got is fine. I've had a hard ride in and got another one ahead of me to get home."

Libby got up and gave Belle the same service she'd given Silas.

Belle looked Silas straight in the eye but didn't linger over looking. Still, he had the sense that she'd taken in everything there was to see about him. There was nothing flirtatious in her glance, and it occurred to Silas that a woman often looked twice at him. He'd gotten used to women being interested.

Belle wasn't.

She turned back to Libby and took the coffee. "Obliged, Lib." She drank it two-fisted, like a man did who had gotten used to savoring the heat on cold nights on the range.

After she'd gotten some of the boiling hot, ink black coffee into her, she turned to Libby. "I'm huntin' hands. Anybody in town need work?" Her voice was deep for a woman. Businesslike. Somber. It tugged on something deep inside of Silas like sometimes beautiful music did.

Libby shook her head. "Cain't think of no one right off hand, Belle, but I can ask around. Most everyone huntin' work signed on with a herd heading for Oregon a month ago. My boys are off hauling freight, or they might help you out. It's late in the season."

"I hadn't heard about the other drive. I haven't been to town in a long time."

Although she kept her voice steady, Silas heard her underlying frustration and knew she needed help.

Libby said uncertainly, "I reckon there's a couple of loafers in the Golden Butte Saloon who might need the money bad enough to work for it."

Belle set her tin cup down with a hard *clink* and pulled her plate of stew closer, plunking her elbows on the table and surrounding the food as if afraid someone would take it from her. "I'll go check, but I don't want anyone who needs babysittin'. I'd rather do it alone."

"How many you need?"

"I want six. A month's work driving a thousand head to Helena."

"You're finally culling your herd that deep? Never thought I'd see the day." Libby poured another cup of coffee for Silas and topped off her own cup.

Nodding, Belle chewed thoughtfully. "I haven't sold more'n ten or twenty head in my life. Always trying to build. But I'm using up my range too fast this year. Had a calf crop I can't believe and didn't count close enough until about a week ago."

Libby refilled Belle's cup. "Uh. . .is your husband in charge then?"

Belle sat quiet for so long that Silas couldn't figure what about that question had stumped her so badly.

He sipped his coffee, watching this new kind of woman closely.

Finally, with a quick glance at Silas and an unreadable look, she said, "Anthony won't be makin' the drive. I'll be in charge."

Silas spit coffee across the table and started choking. Lucky Belle was beside him and Libby straight across from Belle.

Libby jumped up and grabbed a cloth.

Belle gave him a couple of thumps on the back, apparently thinking he'd swallowed his coffee wrong.

Mopping the table, Libby glanced at Silas and didn't quite conceal a smile.

Silas wiped his mouth and shirtfront. A woman in charge of a cattle drive? It sounded like Silas's very own worst nightmare!

Libby's reaction shocked him again. "You'll have more luck getting hands if'n they know Anthony's out, Belle."

Silas decided then not to drink any more coffee until Belle left, because he had no idea what she or Libby would say to surprise him next.

Belle quit beating on him and took her hand back to her coffee, nodding silently.

"Name's Silas Harden. I've punched my share of cows, and I could use a month's work." Silas heard the words come out of his mouth, and he had his third shock in the space of a single minute. He couldn't think of a worse fate than taking orders from a female, a particularly male kind of female at that. What had made his tongue slip loose with that offer?

"I'm Belle Tanner. Thanks for the offer." She angled her body a bit to face him then reached her hand out to shake, like a man would have.

Silas took her hand and felt the tough calluses. It made Silas want to punch somebody that this pretty little woman was running a cattle drive and had been doing hard physical labor for years, judging by her leather-tough hand.

Anthony seemed like a good place to start.

She pulled loose from his grip quickly, but not too quickly.

Just right. Again like a man.

That irritated Silas for some reason.

"I've never heard of you, Silas. You from around here?"

"No, I just drifted into town today. I'm from New Mexico mainly."

"No offense, but I'll be using folks I know or who can be recommended by folks I know." Belle went to scooping up stew with her fork, brushing aside his offer as if he were crumbs she'd found on her shirt.

Silas should have breathed a sigh of relief at his lucky escape. Instead, her rejection bit a fair-sized chunk out of his pride. "It figures a crew run by a woman would be afraid of strangers." Again Silas should have just kept his mouth shut. And challenging her. . .what kind of stupid way was that to talk to a woman? "I've hired on to a dozen outfits in my day with nothing but my word and an understanding that if I couldn't pull my weight I'd be sent down the road. A man's used to proving himself in the West. When you're dealing with women, I suppose it's all about whatever fancy notion she takes in her pretty little head."

Belle looked up from her stew and stared directly into his eyes. No quick, dismissive glance this time.

Silas thought, if he checked later, there'd be singe marks on his skin where her eyes burned a hole through him.

Finally, without taking her eyes off of him, she asked, "Libby, whatta ya think? Has he got the stuff to go with that mouth?"

Silas's eyes shifted to Libby, and she studied him, too. He sat still, being judged by two women, and not for what a woman usually judged him for. He fought the urge to squirm like a schoolboy caught hiding a garter snake in the teacher's desk.

"I think he'd do to ride the river with, Belle." Libby sipped at her coffee. "He's right. You can always show him the trail."

Silas looked back at Belle to tell her he wouldn't work for her even if she decided he measured up.

Before he could cut her down to size, she was talking again. "Well, I reckon I should take your word for it, Lib. Whatever else I am, I am the worst judge of men who ever walked the earth."

Libby started laughing. For a few seconds Silas wondered if the woman would topple off her chair, she was so caught in her laughing fit. Finally, Libby got herself under control. "No one can say that ain't true, Belle. Not knowing Anthony the way we do." Libby started in laughing again.

Belle quit trying to stare Silas to death and looked at the laughing woman and grinned.

Something twisted hard and sweet inside of Silas when he saw that serious face light up with a smile. She was younger than he'd first thought. And although he'd known from the first moment he saw her she was uncommonly beautiful, when she smiled like that, she seemed innocent and approachable. He wondered what kind of fool Anthony was to let his wife go off on a cattle drive with a half dozen men while he stayed home.

He was struck again by the idea that this was a kind of woman he never knew existed. He had no use for women, and he shuddered at the idea of working for one. When he opened his mouth to say he'd rather spend the next month being danced on by a herd of longhorns than work for her, he said instead, "So, am I hired, boss lady?"

Silas gave up any hope of controlling his mouth. It seemed to have struck out on its own for good. He shook his head and wondered at his willingness—no, his eagerness—to do this.

Belle tilted her head to study him. "You're too good-looking and you're too blasted smart—I can see that already. I'll probably have to shoot you down like a foam-at-the-mouth, rabid skunk before we're two days down the trail."

Silas froze. He had no idea how to react to that.

He'd shoot a man for less than calling him a "rabid skunk."

He'd kiss a woman for less than saying he was smart and

350

good-looking.

Their eyes met and the moment stretched. Her shining brown eyes widened, and he felt his own narrow. They were locked together until something almost visible vibrated between them.

Into the dead silence, Libby spoke. "That means you're hired."

CHAPTER 3

"Are you in town for long?" Silas stood from the table, pushing his chair back with a scrape.

"A couple of hours, more'n likely." Belle wished she'd never shaken his hand. The feel of it more than anything else had made her refuse his offer to work. Libby had spoken up in time to keep Belle from foolishly turning down a willing drover. "I'm laying in supplies for the drive, and the general store will be awhile filling the order and packing my horse string."

He nodded and offered her his hand again to seal the deal. "I'll be sleeping at the Golden Butte. Wake me up, and I'll ride out with you."

At mention of the Golden Butte, Belle frowned. She looked at that hand and was tempted to slap it aside. But some people might really sleep at the Golden Butte, and it didn't matter to her what he did. Swatting her new cowhand would have too much to do with Anthony and nothing to do with him. Good manners overcame her reluctance, and she gave him another quick handshake.

He tossed some coins on the table and left her sitting by Libby.

She rubbed her hand on her chaps to get the feeling of him off. She watched him walk away before she turned back to her coffee. "What do you know about him, Lib?"

"He came in huntin' a meal about an hour ago." Libby shrugged. "He's been ridin' the mountain country for a while. He didn't say much. But he saw to his horse before he ate. His outfit looked good and his gun was clean and loaded."

"It ain't much to go on." Belle studied her coffee.

"I liked the look of him. He'll do to ride the river with."

Somehow, Belle was sorely afraid he wouldn't do at all, but not for lack of practice at cowboying. "Keep kickin' over rocks to see if any hands crawl out. We're lightin' out at sunup, but they could catch us if you find anyone who's of a mind to."

"I'll do that." Libby fetched the pot and poured.

While she listened to Libby talk, Belle considered her options. Six hands. She needed that many cowpunchers to make this crossing. Seth had told her the same as Libby, a cattle drive had taken all the men available. But Seth had thought Libby's sons might be in town and they might set aside their mule skinning for a month to make solid cash money.

Belle knew how much help Lindsay and Emma were. And Sarah, though she wasn't big enough yet to bulldog or rope, could haze cattle and stick a saddle like a little burr. But Belle hadn't really counted the girls as hands. She'd more considered them as extra and just thought to bring them along because she couldn't leave them home alone. Now she was going to have to count them. So, she had those three and Silas. That was four hands. She wanted six men besides herself. With a sigh, Belle knew they could make the trip, but it would be as tough as anything any of them would ever endure.

It made her twitchy to sit drinking coffee, but listening to Libby talk was nice. A few more minutes wouldn't hurt, because it wasn't time to head back for a while. She'd left a list with Seth and Muriel at the general store, and it was a long one. She'd pulled a string of packhorses to town rather than bring her buckboard. After nearly giving birth to Betsy on the trail while driving her slow-moving buckboard home, she'd come to prefer the faster pace of the packhorses.

Libby went for the coffeepot again.

While she was gone into the kitchen, the bell tinkled over the door. Belle looked up expecting to see Silas Harden coming—wanting to shake her hand again. Instead, in traipsed a mystery.

Cassie Dawson. A woman forced into marriage who was happy. Impossible.

And yet the woman glowed. She had one hand resting on her stomach, obviously expecting a baby. Her husband swung the door inward then stepped back to let Cassie go first as if she were made out of the most fragile china. Red then followed his wife in.

Then bringing up the rear—of all people—Wade Sawyer. Belle decided she was improving as a judge of men, because she knew Wade Sawyer was bad news. Except he was carrying a little girl with a head full of short black curls, and dark brown eyes, who looked about a year old. Wade smiled down at the child with more pleasure and pride in his eyes than Belle had ever seen from her husbands toward their own children.

The last time she'd seen Wade, he'd had bloodshot eyes and a bad attitude and smelled like a mangy coyote. Now his eyes were clear, and a smile wiped all the cruelty from his face.

"Belle?" Cassie hurried over to the table, her eyes lit up, an excited smile on her face. This young woman had awakened a mother's instinct in Belle from the first. Cassie would have benefited from some of Belle's teachings. But Red got her first, and he'd done right by the little woman.

Belle also noticed that the baby looked the image of Cassie. Belle frowned, wondering how a woman managed such a thing.

Libby came out of the kitchen with her pot.

"I'm just dropping Cass and Susannah off." Red took the baby from Wade and hugged her till she giggled and grabbed at his nose.

"Papa." Susannah squealed and squirmed, and Belle couldn't take her eyes off the little girl surrounded by love. She'd done her best by her girls, but she'd never been able to provide them with a father's love.

"Bye-bye, Suzie." Red settled the baby on Cassie's lap. "I've got work to do. Libby, we'll haul your supplies over as soon as we can. Wade's going to help."

"Thanks, Red. I'll leave the door open. I planned on abandoning the place and having coffee with Cassie and Muriel and Leota over at Muriel's."

"Seth told us Muriel's out doctoring one of Leota's young'uns." Cassie ran her hand over her baby's curls.

Libby gasped. "Is it serious?"

"I think the little boy is running a fever from a cold. Leota hadn't slept all night, so Muriel went to give her a chance to rest." Cassie bounced her little girl on her knee. "They're going to try and get over here before Red comes back from his chores."

Belle looked to be on the verge of getting pulled into a hen party. She hadn't done such a thing in her adult life. Of course, with four daughters, her whole *life* was something of a hen party. But they were a hardworking flock.

Just as she was ready to stand up and walk out, Libby poured coffee and slipped a piece of cake in front of Belle. She knew this dessert wasn't for anyone but Libby's women friends—it was too pretty, with crumbled brown sugar and speckles of sweet-smelling cinnamon.

"That's perfect then." Libby nodded, clearly glad her party was going to grow.

Ruefully, Belle wondered what it would feel like to be welcomed like that. Libby was polite to her, but no friendlier than she'd been with Silas.

Red looked at Belle a long time, a serious expression on his face. "You had your baby, then? Everyone's okay?"

Belle nodded. "We named her Elizabeth. We call her Betsy." Anthony had insisted they name the baby Caterina, of all outlandish names. To keep him happy, they'd tried to call the tyke Caterina, or more often The Baby, when Anthony was within earshot. She and the girls privately called the child Betsy, and since Anthony had been gone more than home, that was pretty much all the time.

Figuring Anthony wasn't long for the world, considering the foolish way he conducted his life, they bided their time and watched their tongues, and now that the man had faced his inevitable death, they were free to call Betsy by her real name all the time.

"Glad to hear it. You were too far out to send to town for Muriel. Cassie, Wade, and I worried some."

Belle's eyes shifted to Wade's. "You're. . .living at Red's place?"

Wade nodded. "When I'm around. I've been doing some scouting for the army, some trapping. Hired on to a couple of cattle drives. I quit working on my dad's ranch. Got sick of living under his thumb." Wade's calm, clear eyes brightened. "Red and Cassie have helped me learn more about God. I'm a believer now."

Libby patted Wade on the arm. "It's been a pleasure having you attend our church. Your pa was in here kicking up a fuss about you living out at the Dawsons'."

Wade shrugged and smiled. "My pa's good at that."

He seemed to be completely at ease with his father's wrath, neither afraid nor angry. Belle had spent most of her married life being one or the other or both.

Belle lived far enough from everyone not to have come up against Mort Sawyer and his legendary temper, but she'd met the man a time or two. He expected everyone to stand aside or be crushed under his boot. Now she realized she had a skilled hand standing right in front of her.

"You're not hunting work, are you?" Belle felt foolish to hire on the son of the area's more powerful ranchers and offer him a dollar a day and campfire meals.

Wade seemed to focus on her for the first time. "Doing what?"

"I'm taking my cattle to market. I could use more hands."

Wade rubbed his thumb over his chin as if considering. "I've got a run to make first, promised to deliver some supplies to a line shack for Linscott. When are you heading out?"

"First light."

"Tomorrow?" Wade asked.

Belle nodded.

"I'll be a few days, but tell me your trail. I can catch up."

Belle would have told anyone who asked that she'd rather do this drive alone than let Wade Sawyer with his coyote eyes help her. But he'd said he was a Christian. More than that—because a man's word didn't mean much to Belle—he looked calm and settled. Much like Silas Harden.

She sighed. She didn't have the luxury of being picky. At least Wade, with his vast holdings, even if he'd walked away from them for now, wouldn't want to marry her to gain Tanner Ranch.

"Fine, we're taking the high trail out of the north side of my ranch."

Wade flinched. "Tough passage. You won't be hard to find. There's not a way off that trail once you start it."

Belle nodded. "I'd welcome the help."

Wade and Red left, jangling the bell behind them.

Belle found herself pulled into talk of babies and husbands and making a home. Three things Belle knew a lot about. And she'd tried to avoid all three with no success.

"So how old is your baby, Belle? I haven't seen. . ." Cassie faltered. "Did you have a boy or a girl?"

"A girl, thank goodness."

Cassie's eyes sharpened, and she held her squirming daughter. "Didn't you want a son?"

Obviously itching to get her hands on the tyke, Libby relieved Cassie of the little girl.

Belle snorted. "I haven't had much luck with men. I'd probably raise 'em up to be as worthless as their pas."

"Pas?" Libby asked. "More than one?"

"Yep, Anthony was my third husband. Uh. . .*is* my third husband."

"Was?" Libby plunked down on the bench next to Cassie. "What happened? Did Anthony die, too?"

Belle felt her neck start to heat. She had no talent for lying. She could skip a subject well enough and not feel the need to blurt out her every thought. But pure, straight-from-the-shoulder lies just didn't sit on her tongue nor her conscience. "I don't want to talk about Anthony."

Libby leaned closer and whispered, "You can tell us, Belle. I knew Anthony. It was only a matter of time until he turned up his toes."

Belle rubbed the back of her neck. "I don't want anyone knowing he's dead, okay?"

"Of course you're not ready." Cassie's eyes shone with compassion. "If he just died, you're still grieving."

"Grieving?" Belle snorted in a way that reminded her of her horse and shook her head. "Not hardly. I just don't want the no-accounts around here to know I'm widowed. They'll be out there pestering me to marry up with them. I'd probably finally just marry one to keep the others away." Belle glared at both women. "And I *don't want another husband.* If you breathe a word, it'll all be ruined."

Libby nodded.

"Why don't you want a husband, Belle?" Cassie's huge eyes were as warm and brown as her coffee.

"I just have a knack for picking a poor lot. It's something wrong with me. I know that. But I can't seem to get it right." Belle didn't like admitting that, but it was her only hope for keeping her secret. "So, I'm quitting."

"Quitting the ranch?" Cassie asked, pure innocence.

Belle should have taken her home and toughened her up, no matter that she was already married. "No!" Instead, Belle had stepped aside and let Red have her, and now look at the little woman, wide-eyed, innocent, sweet, cheerful. Not a brain in her head.

"Quitting men." Belle hadn't meant to shout, but the idea of giving up her ranch startled a yell out of her. "Three times a widow is enough. Now promise me you won't say a word."

Cassie nodded solemnly.

"I'll keep your secret, Belle. But word will get out soon enough," Libby predicted.

"If I can get through this cattle drive then get snowed in for the winter, I'll have a long stretch of peace and quiet. I'll spend my time whipping up a backbone to turn men away." Belle stood, sorry she'd stayed this long. Hoping these women could keep a secret. "I don't have time for jawing. I've got to buy supplies, pick up the hand I hired, and get back to my young'uns. Thanks for the coffee, Lib." Belle tossed a coin onto the table and left before they could ask any more personal questions.

She stalked out of the diner, spurs clinking, the bell over the door tinkling, and her ears ringing from the gossiping she knew the women would do about her. It served her right. She should have brought hardtack and biscuits instead of being so weak as to eat her meal in the diner.

She headed for the general store, determined to hurry Seth up and get out of Divide even if it meant packing her horses herself.

"Sawyer, why haven't you hit the trail yet?" Tom Linscott was already snarling as he rode up to the general store on his thorough-bred black stallion and dismounted.

There'd been plenty in and around Divide who believed Wade

had changed, but some still had their doubts. The difference was Linscott took the time to do it right.

"I've just come from Bates'." Wade jerked his thumb at the general store he'd just exited. "Belle Tanner rode in with a long order, and Seth's gotta finish that up first."

"Well, I want you on the trail today." Linscott wrapped his reins around the hitching post in front of the general store. His black stallion snorted and fought with the rope and tried to take a bite out of Tom's shoulder, but Linscott dodged; he'd reinforced all the hitching posts in Divide long ago, for this very reason. The stallion was as cranky as his owner.

Wade looked straight into Linscott's cold blue eyes and went on as always, being the best he could be and not worrying about anyone else. Linscott had let him do some work here lately. But even that was the tall Swede rubbing in his contempt. It was a big improvement over the days Wade hadn't been able to keep from goading Linscott until Wade ended up bleeding, sprawled on his backside in the dirt. What Tom felt or believed wasn't Wade's problem. He had enough of his own. "I'll be moving as soon as Seth gets time."

"Then I want you back here. I've got some more work, if you're willing." Linscott said it like he was sure Wade *wouldn't* be willing.

Smiling, enjoying the moment, Wade said, "Belle's driving a herd to Helena, and I signed on with her. Once I'm back from the drive, I'll stop out to the ranch. But it'll be a month or more."

"She's taking a herd to Helena this late in the year?"

"So she said."

Linscott settled his gloved hand on top of his Stetson and adjusted it so it rode low over his eyes. "Who's she finding to work for her? If she's askin' you, she must be scraping the bottom of the barrel."

Wade knew better than to even clench a fist. He was a believer now. A man of faith. Getting into a fistfight on Main Street wasn't part of the way he conducted himself. "Lucky for me she is. I need the work."

With a snort that probably charmed the black stallion, Linscott showed clearly that by *not* defending himself, Wade had just proved he was a weakling.

That didn't upset Wade much either. Much. He had so many weaknesses he couldn't count 'em all. That's why he needed God. Trouble was everyone needed God. Linscott included. And since the man didn't believe himself one bit weak, he'd be hard pressed to ever figure it out. That reminded Wade of his father—a man who thought he didn't need anything and had never admitted to a weakness in his life.

"Just get the supplies out to that line shack." Linscott stripped his gloves off his hands and tucked them in the pocket of his fringed buckskin coat. My men're running out of food by now." Linscott brushed past Wade and stomped into the store.

The horse snorted, speaking Linscott's language.

Wade stared at the beautiful beast for a few long seconds. "What do you think, boy? You like takin' orders from that grouch?"

The thoroughbred's midnight black eyes flashed, almost like an answer, and Wade knew the horse didn't take orders from anyone. He lived on his own terms, and he'd judged Tom Linscott to be worthy, or the horse would have stomped the man to death by now.

It occurred to Wade that the horse had the same temperament as Wade's father. Then Wade mentally apologized to the stallion.

CHAPTER 4

Belle conducted her business, doing half of Seth's work for him to move things along. Then she headed over to the saloon where Silas would be sleeping above stairs.

Belle strode into the Golden Butte, a place two of her husbands—one a drunk, the other a cheat—had taught her to hate. Two flouncy-dressed women sat playing poker with a couple of no-accounts. She had no idea how many women worked here, but since there was no sign of Silas down here, he might have been telling the truth about wanting to sleep.

"I'm heading out, Harden!" she hollered up the stairs. "You awake?"

Silas was only a few seconds coming out. He must have been sleeping with his boots on.

"What are you doing in here?" Silas clumped down the steps, scowling at her. No woman followed after him. Belle didn't care, but she noticed. "This is no place for a respectable woman." He glanced at the scantily clad females. "No offense."

One of them raised her glass. The other crossed her legs and hooked her arm over the back of her chair. "None taken, cowboy."

"I'm in here to get you. How'd you think I was supposed to get you without coming in?" Belle supposed her behavior was shocking. She didn't care much, but she could see he did. She took a long look at the two women and was tempted to take them with her, get them away from these men, teach them to work, to grow up, to have some shame.

He clapped his hat on his head. "You should have sent someone up for me."

"I reckon you're right." She didn't respond beyond that. Instead, she gave up on the women, turned on her heels, and led the way out of the saloon. She had her string of pack horses lined up out front.

Silas had a buckskin standing at the hitching post. He swung up, and the feisty little horse perked up its head like it was rested and rarin' to be on the move.

The buckskin had the look of a mustang that'd run wild for a time, and Belle knew the sure-footed mare would make the treacherous cattle drive with ease. The horse also looked well fed, and it had no ugly scars where a cruel man might work his mount with a whip or spurs. It raised Belle's opinion of Silas. She did a quick check of the ropes tying her four heavily laden horses to her roan and tested that her supplies were well secured.

Silas rode up beside her. "Did you find any more drovers?"

"Nope. Well one, maybe, who might come along later." It grated on Belle to think she might have to settle for help from that low-down Wade Sawyer. "I found a few no-accounts here and there. None of 'em needed work." She wondered angrily if she'd told them she was widowed would they come slithering out from under rocks and come along out to the place. She probably could have had those two bums from the saloon.

She glanced at Silas, knowing he might figure out Anthony was dead sooner or later. His well-groomed horse stretched out to a brisk walk beside her.

Silas had brown hair and eyes and was just under six feet tall. Belle had the strange thought that if she had a baby with this man and it looked like *him*, at least some of the time she could convince herself it looked like her, too.

Then she realized what she was thinking and almost spurred her horse into a gallop. The string of ponies she was dragging along kept her from running.

"Okay, what about the trail we're taking?"

The question thankfully took Belle's mind off nonsense. "It's a killer. There's a canyon near my cabin that has a high pass out of the north side. We're going in on the south—that's the only other trail in, and it's a few hundred feet lower in altitude than the one we'll take tomorrow. I've got the cattle settled in that grassy pasture, and they'll fight us leaving it and climbing up the side of a cliff to get out."

A thin whistle escaped Silas's lips as he listened.

"Then is when it gets really bad."

Silas shook his head. "Sounds like a killer all right."

"Yep, we've got a hundred miles of treacherous turns, flanked by steep cliffs a good part of the time and going up and down one mountain after another. The trails are blocked in places with talus slides. The landslide areas seem like they're looking for a horse's leg to break."

"A hundred miles isn't much as cattle drives go."

"Nope, we'll make it. But where there aren't cliffs, there are heavily wooded mountainsides that will have to be constantly combed for bunch quitters. This trail is part of the backbone of the Rockies. The herd will be strung out over miles. The—" Belle faltered. She'd almost said "the girls," but she'd let him find out about the girls when they were well away from Divide. "The drovers will be forced to move constantly, circling, pushing."

"And we're heading out tomorrow?"

"Yep. I already have the cattle cut out. Old stuff and almost all my steers, plus a few head of heifers just to cull the herd down to a level that won't ruin my pasture. The cattle have been getting fat and lazy for the last week. I've also scouted the trail a bit, and the start's not so bad. I've cleared the first couple of slides and found some likely pastureland. We should be able to keep the herd well fed and content for the first couple of days. By then they'll be trail broke, and hopefully, when they have to scale the rugged pass along Mount Jack, the cows and my. . .my cowhands will come through."

"How many hands did you find? You wanted six."

"There'll be five of us. And I talked to one man who had a couple of days' work to finish, but he might catch up to us along the drive."

"That's still a short-handed drive. But we should manage since it's so short." Silas settled his hat more firmly on his head as if he were ready to shoulder the work.

Belle doubted he'd be one that came though—he was a man after all—but she could hope. Right at this moment she was worried enough that she almost wished for all three of her husbands back just because she could make them come along at least and add their body count to the number. In the end she knew they'd just be extra, ornery bulls to deal with, so all in all, she decided their being dead was for the best.

"Now tell me details about this trail. Tell me everything." Silas looked back, as if checking on the horse string was his job. The man had knowing eyes, studying the ropes and packs. Then, apparently satisfied, he turned back to her.

As they made the trek home, she did more talking than she'd ever done with a man, and that certainly included her husbands.

As she talked, he asked questions and impressed her with his knowledge of cattle. By the time they rode up to the ranch, they were talking like old friends.

Silas swung off his horse and paused for a moment to look at her house.

It was a ramshackle, leaking wreck, and Belle knew it. But she didn't know how to fix it. Mostly she was used to it, but having Silas stare at her house made her cheeks warm. When was the last time she'd given a whit what anyone else thought of her? Then she remembered that she'd blushed in front of Cassie and Libby today and hoped her tanned skin didn't show red.

"Let me unload the supplies. Then I'll put the horses up."

Belle glanced up, startled. She'd never expected help. When Lindsay and Emma came out and started hauling, Silas was helpful and respectful—two traits Belle didn't know existed in a man.

Silas picked up the reins of two horses then reached for a third, obviously to lead the horses toward her crumbling barn and makeshift corral. Belle and the older girls each grabbed a horse before he could collect them all. Then there were horses to rub down, hay to pitch, a cow to milk, and eggs to gather. With Silas helping, evening chores were done in quick time.

"Supper!" Sarah's little voice called.

All four went toward that homey call.

Belle stepped into the house through the sagging door.

"I put the same amount of potatoes in the pot I did afore Anthony turned up his toes," Sarah spoke from the stove.

Belle gasped and glanced at Silas who was visibly surprised by the news.

He arched one brow at her in an unasked question.

She resolutely looked away. She had learned a long time ago not to give too much away about what she was thinking and feeling. She'd discovered that a husband often made himself feel more like a man by battering on a woman's feelings, and men not used to doing business with women dealt better when there was no feminine behavior on the woman's part.

She scoffed inwardly at her foolishness. She had assumed that whoever she hired would know that Anthony was dead—probably before they got on the trail. Word would eventually get back to town. But since the only man who'd come with her wasn't from around here, she'd been sifting ideas in her head about claiming Anthony was just away.

Not a complete lie. God had definitely come and taken Anthony away. Chances were she could pull off Anthony being somewhere just for overnight. Then the drive would start and there was no reason Silas would have to know anything more about the missing husband.

She'd never considered it before she left for town, so she hadn't had a chance to mention it to the girls, and for all her mental gyrations, she'd known there was a good chance Anthony being dead would come out. So why did she feel her face heat up? This was the second time it had happened since she'd gotten home and the third time today.

Also the third time in her adult life.

To conceal her overly warm cheeks, she headed for the washbasin to stand in line behind Emma.

Lindsay was already washed up and putting bowls of food on the table.

Sarah had contrived fried chicken, mashed potatoes, a baking of bread, and the last of the green beans from their kitchen garden. A custard stood cooling by the window, rich with their own eggs and cream and honey.

They were seated at the table, and Belle said grace quickly but from the heart, because she considered being spared a husband's company the act of a loving God.

When the food had been passed and everyone was settled in to eat, Silas asked casually, "So what exactly did Anthony die of?"

Belle thought he was looking at his food rather suspiciously, like maybe it was poisoned.

She almost smiled. Then he caught her eye and did smile, and she knew he was teasing her. She looked back at her plate. That moment of mutual amusement might well constitute the nicest exchange she'd ever had with a man. And that definitely included the four times she'd gotten pregnant.

Sarah, always helpful, piped up. "He claimed to be looking for leaks, but he were hiding out from work like always. He fell off the roof."

Silas quirked the corner of his mouth but managed not to smile. "That's terrible."

Without looking up from her food, Sarah responded, "Not really."

Silas pressed his hand to his mouth for a second. "How long has he been gone?"

"A couple months, I reckon." Emma was, as a rule, shy around strangers. Not today, more's the pity. But then Anthony's worthless-ness was one of her favorite subjects. "Didn't rightly notice what day it was. We planted him by the Husband Tree with the other husbands. Lost nearly a quarter of a day of work, but we made it up soon enough."

Sarah said with overly solemn dignity, "They was a worthless lot. Anthony Santoni was Betsy's pa." Sarah pointed her fork at the dark-haired, dark-eyed toddler.

Sarah shook her head of red curls and yanked on one of the corkscrews, pulling it down past her eyes before letting it spring back. "My pa, Gerald O'Roarke, was drunk when he died, as usual. He fell off his horse on his way home from the Golden Butte and let hisself get dragged for nigh onto twenty miles. Ma says he was no great loss 'ceptin' it was right hard on the poor horse."

Silas coughed into his napkin for far too long. "Husband Tree?"

Somehow Belle had never heard her words echoed back at her in quite this way before. Her neck was getting warm again, and she thought desperately of something to say to change the subject. The best she could come up with was, *Let's talk about something else.* She opened her mouth to say it, but before she could. . .

"My and Emma's pa was William Svendsen." Lindsay, who had been mercifully silent until now, smoothed her white blond hair, pulled back in a single, waist-length braid, and spoke. "He got hisself gored by Rudolph."

"And Rudolph is. . ." Silas waited.

"Our bull. Maybe a ten-foot spread of horns. Getting old now, but he's been a good bull. Wasn't his fault William went right into his pen." Lindsay rolled her eyes.

Emma arched her blond brows over her crystal blue eyes. "Any idiot knew better than to climb in that pen with Rudolph."

Silas covered his mouth with his napkin and seemed to be having a problem breathing.

Belle was pretty sure he was choking to death, and she wished he'd get on with it.

"Any other husbands planted around here?"

Sarah mulled it over for a moment. "Umm. . .no, I think that's the lot of 'em. . .so far. Likely another one'll come sniffin' around now that ma's a widow lady again."

"They always do," Emma said with heavy resignation.

"We've learned our lesson." Very sternly, Lindsey added, "Haven't we, Ma?"

Belle rubbed her forehead and stared at her plate as she nodded without saying a word.

"Yep, don't care how many of the mangy varmints come a-courtin'," Sarah said blithely. "We finally got shut of husbands for good. Now we can settle down and run this ranch right."

"We always did run it right," Emma added. "The husbands just slowed us down some."

Finally, far too late, Belle said weakly, "Let's talk about something else."

Betsy chose that moment to whack her spoon against the table and splatter mashed potatoes across Silas's face. He was at the foot of the table and Belle at the head, with Betsy beside her, so the man was clear across the table from the baby. Even at that distance, the potatoes hit him square in the eye.

Belle snatched the spoon out of Betsy's hand and began wiping her messy face while Silas cleared his vision.

Betsy grinned straight at the poor man. "Papa!"

Glancing up, Belle saw mute horror in Silas's eyes as his face turned a startling shade of pink under his deep tan. He rose from the table, knocking his chair over backward in his haste.

The girls didn't seem to notice and started cleaning up the supper dishes.

"Thank you for the fine meal." He set the chair back up. "I'll bunk down with the buckskin in the barn." Silas backed toward the door, grabbed the knob, and wrenched the door open. "I'll be ready to move out with the herd an hour before first light." He practically ran out of the house and slammed the door so hard Belle waited to see if it would fall in.

As soon as Belle could get her humiliation under control, it occurred to her that Silas had known she was a widow lady for several minutes now, and instead of proposing to her on the spot, he'd run like a rooster with his tail feathers afire. That man was horrified at the very thought of marrying her.

It was the nicest thing a man had ever done for her.

She cheered right up and even sang with the girls while they cleaned the kitchen.

It looked like, when it came to men, hiring Silas was the smartest thing she'd ever done.

That wasn't saying much.

Taking this job was the dumbest thing he'd ever done!

He hunkered down in the barn and wondered whether Belle had set her cap for him already.

The Husband Tree?

He was tempted to cut and run, and likely he'd've done it if he hadn't given his word.

The Husband Tree

Papa!

That child had called him Papa, and Silas had nearly turned tail and run out of the cabin.

But wait a minute! He remembered the way Belle got all embarrassed. It was the most womanly thing she'd done so far.

Except she loosened up on the ride home and talked to him intelligently and smiled real regular.

He couldn't recall having a better time talking to anyone, let alone a woman. He caught himself thinking about how pretty she was, and he remembered a couple of times he'd gotten close to her accidental-like and he'd noticed how good she smelled. He considered on that for a while, how a woman could dress like a man, ride a horse like a man, work like a man, and still have something so purely female about her.

Belle Santoni—or was it Belle Tanner? Silas hadn't gotten it all straightened out in his head yet. Belle Whoever. . .worked this place like any man rancher would. And Silas would bet his life the woman didn't even own a drop of perfume or a bar of sweet-smellin' soap. But she still smelled like 100 percent, genuine woman.

Silas sat in the cold barn and remembered how she felt when he shook her hand. Strong and soft and. . . Silas rubbed his hand on his pant leg, trying to put into words what else she was. The best way he could describe her was honest, although the woman had already lied to him at least once about Anthony being dead. But there was honesty in Belle's handshake and in her eyes. Or maybe a better word was *directness*. She didn't have any of the women's wiles that had pitched him such fits in his life.

So, if she was direct, then Silas had to believe she meant what she said. She was foreman of the cattle drive. She'd said she had more hands, but they must be coming in the morning, because there was no one else around. She'd said one of the drovers might be late, meet up with them along the trail. Was she meeting the others that way, too? If so, it might be that he and Belle would have to at least get the drive started alone.

He had no illusions about long, romantic nights by the fire. There would be none of that with a shorthanded cattle drive. He didn't want to think of the brutal month of hard work ahead of them.

He also realized that meant she was leaving the girls home alone. That was the one thing so far about Belle he didn't respect. Even the lying didn't bother him too much, because she hadn't really lied. She just hadn't mentioned a few important details.

But leaving those girls. Silas shook his head. The two older ones were as tall or taller than Belle—but they were still young girls. Rough, dangerous men prowled this wild country, and even an occasional band of Indians. It was no place for a gaggle of little girls to be left alone.

He lay awake, thinking about the drive ahead. He dozed lightly several times and knew the day was coming soon when he'd look back on this night's lost sleep with regret.

Finally, he decided to declare it officially morning. He tossed his blanket aside and went to saddle up in the early hours of the morning. He started with his own. Then he started making packs out of the grub Belle had brought back on her string of ponies.

As he worked around the place in the bright moonlight, he began to really see the Tanner ranch. It was a mess.

He remembered what Lindsay—or was it Sarah?—had said about Anthony falling off the roof checking for leaks. In the glow of the full moon, Silas could see the patched, shoddy job Belle's husbands had done building this place. The fences sagged and were braced haphazardly with tree branches and strips of rawhide. The door to the barn hung from drooping leather thongs, and the logs on the barn and the house were all small ones, as if someone didn't have the gumption to go cut down the big trees a solid house needed.

He started tying a line of horses to the hitching post in front of the barn, and the top rail fell off in his hands. He spent long minutes repairing it, and his fingers itched to set the rest of the property to rights. It was a beautiful site Belle's husband had picked to settle, but the house was set wrong for the winter winds and the warm summer sun. The man who built this had been a poor excuse for a carpenter.

In a brief instant, Silas could see how it was for Belle. He knew how much a woman needed a husband in the West. Someone to lift heavy things. Someone to saddle the broncos. Someone to sign legal documents and deal with the rough characters who were the only kind of men who lived in an area like this.

So, she'd been widowed. The country was hard on people and there were a thousand ways to die that had nothing to do with outlaws or marauding Indians. And once widowed...well...women were rare out here, especially women as pretty as Belle Tanner. Especially pretty women who owned a valley as rich and fertile as this. The men came calling. And like any wise woman, Belle had said yes. But it sounded like she was no judge of men, because her three husbands, to quote Sarah—or was it Lindsay?—were "a worthless lot."

As Silas moved around the yard feeding the chickens, collecting eggs, and milking the cow, the work helped ease out the snarls in his mind. He remembered Lindsay, he was sure it was the oldest girl, saying, "We've learned our lesson. Haven't we, Ma?"

And one of the other girls had responded, "We can settle down and run this ranch right." A weight lifted off his back as he realized that Belle Tanner had *not* set her cap for him. In fact, it was just the opposite.

That's why she'd hidden the fact that Anthony was dead. That's why she spent the whole mealtime last night blushing like a nun in a dance hall. The last thing Belle wanted was another husband, and she was doing everything she could think of to keep from acquiring one.

Grinning, Silas carried hay and water to the milk cow. He glanced up when a lantern flickered to life in the house. He smiled when he thought about the houseful of womenfolk, everyone of whom agreed that keeping men out of their lives was the only way to run the ranch right.

He picked up the basket of eggs and the bucket of milk and headed in with them and knew he'd finally found a woman he could stand to be around.

At least he thought he could stand it. . .for a month.

CHAPTER 5

Silas showed up at the door with milk and eggs. Belle was dressed and on her way out, and they almost collided.

"The morning chores are done." Silas hoisted the milk bucket a few inches to prove it. "But you'd better check. I may not do things your way."

"You gathered eggs?" Belle stared up at him as if he were speaking Flathead.

"Yeah, and milked the cow. And I've got the packhorses ready to go."

Without another word, Belle dodged around him and darted out the door.

Lindsay came close, acting wary, and snatched the egg bucket almost as if she expected him to fight to hang on to it. Sending him a suspicious look, she relieved him of the milk, too, and took both buckets over to Sarah.

Emma was busy in the corner of the one-room cabin, changing the baby's diaper, but she glanced over her shoulder and arched a brow.

Sarah had a cast-iron skillet on the stove heating, and as soon as Lindsay set the buckets on the wobbly counter next to Sarah, the little redhead began cracking the two dozen or so eggs and dropping them with a homey sizzle into the frying pan.

Emma finished with the baby and pulled some contraption onto her back. Then Lindsay stuck the baby in while Emma adjusted the little pack. Dressed in boots, chaps over a riding skirt, and a fringed jacket just like her ma's, and with the baby strapped on her back in a little leather sling the way an Indian carries a papoose, Emma headed for the door.

Lindsay said, "He done the chores already."

Emma stopped short and stared at Lindsay. Silas had the impression Emma didn't understand, as if *Lindsay* had begun speaking Flathead. Finally, Emma shifted her eyes to Silas. She looked so skeptical he almost grinned.

Sarah flipped open the door on the potbellied stove and stirred the fire with a poker, then went back to breaking eggs. She seemed bent on cooking them all up, and he bit back the urge to tell Sarah to go easy and save some eggs for the rest of the day.

Without looking at him, Sarah said matter-of-factly, "She ain't marryin' you. So don't even think about it."

At Sarah's comment, the two older girls turned on him like starving wolves that'd spotted a three-legged mule deer.

Silas was momentarily speechless. Then he remembered last night and set right out to put their fussy female minds at ease. "I wouldn't marry your ma if you wrapped her up in ribbons and tissue paper and gave her to me as a Christmas present."

"And I wouldn't marry you either, Mr. Harden."

Silas let his eyes drop closed at the belligerent tone of Belle's voice. He collected his thoughts, turned to face her, and went right to setting *her* mind at ease, too. "Good. So we understand each other. Now explain it to your girls so we can get these cattle on the trail."

He saw that reddish tint start crawling up her neck again,

376

and he wanted to laugh. He didn't think Belle was a woman who blushed very often, but she'd spent most of her time with him all pink and embarrassed.

She looked past him. "Girls, we've finally found a man we can stand to have around. I promise not to marry him. Now don't scare him off until after the drive. Then I'll *help* you scare him off."

Silas turned to see how the girls took the news.

Sarah was still scrambling eggs.

Emma shrugged and set to untangling Betsy's fingers from her braided hair.

Lindsay looked between the two of them, then, with a resigned sigh, she said, "You never learn, Ma." She started setting the table.

Belle came up beside Silas with her arms crossed. The two of them exchanged a look that was in complete accord.

Children!

Then Belle said, "I let the milk cow out with the herd. She's due to calf in about six weeks, so it's the perfect time to dry her up. I penned the chickens up in the barn and gave them plenty of feed. They should spend this time setting chicks. I hope so, because if they don't, they're bound to escape that wreck of a barn and the coyotes will be thinning them out the whole time we're gone. Otherwise everything was done. We're going to get an hour's jump on the sun thanks to you, Mr. Harden."

"Go back to Silas. I had a schoolmarm who used to call me Mr. Harden when she scolded me. I keep half expecting you to take a ruler to my knuckles."

Belle nodded.

Silas grinned.

Sarah fried.

Emma played with Betsy.

Lindsay sighed again.

"Eat up quick, girls," Belle said. "I want you all saddled so we can start punching those cattle up that high pass in fifteen minutes."

Silas was a man who thought things through. Who considered angles before he acted or spoke. He was a man with a temper, but it wasn't explosive. All of a sudden he figured something out he should have known all along. "We aren't taking a baby on a cattle drive!"

The whole gaggle of women froze. Even baby Elizabeth stopped her cheerful torment of Emma and stared at Silas.

Belle stepped away from his side, where just a second before he'd decided it was to be the two of them against the girls and liked that just fine. She lined up with her daughters.

Sarah took the eggs off the stove and, with a towel wrapped around its handle, held the hot pan like it was a weapon. Lindsay set down the tin plates she was laying out with a sharp click.

The five women stood shoulder to shoulder against him.

They didn't look much alike. Lindsay and Emma some, but otherwise they were as different from each other as if they shared not a drop of blood. But their eyes, whatever the color, held the same cold glare.

Belle could have slit his gullet with the sharp look she was giving him. She said quietly, but with a voice that spelled Silas's doom, "There's no question about the girls going on the drive. The only question is, are you going with us?"

Not his doom as in he was fired. His doom as in he was going to have to go on a cattle drive with a passel of women. One of 'em wearing diapers!

"B–but. . .but we have one hundred of the hardest miles of—" Silas sputtered to a stop.

"What kind of person *are* you who would go off and leave children home alone for that long?" Belle spoke with a rage that was deadlier for being quiet.

Silas had thought that about Belle earlier; still he had never considered— "You have. . .I thought you said one thousand steers. . .none trail broke. . .we. . .four cowhands. . ." He couldn't give voice to the impossibility of what Belle was proposing.

"My older girls can ride circles around any man."

Suddenly Silas quit being stunned. He was furious. He stepped forward and grabbed Belle by the arm and dragged her out of the house in a single motion and slammed the door behind them. He dragged her a dozen long strides from the cabin then turned her to face him and leaned down so his nose almost touched hers. "Don't you mean they can ride circles around any man you've ever been so stupid as to let crawl into your bed?"

He saw the cold anger in Belle's eyes switch over, all of a sudden, to blazing hot. "I owe you for your work, Mr. Harden. Thirty a month. You've worked one hour. I'll get you your *nickel* and you can be on your way!"

Silas jerked her fully against him. "I can't let you and a bunch of baby girls go off on a cattle drive alone. What kind of man do you think I am?"

"The usual kind, Mr. Harden." Belle jerked against his hold, but he hung on. "Isn't there only one kind?"

The door to the cabin opened, and in the gray light of the approaching dawn, Silas saw Lindsay standing in the door with a rifle. She had it aimed at him, and he had no doubt the girl could pull the trigger. Except for the part where he might end up with a belly full of lead, it made him feel a little better to see the young'un be so salty.

"Get your hands offa my ma and get away from her." Lindsay levered a shell into the chamber with a sharp crack. It was a Winchester .44.

It occurred to Silas that this was the second gun pulled on him in recent months. The first one, bandied by Hank Tool, was to force Silas to stay close to Lulamae. This one was the exact opposite.

Silas let Belle go, raised his hands slowly, and stepped away. But he wasn't done talking, regardless of the feisty young'un with the fire iron. "You can't take them, Belle. You'll have to wait. Find more drovers and send *them* on the drive." Then he got slightly less reasonable as he thought of what the crazy woman was proposing. "You stay home and take care of your children the way a decent woman should!"

Belle took a step closer to him, which was just what Lindsay had been threatening to shoot him for. "Go back inside, girls. Mr. Harden and I are having an argument, but he won't hurt me."

Silas glanced up and saw four girls watching him yell at their mother and manhandle her. It made him feel like the lowest form of life that ever slithered across the face of the earth.

"Men have hurt you before, Ma," Lindsay said evenly.

Silas's stomach twisted at the hardness in Lindsay's voice. He'd heard the girls' hostility toward men last night, but it had all been talk about men being lazy and worthless. None of them had indicated a man had laid his hands on Belle in anger.

"Only Gerald when he was drunk. I took care of it then, and I can take care of this now." Belle added, "Anyway, Silas won't."

Lindsay hesitated, the gun still raised.

"I won't, Lindsay. Your ma and I might fight with words, but I'd never harm a woman."

Lindsay kept the gun up.

"Go, Lindsay. Mind me." Belle had the voice of a mother who'd had a lot of practice ruling the roost.

Lindsay gave them both a long look, then reluctantly she lowered the gun, backed into the cabin, and shut the rickety door.

Belle surprised him because she spoke softly. He assumed it was because she was afraid the girls might be listening, because her expression and the fire in her eyes were pure rage. "I may not be what you think of as a decent woman, Silas Harden, but I wasn't born being what I am. Looking and acting like a man wasn't something that I planned on. I didn't ask to have to do everything alone. And it wasn't my wish to raise up girls who wanted to be just like me. I know I'm doing wrong by my young'uns. I know I'm not a—not a decent woman." Belle's voice broke, and she fell silent.

It was then he realized she was speaking softly because his words had struck home hard.

After a second she continued. "But I have to make this drive. My cattle have to be driven to market. *Now.* Without delay. To avoid the winter. If I don't go, all of them will starve to death by spring. My range will be ruined from overgrazing. My way to provide for my daughters will be destroyed. My girls can go with me and face hardship and danger by my side, or I can abandon them to the hazards of staying here without me to protect them." Her hands clenched at her sides.

Silas imagined some of the peril the girls could face. No, they couldn't stay here alone.

Belle lifted her fists and laid them on his chest without striking him. All she needed to do was to entwine her hands and she would be begging.

He hated himself for reducing this proud woman to that.

"The choices I make aren't ones I'm proud of." She tilted her head back to look up at him, her eyes almost level with his chin. He saw those eyes fill with tears. "They're just the only ones I can live with."

He hated himself for making her say she wasn't a decent woman. So far she was the most decent woman he'd ever met.

"The worst part of all of this is you're right. I can't do it without you. I have my doubts if I can do it *with* you. But *without* you we're beat before we start. I need you to go with me, Silas. To go with me and my girls."

The tears and the pleading in her voice and the softening of the sky and the mourning dove's song were all too much. Without any good reason why he would do such a fool thing, he leaned over and kissed her.

381

Belle gasped and jerked her head away.

For a long second their eyes met, as if a force stronger than both of them was binding them together.

A rooster crowed in the barn. The sun sent its first rays over the horizon. A lazy cow mooed in the morning breeze.

Silas's hand went around the back of her neck and sunk into her long, chocolate brown braid and pulled her mouth back against his.

Her clenched fists held them apart until her hands opened and lay flat against his shirt. She tilted her head and let her neck drop back under the force of his kiss as she opened her mouth. Her hands slid up his chest to his shoulders and around his neck.

Silas slid one strong arm around her waist.

"Ma! You promised!"

Glowing Sun ducked under the low branches of the outstretched ponderosa pine, covering her mouth to still her laughter. She watched her little sister scamper about hunting. Hide-and-seek. A game Glowing Sun remembered from when her parents were alive. It was much like the one she now played with her new family, the Salish. Her parents had called them the Flathead tribe.

When yellow fever had taken the rest of the family, leaving Glowing Sun, nearly ten years old, alive and alone in the remote mountain cabin, a band of Salish warriors had found her, taken her home, and cared for her as one of their own.

Watching her little sister head in the wrong direction, back toward the village, Glowing Sun snickered. Then she realized she'd run too far away. Fear twinged her belly. Her Flathead mother had warned her often enough about leaving the safety of the village. She'd head back in soon, but not quite yet. She waited, grinning, for her chance to dart into the open and touch the base.

A hard hand clamped over her mouth.

The Husband Tree

Glowing Sun screamed, but no sound got past those hard fingers.

An arm circled her waist like a vise.

She reached behind her head, clawing. She kicked and twisted her body. Wrenching wildly, she tried to break the iron grasp. Then she thought of her knife.

As she reached for it, the man shifted his grip and trapped both her arms, locking her hands to her sides so she couldn't get to the razor-sharp blade. The man holding her grunted in pain but kept a firm hold. "She's wild. She don't know we're savin' her." Rasping breaths and vague, mostly unknown words sounded from behind her, not far up. The man seemed to be only a little taller than Glowing Sun.

From a foot or so farther behind, someone whispered, "Let's put some distance between us and them Flathead."

She jerked violently and nearly slipped from his grasp, but then his arms tightened. His smothering hand stayed in place, and her arms were bound even more firmly to her sides.

If she could just scream once, her father would come. Wild Eagle, too. They were promised to each other. Even her younger brother, Thunder Light. Her mother and sister would fight for her. The whole village. They had always protected her.

She hadn't heard the white language for nearly eight summers, and few of their words were clear.

"I'll grab her feet. Then we'll make tracks for the nearest settlement."

The second man rounded her, and she saw one of her assailants for the first time. His ugly, heavily furred face, his stinking body covered in crudely cut furs, his filthy hands reaching for her.

She lashed out a foot, and he grabbed it, then caught the other and wrapped his arms around her knee-high moccasins. He caught her deerskin dress, wrapping it around her legs like binding. He sneered. A thick scar glowed red across one eye, down into his beard, and up his forehead into his heavy beaver-skin cap.

The man behind her kept a tight hold, solid as an iron clamp on her waist, never releasing her mouth.

She fought them and saw the beading of her dress snap. The pretty beads she'd sewn so painstakingly along her neckline scattered. She wanted to cry. The beads were so dear. She yanked at the man's arm, substituting rage for sorrow. Rage made her strong, sorrow weak. She'd learned that well, despite the words of the kindly missionaries who told her anger was a sin. Surely it wasn't a sin to hate men such as these. She cried out in her heart for God to send her family, the Salish.

God save me. Save me from whatever these vile men have in store.

She shouted her fury, but the words remained buried behind the suffocating hand.

The men carried her at a near run away from her village.

Oh why hadn't she listened to her parents and stayed near safety? She clawed at the wrist of the captor behind her, but he began nearly crushing her, and she quit so she could breathe.

They slipped along, dodging trees, sliding more than walking down the steep, heavily wooded mountain that surrounded her village.

A cold wind warned of approaching winter. If they took her far, her family would have to leave for the winter campgrounds. She would never find them again.

Their tepees were set up along the low valley, surrounding the crystal water rushing through this part of the Bitterroots. It was the tribe's favorite fall hunting ground. Trout swam thick in the rushing stream, and elk and bighorn sheep were abundant. They could gather food for the harsh winter months ahead.

She left that safety farther behind with every step. Her muffled shouts did nothing to stop the men. Rescue became more and more distant.

A desperate jerk pulled her foot loose. She drove her heel into the man's belly.

His eyes turned wicked, furious. He snagged her flailing foot and wrapped one arm around her feet so tightly she cried out in pain, but no sound escaped.

The man at her feet swung back a fist.

"Not now." The man gagging her lifted her higher against his chest, her breath nearly cut off. "How're ya gonna hit her without hitting me? Knock my hand away, and she'll get loose hollarin'. We'll be out the reward her family'll pay."

Family. She recognized that word. What were they saying about her family? She couldn't bring in a breath. The men roughly pulled her this way and that as they stumbled and ran and moved, moved, moved ever farther from home.

Emerging from the thickest trees, the men picked up their pace. She'd heard horrid tales of the white man, especially from Wild Eagle and Thunder Light, who delighted in scaring her to death. She was old enough to remember that her real parents were good. She understood the Salish people's fear yet knew the wild tales of evil didn't apply to all whites. But these looked like the kind her white mother would have feared and her white father would have watched with cautious eyes. She had no doubt they meant her ill.

Too long without a deep breath of air. Too long fighting and turning. Too long terrified. Her head began to spin. She wrenched her neck, trying to find even a small bit of air.

The man stifling her breath gripped her face harder.

Her cheeks burned from the fight. Her thoughts slowed until she felt dull and stupid. The edges of her vision grew dark until she was looking down a tunnel.

No, Lord, I have to stay awake. I have to be ready if there is a chance to escape.

But the hand tightened more. The arm around her waist

weighed on her lungs like stone. The eyes of the man at her feet burned evil, as if he only waited for his chance to repay her for that kick.

She shook her head, trying to say no without the ability to speak. Trying to beg for air.

"Horses just ahead. We'll gag her, and I'll carry her on my pack mule. We can be far from her village before they know she's gone."

"Far. . .village. . ."

Those were words she understood. She'd been alone before. She'd lived for weeks in her family's cabin after her parents died. She'd buried them one by one in the hard, rocky ground. Digging those graves nearly killed her, and she'd prayed that the sickness that was taking her mother, father, and two little brothers would take her, too.

She'd stayed healthy in that house of death, with no idea how to exist except one day at a time. The aloneness after her real family's death haunted her. To this day, she often woke up screaming to find she'd been trapped back in that deserted cabin.

Into that monstrous aloneness, her new father had come. Though she remembered her terror of the huge, dark-skinned warrior, she had been given no choice. He'd swung her high on his horse and taken her to a new home. A home with so many people she could never be alone again.

"Far. . .village. . ."

No air. No hope. No family.

No, no, God, please no.

The swirling darkness came closer and faded to only the red eyes of the man who held her legs. The rest of the world faded to black, but those glowing eyes followed her.

Burning in the darkness like the eyes of Satan.

CHAPTER 6

Belle jerked away from Silas as if she'd been burned.

He wasn't sure he wasn't on fire himself.

His eyes went to that doorway and that gun aimed at him. Again.

Lindsay aimed that rifle at his chest as if he were wearing a big fat target that had been pinned on him for the sole purpose of collecting bullets.

Belle wrenched away from Silas, muttered, "What is happening to me?" and practically ran to the house, ignoring Silas and Lindsay. Then, in a slightly throaty voice, she called out, "Breakfast is ready."

Silas could smell the eggs and biscuits. He had a long day ahead of him. He'd barely slept the night before. Now he decided without one split second of hesitation to start the day without eating. There was no force short of God Almighty Himself—coming down from heaven with a big stick—that was powerful enough to get him to go into that house and sit all cozy with the Wild Bunch.

He mumbled something about already having eaten and rode out to the steers without looking back, although his hair tingled with the feel of Lindsay and her fire iron drawing a bead on his backside. He was almost out of the yard when he finally heard the door swinging shut.

Just before it closed, he heard Lindsay say, "Ma! How could you—" The door slammed, and whatever else she said was cut off, which didn't matter, because he was riding away so fast he couldn't have heard anyway.

He rode into a lush canyon full of fat, lazy cattle, mostly lying down like the contented beasts they were. Belle had a knack for tending cattle; there was no denying that this all-girl crew was doing a good job.

Silas began hollering to wake the herd up, and as they rose he hazed the glossy herd of T Bar cattle toward the notch in the high side of the canyon where Belle had said they had to take the trail out. He admired the healthy animals as he stirred them from their sleep.

Belle had contrived a rickety fence and held them in a box canyon that seemed to have only one entrance. But on the far north side, a fissure cut into the looming cliffs surrounding the canyon.

Silas could see the rubble, some stones as big as a man, that had caved off that fissure over the years. He knew the trail up had been cleared by hand, and he knew, after listening to Belle and her girls at supper last night, that none of her husbands had done the backbreaking work.

Emma was the first of the girls to show up. She had the baby strapped on her back, and Silas had his hands full with not starting to scream. She set right to work without speaking to him. Lindsay was close behind. Then Belle came with Sarah.

No one had spoken; they'd just fallen to work, Sarah included, on a wiry little cow pony that she handled like an old puncher. Belle came and took the baby from Emma, but even carrying an infant on her back, she gave herself no quarter that Silas could see. Still, the sight of that baby and what lay ahead of Silas almost set him to screaming and running.

With his jaw tightly clenched, he kept working until he had all the steers on their feet. A good number of them had already finished filling their bellies with water from the pond that had been dammed up behind a creek. They were starting to crunch on the shoulder-high prairie grass. Silas had shooed them toward the back of the canyon.

Sarah rode straight for the high trail, pushing a few cattle along in front of her. That trail was so narrow and steep the cattle had to go up single file. The stretch wasn't long but high and treacherous as anything they'd face. Sarah led the string of pack animals and spare mounts tied together on a long rope. That along with a few cattle she pushed left a marked trail for the herd. They liked none of it, but with Silas and the womenfolk punching, once the lazy things began moving, they were contented enough to go where they were told.

The cattle weren't the only thing being hazed. Silas had been in a haze since Lindsay had broken up whatever madness was going on between him and his boss. He pushed himself harder, hoping to keep himself busy enough to forget those minutes alone with Belle.

With the girls working with him, they had the herd headed in the right direction in minutes. Sarah took the lead with the horses. The cattle trailed after her.

Belle took the drag, and taking his life in his hands, he rode up to her.

"Let me do this." Every drover knew drag was the worst. Dirty, hot, slow, exhausting. It was a man's job, and that was the long and short of it.

"I've got it." Belle didn't look him in the eye.

He wanted to argue. He was all set to argue. Then he saw the stubborn set of her jaw and gave up without a fight. "Fine, you take the first shift."

"The boss rides drag. I don't take shifts. Get back to work, unless you're already tired of the hard labor." She finally lifted that clenched jaw and looked him in the eye.

"Look, there were two people back there. It wasn't only me—"

"You asking for your time already, Mr. Harden? I'd hoped you'd stick with us longer than midmorning the first day, but I can't say I'm surprised."

Narrowing his eyes, he thought maybe there was going to be a fight after all. "I'm staying." He wheeled his horse and rode away before he had to share one more word with the stubborn woman.

Drag wasn't too hard now, but when they got off grassland and the herd kicked up dust, it would be choking, bitter work. Silas let her stay, although his instinct was to take the worst spot himself. He'd relieve her later when the conditions were worse, and maybe she'd accept it as his duty to take a turn. On a normal cattle drive, everyone rode drag for a spell, but Belle and her prickly pride might make it hard for her to give up the job.

Besides, to take over he'd have to stay there and argue, and right now that was beyond him because he didn't know what to say. He couldn't remember ever kissing anyone who made him lose his senses quite so thoroughly.

Silas shifted on the saddle and noticed a feisty longhorn with a rack almost six feet across trying to drop back behind the herd and return to the easy living of that valley. He spurred his horse toward the troublemaker, glad for a chance to keep busy dodging horns and hooves. The drive should have been demanding every ounce of his attention anyway. He got to work and firmly ignored the whole Tanner family.

He probably ought to be grateful he didn't have to take a turn carrying the baby.

❧

Wade pushed to make his trip to the line shack in record time.

He couldn't pull his mind away from Belle Tanner and that cattle drive.

Everyone who knew Belle knew she'd take her little girls along. Wade shuddered at the thought, remembering the times his father had forced him to do things beyond his ability and drive his horse even harder.

It was late in the day, and he wasn't going to make the line shack tonight. First, Seth had been slow getting the supplies packed. Linscott seemed to stay in town for the pure pleasure of goading him. Wade finally got out of Divide, and a horse came up lame five miles down the trail. He had to go back and get a new critter. The sun had been high in the sky before Wade was laying tracks at a good clip.

As he crested a rise, still with many miles of rugged riding ahead into the wooded area that abutted Sawyer and Linscott land, a silhouetted figure came riding out of the setting sun.

Wade didn't have to see a face to know who it was. Nobody sat a horse like his pa.

They rode toward each other on the narrow, heavily wooded mountain trail. Wade had the sense of a showdown. It wasn't on Main Street at high noon, but the tension drummed in Wade's ears at the sound of hoofbeats.

His father pulled to a stop, and Wade did the same. To pass each other on the trail would be a close thing. Wade had seen his father in Divide a time or two since he'd left the ranch, but they'd never been alone. All Wade could think was, if he rode on past, for a few paces, he'd be within striking distance.

Please, Lord, help me be a real man. Help me respond to my father with love and strength. I know only a pure miracle could make Pa love me, but can You somehow make him respect me just a bit? Or at least help me get out of here without a black eye?

Facing his father, he recognized the gunslinger eyes, even though to Wade's knowledge his father had never killed anyone.

Wade nodded a greeting.

"What are you doing out this way, boy?"

Wade thought of several evasive answers. Pa would hate that his son was working for Linscott, another big rancher. He'd hate that Wade was living with Red Dawson, working as a hired hand. He'd hate that Wade had plans to meet Belle Tanner along the trail and throw in as a drover.

The fact wasn't lost on Wade that, no matter what he said right now, his father's reaction would be to hate.

There was freedom in that, knowing that nothing would make his father happy. Happiness had to come from inside, from God. So since no answer was going to please the old goat, Wade told the simple truth. "I'm taking supplies to Linscott's line shack. After that, I'm going to hunt up Belle Tanner's cattle drive. She's culling her herd and driving a bunch to Helena."

Mort's face darkened. His fists clenched on the reins, and his horse shook its head nervously and snorted, rattling the metal in its bridle. "You'll be an errand boy for Linscott and work as a cowhand for a woman boss, but you won't come home to take your place?"

Wade nodded. "That's right, I won't." He had ten excuses, or rather reasons, the main one being he wasn't going to put himself under a tyrant's iron fist ever again. But his father had heard this before.

"I'm cutting you out of my will if you don't come home and mind your responsibilities."

Wade knew the ranch and cattle were worth a fortune, and he was working hard now, earning enough to get by with none to spare. But he couldn't bring himself to give one whit about that fortune his pa dangled in front of him. "It's your ranch to do with as you please." Wade swallowed and forced himself to speak the truth. "You've always said you were ashamed of me. Well, I've finally done the growing up I needed to do. I can't be a man with you ruling over me. And you don't know how to be anything but a tyrant. So forget about me. Forget I'm your son. Cut me out of your will. I won't take that land and those cattle and your money even if you do leave it to me."

Wade had a softening of his heart as he said those words. Not because he was changing his mind, but because somewhere deep inside, buried in fear and even shadows of hatred, he still loved his father, still wanted his father's respect. He cared enough to speak of what was important. "You know I've made my peace with God now. No more drinking, no more cards, no more looking for notches in my gun. I'm a man now that *I* can respect, even if you can't. You're getting older, Pa. You need to start coming in to Red's church. You're long past time preparing for the next life."

Mort spurred his horse and rammed into Wade, nearly unseating him. "I don't want to hear about what a weakling I've raised."

Wade's horse pranced sideways, nearly smashing Wade's leg between the saddle and a stout oak. He had his hands full settling the startled animal.

"I want you back on the ranch." Pa jabbed his finger like a knife aiming for Wade's heart. "I want a son I can be proud of, not ashamed of."

"I *am* a son you can be proud of." Wade fought with his horse until he brought it under control. "If you'd stop and listen to me, you'd know that, but you're too stiff-necked to admit it. If I come home, it'll be more of the same bullying, just like what you're doing now, just like what you've done all your life. I refuse to live like that. No *man* would put up with being knocked down and kicked, yelled at and insulted."

Wade's shoulders squared, and he said the awful ugly truth. "You *hate* me for leaving, but you hated me for staying, too. Admit it, Pa. You just plain hate me." A piece of Wade died with that simple statement.

Then Wade thought of a bigger truth. "And it's not just me. You hate everybody. What joy has all your money and land bought you? You're the most miserable man I've ever known."

"Why, you little whelp." Mort guided his horse closer, his fist clenched and raised.

"You're going to hit me, Pa?" Wade got ready to duck. He wasn't having a fistfight with his pa, but he wasn't going to stay still and let himself be beaten either. "Just for refusing to come home? Well, that'll sure convince me I should come, won't it?" Bitterly, Wade laughed at what a stubborn old coot his pa was. And what a fool Wade was for still loving him.

"I don't have to do much to earn a beating from you, do I? I think you oughta know I'm ashamed you're my *father*." Not the loving words Wade had hoped to share with his pa. Not the gentle call to turn to God. "*You're* a poor excuse for a man." The anger poured out of Wade with such venom it surprised even him. "Once I started growing up, once I got to know what being a man really meant, once I found God, I knew *you* were someone to be ashamed of."

Mort froze, his elbow bent, his fist drawn back.

God, I know it's wrong to tell him I'm ashamed of him. I know I'm supposed to reach him with love. Forgive me. Make me wise and kind. Let my boldness be from You and for You.

His father, eyes blazing, lowered his arm. "I'm doing it. I'm changing my will. You'll be penniless."

Wade had already said his piece. He had only one thing left to add. "I love you, Pa. If you ever get to the day when you think you can love me back, I'd be obliged to try and get along. But I'll *never* live on the ranch again, and I'll wish whoever gets it after you die good luck. It'll be broken up, I reckon. It'll make good homes for a whole lotta people."

Mort sneered and jerked the reins, guiding his horse past Wade without swinging a fist.

The Husband Tree

Wade looked after his father and felt the loss of a parent's love. Even worse, the loss of a man's soul. All of that burned like tears made of brimstone as Pa rode away without looking back.

Silas checked on the girls a thousand times throughout that first relentless day.

They were fine.

He couldn't have helped them if they weren't, because he didn't have a moment to spare beyond seeing that they were still in the saddle and working. By the time they got the last steer driven out of the canyon, the whole herd had spread itself across the rugged, rocky plain, hunting succulent young plants that were a sad comedown from their rich grasslands. Silas didn't think there was a single steer that hadn't tried ten times to go back into that canyon, and he swore the critters were working together at times, one to distract him while ten made a break down the back trail for home.

There was no thought of a noontime meal; the cattle would have been back at the ranch by the time the coffee boiled. Silas ate hardtack and jerked beef that he'd packed in his saddlebag, and he saw the girls and Belle doing the same.

He saw Belle swing the baby around to the front from time to time and drop back slightly at drag to attend to Elizabeth's diaper, or whatever else a baby needed.

Silas had kept a lot of space between him and the rest of the crew, but once in the late afternoon, when Silas was so tired he was beginning to forget why he had to avoid the other cowpunchers, a steer cut from the herd and ran within a few feet of Belle while she held the baby in front of her.

Belle, without hesitation, worked her cow pony to stop the steer.

Silas raced his horse over to her, and with a quick glance and nod at Belle so she knew he had things under control, he hazed it back in the right direction. It was only after he had settled in a couple of hundred yards away from Belle that he thought about the way she'd handled her cow pony with one hand on the reins while she clutched Elizabeth to her chest with the other arm. His stomach dropped all the way down to below his belly when he realized Belle had held the baby just so to feed her.

Silas's logical mind told him that, although he hadn't thought of it, of course a woman fed her baby that way, and really it was more convenient than driving a milk cow along on the trail and taking time to milk her several times a day. But no amount of logic could stop his stomach from tap dancing around inside him. It was just too crazy a situation to grab ahold of. No one would ever believe it.

And with that thought, Silas knew he was a dead man.

Even if they all survived the trip without a scratch—which seemed unlikely—he was going to have to spend the rest of his life on the dodge against the chance that the other hard, lonely men who worked cattle in the West would hear he'd signed on for a drive with a baby, a breast-feeding mother, and three little girls. He was never going to be able to live it down.

As soon as they had the cattle safe in Helena, he'd just go ahead and shoot himself.

Silas watched Belle ride right up despite that kiss this morning and look him square in the eye.

Working like a dog and being ten steps beyond exhausted must help a woman get over things.

"I'll take first watch," she said. "The cattle will hold here because of the water."

Exhaustion hadn't been enough for him. He couldn't look at her without remembering and wondering and wanting. "You go get some supper. I'm fine for a while."

"No." Belle shook her head. The boss, clear as could be. "I need time later seeing to Betsy. You go."

Silas glanced at the camp and saw Lindsay and Sarah. Emma was riding a slow, wide circle around the thirsty cattle lining the narrow mountain stream. Belle had left Elizabeth with Lindsay, who already had a fire going.

Silas thought about what "seeing to Betsy" meant. He wanted to be a hundred yards away from the camp when that event took place. Make that a hundred *miles*. "Fine, I'll eat now and take next watch."

Then as he rode into the roughly made camp, he quit thinking about babies and kissing and remembered this morning and the angry girls he'd faced. Wishing there was another choice but to eat with them, he admitted he was starving. Stiffening up his backbone, he rode in, cool as a Montana winter. Then he went to work making the fire smaller and hotter.

The cattle were drinking out of the creek, so he went upstream a piece and fetched back water. He stripped his saddle off his horse and rubbed him down with a handful of grass then slapped him on the flank to send him off with the horses. He proceeded to do the same with Lindsay's horse.

Lindsay came up beside him, carrying Betsy on her back. With hostility that didn't conceal the girl's fatigue, she said, "I care for my own horse."

Silas glanced over his shoulder at the thin, pretty woman-child with the glowing golden hair coated in dirt and sweat and the too-old eyes. He had a burst of insight as to what might convince the girl to let him help her. "I know you can do it, Linz, but I think Sarah's about all in. Let her see me do your horse, then she'll let me do hers. I'm almost finished here. By the time you get supper on, I can have the rest of the camp set."

Lindsay hesitated. It reminded Silas of the way she'd gone

397

about taking her rifle off of him this morning. At last she looked over her shoulder at Sarah, her face contorted from the effort, heaving a heavy pot full of cut-up dried beef and water onto the fire. Silas realized he had been right on target about how tired Sarah was.

Lindsay looked back at him with weary eyes rimmed in dark shadows. "Thanks." She turned back to the camp.

Before she stepped away, Silas had to ask, "Did just one of her husbands hurt her once, Linz? Or was it more husbands, and more than once?"

Lindsay didn't turn around, but she quit walking. The baby stared at him from Lindsay's back, and he braced himself to be called Papa again.

Finally, Lindsay looked him in the eye over her shoulder. "Gerald tried it from time to time, but he only laid his hands on her once I ever knew about. Ma. . .well, Ma was sober and tough as a boot and Gerald was just a no-account drunk. The reason they were having a fight to begin with was because she didn't like the way he was cussin' us girls. After he swung on her, Ma picked herself up offa the floor."

Silas wanted to go dig Gerald up and kill him all over again.

"She just laid him out flat with the kitchen skillet. The fat lip he gave her quit bleeding and healed in no time. After that, she just let him drink, and we girls learned to lay low when he came home. He weren't a smart man on his best day. Hiding from him was easy."

Silas's heart ached at her acceptance of that kind of life. "Lindsay, not all men are like the ones who married your ma."

Lindsay shrugged and a sad smile crossed her face. "I know that's true. So I guess it's something wrong with Ma that she picks men who are useless. I think it's easier to think bad of all men than to think bad of my ma."

Silas didn't know what to say to that.

The Husband Tree

"It ain't all her fault, though," Lindsay continued. "I was seven or so when Gerald come a-courtin'. I know what it was like. There were men all the time. Every day someone else would come, and the ones who'd been by before stopped back. Sometimes they'd fight over her, and I know Ma was scared. She had me and Emma and the ranch to run alone. There were always men coming by, and some of 'em not very nice. I think one day she just snapped. She grabbed at the closest man to get the others to stand off. And that ended up being Gerald.

"With Anthony it was the same only worse. Everyone just assumed she'd marry someone, and they acted like she was a nuisance, making them ride all the way from town over and over. She didn't want another man. She wasn't scared of being alone anymore, but she finally just caved under the pressure, and Anthony was there. 'A good-lookin' devil,' Ma said. Looked a lot like Betsy, and easy to boss around. And Ma just thought she had to. So many people said, 'A woman's got to be married.' Like it was in the United States Constitution or something, and Ma went along."

Silas did his best not to roll his eyes. What was the woman thinking to keep picking bums? Surely good men had come courting.

"This time, when Anthony died, she was gonna hold firm. She promised us." Lindsay scowled at Silas. Then after a long silence, she said, "And now you're here."

Silas didn't know what to say. He had no intention of marrying Belle, but he'd been kissing her this very morning in front of all her girls. He couldn't blame Lindsay for thinking what she did. And a part of him wanted to trot out his virtues as if he were speaking to Belle's father. He wanted to say, *My intentions are honorable. I respect your ma. I don't drink. I'm a hardworking man. I'd never hit a woman or cuss you girls.* But why would he say all that to Lindsay except if he was thinking to marry her ma? Which he wasn't.

Except every time he'd seen Belle today, he'd wanted to ride up next to her, drag her off her horse onto his, and taste her all over

399

again. He couldn't explain that to a young girl when he couldn't even understand it himself. "I'd never hurt your ma, Lindsay."

Lindsay looked away from him. "There's lots of kinds of hurt, Mr. Harden. It ain't all done with fists." She turned her back on him and walked over to the fire.

Silas watched Lindsay urge Sarah down onto the ground so she could lean back against a fallen log. She put Betsy in her little sister's arms and eased the two little girls around until they were practically lying down.

He heard Lindsay say softly, "I need help, Sarah. I need you to sit still and cuddle the baby up, or she'll cry for Ma, and Ma's riding herd. And if Ma comes by on a circuit, she'll have to stop. You know how tired Ma is. You've got to do this to help her."

"Getting grub's my job, Lindsay. And Betsy don't cry none. You take Betsy and sit."

"Please do it for me, sweetie. My back is tired from carrying her."

Sarah subsided with the baby in her arms.

By the time Lindsay began stirring the stew, Sarah was fast asleep, the baby awake in her arms, looking around and kicking. Lindsay came over and lifted the baby away, strapped Betsy on her own back, and went back to the campfire to work.

Silas hurried through the horse chores so he could help her, but by the time he was finished, Lindsay had a plate ready to hand him.

"Eat quick and go spell Emma." The look in her eye told him not to offer any help.

He sat and ate, and finally Lindsay ate beside him, feeding bits to the baby. Silas went to find a fresh horse and another tired little girl.

CHAPTER 7

W ade rode up to the line shack and was surprised at the number of horses: four in the corral behind the little log building, three tied out front.

His hand stayed cautiously near his six-gun and prayed there wasn't trouble. One of the things he'd never managed to hand over to God was the deep sense of his own cowardice.

When he'd been drinking and carousing, he'd wanted to put a notch in his gun to prove himself a man. He'd never been able to pull the trigger though. Now he was glad. Glad he didn't have a death on his conscience.

And now he knew better than to judge his courage against so false a standard as the ability to kill. But his heart still contained a seed of sickness deep inside, calling himself a coward.

What if he needed to defend himself? What if one day he took a wife and had a child and they were in danger and only Wade and his gun stood between his family and death? Seeing these strange horses reminded him that in this rugged land death was just one dumb move away. And a life-and-death decision, like drawing and shooting a gun, was the only thing keeping a man on this side of the pearly gates.

Wade no longer worried about those gates; he knew where he'd spend eternity. But it fretted him like an itch he couldn't scratch to know he was a coward.

He rode his horse to a grassy area back a ways from the shack. He swung down and ground-hitched his mount. That kept the pack animals, which were tied up in a line behind Wade's cow pony, together. The animals went to chomping grass, and Wade walked toward the house, wary. Before he got close, the door swung open and five men sauntered out. Wade knew two of them; Linscott's hands seemed at ease, not worrying about the three strangers.

"You brung vittles." An old drover, one of Linscott's longtime cowpokes, rubbed his hands together like he was eyeing a feast.

Wade smiled. "Yep, oughta be enough supplies in those packs to keep you fat all winter."

"I'm Buck Adams." One of the strangers stepped forward and extended a hand. His eyes were clear and his expression pleasant. Buck was the tallest of the bunch. He looked to be nearing forty. A man at the height of his strength and ability.

"Wade Sawyer." While they shook, Wade wondered if, like so many men, Buck had heard of Wade's pa. Often men would be extra friendly to him, thinking to befriend the son of a wealthy, powerful rancher they'd heard of by reputation. Others would immediately be hostile, and Wade figured they'd been stomped on by his pa or knew someone who had. There were plenty of 'em out there.

Buck nodded but didn't react, which meant Wade didn't have to live up or down to his father with these men.

"This here's Shorty."

Shorty was gray-haired and had a quick laugh and didn't speak a sentence when a syllable would do. But he had eyes that told a hard story of a life in an unsettled land and a toughness no one could earn except by facing a thousand dangers and surviving.

Wade saw a lifetime of wisdom in Shorty's watchful eyes.

"And this is my son, Roy." Buck clapped a skinny kid on the back who had a man's height but not a spare ounce of meat on his bones.

Roy seemed to practically buzz with nervous energy. He used that energy to throw himself into the unpacking with a good nature.

The men, all six of them, fell to unpacking and stowing away the food. The tiny shack was lined with cans and bags before long.

"These fellas are just passing through," Linscott's old drover said.

From the look of their well-kept horses and the way they threw in to help work, Wade was impressed with the trio.

When the work was done, Roy twitched and looked around, bouncing his knee as if sitting still made him crazy.

Wade had to control a grin as he remembered being so young he thought resting was wasting his life. He was only twenty years old, and he'd already grown out of that.

"Come on in and set a spell. Stay a few days." The old drover picked up the coffeepot.

Wade looked out at the cold fall wind. He'd much prefer to stay. It was going on evening and he'd have a cold night outside. But he could ride a few hours toward Belle's drive, and he felt rushed to get there. She'd already be two days down the trail by now.

He deliberately didn't refer to the drive being run by a woman. "I told the Tanner outfit I'd help run their herd up to Helena. They're trying to beat the winter. You know that mountain valley the Tanners live in. It's a late start, and they need to push hard and get back home before the gap snows shut for the winter. I'd better hit the trail."

Buck straightened from where he'd settled on the floor. "We could use a month's work." He tipped his head at his son and Shorty.

Roy got to his feet as if he was dying to hit the trail right now. No doubt he was.

"It'll be a hard drive because they're shorthanded. I told 'em I'd come along as quick as I could." Wade was uncomfortable hiring three men on for Belle, but by the time they rode the trail to catch her, Wade would have a good idea of what they were made of. And he'd be there to help her run 'em off if necessary. Belle'd most likely welcome them.

"I can't make promises for the Tanners. . . ."

Shorty frowned but remained silent.

"Let's do it, Pa." Roy began pulling on his buckskin coat. The boy looked like he planned to hunt Belle down himself if Wade didn't lead the way.

"It's a hard ride through mean, cold country. We'll be days catching up." Wade waited to see what the men were made of.

Buck grinned. "We'll partner with you for the ride over. If we don't get hired on, we'll just keep drifting."

Wade looked at the three men. Considering he was taking three strangers toward a pack of females. . .he knew Belle well enough to know those salty daughters of hers would be along. . . Was he turning wolves loose on a herd of lambs?

He thought of Belle, those direct eyes and scarred hands. Not all lambs, not even close.

"Saddle up. We can put a lot of miles behind us before we sleep."

The Tanner girls were tough, Silas'd give 'em that.

Lindsay was the leader. He saw countless instances of the oldest girl bossing her little sisters around, and sometimes even him and Belle. For the most part, they all did as Lindsay told them because the girl was organized and uncommon smart.

When it came right down to it, Belle was the boss. Silas had noticed that the girls listened to him when he thought things should be done a certain way. But for the regular stuff where no out-of-the-ordinary decisions needed to be made—which described almost everything on a cattle drive—Lindsay was the one in charge.

Emma was the natural horsewoman—so confident in the saddle that Silas rarely quit wondering at it. The first to mount up in the morning and the last to quit the saddle come suppertime, she seemed to have limitless energy. She was also a quiet kid, not prone to much give-and-take with the rest of them. Emma reminded Silas of a lot of cattlemen he'd known in his day who worked and ate and slept and worked some more without having much to say that wasn't about the job.

Sarah was the talker. She was the one often as not who made them laugh or made Silas squirm with her straight talk. The eight-year-old could ride like an Indian, and she did her share in the saddle, often with the baby on her back. But in many ways, Sarah was like the mother. She was quick with a word of sympathy for cuts and bruises. She changed the baby's diaper more than her share. She ran circles around most chuckwagon cooks he'd known.

Belle's contribution to the order was in the way she respected her daughters. She didn't shout words of caution or advice. She expected her girls to be capable, and they were. Silas could see the proud, confident way the girls rose to their mother's expectations. And while they were at it, Belle was outworking them all.

Silas pushed himself hard. At first he thought it was to take up the slack for a bunch of womenfolk. But he soon admitted it was to keep from being the slacker of the group.

The second day, at the fire at night, Silas noticed Emma had bound her three middle fingers together with a leather thong cut off her deerskin coat. "What happened to your hand?" He sat on a fallen log with a plate of beans and beef Sarah dished up.

Emma shrugged as she got her food. "Broke my finger." She

scooped up the first bite of beans without further comment.

None of the rest of them spared the broken bone a glance.

Silas felt a spark of annoyance at the unsympathetic group.

Sarah kept stirring the beans. Lindsay was feeding the baby. Belle was still riding herd.

"Let me have a look at it."

Emma arched a blond brow at him. "Why?"

With a snort of disgust, Silas set his plate aside. "Just do it."

Emma shrugged and untied her fingers. "I checked to see if the bone was lined up proper before I strapped it down."

Silas took her hand gently. The girl was right. The middle finger was swollen but straight. Emma was patient, but she acted as if he were just putting off her getting to eat.

The next morning, Lindsay's horse bucked her off twice, while Silas had his hands full saddling his own bronco. Each time she hit the ground with a dull *thud* and a kicked-up swirl of dust. Then she got to her feet, rounded the contrary beast up, and jumped on his back again before Silas could help.

After the horse kicked its morning kinks out and settled down, Silas noticed a vivid red streak of blood running down the side of her face. He rode over. "Are you okay?"

She was attending to her horse and looked up surprised. Following the direction he was looking, she swiped the back of her leather glove over the cut, smearing blood across the whole side of her face. She glanced down at the bright red on her hand without much interest. "Cuts on the head bleed something fierce," she said matter-of-factly. "I'll be fine." She rode off without further comment.

Silas had to grind his teeth to keep from telling her to get down and let him doctor the cut.

Belle almost got gored by a longhorn steer that same day. She caught the uncooperative critter diving into the brush and woods that came most of the way up to the trail. She harried him with her nimble cow pony, dodging his flashing heels and wicked horns.

Silas was busy with his own side of the herd, but when he saw Belle tangling with that desert brown monster with the white lightning blaze on his face—the brute had given him trouble since the first day—he spurred his horse to get between Belle and certain death.

He got there just in time to see the steer wheel and charge Belle and her horse. The horse jumped out of the way so quickly it almost unseated Belle, riding with Betsy, but she hung on. The razor-sharp horns slashed within inches of Belle's left leg.

Silas snagged his rope off his pommel. He whipped out a loop and sent it flying toward the steer's head. Silas's horse skidded hard to snap the steer off its feet. Silas hit the ground and had the animal's legs hog-tied within seconds.

Silas was riding his own buckskin, and that horse was as good a hand as any of the people he'd ever worked with. Every time the steer tried to regain its feet, the buckskin backed fast enough to keep him laid flat.

"I am sick of this old he-grizzly." Silas took a quick glance at Belle, who still sat on horseback, breathing hard, her expression calm, but Silas thought he saw a tinge of fear and, probably his imagination, just a hint of gratitude.

Silas tied the blazed-face steer's head down to his foreleg with rapid twists of his pigging string and then released the string hog-tying his legs together. Silas released his lasso from the broad horns and jumped free before the spooky mossy-horn knew what had hit him. Silas stepped back into his saddle.

Hazing the beast back toward the herd with his head strapped down to his foreleg, Silas waited until he was satisfied the steer wasn't going to attack; then he turned and rode back to Belle. "We'll leave him like that till he settles in for the night. It won't hurt him, and it might gentle him some."

Belle stared after the steer. "I've seen that done a time or two, but I've never done it."

"You can't throw a steer like that."

Belle looked at him and shrugged. "Sure I can. I run a branding iron every spring, but that's mostly calves. Still, you can't run a ranch without busting cattle."

Silas couldn't seem to get his mind to twist around the sight of Belle doing something like he'd just done. Cold fear shook him at the thought of Belle wading into that mass of churning hooves and stabbing horns. "I don't believe it. You're too small to throw a steer."

"Are you calling me a liar?" Belle dropped the question into the space between them like a drawn six-gun.

Silas'd seen that level, challenging look before out West. A man's word was everything out here, where thousands of acres or whole herds of cattle might change owners on a handshake. To call a man a liar was to cause his reputation damage that might destroy his ability to make a living and follow him to his grave. Silas knew better than to call anyone a liar. And he hadn't meant that now, but judging from the golden lightning flashing out of her eyes, Belle didn't see it that way.

His Western learning kicked in. "No, I apologize for that. I haven't done much this whole trip but underestimate you, and I'm sorry. I just thought as little as you are. . ."

"How much do you weigh?" Belle asked through clenched teeth.

Silas shrugged. "Don't rightly know. A hundred and eighty, or two hundred pounds, I guess."

"And how much does that steer you just threw weigh?"

"A ton. At least."

"I'd say more like twenty-three hundred pounds."

Silas was a good judge of cattle, and he'd say that steer weighed within twenty pounds of Belle's estimate. "What about it?"

"Throwing cattle isn't about *weight*. If it was, the few pounds difference in ours wouldn't matter."

"It's more than a few pounds, Belle. You're a skinny little thing, and I—"

"It's about leverage and quickness." Belle cut him off. "And, more than anything, a good cow pony. You know your horse did most of the work there, and mine is just as good. All of my horses are well trained to work cattle. Emma can bust a steer better than I can. Lindsay just as well. This is the second year Sarah has bulldogged calves at branding time."

Belle rode her horse straight up to Silas's side. "Don't *ever* tell me what I can and cannot do."

Belle's voice was so cold it sent shivers up Silas's spine. "I'll try and watch my mouth, boss. But I'm trying to learn about a new kind of woman here. The two I almost married weren't a thing like you."

Belle's chin lowered, and the anger left her eyes. Silas knew that was the very reason he'd spoken of such foolish things. Belle was a woman after all. She'd forget about whatever was going on inside her head if she could listen to his mistakes.

She didn't ask, not out loud, but her eyes burned with curiosity.

"The first one was the tough one. I really thought I was set in life. I owned a nice spread in New Mexico. I had a house built, a good herd started, and I had a woman set to marry me. I got caught in the middle of the Lincoln County War. Ever heard of it?"

"I've heard a little. Mainly I've heard of Billy the Kid."

"I met him. I wasn't even involved with that fight. It was between two other bunches of hotheads. But when the bullets started flying, they were none too particular who got caught in the crossfire. My girl thought she saw the future and hitched her wagon to another star. I still thought I'd win her back until the day I came on a group of men on my property. I rode up to order them off."

Silas could still feel the icy chill running down his spine. "One was Billy the Kid. The way he stared at me. . .killing-mean eyes." Silas paused to swallow. He was a coward, no denying it. "I knew it wasn't a fight I could win. The Kid didn't say much. He didn't have to. The law'd broken down, and Billy and his outfit were taking whatever they wanted. The only way to stop him was to kill him, and he was a mighty hard man to kill."

Silas rubbed the back of his neck and forced himself to admit the truth. "Too hard for me." Silas looked at the ground between their cow ponies, not wanting to see what was in Belle's eyes. "They let me ride off."

He'd seen contempt before because he'd ridden to Millicent's pa's ranch and told her he was leaving the country. He'd asked her to come with him.

Contempt. She'd figured out before Silas had that he was a coward.

Millicent had turned Silas down. She'd dealt her cards into another game and she'd made what she saw as the best choice. Later Silas heard the man she'd taken up with had died in the fighting. . .so she'd backed another loser. He was well rid of her, but it still hurt. It was all part of the shame. The failure.

Belle might as well know the truth. She'd know what Millicent had known. Silas wasn't a good bet for a woman. "I quit the country. Went home and paid off my hands and fired 'em. I rode out with what supplies I could pack on a string of horses and what cash I could scrape together. I didn't even try to move my herd. I knew I wouldn't live long enough to enjoy 'em."

"Smart man."

Silas looked up, figuring she was making a joke.

She looked dead serious. Then she smiled. "Did you think I'd say you should have shot it out with Billy the Kid—backed by a pack of his friends? My life has little time for fancy dreams, Silas.

You did the right thing, and you know it. You've been drifting ever since? What, two years? Three? That's when that trouble was brewing, right?"

When she put it like that, walking away from Billy the Kid sounded like an act of wisdom. The next wasn't so easy. Running from Lulamae. Belle might as well know.

"I started a new spread in the far corner of northwest New Mexico Territory and got run out of there by a woman. Not as exciting as Billy the Kid."

Belle laughed. "What happened?"

"I got caught kissing her in the stable."

Belle narrowed her eyes, and the smile faded from her pink lips.

Silas wasn't above feeling ashamed.

"And when you were caught you refused to do the right thing?"

Silas well remembered Belle had four daughters. This wasn't a woman who liked seeing young women treated wrong. "She set me up. She grabbed me and kissed me. Her pa was there, handy with his rifle, yelling about my mistreating his daughter before he could even see us, so I knew the two of 'em had it planned. He had friends right behind him, and they took his word against mine. He demanded a wedding. I guess Lulamae was ornery enough that they'd given up finding a husband for her by the regular means."

Belle shook her head. "Overpowered by a girl, huh? I feel *real* sorry for you."

"Well, don't. I've learned my lesson. If you haven't figured it out by now. . .well, I get that same message right back from you, so you understand. I'm *not* gettin' tangled up with a female. Never again. I'm drifting now because it suits me. But I like having land I can call my own. I like a nice spread, and I aim to build myself another one of these days."

"We understand each other then. That. . .that first morning. Just a stupid, weak moment on my part. I don't have many."

Silas remembered that moment. He'd spent far too much time remembering that moment. *Weak* and *stupid* about explained it. And he knew she didn't have many. That was the honest truth.

"Let's get back to work." Belle looked at the cattle spread out in front of them. Almost trail broke, except for a few like that blazed-face steer. "The sun's moving low in the sky, and there's good grazing up ahead with plenty of water. I might let the cattle stay put for a day or two so the girls can rest."

"After only three days on the trail?" It just came blabbing out of his mouth without a thought. He'd like to let the girls rest, too. He could see that Emma had already lost weight. Lindsay had a gaunt, hard look around her eyes, and Sarah had cried when they woke her up this morning, though only until she was fully awake. Then she cut the tears off instantly and went straight to work setting up breakfast for the camp.

Before Belle could cut him off at the knees, he said, "I think they need it. The first few days on the trail are rough. The cattle are almost trail broke, so it won't be as hard from here on. And we've got that mountain pass ahead of us. We'd better rest now, because there'll be no stopping then."

When he'd first opened his stupid mouth, Belle had looked like she was ready to bite his head off, and he wanted to save his neck. Then, when he'd changed his tune about stopping, she got that soft, sad look in her eyes. The one that'd made him kiss her that first morning, and he wanted none of that either.

Well, that wasn't strictly true. He wanted it something fierce. It just wasn't going to be one of those things he let himself have. He decided maybe he was safer when she was mad.

Before he could think of some way to get her hackles up, she said, "It's so hard on them. They're game as any man, and they'd never ask for me to give them any kind of break. But I'm worried about them. And I don't know if you've noticed, but. . ." Belle stopped talking, and with practiced ease she swung the baby around to her front and looked down at the wide-eyed little girl who rode so patiently day after day. "Betsy has changed."

Silas thought of diapers. "Changed how?"

Belle ran her hand over the baby's cheek. "She doesn't cry anymore."

Silas leaned over and looked at that pretty baby, smudged with dirt and so quiet. Her huge black eyes, lined with lashes too thick for any baby, blinked up at her mama. Silas followed the baby's gaze and saw the feminine side of Belle. He saw the mother in her and wished almost violently that she didn't have to work so hard and that men hadn't done her so wrong.

"Is she sick?" Silas nudged his horse forward to stand side by side with Belle, facing opposite directions, and looked at the little one.

Betsy turned her eyes on Silas, but she didn't smile. Just watched.

Belle shook her head. "All the girls did this. They started out being these pink, perfect little babies. Then I'd carry them along with me while I did chores, and they'd get quiet and watchful. I've seen Indian babies act like this." Belle raised the little one so she could look directly into her eyes.

Betsy reached for Belle's nose, and Belle kissed the little grabbing fingers.

"I don't suppose it's bad. It just doesn't seem quite normal to me. I don't know what else to do than. . .than br–bringing them along."

Silas heard that break in her voice again.

Belle pulled Betsy into her arms and hugged her tight, burying her face in the baby's neck and rocking her gently.

"Betsy has been cared for more gently than the others were in a lot of ways, because Sarah stays in the house with her most of

413

the time. But after only a few days, this drive has changed her."

Silas looked at Belle holding her baby, and something burned in him that almost overwhelmed every lick of sense he had. And right at that moment it was a good thing they had two horses, a thousand head of cattle, a baby, and three suspicious girls between them, or he'd have dragged Belle Tanner into the nearest town and married her without another thought just so she could spend a little time sitting in a rocking chair, tending her baby, while someone took care of her and her girls. And while he was at it, he'd make sure her roof didn't leak!

Belle hoisted Betsy into the crook of her arm and shook her head as if to clear it. "You have a knack for making me doubt myself, Silas. I don't thank you for that."

Silas sat silently, afraid of what might come out of his mouth if he spoke.

Belle turned her gaze on him. "I do thank you for saving me from that steer though." She tucked Betsy back into her sling, lifted the reins with one hand, and squeezed her knees on the sides of her horse. With a soft clucking sound she rode away.

Silas turned to look after her as she rode away, and he surely enjoyed the sight of her working that horse.

Belle Tanner might be the toughest cowpoke he'd ever partnered with. She might talk and work and even think like a man. But Belle Tanner was 100 percent, through and through, pure female, and no one who got within ten feet of her ever doubted it for a moment. He had no doubt that when Belle turned up widowed each time, men came a-runnin', and it wouldn't be any different when word got out about Anthony. The thought of droves of no-good saddle tramps trying to get their hands on Belle didn't sit well with him.

If she was going to get herself mixed up with a no-account saddle tramp, it might as well be him.

He tore his gaze away from her, and it was almost physically painful. Then he spurred his horse for the far side of the herd and worked himself hard the rest of the afternoon just to keep his mind off those hordes of worthless men. . .and the way Belle sat in a saddle.

CHAPTER 8

Resting a day was a poor excuse for an idea.

Rest was not agreeing with her. Instead, rest was giving her the energy to have her imagination running wild.

"I'll go ride a circuit." Silas bent over the basin of warm water and slid his scraped-clean plate in. Belle watched every move. What the man did to a pair of chaps was exactly why resting a day was a poor excuse for an idea.

Silas walked away from the camp, and she almost went after him. She felt her muscles bunch to rise and chase that man down right there on the mountainside.

It wasn't the first time. She'd started toward him every time she came within seeing distance of him. She stopped herself before she could do anything foolish like catch the man alone and kiss him again, but she was fighting some powerful instincts. In the end, only the girls being there kept her from chasing him.

The cattle spread out across a high valley in the foothills of the Bitterroot Mountain Range. They would swing the herd slightly east after this and scale a saddleback pass that took them on the east side of a rugged peak Belle had heard called Mount Jack. That was the worst stretch of the trail. The herd would move slow, wear itself out climbing, line up mostly single file, and trudge at the most two or three miles a day for the next week. Then they'd drop down off the peaks to an easier trek with plenty of water but poor eating for the most part, which would take weight off her steers and make them edgy and difficult to handle for the last two weeks of the drive. The herd needed a few days to fill their bellies and rest up for what was ahead, just as her daughters did.

Belle thought of Silas, out there riding in slow circles around her cattle. She thought of the way he'd worked without asking fool questions or making excuses. She knew in her heart he was a different kind of man than the ones she'd gotten tangled up with before. But she also knew that Gerald had shown no signs of being a drinker before they'd married. And William had seemed like an eager, hardworking young rancher when he thought he'd be getting Belle's pa's ranch. And Anthony. . .well, she'd been down on men by the time she agreed to marry him. She wanted to stop the crowd of suitors, and beyond that, she had expected very little. And that was exactly what she'd gotten.

So, even though she thought Silas was different, she didn't trust her judgment, having proved to be sorely lacking in that ability in the past. Belle spent a moment in silent prayer, asking God to forgive her for the life she'd provided for her girls and the sins she'd committed by marrying men who weren't decent Christians.

It was her. She knew it.

Maybe God could give her a miracle and make her smarter, but so far the miracle hadn't happened. She'd always thought she'd just had bad luck until near the end of her marriage to Anthony when the man had left her on the trail in the midst of giving birth to his child. Anthony was more than worthless; he was evil. And she'd picked him and exposed her children to him.

There was something broken inside her. It wasn't bad luck. She was a pure fool when it came to men; or worse yet, there was something in her that brought out the worst in a man. Maybe Gerald had taken to the bottle because of the way Belle acted. Maybe Anthony had been driven to other women when Belle pushed him aside and did everything herself.

Belle knew there was some truth in it. More likely though, she picked men who were weak because she was used to being in charge, and men who could be pushed around tended to be shiftless from the start. Then she'd run roughshod over them.

"Why be surprised that they ended up being exactly what I expected?" she asked no one, or maybe God. Her question drifted on the air unanswered, but Betsy, who sat on her lap, looked up and raised her pretty dark brows.

The older girls were all away from camp, so Belle smiled at her baby and kept talking. "Maybe if Gerald had needed to get the chores done, he'd have sobered up. You think so, baby? You think I should have let the cattle next thing to starve in the hopes Gerald would take charge?"

Belle's jaw clenched at the very idea. Betsy swatted her playfully on the chin, and she relaxed. "Maybe if, when William wanted to spend the few dollars my pa gave me on foolishness, I hadn't stepped in and told him how it was going to be, William would have had to grow up and do something to put food on the table."

"Mama." Betsy kicked her feet, and Belle felt almost as female holding this baby as she did looking after Silas.

"It makes sense, doesn't it?"

Betsy smiled.

The more Belle thought on it, the more she believed it. "I didn't want a man to take charge, so I got exactly what I deserved, didn't I? I've got no business complaining when my husbands turn out to be exactly like I knew they were. But that doesn't mean I want a man bossing me around, now does it?"

Belle shook her head and tickled Betsy's nose. Maybe resting a day wasn't so bad if she could spend a few minutes playing with her baby. "What it boils down to, little girl, is that I am more determined than ever to stay unmarried."

Betsy smiled and clapped her hands as if applauding Belle's good sense. Or maybe the child was playing, but Belle didn't see it that way.

Looking around to make sure no one was near enough to overhear her little conversation with the only person she dared tell, Belle leaned close and whispered, "But the way that man kissed me, Betsy darlin'"—Belle drew in a deep breath as she recalled it oh, so clearly—"well, it does make me forget some of the hard lessons I've learned about my complete lack of skill at picking husbands. It makes me want to just hunt that man right down on the range and kiss him all over again."

Saying those scandalous words—at least scandalous considering she was determined never to remarry—made Belle look up and search the mountain valley for *that man*. She saw him just as he pulled out his lariat, dabbed a loop on a yearling calf, and started dragging it out of the herd. The herd scattered a bit, but they were too tired and too busy eating to worry about one of their own being hauled away.

He backed the steer a good distance away from the others then busted it and hog-tied it.

"What's the man up to now?" Belle gave Betsy a final bounce then settled her into the carrier.

Before Belle got her horse saddled, Silas got the young longhorn in the clear, busted it, hog-tied it, and knelt on the ground by its head. Emma rode up beside him and got off, kneeling on the steer's back. Belle rode over just as they were releasing the steer. It was skinnier than most. She'd noticed it as a straggler almost from the first.

It jogged away from her when she got close. Then, after a running start, it kicked up his heels the way young cattle do in the spring.

"What was that about?" Belle asked as she pulled her horse to a halt and crossed her arms over the saddle horn.

Silas pulled himself onto his horse's back with a single smooth motion, not using the stirrup. Belle noticed that Emma mounted her horse like Silas did. Her daughter, the best horsewoman among them, was imitating Silas.

"I've been thinking that critter was doing poorly. I wanted to see him up close. I found a goiter growing in his throat and cut it out." Silas turned to Emma. "Thanks for the hand."

Emma nodded wordlessly and turned her mount toward the head of the herd.

Belle said, "Take a break, Emma. It's almost time for my watch and the noon meal is on."

"I want to check the horses first." Emma nodded at the horses. "Some of the green brokes've been harassing the cattle toward the front of the herd. I might have to hobble 'em."

"I've noticed them doing it," Silas said. "I'll go check. We'll need you rested later when your ma has to see to the baby."

Emma hesitated and studied them both for a long minute. Finally, she shrugged and headed toward camp.

When Emma was out of hearing range, Silas laughed softly. "I don't think your daughter trusts us to stand watch together."

Belle smiled. "I can't say I blame her."

"Not with your history of killin' off husbands, then turnin' around and marryin' the first man what comes along."

Belle turned angry eyes on Silas.

"Gotcha." He grinned at her.

Anger twisted into laughter, leaving Belle sputtering as he turned his horse away from her and started riding toward the front of the herd to check the riding stock.

Belle clenched her hands so tightly on the reins, her horse skittered sideways a piece. It was only through pure force of will that Belle kept herself from riding after the confounded man and kissing the daylights out of him.

She was extra careful not to share the night watch with Silas, just because she wanted so much to ride alongside him in the dark. From the first, either she or Silas was riding herd at night, never together at the campfire, never alone in the night. It was exhausting for both of them.

The daylong break was good for the girls and good for the cattle.

But it was the longest day of Belle's life.

Glowing Sun hit the ground hard. The world twisted around, made no sense. Gasping in pain at the collision, she noticed the world was black. She blinked her eyes but couldn't see. Even in the dark of night her eyes should have picked up something.

A hard jerk and something was pulled off her head.

Suddenly she realized she was on her back on the ground. Light blinded her and she blinked and squinted at the pain. Sunlight filtered through towering trees.

Then two dark heads blocked the light. Evil men.

She attacked to find her hands tied.

She screamed to find her mouth gagged.

She jumped to find her feet bound.

So she lay still, inhaling terror.

The one man she'd seen before, holding her feet. His angry eyes had followed her into unconsciousness.

The other, the one who'd cut off her breath, was shorter but otherwise like the angry man, full beard, dark hair, fur coat and hat. The shorter one reached for her with scarred, ugly hands. He lifted her up, steadying her. His grip didn't hurt. His eyes didn't glow with cruelty. He seemed a bit kinder than the other man. Of course, she'd kicked the bigger man. But in fairness, the shorter man's face bore the marks of her fingernails, so if their cruelty was over her behavior, this one had as much cause as the other.

"We're just takin' you back to yer people, miss," the shorter man said. "You've been caught by the Flathead Indians, and we're doing our duty to return you to whites."

Whites. Glowing Sun understood *whites* and *Flathead.* She'd heard that word used for her village.

She shook her head frantically, hoping they'd understand she couldn't speak this language. Maybe if they went slow. Maybe some of her white parents' tongue would return to her. So many years since she'd heard it. Even the missionary to her village spoke the tribal language. The missionary was one of their own people who had learned about God from another village.

The smaller, kinder man said, "We've put a far distance between us and your village. But we're not lettin' you loose, and we're not takin' off the gag. You don't know what's best for you, missy. So we'll keep you bound until we can turn you over to your own kind. It'll only be another day, so missing a meal won't hurt you none."

Glowing Sun had no idea what it meant. She heard "far." She heard "village."

The two men set her back on the ground so her back could lean against a tree.

When she leaned on that tree, something poked into her back, and suddenly she knew what she needed to do.

She waited until they were settled down to eat a cold supper in the fading light. The hard jerked beef made her stomach growl. Studying the area, she noted the moss on the north side of the tree, the slant of the sun, the slope of the mountain. She could see a distant peak and recognized it. She had no idea how far she'd come, but she knew where she needed to go. All she needed was a running start.

God, do not take another family from me. Help me find freedom. Help me find my way home once that freedom is mine.

She watched the men and prayed fervently to bear what pain

might be coming her way with her reckless plan.

She waited until the men were done eating and busy setting up their night camp. Then, when their attention was diverted, she grabbed the kerchief knotted so tightly over her mouth and jerked it down to her chin and screamed.

The two men whirled and dashed at her. The short one clamped his hand on her mouth as he had earlier, knocking her head back against the tree.

The other muttered. Unintelligible words growled back and forth between the two of them. Then the tall man untied her hands and twisted her arms painfully behind her back.

The man holding her mouth jerked the gag back into place. "I'd hoped we could leave you with your arms tied in front. You'd sleep better." He shook his head.

The other man took pleasure in jerking the binding tight and pulled so hard on her arms her shoulders ached.

"Hey be careful of her," the shorter man said. "We have to keep her tied, but you don't have to hurt her. She don't know no better than to run back to her tribe."

Glowing Sun cried out in pain. She could have controlled it and normally would have. It wasn't her nature to fuss over a bit of pain. But she wanted them to think she was weak and defeated. She wanted them to be confident. She wanted them to sleep deeply.

The tall man dropped her roughly so her head struck the tree behind her. Stars burst from behind her eyes, and she did a good job of acting hurt. As embarrassing as it was, she faked that she was crying, sobbing. Though it wasn't hard to fake it, because she was afraid and the ropes cut into her wrists and her stomach growled and her village was far over the next mountain.

The tall man laughed in triumph as he went back to his side of the camp, leaving space around her as if *she* were the one who smelled bad.

The other man crouched down, and she withdrew to the

extent she was able. Eyes wide, doing her best to look terrified and defeated, she whimpered a bit.

"We only mean to help you, miss. Don't worry. We'll get you back to your people." The man seemed kind, though he smelled bad enough.

She nodded just to let the man think he'd won. None of her triumph showed in her eyes. But now her hands were tied behind her back just as she'd hoped. She'd wait. Bide her time. As soon as the men had settled for the night, Glowing Sun would move her bound fingers to the hidden seam in her skirt, in the middle of her back.

And get her hands on her razor-sharp blade.

CHAPTER 9

Wade set a fast pace, and the men who came with him kept up. They rode well beyond the setting sun.

"We've got to lay up, I know." Wade turned to the men who had stayed with him so faithfully. "Let's find a spot to camp."

"We've ridden hard before," Buck said genially.

Wade found himself liking all three of these men. They shaped up to be decent, hardworking, and tough. He hoped as much could be said about him.

Shorty had a campfire going and coffee on by the time the horses were stripped of their leather and pegged out to graze.

Settling in with a cup of what was, at this point, barely warm brownish water, Wade marveled at the comfort of it in his hands. "Thanks, Shorty. I figured to make a cold camp. This is mighty nice."

Shorty grunted.

Roy got out a brush and worked on all four horses as if he couldn't quite sit still.

"Your son's a workin' man, Buck. A fine youngster." Wade wasn't that much older than Roy, but the four years seemed like twenty.

Buck smiled, as if he knew just how old Wade was. "You're in a hurry to get to this drive. Any reason?"

"I know—" Wade stumbled. He'd almost said Belle's name. He concealed a smile. No reason not to tell the truth. The men could stick or not. Probably would. But he decided to leave them to the surprise. "I'm not sure what's riding me, really." Wade studied Buck a moment. "There is no reason to feel this strange burden for them, but I feel like God Himself is pushing me to hurry." Wade wondered what this three would make of that.

Buck nodded. Shorty kept pouring coffee. Both of them acted as if it were the most natural thing in the world.

"I know they're shorthanded. I'm sure they're handling things. It's a crew that takes care of itself." Wade had seen the Tanner girls once because he'd been roaming the high country and ridden into their range. Belle kept them so secluded there were some who weren't quite sure even how many children she had. All of those girls were tough. Tougher than him by a long shot.

It occurred to Wade that this might be more of his need to rescue, as he'd felt for Cassie Dawson. The fever to protect her had calmed once he'd seen how happy Cassie was with Red. He'd never have gotten over her without God filling the awful, empty places in his life.

Now this urgency to get to Belle reminded him a little of that desperate need to rescue Cassie. The main difference being, if he implied to Belle she needed to be rescued, she'd rip his arm off and beat him to death with it. "But I'm also sure they're all pushing themselves to the limit. They need help, and I said I'd give it. I guess I'm just bent on keeping that promise. And wanting to get there before they wear themselves down to the bone."

"Good enough for me." Buck finished his coffee and a piece of jerked beef he was gnawing. He turned to Roy. "Son, hit the blankets. We'll be up riding hard before daybreak."

Roy left his fussing with the horses and came to where he'd

laid out his bedroll, collapsed on it, and was out almost instantly.

Wade finished his coffee and took Buck's advice, too.

The next morning they kept up the ground-eating lope, slowing only when the tortuous trail twisted across talus slides or was so steep Wade and the others dismounted to walk.

They'd put hours behind them before the sun rose, and as they reached the bottom of a treacherous slope, Wade saw the flickering light of sun on water and knew it was time to give the horses a rest—a brief rest. He raised his hand, signaling halt, just as a deer darted between two bushes straight ahead. He barely saw its form, but it was fawn-colored and quick. He reached for his rifle, thinking to bring grub to Belle along with helping hands.

He heard a shell snapped into a rifle behind him and knew Shorty was taking aim.

Something else moved, something bigger. Something human. "Hold up." Wade spurred his horse forward just as what he thought was a deer raced out of the underbrush.

A woman, looking back, ran straight into the side of his horse. She cried out and fell backward. White blond hair flying. Ropes dangling from her wrists.

Not far behind, two men crashed toward Wade through the trees and brush.

Wade swung himself to the ground to stand between the woman and two men on her trail. They emerged just as Wade leveled his rifle on them. The one in front skidded to a halt. The one behind nearly knocked his partner down.

Wade had two seconds to wonder if he'd have the guts to pull his trigger. Rifles cocked. Buck, Shorty, and Roy were ready, backing him.

"She's ours," the taller pursuer shouted while he gasped for breath, looking from gun to gun, all beaded on him or his saddle partner.

A barrage of words escaped from the woman who was scrambling to her feet.

Wade saw her take one running step away from him. Snaking out a hand, he caught hold of her wrist.

The girl fought his grip.

He never took his eyes off the men who were after her.

Buck came up beside him. "I've got 'em covered, Wade. See to the girl."

Wade turned to study his prisoner. She clawed at his gloved hand. A white girl—woman rather—but young. Dressed in Indian clothing. "I mean you no harm."

She moaned and crouched low, like a cornered animal. Words erupted from her lips Wade recognized as Flathead, but he didn't know enough of the language to respond.

"*Hau.*" Shorty spoke to the woman, kneeling beside her.

She didn't respond.

Wade shook his head. "That's Sioux. She won't know it."

"She might." Shorty came up beside Wade and looked at the gasping, trembling woman.

Wade could well imagine what she thought. Two men were after her, but she'd been running free. Now there were six, and she was caught. "Can you tell her we won't hurt her?"

Shorty shook his head. "I know a few words of Sioux and a little Cheyenne, but I've only been in Montana a coupl-a years. I can tell she's Flathead because of her clothes, but I don't know any of the lingo. But maybe. . . *Okiye niye?*"

"What's that?" Wade wanted the old man to get on with helping her.

"It's Sioux. Their territories overlapped years back. She might know a few words. I think it means 'help you.' Or 'help me' maybe."

"Great, she'll think we want *her* to help *us.*"

The woman made a sudden move, darting to her feet. Wade grabbed her. She lashed out with her feet and raked fingernails across his face.

Wade held up both hands to protect his face and crowded her

toward an outcropping of rock, cornering her. "We can't just leave you here. Let us help you. We won't hurt you."

A hard fist slammed into Wade's jaw. Grabbing at her flying hands, dodging her thrashing feet, doing his best not to hurt her, he wrestled with her until she jumped back, pressing against the rock.

"She's wild but she's white," one of her pursuers said. "We found her with the Indians, and we were taking her home. We weren't hurtin' her."

Wade registered the men's statement. It might be true, but it didn't mesh with the bleeding scrapes oozing from behind the leather strips dangling from each arm. They'd tied her up for her own good? There was a laugh. "Do you know where her home is?" Wade asked. "Does she have a white family waiting for her?"

"We don't know. But it stands to reason she belongs with her own kind, not a bunch of heathen savages."

Wade's jaw tightened. He'd known a few of the natives. The ones he'd met were often Christians and often gentle people. Oh, he knew there had been massacres. But there were bad seeds among all people.

The woman collapsed on the ground, wailing. Her eyes, so blue, tears drenching her face, though she seemed more fierce than sad. She was too angry, too combative. Her tears were ones of rage.

"Home? Home to your village?" Wade stood over her, feeling like a brute for making her stay when she so obviously wanted to run. He touched his cheek and pulled his fingers away bloody.

Her cry faded and her eyes locked on Wade. She pulled in a deep breath. "V–v–village? Salish village?"

Wade felt his eyes narrow. "You speak English?"

Her voice riveted everyone's attention. Only when Wade heard running footsteps did he realize they'd allowed her assailants to escape.

Roy whirled around.

429

"Let them go." Wade decided. "What are we gonna do with 'em?"

Her gaze slid past Wade to the men. If it was true—that they were attempting some kind of rescue—then they hadn't broken any laws. Even though any fool could see the woman wanted her village, her Indian village, plenty of whites would think she should be taken back to her own kind. Studying her, Wade could see that her clothes weren't torn and her bruises weren't serious or plentiful.

"I've heard the Flatheads called Salish." Buck stepped to his horse and slid his rifle into the saddle boot. "We'd been roaming these hills, and one day hunting I noticed an Indian village. . .must be two days' ride from here. They're camped along a river. Maybe if we pushed hard we could get her home before nightfall. You reckon they took her from there?"

Roy stepped closer. "B–but she's white. Doesn't she need to be with white people?"

Wade watched the woman. Her eyes shifted. She looked constantly for escape. If they let her go, could she get back to her village on foot? If her home was, as Buck thought, a long day's ride on a horse, she'd be three or four days walking it, alone in the wilderness. He dropped to both knees beside her. "Wade." He touched his chest. He pointed at Shorty, Buck, and Roy in turn, saying their names. "Salish? Flathead?" He waited.

"Salish village. Far." She stared at him, some of the terror fading from her eyes.

"Speak English?"

She shrugged then pointed at him. "Wade."

"We" —Wade circled his hands to try to include himself and the other men—"take you"—he pointed at the woman—"Salish village."

"You can't do that," Roy shouted, clenching his fists. "You can't turn her back over to them."

The Husband Tree

Wade looked from one man to another, his face stinging in the brisk morning breeze. "What do you think?"

Shorty shrugged. "She looks like she's been hurt more at the hands of white men than the Flatheads."

"The clothes, her inability to speak English, she's obviously lived with them for a long time. Some tribes take in children of whites and raise them. She'd think of them as her family." Wade watched, sure she planned to run off at the first chance. But that wasn't the only reason he watched. Despite her wild hair and bruised and dirty face, she was beautiful. Those eyes, as blue as the wide Montana sky, brimmed with tears and terror.

The vulnerability touched something deep inside him. The same kind of thing that had driven him to want to rescue Cassie. But Cassie hadn't needed rescuing. Belle would pound on him if he suggested she needed rescuing. It was Wade's own mixed-up desire to save someone. . .anyone. . .the way he wished someone would have saved him from his father. And now this woman most likely didn't need rescuing either. But it went against the grain to return a white woman to an Indian village.

She blinked and two tears escaped her shining eyes and slid down her grimy face. "Wade." She touched her own chest. "Glowing Sun."

"She spoke English." Wade looked up at Shorty. "She knows her name in English."

The man was quiet, but he was savvy. "Someone must have taught it to her. Or she maybe spoke English when she was young and a bit of it is coming back."

"That's your name?" Wade asked. "Glowing Sun?"

"Glowing Sun. Village far."

Wade's heart ached to see her cry. But the pain was almost pleasure, because she was so lovely and fragile yet ready to fight a crowd of men if it meant freedom.

"I think we need to calm her down before we take her back."

Buck came around the horse and patted his son's shoulder. "Make sure she knows she has a choice."

"She can't want to live with Indians, Pa." Roy looked frantic, as if considering saving the woman from his own father.

Wade smiled, recognizing the reflex. "We could take her with us to the Tanner drive. If we ride hard, we could get *there* tonight. Treat her gently and she might decide she doesn't want to go back with the tribe."

"Cold weather's comin' on." Shorty scratched his chin. "Her people might be ready to move to winter hunting grounds, and we'd have a tough time finding them in the middle of a Montana winter. If we don't take her back now, she might never be reunited with them."

Wade couldn't take his eyes from Glowing Sun—such a perfect name for a girl with billowed white gold hair. Her native family could hardly have named her anything else. Moonlight maybe, or Snowbird. She was filthy, her face bruised and bleeding. Even with all that, she was the most beautiful woman Wade had ever seen. Wade watched her eyes, hoping he could head off an escape as he slowly gripped her arm and pulled her to her feet.

She flinched and gasped in pain. He looked down at her battered, bleeding wrists and immediately released her, cornering her between himself and the rock. She crouched again.

Wade held a hand out in front of him, shaking his head. "Don't run, please."

She narrowed her eyes as if searching deep in her memory. "Please?"

Wade's heart lifted. She did know English, at least a little. It might come back if she'd just talk with them for a time. He nodded. "Please."

"Thank you," she said, as if the words just came. She'd been trained in good manners at one time.

Wade smiled. She frowned and jerked her head at him as if she disapproved. Of what? *His* manners maybe?

If someone said thank you, he should respond. . . . "You're welcome?"

She smiled.

Wade motioned to his horse. "Ride?"

She looked from him to the horse.

"Please?"

She jerked her chin as if in agreement. "Village." She swung up on the horse so lightly, it was almost like a moment of flight.

"Well, where are we going?" Wade held the reins tight. He wasn't fooling himself that she was content to be with them.

The two older men sighed and hesitated.

"The Tanner drive." Roy was most adamant. Too bad he knew less about this than the rest of them.

"She's gonna be mad. She thinks we're takin' her to. . .you know." Shorty looked worried and was smart enough not to say the word *village*.

"Yeah, and when she gets mad, it's something to see." Wade pulled a kerchief out of his hip pocket and dabbed at the raw wound on his face.

"Will she catch on right away?" Buck asked.

"Depends on how far she is from home. She might be lost with no idea what direction to head. But Indians are mighty savvy about the land. She could have her eye on a mountain peak or some other landmark, know she needs to head west and we're going east." Wade lifted both hands in surrender. If his kerchief had been white instead of blue, he'd have been waving the white flag of surrender. "Let's head for the Tanners for now. We can change our minds later. We've got time before winter shuts down on us."

"Sounds good." Shorty mounted up.

Buck and Roy followed suit.

"Can we make room on the packhorse for another man?" Wade looked at the woman occupying his saddle. He touched his bloody face again.

"Not without dropping most of the supplies." Shorty started down the trail.

"If she don't wanna ride double with you, you'll find out soon enough." Buck laughed and kicked his horse.

Wade produced his knife and made sure Glowing Sun saw it. Then very carefully he reached for her wrist and cut the rope dangling there.

She nodded. "Thank you."

He tore a strip off his shirt and bound her wounds. "You're welcome." He didn't know the words to warn her they were sharing a horse. Wade reached for the saddle horn and braced himself to get clawed again.

CHAPTER 10

Belle had the herd moving at first light.

By midday they were climbing steadily and the mountain pass was getting narrow. Silas rode ahead to scout the trail, and because the pass was treacherous, Belle wouldn't let anyone carry Betsy but her.

The cattle were unhappy about the steep, rugged climb, so Belle rode drag to badger the stragglers. She made Sarah give over the lead to Emma because there were talus slides in spots that might give way under a horse's hooves, and Emma would be better able to stick her saddle. The cattle walked with ever fewer abreast, and the slow-moving herd strung out over several miles.

The sun rose high in the sky, and the mountain trail was ground into a cloud of dust as the cattle churned up the earth. Belle pulled her kerchief over her mouth and nose and fixed one for Betsy, who spent most of her days lulled to sleep from the monotony of the steady rocking of the horse. A fine white dust hung in the air and coated all of them. The cattle all began to look the same under the sifting powder. Belle's eyes burned and watered, and she wiped the grit from her face wearily until she gave up and let it blanket her.

She bullied and whipped the stragglers as they balked. They were especially cantankerous at places they needed to scramble over rock slides. She saw in the cattle a desire to quit, and she knew how they felt. Still, she pressed them onward, each step an effort. Each inch gained a triumph.

Belle knew that when they got through the pass ahead that dipped low on the mountain like a saddleback, the trail dropped steeply. She watched her first cattle, over two miles further on, reach the summit ahead, skyline themselves, then drop over the lip of the mountaintop. Hours later, when Belle finally reached the top, she looked at the rugged trail going down and back up the mountain. Her stomach swooped at the sight of it. It was late afternoon already and they had to get over it before they could stop for the night.

She took a moment to ask God for strength and to thank Him that she hadn't realized what this trail looked like until now.

Far down the path, Belle saw her cattle plod through the choking dust. Here at the top, with the wind blowing unchecked, the dust had been dispersed. But she looked down that tortuous trail full of switchbacks and drop-offs into what looked like a bowl full of dust. In some places, it hung so thick Belle couldn't see the cattle. These animals were the work of nearly sixteen years of her life. Now here it was before her. Her life's work, moving slowly along, no more than three or four abreast, trailing an older steer as cattle are prone to do. She saw Emma in the lead and she saw Silas appear from over the pass far ahead, where he'd been scouting the trail.

The whole day's journey had been almost no forward progress because of the twisting trail that went around every craggy outcropping. Belle knew the next week would be filled with slow days that accomplished little.

Silas came up to Emma then turned to walk alongside her. They were so far from Belle they looked like miniatures. They walked into a thick cloud of dust and were invisible for a time.

Then there must have been a place the wind would whip in because they were visible again. Emma was turned toward Silas. Belle wondered what they were talking about. Knowing Emma, Belle assumed it was work.

After a time, Silas started to drop back along the herd. Emma picked up her pace a bit, and Silas urged the cattle to do likewise, cracking a bullwhip in the air over their heads and hollering, driving them until the whole line was nearly trotting. He let them pass him until Sarah drew even with him. She walked along with the cattle, following at their new pace. Sarah started moving faster, pushing the herd, passing a few of them as she gained the higher elevations.

Next, Silas dropped back again until Lindsay, who was nearly three quarters of the way to the back, eating as much dust as Belle, rode up beside him. Belle saw Lindsay pick up a little speed and trot her horse toward the front of the line. Lindsay was halfway up the mountain when Emma reached the top. After hanging, skylined against the lowering sun for a moment, Emma dropped out of sight. Then the cattle steadily passing over, out of sight as Belle still trudged downward with a long way yet to go, soon made the top of the hills. Then later Lindsay disappeared.

Belle would be hours making her way to that peak where she could watch her girls again. She knew that Silas had told them everything they needed to know.

The day droned on, and Silas dropped closer to her, urging the herd on as he went. Belle picked up his need to hurry and pushed her stragglers a little harder.

When Silas finally came even with her, he said, behind his own kerchief, "The girls should be making camp by now. There's a passing fair spot over the hill. Not great, but a little grazing and enough water. The cattle will be tired. I think they'll be content to stand pat there for the night. But it will be full dark by the time we've pushed the rest of them over that hump."

437

Belle nodded. The day was getting long for her. There had been no place along the trail to so much as step off the horse and stretch her legs. She'd eaten beef jerky in the saddle, gulped tepid canteen water, and nursed her baby with the kerchief tied over Betsy's face.

"Have you fed her lately?"

Belle looked at him. His eyes were red-rimmed and bloodshot. He was coated with the same white powdered dirt she was. She couldn't make sense of his question, and she knew she must look stupid. "Fed who?"

"Betsy. Is it close to feeding time? You could drop back a piece and sit down and do it. Get out of the dirt. I can take the herd for a while. You look all in, Belle. Riding drag in this dirt is about all a man's. . .I mean. . .about all a *person's* life is worth."

Belle had a moment of wondering how they would have gotten through this drive without him. She had no doubt they'd have done it, but she knew they'd have all been breaking their backs and their hearts to survive it. "It's okay. She's just done eating. I'll finish the drag."

She thought she saw concern and maybe anger flash across Silas's face, but both impressions were gone so swiftly she might have imagined it. She was too tired to wonder anyway.

Without saying a word, he reached behind her back, and with swift movements, he unhitched the sling and took it, baby and all, away from her. He hung the carrier over his own back, double-checking with his hands to make sure Betsy was secure, then trotted his horse forward, calling over his shoulder, "I'll carry her for a while."

Before her slow reactions could overcome her surprise, Silas was out of earshot. Or at least he didn't respond when she yelled, "Give her back."

He rode slightly faster than the cattle, and he gained the high pass and vanished. The summit never seemed to draw any nearer to Belle. He came back after a time, just as Belle was near to reaching the bottom of the trail with the long climb upward left. He didn't have Betsy.

It had been a good idea to get the baby back to camp and let the girls care for her. She'd never have asked him to do it, but she was glad he had and glad for the weight of the growing baby to be off her shoulders for these last grim hours of the day.

He rode in a steady canter down the hill on a fresh horse. The cattle were so deadened that they didn't react to the fast-moving roan. When he reached her side, he said, "Go on up. The girls need some help."

"The girls don't need my help with anything." He was just trying to take over the dusty job of bringing up the rear.

"They didn't tell me what it was. I got the impression it was. . .a. . ."

Belle saw him start to blush. She flickered her eyes open and shut to clear her vision. Silas? Blushing? The man was darkly tanned and coated with dirt, and she couldn't be sure, but she could swear his cheeks were slightly reddened with embarrassment.

"I think it's a. . .female thing. You'd better go."

Belle knew of all the lies he might tell to get her to give up the job, that would never occur to him. They really must need her. "Okay, I'd better go see what's wrong."

Silas nodded, and his eyes didn't quite make contact with hers. The embarrassment again.

Belle rode on up the winding trail, covering it in minutes instead of the hour or two Silas had left to face. The sun was just dropping over the high mountain slope on her left when she crested the hill. She came down into a heavily wooded, steeply canted area with a rippling creek at the bottom.

She saw yet another hard climb, this one narrower than today's, ahead of them. They'd face it together tomorrow.

Lindsay was giving Elizabeth a bath in the creek upstream of the milling cattle. Sarah had a campfire going and stew made from their endless supply of dried beef on to boil.

Emma was on horseback.

The girls all looked just fine.

What did that low-down man mean by "a female thing"?

Well, that was about as low as he'd ever stooped.

Silas pulled his kerchief up to protect his mouth as he thought of Belle's expression. He would have laughed if it wouldn't have made him eat a mouthful of dirt—even with his mouth covered.

It was the only thing he could think of that would have made that blasted woman move out of this dirt. He'd only thought of it because of the way he'd been brought up. He was a man who had been surrounded by dance-hall girls all his young life, and there wasn't much he hadn't learned too young and too well. And one thing he'd learned was the phrase "female thing" would gain a woman instant sympathy from the other women and set a man running in the opposite direction. In both cases, it was the perfect lie. He hadn't been able to say it without feeling like six kinds of fool, but feeling embarrassed played into his hands.

Of course now he was a liar—although a "female thing" could include cooking supper, now couldn't it?

He prayed for forgiveness and had the sense that not only did the Almighty forgive Him, but the good Lord sympathized. Maybe even laughed.

It wasn't that hard to quit thinking about his stubborn boss, considering he was half dead from exhaustion. He shooed the loafers along faster. The sun set before he was halfway up. But the worst of the slides and cliffs were behind him. The cattle could smell water now, and that picked up their speed more than all his hard riding.

By the time he topped the mountain, it was full dark. The stars were out and the temperature had plunged like it always did in the high country. He practically stumbled when he unsaddled his horse.

Then Emma was beside him, working on the roan with a handful of grass and cutting his work in half.

"I don't know what you told Ma, but she's riding night herd right now, and I'd eat and get to sleep before she comes in. She was right prickly with us when none of us were sick."

"I made it up so she'd come into camp quicker. She'd been back there all day."

"Ma always rides drag. It's the boss's job."

"Your ma says that so you won't have to take a turn, and I agree with her when it comes to you girls. And it's no big deal for her to do it when you've just driven a dozen or so head into Helena. But it's *not* the boss's job. In a regular outfit, everyone takes turns, and I'm from a regular outfit. But I can't convince her to let me spell her. So, I made something up, and now she's mad at me again. I reckon I deserve that."

Emma looked over the back of the roan they were working on and smiled at him. Her teeth glowed white out of her dirty face. It was the first time he'd seen the girl be anything but dead serious. It occurred to him in that moment that he was really starting to like the game little girl with the outsized horse skills.

Emma said, "I reckon you do deserve it, but if she asks me again if I'm okay, I'll try and act sick if'n ya want."

Silas started laughing then and shook his head. "Better let her get after me for lying instead. Me lying she might forgive. Me getting one of her girls to lie for me, well, she'd be after my head for sure."

Emma smiled again. "I 'spect that's right."

They finished the horse in double the normal time because they worked so well together. Then they went to the camp and Sarah had a plate of food ready for Silas. He swallowed it fast then dove for his bedroll as quickly as possible to avoid getting scolded by Belle.

He meant to lay awake and watch for her to see if she still looked mad, but he was asleep as soon as his head hit his saddle.

The next day was a repeat of the first, except this time Belle hoped Silas would spell her at drag. He rode up after two hours of watching her eat dust.

"My turn back here." He glared at her and braced himself for what was to come.

"You must really want to do it to make such a fool of yourself last night. Have at it." She rode away without further comment.

Silas managed to smile as she rode down into more of the same monotonous dust.

The trail twisted back and forth, up and down the mountain-side like a prairie rattler, only meaner. When they crested the next ridge, they'd gone half as far as yesterday and the sun was setting on them. In the waning light from the mountaintop, Silas saw what looked like an endless series of ridges out in front of them, and he almost fell into bed, he was so exhausted from thinking about what lay ahead.

Wade's body had been too close as they'd ridden. Glowing Sun didn't like it. But he was strong and she was exhausted, and her stiff back finally relaxed against him.

She awakened as he lifted her off the horse. She struggled against him, and he quickly set her on her feet. Her knees gave out. He caught her before she sank to the ground. Then he escorted her to a log and sat beside her.

The sun had been lost behind clouds, leaving a cold, murky day that pulled at her to sleep again and confused her about their direction. She couldn't tell how long they'd traveled, but if this was the midday meal, she'd slept for hours. She hoped they'd get to her village soon.

Glowing Sun sat at the warm fire on this cold day. The men

442

produced jerked beef and hard biscuits from their packs and shared with her until her stomach was stretched and full.

Wade opened a tin can and gave her a half of a yellow fruit. "Peaches," Wade said. He stabbed at the fruit with the same knife he'd used to open the can and extended the dripping fruit to her.

She carefully pulled it off the knife with her teeth. The juicy sweetness nearly brought tears to her eyes.

"Have some more." Wade speared another slice, holding it carefully over the can.

She reached out to steady the knife as she bit. The warmth of his hand mingled with the sweetness startled her into looking away from the treat.

Her gaze met his and was captured. The moment lingered. His hard, calloused, gentle hand remained joined with hers. She slowly took the peach, and his eyes flickered to her lips in a way that made her hand tighten on his.

At last she blinked and pulled her eyes away and spoke to the ground. "Thank you, Wade."

He touched her chin so she had to look at him again. "You're welcome, Glowing Sun."

"Wade." She puzzled the name over. "Wade in water." She arched her brows.

Wade nodded. "Wade in water." He smiled and offered her more fruit. "Peach."

"Peach." The word tickled her brain, but she couldn't remember it from before. However, she was sure she'd never forget this delicious dessert.

"Horse." Wade pointed at the buckskin they'd shared.

"Horse."

He seemed to enjoy this game of making her say his white words, so she'd play it. But the words made some sense. *Horse.* She remembered that now.

She wondered if she should tell Wild Eagle that she'd slept

in another man's arms. Would he be angry? He was a warrior and possessive of her. The springtime would see them wed.

"Beef." Wade extended more of the salty, tough meat to her.

She shook her head and rubbed her stomach. "Thank you."

"No, thank you," Wade said.

Glowing Sun smiled. She remembered that, too.

They had a halting conversation over the meal, then Wade stood and began packing the scanty camp.

She did her best to help, eager to be on her way home.

Wade crouched down on the heavily traveled trail. "They've already gotten through this pass." He shook his head. "They're making good time."

Shorty came back from scouting around in the fading light of sunset. "I thought you said they needed hands."

"They do." Wade looked up from tracks that were obviously at least a day old.

"I can read sign. They've got five seasoned hands. They might need another hand or two, but not all four of us."

Wade hadn't looked that close, but he could tell the herd moved steadily, and it was obvious they were making good time. He'd also bet his hat that the seasoned hands were Belle's daughters, but he didn't mention it. He'd come to trust these men though, so he didn't worry that they'd hurt the Tanner women.

He looked up at Shorty. "I guess we can go on and check. It sounded like they were taking this herd with almost no help. That was the day before they started. I hope they did find more help. I've been worrying."

"Can we catch 'em tonight?" Roy asked, always full of energy, eager to work and push. A good trait in a boy.

Wade shook his head, looking up at Glowing Sun, sitting perched on his horse. She watched him closely, her eyes narrow. She seemed to be listening, but Wade doubted the woman had learned enough English in an afternoon to follow their conversation.

He didn't like keeping her out overnight with four men. It wasn't proper. But nothing about this situation was normal. "I know this trail. It's a killer in the dark. Rock slides and cliffs especially on this side, going down. We've got to wait until morning."

They went back down the trail a ways until they got out of the wind and set up camp. They ate well. Wade had brought plenty with him, planning to join the drive after he'd left a winter's worth of supplies at the line shack.

Glowing Sun ate as if she were a bear storing up fat for the winter. He wondered how long those men had kept her prisoner.

He kept after her to talk English, and she'd gotten better through the afternoon. She was speaking in broken sentences and learning so fast, Wade knew she'd been familiar with the tongue in the past.

He settled into his cold, blanketless bed—Glowing Sun had his only cover. He fell asleep instantly. He woke in the wee hours of the night to find her gone. "Wake up." Wade lunged to his feet. "Glowing Sun ran off."

Shorty shook his head as he sat up. "She must have figured out we weren't taking her home."

"So we took her another day's ride farther from her village." Buck stood from his bedroll.

"And now," Roy added, "she's alone out there."

"With wolves. Both the two-legged and four-legged kind." Wade felt sick. This was his fault. And now he had to make it right.

He should just let her go with his best wishes. She was probably better equipped to take this journey than he was. But he knew God wanted more from him than just wishing her well. He couldn't live with himself not knowing if she made it to her village.

The worry for Belle rode him for some reason Wade couldn't

understand. God seemed to urge him to ride quickly to the cattle drive. He paused and opened his heart and mind to the still, small voice of God.

And he had an idea.

He turned to his three saddle companions. "I'm going after her. And this time I'm taking her home. I think you three oughta go on and help handle this drive."

"You can't do that. It ain't right," Roy fretted.

"I promise to ask her, Roy. I'll keep at it until she understands. I'll give her the choice to leave the tribe."

Roy didn't speak, but his jaw hardened in obvious dissatisfaction.

Shorty shrugged and pointed down the trail they'd followed. It was the only way over this mountain. "I reckon you can catch her. And if she doesn't want any part of you, you can just tag along to make sure she gets home safe."

"It's settled then." Wade saddled up while Shorty studied Glowing Sun's tracks.

Buck explained where he'd seen the village as Wade strapped down his saddlebags.

Before he was done, Wade started to laugh out loud.

"What is it?" Roy asked. "What's so funny?"

"That little maiden we're all so worried about?"

"Yeah. . ." Roy looked down the trail. "Do you see her? Is she coming back so we can help her?"

"I doubt she's coming back, Roy."

"Why do you doubt it?"

Wade started laughing again. "Because I just noticed she's stolen half my beef jerky."

He laughed as he mounted up and struck out to help poor, helpless Glowing Sun. While he rode away, he hoped when he found her, she didn't kill him.

CHAPTER 11

Silas got to ride drag so much he was sorry he'd ever pushed for the job. He couldn't decide if Belle was punishing him or if she'd had the tiniest of female reflexes spring to life and was looking on the hardest jobs as "men's work."

No sense hoping for the second, so he decided she was punishing him. Always best to put bad motives onto the way Belle treated him.

They pushed the herd on through another long day, with Silas eating dust and squinting against dirt in his eyes. It was late in the season. The daytime was hot, but the nights were frigid, and it snowed on them once. The women cuddled up together, and Silas resented that he was rejected from their little bevy of warmth while he shivered under his blanket alone.

They lost several head of cattle that slipped on washouts along the narrow pass and fell, bawling horribly for hundreds of feet. One steer skidded across a shale slide and broke its leg.

Silas saw Belle preparing to shoot it with hands that visibly trembled. He spurred his horse toward her and shouted, "Hold up!"

She lowered her gun so willingly Silas worried about her. He also knew she wouldn't thank him for trying to take this tough job.

"Belle, let me drive him away so the girls don't have to see." Ah, he was beginning to know how to handle her. He almost patted himself on the back when her furrowed brow smoothed.

"Yes, that's a good idea. The girls." She made no word of protest.

That worried him some. She must be nearing the end of her strength. Belle argued over everything.

He came back with a haunch of beef. The fresh sizzling steaks for supper that night and again the next morning lifted all their spirits.

By the time they'd ridden through another day, the warm, encouraging meal was long forgotten. Silas hated to see how quiet and gaunt the girls were getting. When the two older ones stood side by side, their skin was as white with dust as their hair.

Silas rode ahead and found a trail that led to the best grass he'd seen in a week. He came back to find Belle holding her quiet little baby in front of her, talking to her. Probably whispering endless apologies for bringing Betsy into this bleak world of craggy points and smothering dirt.

At sunset they started coming down out of the high peaks. He worked the herd well away from Belle until Betsy was back in her sling; then he rode up. "Grass ahead. It'll make a terrible long day, but once we're there, let's hold the cattle a day and let them eat." *And let the girls rest.* Silas would say it if he had to.

"How long a day?" Belle's eyes rose to his as if it took all her energy just to lift her chin.

"I could barely see the grass through the next pass; I didn't come close to riding all the way to it. We'll be pushing them in full dark for a couple of hours. But the uphill side of the trail to get there is clear, no slides or drop-offs."

Belle nodded silently for far too long. Then she squared her shoulders and lifted her reins.

"We're going to make it, Belle." Silas wanted to give her a hug for encouragement and to thank her for being so steady.

"I know." Her eyes flashed. The first sign of spirit she'd shown, and Silas decided she needed him to pester her into having some gumption.

"You womenfolk have held up pretty well. I'm mighty proud of you."

Those words might seem like a compliment to some. To Belle they were fighting words.

She rammed her gaze into him like the tip of a bullwhip. "Well, Silas, for a man, you're holding up pretty well, too. I'm mighty proud of *you*. And may I say, surprised."

He could set her off, all the way off. She'd be scolding and yelling and maybe threatening with about one more well-chosen word from him. Instead, he laughed. "That's the spirit."

Belle's temper melted and she managed to smile. Then laugh. "We're going to make it, Silas. No doubt about it. And. . .well. . .I will say. . ."

Silas waited. Yes, she could compliment him. She could thank him. She could even say she liked him a little.

"I will say you haven't slowed us down overly." She smirked.

Silas laughed out loud and decided he might make it through this cattle drive yet.

Still smiling, Belle reined her horse aside and rode down the trail.

Betsy waved bye-bye from her place on Belle's back.

They kept the cattle moving well into the night. They had two more passes to go through before Helena. Both shorter, but also higher and more perilous. Bringing up the rear, Silas was long after the others getting to camp.

Belle was already on the first watch. Emma and Sarah were asleep, cuddled up next to Betsy on the far side of the fire.

He ate stew from a warm pot and tumbled straightaway

into bed to get a couple of hours' sleep before taking midnight watch. He knew, even as he collapsed, that just as he was trying to carry as much of the weight of this trip as possible, the women-folk were trying to ease things for him. And for all their efforts, they were all almost dead. He knew he should insist on taking the first watch part of the time, but his eyes fell shut before he gathered the strength to stand.

The next time his eyes opened it was full daylight. He jumped up, alarmed to realize he'd slept through his shift. He immediately scanned the camp and saw all the girls sleeping soundly.

Except Belle. She'd been on the first watch last night. She couldn't have done the whole night alone. Silas was moving toward the nearest saddle horse before he'd finished stepping into his boots.

God, what happened? Where is she? His prayers were hard and desperate and laced with dread.

He rode out, afraid he'd find Belle trampled to death or thrown from her horse with her neck broken. He moved soundlessly, unwilling to wake the girls and have them go with him for fear of what they might find.

He had been riding half an hour through the wooded grazing land when he saw Belle's saddled horse standing with its head down. Silas spurred his buckskin, scattering a few standing cattle, but the stock were tired and they didn't pay him much mind beyond getting out of his way. He got through the herd and, with desperate eyes, scanned the ground around the horse.

A hundred yards away, in a notch between two trees, he saw Belle's boots sticking out. He galloped toward her, his heart pounding. As he pulled up, Belle cried out softly and sat up.

"Belle, what happened? Were you thrown?" Silas leaped off his horse and knelt by her side. He ran his hands over her arms and legs, looking for bleeding or broken bones.

Belle looked at him, her eyes dazed. He ran his hands over

her head, looking for the bump that must have knocked her cold.

Suddenly she swatted his hands away. "I'm fine. I. . .I guess I fell asleep. I remember getting off my horse to sit by that rock because I was getting so saddle sore. The next thing I knew you were waking me."

She looked over Silas's shoulder and seemed to register the rest of the world. "It's morning! I slept all night?" She stood and pushed past him. "I fell asleep before midnight. I've got to check the cattle. They could have stampeded all the way back home by now. I've got to—"

"They're fine, Belle." Silas got off his knees and cut off her rising panic. He knew just how she felt. "I rode through most of them getting here. We'll check on them in a minute, but I didn't see any sign of trouble."

Belle looked at the steers scattered in the woodlands around the stream and shook her head as if to knock away the last vestiges of sleep. "I can't believe I did that. Anything could have happened. The whole herd could have been rustled. Someone could have come up to the camp and killed all of you in your sleep. The cattle could have trampled you all to death without—"

"Stop!" Silas grabbed her shoulders. "Stop making things up to panic about. None of that happened. We're fine. And we all needed the rest. I haven't slept a night through in probably twenty years. I wake up a couple of times an hour no matter where I am. I should have known something was wrong hours ago. But we got away with it, Belle. We'll start making shorter days of it and resting up a day every chance we get. The drive will take a few days longer, but it won't matter. You're smart enough and *tough* enough to know we can't go back and stay awake last night. So what's the sense of getting all twisted up about it?"

"Tough." Belle laughed. "I guess you could say I'm tough."

"A woman would have to be to live the life you've lived, survive all you've survived."

"And I've thrived with it."

"You've done a lot better than your husbands, I'd say. How'd you find your way to this rugged place anyway?"

Chuckling, Belle rubbed the sleep from her eyes. "You want to know how I ended up here, way out in the wild, living alone."

"Your husbands died. Your worthless husbands. Your girls told me too much about it that first night."

"They didn't tell you the half of it." Belle smiled. "My ranch sits in the most beautiful mountain valley God ever put on this earth. William, my first husband, claimed one hundred and sixty acres of that valley. Gerald claimed another one hundred and sixty because I nagged him until he did it."

"Gerald's the one the girls said hit—"

"I don't talk about Gerald much." Belle cut Silas off and pulled away from him, crossing her arms tight. "Makes me want to grab for my shootin' iron, but yeah, he's the one."

"I'd like to grab for my shootin' iron myself." His fingers itched with the wanting. Or maybe they itched because he missed holding on to Belle. "How many husbands are you up to now?"

"Anthony was third and last. I had to browbeat him until he claimed a hundred and sixty acres. I selected each claim, and they are sitting square on top of the richest grasslands and most reliable springs west of the Colorado River. Plus, now I've got use of thousands more acres because I've got the only water, making it useless to anyone else. All rugged mountainside, but there's feed enough to keep my cows thriving. I'd say I control around twenty thousand acres all told."

Staggered by the amount, Silas looked at the husky, lazy cattle—not as fat as when they started but a good, healthy herd. "Sure enough looks like they're thriving."

"I own three thousand head of fine longhorn cattle." Belle's arms relaxed, and she leaned against the tree she'd been sleeping beside. "I built the herd up from the fifty William and I herded into

Montana along the Boseman Trail. We came out here a couple of years after the 1862 Gold Rush. I had the bright idea all those men hunting gold'd get almighty hungry. And there stood underpriced beef in Colorado just begging to be pushed into the mountains."

"Pushed." Silas laughed. "Probably as backbreaking as this drive."

"It was tough and a lot longer, but with only fifty head it was nothing like this."

"So William wasn't so bad of a husband then?"

"None of this was his idea." Belle snorted. "It was mine and mine alone. And with all the knowledge I'd gained growing up in Texas working alongside Pa, we prospered."

"Why didn't you just stay there with your family in Texas?"

Belle frowned, clearly annoyed by the question. "For the first fifteen years of my life, Pa made do without a son. My ma wasn't well and spent most of her days ailing, so Pa let me tag after him. He shared all his know-how with me, figuring it would all be mine someday. When I was about thirteen, Ma up and died. Pa's second wife was a spoiled, vain thing that didn't know the kickin' end of a horse from the bitin' end. But she did manage to present Pa with a son. The boy was born about six months after William and I got married. We'd gone into it thinking William would step in for Pa and run his ranch. Now, with a son, William and I were just in the way."

"Your pa threw you out?" Silas had never had a pa, not one he'd known and met, but the thought of a daughter being cast aside disgusted him.

Scowling, Belle nodded. "Without a second thought. William married me thinking Pa's land was part of the deal. But with a son and heir, even though the ink had barely dried on the marriage license, Pa showed me the road. He gave me a pat on my pretty little head, two hundred and fifty dollars—called it my inheritance—and let me take my clothes."

"What about William? Couldn't he find work in Texas? Why'd he drag you to Montana of all places?"

"William never had much of a backbone, and he wasn't one to work if it could be avoided. Since I seemed to be the strong-minded one in the family, William just trailed along with whatever I decided. Well, I was mad as a rabid Texas sidewinder and out to prove I didn't need Pa to make my way. So we headed for Colorado and spent every penny of my pa's money, plus every other penny I'd saved, on cattle. Then we herded them to Montana."

"I can't believe if William was so lazy he went along. Didn't he know what working a ranch was like?"

Belle shrugged. "What he knew was he wanted to put half a continent betwixt him and the War Between the States. That was enough to keep him moving west. Once we got to Montana and filed a claim, William discovered a troublesome back—or no, that was Anthony." Belle seemed to hunt around inside her head awhile then give up. "Well, both of them were laid up for one reason or another. I had to build our cabin, and even though I did a terrible job, William didn't help. He probably knew less about building than I did. I dammed up a creek and cleared brush and built fence. In an act of spite, I registered our herd brand as the Lazy S, but William never seemed to get that."

Silas had to laugh.

"The cattle thrived. The roof leaked. Two babies were born. And then William ran afoul of Rudolph and I hauled him up to the Husband Tree and buried him."

"The Husband Tree, Belle? Shame on you." Silas rolled his eyes.

Defensively, Belle said, "We didn't exactly *name* it that. It's just. . .what it is. So we *call* it that. You're the one who asked to hear all this."

"You're right. Go on." Scrubbing his whiskered face to keep from saying more, Silas smiled behind his hands.

The Husband Tree

"A new husband joined the family. Sarah's pa. Gerald O'Rourke sat on the porch and contemplated his whiskey supply and nurtured his annoyance at all the injustices that had been done to him in his life, whilst I learned to dodge drunken fists and increased the herd by hunting down mavericks running wild in the high-up hills."

"Gerald." Silas lost any urge he had to laugh.

"Then with Gerald just barely finished twitchin' from his untimely horse ride, I had a brain spasm I'm still kicking myself for and found myself married to Anthony."

"Which all just proves you're tough. So why are you so mad at yourself for sleeping through one night? What difference does it make if we slow down covering this trail? We can rest up. A few days more won't matter."

"Yes, it will matter," Belle snapped. "For one thing, heavy snow could come at any time. It can snow year-round in these mountains, but the heavy snows haven't started yet. The first one will block these passes, and they won't open up again until spring. I'm not feeling pushed to get to Helena so much as I'm feeling pushed to get home. My herd will be food for the wolves if I'm not there to bring 'em down closer to the cabin. The pond freezes over, and I need to take the ax to it and keep it open. I can't risk being snowed out of my ranch. I can feel winter in the air. The first storm could come any day."

"I know, but that doesn't mean—"

"For another thing," Belle interrupted, "we are already stopping at every half-decent camp we find. There just aren't that many. Once we start out for the day, the place we're going to stop at is already set. We can't hold this herd on one of those dangerous mountain trails overnight, and you know it. So having shorter days isn't possible."

"Belle, we're going to be fine. We're almost—"

"I should never have tried this. I didn't realize how much the herd had increased this spring. A bunch of older cattle moved up into the highest valley. I don't check that pasture very often because it's an overnight ride, and Betsy was newborn and I just couldn't cut it. I didn't want to let the girls go alone, and I just plain didn't feel up to making the trip." She fisted her hands as if she were ready to begin punching herself for her weakness.

Silas couldn't stand it when Belle got in one of these infernal female moods. She was tough and game and made of nothing but gristle and nerve. "Belle, honey, now—"

"When that grass wore out in the late summer, I was surprised to see how many cattle were coming to the lowlands from that way. A lot of yearlings that weren't branded. I had no idea the herd had thrived so. I rode up and was shocked. I not only undercounted, I was planning on that high grass for my herd this winter. I realized I couldn't feed them. I was sloppy."

"You have ten times the courage of any man I've ever known. And then you go and pull this female stuff." Maybe if he could make her mad at him instead of herself, she'd calm down. She seemed to enjoy hollering at him.

"I cut corners."

She hadn't even reacted to his reminding her she was a female. This was serious.

"I took the easy way out, and now I'm risking my girls' lives on this trail drive and—"

"Belle, you are the toughest woman—no, no, who am I kidding—the toughest *person* I've ever known."

She jabbed him in the chest, which was a good sign. "I wasn't tough enough to check—"

"Then you go and start beating on yourself—"

"My own herd, and I'm honest enough to admit when I—"

"For not working hard enough and before I know it, I'm—"

CHAPTER 12

Kissing her.

Silas was kissing her.

Belle didn't even fight him when he pulled her into his arms. Honestly, she moved toward him the second she saw that fire in his eyes. And she didn't know how to judge such things, but she was pretty sure she got to his lips before he got to hers. Except that wasn't possible, because their lips got to each other at the same second and they stayed together with the full cooperation of both parties involved.

Silas's hands pulled her firmly against him.

Belle didn't stop him. In truth, she grabbed ahold, tight, and hung on like it could be forever. Stopping him was the furthest thing from her mind.

"Breakfast is ready, you two." Sarah did it for her. "Knock it off and come eat."

Silas staggered back.

Belle whirled around. Sarah's horse nudged Belle's shoulder. Sarah had ridden right up to them, and Belle had never noticed. Belle's knees sagged, and she had to grab the saddle horn on

Sarah's horse to hold herself up.

Silas moved again, and Belle looked over her shoulder to see he'd backed away about ten yards. Their eyes met, and his were wild. He turned away and ran both hands through his hair with a motion that spoke of the depths of his frustration.

Belle knew just how he felt.

"Ma, should you be kissing a man you're not married to that-away?" Sarah's face creased into a worried frown.

Belle shook her head back and forth slowly. With complete honesty and a husky voice she didn't recognize, she said, "Absolutely not."

"Then why are you doing it, Ma? If you do it, it must be okay, 'cuz you wouldn't do anything that was bad. So—"

"Sarah?" Silas cut in, still with his back to them.

"Yeah?" She sounded vulnerable and confused.

Belle braced herself to repair the damage of whatever ridiculous excuse Silas might have for their behavior.

"Give your ma a ride back to camp. I'll catch up her horse and my own and be right in. We're giving the cattle a day to rest up." And themselves, but Silas didn't admit that out loud. "And Sarah?"

"Yeah?"

Silas turned so he could look in Sarah's eyes. "Your ma is right. We shouldn't have oughta been kissing like that." Silas sighed deeply then forged on. "That's for two people who are married, or soon to be married, and no one else. I was worried about your ma because she didn't wake me for my turn riding herd. I found her asleep out here. For a minute I was plumb scared that she'd been hurt. Then when she was okay, well, I kinda got carried away because I was so. . .relieved. And that kiss, well, it shouldn't have happened, but it did. And it was wrong of me, and it won't happen again, because we are *not* going to get married. I apologize to you and your ma."

Belle listened to his neat little explanation with growing anger. With a sharp twist of dismay, she realized that when she'd decided letting Silas kiss her was too tempting to resist, she'd also known she was accepting the idea that she'd take the leap again and get married to the confounded man. But it didn't sound like Silas was interested. She'd known plenty of men who wanted what Silas wanted but weren't interested in offering marriage. And every one of them was a low-down, dirty, stinking polecat. And she'd slapped every one of them down hard.

Listening to Silas brush aside what had passed between them with his fumbling apology was humiliating, because while he'd been playing a man's game, she'd been falling in love.

Falling in love with Silas?

No!

Belle had been down the husband road too many times. She had learned that marriage was, at its most basic, a business deal. It took two people to make a baby. It took two people to run a home. She had the babies to prove the first. And Belle had survived when the scoundrels had disproved the second. But just because her husbands hadn't come through for her didn't mean it wasn't the way it was supposed to be. People got married for sensible reasons, and if they were lucky, they'd have some affection for each other and call it love. But it wasn't *required.* It wasn't even good, especially if one had affection and the other didn't.

Belle knew without a doubt she'd never felt anything close to love for her husbands. She'd thought she cared for William, but that had died on the vine shortly after their marriage when William realized he was getting a few hundred dollars instead of a ranch.

A husband had his rights in marriage, and she'd endured it when she couldn't think of a way to take the starch out of 'em. That was part of the business of being married.

But love? *Love!* What if she'd loved her husbands and then

they'd treated her so badly? Remembering Gerald's fists, remembering the way Anthony had abandoned her to her fate when she'd gone into labor on the trail. . .the hurt was staggering and she hadn't cared a whit for either man. If she'd have loved them, it would have destroyed her.

Just listening to Silas say there would be no marriage between them was breaking her heart.

My heart will not be involved, Lord. Please protect me from love.

Her backbone stiffened. It was *not* breaking her heart. She *wouldn't* love Silas. She wouldn't love *anyone*! She'd been thinking she'd marry him, but that was another matter altogether from love. And now it looked like he thought Belle was one of those women who. . .who would be willing to be with a man. . .share passion with a man. . .because Silas's kisses were more passion that she'd ever felt with a man. And he thought they'd share such without wedding vows.

Realizing that stung badly. Tears burned Belle's eyes, but she blinked them away. "Let's go, Sarah."

Sarah studied Silas for a minute before she clucked gently to her horse and removed Belle from temptation yet again. They rode back to the camp in silence.

Silas watched after the two womenfolk until the herd swallowed them up. Then he stared sightlessly at the T Bar cattle.

Belle.

He couldn't be around her. He couldn't stay here knowing how she responded to him. He couldn't stay.

And he couldn't leave.

He thought back to Lulamae and knew now the sheer depths of the little liar's sham desire for him. She'd held him tight, and he'd believed she welcomed a kiss—until her pa came in. But compared to the way Belle melted in his arms. . .

The Husband Tree

Silas turned away from the steers and tried to gather his senses. He looked around for his horse, and at his shrill whistle, it and Belle's black gelding ambled over to meet him. He didn't mount up but instead led them along while he headed for camp on foot. He didn't want to go back and face the hen posse that might be shaking out a loop and looking for a low-hanging branch right this minute.

There'd be a new kind of Husband Tree for this crew.

More than that, he didn't want to see the confused look on Sarah's face as she asked him about men and women and whether her ma was being good or bad. Silas shook his head in disgust. He had more to think about on this trip than how warm and passionate Belle Tanner was. How warm and passionate and vulnerable and beautiful and strong and tired—

He shook his head again. He had four little girls to think about. Their welfare had to be his first priority. And taking care of Belle was important, too. But he was *not* getting married. He didn't trust women, and Belle was one of the orneriest critters he'd ever seen, even if she *was* a different sort.

Except, for the first time, he wasn't going to marry her for a different reason than the one he'd had before—that reason being a fear and disgust for the two women he'd run afoul of. No. He wasn't going to marry her because *he* was worthless. He was penniless, and he had run like a coward from two ranches. He had to make something of himself before he could tangle himself up with a woman as fine as Belle.

To go into a marriage without a way to support a wife was dishonorable. Oh, he knew he could make a place for himself at Belle's, but even if he worked the land hard, it would never be his.

The Tanner Ranch. In Divide, that's what they called it. Not a single name of one of her husbands had stuck. He could move in and claim his place and set the holding to rights and make Belle's life easier, but none of it would ever be his.

He knew as he thought it all through that he was making excuses. The idea of being sucked into Belle's all-girl household reminded him too much of the way he'd been raised, surrounded by women. It had been smothering. He'd escaped that life at the earliest possible moment, and he couldn't willingly sign up for another hitch of it.

He thought of Emma's toughness. Lindsay's quiet confidence. Sarah's homey mothering. Betsy's silent watchfulness. Sure he liked them. Not wanting to be the only rooster at a hen party didn't mean he thought there was anything wrong with the girls. As a matter of fact, he'd gladly thrash anyone who said there was anything wrong with his girls. But that didn't mean he wanted to buy into their brood.

He caught a handful of mane on his own horse and jumped onto its back. He set out to circle the herd and take stock. He was ready to face the Tanner women again, but just to be on the safe side—what with the way Lindsay handled a gun and all—he started his inspection in the direction that led him directly away from them.

Silas didn't return to camp until close to noon. The cattle were fine, munching away on a fair stand of native grass and young pine boughs.

He ran into Emma once and noticed she must have bathed in the creek, because he could see her instead of dirt. She was out doing her own inspection. She nodded to him without saying much, but normally she'd have come up and talked to him for a minute, so he wondered what had gone on back in camp.

His inspection led him near the camp, and he was debating whether to face the Tanner women or starve to death. He was having a hard time picking.

Then three riders came over the top of the draw they'd punched the cattle over yesterday.

Silas headed for camp and got there while the riders were still a half mile away, winding down the steep trail. He watched them from a distance, and although they looked like average cowpokes, he didn't trust anyone around his women.

He was swinging off his horse when he realized he thought of Belle and her girls as his. He was lucky he didn't fall all the way to the ground. He might have if there'd been time. For now, he stepped over to Belle. She'd cleaned up in the creek and was all sweet-smelling and pink along with the girls and was now busy spreading a batch of washing on bushes near their camp. This wasn't the usual batch of diapers they did every night. This was a full washing.

He grabbed Belle's arm to get her attention. "I'm going to say you're my wife. I don't want these men to think you're an unmarried woman. Let me deal with them. Go along with me."

Belle looked shocked at his suggestion. "Silas, I'm not going to—"

"Just do it." Silas talked over top of her then stepped quickly over to Lindsay who was peeling spuds along with Sarah.

Belle went on protesting, but he ignored her. "Lindsay!"

Lindsay turned to him, her eyes narrow. So she'd heard what went on between Silas and Belle this morning, too. Well, he didn't have time to talk about that now.

"I want you girls to call me Pa while these men are around."

Startled, Lindsay exchanged a look with Sarah. Then the two of them looked over their shoulders at the approaching men. They'd all noticed the strangers and were wary. But Silas's order surprised them.

"Sure, Pa." Lindsay shook her head and grinned. "That's a good idea. I've been trying to get the potatoes peeled before I went for my gun." Lindsay was a practical girl.

Silas admired that. "You too, Sarah."

"Silas," Belle scolded. "We are not going to lie to—"

"Put a few more potatoes in the pot. If they're just passing through we'll let them sit up to a meal."

Sarah giggled. "Glad to help, Pa."

Betsy was tied onto Lindsay's back. She waved her arms at Silas and said gleefully, "Papa."

Silas bit back a grin at Betsy. He'd have laughed out loud at the little imp if he hadn't been in such a hurry.

"Now, Silas. . ." Belle caught his arm.

"Wait just a second, Belle." Silas patted her arm and kept giving the girls orders. "Lindsay, ride out and tell Emma so she doesn't come busting into camp and give us away. I'm not saying there's anything wrong with these men. But it's best to keep a careful eye at first. And even if they're decent men. . .well, men are notional critters when there are beautiful women to hand. So, I want you especially to ride careful around them. Don't ever be out of my sight while they're here. I may try and hire them to help with the herd if they measure up. If they do, you'll have to keep calling me Pa until they leave."

Lindsay's chin lifted, and her eyes shone as she asked breathlessly, "You think I'm a beautiful woman?" She stuttered and shook her head and looked at the ground in embarrassment. "Or, no, you're talking about Ma."

"You're as pretty a little thing as any man has ever set eyes on," Silas said in pure disgust. "And I don't want those men thinking you don't have a pa around to fill them full of buckshot if they so much as look at you sideways! And it ain't a compliment, Lindsay. Being pretty can be a blasted nuisance. Ask your ma."

"You do." Lindsay looked back at Silas, her face glowing with pleasure. "You think I'm pretty. You think Ma's pretty, too."

Silas could have sworn Lindsay grew about two inches right there in front of him. She stood up taller. A different expression was on her face than he'd ever seen before. She squared her shoulders. "I'll find Emma and let her know what's going on." She lifted Betsy out of her carrier. "Sarah, you take Betsy."

"I've got her." Silas took the baby without thinking about it.

He was too worried about what ideas he'd just planted in Lindsay's head. "Lindsay, I won't have you making any sheep's eyes at these *hombres*. Don't go gettin' ideas."

"I won't, Pa," Lindsay said fervently. "You can count on me to behave myself." She turned and walked quickly toward the closest horse.

The men were drawing nearer, so Silas hissed after her, "I don't want you riding out any farther than where I can see you. And get Emma back to camp, too. And your name's Harden, every one of you."

Lindsay hung a bridle on the horse and jumped on it bareback. "Harden. Yes, Pa. I'll tell Emma her name. We'll both be careful. . . Pa." She kicked the horse and rode toward Emma, who was way down the hill but clearly visible.

"Hello, the camp," the men called out, pulling to a stop from a decent distance. Silas felt better knowing these men were wise in the ways of approaching a cow herd.

"Silas," Belle said quietly enough the men couldn't hear her, "I've handled men many a time. I don't need you to pretend—"

"You mind me woman"—Silas spun around and jabbed a finger right at her nose—"or I'll tan your backside right in front of these cowpokes."

Belle opened her mouth, but no words came out, which suited Silas right down to the ground.

"You want me to take the baby, Pa?" Sarah asked.

Silas hoisted Betsy up against his chest, barely noticing he held her. "She's fine. Get on with your chores."

"Yes, Pa."

"Silas—" Belle started in yapping.

Silas turned on her and saw pure spitfire in her eyes. Well, there wasn't time to palaver about it. She'd just have to do as she was told by her husband the way the good Lord intended. "If these girls call me Pa and you Ma but you say we aren't married, what kind of loose woman does that make you?"

Belle gasped.

"What are those men going to think?"

Silas closed her mouth by giving her a sound kiss. He pulled away and said in a voice that brooked no objection, "You're Belle Harden. Don't forget it no matter how many last names you've had before."

Then the men rode up and Silas turned to them with one of his arms around Belle and Betsy perched on his shoulder.

The very image of a happy family man.

CHAPTER 13

That coffee smells mighty good, ma'am." The middle-aged man, riding between an old grizzled cowpoke and a boy, did the talking, and Silas pegged him for the leader of the group. "I'm Buck, and this is my son, Roy, and my saddle partner, Shorty."

Their gear was clean and neatly packed, and their horses looked well cared for. The men themselves looked a little rough, but riding a long trail would do that. Silas didn't like that they'd addressed his wife before asking his permission. Still, a woman was a wonderful thing, and the men were probably so fascinated by Belle that they could barely remember Silas was there.

"You're welcome to join—"

Silas dug his hand into her waist and squeezed so hard she quit talking. "Get back to the meal, woman. These men aren't here to talk no hen talk." Which was probably wrong. These men would no doubt welcome hen talk—or anything else Belle suggested—just to hear the sound of her voice.

Belle looked at him, and Silas wondered if she hadn't just left burn marks on his skin with the fire in her eyes. He grinned and eased up the grip on her waist then caressed her stomach with a little circular motion of his thumb. She looked confused for a second. Then she turned to help Sarah with the noon meal.

Obedient. Belle Tanner. . .Harden, he amended. . .was obeying him.

Silas could have wrestled a grizzly bear he felt so powerful. "And take this young'un off my hands," Silas added gruffly.

Belle turned back and took Betsy without speaking a word.

Silas wondered if it was because his behavior had left "his little woman" speechless. The thought almost made him smile. More likely she was too busy plotting his slow, painful death to talk.

Silas looked back at the men. They'd ridden closer but still waited a respectful distance, which spoke well of them. "Light and sit. No one ever walked away from the Harden campfire hungry."

He watched every move they made, conscious of how close a gun hand got to a trigger and whether he saw something behind the eyes of any of the men that made him uneasy. Silas had been down the river and back more than a time or two. He'd seen every kind of low-down trash the earth had to offer in the men who came to see his ma and her friends. He'd seen fine, hardworking, honest men who dressed in rags and smelled worse than their horses. He'd seen well-dressed, prosperous men with eyes like snakes and hearts dripping with filth. He'd ridden hard miles and dug a living out of a hard country, and he trusted his judgment when it came to sizing up a man.

The riders settled into the camp, resting against a fallen log one of the girls must have dragged in while he was busy kissing the daylights out of Belle. They introduced themselves, as did Silas sitting across from them on the other side of the fire. He never mentioned Belle's or Sarah's names.

Belle served coffee, careful to stay a healthy arm's length away from the men. Then she removed herself from the circle as quickly as possible. She was acting for all the world like a proper, demure, and obedient wife.

Silas wondered when she'd learned to fake that.

"We've been riding with Wade Sawyer." Buck held the coffee cup cradled in two hands like he needed to warm himself. Silas held his the same way. So did every experienced cowhand in cold country. "He said you'd asked him to help with the drive. We were Tom Linscott's line camp, just passing through, when Sawyer delivered supplies. He said maybe you needed more hands. He didn't make any promises about hiring us. We understand that, and we'll ride on if you say the word."

Silas had no idea who Wade Sawyer was. He didn't mention that.

Belle came up beside him and actually wrung her hands a bit as if she were afraid of displeasing him, when what she was probably really thinking was she'd like to wring his neck.

Who'd a guessed the little woman was an actress?

"Remember, I told you I saw Wade at the diner, just after you left? I told him we were shorthanded, but he had already hired on to deliver Linscott's supplies. He said he'd ride out this way if he made good time."

She had talked about asking others in town to ride herd. Maybe she'd mentioned Wade in passing. Silas couldn't be sure, but he appreciated his little woman filling in the gaps. He looked at Buck. "So why isn't he with you?"

"The strangest thing," Buck said. "There was a white woman dressed in Indian clothes running from. . ."

The men talked openly as men did who weren't on the dodge.

After they'd finished their tale of Glowing Sun, Silas noticed they all said their pleases and thank yous as if it came straight from their heart when Belle poured more coffee. Silas didn't doubt that they were sincere. Coffee being poured from the soft hand of a pretty woman was mighty rare in the wilderness.

With coffee refilled, Buck went on. "We were riding out from the goldfields near Helena."

Buck eased back as if settling in for his storytelling. "The mines played out a decade ago, but dreamers still came and tried to hammer wealth out of the tightfisted ground. Us among 'em. Roy was just a boy then."

Buck wove that tale with Shorty chiming in—a man of few words, but the ones he spoke were worth hearing.

Silas liked the look of them. He wanted to tell them they were hired but decided to wait until Lindsay and Emma came back to camp. He needed to see how they acted when they saw "his girls." The boy drank his coffee quickly and asked for more before Belle offered. He kept looking at Betsy like he was hungry for the sight of a baby.

When Sarah took the baby from Belle's carrier and bounced her, Roy got up from the fire and went to stand by the womenfolk as if he were being drawn in by a magnet.

"Don't mind the boy," Buck said quietly. "He's never seen a baby before. Not up close. Maybe an Indian baby a time or two from a distance. I had a spread on the Musselshell in the foothills of the Rockies for a while, but we got driven out by the Sioux seven years ago when the boy was ten. Found my wife and two older daughters massacred and my home burned. My cattle driven off, too, all while the young'un and I were riding the range. Didn't have the belly for startin' over without my woman to make a home of it. We've been driftin' ever since. Shorty was working for me when it happened, and now we ride the trail together. It's been mostly line shacks and frontier towns for my son. We've lived a far piece away from folks out here. That baby. . .well. . .Roy wouldn't be any more fascinated if a leprechaun came sliding down a rainbow with a pot of gold."

Silas nodded, but he made sure he knew where Roy was every minute.

Lindsay and Emma rode up about the time Belle was stirring the beef stew for the last time.

Roy's blue eyes lit up, and he quit looking at the baby.

"I found lion tracks back a ways, Pa." Emma dismounted and began stripping the leather from her horse.

Something big and strong grew in Silas's heart at the sound of Emma calling him "Pa."

"I trailed him a spell, but I never caught sight of him." Emma's knowing eyes took in the men, their horses, their guns, and the look in her ma's eyes all in one sweeping glance. She must have liked what she saw, because she kept talking and working. "The tracks look a couple of days old, but this is probably his range."

"I'll take the next look around." Silas noticed Roy edging close to Lindsay as she began working with her mount. "Lion meat would surely add something to our kettle."

Belle said with a meek voice Silas had never heard her use before, "Silas, there's plenty of stew and biscuits for these folks if it's all right with you."

That big, strong feeling Emma had awakened was nothing compared to how powerful it was to hear Belle, however much she wanted to kill him, pretending to be a submissive wife. He knew enough to enjoy it while he had the chance. "My Belle's a rare cook." He didn't really know that for a fact since Sarah had done most of the cooking, but the girl had to learn it from somewhere, so it stood to reason.

"We've been eating hardtack and jerked beef, with a venison steak thrown in once in a while. I can't remember what a warm meal served by a woman tastes like," Buck said. "We'd be proud to have a meal with you."

Silas heard the respect and honest appreciation in Buck's voice and, with some misgivings based on the way Roy was looking at Lindsay, asked, "Are you boys looking for work? We've got another two weeks on this drive into Helena. I left it too late because I couldn't find hands. Now we're trying to drive on our own, and though my womenfolk are good, handy girls, all of 'em, we could surely use the help."

Shorty nodded. "Reckon I can go that way as soon as another. How many hands have you got riding herd?"

Silas was surprised Wade hadn't told them. His respect for the unknown man rose for not telling strangers about the nearly all-female crew. He also decided the reaction he got from these men would decide the near future. "This is the lot of us. My girls and I are taking this herd alone."

Shorty's eyes narrowed.

Buck leaned forward. "Just the womenfolk and you? And you've moved them through these mountain trails?"

Silas didn't answer. Buck knew full well that was a fact, because he'd just come down the trail, and no one could miss that a thousand head of cattle had passed that way.

Buck shoved his hat back and smiled. "They grow 'em tough in Montana, I'd say. Women as well as men. You should have seen that little spitfire giving Wade all he could handle."

Roy's face had now turned an alarming shade of pink, and he was staring straight at the ground as if his feet fascinated him. Every once in a while he'd take a quick glance up at Lindsay then go right back to inspecting his boots.

"Can we hire on, Pa?" He pulled off his well-worn hat and finger-combed his overly long, dark blond hair as if suddenly worried about his appearance.

Lindsay walked to her horse to rub it down.

Roy trailed a good twenty feet behind, not speaking to her and not listening to his father's answer.

Silas's eyes narrowed as he watched Roy. He clenched his hands between his splayed knees until his knuckles turned white and considered rescinding the offer of work. He looked back at Buck and made sure the man saw his displeasure.

Buck looked from his son to Silas. He leaned forward and said low, "I'll see to the boy. Don't worry none about him. He's a good 'un. Just young."

"I know what goes on in a young man's mind." Silas frowned. "It's not that I don't understand. But it's different when you're a man with pretty little girls like mine, Buck. Real different. I won't put up with a single wrong word from your boy."

Buck nodded. "I'll be right beside you if he steps out of line." Then he grinned. "But the day will come when you're gonna have to let the fellers near your girls."

Silas couldn't manage a smile, but he did nod.

"Your oldest is marryin' age, I'd say," Buck added. "And the next, well, I've known gals hitched that young, too."

Silas's stomach did a dive that almost brought him up off the ground. He didn't respond, but he wanted to grab Lindsay and drag her back home and lock her in the house. He stared hard at Roy. "It's not that I won't let 'em near. I will when the time comes a few years from now, but I'll be near, too. Standing close at hand with my shotgun."

Then Silas thought of the way Hank Tool acted when he caught Lulamae in the barn. Hank had set the whole thing up with Lulamae, not just *allowing* her to be treated in such a way but most likely instructing the poor dumb cluck to behave so. Silas was suddenly furious with Hank Tool for being so cavalier with his daughter, and only the distance of four states kept Silas from hunting the man down and thrashing him.

Buck laughed. "A man after my own heart. If you're still interested, we'd appreciate the work."

Silas leaned forward and offered the man his hand. "You're hired."

Buck leaned across the campfire and shook Silas's hand. Shorty nodded from where he sat, leaning lazily against a tree trunk. "I think we'd be willing to take the job just to eat at your campfire."

"Well, you'll do that and earn thirty a month, too. Although the job's only got two weeks left."

"Done," Buck said. "It's a pretty country, but it's a hard route you're takin'. God made most of the land stand on end instead of lyin' flat like a decent piece of land had oughta."

Silas nodded with a wry smile. "You've just come over the trail. You know what the last few days have been like. We've got one blazed-faced steer who spends all his time trying to go home."

"We rode through some of the herd. It's a good-looking bunch you got. Fat and sassy. They've been well tended. A lot of steers are mighty gaunt by the time they've been on the trail a few weeks. You must know ranching."

Careful not to crack a smile, he said deliberately to goad Belle, "Thanks. I put a lot of care into fattening them for market. I'm really pleased with the way they've stood up. We've driven them hard. We had one spell. . ."

Silas sat ignoring his obedient little Belle and taking all the credit for her hard work. He imagined her going for his throat and somehow ending up with her arms around his neck. It took all his will to pay attention to cow talk about the hills behind and the hills ahead.

Belle handed Buck and Shorty plates of food with a kind word and a demure smile then turned back to the fire and returned quickly with food for Silas. He thought she slapped it a little hard in his lap, but she didn't dump it on his head, so he silently thanked the Lord for looking out for him and ate his meal.

Roy was helping Lindsay rub down Emma's bay. He was working energetically on the off side of the horse, occasionally glancing over the animal's back at Lindsay. It occurred to Silas grudgingly that a young man who tried to impress a young lady by working hard by her side wasn't a bad sort. He also made a mental note to keep his shotgun at hand while he slept.

Silas went out to ride the circuit with all three men. He wasn't about to leave a single one of them alone with his girls. He did remember, as his thoughts ranged over how he'd defend his women, that his women could probably outrope, outride, and outshoot most of the men in Montana. It made him smile with pride to think of it.

The four men rousted strays out of the thickening brush that grew up the mountainside. They got the cattle settled in for the night, and Shorty trailed the mountain lion off a few miles into the hills and came back to report it seemed to have been on its way out of the country.

When the sun set, the night had more than the normal bite of cold, and white began sifting down out of the sky. Silas knew the heavier snow wouldn't be long in coming. He thought for the first time that if he rode back to Belle's ranch with her, and as a gentleman he would have to escort her home, he might accidentally get himself snowed in with the Tanners for the winter. The idea made Silas feel so good inside it scared him right down to his boots.

Belle and the two older girls went out after supper to stand first watch.

"I don't rightly know when I've let a woman ride herd while I warmed my toes by a fireside," Buck said with a furrowed brow. "It don't seem right."

Silas could have taken that as an insult, but he knew exactly what Buck meant. "The Lord hasn't seen fit to give me a son yet." And the thought of having a son with Belle made him so restless he could barely continue the conversation. Clearing his throat, he said, "I need the help, and the women are top hands with a horse. My Emma can hold her own with any man, and that includes me, and they love it. All of them would rather sit a horse than sew a dress. I don't know if that's the proper way to raise a girl, but we're all to ourselves most of the time, and we just go our own way. When a man comes along for the girls, well, he'll take 'em as they are or he won't get near 'em. If there's any changin' to be done, he'll be doin' it."

Shorty leaned back against his bedroll, using his saddle as a pillow. He tilted his trail-worn Stetson over his eyes. "I'll take second watch with Roy. I'd like to get a little sleep before then if you two are done yammerin'."

Buck settled back, too. "You'd better stay in and keep watch over the girls, Silas. We'll take this first night."

Silas said cordial-like, "Appreciate it, Buck. I sleep light, so I'll ride out time to time." It was the barest of warnings, but Buck grunted his approval as he rested his head on his saddle and pulled his blanket over himself in the flicker of the campfire. No one would respect a man who didn't watch over his daughters and his herd with equal vigilance.

Silas settled into his own bedroll, thinking of the soft snow and the winter closing in and how much he enjoyed the idea of Belle giving him a son. . .or another daughter. Yes, he'd be contented with a girl all right.

Then he did his best to turn his thoughts to something else before it became impossible to sleep. He wasn't all that successful. In fact, he was as bothered as a man could be and almost went out to ride, since he wasn't sleeping anyway. But he couldn't leave.

Shorty woke Roy, and the two of them left the camp quietly. Silas heard them go and lay awake until Belle, Lindsay, and Emma all came riding in. The snow had stopped, and the night was sharply cold but not bitter. The women went straight to caring for their horses.

Silas pushed aside his blanket, stood, and walked over to Belle. He rested his hand on her elbow. "Let's step away from the campfire for a second."

Belle nodded and followed him as the girls worked their horses. Silas stayed where the sleeping girls and Lindsay and Emma working with their mounts were in their line of sight.

Silas whispered, "I just wanted to remind you that you have to show me a bit of affection from time to time to keep this idea in these men's heads that we're married."

"What?" Belle's shocked question rang out clearly enough to be heard down the whole mountainside.

Silas squeezed her elbow. "Shh. What else? A wife gives her husband a kiss now and then. You'll do it, too!"

"Silas," she began sternly, but at least she wasn't yelling, "I am not—"

Silas shut her up by kissing her, and when she melted against him, it occurred to Silas that this was the most fun he'd ever had in his life. It was the plain honest truth that he was a happy man when he was tormenting Belle Tanner. He eased his lips away from her and said with his mouth a bare inch from her ear, "I'll sleep with the men."

Belle shuddered and Silas breathed softly against her ear again to see if she'd repeat the telltale movement. She did.

"Silas," Belle said with reluctant protest, "what about the girls? They can't see us behaving in a way that's not proper. They'll think—"

"I already told them what we had to do. They understand." Silas leaned closer again and murmured, "Now think, darlin', the yarn I spun these boys is the only one we could have told. When it gets down to it, me being along on this drive with you is about as improper as anything can be."

"No, it's not. The girls are better chaperones than a fire-and-brimstone preacher backed by a convent full of nuns."

Silas grinned. "That is the honest truth. But I'm here as your husband while these men are with us. We have to make do as best we can."

"But it's all a lie, Silas. I'll spend my night praying for forgiveness for this nonsense. All you had to do was be honest."

He kissed her again because it seemed to quiet her down. "Now I've been calling you *my woman* and the girls *my girls*. I've been real careful not to say the word *wife* and *daughters*."

"You told the girls to call you Pa. Don't try and pretend that's not a lie."

He was holding a smart woman in his arms. He found it suited him. "Well, I've already asked for forgiveness, and I feel like God understands. Which means you're more stubborn than God, and why am I not surprised?"

Belle jerked her arm out of his grip, but Silas caught it and reeled her back in for one last kiss. When she'd calmed clear down to being limp in his arms, he pulled back just enough to whisper in her pretty ear, "I think we've been over here long enough." He said it all scoldinglike, as if Belle was keeping him over here just because she wanted a few minutes of privacy to smooch. "Now you go on back to camp and behave yourself."

Silas pressed his bristly cheek to her smooth one and slid his arms snug around her waist. "We have to do this, darlin'." He nodded, his face nudging her chin up and down. "It's to protect you and the girls. You can see that, can't you?" He kept nodding, kept her close, marveled at the woman smell of her.

Finally, she nodded, too.

Pulling back, he thought her eyes looked a bit dazed, and she flickered a glance at his lips that made Silas step back before he had to do any more explaining to the girls. He took her hand and led her back to the campfire where she'd sleep well away from him.

He felt a niggling of guilt for not being honest with the new hired hands, and he especially worried about letting the girls call him Pa. Was he teaching the girls sinful lessons? He opened his eyes to see snowflakes drifting down again.

Silas asked God to help him figure out his feelings for Belle and how they matched up with his feelings for women in general.

This being a father business is complicated, Lord. I don't know how You've managed it for all these years. I'd appreciate some guidance.

A breeze moved over him, and the wind carried a whisper that he knew he imagined. It whispered something like, *"If you married her, none of this would be a lie."*

That whisper cracked like a bullwhip in the air and jolted Silas wide awake. He lay there, watching it snow for two hours, his prayers mixed up with remembering the scent of Belle's hair.

When he finally drifted off, he woke up every few minutes all night long. And it had nothing to do with being suspicious of the new cowhands.

CHAPTER 14

The little minx barely left a trail. And Wade considered himself a fair hand with tracking.

Since he'd left his father's ranch, he'd spent long weeks living off the land in these very mountains. He felt close to God up here. The big sky felt wide enough to hold heaven, and the mountains would make a grand footstool as God watched over His children. Finding he could survive with the strength of his own hands gave him hope that he was a worthy man. It tore down all the mountains of self-contempt his father heaped on him with constant criticism and hard fists. This land made him believe in his own worth.

So Wade didn't expect to have trouble keeping track of Glowing Sun.

But he did.

She was easy to follow for the first day. The only trail she could take was the one they'd been on.

He pushed his horse and hoped to close the gap between them. But once he was through the toughest passages, there were choices. Scared he'd choose wrong, Wade studied the ground often until he assured himself he was still on Glowing Sun's trail.

The Husband Tree

Buck had given him detailed directions to the Flathead camp, and Wade considered several times just riding straight for it as the second day stretched to three, then four. He could go to her village, stay back from it but remain watchful, and wait for Glowing Sun. All he needed was to see her arrive safely.

His common sense told him the woman was well equipped to survive in these rugged mountains.

But if he was so sure she'd be fine, then he might as well go throw in with Belle's cattle drive and be done with the wild-goose chase. His reason for following after Glowing Sun was to protect her. Abandoning her trail didn't figure in.

He swung to the ground, checking what looked like the pad of a moccasin on a stretch of damp forest soil, when his horse reared with a wild squeal and jerked the reins out of his hands. Wade made a dive for the suddenly frantic animal and managed to swing himself up onto the buckskin. Even with Wade's hand pulling hard on the reins, the horse ran nearly a hundred yards back in the direction they'd just come. Only then did Wade manage to halt his gelding. Snorting and wheeling, the horse must have been far enough from whatever upset him because, though he fidgeted, he let Wade take charge and hold him nearly in place.

"Wade!" A woman's voice. Glowing Sun.

Wade turned, trying to locate her.

The horse stopped and perked its ears forward.

A snarling grizzly lumbered out of a clump of quaking aspens near where Wade had stood just seconds ago.

His horse whinnied and backed away.

Wade patted the horse on the neck to show his thanks. As the bear charged forward a dozen feet, baring its teeth, Wade pulled his rifle from its sling on his saddle and snapped a shell in place.

The bear skidded to a stop. The wily animal had obviously seen and heard a gun before.

"Wade! Help!" She spoke English. Granted, it was only two

481

words, but he'd taught her those words. He didn't look away from
the roaring brute, but the direction of her voice told him Glowing
Sun was in the upper branches of a tree just behind the bear.
"Hang on. I'll. . .save you." Wade knew it was foolish, but he felt
himself grow taller when he shouted the words. His shoulders
squared, his chin lifted. Pathetic as it was, he had to grin as he
sighted down the length of his rifle.

Sorry, Lord. I know I've got a problem with rescuing women.
Most of 'em don't need rescuing one whit. But just maybe this one does.

The grizzly shook its head as if forbidding Wade to take a
shot.

Wade waited. If the old grizz didn't want a fight, it'd have to
turn tail and run.

With a furious roar. . .that's just what it did. The bear, nearly
as tall in the shoulders as Wade's horse, whirled and vanished into
the thickly wooded mountainside.

Wade wasn't about to go after the old monster, but he'd gotten
to know Glowing Sun well enough in their time together that
he reckoned if he waited too long she'd climb down from the
treetops and run. Trusting his mount, Wade waited until his horse
settled down before he approached.

She wasn't in the copse of aspens. He moved on into the forest,
watching the treetops, until he saw her peeking out between the
thinning leaves. Looking disgruntled, she sat on a branch so high
she should have had a nosebleed. The tree, an oak, magnificent
in its fall dressing of red leaves, nearly concealed her, but enough
leaves had fallen that he could catch a glimpse.

The claw marks told their story. The grizzly had followed her
up a long way, forcing her into the slender upper branches. She
clung there now, hanging on to the trunk so far up that the tree
bent under her weight.

When she saw him she gasped in relief. He saw her release
the trunk then frantically grab it back. Even as far up as she was,

The Husband Tree

Wade could see that terror had her in its grip.

"Just take one step at a time." He could see her whole body trembling.

"P–please. H–help." Her voice shook and Wade heard the tears making her voice waver. "W–Wade, help me!"

Wade didn't think the tree would hold both of them up that high, but the vulnerability in her usually strong voice forced his hand. Grimly determined to get her before she fell, he tied his horse to the tree, said a quick prayer that the grizzly had quit the country, and began climbing.

The ancient oak was as easy to scale as a staircase. It had limbs low to the ground. Probably why Glowing Sun had chosen it to escape the bear.

"Oak tree," Wade called up.

Maybe if she would talk, her panic would ease. Glowing Sun had been terrified when he'd first found her running from those men, but even then she'd been fighting mad.

How long had she been up here? Wade had set a slow pace. He couldn't guess how far ahead of him she'd gotten. It was possible she'd been treed overnight, even longer. She must be exhausted, her muscles cramped and cold.

"Oak tree," she answered, but her face was pressed to the bark, and he could barely hear her.

"I'm coming."

She risked a glance down and saw him, still with yards to go. But her eyes locked on his, and Wade saw relief. Then her gaze slid to the ground, so far below, and she turned back to the tree, her trembling arms clamped even more tightly around the trunk.

Wade felt like he was scaling a castle wall or climbing a prison tower. Very heroic. Very white-knightlike. He grinned and climbed faster. "Grizzly bear."

She looked down again and nodded wildly. "Grizzly bear." She put enough feeling in those words to fill a book.

Wade remembered his mother reading fairy tales to him when he was very young. *Rapunzel* was one of his favorites. Wade had pictured himself climbing to rescue the princess trapped in the tower. He remembered his father's unkindness to his mother, though he'd been very young when she died and wished he could have rescued her.

The reality of the bark under his hands and the maiden overhead furrowed his brow. *Did* he remember his mother? Maybe he just regarded everyone with the same cruelty his father did.

Wade shook his head and paid attention to his very own imprisoned princess. "I'm coming to save you, my little damsel in distress." He grinned at his nonsense. Glowing Sun would probably pull her knife on him and try to run away as soon as her feet hit the ground, so he might as well enjoy the moment.

Glowing Sun frowned, clearly not understanding his words. He noticed she didn't look away. Maybe if he just chattered she'd forget her long hours of terror.

"I know you must have been kidnapped from your family years ago. From your ma and pa."

Her forehead furrowed. "Ma? Pa?"

Wade moved up to the next branch. For the first time, the branch he stood on protested at holding his weight. The leaves had turned a stunning glorious red, and some fell as Wade jiggled branches. Still, he felt surrounded by God's glory in the middle of these leaves. "I'll slay the dragon for you, release you from your tower prison, and return you to your home." Wade's heart fluttered as the next branch he grabbed cracked. He spread his weight. A branch under each foot and one in each hand; he hoped the combination would hold him.

God, lift me up. Bear my weight.

Wade silently prayed with every move. The Bible was full of stories like that. And he decided maybe praying aloud would be for the best.

" 'The Lord is my shepherd; I shall not want.' "

The terror faded from Glowing Sun's eyes, and she focused on Wade in a new, sharper way. She said, " 'He maketh me to lie down in green pastures: he leadeth me beside the still waters.' "

"You know that verse?"

Glowing Sun looked at him as if she were irritated.

Wade wanted to laugh. He'd interrupted her. "I'm sorry."

"I forgive you."

The girl had definitely been raised as a Christian, both before and after she'd lived with the Flatheads.

She went on. " 'He restoreth my soul: he leadeth me in the paths of right–right–ness. . .' " Faltering, she quit and scowled.

" 'Righteousness for his name's sake.' "

Her voice joined his. " 'Yea, though I walk through the valley of the shadow of death, I will fear no evil.' "

This was about the most perfect verse they could have chosen for all Glowing Sun's troubles. His, too, more'n likely.

Wade thought of his father and how deeply the old man needed God. Wade had no doubt God had led his father in the path of righteousness. But Mort Sawyer had gone his own way.

While he was distracted by thoughts of his tyrannical father, Glowing Sun went on reciting. " 'For thou art with me; thy rod and thy staff they comfort me. Thou pre–pre. . .' " She stumbled over the words.

He added his voice. " 'Thou preparest a table before me in the presence of mine enemies.' "

It occurred to Wade that if he took Glowing Sun all the way home, he'd have to face an Indian tribe, and they weren't all friendly. He might well be asking God to prepare a table in the presence of his enemies before the day was out.

" 'Thou anointest my head with oil; my cup runneth over.' "

The branch under his left hand was about double the width of a pencil. It bent but didn't break. Wade moved as quickly as possible up the ever-narrowing trunk, hoping that if he didn't leave his weight on any one branch for long, it'd hold. Each one that broke or was even cracked would add to the challenge of getting back down.

" 'Surely goodness and mercy shall follow me all the days of my life: and I will dwell in the house of the Lord for ever.' "

And with those words, Wade's fear evaporated. Yes, God's goodness and mercy followed him. Since he'd found the Lord, he'd found the courage to leave his father's house, and his life had been so much better.

It gave him courage to know that if the worst happened and he and Glowing Sun fell, then they'd dwell in the house of the Lord forever. There was nothing to fear.

Considering Wade believed himself to be a coward, that was a powerful notion to settle in his heart.

He looked away from his handhold as he drew even with Glowing Sun's feet. She stared deep into his eyes. It was clear she understood the scripture and it had calmed her. He reached his hand up for hers. She reached down and held fast. Wade nodded, and Glowing Sun lifted a trembling foot from the slender twig it was perched on. She took her first step down.

He went lower. The trunk was leaning too far in one direction, and Wade shifted his weight so he was on the opposite side from Glowing Sun. He descended a step, then another. She came along.

Wade felt the violent trembling of her hand and suspected it was as much exhaustion as fear.

"Just about ten more feet down and we'll get to the strong branches."

Glowing Sun looked at him, confused.

Wade touched their joined hands to a branch between them. "Branch."

She smiled. "Branch. Oak tree branch."

Another step, then another, one more and Wade got his foot

on a sturdy limb for the first time. He breathed a sigh of relief. He descended until that sturdy limb was under his hand instead of his foot.

Glowing Sun sighed in an almost perfect imitation of him. Did she think he'd been teaching her that as a word?

He looked over at her and smiled. "We're safe now."

True, the ground was still fifty feet away, but they *were* safe.

A bit more climbing down and Wade felt Glowing Sun recover her courage. She let go of his hand, which Wade didn't like, but they made better time and were on the ground in just a few more minutes. When she landed beside him, light on her feet, he laughed. She smiled then threw her arms around his neck and laughed with him.

He lifted her and swung her around. "My very own damsel in distress. I've finally saved someone."

Her head dropped back as he whirled her around. Her wild, blond hair whipped in the fall breeze. A fluttering of crimson leaves rained on them as he lowered her to the ground and grinned down into her sky blue eyes.

Their gaze caught.

Wade's arms tightened involuntarily.

The smile faded from Glowing Sun's face, replaced by a fascination with his lips.

Suddenly his whole life made sense. He had a future, and he could see it. . .with Glowing Sun. They'd start their own ranch. They'd have beautiful little blond daughters as wild and courageous as their mother. He'd be a father and a husband. A strong, courageous man with God fully in his life.

He leaned down to kiss her.

"Not so fast."

The voice, accompanied by the *crack* of a jacked shotgun jerked Wade's head around.

CHAPTER 15

Every time she woke, Belle remembered Silas's kiss.

It was infuriating the way he'd ordered her around. But his bossiness warmed her heart, too. No man had ever cared enough to take his place at the head of her household. She'd hated it at the same time she felt drawn to that strength.

Belle woke up in the first light of dawn and didn't know who she was anymore. She was lying with Betsy in her arms, and the little girl was wriggling. That had no doubt awakened her. She looked around and saw Sarah quietly tending the fire. In the distance, Emma was filling the coffeepot with water from the stream. Lindsay was saddling her horse with help from Roy.

Since when did Lindsay need help saddling her horse?

Belle should get up and run that young whelp off, but Betsy swatted her in the face and fussed, and Belle put off rescuing her oldest daughter—who was surely fully capable of rescuing herself—and tended her youngest.

"Mornin', Ma." Sarah smiled. "I'm gonna gather more wood."

Belle nodded and got Betsy into a dry diaper then settled in with the fallen log at her back to get the baby her breakfast. Alone for a few moments, all Belle could think about was what Silas had made her feel.

God, I want more of that. I want his attention and his strength and even his bossiness. I want a man who cares enough to want to run his own family.

As she sat there, her child in her arms, memories of Anthony and Gerald and especially William crowded her thoughts. All the times she pushed them around and they'd just take it.

"They didn't care." Belle spoke to her baby, sad for the hard life she'd brought to her child. "They didn't care one whit if I liked them or respected them or loved them. Your pa was probably the worst of the lot, and that's saying something after Gerald, but he was a low-down coyote of a man. The only decent thing he ever did in his life was to give me you, beautiful girl."

And the giving had been dreadful, and it hadn't happened at all after the first time he came home smelling of another woman's perfume.

"They weren't men. To say they were children is an insult to you and my other girls, because they work hard and respect me and love me, and I them." Belle ran her hand over Betsy's lustrous curls. No, she couldn't love Anthony, couldn't stand the man, but she did adore this pretty baby.

Would Silas make babies as lovely?

Her head filled with images of her cooking for him and jumping to do his bidding, saying, "Yes, Silas," and, "Whatever you say, Silas." And letting him lead her away into the dark from any campfire they were ever near.

"I can actually imagine doing that." Betsy stared at Belle silently. Belle needed to talk to the baby more. Sing to her. Cradle her and rock her. She could do that, at least some, if she was really married to Silas. She yearned for that, and yet that wasn't who she was. Belle had learned to trust no man to take care of her. She'd learned to please herself, and any man could follow or get out of the way. They'd always been plenty willing.

She thought of the things Silas had said to Sarah yesterday about not marrying, and it occurred to Belle that, for the first time, she might have to do something to bring a man around. She'd never had to consider enticing a man before. She'd spent most of her life trying to discourage them. She had no practice in convincing a man he should propose.

"How does a woman fetch a man to marrying her, Betsy? I've never had to do such a thing in my life." She sat there thinking how to please Silas. Wondering how to dab a loop on this one particular man. She thought of his kisses and the stern way he'd dictated to her, and she wanted him to belong to her.

And he'd told Sarah he wasn't going to marry her. He'd said it like a man who knew his own mind.

So, did she catch him by being a submissive little wife? Or did she lasso him and toss him over her saddle and drag him to a preacherman?

The sharp cold of the morning made Belle wonder if they could get home before her mountain valley became locked away from the world for the winter. There had been snow already in the heights. She could see the white peaks from where she lay. She thought of her cattle back at her ranch and the ones on this trail and the extra help they now had, and forcing her mind to practical matters, she jiggled a burp out of Betsy and got to her feet to help build up the fire.

If she fussed with her hair a little longer than usual and started to make a couple of apple pies from the dried apples they packed along, well, that didn't have anything to do with snagging Silas. She just had time for once was all.

She was pulling the last pie out of the fire and had just started mixing hotcakes when Buck rode up in the first full light of morning. "Silas says we're pulling out. Shorty rode ahead and found good grazing not too far up the trail. We'll make a short day of it. He says your girls have been pushing too hard and need the rest."

Belle offered Buck a cup of coffee and a slice of pie. The man dismounted and ground-hitched his horse. He was taking a bite of the warm pie almost before the reins hit the dirt. Buck talked pleasantly of the good condition of the cattle, which warmed Belle's heart.

He polished off the pie within a couple of minutes. Then he got up reluctantly from the fire and said, "Mighty fine eatin', ma'am. Mighty fine. Thank you."

Belle knew an admiring look when she got one, because she'd gotten hundreds of them—thousands of them—in her life. But there was nothing improper in Buck's glance. It was just a look that said, *I'd marry you in a heartbeat just for this slice of pie if it wasn't for your husband.*

Belle could have corrected him. Yet her silence wasn't a lie.

I'm sorry, God. I know we're doing wrong.

He took one last swallow of coffee. "We'll be on the trail right after we eat. Silas said to tear down the camp."

"I'll have a proper breakfast of hotcakes ready in ten minutes then have the camp stowed away in half an hour. And tell the others there's pie and coffee to go with breakfast."

Buck laughed and tipped his hat. "It'll start a stampede, but I'll tell 'em, Miz Harden."

Belle fed the hands and had the strange sensation of being left out of the hard work. She didn't mind. It felt kind of nice to have time to make a meal special and pack up the camp for everyone. But it made her nervous to turn such a huge part of her life over to someone else. Even if the girls were riding along and watching out for the Tanner interests.

They started punching the herd along by midmorning and found the going easy. The sun rose high in the sky, but it didn't drive away the sharpness of the cold like it would have earlier in the season. There were narrow trails and some spots with bad footing, but those were less frequent than before.

With the three extra hands, Sarah never even forked a horse to tend the herd but just stayed with the packhorses, seeing to Betsy. And the older girls got a long break during the day.

Silas found the water and grazing Shorty had spoken of early. They made good enough time that they could set up a camp and get a meal on with some light left in the sky.

Lindsay came riding in just a few minutes after the others, and she was alongside of Roy. The two of them seemed to be talking and smiling at each other. Belle felt a pang of dread in her stomach to think a boy had caught her little girl's interest. She had to control the urge to fetch her skillet.

There was plenty of dead wood at hand, and they built a huge, roaring fire to ward off the ever-increasing chill. Shorty had brought a haunch of bighorn sheep back from his scouting, and they broiled mutton steaks over the fire and had fresh-baked bread instead of the usual sourdough biscuits. And they ate the last of Belle's pie.

Shorty had a fine singing voice, and he started in on one song after another, finally lifting himself off the comfortable softness of the pine boughs they gathered for bedding to stand the first watch.

The days fell into a rhythm after they had cowhands. Although Belle rode out every day, she did little more than take a couple of circuits around the slowly plodding animals and go back up front to the string of pack animals. As the trip stretched out and the responsibility eased more and more from her shoulders, Belle felt herself relax more completely than she had in years. She took pleasure in cooking good meals, with lots of help from the increasingly idle girls. She relished the time she had to cuddle Betsy in her arms. She accepted Silas's strong arms around her every night and the sweet kisses he insisted were necessary for the sake of the cowhands. That didn't exactly make sense to her, especially since he often kissed her when none of the men were around. But she trusted him, so if he said a kiss or two was necessary, she went along. Then they went to their separate sides of the camp.

They had a few more days of needle-sharp peaks to scale, but with Buck, Roy, and Shorty helping, they went smoothly. Belle took on the job of scouting the trail. She rode ahead with the camp gear, chose a site, and set up early, without eating a drop of dust.

The twenty-fifth day on the trail, Belle descended a high peak well ahead of the others, with Betsy on her back and Sarah by her side, and saw the raw little town of Helena that had been named the territorial capital just recently. From their high perch, they could see many miles across the lower mountainside and the sweeping valley around the town. But it was close, so they'd be there in two days. One day if they pushed hard.

They'd made it. She'd gotten her herd to market. She'd saved her ranch. Joy caught so hard in Belle's throat she almost cried, which was too embarrassing to contemplate. Choking back the pride at making this trek successfully, she scouted out a spot to bed down the cattle for what might be their last night on the trail.

She and Sarah pushed past several likely camping sites as she longed to get her cattle as close as possible to trail's end. They finally found a lush valley so beautiful it awakened a longing in Belle to own it.

"We'll camp here." Belle looked at Sarah, and they smiled at each other.

"This is a beautiful place, Ma." Sarah looked around almost reverently.

A tumbling stream poured out of a fissure in one of the snowcapped mountain peaks that stood like sentinels around the valley. The creek cut across the lowest spot in the valley and spilled down a ledge and out of sight.

"Look up there." Belle pointed overhead. "A bald eagle." It

screamed as it soared around the cliff sides, catching updrafts and diving for what looked like pure joy.

A herd of bighorn sheep spotted them and leaped up the mountainside so gracefully that they might have been flying. Grass grew belly deep to her horse, and the woods didn't encroach onto the grass except in a few places, where they formed islands of shade around the babbling creek.

"I'd never part with my ranch. But this is as close as I've ever been tempted. I believe that if I'd seen this mountain valley first, I might have picked it for myself." She rode her horse around until she found a sheltered spot up against the mountain that would cut the icy, north wind and reflect the heat of their fire back to them when the night grew cold. She did the first stages of her setup for camp, started a rising of bread, hobbled her pack animals, and turned them loose. Then she and Sarah started back up the trail, finding Silas.

"I want to push farther tonight."

"There's no need, Belle." Silas had that gruff, bossy tone she was starting to love. "We'll be in Helena in just a couple of days."

"I found good grass."

Silas looked at the lowering sun and the ample grass along the trail where they now stood. "Belle. . ."

She smiled and rode her horse right over to him, thinking of a few times he'd persuaded her to do his bidding with a well-timed kiss. She decided to try that for herself. "Please, Silas. I've already set the camp up. It'll be hard work to go all that way and tear things down."

She leaned forward, caught the front of his shirt in a fist, and pulled him toward her. He came along so willingly she knew she had him.

By the time she was done kissing him, she'd've probably, judging by the stunned look on his face, been able to convince him to drive the herd all the way into Helena without stopping.

The Husband Tree

God forgive me, I'm wheedling just like a woman.

Belle was half horrified at herself, half elated to know she possessed such a skill. Manipulative, too, as if Silas was saving her work by driving himself into the night.

"We can go farther if it'll make things easier for you." Silas had a heavy-lidded look in his eyes and a strange, satisfied smile on his face.

But Belle was pleased, too. She wondered if she looked just like him.

There was still a bit of dusk left when the thousand head of cattle waded into the grass. She looked at Silas, and he smiled. It was a sweet moment, an intimate moment, shared by the two of them alone. Well, alone except for four children, three drovers, and one thousand cattle.

But sweet.

CHAPTER 16

I wonder if it's been claimed," Silas muttered.

Belle heard him and had a flash of worry. Was he thinking of leaving her? He'd been adamant to Sarah that morning about not getting married. Maybe he'd finish the drive, stake a claim, and come straight back here to live forever.

"Great location," Buck said. "A short ride to the territorial capital."

"But still wilderness," Shorty said, as if *wilderness* was the same word as *heaven*.

Belle noticed that Roy didn't join in the talk. He was sitting on his horse, alongside Lindsay, as he'd taken to doing all the time. They were apart from the group, talking quietly.

Belle marveled at her daughter's shy smiles and easy conversation with the boy. Belle knew Silas kept an eye on the two youngsters. She'd suggested it, and the serious look in Silas's eyes as he agreed wholeheartedly helped Belle put her concerns in Silas's capable hands.

Silas hadn't let the men go out riding herd with the girls for the first few days, but Belle could see that he'd eased his watchfulness after a bit, and Belle allowed it because she trusted Silas's judgment.

Lindsay and Roy put up their horses. Belle was busy bending over her coffeepot, and when she straightened, she noticed the two were gone. Curious and uncomfortable with their budding friendship, Belle headed into the wooded area near where their horses stood grazing. She wandered without a direction for a time. Then she rounded a thicket and came upon Roy kissing Lindsay.

"Roy! Lindsay!" Belle cried.

The two of them jumped apart.

Lindsay tried to say something, but her face went crimson and she brushed her hands over her skirt and hair. Finally, to get her hands to stop fidgeting, she clenched them in front of her.

"I reckon I owe you an apology, Miz Harden. I just. . .Lindsay and me. . .we were only. . ." Roy's voice faded to nothing, and he lifted his hat and pulled it forward on his head until it shaded his eyes.

"Roy, you go back to camp right now," Belle ordered.

"Miz Harden, please don't take none of this out on Lindsay." He laid his hand on Belle's daughter's shoulder, and Belle wished for her skillet. "She's a fine girl and I wouldn't shame her. Nothin' happened. We were talking and. . ."

"Roy!" Belle cut him off and crossed her arms. "I'll leave your father to talk with you. Right now I'd like a word with my daughter. Alone!"

Roy looked at Lindsay, who glanced at him then looked back at the ground. Roy started to the camp. He had to walk past Belle to get there. When he was only a few feet in front of Belle, he stopped and pushed his hat back. "Lindsay and me. . .I know we're young, ma'am, but we have decided we're gonna get hitched."

He'd have done less harm if he'd punched Belle right in the stomach. "No you are not. Now go!"

MARY CONNEALY

She jabbed her finger behind her.

He didn't budge.

"I'll say my piece first. If you're mad, then yell at me, not Lindsay. She's a good girl, and I haven't behaved in a dishonorable way to her." Roy looked Belle square in the eye.

Although he was young, Belle was reluctantly impressed with his desire to take whatever anger Belle might have upon himself to protect Lindsay.

"We're getting married in Helena tomorrow if we get into town early enough."

"You are not!" Belle interrupted.

Roy kept talking as if she hadn't spoken. "If not tomorrow, then the next day. I haven't talked to my pa yet, but if he's agreeable, the two of us will stake claims, along with Shorty, that would cover this whole valley. Pa and I talked about the claims some, but I didn't say a thing about Lindsay because I hadn't spoken to her yet. But now Lindsay has said she'll marry me. We'll set up our own spread here if the valley isn't claimed. If not here, then somewhere else close by. We've ridden through some likely spots."

Belle's heart pounded harder with every word. Roy was determined and Belle was terrified.

"I had just convinced her to say yes when you came upon us. That kiss is the first and the last one she'll get from me before we're married. I love Lindsay, ma'am, and I respect her too much to dishonor her."

Belle's mind unwillingly skittered to the way Silas and she had kissed. Without intention to marry. *That* had been dishonor. As their lies about being married had been. Roy's behavior was better than Belle's.

"I'll always see to her safety and happiness above my own. I promise you that."

Roy stared at Belle for a moment longer, and Belle saw clearly that he wished she'd say something so they'd have her blessing...

498

or at least her permission, however grudgingly given. Belle just couldn't do it. At last he nodded his head firmly and walked on past her without further comment.

Belle turned to Lindsay who was still fixated on the ground. Belle chided, "Lindsay."

Lindsay looked up from the ground then stared past Belle's shoulder. Belle could tell the minute Roy disappeared from sight, because Lindsay suddenly had a huge grin on her face, and with a few running steps, she crossed the distance between them and threw her arms around Belle's neck. "Oh, Ma, I never knew how it could be. I know now why you keep marrying the low-down varmints." Lindsay laughed then pulled back to arm's length to look at Belle. "Only Roy isn't no varmint. He's a good 'un. He is, isn't he?" Lindsay asked fiercely. "He will treat me right and work hard. I'm as old as you were when you got married. And I think his pa will stay with us, so it won't be the two of us alone in the world like it was with you and my pa."

"Lindsay, you're only fifteen—" Belle began somberly.

"I'm sixteen in a few months, Ma," Lindsay interjected. "You were fifteen when you married my pa. And now you have Silas." Lindsay's voice dropped to a whisper. "I haven't told Roy about him not bein' my real pa, and I won't until after you and Pa are married. Roy won't mind, but I don't want I should embarrass you none, what with all your kissing and such."

Belle was struck speechless by the way Lindsay so casually mentioned the. . .the play acting she and Silas had been doing. Silas had said he'd talked to her, but what had he really said?

"I wouldn't want to leave you with no help," Lindsay went on. "But with Pa around, you'll be okay. Aren't you happy for me, Ma? I love Roy so!" Lindsay wrapped her arms around Belle's neck again and almost strangled her with her enthusiasm. She seemed oblivious to Belle's dismay. She was walking on a cloud and couldn't believe anyone could be less than thrilled.

Well, Belle was a whole lot less. "You're too young to get married."

Lindsay laughed. "I'm young, I know. So's Roy. But we're old enough to start a life together. Roy will be tellin' his pa right now." Lindsay turned toward the camp, grabbed Belle's hand in hers, and towed her along. "I want to go stand by his side when Roy tells him, like Roy stood by me."

Belle couldn't think what to say. Hoping and praying Buck or Silas would talk some sense into the young couple, she went along.

They got to camp in time to see Buck shaking Roy's hand and laughing. Silas was standing beside the father and son, looking very serious.

Belle met his eyes as soon as she saw him and knew he was of the same opinion she was. She went straight to his side, and as soon as Buck's hearty congratulations were finished, Silas said bluntly, "Belle and I think Roy is a good boy, Buck. But how can he marry Lindsay when he doesn't have so much as a roof over his head?" Silas's curt announcement brought the festive mood to an abrupt halt.

"Now we. . .we *might* agree to Roy courting Lindsay, but we want him to have a start for the two of them before there's any wedding.

"I have an idea that might work," Silas continued. "Why doesn't Roy come on home with us? He's too young to stake a claim to any land, but he could court Lindsay proper, get to know her this winter. Buck, you and Shorty can stake a claim. In the spring, Roy can come and help you start a herd. When he's twenty-one and old enough to claim some land, he and Lindsay can get married."

"I do the work of a man right now," Roy objected. "Age is just a number you write on paper. I'll stake my claim now and prove up on it by the time I'm twenty-one. That's five years from now. We're not waiting that long. We're not waiting another week!"

"Well, son"—Silas tilted his hand low over his eyes—"maybe you don't need to wait *five* years to marry, but you could wait say...two years. Lindsay's only fifteen. She's not—"

"Ma was fifteen when she got married," Lindsay interrupted. "I'll be sixteen in a couple of months. And Roy is going to be a lot better for me than—"

"Lindsay!" Silas cut off Lindsay's yelling and threw her a warning look. Lindsay covered her mouth before she blurted out something about Belle having a different husband than Silas all those long years ago.

Then a gleam appeared in Lindsay's eyes that made Belle nervous. "And how old were you, Pa? You and Ma are about the same age. Ma was fifteen and you were...sixteen if I remember. Same age as Roy. And you had nothing or the next thing to it. Didn't you say, Ma, that Grandpa Tanner gave you two hundred dollars and the two of you set out and crossed practically the whole country? Ran fifty cattle across most of the Rockies because you'd heard of the gold strike in Helena and heard they were hungry for beef and paying prime dollar for it?"

Belle felt Silas clutch her hand tightly. She said, "We did start out that way, Lindsay. That's why we know it's hard. I'd like something better for you."

Buck added his voice to the mess. "The boy and I talked about claiming that high valley. The two of us'll do it, and Shorty will throw in and get himself another one hundred and sixty acres right next to it. We've been riding the grub line long enough. We can have a roof over our heads by snowfall, and I can make it tight and comfortable. I've got enough money to buy a few head of cattle to start up a herd, and with all of us working together, we'll be okay. Now, I know they're young. But folks marry young out here. My Caroline and I were settled young, and I think that's the best way to do it. Having Lindsay with us, well, that would make starting a home something worth doing. Silas, I'd help Roy take care of your girl. You have my word on it."

"Maybe in the spring we can—"

"I don't want to wait until spring. . .*Pa*," Lindsay said with clenched fists.

Belle heard the threat in Lindsay's voice, but she wasn't going to let her daughter threaten her into doing something Belle thought was wrong, no matter how much disgrace she brought down on her own head. Silas squeezed her hand again before Belle could angrily confess their lies. She looked sideways at him.

"Folks *do* settle young out here, Belle." Silas looked over at Lindsay and said with open longing, "I don't want to let her go. I wanted to spend more time with our girl. I'm not ready to give her up. But however much we don't like it, Roy's a good boy, and Buck and Shorty will be there to take care of her."

Lindsay's eyes filled with tears as Silas spoke. She took two uncertain steps then ran the short distance between them and threw her arms around Silas's neck. "I don't want to leave you either, Pa. I love you."

Lindsay cried into Silas's neck, and he hugged her tight. Then Lindsay let go of Silas and turned to cling to Belle.

"I love you, Ma. I don't want you to be unhappy, but my heart is telling me to go with him. You know I do the work of an adult woman. I have for years. I *am* an adult woman. And adult women get married. What I feel for Roy—it's so strong and good, I don't want to let him go, not even for the winter."

Belle looked over Lindsay's shoulder to meet Silas's eyes.

Silas seemed to have made up his mind for both of them.

Belle felt a scream gathering deep in her belly.

Wade shoved Glowing Sun behind him as he whirled around.

It was one of the men who'd held her captive. With a shotgun out and level and cocked.

A distressed moan came from Glowing Sun.

Wade didn't move his hand toward his gun. This man had the

draw on him, and not even a fast draw—which Wade wasn't—could beat a pointed shotgun.

You wouldn't be able to pull the trigger anyway, coward.

An inner voice reminded Wade he was a weakling. He'd been no different before he turned his life over to God, but the cowardice had tormented him back then because his measure of a man was whether he had the guts to kill. Now Wade found comfort in knowing he didn't have a killer instinct. He'd shoved away the knowledge of his yellow belly and mostly forgotten it.

Until now.

Now, when his ability to pull the trigger might be the difference between life and death, not for himself, but for the woman he'd just realized he loved—that taunting voice came back and reminded him he had no guts.

"Move away from the girl." The man stayed across the small clearing, well out of reach but not so far he could miss with a shotgun.

"We're going back to her village." Trying to talk sense to the man, Wade saw the viciousness in the gunman's eyes.

"I've given her the choice whether to live with her Flathead family or not, and she's chosen them." Wade knew he intended to try harder to convince her. If he'd kissed her, held her, spoken of love and marriage, would she stay in his world? If she wanted him to, would he join hers? If her tribe would allow it, Wade knew he'd go with Glowing Sun.

"That ain't no choice. She's wild. She don't have the sense to pick right. She's going with me. I want her, and she'll be mine." The greedy, hungry eyes told Wade that this man wasn't interested in rescuing Glowing Sun at all. He had terrible plans for her.

Something hardened inside of Wade…pushed out the taunting voice and brought his courage forward in a way he'd never felt. He could do it. To save Glowing Sun from the dreadful fate this man had in mind, he could pull the trigger.

Dear God, help me protect her. Help me save her.

Wade knew he would die for this. This man would get his gun fired first. But Wade would take that lead shot and still get his own gun into play. He'd give his life to protect this beautiful woman.

"Please, just go." Wade had to try reason again. "I won't let you take her."

Cruelty leeched through the man's laughter.

Wade flexed his fingers, close to his holster, but not close enough. The man raised his gun.

Wade slapped leather. A shot rang out before Wade could get his hand on his gun.

So intent on rescuing Glowing Sun, Wade fought through the expected impact. He pulled his gun and leveled it—to see the man drop to his knees.

Stunned, suddenly aware that no bullet had struck him, Wade watched the man fall, and as he dropped, Wade saw a man behind him holding a smoking pistol. The saddle partner who'd helped capture Glowing Sun to begin with.

The man slipped his six-gun into his holster and raised his hands. "Don't shoot."

Wade realized he had his gun leveled straight at the man's heart. He lowered his weapon.

"I knew he was up to no good." The man walked up to his partner and prodded him with his toe. "We split up right after you'd taken the girl back. I'd only been riding with him for a couple of weeks since we finished a cattle drive. I didn't like the way he treated the girl, but I thought it was right to take her back to her own people, so I went along."

"He wasn't here to return her to anyone." Wade felt his hand begin to tremble. He hadn't needed to take that shot, but he knew, deep in his gut, that he would have. He should have been proud of that. Instead, he felt changed, scarred, ashamed. "He wanted her for himself."

"I heard. And I'd figured it out myself. He was loco to beat all when you took her. Way too hornet mad to explain him wantin' to help her."

"Thank you. You saved my life. You saved both of us."

The other man nodded. "I'll stay to bury him. Reckon I can do that one thing for him. You go along and take the girl home."

Wade nodded then looked once more at the man who now lay still and lifeless on the ground. It was awful to kill a man. A terrible thing to carry on your soul. Wade thanked God he didn't have to do it. Knowing he would have done it was burden enough.

He prayed silently for the man who did take that shot.

Then he turned.

In time to see Glowing Sun vanish into the woods.

Chapter 17

Belle didn't scream. Mainly because she took one look in Lindsay's eyes and knew it would do no good.

It wasn't just determination, though there was plenty of that. In fact, more than determination, Lindsay just had a solid, settled look that said she was getting married. With or without Belle's blessing.

Belle could go along or be trampled, so the only real choice Belle had here was in how much she hurt her relationship with Lindsay.

But even that wasn't the look that stopped Belle in her tracks. Lindsay was in love. It shone out of her.

For one second, Belle remembered how she'd felt about William at the very beginning. No one could have stopped her. And William wasn't half the man Roy was. Whether Belle liked it or not, her daughter was getting married.

Silas's firm hold on Belle's hand grew tighter until he might have been the only thing holding her up. Belle gave one hard jerk of her chin, and that was all she could manage.

Lindsay laughed and threw herself into Roy's arms as joyfully as if Belle had clapped and yelled with delight at this wedding. A bright girl, Lindsay knew this was the best she was going to get from her man-hating ma.

"Let's get settled for the night so we can get into Helena in time to sell these cattle tomorrow." Silas kept hold of Belle's hand and dragged her away from the tight circle of people talking and laughing and planning.

As Belle moved, she landed her eyes on Emma.

She saw frightened eyes. And Emma never showed fear. Belle tried to tug loose of Silas, but rather than let her go, Silas let himself be dragged to Emma's side.

"What's she doing this for, Ma?" Emma let Belle slide her arm around her waist. Looking past Emma, Belle saw Sarah tending the campfire with Betsy on her back. Sarah was crying and salting the stew with her tears.

And why shouldn't they be terribly upset? Belle had spent all her years as a mother filling her girls' heads full of dire warnings about men.

"Lindsay will be okay, girls." Belle didn't believe it, but she tried to sound convincing. "Roy's a good man."

A boy. A young one at that. God, how did this happen? I'm losing my daughters. She's starting her life out as bad as I did. All my warnings and she up and marries the first man her age she's ever seen.

Emma didn't answer.

Sarah kept stirring.

Silas led them back to the campfire in the dusk. "He is a good man, Belle. I've taken his measure, and I trust him to do right by our girl."

It was no comfort. The man who wanted to hold her and kiss her but didn't want marriage earned no trust in Belle's book.

"I'll make the best of it." Belle pulled away from Silas. "And so will Lindsay. That's all a woman can do in this life."

Silas gave her a long look. Then he nodded. "That's all any of us can do, Belle." He strode toward his horse. "I'm going to ride a circuit. I'll be back in time for supper."

They drove the herd up to Helena late the next night and held them on the flatland south of town.

"Shorty and I're gonna go into town and hunt cattle buyers." Silas's voice from behind her turned Belle around.

He'd quit with his kissing nonsense ever since Lindsay and Roy had announced their engagement. Belle was too upset to miss it.

Truth was, Belle had come to think of Silas as Lindsay's pa, looking to him whenever her doubts were too much for her. His shared concern gave her strength. He quietly assured her that allowing the marriage was the only real choice. That alone kept her from screaming.

It occurred to Belle to protest Silas handling the sale of her cattle. But she trusted him. It was that simple. "Thank you. I'll get the camp set up and have supper waiting when you get back."

"We could be late."

"We'll expect you when we see you then." Belle was struck by this quiet, reasonable conversation. She couldn't remember talking with any of her husbands like this. She gave orders. They followed them or lit out to hide until mealtime. There was no relaxed discussion of plans and duties. Silas was a good man. She'd finally found one.

And he wanted no part of marriage.

Silas rode off with Shorty.

Belle watched Lindsay and Roy sharing every chore, whispering, excited.

"Let me get that." Buck came to where she was dipping water from a quiet stream. He reached for a bucket she already had filled.

"You know they're too young." Belle scooped the water without looking at the man.

Buck took the pail from her and straightened, holding both, leaving her hands free.

Why had she never been able to find a man who would work beside her?

"I know they're young. I do. But my son does a man's work every day. He's honest, with no vices. I've raised him to be a Christian, and he's taken it to heart. He'll give full weight to his marriage and keep his vows. And I've never seen him so happy. He's got a powerful love for your daughter."

Belle heard a twinge of resentment in Buck's voice. Resentment aimed at Belle because she wasn't excited about Roy marrying Lindsay. The two of them turned to watch Lindsay and Roy in the distance, chattering and smiling as they rode a circle around the herd.

"It's not about Roy." Belle looked seriously at Buck. "He's a fine young man. You know I like him. It's just. . .I married so young. The work was hard and relentless. I wanted my daughter to be a child for a little longer."

"I've been riding with you for two weeks now. Lindsay's already not a child. She works her heart out for you. I wouldn't be surprised if her life with us was easier than her life with you."

"Most likely will be." Belle sighed. "Her life with me is hard, but it's. . .safe. I love her and treat her with respect."

"I won't—"

Belle held up her hand. "I'm not insulting you, Buck. I promise I'm not. It's not you and Roy and Shorty. I'd feel this way no matter who staked a claim on my girl's heart. I can't stop this wedding, but I think I'm allowed to hurt a little having to let my girl go."

Smiling, Buck nodded as they turned together and walked toward the camp. "How about next spring, as soon as calving is done and the snow melts, I send Lindsay and Roy over for a visit. Say the first of June. They can stay for two weeks."

Belle thought of her ramshackle cabin and wondered where

they'd sleep. Maybe Silas would help her add a room. No, Silas would be gone. He'd sell these cattle and ride away. Her hurt over Lindsay multiplied by her hurt over finally caring about a man.

She was tempted to tell Buck the truth, not wanting falsehood between her and Lindsay's new family. But even that was beyond her as she watched Lindsay and Roy and ached for what lay ahead for her daughter.

Buck didn't wait for Belle to agree to the visit. He seemed to be satisfied that he'd had his say. He set down the water. "I'll go spell Emma."

Belle's other girl rode the far side of the herd. Sarah puttered around the camp, going about business as usual, talking and being herself. Belle wished herself eight years old again, without a care in the world. . .except for feeding nine people every day using scant supplies and an open fire, of course.

Emma rode in.

Belle went to her quiet, horse-crazy daughter.

Emma hadn't said much about losing her big sister. Of course, Emma was quiet in the normal course of things. But she'd been even more so today.

"We'll miss her, won't we?"

Emma kept busy stripping the leather off her horse. "I reckon we will."

"She'll be okay, you know."

Emma shrugged then looked up at Belle. "Running the Tanner Ranch took all our energy every day. How can we get by without her? Will Silas stay?"

"I don't figure that Silas will stay, no. We talked about marriage, Emma. Silas isn't interested."

Emma shook her head. "The two of you act married already. Why doesn't he want us, Ma?"

Belle didn't know what to say. She'd expected to talk about Lindsay, not Silas. But she'd known from the first that Emma and

Silas were close. Emma had opened up to him as she had to no other person. As for wringing a marriage proposal out of the man, Belle had no idea how. No man had ever *not* wanted her. "I don't know, Em. But he doesn't, and that's the end of it."

Emma's face crumpled, but she didn't cry. Belle didn't think Emma had cried since she was three years old. "I'll help get the meal." Emma walked away, her shoulders slumped, shut off from Belle and the whole world. She turned as she reached for the boiling coffeepot and stared at Lindsay and Roy for a minute before she poured herself a cup of the blazing hot brew.

Sarah hummed as she worked over a stew using the last of their jerked beef and potatoes. She mixed up sourdough biscuits and talked at Emma. Emma released Betsy from the pack on Sarah's back then fussed with her, teasing a smile out of the little one while she sipped her coffee.

Silas and Shorty didn't come back. The rest of them ate a quiet dinner, and the night sky spread over them and gleamed with a million stars. They all took to their bedrolls except Buck and Roy. Buck adamantly refused to let Emma ride a watch so close to a settlement where strangers might happen by, and he didn't believe it proper to let Roy stay in with the womenfolk alone.

Belle knew that no chaperone besides herself was necessary. She'd make such a strict watchdog Roy might not survive it.

After the men rode out, Belle heard singing wafting across the night air. The steady noise wasn't cattle drovers being whimsical, singing the cows to sleep. It covered strange night sounds apt to startle the herd. But it felt like a lullaby. Like a long-lost chance to be a child again and have her mother crooning over her, protecting her against all that was big and bad in the dark of the night.

That kind of safety had ended too soon for Belle with her mother's death. And now it was ending too soon for Lindsay.

In the sleepless night, Belle was left thinking of her father's cavalier dismissal of her when he had his long-desired son.

Thinking of William's unkindness after Belle's inheritance was lost.

Thinking of Gerald's drunkenness and his raised fists that she hadn't dodged nearly as often as she'd let on to her daughters. Too many times she'd stayed behind to give them a chance to run.

Thinking of Anthony's unfaithfulness and the way he flaunted it, shaming Belle as often and as publicly as he could.

Thinking of Silas and his strength and warmth. . .and rejection.

It wasn't fair to measure Roy with such a wretched yardstick, but it was the only one Belle had. She was giving her daughter over to a man because no other choice was forthcoming.

Belle lay on her side, stared into the crackling, glowing embers of the fire, and cried. Tears soaked into her sleeve where she rested her head on her arm. She was letting her firstborn go. With her tears, Belle came to see she'd accepted the situation. She was going to give Lindsay and Roy her blessing.

Crying silently, Belle fell asleep praying for life to be kinder to Lindsay than it had been to her.

Glowing Sun saw her chance and ran.

Her village was only miles away now. She was in territory she recognized. She was home.

But even as she dashed up a steep incline, she admitted she wasn't running from those evil men. She ran because she feared what Wade made her feel.

She had taken a direct route no horse could follow and had gone nearly a mile when the thudding of hooves sounded behind her. She didn't have to turn around to know he'd come. Wade, with his warm, kind eyes that spoke of dreams and a future, would always come.

And he'd take Glowing Sun away from the only world she understood.

Away from the man she'd promised herself to. She couldn't betray that promise, even if now the thought of marrying Wild Eagle frightened her. How could she marry him when she'd been willing—no, eager—for Wade to kiss her?

She didn't dart into the woodlands or scale the rocks. She'd been riding with Wade long enough to know he wouldn't stop until he caught her. He'd want to hold her again.

She didn't think she could say no.

Finally, as she ran alongside a trickling brook, the horse drew up beside her and she stopped. Turning, she saw Wade rein in his horse and swing down to the ground with a jingle of spurs and the creak of leather. "You're safe. That man is dead." He said it with such kindness, as if she were running for her life, not from her emotions.

Glowing Sun nodded. Much of her white language had come back to her as they'd talked. "Safe" she knew. "Dead" she knew.

Wade dropped his reins to the ground, which kept his well-trained horse in place. The animal turned its muzzle to the crystal stream and drank noisily.

Coming until they stood toe to toe, he tipped his hat back so his eyes weren't shaded and smiled down at her. "The saddle partner, the other man who held you prisoner, took care of the outlaw who got the drop on us. He's a decent man who means you no harm. He's not following us. You're safe now."

Those words meant the world to her. Except she was only safe from that man, not from Wade. Not from herself.

"Go home to Salish village." Glowing Sun nodded.

Wade shook his head. "Stay."

Glowing Sun understood that, too. "Home."

"Come home with *me*. Marry me, Glowing Sun. I love you."

She understood every word. She loved him, too. But his world frightened her. His world had killed her white family, and it threatened her Indian family every day. And she'd made promises. "No."

Wade smiled. "Yes. Please."

"Thank you." That wasn't exactly right, except in her heart the words were perfect because she was so thankful a man as fine as Wade wanted her.

Cradling her hands in his, he dropped down on one knee. Glowing Sun had no idea what that meant. She only knew it looked like begging. Such a proud man, so strong, so courageous, and she was making him beg. She felt shame and tugged on his hands.

"I love you. I know we haven't known each other long. . ." He fell silent, struggling.

Glowing Sun knew he searched for simple words that made sense to her.

"Time." He swiped at his hat and threw it to the ground beside them and his eyes gleamed with hope. "Give me time. Come back to *my* village. I've got a safe place you can stay until you. . .you're. . . uh. . .until you love me, too. My friends, the Dawsons, will let you stay there, safe. We can get to know each other better. Please just give me a chance."

He seemed so sure. And why wouldn't he be? He'd held her after he'd guided her down from the tree, felt her respond, felt her longing to kiss him. What else could a man think?

Glowing Sun pulled harder on his hands, and he stood, as if he'd do anything she asked of him, devote his life to pleasing her.

Wild Eagle wasn't a man like this. He wouldn't think of her pleasure. He was strong, harsh even, a great warrior who would give her strong sons. An Indian woman wanted that in her husband.

Not this softness, the kind eyes and sweetness and concern. Glowing Sun's heart ached to think she'd have none of this in her life.

Wade stood before her, waiting.

"I have remembered much white words." She squeezed his hands, wishing he would let go. Wishing she could want him to.

The Husband Tree

"Abby. Abigail. My white name. My family dead. Fever. I—ten. Ten summers. Salish father found me. Took me from house of death. Went to Salish village."

"They saved you." Wade smiled, listening to every word.

Had Wild Eagle ever listened to her this way?

"I have to go home. To my Salish village. I—" She fumbled for the right word. "Promised. I would keep my promises to my people." Her heart cut like a knife, each beat a stab to her chest. "No, Wade. I will not marry you. No." She had to force the next breath through the thickness of tears clogging her throat. "Thank you."

Wade shook his head as if her words made no sense.

Perhaps they didn't. Perhaps she'd spoken them wrong.

"Come home with me. Marry me. I love you."

Glowing Sun jerked her hands free, shaking her head. She took two steps backward, planning to run. He'd catch her. Maybe his arms would wrap around her. Maybe he'd kidnap her this time and force her to do the thing she wanted most—be with him.

The betrayal of Wild Eagle and her people wouldn't be her choice then. She could live with the decision if Wade made it for her.

She took another step, and joyfully, she braced to have her future decided for her. . .by Wade.

CHAPTER 18

Belle was barely aware of it when Silas came back to camp, ate quickly, and crawled into a bedroll on the far side of the fire. She should have gotten up and asked about the sale, but her head ached from her tears, and she was groggy and stupid with exhaustion.

When morning came, there was no time for sorrow or second thoughts.

Silas got twenty-five dollars a head for the cattle. Cash money. He'd ridden back to camp with twenty-five thousand dollars in his saddlebags and slept light with his shotgun close to hand.

Riders came and drove the herd away before breakfast.

Silas took charge of the morning camp. "We've got to see to the wedding then hit the trail for home before the mountain passes close up on us. Let's go into town."

"I'll see to the preacher," Belle said.

Silas doused the barely smoldering fire. "Let's meet at the Cattleman's Diner for lunch and have the wedding right afterward. We can start making tracks before the day is done."

Which meant Silas was going back with her. Or was he going as far as Lindsay's valley? Maybe he planned to stake a claim there, too.

The Husband Tree

It didn't matter. With him or not, getting back home before her valley snowed shut for the winter was still a worry.

The men planned to head for the land office and stake their claims, sixteen-year-old Roy included.

Before they rode off, Belle pulled Silas aside. "I'm planning on buying some things to help Lindsay run a household. We'll have some cattle to herd and a wagonload of goods at least."

Silas nodded as if Belle was asking him permission, when in fact she was just warning him of more work. But she liked having him in agreement. He tugged on the brim of his hat. "Good thinking. Lindsay's earned a share of the herd, so don't be tightfisted." He rode off before Belle could punch him.

Belle and the girls went to the mercantile, and Belle went on a shopping spree.

"We need to set you up for housekeeping, Lindsay. It will be my wedding present to you and Roy."

"How do you do that, Ma?"

Belle realized that Lindsay had hardly ever been to a town. For their own safety, Belle had left the girls home when she'd bought supplies. And Belle had bought only the most basic goods, living off the land for the most part. Salt, sugar, flour, little else. Smiling, Belle said, "I'll show you."

She bought a winter's worth of food for four hungry people. There would be no garden supplying them, so she bought canned vegetables and fruit. Salt pork, salted fish, slabs of bacon and ham, and anything else that caught her fancy. Then she turned to yard goods for curtains and sheets and bed ticking, heavy cloth for winter clothes and lighter fabric for summer. She also found several ready-made dresses for Lindsay, since she wouldn't be coming home to pack, and several pairs of wool pants and flannel shirts for Roy. Belle also threw in new outfits for Buck and Shorty, worried that a man might not think of such things. Needles and thread, pails and tools. She added dishes and pots and pans, including, of course, a good-sized cast-iron skillet. She threw in an extra just to be on the safe side.

The list kept growing, but Belle didn't hesitate. Nor did she restrict herself to household goods. She found a livery that sold her two teams of oxen and two big freight wagons to carry the ever-growing load.

Belle found chickens and a milk cow with a calf and a pair of suckling pigs, though they were expensive. She bought a fine Hereford bull and ten head of cows.

She'd spent nearly five thousand of her twenty-five thousand dollars before midday.

She ordered the supplies loaded then headed for the land office to buy several tracts of land. She already controlled them because of her water rights. She also owned the passes into the valley, so she could block anyone else from entering. She considered the land hers, but she wanted a clear title. Pointing to a map, she described the acres she wanted to the slender clerk.

Wire-rimmed glasses perched on his hawkish nose. His skin had a pallor that said he rarely stepped outside. "All of this is fine except for this one parcel. Someone staked a claim on it." He indicated the high valley where she'd lost track of so many cattle last spring. "I'm sorry, but that's already taken."

"But there's not water up there. I own the springs and the gap into the valley. No one can live there."

The man shrugged. "I didn't quibble with the buyer. I expect a man to know what he's claiming. Maybe once your new neighbor finds out the lay of the land, he'll sell to you."

Belle's heart pounded at the thought of some man invading her home. "Who bought it? Is he here in Helena?"

"Now, ma'am, I can't tell you any of this." The land agent lifted his nose at her. "It's not my business to go blabbing about land sales. Trouble can come of it."

Belle fought the urge to grab the smug man by his shirtfront.

She'd show him trouble. "Just give me a name. I'll ask around and see if he's still in town."

"I'll figure out what you owe for the rest of this property, though it's irregular to sell to a woman." The haughty tone grated on Belle's already-shredded temper.

Clamping her mouth shut, Belle produced the note she'd carried for years from her lawyer, giving her authority over the fund she'd created for her daughters. That authority granted her the right to buy land.

The man sniffed but let the sale go through.

As she signed the papers and handed over her money, she thought of that piece she wanted most, a high valley that stretched itself down almost to her ranch house, the one that she used for a summer range. Fear twisted Belle's stomach. She had used that valley for sixteen years.

When she produced five thousand in cash, the land agent was slightly less rude. The purchase brought her holdings to over twenty thousand acres. A lot of it was rugged and next to useless. Still, it connected her ranch into one solid block of property.

She walked out of the land office shaken from leaving it too late to get hold of the high valley. Her cattle could winter over in it, unless she got home to find a settler had moved in already, but she'd have to cull the herd sharply again next year or she'd hurt her range from overgrazing.

Whoever lived there would be a close neighbor and might dispute some of the water rights Belle owned. The titles were all clearly in her hands. But the law didn't mean much when you lived as far out as Belle. Strength held land more than a deed. She could only hope that whoever her new neighbor was, he would be friendly. With a clenched jaw, she wondered if she'd be able to keep the buyer out by refusing permission to cross through the gap. But that gap was a fair ride from home, and she couldn't guard it day and night.

With her grazing land reduced, that meant a repeat of this blasted cattle drive next year. With a catch in her throat, she realized it also meant she'd get to visit Lindsay. If Lindsay and Roy came for a visit in the spring and Belle drove past their valley later in the summer, she'd see her daughter twice this year. Only twice.

Only years of self-discipline kept Belle from crying her heart out.

Her girls quietly followed her out of the office. They'd sat waiting on a bench near the front door, out of earshot. Belle didn't share her worry with them. Emma would have to know eventually, but why burden Lindsay with these problems? She'd soon enough have her own.

"Now we'll go see about the preacher."

Lindsay giggled. Emma rolled her eyes. Sarah bounced Betsy and tickled her chin.

Everything was in order in time for lunch at the Cattleman's Diner. Lindsay was wearing a new dress, and they'd all cleaned up, though Belle refused to buy a skirt that wasn't split for riding, so she knew she probably still looked like a cowhand.

As Belle slipped into her chair, she announced, "The wedding is right after we eat. The parson will be waiting for us at the church."

Roy sat next to Lindsay, looking at her with a gleam of joy. The rest of the table was pretty quiet.

At the end of the strained meal, Belle led the way back to the preacher.

There were nine people in attendance. Ten, counting the preacher. Rather than sit down, the women lined up beside Lindsay and the men lined up beside Roy.

With the preacher, it was six men to four women. Maybe that's why Belle felt defeated. She was outnumbered.

"Dearly beloved." The pastor had a shining bald head and kind eyes. Small golden wires framed a pair of spectacles, and he held the Good Book open in his broad hands.

Lindsay and Roy exchanged smiles and clung to each other's hands.

The parson droned on a bit, and Belle looked past her daughter and the man who was tricking her into marriage to see Silas next to Roy. Just as Belle was beside Lindsay. The two of them, both against this marriage, were the worst possible choices to stand up for this marriage.

Lindsay never looked away from Roy, her face set in happy, determined lines, and Belle knew this was no accident. Lindsay could have asked Emma to stand beside her. Roy could have chosen Buck. By selecting Belle and Silas, Lindsay was forcing them to bless this union.

It was tempting to turn the little imp over her knee.

"Do you, Roy Adams, take this woman to be your lawful-wedded wife? To have and to hold from this day forward, for better or for worse, for richer, for poorer, in sickness and in health, to love and to cherish, from this day forward as long as you both shall live?"

The parson looked at Roy, who didn't so much as glance at the man of God. "I do."

Belle had to admit that none of her husbands had ever sounded as fervent as young Roy here.

"And, Lindsay Harden, do you take this man to be your lawful-wedded husband? To have and to hold from this day forward, for better or for worse, for richer, for poorer, in sickness and in health, to love and to cherish, from this day forward as long as you both shall live?"

That wasn't even Lindsay's name. Belle opened her mouth, but she caught a look from Silas and a tiny shake of his head. Well, what did it matter? Lindsay's name wasn't Harden anymore anyway. And these vows before God had the power of a lifetime commitment, if Roy could manage to stay alive.

"My real name is Lindsay Svendsen, I reckon. Ma was married to another man before my pa. Though I think of him as my father and call myself by his name. But I want to do this right." She smiled at Roy who didn't look a bit concerned. "I do." Lindsay said it loud enough to stab Belle right in the ears.

"Then before God and these witnesses. . ." The parson blessed the union, just as parsons had blessed all three of Belle's.

But Belle felt God here in this room, between her daughter and this young man. She'd never felt such from the men she'd married. Yet another sin to pile on her conscience that she hadn't insisted on a man of faith to marry.

Tears burned in her eyes as Belle watched her daughter make a better, more intelligent choice for a husband than Belle ever had.

Belle managed to hug her daughter once the vows were finished, and they all walked out of the church, Belle on Silas's arm. She realized she was leaning hard. The loaded wagons had been hitched up so they could ride straight out to Lindsay's new home.

Roy took one look and frowned. "We aren't accepting charity from you." Roy squared off in front of Silas.

Silas looked straight into Belle's eyes, and she could tell he was apologizing for Roy's assumption.

"Lindsay isn't a hired hand, Roy." Silas answered the question knowing Roy wouldn't understand his deferring to Belle. "She's been a full working partner in the Tan. . .uh. . .that is the *Harden Ranch*—"

Belle did her best to burn him to the ground with her eyes for claiming the ranch as his own. This was a bad day all around, and she needed to take that out on somebody. She decided right then it might as well be Silas.

Silas continued. "She's a partner and she's leaving the partnership. Now that might not make sense to you, but that's the way we run our place. So this is her part of the partnership paid out in supplies and livestock. It's not charity. She's fully earned this. I expect you to let her have every bit of it."

Roy held Silas's gaze.

Belle had a fight on her hands to keep from shoving between the two of them and taking charge.

In the end, without Belle sticking her nose in at all, Roy gave an uncertain jerk of his chin. "I've seen Lindsay work, and it's true." He looked at Lindsay. "You really are a partner. That's one of the things I love most about you—your strength."

Buck said, "A wedding gift is a traditional thing, son. It'll help smooth out the first months up there, make things easier for Lindsay. Take 'em for her if not for yourself."

Nodding, Roy reached out a hand to Silas. "Obliged, sir."

"Her ma is the one who figured all this out, bought it all, and helped raise up our girl to be the woman you love. Thank her."

"I've missed my ma something fierce over the years. I'm glad to be in your family, ma'am." Roy turned to Belle and, after a second of hesitation, launched himself into her arms.

Belle caught him close, her eyes wide with shock. She saw Silas suppress a smile.

It was strange holding a young man. Belle had always been determined to have daughters, and if determination could decide such a thing, she'd gotten her way. But maybe a son wouldn't have been so bad. If she could keep him from growing up to be a man.

She hugged him back mostly to get him to let go of her. Then they set out with the cows and supplies. It eased Belle's mind to know what could have been a hard beginning for Lindsay's married life would be comfortable. They'd have a good start, partially because of Belle's gifts.

Buck had bought a few head of cattle, too, not knowing of Belle's plans. They all rode out of town together, driving the horses and Lindsay's beeves ahead of them, with Buck and Shorty driving the freight wagons.

It wasn't easy to pry Lindsay loose of Roy's side, but Belle contrived to have a private talk with her daughter. Riding abreast, Belle nervously began her talk. "I want you to know what to expect of a wedding night."

"I know what goes on with a man and a woman, Ma."

"How do you know that?"

"Well, Ma, I've watched the animals mating over the years, and you and the husbands all shared the same little room we slept in. I think I know what's coming."

Belle was horrified to think her children had overheard her and her husbands. Heaven knew she'd done her best to keep the men at arm's length. Even to the extent of sleeping in a separate bed and keeping a baby with her whenever possible, the soggier the baby the better. Belle had found wet diapers to be a powerful deterrent to a man. "There may be things you...uh...don't know...exactly."

With a firm squaring of her shoulders, Lindsay said bravely, "All that happens is I do my best to get away." Lindsay added sadly, "Except I guess after all is said and done, no woman, nor no female animal, ever gets away, does she, Ma?"

"Lindsay," Belle said, barely able to speak past her surprise, "the thing is. . .I didn't. . .um, care overly much for any of the husbands. I think if'n you *liked* your husband, and you say you like Roy—"

"Oh, I do like him, Ma, I really do!"

"Then, well...you might not *want* to get away. And anyway, it's a little...different than animals because of...the hooves and such, I reckon. You just...you just...well, a man has his rights." Belle felt her neck heat up. She rested her hand on Lindsay's shoulder, and Lindsay looked up at her, her face as pink as Belle's felt.

"I've been able to teach you a lot of things in my life, Lindsay," Belle said solemnly. "But I'm not one to teach a young girl about how to love a husband. I think you already know more about that than I ever will. I think you're gonna be real happy."

"I think so, too, Ma," Lindsay said fervently.

"And if Roy is ever bad to you, well, just remember you can outshoot any man I ever knew," Belle stated firmly. "And if you can't get to your shotgun, I bought you a cast-iron skillet. So you can—"

"Belle!"

Belle and Lindsay twisted in their saddles to look behind them.

Silas had ridden up and looked outraged.

Belle wondered how much of their conversation he'd heard.

"Belle, you ride on ahead. Lindsay and I need to have a talk."

Belle exchanged a wild look with Lindsay then looked back at Silas. She might have protested if she hadn't fallen into the habit of pretending to be an obedient little wife over the last few days... and if he hadn't looked as if he were considering killing her.

Spurring her horse a ways, she looked back and saw Silas talking. He and Lindsay rode together for the better part of an hour and seemed to be having a nice conversation. Belle knew it couldn't be about a wedding night, because there just wasn't that much to know, so she decided it had something to do with the cattle they'd bought and she left them to it.

Later, she noticed Silas talking long and hard to Roy, so she was sure it was about setting up ranching. She almost went over and offered to give them her own advice, believing she was a better rancher than either of them, but she remembered her role as a submissive wife and stayed away.

CHAPTER 19

Glowing Sun took a single step to run, to force Wade's hand, to make him decide for both of them.

A loud cry broke the silence. A scream as wild and fierce as a soaring eagle. Her eyes lifted to the mountaintop and she saw her. . .future.

Wild Eagle. He rode his horse without reins or saddle, carrying a spear, painted for war.

Wade tried to push her behind him.

"No, don't touch me. He'll kill you."

Wade raised his hands away from her.

Glowing Sun moved quickly so her body blocked Wade's from the possibility of a hurling spear.

In her own tongue she called a greeting. "I'm safe. This man brought me home."

To Wade she said, "I am to marry him. This is why I say no to you." She looked over her shoulder and saw Wade's shock.

He shook his head, denying it.

"Yes, I will go with him to my village. We must never see each other again." She turned back to face the Salish man she respected but now knew she could never love. "Do not harm him, Wild Eagle. The man who took me is dead."

Wild Eagle rode up until his horse nearly knocked her back. Her warrior husband-to-be landed on the ground with the grace that had drawn her to him from the beginning. Wild Eagle poured a torrent of words over her. She'd gotten so used to the white words that it took her a moment to understand what Wild Eagle said. He spoke of anger that she'd been taken, as if his possession had been stolen. There was nothing of love or fear. He caught her around the waist and nearly threw her onto his horse. No gentleness, no kindness, no love. Without a look at Wade, as if rescuing her wasn't worthy of a single thank you, Wild Eagle vaulted up in front of her.

She thought of the way Wade had lifted her onto his horse. The way he'd sat behind her, holding her, letting her sleep in his arms.

Wild Eagle wheeled his horse and, with another war cry, charged up the mountainside he'd just descended. She'd have fallen if she hadn't known what to expect and been ready.

Glowing Sun couldn't stop from looking back.

Wade watched her, still shaking his head. His heart in his eyes.

"No!" His cry echoed across the land.

She heard it, but if Wild Eagle did, he showed no sign. Her only answer to Wade was prayer.

Please, God, let him understand.

She turned away and put her arms around her man.

The wrong man.

Because the winter sky was threatening, Belle pushed hard.

They reached the high valley by early that evening, making much faster time without a thousand cattle to prod. The freight wagons had lagged behind, but they were pulling up by the time a fire was crackling and supper was ready.

They bedded down for the night, Roy and Lindsay picking a spot well away from the rest of them, even starting their own campfire. Belle with her three remaining girls. Silas with Buck and Shorty.

The next morning, despite the urgency Belle felt to hurry home to the Tanner Ranch, she didn't for one second want to leave before Lindsay had a roof over her head.

The men were master carpenters, at least to Belle's inexpert eye. Shorty tirelessly hewed down logs. Roy and Buck dragged the logs on horseback and threw their backs into lifting, working like no men Belle had ever seen. Silas was the unquestioned boss of the job. He showed a knack for turning a stack of logs into a sturdy, tight little house.

Belle envied her daughter the nice cabin. Belle planned to spend a piece of what remained of her money having her own cabin repaired or maybe a whole new ranch house built, but that would have to wait until spring. She and the girls would need to spend another winter in her rickety cabin, struggling with the bitter cold. She'd chink the cracks with straw as Red Dawson had taught her, but that only slowed the wind. It didn't stop it.

She spent the whole day setting up a camp and unloading the wagons. She and the girls rode herd on the livestock and helped whenever possible with the house. Belle gave one piece of advice after another to Lindsay, always followed by the thought that maybe Lindsay knew better how to do things than Belle.

Lindsay kept working hard, but her eyes strayed to her new husband every few minutes, and sometimes Roy would be looking back at Lindsay. The two of them would stare at each other as if there were no other people alive in the world. They'd had their wedding night together, and already Belle could see that Lindsay was no longer a girl. She was a woman and might one day soon be a mother.

By nightfall the one-room cabin stood, doorless, windowless, but with a roof atop it and a big stone chimney dry enough to hold a fire. There was also a good start on a stable, enough to keep the pigs, milk cow, and calf from wandering. Lindsay and Roy slept in the house, but the rest of them stayed outside. This would be their last night in the majestic mountain valley that would be her daughter's home.

The next morning they rolled out of bed to a light sprinkling of snow. With the snow came a renewed urgency for the Tanners and Silas to move on. Belle hugged Lindsay good-bye with tears streaming down her face.

Lindsay had the serene look of a woman in love, and though her good-byes were tearful, she never wavered from her new husband's side. Silas hugged Lindsay as if she had been his child every minute of her almost sixteen years. Belle saw Silas and Lindsay whispering together and felt strangely left out even though Lindsay's good-byes to her were fervent and loving.

Just as they were leaving, Lindsay pulled her aside. "I want you to know how much I respect the sacrifices you've made for me all my life, Ma. Watching all the menfolk work so hard to build this cabin has made me realize how hard you've worked to make a home for us with no help. I'm trying to imagine what I'd do in this lonely valley with a herd of cows and a no-account husband. Building a cabin myself. Tending the herd myself. Doing everything alone with a baby on my back and another on the way." Lindsay laid her hands on Belle's arms.

Belle was shocked to realize her daughter felt sorry for her.

"I'm sorry you ended up with the husbands you did, Ma."

Belle was sorry herself.

"But I'm glad I was born, and I'm glad for my sisters."

Belle nodded. She'd always known that whatever lousy things her husbands had given her, they'd also given her the loves of her life and a reason to live and be strong.

"I think, Ma, that. . .things. . .don't have to be so hard between a man and a woman as they were for you. Silas knew things that I reckon you don't know. And he explained things to Roy so. . .well, Roy was wonderful."

Belle tried to keep up with what Lindsay was saying. What things could her daughter possibly be referring to?

"I hope someday you'll know what it's like to. . .be with. . .a man you love. And who loves you enough to be gentle with you." Lindsay hugged her tight.

Well, Belle knew she was already with a man she loved. And it hurt more than anything she'd ever known, short of saying goodbye to her daughter.

They hugged, and finally Belle let go, swiping at her tears while Lindsay turned to Roy. Belle's last sight of her daughter was Lindsay crying her eyes out and being held and comforted in the strong arms of the man she loved. Each of their two blond heads rested on the other's shoulder. Their tall, lithe frames clung to each other. It occurred to Belle that they would have beautiful children. And Lindsay would at least *think* they looked like her.

Belle's heart threatened to break. There would be other cattle drives, and the rugged mountain passes couldn't stop a determined woman who wanted to visit her daughter, but the West had a way of swallowing people up. There was a chance she'd never see her daughter again. But she also knew that the girl could have waited a long time and searched the world over and found no better husband.

It was small comfort.

The snow fell more heavily, and the Tanner-Harden party headed up the mountain pass at a sharp trot.

"We'll be home in four days if I have anything to say about it," Silas yelled from where he brought up the rear, leading the spare horses. They'd eaten all their supplies on the trip and brought very little home. Belle had put in stores for the winter before the drive started.

Heartbroken at leaving Lindsay, Belle looked back; she had Betsy on her back and trailed Sarah and then Emma, who was in the lead. She decided bickering might be just the ticket to get her gumption back.

"A hundred miles in four days? You're crazy. It took us a month to come in to Helena."

Flashing a grin at her, Silas said, "We pushed a thousand head of cattle over this trail. Reckon that slowed us down some."

"This is a mean trail, with cattle or without." Belle had made this trip in four days before, but in good weather, and it had been a hard, heartbreaking ride. She'd done it before she'd married Anthony, to find a good lawyer and write a will that favored her children and cut off her husband. It wasn't easy finding the right man for that will, because most lawyers barely recognized a woman as having legal rights. But she'd done it.

"I think four days in the snow is mighty bold talk, Pa." Emma could probably stop calling Silas Pa now. Belle didn't remind her.

"Well, men could do it. But with you womenfolk slowing me down, maybe you're right."

Emma flashed him a smile over her shoulder. "We'll see who has to hustle to keep up." She leaned low over her horse and pushed to the limit of safety and perhaps a bit beyond.

The race was on. Against men, against time, against nature.

It gave Belle something to focus on, and she needed that bad. All of 'em had their hands full keeping up with Emma.

Late that night, long after the stars were out, Silas finally let up pushing them.

They got a hot fire blazing high, the girls on one side, Silas alone on the other. It hurt Belle to think of how cold he was over there alone. There was no way she could think of to convince him he belonged with her. Remembering his certainty that they weren't going to get married, she quit her foolish daydreaming and slept.

Come morning, they were up, building the fire and starting coffee. They had a warm meal in their bellies and were on the trail hours before first light.

The next stretch of the trip was a repeat of the harrowing series of passes that had taken them five days coming across. The wind picked up through the day, and snow drifted down occasionally, especially when they'd crest a peak.

They neared the top of one of those dizzying trails, and in a wide spot, Silas rode up beside her, their horses wading in three inches of snow. "We've got to get through this whole stretch today, Belle."

"It was five days coming across." Belle hated the way she sounded—whiny. But the cold was like taking a beating. She hated that she was putting her girls through this.

"These peaks get higher with each one we cross. Look how deep the snow is already." Silas looked up at the whirling white that sifted down steadily on the higher elevations. "And this doesn't come close to a heavy snow."

Belle stiffened her backbone. "We'll make it." She pulled the front of her buckskin jacket tight at the neck to keep out the biting cold.

Nodding, Silas reached over, even as they trotted side by side, and flipped up the collar of her coat. He gave her flat-brimmed Stetson a tug as if to pull it to cover more of her head.

They exchanged a smile, and Belle wondered, maybe, if they weren't half dead from cold and exhaustion and separated by the space between two horses, with three children looking on, if he might kiss her again.

Smiling, he said, "Sure as certain we'll make it. I've never been with a tougher bunch of cowhands. I'll go tell your girls to pick up the pace."

Once they got through that stretch, it was lower, except for that one last sky-high peak they had to climb to get into her valley. The first one they'd driven the cattle up when leaving home.

The day wore on and the peaks rose and fell. The cold wore on her. They ate beef jerky in the saddle, and Belle fed Betsy and changed her diaper with almost no break in the pace. They had to stop, water the horses, and switch saddles to fresh mounts, but it was never for long, and they pushed on hard.

As the sun set, they began the long climb up the last treacherous trail they'd tackle tonight. The snow had stopped, but the wind cut and howled. Belle wanted to beg for mercy, but she clamped her mouth shut.

Silas tied the horses onto Belle's saddle. "I'm going to spell Emma—take the lead. The snow looks deep ahead. If a trail needs to be broken, especially where there are drop-offs, I want to do it."

Belle wanted to beg him to be careful, but she didn't have the energy. He passed Sarah, talked to her, coaxing a smile out of Belle's little redhead, then rode up, patted Emma on the shoulder, and passed her. Belle brought up the rear carrying Betsy. Belle saw Sarah's head nodding, but she was too stupid from exhaustion to react. Her mind wanted to yell, her heels wanted to goad her horse, but she had no strength to do it. She just sat her horse and watched in numb horror as Sarah slid sideways, falling, which was unheard of for one of her girls, short of being tossed by a bronco.

Silas glanced back, as he did constantly, and spurred his horse to Sarah's side. He caught her in time.

Belle breathed a prayer of thanks into the bitter night.

Silas's gently muttered words blew back to Belle on the cold wind. "Here, ride with me." Her heart ached as she saw the careful way he lifted the little girl onto his lap and let her sleep in his arms. He strung a rope between himself and Sarah's horse and pushed past Emma to take the lead again, all without letting up the pace. The rest of the nearly dozen horses were tied onto the back of Belle's saddle, and they plodded along in a line, one behind the other. The three riders—Silas, Emma, and Belle—struggled on up the last peak they had to face today.

Snow started sifting down when they still had a mile to go up and several miles on the other side to descend before it was safe to camp. With the slippery snow, the downhill side might be more treacherous than the switchbacks they were climbing.

Silas led the way through the deepening snow, breaking the trail. Belle constantly checked Betsy, strapped on her back, to see that she wasn't being smothered by her blanket and that she hadn't let so much as a finger slip out from under the covers. Emma rode in the middle, a quiet, intense little girl who hadn't said much since she'd hugged her big sister good-bye.

Belle sensed a world of sadness in Emma and didn't know how to get her taciturn daughter to speak of her hurt. Belle wasn't sure speaking of it was a good idea anyway. And good or bad didn't matter much, because there was no time now for talking.

Belle couldn't remember when there'd been time for anything in her life except work and more work with Emma always at her side, doing a man's share. And Lindsay. And now they'd have to do it all with one less pair of hands.

They reached the peak at last, the horses floundering in knee-deep snow that came light and blew with the sheltered wind into drifts against the side of the trail. A white world against a coal dark sky, filled with blinding snow and whipping wind, surrounded them.

When the trail was wide enough, Silas dropped back to speak a word of encouragement.

As they began the downward slope, the sure-footed horses slid often, sometimes sitting on their haunches to stop. One switchback would lead them so close to a sheer drop, Belle's legs would dangle out over thin air while the other scraped the mountain. Another would take them into the side of the mountain where the snow was deeper and the winds whipped stronger, sapping their strength with its clawing cold.

The Husband Tree

They dropped lower and the snow got deeper. For a while, Belle wasn't aware of anything beyond her horse putting one hoof in front of the other. She knew if they didn't get below the snow line soon, they'd have to get off and walk the horses, because their mounts were spent.

Then, just when Belle began to think there wasn't a place in the whole world that wasn't icy and white, they passed a sheltered spot and the snow wasn't so deep there. They moved out into a more difficult stretch again, but they could see ahead that the trail was improving. The snow slowed and stopped, and stars shone overhead. The horses seemed to sense relief ahead. Their ears pricked forward and they picked up their pace.

At last, after making more demands on the animals and the people than seemed possible, the trail widened. The going became easy enough for Silas to drop back beside Belle. "The trail clears ahead, and we can camp just as soon as I find a good spot."

Silas laid his hand on her shoulder, and feeling numb and stupid, Belle looked sideways at him in the moonlight. She realized she hadn't reacted when he'd spoken to her. Sarah was sleeping on the saddle in front of him, wrapped up as tightly as the baby on Belle's back. The sight of her daughter in his arms almost shook loose some useless tears, but she held them off.

"Emma's all in, Belle."

Their eyes met. Her throat ached from what they'd put her children through today.

"I don't think she can hang on to her horse much longer." He leaned closer, and Belle wondered if her eyes were focused, because he seemed unsure if she understood him.

She forced her head up and down. Words were beyond her.

"I can't handle both of them. I'm sorry, but you're going to have to take Sarah. We can't stop, not yet. Can you do it? Can you hold her?"

Belle didn't know where she found the strength, but she checked Betsy quickly, realizing in her exhaustion she'd forgotten

535

she had a baby on her back. Betsy blinked her eyes owlishly up at her, and Belle could see that the little girl had weathered the storm better than the rest of them. Tucking the baby back in quickly so no heat would escape, Belle accepted Sarah into her arms.

Silas helped balance Sarah so all her weight was on the horse, not on Belle's tired arms. Sarah moaned and shifted her body around a bit, but she never woke up as she was passed between the two of them.

"Are you okay?"

Belle nodded again but didn't speak.

Silas rode forward and bent over Emma. Only when Silas reached for Emma's hands did Belle realize Emma had lashed herself to the saddle horn and now rode along in her sleep. Silas untied Emma's hands and lifted her gently into his arms. Emma was as tall as Belle, yet Silas lifted her as though she were a small child.

Belle's throat closed. Tears bit at her eyes with their salty heat. The valor of her daughter and the kindness and strength of a man they didn't even know a month ago swelled her heart. And if she wasn't in love with him already, she fell in love in that instant.

She quit fighting her fear of love and the danger to her heart. She couldn't stop her feelings anyway—so the only thing she really quit was denying them.

Belle knew now that she had loved him for a long time. Maybe it wasn't love when she'd been afraid to hire him the first moment she saw him. Maybe it wasn't love when she discussed her plans and problems with him on that long ride from Divide to her ranch. Maybe it wasn't love when she melted under his kisses. But it had been the beginning. From the first instant, love had been growing in her heart until tonight. As he worked to care for them to the limit of his strength with an unending reserve of gentleness, it had bloomed into something that would live in her forever.

She loved Silas Harden. She was his.

And he didn't want her.

They plodded along the last mile of ever-thinning snow until the white on the trail vanished as if it had never been. The going was still too steep for a camp, but once they dropped into the tree line, Belle found a reserve of strength without the wind that deepened the cold.

Silas checked over his shoulder to see if she was still with him. With the moon and stars overhead, she could see him as clear as day, even in the mottled light of the forest. She nodded, and he smiled and turned back to the winding trail. At last they reached a plateau that was level and had a water supply.

Silas rode his horse to a sheltered spot under an overhanging cliff and dismounted with Emma in his arms. He jerked his bedroll off his horse, and with a few flicks of his wrist, he had Emma settled, asleep on the ground. Belle was still trying to swing her leg over the back of her horse when Silas was at her side.

He lifted her down, and when her legs buckled, he kept one hand on Sarah and lowered Belle to the grassy floor. "Just rest," he whispered. "Let me get Sarah settled and I'll help you with Betsy." He led the horse a few steps away so a nervous movement wouldn't allow them to trample Belle.

Belle heard the exhaustion in Silas's voice and forced herself to sit up and, with clumsy fingers, lift Betsy around to the front. Betsy was wide awake when Belle uncovered her. The quiet baby made sounds of distress that reminded Belle the child hadn't eaten or had her diaper changed for hours. Belle saw to the diaper.

Silas was by her side, helping her to her feet and guiding her to a felled log to rest her back. "You feed her and put her to sleep. I'll get a fire going and see to the horses."

Belle nodded dumbly, and as soon as he stepped away, she nursed Betsy then tucked her little girl back into her blankets for the night.

She awoke briefly as Silas eased her from a sitting position to the ground. He murmured, "I'm sorry. I'm sorry I put you through this, baby. You're the bravest thing I've ever seen." It might have been a dream, but she thought he pressed his lips to the top of her head as he eased her close to the fire. And she must have been dreaming when she heard him whisper, "I love you."

Silas moved away to his lonely side of the camp, and as she dozed off, Belle wondered briefly if she'd heard it but convinced herself he was talking to Betsy. Of course he was. Betsy was a baby after all, and who wouldn't love her? But why say that when the baby was sound asleep?

She wished with everything in her heart that he would have said those words to her. And she wished she had the nerve to say them back. He deserved to know how much she loved him.

Though she was too tired and too afraid to say any of it out loud, in her dreams she told him everything in her heart.

CHAPTER 20

I love you, Silas. So much."

Silas sat up on his bedroll, stunned.

"I've never known a man as strong." Her voice slurred.

But Silas could hear every word. "You're so steady. So smart. I wish I'd married you. Not the others. Only you. Love you. Love you so much."

Narrowing his sleep-heavy eyes, he couldn't see Belle in the dim light. She was talking in her sleep, or maybe it was a stupor rather than sleep, but she'd said it. And that meant she'd thought it. And, whether she'd ever admit it or not, somewhere, some part of her had those words to share.

He was so thrilled he would have asked her to marry him right then and there—except she was fast asleep, and he was tired all the way to his bones. He forced himself to lie back down, and within seconds sleep dragged him under.

He jerked awake to see stars hanging like an explosion of diamonds high overhead. The moon was low in the sky. Dawn would begin to blot out the stars very soon.

Every muscle in his body objected and every sensible cell in his brain hollered, *No!* but he held his eyes open anyway.

God, I almost killed my girls yesterday. I'm sorry I forced them through that. But it had to be done.

He knew from the conditions last night that they'd never have gotten through today. Silas thought of how battered his girls were and how they'd bedded down for the night closer to unconscious than asleep. He thought about the glazed look in Belle's eyes as Silas added to her burden by making her carry Sarah. He remembered the heart-wrenching sight of Emma's wrists strapped to her saddle. The only reason he didn't break down and cry was because he was a man. He got mad instead.

He aimed his anger at himself mostly for staying that extra day to help Lindsay when she had three able-bodied men to see to her needs while Belle only had him and three young children to boot. But Silas had needed to be sure there was a roof over Lindsay's head. Whether or not it was smart didn't matter. He'd had it to do and he'd done it.

He spent awhile raging in his mind at Belle's worthless husbands. They were lucky to be dead and beyond his reach, or he'd have hunted them up and beaten them within an inch of their lives. Fury built in him at Belle, too. She hadn't needed to choose such a hard road for herself and her girls. She could have easily stayed in Texas, even if she didn't stand to inherit a ranch. Her pa would have made sure she got by, even with that no-account husband. And she could have just left it to the worthless bum of a husband to eke out a living while she stayed to a woman's place and cared for her children.

When he was in full mental rant at Belle, he knew it was exhaustion talking, because everything about her spoke to his heart. Every tough, courageous choice she made touched him all the way to his soul. He'd finally worked up the nerve to tell her he loved her last night, and she'd said the words back. Trouble was, he hadn't realized his feelings until they came out of his mouth.

The Husband Tree

He should have married her in Helena. Instead, he'd still been stuck in his fool notion that he didn't want any part of marriage.

Now they had trouble. Silas couldn't think of a way to marry her and still get back to the ranch ahead of the snow.

He could do it without shame now. He might have been a coward before, but no more. His days of running were over, and with Belle at his side, he'd never need to run anyway. She was tough enough to handle whatever came along.

And he had plans that would make him worthy of her. But he needed to do that work before he could present himself to Belle as a husband fit for her and the girls. Of course, Belle would go ahead and marry him most likely. She'd shown a bent for marrying all and sundry.

The right thing to do would be to take her home, climb out of that valley of hers any way possible, then come courting in the spring. But spring seemed like an eternity away. No matter how Silas worked it around in his head, he couldn't fit a trip to Divide for a preacher into their plans before the long Montana winter shut down on their heads.

Maybe once they were home, if it looked like the weather was going to hold, they might make a run for town. But they didn't dare ride away from the place and leave the girls, and they didn't dare take the whole family out and leave the herd.

Silas thought again of his girls' hard lives and got angry all over again. And that was just as well, because nothing else could have kept him awake.

Today wouldn't be so brutally hard, but it would be hard enough. They had to press on and get close enough to the pass near the Tanner Ranch to get over it the next day. They'd come twenty miles from Lindsay's valley, and that valley was nearly fifteen miles from Helena. They would ride forty miles today because the going was better, but the day had to start now, and it had to last until well after dark.

That left ten miles of clawing their way straight up and down the mountain that sheltered the Tanner Ranch at the same time it cut it off from the rest of the world. He knew that what they passed through yesterday was a sign of things to come. The gap into Belle's place would still be open, he hoped, but it was just a matter of time. There was a lower pass on the south end of the Tanner Ranch, but they'd have to ride three days around the mountain to get to it, and by then *it* might be closed off.

No, they had to make the north pass today or tomorrow or a winter storm could lock Belle away from her ranch for the whole winter. And Silas knew Belle. He knew the stuff she was made of. He knew she'd do whatever it took to get home. If it meant risking her life and the lives of her children, she'd scale that mountain on her belly in snow that'd bury Goliath and get home. The woman didn't have an ounce of backup in her. His only goal was to get her there before it came down to life and death.

Throwing back his blanket, he rolled to his knees, aching in every joint, and crawled to the fire. He stirred up the flames and had coffee going and the horses saddled before he woke his girls. They moaned and groaned, and Sarah cried and begged him to leave her alone. Silas could have let it break his heart to hear his sturdy female ranch hands whining up a storm, but he teased them and called them lazy. It didn't take long until their grit kicked in.

They were on the trail an hour before first light. As soon as the first blush of dawn brightened the sky, Silas set the pace at a ground-eating trot. They switched their saddles to fresh horses twice during the morning, never letting up the pace. The horses seemed able to trot along forever as long as they got a break from the weight of a rider.

"Silas, we've got to walk a spell," Belle yelled from behind Sarah and Emma.

Wanting to snarl at the delay, Silas knew this was for Betsy, not Belle. Belle never asked for a break for herself.

The Husband Tree

They walked along for close to half an hour, Silas careful not to look back but smiling at his unlikely cowhands.

"Let's move out," Belle hollered as soon as the little tyke was returned to her carrier.

Silas pushed on again.

They made a quick cold lunch, and Silas insisted the girls walk briskly around the little clearing he'd found so their abused muscles would loosen up some. "Let me carry Betsy for a while, Belle."

She shook her head.

Silas caught her chin. "You know how bad it got last night."

"Betsy's my responsibility."

Silas looked over at Emma and Sarah, walking along briskly, out of earshot. "Please, can you just this once mind me, woman?"

Belle's eyes flashed. "Mind you?"

Smiling, Silas said, "Nice to see you've still got some spunk."

He stole a long, deep kiss. "You'll probably end up with Sarah and Betsy both by nightfall. It'll be all I can do to handle Emma. This will help you save your strength now."

Looking bemused by the kiss, Belle said, "Okay," and handed the baby over.

Silas decided he'd remember this method for persuading the stubborn woman. It would be his pleasure to convince her to do things his way from now on.

"I'll give her back come feeding time." He took the carrier and strapped it on his own back. "Girls! Let's hit the trail."

By late afternoon, Belle had taken Betsy back for a while. Then Silas retrieved the baby during a saddle switch.

The horizon filled with the last mountain they needed to climb. Silas knew it was still far away, but he watched it loom over his head and wondered how they'd ever scared those cattle up and down this twisting trail.

Just as the sun set, they started climbing from the base of their last obstacle. Silas considered laying up to sleep right then, but he

543

felt the lowering sky and smelled snow in the wind, and he wasn't bold enough to stop and dare the winter to swallow them up.

An hour later, no more than a quarter of the way up this massive climb, Silas saw Sarah's head bob forward. He lifted her out of her saddle over feeble protests.

As full dark came over them, they reached a level spot that would have worked for a camp. But the horses were jumpy and Silas was, too. He saw the fear in Belle as she looked over her head at the sky. Looking behind her, she saw darkness pile on top of the stars. They slowly blinked out, and the moon disappeared behind the encroaching snow clouds.

Silas dropped back and yelled over the rising wind, "We'll be riding all night, but I don't think the weather's gonna hold till morning. Let's change saddles again and try to make it to the top and over."

Even in the darkness, Silas could see the dark rings around Belle's heavy-lidded eyes. She nodded her head. "Let me take Betsy. Sarah's enough for you."

The woman was pure heart, with more guts than any man Silas ever knew. Silas dismounted, lay Sarah down, and dragged Belle off the saddle, lowering her to a sitting position. He made sure she had a firm grip on the baby; then he eased Emma off her horse. He changed the saddles, handed out some beef jerky, and got them mounted up. Emma looked about all in, but he didn't think Belle had it in her to carry Sarah as she had the night before, so he left Emma riding alone. Betsy rode on Belle's back because she'd need to feed the little girl. Silas carried Sarah in his arms. Belle was so tired she was actually just taking orders at this point. Silas decided to enjoy it as it wasn't likely to happen again.

They started the frisky mounts up the trail. The horses smelled the storm, or maybe they knew they were close to home, because they seemed to be as fresh as if they had just started the day. The lively horses roused Belle and Emma somewhat, and they fell into line behind Silas. Every few steps he checked to make sure they were still with him. As they reached the halfway point on the climb, snow began to filter down from the sky, and Silas pushed the horses harder, knowing that when the snow accumulated it would make the going slippery.

But it wasn't soft snow like they'd had on the high ground. This was heavy. And it was coming from behind them, snowing even in the lowlands. Snow could come by the foot up here rather than by the inch. Add in drifting winds, and the pass still high overhead could be closing up even now.

His mount nickered and fidgeted, sending the metal in its bridal clinking. But it was a good horse and it minded. Silas remembered a series of dead drops near the peak where they'd lost a few head of cattle who stumbled at the wrong time. He wanted to get past those before the drifts started to form.

The snow began to collect until it covered the horse's hooves with every step. They trotted on through shelter where the snow hadn't covered the trail, along wind-whipped cliffs that cut through their woolen clothing, along rock faces that rose high overhead, and caught every flake of snow, dropping it down and deepening the going.

Silas looked back steadily, worried about the womenfolk. Time to time he'd see Belle pull little Betsy off her back and tend to her. Silas knew Belle wouldn't neglect her baby, but he couldn't quite imagine how the woman managed to feed and change a baby without once getting off her horse.

The last of the stars were blotted out as the clouds moved ahead of them. The wind rose until it whined eerily among the thinning trees.

Silas looked back to see Emma tying her hands on the saddle again. Behind Emma was Belle with their horses strung out behind her.

Silas dropped back. "Give me your reins."

Emma looked up, her blue eyes vague, her lids heavy. She didn't obey him. In the normal course of things, Emma would have refused to let anyone do anything for her. But right now, Silas was sure she disobeyed simply because her head was too foggy from exhaustion to understand his request.

He unwound the reins without waiting for her to respond and guided her horse. This time he didn't carry her. He didn't think he had the strength.

As they climbed higher, the wind cut more sharply as if to punish them for daring to be abroad in this weather. Silas caught himself dozing. Scared to his boots because the sheer drop-offs that were so treacherous were just ahead, he grabbed a handful of snow off a rock and smeared it on his face. He was already so cold he barely felt it.

"Belle!" Silas looked behind him. Emma sat with her head bowed forward, almost certainly asleep. But he had her reins. He could control her horse. But Belle had to be alert.

Belle didn't respond.

"Wake up, Belle. Listen to me," Silas hollered. The trail was too narrow for him to drop back. The wind was so high his voice barely carried. "Belle Tanner, you stop lazing around and wake up and ride that horse!"

He continued shouting until Belle lifted her head. With a jerk, she looked around and realized how dangerous the trail was. Her hands tightened on the reins. "I'm awake." She shook her head. "Lazing around?"

Silas thought he heard a little spitfire in her voice. Well, if calling her lazy didn't set her off, nothing would.

"I'm paying attention, Silas."

"You'd better be, woman," Silas shouted back. He kept shouting pure nonsense, whatever his thick head could think of, about the cold and the climb and the cattle. Anything to keep himself and Belle going. Finally sure Belle and even Emma after a while were alert, he rode on, talking with them, making his voice carry above the wind.

They were tough women, and they worked as hard as he did to keep their group going, encouraging each other and pushing each other to go on, even when sometimes it didn't seem like the next step was possible.

Then suddenly, they were at the summit.

"We made it!" Silas shouted and looked back to see Emma and Belle crane their necks to see ahead in the darkness.

"We're home!" Belle smiled, pure triumph.

"Home." Emma spoke more quietly, but she squared her shoulders and looked down to realize she didn't have her reins anymore. She looked up, straight into Silas's eyes. "Thank you."

He felt more than heard those words. They filled his heart until his throat clogged with something that *could not* be tears.

Silas turned back and looked down in his arms at Sarah with her eyes open, smiling up at him. He boosted her around so she sat, looking forward, while he minded his horse. The vast canyon where Belle had held her steers before the drive was before them. There was still a long climb down to get below the snow line and another ten-mile ride to get to the cabin, but they were home. Silas felt a weight lift off his back.

After the first dangerously steep yards off the peak, the trail widened. In the heavily falling snow, Silas was able to ride back and untie the horses. He unhitched them from Belle's saddle and from each other. "Hyah!" he yelled and slapped the closest horse on the rump. These critters were almost asleep, too. Just like the people traveling with them. First they walked, speeding up on the wider trail. They passed Belle and Emma. Then they picked up speed, trotting at first, then, when Silas saw them pass the snow-clad ground far below and gain more solid footing, they broke into a gallop. They charged down the mountain. He knew they'd run until they got to the cabin. There was no longer a need to watch them.

He looked down at Sarah in his arms and chucked one gloved hand under her chin. "We made it home, Sarie."

She smiled and nodded then lay her head back against his chest and went back to sleep.

He rode on up to Belle's side. "We're almost below the storm. I don't have it in me to ride until we get home. I'll find a place and we'll camp one more night on the trail."

Belle nodded.

Sarah stirred slightly and murmured, "'K, Pa."

Silas dropped a quick kiss on her curly red head and hugged her close as the horse dropped down out of the rugged peak.

Finally, the snow was behind them.

Belle rode up beside him. "I know where to camp."

"Lead on, darlin'."

Belle smiled at him and urged her mount ahead. Belle didn't go much farther. She picked a well-sheltered spot with an icy cold spring trickling down out of a crack in the mountain.

Silas used the last energy he possessed to get the horses picketed for fear they'd head for home with the other horses. Silas had no interest in taking a ten-mile hike in the morning. Then he built up a roaring fire to make the bitterly cold night bearable.

Belle sat feeding Betsy, both of them mostly asleep, while he did everything to prepare the camp, including finding the last of the beef jerky and urging them to eat it and drink some water.

He settled Emma and Sarah next to each other and covered them with a blanket to share their body heat. He found Belle asleep with a dozing Betsy in her arms. He woke her enough to urge her into the nest of warmth with her girls, resenting that he didn't have the right to share that warmth.

He intended to fix that—and soon.

Belle stirred awake as Silas covered her, and struggled to sit up. In a voice rusty with sleep, she said, "Silas, we're home. We made it. Thanks to you."

"We're going to be married, Belle, just as soon as I can figure out how to get us to a preacher."

"But Silas—"

"Go to sleep. Just sleep. Tomorrow we'll be home, and we'll figure everything out then." He stalked away from her, knowing he was already her husband in his heart. But they needed the vows to be said before God.

Belle murmured, "Home." From across the camp he heard her utter, "I love you."

Silas lay awake for several minutes trying to believe the other lower pass, nearer Belle's cabin, would still be open and he could risk taking her to Divide for a wedding. He knew, unless it was completely impossible, he was going to try first thing tomorrow, because he knew he had reached the day when he could no longer be near Belle Tanner and not be her husband.

Rather than having even the slightest twinge of regret at the loss of his freedom, he fell asleep excited about the future and eager to get on with it.

The wind moaned and howled, and the snow fell in the high altitudes, but they were safe. Silas and his girls had made it home.

God, help me get out of here tomorrow. Help me find a way to marry this woman now.

CHAPTER 21

Belle slept late the next morning.

The sun was already brightening the horizon in the east when her eyes flickered open. The first sight she saw was Silas, crouching by the fire, lifting a coffeepot.

They'd made it. This was her valley.

"Silas, we're home."

He looked up and smiled. His face was wind burned, his hair knotted and flattened by his Stetson, though he wasn't wearing it now. He had a week's worth of stubble on his face because he hadn't shaved since the day Lindsay had gotten married.

And he was the most wonderful thing she'd ever seen.

"We made it, didn't we, darlin'?" A dark look in his eyes reminded her of warm words she'd dreamed in the night.

"Because of you." She pressed against the ground to sit up, wondering what kind of mess she must be. It was a wonder the man didn't turn tail and run. She smiled and wondered when the last time was she'd cared about her appearance.

"Because of all of us." His eyes went past Belle's shoulders.

Nodding, she glanced to see all three of her girls, still fast asleep. And with the sun well up in the sky. Shameful. "A pretty tough bunch, huh?" She looked back at him and smiled.

He was wonderful and brave and strong. He was everything a man should be.

And she might have dreamed it, but she thought the man had asked her to marry him last night. She wondered if he'd ask again just so she could be sure. Lowering the coffeepot back onto the fire, their eyes held. "So are you going to quit wasting the day away and get going?" Belle challenged.

A smile spread wider. "So we can get married?"

Silas hadn't spent much time smiling on this cattle drive. All things considered, that was understandable. Belle hadn't done much of it herself. So now she looked at his smiling face and noticed for the first time that he had a dimple. A single dimple on the left side that for some reason fascinated her. Then she shook off her bemused state as she thought of what he'd said. Belle sat all the way up. "Silas Harden, I've had a lot of proposals in my day."

Silas said dryly, "I'll bet that's right."

"And that is the worst one I've *ever* heard, bar none."

"Is that so?" He stood and came straight for her.

Belle's eyes widened. "Now, Silas. I haven't said yes yet."

Dropping to his knees, he leaned in and kissed her hard with his whiskery face, still grinning. Then staring straight into her eyes, he asked, "Don't you think I oughta marry her, Emma?"

Belle thought that seemed like yet another strange proposal.

"I think you're gonna hafta, Pa," Emma said solemnly.

Belle looked over her shoulder and saw Sarah and Emma had joined the living. They were standing behind her, watching the man kiss the living daylights out of her. Even Betsy was awake and watching.

"We talked it over, Ma," Sarah said earnestly. "We think you and Pa oughta get married. I mean, I know we didn't want anymore husbands. Heaven knows up till now you've picked a useless lot. But we're all fond of Pa and kind of used to calling him Pa, and we talked it over with Lindsay, and she's for it. So we vote for you marryin' him."

"You talked it over with Lindsay?" *How long ago?* she wondered.

Emma said gravely, "It was unanimous."

Betsy, perched in Sarah's arms, waved wildly and bounced until Sarah almost dropped her. She yelled, "Papa! Papa!"

Sarah tilted her head in Betsy's direction and nodded ruefully. "Completely unanimous."

"Thanks." Silas smiled at the girls. "I'm mighty proud to be your pa, too. And I'm glad to hear I've won the election. Majority rules." Then he looked back at Belle. "You don't even have to vote. I *am* their pa. You heard 'em, and that's the way it is. Now, *Ma*, isn't it high time you married their pa?"

"Silas, you're not their...*mmmph*..."

When Silas quit kissing her into silence, he said, "And you hadn't oughta carry on, kissin' and such, in front of youngsters. Not with any man, but for sure not with a man you don't plan to marry. So, it's settled."

"Can I say something?" Belle snapped.

Eyeing her mouth as if prepared to silence her again, Silas said warily, "Depends."

Belle narrowed her eyes at him. "I had no intention of letting you get away without marryin' me, Silas Harden."

Then Silas laughed out loud and kissed the daylights out of her, and the girls jumped on his back, and pretty soon the whole family was within a gnat's eyelash of rolling right off the mountainside.

When the jubilee was over, Silas poured coffee all around and doused the fire. Then he started saddling horses while the women gathered bedrolls. Then he herded them all toward the horses. "We've got to get back to the ranch and get to Divide before winter closes in. I'm not spendin' the winter in the barn. And while we're there, we can get some lumber to patch up that sad excuse for a cabin."

The Husband Tree

"Silas," Belle said uncertainly. His eyes dropped to her lips again, so she thought over what she had to say with some care. "The thing is, what if we get snowed away? I can't risk leaving the herd, and I can't drag these girls over that south pass when they're so exhausted. But I dare not leave them, in case we don't get back."

Silas said shortly, "Just get in the saddle. We'll be home in four hours. . .three and a half if we push hard. And we can talk about it then. But we're going to be married if we have to ordain Emma and have her perform the ceremony."

Sarah said pertly, "*I* want to perform the ceremony. I'm more religiouser than Emma."

Emma slapped Sarah on the arm. "You're not religiouser than me. Why, I'm the most Bible-believin' person in this family by far. And I'm oldest."

"You're not oldest. Lindsay's oldest."

"Lindsay's not oldest no more, 'cuz Lindsay's not here. In a family where the ma and pa ain't married, it's the oldest child's job to do everything she can to fetch 'em both around to doing the right thing."

Belle interrupted, "Emma, you shouldn't say your ma and pa ain't married."

Emma said, "I know, I know. My ma and pa *aren't* married. I knows grammar rightly enough."

"No, it's not the *grammar*. It's saying Silas is your pa but I'm not married to him. That makes it sound like I've got a twelve-year-old child and have had. . ." Belle shut up before she dug herself in any deeper.

Emma went back to fighting with Sarah.

Silas dug a few forgotten, beat-up pieces of jerky out of one of the packs, picked the horse hair off of them, and gave them to Sarah and Emma.

The girls still bickered as the family started down the trail.

It occurred to Belle that the girls didn't fight much. The good-natured sniping seemed childish to her. Her daughters had never had much chance to be children. Maybe with Silas to carry part of the load, her girls could have a little taste of being young before they found themselves married with adult responsibilities to shoulder.

Belle thought of Lindsay and had a wave of loneliness for her oldest child. Lindsay had been forced to grow up far too soon. But on the other hand, if ever a fifteen-year-old was mature enough for marriage, Lindsay was.

Belle breathed in and out evenly until any risk of sentimental tears passed. Then she spurred her horse into a trot and passed Silas on the trail. As she went by him, she grinned. "A woman might think you're not in that all-fired of a hurry to get married, the way you're doggin' it."

He laughed. "Don't you believe it, woman." He urged his horse to a faster pace to keep up with her.

She set her horse to a ground-eating trot, and proving Silas didn't know her range as well as he thought he did, they were home in two and a half hours.

Silas told all his girls to get in the cabin and go to sleep. He'd be back before nightfall with a preacher if he had to crawl a hundred miles on his hands and knees across bitter cold snow.

Belle said, "No, I'll just go along. But I'll have to take Betsy. She'll need to eat."

Silas dragged Belle out of hearing distance of the girls. "Here's how it is, Belle. If we go together, there is a chance we won't get back and the girls could spend the winter alone. They'd probably survive it because they're good strong girls, but neither of us wants to test that. If we take the girls, there's a chance the whole family won't get back and the cattle won't survive the winter, which wipes out your years of work, and I won't let our marriage cost you so much."

The Husband Tree

Then Silas lifted Belle onto her tiptoes. "If I don't go, there is no way I can spend the winter here with you and not. . .not be. . . be with you as a husband. It would be better if I go alone, and if I can't get back, at least the snow would preserve your honor. If I *can* get back, we'll be married and I'll hustle the preacher out of here the minute the ceremony is over. You can ride out to the low pass and meet me and the parson. Figuring a six-hour ride, I should be back about midafternoon. Me going alone is the only thing that makes sense."

"But what if you get to the pass and can't get out?" Belle asked worriedly. "I love you, and I don't want you to risk your life trying to get us married."

It was all Silas could do not to drag her into his arms and kiss her, but he just didn't have the time. Instead, he tugged his hat low on his forehead. "I'll be back before nightfall with a preacher. Be waiting at the pass so we can send the poor man straightaway back to Divide. If I don't make it, I'll be in here the minute the pass opens up in the spring. Whatever it takes, however long I have to wait, I'm marrying you."

He gave her one hard kiss because he couldn't resist; then he turned his back, grabbed up a horse, saddled it, and was running it at a full gallop before he was out of the ranch yard.

She'd had a lot of men eager to marry her. Dozens. Hundreds! But none more so than Silas Harden. And for a fact, she'd never been anywhere near so eager to marry one of them.

She shooed the girls into the house and started heating water for baths. One by one she dunked her girls in the water and scrubbed a month's worth of trail dust off of them. By the time she was done, their nails were clean, their hair squeaked, and even the tips of their toes were shining. They all went to sleep with very little urging, even though it was the middle of the day.

Then Belle, knowing she had hours before the time came to leave for the south pass, rode out and inspected her herd. She rounded up the horses Silas had sent running ahead and herded them into the corral. She found the milk cow and roped her and coaxed her back to the barn so the animal would gentle down some before her baby came and she needed milking again. She found a goodly number of the chickens brooding in the barn. She moved the ones who weren't nesting back to the chicken coop so she could be sure any eggs they laid were fresh. She found enough work to do to keep her busy all afternoon and into the next week, but finally she had to turn her back on it and take her own bath and get the girls moving, because she wanted them at the wedding.

She dressed all of them, including herself, in their prettiest dresses—which weren't all that pretty, but it was all they had— and headed out. They were just starting the steep climb toward the snow line when she saw Silas coming down the hill with another man. A thrill of excitement made Belle shiver, and she tried to control the smile that kept breaking out on her face.

"You really love him, don't ya, Ma?" Emma asked with hushed pleasure.

Belle watched him come, still over a mile away on the winding path. She knew the minute he spotted her, because his horse broke into a trot. It warmed her heart till she thought it might catch on fire. She said quietly, "I think I finally got it right, girls. I think I've found a husband to be proud of and a father for the lot of you to love."

"I hope it's the other way around, Ma," Sarah said. "I want him to be a husband for you to love and a father for us to be proud of."

Belle laughed. "Maybe we can have it all."

She saw Sarah nodding with quiet satisfaction, and at the same instant, all three of them, with Betsy on Emma's back, started trotting forward.

The Husband Tree

The two parties met at an unlikely spot on the trail. There wasn't a spot wide enough for them to dismount and stand before the preacher. And the preacher had a disgruntled, kidnapped look to him. The horses looked exhausted, and there was snow clinging to the preacher's boots.

"It's snowing in the highlands. Let's make this quick so the man can get back through the pass," Silas said.

It might not have been the shortest wedding ceremony on record, but that's only because no one kept records of such things. It had to be in contention.

The preacher was still pulling his horse to a stop when he said, "Silas Harden, do you take this woman to be your lawful-wedded wife?"

Silas grinned as he dragged his Stetson off his head, "Well, why else did I drag you all the way up here?"

"Just answer, 'I do.'" The preacher glared at him in a way that didn't strike Belle as all that holy.

"I do."

"And do you, Belle Tanner, take this man to be your lawful-wedded husband?" The preacher wheeled his horse to face Belle who was just riding up and turning her horse so she was beside Silas. She'd heard the first question put to Silas, though, so it counted.

Before she could answer, Silas reached over and grabbed her hand. "Aren't you gonna tell her to obey me? I think you oughta say it 'cuz she's a headstrong little thing."

The preacher snapped at Belle, "Are you gonna obey him?" His horse danced sideways toward the edge of a fifty-foot drop-off at the unusually testy voice coming from the peaceful, God-loving man who sat on his back.

Belle leaned across her horse and subdued the fractious mount before they lost their parson. "Not likely, unless he orders me to do something I was gonna do anyway."

The preacher looked at Silas. "I've known Belle for a while now. I could have told you that."

"But it's a promise before God, isn't it?" Silas asked in astonishment. "It's required."

Since Belle had his horse, the preacher felt safe enough to take off his broad-brimmed felt hat as was due respect for the current occasion. He tapped it impatiently on his Bible. "Now there's no sense making Belle take a vow before God that she doesn't have a ghost of a chance of keeping. It'd be a sin to my way of thinking. So, if you want her so all-fired bad—and the way you as good as stole me out of the diner in Divide tells me you do—then take her without 'obey' and shut up about it. It's all the same to me, and I'm leaving here in thirty seconds whether you're hitched or not. Now, no offense, folks, but I don't want to spend my winter with you. Do you know I've got a wife expecting a baby in January?"

"I already said I'd take her," Silas protested. "It's her vows we're speaking of now."

Belle said, "I do."

"I do what?" Silas growled. "I do take this man, or I do know about his wife having a baby?"

The preacher slapped his hat back on his head, leaned over, and wrested his reins out of Belle's hand. "Thank you kindly for holding Blackie, Belle. Much obliged. Try to keep this one alive for a while. These weddings are wearing me out." The preacher turned his horse and started up the trail. After about twenty yards, he stopped and turned around and yelled, "I almost forgot. I now pronounce you man and wife!" He wheeled his horse around and headed at a gallop for the summit.

"Will he make it? How bad is the pass?" Belle worried. "We should follow him and make sure he's all right."

"It's not bad and the snow's not real heavy. With the trail we broke, he'll be fine. Besides, his wife found out I was hauling him out of town, and she was after me with a posse before we were out of sight. We stayed ahead of her, but she'll be waiting to haul him down off the mountain if he should run into trouble. That is one tough woman!" Silas leaned across the space between his horse and Belle's. Sliding one hand firmly behind Belle's neck, he said, "You may now kiss the bride." And he did just that.

Sarah yelled, "Hurray!"

Betsy clapped her hands together and yelled, "Papa."

"High time," Emma said. "We got evening chores. Let's get back to the ranch."

Silas let go of Belle, and she touched her lips to keep the warmth in them. "Yeah," Silas said with a sparkle in his eye. "Let's go home, girls."

Belle smiled at him with a heart that felt younger and a spirit that felt lighter than it had since before her pa had given her to William. "Yes, girls, let's take the new husband and go home."

Silas laughed and kissed her again. When he was close enough that only she could hear, he said, "You're gonna forget you ever had another husband 'sides me before I'm done with you, Mrs. Harden."

"I already have," Belle said peacefully.

They all turned their horses for home, and the animals were anxious to get out of the sharp winter weather in the highlands, so they moved along willingly.

It was the happiest day of Belle's life.

CHAPTER 22

Belle was furious.

She'd been cheated. She had been done so wrong she thought she might dig up all three of her no-account husbands and beat the daylights out of whatever was left of their worthless hides.

Nestling closer to Silas as he slept, she knew, after three earlier marriages, she'd never known what went on between a man and a woman!

Silas's eye flickered open when she moved, and she forgot all about being mad. "Good morning, wife. You enjoying our honeymoon?" He'd made up a warm little bed for them in the barn and teased the girls that he was taking their ma on a honeymoon. Now they lay here, toasty warm, wrapped in blankets, wrapped in each other.

"Morning, Silas."

He pulled her closer till her cheek rested on his shoulder, close enough that when he looked into her eyes there was nothing else in the world. Then he leaned close and kissed her. No whiskers. He'd looked like a wild man when she married him. He hadn't taken a second to bathe or shave or even change into clean clothes before the wedding. But he'd done all that later, after that poor excuse for a ceremony but long before the wedding night. He'd cleaned up real good.

Wrapping one strong arm around her shoulders, he pulled her still closer. "You're not ready to plant me under the Husband Tree yet, are you?" He kissed her, probably to help get the answer he wanted.

He needn't have bothered.

"Nope, I'm going to keep you above ground. I like you all warm and—" Their eyes met and her nonsense suddenly seemed unworthy. The smile melted off her face. "Don't speak of such things, Silas." She slid one hand into his overly long hair. "I want you with me for the rest of my life. I can't bear to think of that tree right now."

Moving with almost desperate speed, she flung her arms around his neck and kissed him. His arms closed around hers and held her tight. "You're not getting rid of me, Belle."

His words were interrupted by her lips. "I've survived—" He went on, in broken sentences, "A long time in this land." He tossed in words between the kissing. "I know my way around." The gleam in his eyes made her wonder if they were still talking about ranching and his long life. "You're stuck with me."

"I am, aren't I?" She thought now of the glow in Lindsay's eyes the morning after her wedding and knew that Lindsay was already more of a woman than Belle had ever been.

But that was before last night.

"This is my first real wedding night." She turned her thoughts from the others, only able to control a shudder at those memories because of where she was now and the strength and warmth of Silas's arms.

And although she was furious at her husbands, she wasn't going to dig them up after all, because she was too contented to move.

"We need to get going," Belle murmured. "The girls will have breakfast on by now. We're sleeping the day away."

"We're not sleeping, darlin'."

Which Belle had to admit was the plain truth. "But I need to check the herd. And I never did a good check on the saddle stock yesterday and—"

Silas quieted her right down. He drove every thought of work and the ranch and even her girls from her mind.

They got into breakfast late.

The girls were dressed and cooking. Sarah had outdone herself to make it a celebration. They had eggs she'd scrounged up just this morning. There were hotcakes on the grill. She'd sliced into a new side of bacon and shredded raw potatoes and onions into hash browns. They were all so starving for food that wasn't laced with the flavor of trail dust that they ate like field hands, which, when it came right down to it, was exactly what they all were.

After they were sitting over their second cups of coffee, Silas announced, "This cabin is a disaster. It needs at least one more bedroom, and I've got to patch the holes in it before the snow falls. Which one of your worthless husbands built this wreck for you, Belle honey?"

An extended silence filled the room. Sarah's eyes widened, and Belle could see she was trying to think of a way to warn Silas off dangerous ground. Emma slumped low in her chair as if she had been awaiting the first fight—and now here it came.

Belle set her coffee cup down with the sharp *click* of tin on wood. "I built it myself."

Silas looked around for a long minute. "Well, in that case, I think it's wonderful. In fact, I wouldn't change a thing."

"You wouldn't change a thing?" Belle roared. "Why, this place is falling down around our ears."

Silas grinned at her until she quit snarling. When she finally did, he started chuckling, softly at first then louder. He gasped over his laughter, "You said it. I didn't." Then he started laughing again.

Belle threw her coffee cup at him. But no one took it seriously, because it was both tin and empty. Silas just ducked and kept laughing. Before long the whole table was laughing along with him.

Silas finally managed to say, "Then I have your permission to fix a few things, Mrs. Harden?"

"Oh, Silas," Belle said ardently, "if only you would."

Silas rose from his end of the table and rounded it to pull Belle out of her chair. He took the seat she'd just vacated and dropped her right onto his lap. He kissed her with a resounding *smack*, then stood and returned her to the seat and just as easily returned to his own chair. "I'll have the frame up before nightfall or your name isn't. . . C'mon, sweetheart, this is a test. What's your name these days?"

"It's Belle Harden. *Mrs. Silas Harden.*" Her heart pounded from that kiss and from how much she loved her new name. "And from this day forward, all the girls are Hardens, too." Belle nodded firmly to her girls, and they all nodded back just as confidently. No fussy legal formalities needed for the Harden clan.

Silas said with exaggerated severity, "And don't any of you ever forget it."

He got up from the table, dusting his hands as if one chore was done—naming his family. "Point me to the tools. Have you got an ax? I need to cut some trees."

Silas clamped his Stetson on his head and started for the door. He stopped suddenly. "No, the house isn't first. I need to ride out and check the cattle. We need to get them closer in, off the summer pasture, before their grazing in the highlands is buried under ten feet of snow. I need to check them over and make sure none are sick or injured, and I ought to do a tally before winter so we have some idea of what to expect for calves in the spring." Silas dragged his hat off his head as he stood in front of the open door and stared across the rugged land.

"I'll get started on all of that." Belle got up from the table and went to his side. "Let me do it while you work on the house."

"It's not gonna be that way, Belle." Silas shook his head. "You are done doing a man's work around here. I'll just have to push hard with the tally and get to the cabin later. We've got two months before the weather closes in on us, maybe more."

"No!" Belle shouted.

Silas jumped and gave her a wary look. "Belle, I know what the preacher said about obeying, and I know you're not used to stepping aside when there's work to be done. That's one of the things I love most about you. And I'm not trying to give you orders. I'm just trying to begin this marriage as I mean for it to go on. I want to make your life easier."

"I didn't mean to holler at you, Silas. I'm not fighting with you over giving up my work. Believe me, I'd like nothing better than to run this house and leave most of the outdoor chores to you. The problem is, if we mean to have this house enlarged and sealed up before winter, you're going to have to hurry. We *might* have two months, but sometimes we get an early snow that surprises us. Let me keep on at the cattle chores for a few days. A week or two while you set yourself to working on the house. I can do the cattle, but I am a poor excuse for a carpenter. I guess I yelled because we don't have much time and. . ." Belle leaned so close her chin rested on his chest, and murmured so the girls couldn't hear, "I want our own room so bad."

Silas pulled his gaze away from the horizon and looked down at her. Somehow, even though he wasn't a huge man, not as tall as any of her other husbands, he made her feel small and feminine. He rested his open hand on her cheek. "You've done better here than any woman could have. Better than most *men* could have.

The Husband Tree

Don't you speak badly of yourself because the house you built with your own hands isn't good enough. Look what you've built here, and I'm not talking just about the cabin and barn. I'm talking about the sweet bunch of daughters, the herd, the money you've earned, plenty more things; all of this is yours and your girls', and it's something to be proud of. I wish. . ." Silas's chin dropped and he didn't meet her eyes. "I wish I could have brought more into this marriage, Belle. It isn't honorable for a poor man to come to a rich woman with his hands empty."

"Rich woman?" Belle had never thought of herself in such a way.

"Yes, that's exactly what you are. You have this whole spread paid for and two thousand-plus head of cattle and fifteen thousand dollars cash money in that bag you brought home. I reckon you're as rich as anyone in the state these days. I reckon I'm just another sorry excuse for a husband around here. This"—he waved his hand at the expanse of open pasture broken by clumps of trees and rocky outcroppings that spread out before them—"all this is yours. I want to contribute something more than I can right now. I'm going to add to it and put everything I have of myself in it, but it'll take time, and I. . .well, I have an idea." He looked up at her like he was almost scared.

Belle's heart turned over to see him so vulnerable.

"I'm not sure if it'll work, and I want to accomplish it before I talk about it."

"What idea, Silas?"

Silas lay his hand over hers where it rested on his chest. More than ever she wanted that new bedroom built on. The barn was going to get mighty cold before long.

"Hush now." Silas lay his finger over her lips. "I'll tell you about it when I'm ready. If I tell you now, knowing you, little woman, you'll just treat my idea like it's a cantankerous bull. You'll grab it by the horns and wrestle it right into line all on your own. For now, I'll. . ." A shadow passed over his expression, and Belle knew he was unhappy about what he was going to say. "I'll do it your way and let you keep on with the cattle, but only for the time it takes me to get this place spruced up and get some headway on"—he hunched one shoulder and said dismissively in a way that made Belle worry that she'd somehow wounded his pride—"my idea."

His touch was so tender and his eyes so full of regret at letting her work at her cattle and having so little to contribute to their marriage that Belle wanted to take him off somewhere where they could be alone and cheer him right up.

He seemed to read her mind, because the wistfulness was gone out of his eyes. He leaned over and kissed her. "Just promise me you'll leave all the real hard labor to me. Just do your tally and keep track of any animals that need attention. I'll do the rest." With what sounded like honest regret, he added, "At first, I reckon I'm going to end up being as worthless as your other husbands, but only for a while. . . ."

"Don't you dare say that, Silas Harden. You've already done more for me than all three of those worthless old coots put together, so don't you ever lump yourself in with them again."

"Yeah, I noticed you enjoyed our. . .honeymoon." He smiled with heat in his eyes.

She slapped his shoulder. "I meant on the cattle drive."

Laughing, Silas said, "Oh, that's right. I do remember helping you out a bit during that."

"You work on the cabin, and whatever this idea is of yours, you go do it with my blessing."

Silas tucked one finger under her chin and tilted her face a bit and looked into her eyes for a long moment. Then, as if satisfied with her sincerity, he gave her a brisk nod and slapped his hat on his head. "I'll get on with chopping down some timber."

"I can help, Pa." Emma got up from the table. "I can hook a line to the logs and drag them back here."

The Husband Tree.

Silas looked over at the girls, and Belle had the impression that Silas had forgotten they had an audience. She knew how he felt. Sometimes it seemed as if they were alone in the world.

"*Pa*," Silas said with quiet satisfaction. "I really like that, Emma. I'm mighty proud to have you call me that." He took two steps to where the girls had stood watching them hash out their chores and wrapped Emma and Sarah, with Betsy in Sarah's arms, in a bear hug. He even growled while he did it. He hugged them long and hard, and for just a second, with an especially big growl, he lifted all three of them off the floor. Sarah giggled.

He set them all down and said to Emma, "No, you're not helping. Those logs have a way of rolling wild on a person. I don't want you in the way. I can use your help when I'm back here, but I don't want you on that mountainside with falling trees."

Belle saw Emma's eyes shine. No man had ever told her no when she offered to work before, and no man had ever acted like her safety was more important than the strength in her back.

Belle remembered how she'd struggled with trees, bringing them down here. One of the reasons she'd built where she did was because there was a nice stand of young growth ponderosa pines at this spot and she could get the logs from where they fell to the house site.

Later she found out this area had a stream of water flowing through it in the rainy season that turned the ranch yard into a mud hole and the corral and barn into a swamp. The wind whipped into the cabin with nothing to stop it, but a couple of miles of clear sailing to pick up speed. The snow tended to blow into deep drifts all around them, and they didn't get any afternoon sun at all.

She'd had Lindsay on her back or toddling around her feet while she built it. Before she was done with the barn, she'd had Emma growing big in her belly. She'd only wanted a roof over her head, and she never thought to consider such things as spring flooding and afternoon sun when she'd begun struggling with the logs and the ornery horses and the lackadaisical William.

Thinking of Silas's gift for quick, tight construction, as he'd demonstrated on Lindsay's house, she got excited for what was to come and hadn't a single qualm about keeping up her grueling work with the cattle. She didn't have any plans to spare herself work and leave all the toughest jobs for Silas either. He didn't deserve to have every task on this ranch settled on his shoulders from the first minute.

Silas said to Emma, "For now, I hope you don't mind helping your ma with the cattle still. It won't be for long. I promise."

"No. No, Pa. I'll help her gladly. I never figured to quit anyway. I'm happier on horseback than I am in the kitchen. Even when you're done with the house, I want to keep riding herd."

"I'll always need help, I'm afraid." Then Silas looked at Sarah. "And I can't believe someone so young can turn her hand to a kitchen and take such good care of us like you do, Sarie. You're gonna not have much extra help for a while either. I didn't want it to be this way, but for now it's gotta be."

"I like being called Sarie," Sarah said with pink-tinged cheeks. "I never had a nickname before, Pa."

Silas tapped her nose with one finger. "I gotta get on with it or we'll be having snowflakes for breakfast one of these next days. Now, you all"—he tossed a glance around the room that included all of them—"quit making a man want to stay inside to spend time with his pretty girls and let me get to work!"

He flashed them a grin so handsome that Belle's heart seemed to be melting right inside her chest.

He hugged the girls again, and as he passed Belle, he grabbed her and dipped her backward over his arm and kissed away every brain cell she had in her head. He'd been gone for several minutes before any of them thought to get on with the day's work.

Belle heard herself sigh. She had it real bad. Then she smiled at the girls. "Let's get to work."

The Husband Tree

She went out to saddle up a bronco. As the horse crow hopped across the corral to work out its morning kinks, she took a moment to give thanks for Silas Harden. She'd always believed, but now she had actual living proof.

There really was a God.

CHAPTER 23

There really was a devil, too!

The pointy-horned, pitchfork-toting sidewinder had put one over on her again!

Silas Harden and his stupid *idea*! Belle was getting real sick of the fact that she hadn't seen hide nor hair of Silas since she married him. Except at mealtimes and bedtimes, of course. He was always right on time for those.

He'd fixed the house up to a point, tossing together a bedroom and patching a few of the worst cracks to cut the wind. Near as she could figure that had taken him about three days. He'd done nothing since.

Belle and Emma took a few days working the kinks out of their green-broke horses that they'd left behind while on the drive. They'd next thing to gone pure wild again with a month's neglect. Belle hoped to have them gentled by spring. She'd been a steady supplier of well-trained horses for the area ranchers. And Emma had a special gift for it. They'd make good money on this year's horse crop.

Still, it was a spine-jarring business getting into the saddle most mornings. Once the cayuse she picked out for this morning worked out its nerves, she turned to Emma. "Where's Silas?"

"He was gone when I got up." Emma shrugged. "He took the roan today and a bunch of the tools. I reckon he's working on something for the house."

"But *what* for the house? The extra room has been done for a full week."

"Now, Ma, don't go to nagging at Pa. He's been a purely good husband so far."

Belle had to admit that was the honest truth. When she thought about the way Silas had pulled them over that mountain trail with pure grit and iron will, her loved bubbled up like a spring. She'd never met a man she respected more. So, whatever he was doing, she'd trust it was for the best. "He did a good job with that spare room. I don't know much about building. Maybe he's fixing things I don't even notice. I've been gone for long hours. He could come and go ten times and I'd never notice it."

"We could ask Sarah. She's keeping Betsy in the house or around the ranch yard while she works. She'd see him during the day."

"We've got to get going this morning. I'm not going to start in nagging on this one. I promise."

Emma jerked her chin in satisfaction. "What are we workin' on today?"

Belle kicked her horse who seemed content to stretch his legs with her on his back. "That high rise. I've got a herd of longhorns that think they're mountain goats. I wanted to see how many calves are up there."

"Didn't Pa tell you to leave the herds that are hard to get to?"

"He did, but he thinks he's got a long time to work before winter comes. He's new to this area. I'm not going to sit around resting and leave everything to him while he's working so hard on the house. That ain't nice."

"No, it surely ain't. But that's a tough trail up there." Emma fell in beside Belle. "It'd like to scare any sensible cow into a dead faint, but not these critters."

The trail got narrow. Belle and Emma strung out to single file. They quit talking so they could attend to dodging pine trees trying to slap them in the face.

The two of them drove the bulk of those crazy mountain-climbing cattle down closer to the house. All of them took turns trying to go back to the highlands. But once they finally came down and found lush grass, they settled in to eating, and Belle knew they'd stay where the living was easy. Cattle and men: The only real difference was she could sell cattle off and earn real cash money.

This was one of many far-flung groups of cattle Belle needed to check. She'd been burned so badly by miscounting her herd last spring that she was afraid to be slipshod again. She'd check every square inch of her land before the snow fell or know the reason why.

Knowing Silas wouldn't like the brutally hard day she'd had, Belle kept her work to herself in front of him, and so did Emma, to keep from hurting his feelings.

Wade found a line shack far enough from the Flathead village to not be on their hunting ground. The cabin was ramshackle, ten feet by ten feet or so, with a shanty in the back big enough for his horse and nothing else.

He was drawn to Glowing Sun so powerfully that he could go no farther from her. But she'd left him. Gone off, just as Cassie Dawson had. Just as his mother had. Wade had let Cassie torment him until he'd lost his way completely, before finding his way in the end to God.

Tempted to go to Red and Cassie for advice, Wade felt God telling him it was time to stand on his own. Time to focus on his own strange longing to save a woman in need.

Sometimes he caught the slimmest memories of fairy tales his mother had read to him. And maybe he remembered his pa shouting at his ma. The ogres in those fairy tales and the monster that was his father were twisted together and added to by years of fear. The damsels in distress, the heroic white knights. . . Wade couldn't decide what of his memories were true.

Was the shouting from later years? Pa had done plenty of it. And Wade's longing for memories of his mother got mixed in. Whether it was memory or not, Wade knew it was time to stop thinking about saving someone else and find a way to save himself.

Not his soul. God had done that. But he needed wisdom to save himself from making the same mistakes over and over again. He knew he was lonely. It might be because he didn't like his own company. How better to get over that than to force himself to be alone.

This line shack would be a retreat for him. A refuge. He'd winter here, hunt for food, read his Bible, search his soul. He welcomed the coming snow that would trap him inside and keep him from the almost irresistible need to ride to Glowing Sun.

He sank onto the tattered blankets of the single narrow cot. The bed squeaked with protest under his weight, but it held.

Wade buried his face in the Bible clutched in his hands. Why would Glowing Sun choose him? He was a weakling. She'd chosen a warrior.

The strength he needed seemed beyond his grasp, at least for today, and he covered his eyes with one hand and cried.

The snow that would keep him from making a fool of himself over a woman who didn't want him couldn't come soon enough.

Belle raced against the coming winter.

She rode out with Emma most days, though sometimes it

made more sense to split up.

Leaving the cabin right after breakfast, Belle usually didn't even see Silas, who was up and out before dawn. She came back to the cabin to feed Betsy, and he was never around. Some days, if the weather looked to hold decent, she'd head for the farther reaches of her land, and she'd take Betsy along and nurse her on horseback and eat jerked beef and hard biscuits and not get back to the cabin all day.

Silas would be there looking for all the world like a horse that had been rode hard and put up wet.

She was exhausted herself and not given to making idle talk with anyone. And when they were alone, talking was the furthest thing from their minds.

They'd been married for two weeks the first time she'd asked him, sitting at the dinner table, what was keeping him so busy.

Silas laid down his fork as if the food suddenly tasted bad. Then he looked at his plate as if he couldn't meet her eyes. "I'm not ready to talk about it, Belle honey. I'm keeping real busy and my. . . um. . . *idea* is going to work out fine. I won't be long at it"—he looked up, direct, bossy—"so don't start moving the herd down to the low country without me. I don't want you and Emma out on those passes and mountain slopes. Please trust me, Belle, and be patient. There's plenty of time to get everything done."

There wasn't, and she'd already moved a lot of her herd down. But she didn't correct him, because he looked so sad. She somehow felt like her question shamed him. She wished she hadn't brought it up in front of the girls. He might have been willing to tell her his idea if they'd been alone. He had that sad, sweet look in his eyes. And the way he held her that night made her feel so content she didn't care what the man did during the day.

The next morning she and Emma cleared downed branches from the spreader dam Belle had built years ago. There was no way to get the branches out except to wade in after them. Belle wore her oldest clothes.

"There's no reason I can't come in there, too, Ma. It'd go faster."

Shaking her head, Belle said, "Then Sarah would have to come out and drag the windfalls away. Someone has to do that." Belle shuddered to think of Emma in this bitter cold. "I can last for about an hour in here and that's enough. There's no reason for both of us to get soaking wet."

"Did you tell Pa you were doing this today?"

Belle shoved a long, many-limbed branch to the shore.

Emma grabbed hold and dragged it away from the edge so the first good rain wouldn't wash it back in to clog up the dam.

"I was going to, but you saw how he acted last night. What am I supposed to do? Kick up a fuss? Pester him to help me? You're the one who told me not to start in nagging."

"I know I said that. But I never figured him for a lazy man. Not after the cattle drive. And he was a rancher before. He knows what needs doing. Why isn't he helping us?"

Belle heard Emma's concern. It had more to do with frustration because Belle wouldn't let the girl wade into the bitter cold water than with being real upset at Silas.

"I don't know, honey. Why do you think?" Belle was as mystified as Emma.

"Maybe it's a husband thing. Maybe instead of marrying him you should have just kept him around as a hired man. I wonder how Lindsay is doing? You suppose she has to take care of all three of those men?" Emma shook her head and worked quietly while Belle waded out for another clump stuck against the earthen dam she'd mounted up across a spring runoff.

Belle was determined not to nag, so she bided her time. A week later, when they were alone in the tidy little room he'd erected, she'd thought the moment was right. "So, tell me about your idea, Silas. I want to know—" She broke off her question. Because what she wanted to say was, *I want to know what you're doing all day every day when you should be working this ranch.* And there was no way to say that right. So she let the question hang.

Silas smiled at her, came close, and caught her hands. "My idea is coming along great. Today I—" Silas's words cut off as he lifted her hands into his and looked down at the calluses. The glow faded from his eyes, and he ran a thumb over the roughness, as if he were personally responsible.

"Belle, the West is a hard land, and it's particularly hard on women and children. But you're the strongest woman I've ever known." He held her work-roughened hand for a long while, palm up.

He'd been going to talk. She knew that. So whatever he was doing must be all right. She imagined his clearing a pasture of felled trees or building fence, something to surprise her. But her ugly hands distracted him. She wished she could be a pampered and beautiful woman, but it wasn't in her nature.

Lifting her hand, he pressed the palm to his lips. The way she shivered from his touch made her think of being even closer, and she knew she had about five seconds to head that off.

Not that she wanted to. She just wanted to finish questioning him.

She pulled her hands away. "Don't, Silas. I want us to talk. We never spend any time really talking. What do you have planned for tomorrow, because I. . ."

His strong hands tipped her head back. "You are more than just strong. You're beautiful, too." He whispered that nonsense against her windburned cheek and acted as if he were starving hungry for her chapped lips.

"And sweet." Gently, he captured her hands again and pressed her palms against his cheeks.

"And soft where it counts." Turning from her lips, he began kissing each callus, taking a side trip back to her mouth from time to time.

"Your eyes shine like gold." He kissed each eye.

She found that she couldn't open them again after his gentle caress. "Silas," Belle whispered, trying to remember what she'd wanted to talk about.

"I love your hair down, like liquid silk in my hands." He touched her hair, her coarse, neglected hair, as if he couldn't deny himself the pleasure.

They never did go back to their talk.

And she never for a moment considered going after him with a frying pan.

After he was long gone the next day, she remembered.

She needed to move the cattle from a particularly dangerous stretch of high-up pasture, and she didn't want Emma out on the rocky ledges they'd have to traverse. She was especially worried about it because a wolf pack had moved into her mountain valley. They kept her hopping trying to track them down while she rushed ahead of the oncoming winter.

She should probably tell Silas about the troublesome wolves, but she knew he'd say, "Leave it for me." That's all he ever said. But Belle was finished listening to empty promises. Time was short. She'd hoped she could convince him to abandon his *idea* for just a day and come with her.

"I've gotta go to the north high pasture today, Em. I'll take Betsy along." She'd faced that last high ridge alone before. She'd do it again.

"Let me ride with you, Ma. Them wolves are a mean bunch this year."

"We've got to finish the haying. If you stay in and put in a long day on that and I get these cattle tallied, we're done with the worst of the fall chores. I don't like the feel of the wind. I want both of these things done today."

"But you shouldn't go so far alone."

577

"I've done it many times."

Emma stared at her.

Belle stared back. She could boss her children around just fine, but usually they agreed on things together. And Emma could smell snow on the wind as well as Belle.

Finally, Emma nodded. "You'll be late. But I'll be watching for you, too, Ma. We'll put in a tough day today; then things'll calm down. Who knows, maybe even Silas'll stay around once the wind starts blowing. Anthony did."

"Only 'cuz the pass was closed. Whatever Silas is up to must be somewhere inside the valley." Betsy shifted in the pack on Belle's back and cooed through her bundling.

"Are you sure?" Emma eyed the horizon, turning in all directions. "He could be riding into Divide every day."

Belle froze. She'd never considered that. Could he possibly be going in to find whiskey? "No, he's not drinking. I'd know the smell." But if he was careful, would she know? And would she know about dance-hall girls if he was careful to wash their perfume away? Anthony had done that at first.

Belle shook her head. A painful cracking feeling in her heart made her wonder for the first time if Silas might be betraying her. "Well, we'll know for sure one of these days." She briskly pulled on her gloves. "Until we do, I've got cattle to round up."

Emma nodded, her face calm, but Belle had seen that calm falter for a minute. Emma loved Silas, too. "And I've got haying to do."

The two women swung up on horseback. Belle, with Betsy, rode upland. Emma rode down. Heaven only knew where Silas rode.

Belle mused on Silas, denying he would drink or be untrue to her. But where could he be? She'd been all over the range. Then she realized she'd never gone near that high valley someone had claimed. Could Silas be doing something in that direction? She brought all the cattle down from up there before the drive and figured not to check that land again until spring.

For that matter, she'd never told Silas someone had claimed it. If he was working over there, she needed to tell him to quit. But why would he be over there? They'd been home over a month now, and she knew no further progress was being made with the house. When he watched her with those sad eyes, it didn't cut quite so deep.

She traveled up-country with her rifle on her saddle and her six-gun strapped down, because the wolves were coming in closer to the place following the herd. She'd already thinned the pack some, but there were plenty left. She'd had wolves all the years she'd been here, and although the pack this year was especially large and more aggressive than most, she didn't think much of their nonsense. She accepted a certain loss of cattle as the way things were but fought all the time to keep the losses small.

She worked a long, cold day in the rugged hills, dodging longhorns as wild and vicious as any grizzly. She'd be late getting home, but after today there would be no more long, bitter days. Only short, bitter ones with a husband who'd once again failed her. Before she headed home, she sat down in a sheltered spot to build a fire, have some coffee, and see to Betsy.

The little girl had stayed strapped on Belle's back all day with barely a sound—except for a few necessary breaks that had also required a fire. It had slowed Belle down some.

Once Betsy was settled, Belle packed her horse and swung up. She rode a mile downhill until she came to an open meadow. Only then did she realize the weather had turned sharply colder during the day. Up until now the timber had cut the force of the wind. It was already late. Because Belle had no plans to come up here again until spring, she'd stuck it out doing everything that was needed.

She rode on for hours, winding closer to home with still a long, long way to go, when the cold got to be too much. Belle chafed at the delay, but she'd known she had to see to Betsy at least one more time, and she couldn't unwrap the baby without a fire. She found an overhang, got a good fire going, and settled herself comfortably into a corner with the rock wall behind her.

And suddenly she was waking up.

She'd only awakened because Betsy started crying in the bundle of blankets nestled beside her on the ground. Belle sat forward quickly, shocked at herself for falling asleep. Her stomach lurched then dived hard, and she just barely managed to set Betsy down and crawl a few steps away before she threw up in the grass.

When she quit retching, she wiped her mouth and slowly sat back down. Alerted by a particularly loud squall from Betsy, she unwrapped her baby, just over nine months old, and put her to her breast, which Belle noticed now was tender.

Belle was no schoolgirl still in pinafores. She'd been up and down this trail before.

She held Betsy in the waning light and stroked the cheeks that were hollow and too tanned for a baby.

And Belle Harden cried.

She was going to have another one. Another precious little baby. She could already picture a little girl who looked just like Silas. A little girl who was too quiet because she was raised on horseback by a ma who didn't have time to fuss over every little whimper.

God, please let it be a girl.

That same old prayer. The one she'd spoken into so many lonely nights.

Belle remembered what it had been like when she had Emma growing in her and Lindsay strapped on her back. She'd built the cabin in that condition and rode herd for long days just like this. Surviving that year and the one after, with Lindsay a harum-scarum three-year-old and Emma at her breast, had taken every ounce of strength she had.

The Husband Tree

And these two, Betsy and the new one, would be almost that close in age. She thought of the branding time to come in the spring. She would be trying to brand these vicious, wild two-year-old bulls and heifers she'd scared out of the hills as well as the spring calves. Last spring had almost killed her. Dozens of times she'd been kicked or knocked to the ground. She accepted the rough-and-tumble ways of branding. But more than once she'd taken a hard blow to the belly because she was almost due to have Betsy and her stomach was in the way something fierce. More than one night she'd lain in bed and felt pains start then ease off, and she knew it was the brutally hard work that was pushing the baby to come before time.

Anthony had of course done none of the spring work. Claimed he had a bad back.

This spring she wouldn't be quite as close to due, but it would be bad enough. And if the baby did come, unlike Betsy who was close to ready to face the world, this baby would be too young. She stood a good chance of killing the poor little baby with her work.

God, please let it be a girl.

The fear and sorrow of that made her wish the baby away, and Belle hated herself for that. No baby deserved to come into the world with a mother who felt such awful things. She *loved* her girls. She was grateful to God for giving her every one of them, because her life would be empty without them. But she was a bad mother.

Belle admitted the real reason she cried was because she was going to give birth to another little girl who would never know a mother's time or soft hands. A little girl who was going to have to get tough, grow up hard, and quit wanting a mother's tenderness fast.

She looked down at Betsy who was nursing with her eyes wide open, staring at her sobbing mother. Betsy reached her thin, brown hand up and rested it on the swell of Belle's breast and opened and closed her hand as if to massage more milk for herself.

Belle wiped her eyes against the sleeve of her buffalo-hide coat and slid her work-roughened finger into the tiny hand.

Betsy clutched onto Belle and kicked as she nursed.

"I'm sorry I haven't been better to you, baby." With her voice breaking, Belle pulled her knees up to more completely cradle her neglected little angel and tried to sing a lullaby, stopping several times as she sorted through her mind for a song that wasn't one she sang to the cattle on the drive at night. She couldn't think of any, and that made her cry some more.

In the end, she just hummed and cried and let Betsy hold her finger. She tried to remember the last time she'd sung to her baby. And when she couldn't think of a single time, she cried all the harder.

Through her tears she thought of Silas. She thought of his charm with the girls and his gift for making her feel like a beautiful woman when she was so far from being one.

It was all lies. She knew that now. Yes, he'd worked hard beside them on the trail, and he'd been nothing short of heroic helping them get home. But now she could see that it had all been lies. He'd worked his way into her life; then he'd turned into another man who used her.

Exhausted from the early morning and the hard day and from growing a new life inside her, she slid down until she lay on the ground and curled her body around both her hungry old baby and her hungry new baby who was already making demands on her strength.

She'd known keen disappointment with all her husbands, but none had ever hurt like this. And it wasn't because he'd turned out to be lazy. It wasn't because he'd charmed the girls into loving him. They were so starved for a man to admire them that they would have fallen for anyone who spared them a single kind word. And it wasn't because he had lied, at least lied to Belle's way of thinking, because he'd let her believe he would hop out of the cart and pull along with her instead of going along for the ride like the other husbands.

It was because she loved him.

That love cut into her heart now like a dull-edged knife and carved out a piece of herself that Silas had awakened and warmed. Her love for him died along with her hope. She was going to have to go on handling the ranch just as she always had. She had been a fool, weak and stupid to want someone to carry the load. She deserved this. She had long ago learned she had to take care of herself. But now she knew, deep inside of her, she'd always clung to a tiny ray of hope that someone would come along and rescue her like she was some pathetic damsel in distress out of a fairy tale.

Well, there was no rescue coming. And she was no damsel. She was a cowpoke and a good one, and she was never going to be anything else.

Then she thought of the years ahead of her when she was going to have to be strong enough to deny Silas his husbandly rights. That had never been hard with the other husbands, but now the wonderful pleasure he'd introduced her to would have to die, too. If she didn't keep him away, there would be more babies—the ones she took such poor care of. When he'd shown her how it could be between a man and a woman, she had longed for Silas's baby. She had pictured herself with four more little girls, these girls chubby with light brown eyes and tawny brown hair streaked with gold from the sun. Silas's girls wore ruffles and were easy to make smile, and her other girls fit right in with them, learning to laugh and dress pretty and work in the house.

Now she knew that for a fool's dream. It would be impossible, because she didn't have the strength to give Silas all his babies and run this ranch, too. In that moment she hated Silas Harden. She hated him for making her love him and for teaching her about what could pass between a man and a woman and most of all for giving her hope.

She grieved for another neglected little baby girl.

God, please let me be strong enough to survive this new mess I've made of my life. Forgive me for marrying him. Forgive me for being such a fool.

Crooning to Betsy, Belle wished the baby could forgive her. But Betsy would never know what had been taken from her.

Wrenching tears wrung straight out of Belle's heart, until finally she slept before the slowly dying fire.

CHAPTER 24

Silas laughed out loud in the chilly night. He was done.

Well, not all the way done. But close enough he could finally share his idea with his womenfolk. Tell them what he'd been up to for the last month.

Knowing he was hours late for supper, he pushed his horse hard, but the animal was game and rested from lazing the day away while Silas worked. They made good time, and Silas imagined being the hero to his women. Hugs and kisses and all that would come his way when he finally told them about his idea.

He shouldn't have stayed so long today, but the long month of backbreaking work was worth it. He was overflowing with the pleasure of it. He knew he could never give to Belle what she'd given to him, but it was something.

It was a lot.

It was enough.

He thought about all Belle had given him. Of course there was the vast land holdings and impressive herd of cattle. But there was so much more. All of it more important than the ranch.

The girls.

"I'm a father." Silas's horse pricked up its ears when Silas spoke aloud, probably figuring his rider had lost his mind.

Grinning, Silas thought of his pretty, hardworking girls and patted his mount on the neck. "Never gave that much thought before, boy. If I had, I reckon I'd've thought of children as a heavy burden and a big responsibility. But I never figured it for the fun. I love being a pa to all those girls. I love hearin' the word *Pa* from them." He wouldn't mind having a dozen more of them. Thinking about Belle having his baby was enough to make him slap his hand on the rump of his horse and gallop every step of the way back to the cabin.

No, there was no comparison to what Belle had brought to this marriage compared to what one penniless, cowardly cowpoke brought, but he knew Belle loved him. He returned that love in full measure. It was more than any man had given her before. He wished he had more, but yes, it was enough.

He rode up to the ranch yard under a high, full moon. The cabin had its feeble glow shining out of the cracks in the front door. Except there wasn't much light showing—which meant there weren't as many cracks. That meant the cracks had all been patched. He'd told Belle he'd get to it, but she must not have trusted him to do it. Of course he had no intention of doing it, but still she should have trusted him. Frowning with irritation, he almost let his good mood slip but shoved the crankiness aside as he put his horse up and hurried to the ramshackle house to make his announcement to his girls.

Before he could get there, the door flew open, letting the meager heat out of the cabin.

Sarah called out, "Ma, is that you?"

There was something he'd never heard in his stalwart little Sarah's voice before. Fear. The cold night air whipped around him, but it was Sarah's voice that chilled him.

"No, it's Pa, Sarie. Isn't your ma in yet?" Silas increased his already-hurried stride. His pleasure evaporated. Belle should have been home hours ago.

"Her horse came in alone." Sarah's eyes were shaded by the dark, but Silas could see the furrows in her brow and hear the worry in her voice. "Emma is trying to back-trail him, but it was already almost dark when the horse showed up wearing his saddle and bridle. Emma said he came from the far north where Ma was combing those breaks for any hide-out steers today. Emma headed up there."

"Your ma was up in that steep timberland? I told her to leave that for me." Silas forgot his fear for Belle for just a second as he digested this latest bit of proof that Belle didn't want to move aside as boss and make room for him.

"I reckon she thought she was out of time, Silas." Sarah sounded matter-of-fact. She obviously didn't plan on Silas doing that work either. "Snow comes early up here."

"I know when snow comes," Silas snapped, annoyed with the way Sarah called him by his first name instead of saying, "Pa." He looked at his upset little girl more closely. Her worry for her mother was only part of what the little girl was feeling. He detected a note of. . .resignation. Like the little girl had resigned herself to something, but Silas couldn't think what. And under that, so slight he hoped he misunderstood it, he got an impression of disdain. "Follow me to the barn while I saddle a fresh horse."

Sarah trotted to keep up as he rushed toward the barn. "I should have gone with Emma, but she said I should tell you what'd happened. Emma said you might help."

Silas looked at her, not breaking his stride. "What do you mean, I *might* help? Of course I'm going to help."

Sarah shrugged. "We're used to doing for ourselves."

Silas bit back an angry retort. "How long ago did the horse show up?" Silas had been unusually late. He'd thought he'd come bursting into this tumbledown house and make his big announcement and be greeted like a conquering hero. Instead, the house held only one scared, disrespectful little girl.

"Hours. Emma's been gone for hours. She told me which way Ma rode."

"You can't go, Sarie. You need to stay here and take care of Betsy. Does she have enough to eat?" He knew the baby still nursed.

Sarah grabbed a lasso and went out of the barn to the yard where the riding stock was corralled. Over her shoulder, she said, "Betsy's with her."

"With Emma?" Silas followed her and watched Sarah disobey him and lasso a horse. He clenched his jaw but said nothing. If she wanted to come, she could come.

"No, with Ma."

Silas had been leaving earlier than Belle most mornings. He hadn't realized Belle took the baby along. "She takes Betsy with her to work the cattle?"

"Ma has to take her if she's gonna be gone over a feeding time. How else can she manage?" Sarah led her horse into the barn to where her saddle was kept.

Silas felt a twist of fear as he threw a loop over a fresh horse. Not only was his wife missing, but his baby might be in danger, too. Hopefully the horse had just broken its reins while it was tied up, but anything could happen in the wilderness. His fear bloomed into anger at Belle for putting herself in danger.

He and Sarah were saddled and on the trail in minutes. As they rode out of the yard into the cold night, Silas asked, "Do you know where she was headed exactly? Did she tell you?"

"It weren't no secret, Silas." She guided her horse in the direction she'd said Emma went.

Silas caught up and rode alongside his daughter. "Why are you calling me Silas tonight? I thought you were going to call me Pa."

"You're not my pa is all." Sarah didn't look at him. She just urged her horse a little faster and said over her shoulder, "I forgot

that for a while. And I don't like the name Sarie anymore neither."
She took a narrow trail that headed virtually straight up.

Silas couldn't ride alongside her, so he trailed behind an eight-year-old girl. The little slip of a thing was more in charge of this Tanner Ranch than he was.

As they pushed hard up a trail that was treacherous even in the light, he worried and fumed and prayed for Belle to be all right so he could yell at her until she stopped thinking she was the head of this family.

He made Sarah stop so he could check for tracks. Belle's riderless horse had left a clear trail coming home, and Emma's horse was heading out this same direction. He got on his horse, and Sarah took the lead again.

As the trail ride grew long, Silas turned his mind away from the worry gnawing away like a rat in his gut, knowing panic would do no good. His mind wandered to his news. He'd expected all his girls to be excited.

As they rode, he drew his coat more tightly around his neck against a wind that was increasingly bitter. He tried to set his hurt aside as he thought about his wife and his girls and how happy he was going to make them and how wonderful it was to be part of this family. Then a new idea popped into Silas's head. He'd grown up around women—too many women. He knew more about women than any man ever should, including very personal *female* things. He'd wished long and hard as a boy that he'd be spared the knowledge of a woman's ways. No young man wanted to learn such—but he had.

And that led him to his wife and what womanly event *hadn't* occurred with Belle in their month together. She could be expecting their child.

Silas's heart thumped hard as a quiet assurance settled on his heart as if whispered by the mouth of God. Belle was going to have his baby.

Belle, lost in this vast, cold night with a baby on her back, doing all the work of a ranch hand with no help because she was too stubborn to step aside and give him a chance. And she was carrying his child.

When he got that woman home, he was going to nail her chaps to a rocking chair and make her stay in the house! Things were going to change around here!

He didn't care who had built this place up. He was the husband, and it was the Harden Ranch, and Belle could just accept it and obey him, despite ducking the vow to obey with that infernal weak-kneed preacher.

His hands tightened on his reins and his mount sidestepped a bit until Silas brought himself, and his horse, under control. All that yelling would have to wait until he found Belle and made sure she was safe.

They had been on the trail for hours, and only fear was keeping Silas awake. Sarah wasn't speaking to him—which wasn't like her. She was a talkative little thing.

They got past the steepest part of the ride, and Silas rode up beside her. "You're sure she was going to the north timber?"

"You're a husband." Sarah didn't look at him as she pushed her horse faster. "Don't you ever talk to her? She always tells us where she's going."

Silas didn't like the way he'd been dropped back into the pack of husbands. They all talked about "the husbands" as if they were a group, not worthy of being remembered as individuals. He'd never minded that until all of a sudden he was one of them.

They were overdue for giving the horses a breather anyway, so he reached across and grabbed Sarah's reins and pulled her horse to a stop.

Sarah stared straight forward.

Silas leaned over and caught her chin and pulled it around so she faced him. "Give your horse a rest for a minute. What's going on here? Why are you angry with me?"

Sarah stared at him for a long time, and Silas began to believe he'd been speaking in some strange foreign language. "Talk to me, Sarah. If you're upset with me, say so. Don't be like this, all moody and rude. Just say what's on your mind."

Sarah opened her mouth then closed it again. She inhaled slowly then squared her shoulders. "Ma says it don't do no good to talk to husbands. She says men are all alike and there ain't no point trying to change 'em." Sarah tugged at her reins. "Let's get back to hunting for Ma. We don't have time to sit here yammering while Ma might be in trouble."

Silas didn't let her go. He'd been handling women long before this little one had made her way onto the earth, and he'd be hornswoggled if the contrary little filly would get the best of him. He knew the twisting and turning routes a woman's mind could take, and he knew if she was just a few years older, she'd say, *If you don't know what's wrong, I'm not going to tell you.*

But Sarah was still young for that. Silas thought he could handle her. "You haven't said anything to me that makes sense, Sarie. Say it plain. What did I do?"

Sarah looked at him with that disdainful expression, but Silas knew Sarah wanted to love him. He'd seen her light up too many times over little compliments or simple kindness. "Say anything that's in your head. I won't get mad and I won't punish you. I love you, and I want to know what I did to hurt you."

Sarah's gaze dropped, but Silas still had ahold of her chin so she couldn't forget he was nagging her.

"I think you do love me." She looked back at him. "And I don't reckon you've done anything to hurt me. It's just that. . . we. . .I wanted. . .I hoped you wouldn't be. . .lazy like the other husbands."

"Lazy!" Silas exclaimed, thinking of the long, hard hours he'd been working.

"I thought you'd help us some." Sarah plowed on with her explanation. "But Ma and Emma did the regular fall chores, even patching the cabin, which you said you'd do."

"I will do it." He had no intention of doing it, but that was beside the point. "Winter hasn't come yet. I had some things I needed to do first."

"Winter is here." Sarah shrugged in the bitter cold like she'd heard it all before. "It's time for everything to be done, and everything *is* done."

"What do you mean everything is done?"

"We're ready now for winter if we can just find Ma and get her home safe. It's just like last year, only last year she didn't have Betsy, so it was easier. But she said she did it all with the rest of us girls on her back, so it don't matter. Course the herd was smaller when I was a baby and she was a mite younger."

"You mean she's brought all the cattle in from the summer pastures already?" Silas asked incredulously.

"Well, sure. She has to. You know she cut and stacked the hay."

"But I told her to stop that." Silas's stomach twisted with regret. He'd made her promise him. They'd had a big fight over it and. . . Silas thought back to the night they'd had that set-to. He couldn't remember her actually promising. He'd demanded that she do it and. . .he wasn't sure, but he thought she'd given her word. He'd insisted, ordered her to wait. Then he'd kissed her and her arms had gone around his neck.

No woman as agreeable as Belle could be defying him and lying to him. "I told her I'd do it. She said she only did one small patch that filled in with snow real early. I told her to check the herd and do a tally. I didn't mean for her to round everything up. And to be ready for winter, she'd have to dredge out the ponds and do some branding. There are longhorns to bring in by herself before everything is done."

"She's not by *herself*," Sarah said with narrowed eyes. "Emma helps. And I do sometimes."

"I *told* her to leave that for me." Silas's temper snapped. "I know when winter comes up here, and I could have managed. I told her I had something important to do first, and she said she didn't mind waiting."

"You weren't going to help, Silas!" Sarah jerked her chin free of Silas's grip. "Me and Emma figured that out the day after you started disappearing in the morning and not coming back until suppertime."

"You decided I wasn't going to help over a month ago?" Silas couldn't believe it. They'd all been so nice. So loving. And they were thinking terrible things about him.

"I don't rightly think Ma *ever* expected you to pitch in."

"She didn't expect it? After the cattle drive?" Silas fought to keep his temper from cutting loose on a little girl. She wasn't who needed to hear hollering. It was Belle.

"We don't care that much. We're used to no-account husbands."

Although if Sarah wasn't careful, she might hear a cranky word or two.

"And you're a sight friendlier than Gerald who was drunk most days or Anthony who was always off somewhere and had a mean mouth towards Ma. So it don't matter none except for the amount of potatoes I have to peel."

Silas felt like Sarah had just plowed a fist into his belly, only her words packed a mighty big wallop for such a little tyke.

"We'll get over being disappointed. It's just that at first we had hopes you'd help is all. The only thing you did wrong was to get our hopes up."

They'd gotten Silas's hopes up, too. But being disappointed by women seemed to be his lot in life.

"Ma says that's just part of being a man," Sarah added. "It'd be right nice if we don't have to have any babies though, and babies seem to go with husbands. I love Betsy and all, but branding was right hard on Ma when she was almost due to have a baby." Sarah shrugged again. "It don't matter. When it happens, she'll manage. She always does."

"I don't intend to be a no-account husband." Silas thought of the baby most likely already on the way, and he thought of the hard work Belle had been doing, most of it on horseback. He thought of that nasty blazed-faced steer that had almost gored her on the trail. She'd be facing dozens of contrary longhorns out on the range. Even if she didn't get herself killed, she was going to manage to lose his child, but it didn't appear that taking care of his baby was as important as rounding up her herd.

Sarah shrugged. "Reckon no one intends to be no-account."

"I've been working real hard on something that. . .well, I wanted it to be a surprise. I'm not hiding out. Can't you tell I've been working?"

"On what?" Sarah asked.

A well of stubbornness rose up in Silas. It made him mad to have to answer to this little girl. She should just take his word for it that he was working hard and trust him. "I want to tell you when you're all together."

Sarah gave him a look like she didn't much care what his excuse was. "We've got to find Ma. We don't have time to talk right now. You do care enough about her to want her to be okay, don't you?" The way Sarah said it landed another blow. "I mean, you need her to do the chores, right?"

Had it gotten this bad that the girls didn't think he cared if they lived or died except for the work they could do? And it looked likely that they didn't much care if he lived or died either. There was still a side of the Husband Tree lacking a grave, after all.

Sarah pulled on her reins and Silas let go. He fell back in line behind her, and the two of them picked up the pace as they headed into increasingly rugged, cold timberland. Silas studied the vast, trackless woods in the night and didn't know how he could ever find the woman he loved in the midst of all this. And when he did find her, which he would or die trying, he didn't know how he was going to fix things back to the way they'd been when he first married her.

He thought of the unkind, disrespectful things Sarah had said and knew they came straight from Belle's mouth. While he'd been breaking his back trying to make things better for them, she'd been poisoning her children's minds against him.

As he rode on, he began to wonder if he did want to fix things.

CHAPTER 25

Belle woke up so groggy she thought for a while the warmth in front of her was Silas.

Reaching out her hand, she felt heat but no man. It was the fire, burned low, barely casting any heat. She was out on the trail.

She'd done it again. She'd fallen asleep. She didn't jump up because she could feel another roiling bout of nausea. She didn't have morning sickness much when she was carryin'. There just wasn't time for such nonsense.

She threw up from time to time when she was first expecting, often just leaned over so she missed her horse and cast up her food on the ground as she rode on. But she didn't count that as morning sickness because it didn't always hit in the morning. Besides, somehow morning sickness sounded like some big event that changed the pattern of your life, like needing to stay in bed of a morning until it passed. Belle didn't have a prayer of getting to do that, so why bother paying attention or naming the condition?

She rolled onto her back, cradled her sleeping baby in her arms, and stared up through the tree limbs at the stars. She could see it was really late. The girls would be worried, but they knew her days could stretch long. She'd just lay here another minute to let her stomach quit crow hopping around; then she'd grab up her horse and head home.

Silas would probably have to know what she was up to today, because heaven knew he'd be tucked up safe and warm in bed right now. She'd tell him and he'd fuss at her and tell her to leave the fall work for him. Then she'd protest that winter came early and he'd moan about his *idea* and fuss at her, then look sad that she had to work so hard. But Belle was all out of sympathy for him.

She finally felt up to moving and sat up slowly. Her head didn't start spinning and her empty stomach seemed willing to hold itself steady, so she stood and doused the last of her fire. With the fire gone, Belle realized just how cold the night had grown. It was going to be a hard ride home. She tucked Betsy in her pack, careful to make sure the baby was well bundled. Then she walked over to where she'd hitched her horse.

He wasn't there.

She leaned against the gnarled oak tree for a long minute, feeling as if the world had shifted and up was down all of a sudden. Then she looked around, trying to see another twisted-up tree that could be the one she'd picked for a hitchin' post. She looked at the sky again, and she thought of the horse she'd ridden. It was one of her best mountain horses and it was blue blazes as a cow pony. She knew as sure as she was standing here that somehow the contrary beast had broken loose and headed for the barn.

The minute she realized that, she started walking. The girls would be frantic. She had no way of knowing how long ago the horse had taken off, but it would beat her home. Emma and Sarah would assume the worst, and Emma would head for this timberland, leaving Sarah at home in case Belle showed up from an unexpected direction.

Emma was probably out on the trail hunting for her right now, afraid that the hard world had caught up with one of the

Tanner women for a change—instead of a husband. Belle heard the distant howl of her wolf pack and knew it wasn't safe for her girls to be out afoot on the range.

Belle pushed hard. Knowing better than to try and run in her pointed-toed boots, she hiked along at a good pace. Every minute she got closer to the ranch was one minute less the girls would worry. The wolves howled again, and she wished for her rifle, gone along with her horse. She took off one of her work gloves, slipped her hand inside her buffalo coat, and rested her hand on the pistol at her hip. The hard, cold steel comforted her.

There was snow and ice in the air. Belle shuddered as the wind sliced at her face and neck. She knew to stay to the main path, because that's the way Emma would be coming. She thought of those baying wolves, their eerie, unearthly howls closer now than they'd been. She walked faster. She didn't want Emma to meet up with the pack alone.

She pulled Betsy around and strapped her onto her front inside her buffalo coat without breaking stride. Pushed faster by the sound of wolves, she heard a change in the tone of their howls and knew they'd picked up the scent of prey.

She hoped it wasn't Emma.

Her hand went to the sleeping bundle in her arms. She hoped it wasn't her and Betsy.

God, take care of my family tonight.

She thought of the baby she carried inside her and said a prayer for that wee little one, too.

Protect all of us, Lord, and please let this new baby be a girl.

The path wound into a particularly thick clump of trees. The branches almost reached out and grabbed her when she passed. Unmindful of her own comfort, Belle let the windswept branches whip across her face as she picked up her pace to a run.

The wolves were closer now, and a chill that had nothing to do with the weather raced up her spine. They'd found something for their supper—her.

With two babies to care for, she ran faster. She saw a lighter area ahead and knew she needed to make that so she could have a field of fire. In the woods, the wolves could be on her before she knew they were coming. She needed to find a tree to climb or a rock wall to cover her back with a good open area in front of her.

Suddenly the baying of the wolves stopped. She felt the evil in the silence. She knew they were coming.

Now.

Quiet.

Stalking her.

The heavy shroud of trees thinned, and she saw the sky for the first time in a while. There was enough light for her to see a ponderosa pine with branches low enough to grab ahold. The back of her neck prickled as she waited for the first wolf to pounce.

She sprinted for the tree. She heard the nearly soundless rush of something behind her, and she whirled and stared into wicked yellow eyes and bared fangs already airborne. Her hand was on her pistol. She fired without making a conscious decision to shoot.

The noise and the smashing bullet knocked the wolf back. Two wolves behind this one whirled back into the cover of the trees, breaking off the attack. Belle saw eyes glowing in the moonlight. Staring at her. Hungry.

She backed to the tree. Glancing behind her, she holstered her gun and caught the first branch. She swung up. The wolves came at her with a rush. She clung to the branch with her arms and legs. She had surprising speed for a woman with a baby on her chest.

One of the wolves caught her dangling buffalo robe in his teeth. The weight of the wolf almost knocked her to the ground. Belle knew it was hang on or die, and she had the grit to hang on.

Another snarling wolf caught at her coat. With frantic clumsiness she jerked at the leather belt that held her coat on and untied it. She shrugged it off, wrenching her shoulders as the wolves tried to drag it down. The wolves dropped back to the ground and attacked the robe with vicious snarls and ripping jaws.

Belle levered herself up to a sitting position and stared down at a pack of huge gray wolves, at least ten of them. She'd been thinning this pack for a month—probably already killing half a dozen. Her absence for a month because of the cattle drive had made them bold. She had ten to contend with instead of sixteen. That gave her some satisfaction.

Swinging up to a safe height, she pressed her back solidly against the tree, held tight to Betsy with her left arm, and took careful aim with her revolver. She shot two of them, including the one that looked like the leader of the pack. Betsy cried with fear at the loud noise. The wolves ran, and Belle managed to wound a third before they vanished into the woods.

"I'm sorry, baby girl." Belle bounced Betsy as she reloaded. "Don't cry, honey. I know it's loud. Mama has to get rid of these nasty old wolves so we can get home."

Betsy responded to Belle's voice, and like a good little cowpoke, she got ahold of herself.

Belle heard the beasts moving swiftly, circling her from the cover of the trees, just out of her sight. She didn't dare get down. But if she stayed here, she was leading Emma right into the middle of seven savage wolves.

Without the coat, the cold bit into her arms. Betsy, calm now, had a blanket over her, but it wasn't enough to keep her warm for long.

Belle looked down at her coat on the ground, a dead wolf carcass stretched out on top of it. Did she dare climb down for the coat?

The gunshots would warn Emma and make her ride cautiously. They would also bring her running no matter where she was, because the shots carried for miles in the high thin air.

Belle watched the woods with intense concentration, waiting for a shot. She had to thin out the pack before Emma and maybe

Sarah, too, rode into it. One foolishly bold wolf stuck his nose out of the brush. Belle shot him dead. Six to go.

They all dropped back, but Belle heard them out there, pacing, circling. She coddled poor little Betsy who was fretting again. Belle tried to identify the wolves' locations, but they moved like ghosts.

Belle began to shiver, only a little at first, but the cold crept into her muscles, and the shivers started to come from deep inside. She had a glove on her left hand. Her right-hand glove had been in the pocket of her buffalo robe. Even though it didn't fit, she put it onto her right hand. She worked the cold, stiffened fingers of her shooting hand, knowing her gun would save her, but she couldn't shoot with the glove on, so as soon as her hand felt better, she switched the glove back. She held Betsy close and used her body heat to keep the baby warm.

After long minutes, a second wolf emerged with a chilling, low growl. Belle cut down their number once again. Five left. Only five.

This time they seemed to vanish. She didn't hear a noise. She didn't even sense their presence. She doubted very much they'd run off, but maybe they'd been driven back far enough that she could get that coat.

Belle's shivering was becoming so uncontrollable that she soon wouldn't be able to handle her gun. She couldn't sit up here all night. Betsy wouldn't survive it. Her baby started to whimper and fret against Belle's chest, from cold or hunger or fright. Belle had to do something.

She slipped down a branch to see better into the woods and realized her legs barely worked. They were stiff and numb from sitting so long in the treetop. She saw nothing and heard nothing, so with considerable struggle due to numb legs and arms still with cold, Belle climbed lower, her eyes shifting between that blood-soaked buffalo coat and the surrounding forest.

She was to the point of climbing down to the ground to snatch that coat and rush back up into the tree, when suddenly three of them lunged at her from the side, leaping nearly high enough to sink their teeth into her dangling leg.

She whirled, off balance, and fell backward out of the tree. Betsy cried out as they fell. Belle fired as she fell into the raging fangs, until her gun clicked on empty chambers. Taking a second to look for where the next danger would come, she saw three more wolves dead on the ground.

Belle reached for the bullets in her cartridge belt with fingers numb and uncooperative from the cold. A blood-chilling growl sounded from just behind her. She shoved a bullet home and tried to whirl from where she lay, but her feet and legs were useless. They were as dead as if she'd dragged stumps of wood along with her. Her arms were heavy and limp. Even her brain was murky and slow-acting, and she had a strange sense of not caring what happened to her, just wanting to sleep.

Betsy squirmed and cried, and that forced Belle to face the new danger and keep fighting, for Betsy's sake if not her own. She turned and looked into the eyes of a pair of hungry wolves. She raised her gun with only one bullet.

A shot rang out and then another and a third. She blinked her eyes with aching slowness as both wolves slammed sideways with sharp whines of pain, twitching and dying.

Emma rode into the clearing with her rifle drawn and smoking. "Thanks," Belle said, her voice trembling with cold.

Emma looked around at the pile of dead wolves. "Figured when your horse came home alone you was havin' trouble." Emma always got calm in a crisis. Of anyone she knew, Belle would rather have her second daughter at hand when there was trouble. By the utter calm she saw in Emma now, she knew her girl was scared half to death.

Belle wasn't yet ready to stand, but she saw her coat within reaching distance. She dragged her gnawed-up buffalo robe out from under the corpse of a wolf and, ignoring the soaked-in blood, pulled it on over herself and Betsy. Belle tied the coat around her clumsily and started shivering so hard she had trouble sitting upright.

Emma dismounted and led the extra horse she'd brought along over to Belle. "Let me take Betsy. It's warmer inside my coat."

Belle nodded soundlessly and opened her coat to pass the bundled-up baby over, carrier and all.

Emma hooked her sister onto her chest, inside her own heavy coat. Then she boosted her mother to her feet and, doing almost all the work herself, hoisted Belle onto the spare horse. Emma found Belle's second glove and, like she was dressing a child, put it on Belle's hand. Emma steadied Belle on the saddle, took the reins, swung up on her own mount, and headed out, leading Belle's horse.

Silas and Sarah charged out of the woods before they'd gotten out of the clearing.

Silas had his gun drawn. The minute he caught sight of them, he yelled, "I heard wolves. Where are they?"

Emma said in her too-calm voice, "Dead." She nodded her head toward the tree in the center of the clearing.

Silas turned toward the tree.

CHAPTER 26

Silas took one look at the carnage. Death and blood and violence filled the clearing.

He spurred his horse toward his shivering wife, where she sat slumped forward on her horse. "Belle! Where are you hurt? Where's Betsy?" He lifted Belle off her saddle onto his.

"I've got the baby, Silas," Emma said, using his name instead of Pa so calmly Silas wanted to shake her.

Maybe later. Now he pulled Belle's shredded, blood-soaked coat open, expecting to see her covered with bites and claw marks. He couldn't see a one.

He'd heard the wolves baying. Heard the repeated gunshots as he and Sarah had raced in the direction of the commotion.

"I'm cold." Belle pulled her coat closed and said with chattering teeth, "Give me back my coat."

He rode over to the tree, carrying Belle across his lap, and started to shiver himself. He counted until his mind couldn't take in the number. Then he looked down at Belle. Even in the moonlight he could see her skin was ashen and her lips were blue. There were streaks of blood on her face. "You're hurt. Where are you hurt?"

"No, I'm fine. Just cold."

Silas wiped the blood off her chin and held his hand up in front of her face in the moonlight clearing.

The blood was black on his hand, but she knew what it was. "Wolf blood." She shivered and shrugged. "They never got me or Betsy. We were fine, just cold because they tore my coat off."

"Tore!" Silas started snarling himself.

"Your!" He lifted Belle until she was sitting upright.

"Coat!" Her nose was almost pressed against his.

"Off?" His hands tightened on her shoulders.

"Tore it off?" Silas checked himself and said with suppressed violence, "Why were you out here? I *told* you to leave this for me."

His voice kept getting louder as he thought of how close she'd come to being killed. "And by yourself? You didn't even take one of the girls? You're hours late! We thought you were—" Fury clamped his throat shut.

Her pale skin and the tremors that vibrated through her kept him from shaking her until her bones rattled or her brain started working—whichever came first. He bet on the rattling bones, because he had no doubt her brain wouldn't come through for him.

"Silas, you came for me." She said it through a fog, and Silas realized she was dropping off to sleep. She wasn't falling asleep. No matter how tired a person was, no matter what they'd been through, they didn't nod off when someone was shouting right in their face. She was losing consciousness.

He felt the iciness of her skin and saw the blue tinge of her lips, and he forgot about being mad. Well, he didn't forget. He just decided he'd leave it until later.

He'd lived in the high country off and on most of his life, so he knew a hard chill getting a grip on a person could kill. He pulled off her buffalo coat, ignoring her soft cry of protest as she tried to keep it around her. He opened his own coat and his shirt, then unbuttoned hers and pressed her chest against his, separated only

605

by his underwear and her chemise. He pulled off her gloves and tucked her hands between their bodies and shivered himself from the lifeless cold of her fingers. Then he wrapped his own sturdy sheepskin coat around both of them and wrapped Belle's buffalo robe over the top, flinching from the wetness and the smell of blood but using it anyway because Belle needed it.

His horse danced sideways at the unaccustomed activity of two riders on his back.

Emma rode up to hold the horse steady.

"We can't take her all the way home. She's too cold." He looked up at Emma who was studying Belle with a deep furrow of worry between her brows. "How's the baby?"

"Betsy's fine." Emma's hand crossed her chest to hug the completely covered baby. "Ma kept her bundled up."

Trust Belle to protect her children even in the middle of this madness.

Belle started shivering again. Silas couldn't pay attention to Belle's feet on horseback. They might be dangerously frozen by the time he got Belle home. "Scout out a sheltered spot, Emma. Get a fire started. We've got to get your ma warmed up."

Emma's eyes flickered between Silas and her ma. For one long second she hesitated, as if judging for herself if Silas really meant to help.

He kept from yelling by clamping his teeth together hard.

Finally, she turned and headed up the trail toward home with Sarah following.

Silas covered Belle more carefully then rode after his daughters.

When he caught up to Emma, she had sparked a handful of twigs into flame, and Sarah was dragging in a big dead pine branch. Silas knew they'd have a fire big enough to scare off every wolf in the Rockies before long. Emma had chosen wisely as Silas had expected. She'd built a fire a few feet out from an overhanging cliff so the wall was warmed along with the ground between the fire and the wall. The curve of the rock sheltered them from the wind, and the fire was reflected off the rock until it was warmer than the dilapidated cabin they lived in. But the perfect little niche in the rock wasn't large enough for all of them. Sarah threw the dead branch on the flames, and the flames licked and caught and spread.

"We have to find somewhere we can all squeeze in, Emma." Silas was getting worried about Belle's unresponsive state. He swung off his horse and settled Belle on the ground between the roaring fire and the overhang while Emma tied up his horse and Belle's. "No, don't hitch my horse. You keep your ma here. I'll go find somewhere big enough for all of us."

Sarah added another armful of wood.

"No, Silas. I picked this on purpose. It'll heat up fast. Sarah, Betsy, and I are fine. We can make the ride home easy. I can feed Betsy cow's milk for one night."

He'd been called Silas again. This time by his Emma, the one who seemed to love him the most deeply. They'd all turned on him. He should have known better than to try and make a place for himself in this man-hating household. Well, it wasn't the first time he'd been a fool over a woman.

Emma began dragging a dead branch toward the fire, stopping to grab two more smaller bits of kindling as she worked.

"We're wasting time talking. Get in here and start rubbing your ma's arms and legs. It'll take hours for you to ride home, and I don't want you out alone."

Silas turned his attention to Belle. It took him a second to notice that the girls ignored his orders and kept working, building the fire.

He didn't notice them again until Emma spoke. He looked over and saw her across from the now-roaring fire, sitting on her horse. "We'll head in now."

"Emma, I don't want you riding these wolf-infested hills with

607

Sarah and Betsy. We're all staying."

"I know this range better'n you, Silas. Having this place so close was pure good luck. There isn't anything else like it anywhere around." She stared at him suspiciously for a long moment, and Silas got the impression she was trying to decide whether to trust him with Belle's life.

Finally, Emma said, "You can see to her if you want, but if you don't want to do it, I will, and Sarah can get Betsy home."

"Of course I'll take care of her," Silas exploded. "I want to take care of all of you."

"I'm obliged for your help with Ma, Silas. I'll leave her to you then. But I reckon we girls'll be takin' care of ourselves." Emma clucked to her horse and rode down the trail with Sarah trailing after.

"Emma!" Fury almost blew the top of Silas's head off. He surged to his feet. "You get back here right now!"

Emma and Sarah, with Betsy, rode on without a backward glance. They disappeared into the woods as he stood there raging at the empty night.

It was all he could do to stop himself from snagging the mane of his horse and riding those impudent young ladies down and dragging them back. Only Belle's critical condition kept him from fetching Emma and turning her over his knee. Except he wasn't sure he had the right to hand out a spanking to Emma. Yesterday he'd thought he was their pa, and he would have said he had the rights of any father. But today everything had changed. The blazing anger turned into hurt. He *wasn't* their pa. He wasn't *anything* around this place but another one of the husbands. And even though he'd been working his heart out for these women, they didn't trust him to be different than any other man they'd known.

So, Belle kept the reins of the ranch in her hands, and Emma toiled along by her side, and Sarah kept the home fires burning, and none of them even minded much until something like tonight happened. Tonight they couldn't help blaming him. Emma, like Sarah, held him responsible for Belle being out here half frozen and in danger from wolves. It hit him hard that, whatever his excuse, it didn't matter, because they were right. It *was* his fault. He should have told them what he was up to. Fool that he was, he'd thought they trusted him. Just another mistake on his part.

He wanted to go after them. Beg them to forgive him. Beg them to love him again. But his wife was unconscious. She was in mortal danger from the vicious cold. He stared, bitterly ashamed, into the black, windswept night that sheltered treacherous trails and hungry wolves and fractious longhorns. The wilderness swallowed up his daughters.

With no choice, he turned his attention to Belle. He laid the buffalo robe on the ground for a bed then pulled Belle's outer clothes off. She needed every ounce of heat the fire and his body could produce to warm her skin and prevent frostbite. He turned her so her back was toward the fire, being careful not to get her too close to the flames. Then he rubbed her arms and legs with so much vigor that she awoke slightly and swatted at him in protest.

"Let me sleep. I'm tired." Although her eyes didn't open and in her semiconscious state her words were slurred, her attitude was cantankerous. It lifted Silas's heart to hear even that little bit of spirit.

As he massaged her arms and back, he studied her face. It was stark and white under her tan. Her lips were blue and pinched. He rubbed his hands over her strong, clever fingers, which lay lifeless in the flickering light of the fire. He turned back to her feet, which had him the most worried. It made Silas sick to think of people who'd lost toes, even a foot or leg, to frostbite. He hated to think of the horror Belle might go through if her feet were that badly frozen. He held her feet to his chest, hugging them in his arms to warm her ankles. Then, because they didn't seem to be warming, he lifted his shirt and pressed the bottoms of her feet against his bare stomach. They were frigid and set a shudder of cold through him. He held her feet, edging a few inches closer to the fire.

"Belle Harden, this is no time to turn into a weakling." As she drew heat from his body, he talked, hoping she'd respond. "I've got heat to spare, darlin', and strength. This time you're going to have to depend on me. Just like you did on that cattle drive." His belly ached as if her icy feet were absorbing the cold from his deepest core.

Her shivering came again. Her whole body was wracked with it. She began to moan through chattering teeth, and after a while she struggled against him and murmured again. "Feet hurt."

She kicked at him, but it was so feeble his heart clutched to think of her usual strength, now so reduced. He thought it was a good sign that his warmth was causing her pain. He hoped that meant her feet weren't dangerously frozen.

"Wolves!" Belle's hands flew wide, and Silas had to scramble to keep her from getting too close to the fire.

"The wolves are gone, Belle."

"Wolves!" Her arms flew up as if she were dreaming that one sprang at her right now. "No!"

"You're safe, Belle honey. The wolves are gone."

Belle clutched at her chest, the shivering wracking her body. "Betsy!" Her hands flailed at the place she kept Betsy strapped on. Then she cried out in terror.

"Betsy's fine, Belle. She's fine."

Belle twisted as if she planned to get up.

Silas kept a firm grip on her feet. "Emma has Betsy. You shot all the wolves, Belle." Silas crooned to her, afraid to let her feet go when they were so cold. The rest of her seemed to be working just fine. "You won." He reached out and caught one of her thrashing hands that had flopped on the ground too close to the fire. "You're safe." She jerked against the hold, but he wouldn't let go, afraid she'd be burned. "Your girls are safe." He thought there was some pink behind her blue-white fingernails and her hands weren't the flaccid, lifeless cold they'd been earlier.

"Stop! Gerald, stop. Please!" She kicked hard at Silas's stomach and cried out Gerald's name in a voice so laced with fear and pain Silas ground his teeth together to contain his rage at what Belle had suffered at the hands of men. Belle's words were almost begging. To think of strong, courageous Belle being reduced to begging by one of her husbands was infuriating.

"I'm here, Belle. Gerald is gone. This is Silas. I'll take care of you." To think she was mixing Silas up with Gerald was heartbreaking. He continued to talk to her, trying to pierce her muddled thinking.

"You're going to be all right. The girls are safe." Out in this cold night. Without Silas or Belle to protect them. But he was confident in his statement. They'd be fine without any help from him.

At last the tremors eased. Belle at last lay calm, her eyes closed. Silas pulled her feet out from against his stomach and saw that the alarming white had pinked up a bit. He heaved a sigh of relief and pulled on her socks, then carefully arranged her close to the fire. Silas stretched out beside his wife on the side away from the fire to surround her with warmth. He pulled a blanket over them, one he always carried behind his saddle. He held her close, tucked his feet beneath hers, and prayed.

The shivering came again but it didn't last so long. There was more time in between the next bout. The color seeped into her cheeks, and Belle's movements became more languid. With a sigh of utter relaxation, she said, "Silas, I love you."

Some of Silas's anger at Belle for risking her life eased away when she talked to him so sweetly. It reawakened the excitement that had been buzzing through him when he'd ridden home so many hours earlier. He whispered in her ear, "I think we're going to have a baby, Belle Harden."

"I can't have a baby." Belle shook her head frantically, eyes still closed. "I can't." And she started to cry.

Something in Silas turned as cold as the Montana wind that howled outside this little niche of warmth. His wife, cuddled safe in his arms, cried over the thought of having his child.

Belle was just barely conscious. He knew she was only vaguely aware of what she was saying. Did that mean he should pay no mind to what she said? Or did it mean she had no strength for anything but the truth? Did it mean Belle was truly, deeply heartbroken to think she was carrying his child? Whether she was expecting or not, her tears meant she didn't want to be. So why had she let him make love to her? Belle was a grown woman. She knew what caused babies.

Silas knew the answer. Pleasure.

It was new to Belle. She wanted the pleasure and had found it irresistible. But she didn't want to move over and give up being boss of the *Tanner* Ranch, and she didn't want his child growing in her body.

She was using him. She'd support him and feed him, probably even dole out spending money if he asked, all so she could keep him around. But the ranch was hers alone, and his baby was a cause for tears.

Any way Silas thought of it, he came out sounding like. . .like his mother. Earning money in the upstairs of a saloon.

That's what a man got for coming to a rich woman when he had nothing to offer. He'd known it was wrong, but he'd married her anyway because he wanted her so much. And he thought love was enough. And now he had to pay the price of being a man with no honor and no pride.

He'd lost two ranches in his life by turning coward. Running away was getting to be a habit, because right now he hurt so badly from hearing her cry, he wished himself halfway across the country from Belle.

He tested her warm, supple limbs and saw that she'd fallen

into a natural sleep. He checked her toes, and even they were warm and pink in the crackling firelight. Trust Belle to tackle a pack of wolves and freezing cold and then shake it off with no damage to herself.

He wrapped her up good and snug. "You're all right now, Belle. You're going to be all right." Knowing he shouldn't, he held her close, thrilled that she was safely warm.

She wound her arms around his neck. She tilted her head to reach for his lips.

He met her searching lips and thought about the baby she was most likely expecting and never wanted to bear. He broke off the kiss.

She protested but settled back into a deep sleep.

He held her through the long night while he nurtured his anger and vanquished his love and planned how to be a man who could stand to look at himself in the mirror.

It was still dark when Belle woke the next morning.

Silas was shaking her. "We'd best be on the trail home."

She sat up and a wave of nausea lurched in her stomach.

The baby.

Silas was fully dressed. When she moved, he stood away and started quickly packing up the meager camp. She remembered everything. Crying herself to sleep. The wolves. Emma's smoking rifle. Silas.

Things were foggy after Silas had picked her up off her horse and started fussing over her and scolding her for working her ranch. Like she hadn't put up with enough already yesterday.

She'd never had a husband quite like this before. The others had complained and whined and laid low when chores were being handed out. But she'd never had one not only refuse to help but get upset when she did it herself. It was just a new twist on the same old story, but she couldn't figure out why Silas didn't just shut up and let her get on with her work.

Once her stomach settled, she thought of Betsy needing breakfast and got up to start packing the camp.

Silas had everything done except dousing the fire. "You up to the ride home?" Silas almost growled the question.

Belle had beaten back one pack of wolves only to face another this morning. "Yep." She brushed his question aside brusquely.

Beyond that, they didn't talk.

Both horses were already saddled, so they were on the trail within minutes. They had no food, and she was in a hurry to get to Betsy, so they set a brisk pace.

Her husband was obviously angry. Belle assumed it was because she'd gone and done another chore he considered his. She didn't have the strength this morning to deal with his infernal wounded pride.

They made good time in the sharp cold, and the sun wasn't fully up when they rode into the ranch yard.

Without making eye contact, Silas said with tight sarcasm, "If it's all right with you, I'll take care of the horses."

Belle looked at him through narrow eyes, disgusted at his temper. She checked the impulse to tend her own mount because she was eager to be away from his surly company. "Thank you." Tossing him the reins, she dismounted without checking to see if he caught them and headed to the house.

She got inside in time to pick Betsy up where she lay kicking in the wooden crate Belle had fashioned into a bed. She sat down and nursed her baby and fought back tears by building up the fire under her temper. She fumed and rocked and looked down at Betsy, not the youngest anymore.

Emma and Sarah slept on, even though it was well past their normal waking time. The night had been a late one.

Betsy ate and surprised Belle by falling back to sleep in her arms. Just as Belle laid her back down, the front door slammed open with so much force the rickety thing shattered into pieces and fell onto the cabin floor, letting the icy wind blast through into the cabin.

Emma surged out of her bed. Sarah sat up with a startled scream of fear. Betsy awoke with a loud cry. Belle whirled around, and her temper flared to white hot.

She stalked over to face Silas with only inches separating them, ready at last to put him in the place he needed to be. Ready to chalk him up as another mistake. So enraged, she was ready to plant him under the lone oak with the rest of the husbands without waiting for him to turn up his toes!

She'd trusted him! She'd thought she could believe in him! Well, so far he'd been a bigger disappointment than anyone she'd ever married. And in that instant, Belle decided she wasn't going to put up with it. She wasn't going to just accept this lazy, no-good polecat of a man and carry on doing everything herself while he lazed about and lived off her labor.

Silas was going to hear exactly what she thought of his no-account ways. And when she was done with him, he was going to measure up to her idea of what a husband should be or she was going to march him straight down the road. Things were going to change around here! "Silas, things are going to. . .*mmph*."

One hard hand settled over her mouth, and the other clamped over the nape of her neck. He jerked her forward so hard it next to knocked the wind out of her.

Chapter 27

Things are going to change around here!"

Silas leaned down until his nose nearly touched hers. "Do you hear me?"

Belle grabbed his wrist. His arm left her neck and wrapped around her waist as immovable as a band of iron while his other stayed firmly on her mouth. "Settle down and shut up and listen to what your husband has to say for once in your confounded, stubborn, bossy life."

Sarah snatched up the cast-iron skillet and waved it in front of her. Silas thought she looked pretty cute with the skillet in one hand and the baby in the other. Not real threatening.

"You get your hands off of my ma." Emma erupted to her feet and dove for her shotgun.

That impressed Silas more than the skillet. But, unlike when Lindsay had threatened him that first morning, now he wasn't afraid. He could handle all of these women with one hand tied behind his back. He noticed right now it was taking two hands just keeping Belle quiet, so maybe, just to be on the safe side, he wouldn't tie one up. He'd let things go on too long while he worked on his *idea*.

He'd been happily toiling away for them while thinking they loved him and trusted him. But it appeared that wasn't true. Still, he knew Emma. He knew what she was made of. Sure, she might shoot a man who hurt her ma. He'd expect her to. He wouldn't respect her if she didn't. But she wouldn't hurt him.

"Put down that gun." He kept Belle's mouth covered and kept his unshakable grip on her but his whole attention focused on Emma. "I'm not doing anything but making your hardheaded mother listen to me, and you know it."

Emma half raised the gun. She had her eyes riveted on Silas, then glanced at the hold he had on her ma and lowered the muzzle to the floor.

Silas noticed that Belle had quit fighting and squirming. He had the impression she did that because it was upsetting Emma. And just maybe his wife's heart wasn't in having him shot. Either was encouraging.

"And Sarah, you mind Betsy and set that pan aside. You are the most contrary bunch of females I have ever been near. I am going to give you *one more chance* to back up and make room for me in this family."

"Make room?" Sarah said in disgust.

Emma gave Silas a narrow-eyed look, but she didn't raise the gun again.

Good sign.

"Like you haven't been sneaking off every day while we do all the work," Emma said. "Like we wouldn't have let you help."

Belle made a garbled noise of accord with her daughter and gave a firm nod.

Betsy chose that moment to start crying. Silas supposed she could be hungry or wet or have a pin sticking in her little bottom, but he reckoned the truth was she was just female and decided to add to the commotion on principle. Silas wished he had enough hands to shut them all up.

"I don't imagine anyone in this family is interested in seeing the *house* I've been building for the last few weeks."

Dead silence met his announcement, except for the sound of the skillet hitting the floor. Betsy even reacted to the changed atmosphere in the room and stuck both hands into her mouth.

Belle quit fighting against his hold. "Eew ouse?"

Silas uncovered her mouth.

Belle repeated, "New house?"

"Yes. New house. What did you think I'd been doing ever since I got here?"

Silas thought he heard a cricket chirp in the dead silence.

"Never mind. I know what you all think of me." He tugged his Stetson low over his eyes. "But confound it, how could you not trust me better than this? I punched a thousand head of cattle over a hundred of the roughest miles God ever put on this *earth* for you women. I worked eighteen- or twenty-hour days. I hauled you *all* over two mountain passes even though it almost killed me doing it! I—I—" Silas lapsed into silence to match the rest of them and took his arm off of Belle's waist and stepped back.

Finally, he said, "How could you believe I'd—" Surprised at how hurt he was by their easy belief in his worthlessness, he fell silent. Sure, they'd known a lot of no-account men, but he'd next to broken his *heart* getting those cattle to market and building Lindsay her house and getting them all home safe. Didn't that count for anything?

At last he said the only thing he could think of. "I asked you to wait for me with all the winter chores, Belle. And I told you I had an idea I needed to work on. Why didn't you say something if you needed me? Instead, you just assumed the worst of me and did the work yourself. Do I have to prove myself to you every day for the rest of my life? Is that what I can expect from marriage to you?"

He stared at the floor for a while, trying to find in himself the pleasure he'd had at being married and being a father. It was so laced now with hurt it was as if he'd never even known these women. "Well, decide if you want to live here or with me." He stalked out.

He was halfway to the barn when Belle called after him. "New house?"

Afraid of the scalding things he wanted to say to her, Silas ignored her and kept walking.

She hollered, "Where is it?"

He turned back.

Belle stood in her tottering cabin with the door in pieces on the ground. All three girls peeked over her shoulder at him.

He looked back at them for a long time, studying his wife, wondering who she really was. He knew the hardworking rancher and the sweet, loving woman in the night, but underneath the years of disappointment and hard lessons her life had taught her was there someone else? Was there someone who could trust and love, someone who could move over enough to include him in her life and find joy in wanting his child?

The events of the past day told him no. He'd signed on for a lifetime of bouncing off the brick wall of Belle's doubts about all men. It hurt. He didn't like it, and he didn't want to live like that.

If there was a soft side to be coaxed out from under her toughness, he didn't appear to have the knack of doing the coaxing. And he'd reached the point where he didn't have much interest in doing it either. Letting him into her life and opening up to him had to be something Belle did herself.

"It's in the mouth of the high valley near the south pass. I staked a claim to it while we were in Helena. It's mine. I reckon I'm going to go live there." He turned away from her and caught up his horse. Then, without a backward glance, he rode off in the icy cold to his empty home.

❦

All three of them looked at each other. Then they looked around the ramshackle house they lived in.

Hoofbeats faded in the distance.

Belle came out of her trance and whirled back to the door. She stared in the direction he went. "He said he had an idea. He said. . .he said I was a rich woman and it hurt his pride to come to me with nothing."

Belle turned back to the girls. "New house?"

"He claimed that valley you wanted?" Emma asked.

Sarah said wistfully, "I'd kind of like to see it."

"He said he'd do the winter chores," Emma added. "But I never believed him. Not for a minute."

Belle shook her head. It had never occurred to her either. It had never occurred to her to trust the man who had saved their lives several times over. "He worked so hard on the drive, but I just thought he was—I don't know—putting on an act, I guess. Remember how Anthony dug that well for us when he was courting me?"

Emma and Sarah nodded.

Betsy kicked her legs and said, "Papa."

"Anthony dug mighty slow though," Emma said thoughtfully. "Kept on and on about the rocks. Even then we knew he was no-account, didn't we, Ma? We just didn't expect no better."

Belle looked back out the gaping doorway. "Anthony would never have risked his life to haul us over the passes home. He'd have never put in the long days riding herd, and he didn't have an ounce of Silas's skill handling cattle and sticking his cow pony. A man doesn't get good at things like that without practice, and lazy men don't practice. How could I not know all of that after spending a month with Silas?"

"He did a right fine job on Lindsay's house," Emma remembered. "I could tell he knew what he was doing. Reckon any house he built'd be a good 'un."

Sarah said, "Do you think he'll let us live in the new house with him?"

All three of them exchanged a glance. Then they started smiling.

Belle said, "Let's go see."

The girls dressed. They all pulled on their heavy coats, tucked Betsy in the carrier, and headed for the corral.

It was nearly a two-hour ride to the south pass. Belle thought how nice it would be to live two hours closer to Divide. The trail split, one half starting up the mountain to the pass, the other winding into Silas's high valley. They had only gone a mile down that valley trail when they rounded the mouth of the canyon. There, sitting beside a spring, sat the most beautiful ranch house Belle had ever seen. It was all logs. One story high and built in a single straight line. The house was about four times the size of the one they lived in. It had a neat porch across the whole front of it, made with a split-log floor. Evenly spaced saplings formed a railing along the front.

Belle knew Silas hadn't been able to go to town for anything to make his building easier because the pass was snowed shut. There were no glass windows—only shutters pulled firmly closed without a sagging corner in sight. Three chimneys of fieldstones adorned the roof. Only the center one had smoke coming out of it. As they got nearer, she saw the leather hinges on the front door and the tight corners of the log cabin that had been hewn out by hand. She could see the wooden pegs that held the porch and doors and shutters together. It must have taken him forever to do such a lovely job on this big cabin.

She realized the stiff breeze was gone and the snow wasn't as deep as back home. Silas had chosen a spot that cut the north wind. Belle knew the little spring flowed year-round out of a fissure in the cliff close behind the house, so they'd always have

621

fresh water. Silas had thought of everything.

She rode closer and saw Silas's buckskin grazing in a corral behind the house. A big barn stood beside the corral. Built with the same attention to detail. The same *loving* attention to detail.

"He loves me." Belle stared at the proof. "He loves all of us."

Emma nodded. "He'd never've gone to so much trouble elsewhere."

Belle's hand went to her flat stomach, and for the first time in her life she was excited and proud to be expecting a baby. She remembered her tears of yesterday with shame. With ironclad resolve, she decided then and there to be the best mother to this young'un and to the rest of her girls that the world had ever known.

God, I don't mind if it's a boy.

On that shocking thought, she spurred her horse and galloped toward the home he'd made for all of them. She went to the corral to turn her horse loose. Even matters of the heart took second place over caring for her horse.

Emma jumped down beside her and caught Belle's reins. "You'd better go try and cheer him up, Ma. We'll give you awhile to grovel."

Belle looked sharply at Emma.

Emma grinned.

Sarah piped up from behind, "Hand over Betsy, Ma. And don't be shy about crying if need be. That's supposed to soften men up something fierce."

"Where'd you hear that?" Belle asked.

Sarah took Betsy, and the three girls headed for the barn.

Over her shoulder, Emma called, "We won't come in until you come for us, Ma. If you have to be pathetic, then do it, but we don't want to watch. We need to explore the barn anyway. We may set up a camp and spend the night. Even without a fire, this barn'll be warmer than our old cabin. So take whatever time you need to convince Silas to let us live here." Her two smug daughters headed for the barn, giggling.

Belle glared after them for a minute, but it wasn't because she was upset. Her temper was all fake. The truth was she might have to grovel and cry and act pathetic, and if that's what it took, so be it! But that didn't mean it came easy to her.

It took awhile to gather the gumption to admit she was wrong on every count straight down the line. She squared her shoulders and headed for the ranch house.

As soon as she looked where she was going, she saw Silas standing on the porch at the top of the steps, leaning one shoulder against a sturdy support post with his arms folded and one ankle crossed over the other one.

She faltered a bit at the cranky look on his face that told her he wasn't going to settle for any less than an abject apology, but she had the guts to keep moving. Whatever he said, she reckoned she deserved it.

She stopped at the bottom of the steps, and her mind went completely blank. Apologizing wasn't something she did much of. "We...uh...we want to live here."

Silas just stared at her.

"With you."

He cocked his head slightly to the side but didn't speak.

Belle sighed deeply. "We... *I'm* sorry. I can't believe I didn't trust you after all you did for us. I... Even if I didn't, I should have *talked* to you. I should have *told* you what I was thinking, how upset I was."

Still nothing.

"Well, go ahead and yell at me if you want to." Belle was getting tired of being contrite. It just didn't sit well. She tried one more time. "I was wrong, and I'm sorry, and you don't have to prove yourself to me ever again. If you sit down on your tail and never lift a finger to help me again, even if we're married for fifty years, I'll never think you're lazy. I'll never doubt your word, and I'll never breathe a word of criticism."

Still no response.

"I promise that if you say you'll take care of the chores, I'll let the chickens starve and the cattle wander off and the vegetable garden dry up and die before I believe ill of you."

Silas was silent.

Anger stabbed her, but it wasn't her strongest reaction. She was afraid.

What if he never forgave her?

What if he never smiled at her and hugged the girls?

What if he didn't want to have a baby with her and he never came to her again in the night?

"All right!" She flung her arms wide. It burned. It burned bad. But she made herself say the most outrageous, impossible, stupid thing she'd ever said.

"I'll obey you!"

CHAPTER 28

Silas felt his eyebrows shoot up to his hairline.

His arms dropped from the stubborn crossed position he held them in. He stood up straight. "Really?"

Belle nodded.

"You'll let me give you orders?" He had to fight a smile of triumph.

"I said I would, didn't I?" Belle fisted her hands and propped them on her hips defiantly, but her words didn't match her movements. "I'll obey any orders you want. You're the boss of this ranch, and what you say goes."

"Well, that sounds interesting. Let me think." Silas rubbed his chin between his thumb and forefinger and stared at the sky so he wouldn't laugh out loud at the faces she was making while she was trying to be apologetic and submissive.

It was killing her.

He didn't think it was a good idea for her to realize how much he was enjoying the sight. She probably only had so much "obey" in her, and she was likely to start growling any minute.

On the other hand, he thought he had a right to a little getting even with her for all the hurt she'd caused him. "What if I told you I've never cared much for that silly T Bar brand? We're changing it. I registered my own under Circle H in Helena, and starting this spring, all our calves are going to wear it. That's what I used to call my spread down in New Mexico, and it suited me."

Belle swallowed visibly, and Silas thought she was choking over his first order. "The T Bar stands for something out here. I've spent the last sixteen years building that name into—" Then she clenched her jaw shut.

Silas could see her physically trying to stop the words that wanted to escape her lips. She must have gained control of herself, because finally she said rather hoarsely, "Yes, Silas. Circle H sounds fine."

Oh, this was lining itself up to be one of the best days of his life. He wondered how much she'd take. "And I don't like the way you've been breaking the horses. There're none of 'em trained the way good cow ponies should be. I might let Emma help once they're green broke, but I don't want you taking a hand. You teach 'em bad habits it'll take me years training out of 'em."

"Silas! My horses are— I'll have you know—" Belle must've bit her tongue, because she got the words to stop spewing.

Silas tilted his head a bit sideways. He expected nothing less than her trying to do things her way and leave him out. And considering her horses were some of the finest, best-trained stock he'd ever seen, it was reasonable for her to want to help. Still, tormenting her was too good to miss.

She breathed in and out of her nose so loudly he could hear it. Then she said through her bared teeth, "I'll let you take care of that, Silas."

Silas started backing across the porch. He opened the door behind him. "Come in here, woman."

Belle hesitated, and Silas saw some of the flashing rage in her eyes ease.

Silas had the impression she was feeling guilty, like maybe she didn't think she deserved to go into such a fine house as the one he'd spent every waking moment of the last month building just for her. But he didn't give her a break, not when he was having such a good time. He crossed the threshold with her still standing on the ground, and he decided the best way to get her inside was to say, "While we're on the subject of changes, I don't like the way you dress. I'd like my woman to look a mite more like a female."

Belle surged forward up the stairs, so mad Silas thought her hair might stand on end if it weren't caught back in her braid. She stormed into the house. "You listen to me. . .*mmph.*"

Silas shut that yapping mouth right up with his lips. He swung the door shut and broke off the kiss just enough to speak. "Did I mention that I want more children with you than you've given to the other husbands?" He made sure to kiss her so deeply she couldn't respond to that.

Finally, he pulled back. "Combined."

When she was clinging to him, he kissed his way along her jawline and murmured in her pretty little ear, "I won't feel right about it if my young'uns aren't in the majority. So that's five more babies, woman."

"Five more?" Belle asked weakly. "That's nine children."

He silenced her again until she shuddered in his arms. "Did I say just five more? I meant five *boys.* However many babies it takes to get that number of *boys* is what I expect from you."

"I. . .I don't think. . .I may not be able. . .I've shown no talent for birthing boys, Silas." She was almost wailing before she was done.

He slid his hands down her back and pulled her hard up against him. "Are you disobeying me, woman?"

"Umm. . .the other girls all have your name." She was starting to sound wimpy. Like a regular female. He thought he almost had her toeing the line.

Silas kissed her again. He really didn't want to think of Belle going through the dangers of having babies many more times. Besides, he considered the girls to be, in all ways, his own, so there was no point in trying to match up the number of children. But what was the fun in admitting that?

Belle said, when he let her breathe, "I'll do whatever you want, Silas."

"Anything?" She wasn't obedient worth a hoot as a rule, but he remembered how agreeable she always got when they were alone. This sweetness would no doubt wear off. In fact, he was surprised it had lasted this long. And the only reason it had was because he was distracting her.

But obedience aside, as soon as he was done teasing her, he was going to sit her down and apologize for his own foolishness in not telling her he was building a house. Silas admitted he'd been selfish in wanting to impress her. He should have known his hardworking, self-sufficient wife would take care of her land with or without him.

Silas wasn't going to make that mistake again. He'd almost lost his precious wife last night through his own prideful behavior. From now on he'd talk everything over with Belle. But he wasn't going to start apologizing quite yet.

She let her head drop back as he nuzzled his way down her neck. Breathlessly she murmured, "Anything, if you'll just forgive me for mistrusting you. . . ."

Silas didn't know if she noticed or not, but he was acting real forgiving right now.

"And if you'll let me live with you in the beautiful house you worked so hard on."

"Where are the girls?"

"And let me love you again, Silas. Please, will you believe I love you? Please say you'll love me like you did before I was so bad."

The Husband Tree

Now Belle was begging, and as much as Silas loved it, he couldn't stand that he'd reduced his proud, strong wife to that. But he decided to listen for just a second longer because he wasn't likely ever to hear it again.

"I'll do whatever you want, including starting on those five boys. I do believe I've got a start on the first one already."

He paused in his kisses and looked into her eyes. "Really? I wondered. But you cried when you talked about having my baby."

Belle couldn't seem to pay attention. "When was that?"

"Last night in the woods. After the wolves almost got you." Silas shivered as deeply as if he was freezing to death when he thought about it. "You cried. Cried hard and said you didn't want another baby."

"I don't remember saying that, but I know I've been a bad mother to the girls. I've done wrong by 'em, every one. And I regret that more than anything in my life. I don't want to hurt another baby by not having time to love her and hug her and care for her the way she deserves."

The last fear eased itself from Silas's heart when he heard Belle's regret over a baby wasn't because of him. "I'll make sure you have time to do things the way you want with him, Belle. I know the girls have been raised different from most little girls, but I think they're perfect. I think they're the kind of women the West needs to tame it. I'm so proud of them, I'd like to bust every time I hear them call me Pa. And that makes you a wonderful mother."

"They are good girls, aren't they?"

"The very best. And remember I'll be here to make sure they don't get mixed up with any no-account husbands, so we won't have to worry about that." He kissed her again. "Speaking of the girls. . .where are they?"

"The girls promised to stay busy until I called them."

"Oh, yes. They are very good girls."

And that was the last word spoken in the Harden Ranch house for a long time.

EPILOGUE

Belle saw she'd had a boy seconds after his birth and looked at Silas with equal parts pride—at finally producing a son—and fear—at figuring out how to raise one.

"We'll just do exactly what you did with the girls, honey," Silas said.

She'd learned that the man could, on occasion, read her mind.

"They're all as tough and brave as we could ever hope our boy would be."

Tanner would need to be tough indeed to out-tough Betsy, Sarah, Emma, and Lindsay, but from the way he came into the world kicking and screaming, Belle suspected he was up to it.

One warm summer day Belle strapped her son on her back and took a ride to her old cabin. She guided her mount up that steep hill to the Husband Tree and sat to rest and have a little talk with her boy about what she expected in a man.

Tanner slept through it, but Belle had her talk with him anyway, just to get in practice raising a son. She wanted the boy to grow up remembering where his ma had come from and how little she'd had to start and how far a person could go with hard work.

Belle looked down on the pathetic cabin that she'd built with her skinned knuckles and insufficient strength so long ago.

"I can't bring myself to miss a single one of the no-account bums, including William, who I am most likely sitting on right now."

Tanner squirmed a bit in her arms but didn't wake up. "But I'm glad for what I went through, because surely only the steps I took led to the exact place I'm in right now with you and my daughters and your pa. And—sitting on William notwithstanding—it's a very good place."

Rocking Tanner gently, she marveled at the chance she now had to fuss with a baby and sing lullabies.

She saw Silas and watched as he spotted her and rode up to dismount.

"Missing your old husbands and that cabin, Belle honey?" Silas settled with his back against the Husband Tree and smiled right into Belle's light brown eyes.

"Not even one little bit." Belle leaned her shoulder against Silas's. "I'm thinking that I needed these husbands to get my girls. And if I hadn't had all girls and needed to hire cowhands, I'd have never gotten you. It worked out in the end, but could marrying these no-accounts have been part of God's plan?"

"I don't know if either of us took the direct route God had in mind, but in the end it led us both to a good place." Silas reached a work-calloused hand to cradle Tanner's head. It was covered with dark hair, and the boy had brown eyes.

Belle supposed she'd given birth to yet another child who looked just like his pa, but Belle could pretend the tyke looked like her if she wanted to.

"It's possible I needed to go through those early years to understand—or at least accept—the ways of God." Belle's words drew Silas's attention away from Tanner, and their matching brown eyes met and held.

The Husband Tree

Silas leaned forward until their lips met. "Well, however we got here, I like where we ended up real well."

They sat together talking...and not talking...for a long while.

Then Tanner woke up and kicked up a fuss.

They got up to head home.

Before she left, Belle patted the Husband Tree good-bye and good riddance.

Discussion Questions

1. Belle has a really bad attitude about men, and she's passed that on to her children. Talk about how our words, sometimes spoken thoughtlessly, affect how our children see the world.

2. Silas runs out on a trumped-up shotgun wedding. He knows if he does this, he has to abandon his ranch and his money, leaving the area of his home. Talk about how women used to be "protected" by society's rules and how the death of those rules has helped and hurt both women and men.

3. Belle Tanner isn't very old, but she considers herself ancient in life experiences. Were you able to picture her as young when she had such a tough demeanor and such grown up children?

4. Silas considers helping on this cattle drive, with a baby in tow and an all-woman crew, completely humiliating. And yet he feels honor bound to help because he gave his word, even more because he knows they need him. Was it realistic that a man as burned by women as Silas had been would stay and help?

5. Belle and Silas shared their first kiss very early in the book in a completely spontaneous, highly emotional moment. Discuss if that was believable. In your own relationships are you (or have you been) powerfully drawn to the "right man"? Or is a powerful moment like that to be trusted?

6. If you've read *Montana Rose*, discuss Wade's transformation.

7. Many readers of *Montana Rose* despised Wade. Did you? Can you now accept him as a changed man, or do you still despise him? Has God ever changed a person you know this dramatically?

8. There is a lot a documentation of white children raised by Indian tribes as Glowing Sun has been. Very often those children had a terrible time readjusting to the white world. Why do you think that is?

9. Discuss how Lindsay, after a lifetime hearing her mother warn her about men, could so completely fall for a man. Didn't she listen to her mother? Or did Belle's actions, remarrying repeatedly, speak louder than her words? Or is love just that powerful?

10. Discuss Silas and how he handled his "surprise" for Belle. Was he wise to want to surprise her? Was he right that a poor man had a hard time marrying a rich woman?

11. Did you dislike Silas for being so mad at Belle when he should have just told her about his surprise?

Wildflower Bride

DEDICATION

This book is dedicated to my husband, Ivan. He worked so hard for so many years while I was raising our four daughters: Josie, Wendy, Shelly, and Katy. The long hours, early mornings, hard labor, relentless work outside with the cattle in bitter cold and blazing heat—all to support us while I stayed home with the girls. We both really believed it was the right thing to do. Or as Ivan is fond of saying, "I don't suppose it hurt them any to have you around."

So now the girls are grown, and I can help a little more with the money. He still works in the bitter cold and blazing heat. But maybe now he only works as hard as one and a half men instead of two.

Ivan, you are my hero.

"The LORD is my light and my salvation;
whom shall I fear?"
PSALM 27:1

CHAPTER 1

Montana Territory, 1877

Gunfire jerked Wade Sawyer awake.

His feet hit the floor before he made a conscious decision to move. Grabbing his rifle mounted over the door, he rammed his back to the wall, jacked a shell into the chamber, and listened.

Another shot fired, then another. The volley went on and on. Many guns blazing.

Even as he figured that out, he realized the gunfire wasn't close. Wade yanked the shack's door open. In the heavy woods and the dim light of approaching dawn, there wasn't much to see, but he knew the ruckus wasn't aimed at him. It had another target, and from the direction of the sound, he knew what. . .or rather who.

Glowing Sun. And her village.

Already dressed because he slept in his clothes, he yanked his boots on. Snagging his heavily lined buckskin coat off the peg on the wall, he dashed toward his horse, yanking the jacket on while he ran.

Living in a meadow Wade had penned off, his chestnut gelding had his head up, alerted by the shooting, staring toward the noise. Wade lassoed the horse and had leather slapped onto the animal within two minutes. Wade swung up and slid his rifle into the boot of the saddle. Letting loose a yell that'd make a rebel soldier proud, Wade kicked his horse and charged toward death.

The shots kept ringing, echoing from the Flathead village set in the meadow high on the mountaintop.

His horse was game, and terror goaded Wade to risk the treacherous trails at a breakneck pace.

But it was too far. Racing up a deer trail, he knew, no matter how fast he rode and how much he risked, he'd be too late. He was already too late when the shooting started.

The hail of bullets ended. Wade galloped on. The weapons falling silent only made Wade surer that whatever damage was being done was over. In the gray of dawn, that silence ate at him, interrupted only by his horse's thundering hoofbeats. He reached the base of the rise surrounding the Flathead village and tore up the mountainside.

A horse skylined itself, a masked rider atop it. A struggling woman thrown over his lap, screaming, clawing, kicking. A blond woman dressed in Indian garb, her hair catching the rising sun. Screaming as only Glowing Sun could scream.

She was still alive. Wade felt a wash of relief mixed with rage and terror as he goaded his horse forward. He could rescue her. Save her. He was in time.

Wade closed the distance, his horse blowing hard as it galloped up the rugged hillside, hooves thundering. Still a long upward quarter of a mile away, Wade wasn't close enough yet to open fire. Afraid he'd hit Glowing Sun, Wade drew his rifle and carefully fired over the man's head.

At the instant he pulled the trigger, three masked riders topped the hill, riding at full speed.

Wade's bullet slammed the first one backward. The man shouted. His horse reared. A splash of bright red bloomed on the man's shirt. Grabbing at the saddle horn, the outlaw showed great skill by keeping his seat. But he lost control of his mount and plowed into the horse bearing Glowing Sun and her abductor.

Shocked and sickened to have shot a man, Wade grimly raced on toward Glowing Sun.

The masked man just behind the one Wade had wounded swung his gun at Wade in a way that struck Wade as awkward or somehow wrong. The shooter hesitated; then, without firing a shot, he abandoned the fight, whirled, and raced his horse back the way he'd come.

The third man, skinny, but beyond that unrecognizable behind his kerchief, turned to face Wade's gunfire. The instant he saw Wade, he turned coyote like the other outlaw and ran, leaving behind his wounded friend and the man who had Glowing Sun.

Cowards.

Glowing Sun gave an impossible twist of her body and an earsplitting shriek. She kicked herself over backward, landing a bare foot in the man's face.

He must have yanked on the reins, because the horse reared, neighing and fighting the bit, skidding and spinning. As the horse threatened to go over backward, the man threw himself to the ground.

Glowing Sun went with him, screaming but not with fear or pain. It sounded like fury, killing-mean rage. And it sounded strong. Wade prayed she hadn't been hurt.

Wade, still galloping full ahead up the long slope, leveled his rifle one-handedly and fired again, even higher this time.

The man Wade had shot gained control of his horse, wheeled, and dashed after the other bandits.

The fallen man leapt to his feet, still holding on to Glowing Sun. Then Wade realized the masked man wasn't holding her...he was fighting her off.

Shouting Flathead words Wade didn't understand, she had one hand jammed into the man's throat as she slashed with her knife.

With the sharp *smack* of his backhand on Glowing Sun's face, the man broke her grip. Her blade slashed, catching a flare of light from the first beams of the rising sun, cutting the man across his arm and chest. The outlaw yowled in pain.

Staggering back, Glowing Sun screamed an Indian battle cry and dove at him. She caught his kerchief and pulled it down. Then her fingers slipped. She fell and slid down the steep hillside on her back.

Wade fired again, his horse thundering forward.

Stay alive. Stay alive.

He'd be there in seconds. But one bullet, one slash of a blade could rob the world—and Wade—of Glowing Sun's courage and beauty and indomitable spirit.

The outlaw jerked his gun free and shot at Wade. There was no blast. The gun jammed or was empty. Wade thought of the volley of gunfire that had awakened him and suspected the man had emptied his gun already.

Fury twisting his face, the man, his mask dangling around his neck, gave Wade one wild look. Wade saw his face plainly. Blood poured over his thick black beard and down the front of his heavy sheepskin coat. The outlaw snatched up his horse's reins and threw himself into the saddle, and in two leaping strides, his horse vanished over the rim, following the other outlaws into the Flathead valley.

Wade reined hard as he reached Glowing Sun. His horse nearly sat down as it slid to a stop. Wade swung to the ground and raced to Glowing Sun's side.

Blood soaked the front of her dress, coated her hands. She jumped to her feet as he got there.

"Where are you hurt?" Frantic, Wade tried to force her onto the ground.

She fought to stay on her feet and slashed the knife.

He knew her well enough to duck. "It's me! Glowing Sun, it's Wade. Let me help you!" He knew what he must look like. He hadn't shaved all winter or cut his hair. Or bathed for that matter. He had no business expecting her to recognize the wild man he'd become.

She froze. Her knife was raised to strike. Her eyes locked on his face. "Wade?" The rage switched to relief. The knife fell from her fingers and she launched herself into Wade's arms.

He staggered down the hill a few feet as he caught her hard against his chest.

Dear God, dear God, thank You. She's alive. Holding her feels like a taste of heaven. Thank You. Thank You.

Wade's head cleared from the knee-weakening relief. "Where are you bleeding? Were you shot? Did those men hurt you?" She felt vital and strong in his arms, not like a wounded woman should. His hands went to her shoulders, to push her back so he could see where she'd been hurt.

Before he could accomplish that, the smell hit him. Wade whirled with her still in his arms. Her feet flew out as she swung from his neck. He carried her as he dashed to the crest of the rise to see. . .

Devastation.

Smoke and bodies.

The tepees in flames.

Glowing Sun's village laid to waste, people sprawled everywhere. A dozen, maybe two dozen, all still. As death.

Gasping in horror, Wade looked at the village.

He'd made a habit of riding up here through the winter. This was the summer hunting grounds for Glowing Sun's people, and he'd watched and waited for her to return from her village's winter camp. He knew, even as he'd done it, the behavior was too much like what he'd done to Cassie Dawson a few years ago. But he couldn't seem to help it. He'd needed to see Glowing Sun.

As spring had come on, he'd been more careful. Ghosting his way to the rim to study the high mountain valley to see if the Flatheads had returned. Only a week ago he'd ridden up here to find they'd come back. He'd dropped behind a scrub pine and watched until he caught a glimpse of her, alive and well and as beautiful as a dream. Then he'd slunk away like a low-down coyote.

Now, movement caught his eye. The men who'd taken Glowing Sun galloped far across the shallow bowl where this small group of Flatheads, roaming far from their reservation home, spent their summers. Wade's hand clutched at his gun, but he was too far away for a shot.

A shot. He'd shot a man. His stomach churned. He fought nausea.

A wail of torment from Glowing Sun stopped him from dropping to his knees and emptying his stomach. He wanted to get on his horse and run from what he'd done. But he couldn't leave Glowing Sun with this devastation.

A flash of Glowing Sun fighting for her life ran vividly through his mind. What choice did he have but to fight for her? But it left him heartsick.

Then he looked again at the smoldering ruins of the peaceful village. Men, women, children. Killed by those four men. They'd come with rifles and handguns. The Indians were, more often than not, unarmed, at least unarmed beyond knives and spears. The Flatheads were a peaceful people. Their meager weapons were nothing against heavily armed men with repeating rifles.

Wade should be proud he'd shot one of those murdering scum. He should want to kill them all. The shame of that thought made his stomach twist again, and he thought he might vomit. He knew being able to kill wasn't the sign of a man. He'd grown enough in his faith to understand that, but his common sense was fighting a battle with his upbringing.

"Why did this happen?" Wade asked God aloud.

Glowing Sun answered. "A massacre." She still clung to him, but she'd lifted her head and turned to look at the butchery. She'd spoken in Wade's language. He'd taught her English, or rather helped her rediscover her first tongue.

Wade blocked her view of the nightmare by turning and putting his body between her and the destruction. Thinking of her distracted him from his nausea.

Wildflower Bride

Before he could check her for injuries, a cry of pain rose from the village nearly half a mile away in the valley.

Whirling to follow the sound, his weak stomach forgotten, he released Glowing Sun and grabbed at his horse's reins. He jumped on, held his hand out to her. Her hand slapped into his with a sharp *clap*. He swung her up in front of him, remembering how she'd liked to ride.

They raced down the hill and waded into a bloodbath.

Glowing Sun snagged the reins away and swung her leg over the horse's head. She jumped to the ground before the chestnut stopped and raced toward the loudest cries of pain.

Wade followed, relieved to see her moving and unhurt despite the blood.

Glowing Sun dropped to her knees. "Mama!"

Wade's stomach twisted with dread as he saw two gunshot wounds bleeding from the woman's chest. The woman opened her eyes, but they seemed unfocused. She grabbed at Glowing Sun as if fighting her off, screaming.

"No, Mama. Let us help you."

The older woman kept screaming, fighting.

"Flathead, Glowing Sun. Speak Flathead to her."

Glowing Sun looked up, confused.

"You're speaking English." Wade pulled off his coat then tore off his shirt and grabbed his knife out of its sheath in his boot.

Glowing Sun shook her head then turned back to the woman. "*Ten*. . .Mama. . .*Ten*."

Ten? Did that mean "mother"? Wade should have learned the language of the tribes around him. Why had he never tried? His father hated the idea. Indians were to be driven off, not treated as neighbors.

Glowing Sun spoke in the guttural tribal language.

The injured woman calmed and seemed to recognize Glowing Sun. Instead of screaming, she began a chant.

"We've got to get the bleeding stopped." Wade dropped beside

645

Glowing Sun. The chances of saving Glowing Sun's mother were slim, but they had to try. With a loud tearing sound, Wade's shirt split under his blade. Wade handed strips to Glowing Sun, who pressed them against the gushing wounds.

Glowing Sun began to pray in English, frantic petitions to God for mercy. Wade glanced up and saw love in Glowing Sun's eyes. The kind of love Wade had known for his mother. A long-lost love.

Wade knew nothing of the Flathead language, but to him the woman's chant was a dirge. To the extent he could understand, it sounded wordless, just syllables of mourning.

He joined Glowing Sun in her prayers, asking for a miracle, because only a miracle would spare this woman.

"God, please spare her life. Guide our hands. Wisdom, Lord, give us wisdom to know what to do, how to help."

The two of them worked in desperation, one on each side of the stout woman. Stemming the bleeding, binding the wounds. Long black braids, streaked heavily with gray, hung limp. The woman's dark eyes seemed to look beyond the sky. A cry rang from her lips. Her eyes flickered closed, but the dirge continued.

"Press harder." Wade shoved a wad of cloth on top of the one soaked with blood. He moved Glowing Sun's crimson-stained fingers.

The woman didn't react to what had to be excruciating pain. She continued her death chant.

Glowing Sun's mother's song became weaker, quieter, sadder.

At last the noise ended. Wade felt the moment life left the woman and her spirit left her body.

With a cry of grief, Glowing Sun stopped her futile medical treatment and flung herself on the woman.

Wade eased back, staying close but knowing nothing he could say or do would help. Only then did he hear other moans. Other cries for help.

He lurched to his feet, his knees numb from the long time

on the ground. How long had they worked on the dying woman? Were there others they'd neglected in their futile fight to save Glowing Sun's Flathead mother?

He hated to leave Glowing Sun. He couldn't insist she come. He faltered. "I've got to see if there are others who need help."

She didn't raise her eyes. Instead she started her own death chant.

Without even waiting to see if she heard him over her cries of grief, he turned and rushed toward the sound of pain.

CHAPTER 2

Wade dressed the wounds of five people. Three he expected to die within hours. They were gut shot and there was nothing that could be done. Two others had a chance, if infection didn't set in.

He'd counted nineteen dead.

The two who were less seriously wounded were still bad off. One, a half-grown boy, had a bad bullet graze cutting his leg and a gunshot wound in his shoulder. The other was an older woman, gray haired and whipcord lean. She bled from her temple. Wade had figured her for dead until she began moaning. Wade noticed when the moans at last penetrated Glowing Sun's grief.

Wade was surprised she remembered as much English as she did. Though she'd rediscovered much of the language of her birth while they'd been together in the fall, now she seemed to speak it with little effort. He wondered if she'd secretly practiced it over the winter. He also wondered if she'd thought about him.

Glowing Sun ended her chant and lurched to her feet, leaving her mother's side for the first time, turning toward the others who were hurt. "I didn't know anyone else was alive." She rushed toward the old woman just as Wade got to the woman's side and dropped to his knees.

Wildflower Bride

One whole side of the woman's head was matted with blood.

"We need more bandages." Glowing Sun pulled her knife from behind her back and slit the soft doeskin of her skirt. Wade hadn't seen the knife since she'd slashed at her kidnapper.

The woman's eyes fluttered open. She focused on Glowing Sun and struck.

A hard blow knocked Glowing Sun backward. The woman rolled to her side and lunged, shouting words Wade couldn't understand.

Wade caught the woman by the waist and flipped her onto her back on the ground. Assuming she was panicking as Glowing Sun's mother had been, Wade spoke soothing words to the struggling woman. "Glowing Sun, talk to her in Flathead."

Glowing Sun lay on her back as if dazed.

The woman swung a clawed hand at Wade's face.

He caught her wrist in midair and she swung with her other hand. Wade was close enough that the blow landed on his back and did no harm. "Glowing Sun! Make her understand I want to help her."

Then Wade realized the woman, swinging her free fist, pounding on his back as he wrestled with her, was looking at Glowing Sun with clear eyes. Not like Glowing Sun's mother, who was delirious. This woman was absolutely clearheaded in her attempt to hurt both of them. But mainly Glowing Sun.

"What's the matter with her?"

Glowing Sun regained her place at the woman's side and shouted harsh words at the woman.

The woman yelled back.

Pinning the woman's free hand, Glowing Sun continued her war of words.

The woman struggled, kicking and wrenching her body wildly. She screamed as if they were killing her. Wade held on doggedly. Only her wounds kept the woman from possibly winning this fight against both of them. She was older than they but wiry and strong and fierce. At last she quit fighting them. Her muscles went lax and she fell silent.

Glowing Sun spoke more calmly.

The woman listened then replied.

Glowing Sun's face crumpled as if the words stabbed knife wounds into her soul. Releasing her hold on the woman, Glowing Sun looked at Wade. "Let her go."

Wade arched a brow at Glowing Sun and held on. There was no attack from the woman's free hand, so warily, Wade did the same and leaned back on his heels.

The woman closed her eyes, covered her bloody face with both hands, and began the wailing that sounded like grief, much like Glowing Sun's mother had. But Wade knew this woman wasn't crying for her own impending death, but for the death of her people.

Glowing Sun jerked her head in a way that asked Wade to step away from the woman. They moved to the other wounded, accompanied by the death song.

Two of the surviving Flathead people had died while they worked on the angry woman. Wade prayed over the third but held out hope only if God supplied a miracle. As they finished binding the leg of the half-grown boy, Wade finally asked, "What was that back there?"

Glowing Sun gestured and Wade followed her to the far end of the village, away from the singing. "That is the mother of my. . . my. . ." Glowing Sun furrowed her brow as if searching for the English term. "*Naw*."

"*Naw*'? What's that?"

Hesitantly she said, "Husband?"

Wade controlled his expression only because this day had been so laced with shocks he was numb. He remembered all too well Glowing Sun swinging up on the back of a horse and riding away last fall. He'd come only moments after she and Wade shared their first and last kiss. As she rode away, she had looked back with longing, but still she'd made her choice.

It had cut Wade's heart out. He looked around at the devastation and found the man he sought. Dead, sprawled on his back, a tomahawk in his hand and so many bullet wounds it was clear it had taken a lot to kill him. "And she's angry at you?"

"She blames this massacre on me because they didn't hurt me. Instead they tried to take me with them."

"That's ridiculous. If they did leave you alive, they had terrible plans for you. And this killing is because they're evil. That's not your fault."

Glowing Sun looked at the death surrounding them and caught a handful of her white-blond hair, twisting it as if to yank it out of her head.

Wade knew no one could deny what he'd said. The evil was too huge, too ugly. "She's got no reason to hate you."

Glowing Sun yanked that razor-sharp knife with the slender blade from behind her back. "She has objected to me joining her family from the first."

"So you are married? Were married?"

She raised the knife to hack at her hair.

"Stop!" He caught her wrist.

Glowing Sun pulled against his iron grip. "Why do you stop me? Do you wish to *own* me because of my hair? Or *love* me? Or *hate* me because of it? I would rip it from my head, cut it away."

"No, I don't love you because of your hair." Before this morning's madness he would have said he loved her because of her heart, her fiery spirit, her courage, and, yes. . .her beauty. But he'd seen a savage side of Glowing Sun today as she'd slashed at her kidnapper. He realized he didn't know her well enough to claim something as deep and profound as love. But he wanted to know her. Wanted to love her.

"We don't have time for you to fuss with it. Let's bury your dead and tend to the injured." Wade wanted to ask about her husband. Had they been married before he'd rescued her from kidnappers last fall? And what did it matter anyway? Except that it meant he'd kissed a married woman. And more important, at least as it showed her character, the married woman had kissed him back.

"Where did you come from?" Glowing Sun dropped her hair without slashing it off.

"I've been living in the mountains. In a miner's shack."

"Nearby?"

"Near enough to hear the gunfire."

Glowing Sun looked around the village until her eyes landed on her husband. "Wild Eagle." Tears filled Glowing Sun's eyes as she looked away. The tears overflowed as she pointed at two children lying dead, side by side. "And that is my brother and my sister." Her voice broke.

She lifted her chin as if drawing courage straight from her spine. "My father is dead beside him. Better my mother is dead now than to face life without her beloved husband and children."

"And what of you? Now you face life without anyone." Except him. Glowing Sun had him whether she knew it or not.

"You speak truth. There is no time now for anything but seeing to my people."

The sun rose high as they worked, exchanging few words. Glowing Sun carried water as her patients cried out with thirst and pain.

The older woman roused herself soon enough and, despite her ugly head injury, began tending the boy who had a chance at survival. She refused to let Glowing Sun or Wade near him.

The smoke dissipated as the tepees finally burned to the ground, leaving only the reek of ash and the scent of blood.

"We need to bury them." Wade turned from the living to face the dead. "What can we use for a shovel?"

Glowing Sun nodded then squared her shoulders and approached her mother-in-law. They began to speak quickly. Wade wasn't sure anymore if the words they exchanged were harsh or if

Wildflower Bride

the guttural language just sounded like it to his untutored ears.

At last Glowing Sun returned to his side, tears in her eyes that told him all he needed to know. "She refuses to let us touch them. She said she needs to go to the Bitterroot Valley and fetch a holy man to sing for them."

"We can't just go away and leave them lying here."

"It is more the way of my people than to bury them. We believe people return to the earth when they die. Some tribes burn their dead on pyres. Some leave bodies to the elements, allowing the earth to reclaim them."

"Which will you do?"

Glowing Sun shook her head. "It isn't for me to say. She believes they died murdered, their souls stolen. I believe they died in battle. That is a noble death. It will be up to the holy man."

Wade didn't like it. But he wasn't about to add to Glowing Sun's distress. He walked to the side of the unconscious woman who lingered despite her devastating wounds.

"I'll respect your traditions, Glowing Sun." The sun lowered in the sky, and Wade knew it was too late in the day to begin the journey. "We'll head for the Bitterroot Valley tomorrow."

"Do not call me Glowing Sun," she snapped. "Wild Eagle's mother told me I've dishonored the name and my tribe." She walked along beside Wade and knelt by the injured woman's side, glancing over her shoulder to see if this would earn her a rebuke. "I remember my white name and will only answer to it from now on. Abby. I don't remember the rest of it, but maybe it will come back."

Glowing Sun's...Abby's...mother-in-law ignored them, as if she knew the woman they hovered over was beyond being hurt by them. "She can do this, Glow...uh ...Abby? She can decide how to treat *your* parents after their deaths? Decide to strip you of your name?"

"We respect age. To defy her now would only deepen her contempt and anger. And she's badly hurt, despite her refusal to

653

let me help with the boy. I won't make things harder for her."

As they knelt, Wade realized that the woman's shallow breathing had ceased. Her tenacious hold on life had been severed. Glowing Sun drew a blanket over the face of the young woman who had never regained consciousness.

"We've done all we can." Wade rose and came around the woman to Abby's side.

"You would leave me?" Abby looked desperately at him.

"No!" Shocked that she'd even think it, Wade rested his hand on her shoulder. "Let's get some sleep and set out in the morning."

"Set out where?"

"The Bitterroot Valley." Wade would see Abby home, though it hurt to send her so far away.

"Have you nowhere you need to be? Don't you own a ranch?"

"My father owned a ranch, not me. No, I can go along with you and see you safely home."

Abby looked at her village.

High mountains rose up on the north and a waterfall cascaded down into the valley, feeding the stream that cut through the center of the village. That stream flowed red with blood. The smoldering ruins of the village made a mockery of the lush grass and newly leafed forest that grew along the valley's rim.

"There's nothing left here." Wade resisted the urge to pull her into his arms and comfort her. "Not for you, not for anyone."

Sid Garver charged his horse up the last hard mile of the trail into his canyon hideout.

The animal faltered, heaving, exhausted from the hard run as Sid spurred it on, desperate to get under cover after being seen at the Indian village. As he neared the well-concealed crevice that led into the heart of this mountain, he heard a shout from behind.

He reined his horse in, fighting the bit of the mustang that he'd been pushing past its limit for two hours.

Hoofbeats behind him stopped. He wheeled his horse to see Harvey wriggling on the ground like a landed trout.

"How 'bout I just shoot him, Sid?" Paddy O'Donnell had a big smile on his face. He swiped his mouth like the thought of emptying his gun into a friend made him drool with pleasure. "He's gonna be heavy to haul inside, and he's slowing us down."

They hadn't been slowed down at all. Harvey had stuck his saddle for this wild ride away from the Flatheads they'd slaughtered. But Sid wasn't entirely opposed to Harv dying. Harv had bought into this fight by grabbing that woman. They should've killed her like the rest. They could have cleaned out that trash then rode away and come back in a month. No one would have tied them to that massacre.

Sid swung down off his horse, nearly kicking the quiver and arrows that hung from his saddle horn. He'd grabbed them on an impulse, stripped them off the body of a big warrior. It had suited him, taking this trophy of their kill. Sid could understand the bloodlust that led a man to take scalps.

Ground-hitching his horse, Sid strode to Harv's side. It was obvious the man had been bleeding like a stuck pig the whole time they'd been riding. Sid hadn't looked back or offered to help.

Leaning over Harv's blood-soaked form, Sid thought about that beautiful critter this dumb ox had grabbed. All that blond hair stuck there in the middle of that Flathead village. Young and beautiful and feisty and hair glowing like gold.

Hard to blame Harv when Sid had wanted her himself.

But there was golden hair and there was just plain gold. Sid would have killed the woman without hesitation to clear the way to the gold. But he'd wanted those Flathead cleared out of there more and for the only reason Sid was gonna keep Harv alive.

"Grab him, Paddy." Sid didn't bother to ask Boog. The man had a bullet in his shoulder. Sid had been half afraid Boog would fall off his horse before they got home, too. But Boog was a hard man to bring down.

Paddy giggled as he swung down. He came up beside Harv. On opposite sides, the two of them hoisted Harv to his feet.

Harv clenched his jaw—his jaw slit by that wild woman's knife. She'd cut his face and his arm, and she'd opened up wounds on his chest and neck, too. Harvey had to know he was lucky to be alive. "She got my mask off, Sid." Harv grabbed Sid's shirtfront in a death grip. "I'm done riding with you if we can't shut her up."

"You mean she can identify you?" Sid hadn't so much as looked at Harv until they'd crossed the Flathead village and gone over the rim of that valley. Sid assumed Harv had pulled his mask down himself, though none of the rest of them did until they were well clear.

Sid's fingers itched to put a bullet in Harv right now. But Harv had the whole gang over a barrel and knew it. "Yep, we have to shut her up." It went against his grain to kill a woman. But if it came down to life and death, Sid reckoned he could do whatever was necessary.

Boog rode up beside them, his left arm hanging motionless at his side, blood soaking his shirtfront. His face was sheet white, but he still sat tall and steady in the saddle. "The man who shot me and saved the wild woman saw you, too."

Sid's jaw tensed. "You're sure? No one's gonna pay much attention to a half-wild woman been living with the Flatheads. But if a white man saw him. . ."

"I'm sure."

"You'll have to lie low awhile, Harv, till we make sure it's safe." Unless the cut turned septic and killed him. Save Sid the trouble but lose him a fortune.

Now someone had seen Harv's face. If the man who'd shot Boog had a sharp eye, he might recognize them even with their faces covered. Western men knew details—boots, guns, saddles, brands. You didn't always have to see a man's face to recognize him later.

A gritty sound of pain escaped, but Harvey held his own

weight and headed silently for his horse, which Boog had caught and led back. Nursing one arm, Harvey nearly fell as he struggled to remount.

"Just a coupla more miles and we can patch you up."

Harvey nodded, but he didn't unclench his jaw to speak.

Sid set a slower pace. There'd been no sign of pursuit, and they'd put hours and mountains between them and that village. They'd circled around the whole mountain valley because the man coming along had forced them to run for it to the west, but this canyon was on the east side of the Flathead village.

But now they could rest.

And plan.

CHAPTER 3

She was no longer Glowing Sun.

Her eyes flickered open at that thought. She didn't know how to be anyone else.

Abby. No last name to her recollection. Just Abby. She'd been ten. Surely she'd known her last name. But her life with her white family had faded completely.

A flash of her white father laid out in his grave came from somewhere deep in her memory, and she wondered how much else was there.

She pushed back the blanket salvaged from the wreckage of her village. As she sat up from where she'd slept near Wild Eagle's mother, she saw Wade sleeping on the far side of the fire. And no one else. "She's gone!"

Wade was on his feet, his gun drawn, before Abby had finished speaking. Looking around, seeing no gunmen, he holstered his weapon and rubbed his eyes. "Who's gone?" But he figured it out before she could answer. "She must have started out for the Bitterroot without us. They can't go back alone. She's hurt. The boy couldn't even walk yesterday."

"I suppose she decided she'd rather risk death than travel

with me." Abby pulled her knees up to her chest and leaned her face against them, closing her eyes against the pain. She'd known she wasn't her mother-in-law's choice for Wild Eagle. But Wild Eagle had wanted her, and the woman had accepted it. Only now did the woman show contempt. Maybe with the death of her family, all Wild Eagle's mother had left was hate and she'd needed to aim it at someone. Abby would never know.

"We'll catch up to them." Wade began packing his bedroll. "You can go to the larger village to live." Wade appeared eager to be rid of her.

"I won't return to the Salish people. That life is dead to me." She reached for her hair. Usually she carefully tended it, running a comb through it and braiding it every night. Then upon waking, she let the braid free, combing and braiding it again.

It reached nearly to her waist, and she'd had it unbraided when the men attacked yesterday morning. She'd washed it in the cold creek the night before the attack and let it dry in the spring breeze. Then all day yesterday, after Wild Eagle's mother's cruel words, she'd ignored it, hated it. She'd never given a thought to ridding it of its knots. She might as well have a rat's nest on her head for the snarls.

A sudden bitter wildness gripped her, and she pulled her knife. Hating her hair. Hating that her difference had separated her from the life she loved. She slashed a chunk of snarls away and grabbed for another.

Wade's running footsteps warned her, and she turned. He caught her hand. "Stop!"

"You like my hair, then?" She slammed the hank of white snarls against his chest. "Take it. I'd been kidnapped for it last time we met. My village had been slaughtered for it. Wild Eagle's mother hates me for it. My yellow hair affects white men like it is truly gold. It makes you all act like fools. So of course you like it, too, Wade."

"Glowing Sun, I didn't—" Wade held on to her knife-wielding hand.

"No!" She pulled against his grip, eager to fight, to rage instead of hurt. "My name is *Abby*. I will *never* answer to my Salish name again. Strike it from your mind."

Before she could attack, the sound of hoofbeats pulled her eyes toward the rim of the mountain valley.

Two horsemen appeared.

Wade shoved her behind him and pulled his gun with the soft *whoosh* of leather against steel.

They rode silhouetted against the morning sun and appeared only as black shapes, faceless. One led a packhorse behind him.

"Perhaps the men from yesterday have returned." Abby stepped to his left side. "Perhaps the gold of my hair is too much for the fools to resist."

Wade reached for her then looked at her knife. A smile spread across his face. A handsome face, Abby realized, though it was lost behind whiskers. And she remembered she'd thought so when they'd been together last fall. And now he seemed to approve of, even enjoy the fact that she'd drawn a knife.

What a strange heart for a white man. Not a brutish coward like those who had attacked her village. She well remembered from last fall that he'd also been kind when other white men had tried to take her from her village. Wade had come along and protected her. Not that she wasn't doing well at protecting herself, but he'd helped. And he'd been so kind. It was his kindness that had captivated her far more than his looks. His kindness had made her long to stay with him when she was promised to Wild Eagle.

And now he looked like a crazy man, his dark hair flowing, his beard covering every inch of his face. But his kindness was still there in every word and deed.

The disloyalty to Wild Eagle, only hours dead, shocked her into raising her knife toward the men.

"Wade!" one of the men called out.

"Stop!" With a lightning-quick move, Wade caught her hand as she prepared to send her knife whizzing at the intruders. "I know one of them. He's a friend. Red Dawson. These aren't the men who attacked you."

"He is white." She twisted, trying to escape his grip. "He cannot be trusted. You cannot be trusted."

"You trust me already, Abby. You're just mad. I don't blame you." Wade hung on gamely to Abby's wrist with his left hand while he holstered his gun with his right. "They mean us no harm."

Abby had to give Wade credit for not trusting her, because he wrested her knife away from her.

"Ow." He looked at a quarter-inch slit in his thumb, wiped the blood on his shirt, and arched one brow at her as he tucked the knife into his boot. "Behave yourself."

Abby wanted to claw his eyes out. The arrival of the two men intervened.

Red pulled up beside Wade and swung down, the other man just a moment behind him. "What happened here?"

The men studied the carnage and the long row of covered bodies stretched out alongside the stream. "Let me go and give me back my knife. Your friends are safe enough."

Wade gave her a penetrating look then released her and plucked the knife from his boot. "It was a massacre of Glowing Sun's...uh...Abby's..." Wade shook his head and ran his hand through his tousled hair. "This was a Flathead village. This woman, Abby, lived with them and was one of the few left alive." As Wade quickly told them the rest, Abby noticed he'd smeared blood on his forehead; his finger was cut more deeply than she'd realized.

"Glowing Sun?" The other man looked at Abby as he removed his hat. His long brown hair reminded Abby of Wild Eagle. Of course her Salish man's hair had been longer, but it was as thick.

"I've heard of you. I'm Silas Harden. I'm married to Belle Tanner Harden. Some drovers who helped with our cattle drive last fall told of a white woman named Glowing Sun who lived with the Flathead. It must be you."

"My name is no longer Glowing Sun." Abby's eyes narrowed. "With the slaughter of my village, I leave my Salish name behind. My name is Abby. The white name I was born with."

"So Buck made it to help with the drive?" Wade extended his hand. "I sent him. I'm Wade Sawyer."

Silas shook Wade's hand. "Yes, Buck, Roy, Shorty. Roy ended up marrying my daughter Lindsay."

"Honest?" Wade noticed he was bleeding when he left a streak of blood on Silas's hand. "He was just a boy."

Pulling out a handkerchief, Wade pressed the cloth to his wound. Disgusted with his fumbling efforts, Abby jerked the kerchief away from him and tied it tightly against the paltry cut.

"I know." Silas shook his head and crossed his arms in disgust. "And my daughter was too young. But we couldn't talk any sense into 'em."

When Abby was done with her bandaging, she looked up into Wade's eyes. He'd watched her, his head bent low. Now they were too close. Abby stepped back and to his side.

Silas looked at Abby, but there was no evil in his eyes, not like in the men who'd come yesterday. "They told us about the kidnapping and that Wade had gone after you when you ran off. I'm sorry about your village. Who did this?"

Abby shook her head silently.

"We don't know." Wade rubbed his bandaged thumb. "We haven't had time to turn our thoughts to tracking them down. There were wounded to tend. Two other survivors headed back to the main Flathead village in the Bitterroot Valley. What brings you out this way?"

The redheaded man pulled off his hat. Glowing Sun saw his serious expression and knew this wasn't a show of manners so much as a sign of respect for whatever news he carried.

"There's been an accident, Wade. Your pa's hurt bad. He asked for you. There've been people out looking for weeks. No one had seen a sign of you. Then the gap finally opened to the Tanner Ranch—"

"The Harden Ranch," Silas interrupted. "How long do you think it's gonna take for you to remember Belle's married?"

"It's not that I forget she's married. You're standing right here, after all. It's just hard to break the habit of wondering whether one of her husbands will last." Red shrugged one shoulder sheepishly.

One of her husbands will last? Abby had a sudden desire to meet this woman.

"You and half the other people around here." Silas shook his head, looking disgusted.

"Sorry."

"Work on it."

Red turned back to Wade. "Silas knew you'd been up in this country late last winter. The two of us've been scouting around for a week. This morning we finally found a trail and backtracked you here. You need to come home, Wade."

"That's not my home. Not anymore."

Abby was struck by how much Wade sounded like her.

"His back is busted up. He got thrown by a mustang out riding alone and lay there through a cold night."

"My pa fell off his horse?" Wade sounded incredulous.

"He hasn't been able to walk since. He's asking for you."

Wade shook his head. "Not interested."

Red rested one gloved hand on Wade's shoulder. "You can always leave again. Going to see him now is the right thing to do."

"I've told you what he's like. He's the one who—"

"Wade," Red said, cutting him off, "honor your mother and your father. It's as simple as that. Nowhere in that commandment does it say they have to deserve it. He's a broken man. Come, if only to say good-bye. He doesn't have long to live."

"That spiteful old man will live forever."

For the first time, Glowing Sun realized how young Wade was. She'd thought little of his age. But his words now were the words of a boy, not a man. Abby turned and glared at him. "Your father has asked for a chance to say good-bye. I have lost two fathers. You should cherish the father you still have."

"Cherish my father?" Wade looked at her, the kindness gone. It made him a different man, cold and empty, a stranger. "My father was a tyrant who. . .who. . ."

Wade sighed so deeply, Abby could see his whole body nearly empty of breath. He shook his head as if to clear it and shrugged. "Yes, of course I'll go. Let's get packed up."

"We can split what's left of our supplies between us and let Abby ride our packhorse."

He reached for Abby's arm but she evaded his touch. "I have no place with you. Ride away and return to your life."

Wade froze. "No. If you won't go with me, then I'll stay. I won't leave you here alone."

"I am alone, no matter where I go now. I cannot return to my village and I will not fit into the white world."

Wade squared off in front of her, as solid and unmoving as the mountains that surrounded them. "I won't leave you."

Abby stared at him. Their gazes held a long time. Too long. She knew he meant it. And she knew he needed to go home. Well, she'd ride along with him, then, and leave when he was busy saying good-bye to his father. With a snort of pure disgust, she said, "Fine."

They packed up in minutes.

"Don't you want us to stay and bury them?" Red asked.

"Glowing. . .uh. . .Abby. . .said her people would have a special rite for the dead. They'll be back to see to them."

Red looked doubtful, but after a long hesitation, he settled his Stetson firmly on his head and swung up onto his buckskin gelding.

"You've left Cassie alone at the ranch for a week?" Wade asked as he mounted his chestnut.

"I left her to visit Belle."

Wildflower Bride

Wade blew a long, low whistle through his lips. "Do you know Belle Tanner?"

"Harden," Silas said through clenched teeth as he mounted his roan.

"Sure, I know Belle." Red sounded kind of sad.

Wade shook his head. "Cassie's never gonna be the same."

The men looked at each other for a long moment then started laughing.

Abby had no idea why.

They fell into line as the trail narrowed over the edge of the valley. She took one look back. This was the second life taken from her. It must be something about her. God must have created her to be alone.

Well, fine. She'd be alone. That suited her.

As they crested the valley walls, Red took the lead, glancing at Wade as he passed him. "You look like a wild man, Wade. You'd better shave and cut your hair before your pa sees you."

Without comment, Wade fell into place behind Red. He ran one hand into his beard, nodding. "I haven't given it a thought all winter."

Abby noticed that Silas brought up the rear. She wondered if that was because they thought she'd run. She ran her hand across the knife she'd hidden in the pouch at the small of her back. Well, they had the right of it. She would run. But not now. Not until she'd seen Wade home. He'd saved her from that awful murderous brute. In fact, he'd saved her last fall, too. So she was indebted to him, and that didn't sit right.

She'd see him home because she knew he wouldn't go otherwise.

And then they'd be even. She'd owe no white man.

CHAPTER 4

A bull charged straight for Cassie Dawson. She screamed, dropped her lasso, and threw herself sideways. The bull missed her by inches.

Landing on her backside, Cassie whirled around to see the bull skidding and wheeling around. She scrambled to her feet. Her hair came loose from its braid and the dark, waist-length strands blinded her.

Screaming again, she thought, *The fence. I have to get to the fence.*

The bull charged. Its hooves thundered.

There wasn't time. Cassie staggered back.

A rope flashed past Cassie's face so close she felt more than heard the whip of it. The noose snagged the bull around the neck. The animal jerked to a halt instantly, only inches from Cassie.

Cassie staggered backward then turned to see the fence not that far away. On shaky legs, she ran for it. She would have climbed over, but Belle Harden's voice stopped her as surely as if Belle had roped her, too.

"What did I tell you about getting in that pen?"

Cassie turned, pulling her hair back and out of her eyes, an

Wildflower Bride

apology already forming on her lips. But Cassie couldn't speak for the fire in Belle's eyes.

Belle finished hog-tying the bull then stood and strode toward Cassie. "Why'd you come in this pen alone?"

"I. . .I wanted to practice."

"After I told you how William died, gored by a bull?"

"Yes, but that isn't really a bull." She pointed to the calf struggling against the pigging strings.

Emma Harden, Belle's thirteen-year-old daughter, untied the little bull and it jumped to its feet and pawed the ground.

"Git!" Emma waved her arms. "Hiyah!"

The calf bawled like a little spanked baby, turned tail, and ran. Cassie looked at Belle.

Belle narrowed her eyes. "Just because he's only a couple months old doesn't mean he can't knock you down and stomp you into the dirt. He proved it."

Cassie dusted the back of her skirt.

"Red would skin me alive if he found out you were in here alone. He's gonna be mad just findin' out I taught you to rope."

"Dinner's ready." Sarah's voice mercifully pulled attention away from Cassie. Belle's nine-year-old daughter stood just outside the door of the gracious log cabin with the long porch. The house was less than a year old, and Silas had built it big enough to leave room for company. . .or a growing family.

Belle's little girl Betsy clung to Sarah's skirt on one side. Cassie's firstborn, Susannah, had a hold on Sarah's other side. The two girls looked almost like twins. Both had curly black hair. Betsy's from her Italian daddy, Anthony Santoni, Belle's third husband, now mercifully dead. Susannah's hair came straight from Cassie, passed down from her grandmother, a Spanish countess. Susannah was just a few months older than Betsy.

With toddlers clinging to her knees, Sarah held the two babies in her arms. Little Michael, with bright red hair just like Red's, was perched on Sarah's hip. The other, Belle's newborn son,

Tanner, was cradled in Sarah's arm. Even at two weeks old, the child was the image of his pa, Silas Harden.

"I'm sorry. I shouldn't have come in this pen without you." Cassie had to choke out the apology. Honestly, Belle was bossier than Red.

"What'd I tell you, Cassie Dawson?" Belle jammed her fists on her hips.

Cassie suddenly wanted to laugh, but she wasn't going to. Belle had taught her better than that. She lifted her chin and forced herself to glare right into Belle's eyes. "I made a decision that I could handle that calf. Yes, I fell over, but I would have been fine. You"—she jabbed her index finger straight at Belle's chest—"are *not* going to speak to me like I'm a child."

Belle grinned.

"Nice work." Emma patted Cassie on the shoulder. "Real scary."

"Thanks, Em." Cassie's cheeks warmed up she was so pleased with the compliment on her dangerousness.

Belle rolled her eyes.

Sarah, with an entire nursery of children, approached enough to hear Cassie practice using her backbone. "That's real fierce. I'm not funnin' neither. I'd mind you right quick. Wouldn't you, Susannah?"

Susannah, nearly two, poked the fingers of both hands in her mouth as she nodded. Through her drooly fingers, she giggled and said, "Mama scary."

"Good." Belle smiled down at Cassie's little girl. "It's settled. Your mama is as fierce as can be." She turned back to Cassie. "We're getting you toughened up. You may never get onto roping a calf, but you're learning to push back when someone pushes you. That's a good lesson. You won't have Red riding roughshod over you anymore."

"Red's pretty sweet, Belle." Cassie knew it was wrong to think of Belle as her mother. Belle was only about ten years older. But the woman was fifty years smarter and a hundred years stronger. Still, they should be friends. But Belle treated thirteen-year-old Emma like more of an equal than Cassie. "He really doesn't ride roughshod over me."

"Best to be prepared just in case he starts. Now, promise me you'll practice with the calf I built you"—Belle pointed to a sawhorse with a longhorn skull hanging from one end—"instead of going in the pen."

"I promise." Long gone were the days when Cassie sat demurely in her mansion embroidering pillowcases and keeping her skirts tidy while she waited for her tyrant first husband, Lester Griffin, to come home. Since Griff had died and she'd married Red, she worked alongside him whenever possible. Of course, they had two children now and that slowed her down some. And Red had never let her so much as swing a rope, let alone try to hog-tie a steer.

Belle cleared her throat.

Cassie pulled her thoughts back to the lessons Belle was trying to teach her. "I mean, I promise because I *want* to, not because I'm taking orders from anyone." Cassie felt her cheeks heat up. It was just plain embarrassing to speak so rudely, but Belle insisted.

"Good girl." Belle patted her shoulder. "Try it without blushing next time. And you're getting better at roping, too."

"I can drop the rope over the fake calf every time now. From a moving horse, too. That's why I decided it was time to try a real critter."

"Red may be gone for weeks hunting that worthless Wade Sawyer."

"Wade's not worthless. I told you he's changed."

The noise Belle made in response definitely qualified as rude, and there wasn't a single speck of pink on Belle's cheeks. Cassie intended to learn that exact grunting noise.

"We'll work on roping and busting steers and the other chores any decent woman oughta know. It's unbelievable you've never learned bronc riding. What is Red thinking? If we don't get finished, maybe I'll start coming for a visit from time to time. Have you ever cracked a bullwhip?"

Cassie shook her head. She'd never even seen one. "I'd love to have you visit."

Reaching Sarah's side, Cassie took her precious son, Michael, into her arms and smiled down at Susannah. Her skin was as white as a porcelain doll with perfect pink blush painted on. Cassie had that same skin and the cheeks that wanted to blush at the least little provocation. "Hi, sweetie." Every time Cassie saw Michael's riot of red curls, she wanted to laugh and dance a jig. This little boy who looked like Red and her little girl who looked like her—her family was a gift straight from God.

"Hi, Scary Mama." Susannah hugged Cassie's knees.

Cassie laughed.

Emma swung Betsy up into her arms and tickled the dark-eyed toddler who giggled and squirmed.

Belle took her new little son, Tanner, in her arms and ran one gentle finger down his cheek.

Cassie patted Sarah, who had long red curls escaping her braid, thanks to Belle's second husband, Gerald O'Rourke, long dead and not mourned. Sarah and Michael looked like brother and sister though they shared no blood. The Irish bred true. "You're cooking for a crowd with me and my children here. I appreciate it."

"The three of you together don't eat as much as Pa. It's fun having company." Sarah, her arms empty, picked up Susannah.

The bunch of them went inside.

"What are we going to practice on next?" Cassie pulled out a chair for Susannah.

Sarah set the little girl down and tied a towel around her tummy to keep her from falling. Cassie took the chair next to her daughter, holding Michael on her lap.

"Have you ever branded and cut a calf? It's the time of year for it."

"Ma"—Emma washed her hands at the tidy sink—"Pa said

you're not to start branding while he's gone. He said it's too soon after the baby."

"We could just do a few for practice. He'd understand."

Emma wiped her hands, her head shaking. "I'm telling."

"Like he wouldn't notice anyway." Belle smiled. "How about I let you teach Cassie how to handle a branding iron and castrate a calf?"

"That'll work." Emma hung up the towel and went to the stove.

Sarah set a steaming hot bowl on the table. Emma added a teetering mountain of lightly browned biscuits.

"What's *castrated* mean?" Cassie began ladling the chicken stew Sarah had prepared, careful of Michael's grabbing fingers.

"I'll tell you after dinner." Belle sat down at the head of the table with her son tucked into the crook of her elbow.

"Why not now?"

"You need to finish your meal first."

"No, I don't. Tell me what it means?"

Belle stopped reaching for her fork and raised her eyes at Cassie, giving her a level look so daunting Cassie couldn't imagine ever standing up to Belle unless Belle gave permission. . .which wasn't really standing up to her at all. "Trust me, Cassie."

Cassie wondered if this was one of those times she should be rude and pushy. Something sparked in Belle's eyes that helped her decide to be patient. And anyway, the stew smelled good and she was starving.

Dinner got over.

Belle explained.

Cassie decided she'd never question Belle again.

"The bleeding started up the minute I moved this morning." Boog unstrapped his arm, held in a sling by his belt. "We might as well use the branding iron. Get the fire red hot."

Sid didn't think Boog's arm was broken, but Sid was no doctor. He watched Boog grit his teeth as he pulled off his bloody shirt. The blood had soaked through the heavy padding they'd bandaged him with. The man didn't so much as moan. He was tough, no denying it.

Harv had complained all night like a little girl. His cuts were bad, especially where that wild woman had slit his chin, nearly cutting Harv a new smile in his chin hair. But Boog had a bullet pass through his shoulder and he'd never made a sound.

Sid shoved the iron deep into the flames.

"Don't you come near me with that thing." Harv scooted away from the fire, a dirty kerchief tied around his jaw to staunch the bleeding from his face.

"It'd help, Harv."

"No one's gonna close a wound on my face with a runnin' iron."

The running iron with its hooked tip could be used to alter any brand. They didn't rustle big-time, just enough for some odd cash. Sid had a lot bigger dreams than rustling. He aimed to rustle an empire from Mort Sawyer.

But money got tight for whiskey, so sometimes they'd grab a few calves, drive 'em in this dead-end canyon. They'd fix the brands then let 'em grow awhile before they sold 'em so the brand healed and looked pretty good. They'd even registered brands that were easy to twist around and turned Sawyer's M Bar S, Linscott's Double L, and Dawson's D Bar into the brands the gang claimed. Now that the gap had melted and they could get into that high valley the Harden Ranch claimed, they could run off a few cows from there, too.

"It's not like you're purdy'r nuthin'." Paddy laughed as he leaned back against a tree trunk that sat alongside their campfire, looking at Harv.

Harv's fingers twitched, and for a second Sid thought Paddy had pushed himself right into the business end of a shootout. But

Wildflower Bride

Harv didn't draw, and Paddy was too busy laughing to notice he'd almost died.

Boog, who didn't miss much, slid his cold eyes between the two, his six-gun strapped down. His shooting hand still worked just fine. "Let's get this over and done." Boog sat down by the fire and reached for the iron.

"I'll do it." Sid needed Boog, make no mistake about it. He needed Harv, too, and that gnawed at his gut because Harv was slowing them down. "You can't burn your own wound."

"I have before." Boog's ice blue eyes, as cold and dead as coffin nails, flickered away from the iron and steadied on Sid's face.

Sid felt death whisper across his skin like sleet. Sid moved cautiously, as if Boog was a ten-foot rattler. "So you want help or not?"

Boog nodded.

The dull rasp of the iron against the burning wood brought Harv forward, eyes riveted on the red-hot metal. Even Paddy shut up and got serious.

Carefully, Sid barely touched the oozing wound then pulled back the instant Boog's skin hissed.

The four of them were silent as Boog closed his eyes, his teeth clamped shut against any sound of pain. The smell of burnt flesh burrowed into Sid's nose.

Boog looked up at Sid. Killing-mean eyes. Sid's stomach churned. One wrong move right now and Sid would be dead on the ground just because Boog hurt so bad he needed to hurt someone else.

"Now do the other hole." Boog's voice sounded like a thousand miles of jagged rock.

Sid swallowed his fear as he moved around to stab this dangerous man in the back. Again the hiss. Again the silence. Sid had a new appreciation for the steel at the core of his saddle partner.

Sid set the running iron aside and went back to his place by the fire while they all waited silently for Boog to stop wanting to kill someone.

At last Boog spoke. "We need. . .need to get back to Sawyer's." His faltering speech was the only concession he'd make to the pain. "We've been gone long enough. Questions will be asked if we're away longer. But I'll be laid up a couple more days."

Sid suspected Boog should have been laid up in bed, with a doctor's care, for two weeks. Instead he asked for two days.

"I'll go back now with Paddy." Sid was glad for the excuse to be rid of both wounded men. "We'll leave you and Harv here to heal and tell the cowhands you got sidetracked and'll be along shortly."

Boog's eyes slid to Harv. "No, I'm not sittin' here listenin' to Harv whine like a little girl for days. I'll kill him just to shut him up. And there goes that gold you're so hungry for, Sid. I'm going along with you. We'll tell 'em we had a run-in with rustlers. Tell 'em they dry-gulched us and got away."

"What if we see that spitfire of a girl? She can identify me." Harv plucked at the caked blood in his black beard and fell silent.

Sid had no doubt Harv wouldn't survive being left behind with a wounded, surly Boog. The only reason Sid hadn't plugged him was that gold. "We're biding our time until the boss dies. No heirs since he cut that worthless bum of a son out of his will. Once Mort is gone, I'll stake my claim to the ranch."

"There'll be some others that want it for themselves," Boog warned.

Sid nodded. "And they can fall off their horses just as easy as Mort did." Sid stood and started saddling Boog's horse. He knew better than to ask, because Boog wouldn't accept help from any man. He'd saddle his own bronc if he were hog-tied and buried up to his neck in scorpions.

Boog's eyes narrowed but he let Sid work.

"What about the gold? We don't need the ranch if we get the gold." Harv's shifty eyes darted between Sid and Boog. He was a man without honor, so he expected none from anyone else. Sid knew that Harv realized his knowledge of that cache of gold was the only thing keeping him alive.

Sid suspected Harv had the situation with the gold and the ranch about right. "I want both. The ranch and the gold. And if Mort don't up and die pretty soon, I might just give him a shove right through the Pearly Gates."

Boog made a sound Sid had never heard from the man before. Narrowing his eyes, Sid said, "What?"

"Mort Sawyer in heaven." Boog snorted, shook his head, and then snorted with amusement again. It was as close to a laugh as Boog had ever come in Sid's presence.

CHAPTER 5

Y ou sure you don't want anything from your cabin?" Red asked Wade for the fourth time.

"Nothing there. Food for a few days, nothing I want."

"We can lay up at my place overnight." Silas pulled up as the four riders reached a trail that climbed up a treacherous, snaking path. "See what the womenfolk are up to."

Wade looked up that narrow trail, dreading the journey home. He'd ridden in near silence all day, switching between his imagination—dreading what his father would have to say—and prayer. The afternoon was wearing on and it'd be deep into the night before they got to Pa's ranch, if Wade rode straight through.

The June days were getting longer, but in the Rockies the sun set early if a body stood in the shade of the mountain. And the shade of the mountain was everywhere. Staying at the Tanner Ranch was a one-day reprieve. It'd give him a chance to clean up, shave, wash his clothes, and work up his nerve. "Sounds good to me."

"Agreed." Red tugged on his hat brim. "It's too far to travel to your ranch tonight."

"Pa's ranch. Not mine."

Red gave Wade a sharp look. "Tomorrow I'll go on with you,

Wade. I told Mort I'd see you all the way home."

Wade couldn't hide much from Red. The Dawsons were the best friends he'd ever had in his whole miserable, friendless life. "I don't need a babysitter, Red." Wade could barely speak through a jaw that seemed permanently locked in a grim line.

"No"—Red clucked to his buckskin and headed up a trail that'd scare a mountain goat into a dead faint—"but you could use a friend."

Wade nodded silently and veered his thoughts away from whatever ugliness his father would have waiting. Red knew him well enough that no thanks were needed.

Glowing Sun. . .no, Abby. . .sat her horse quietly while the men talked. Today her name was Abby, so he'd use it, even make himself think it. Abby had to come along to Pa's ranch. Wade had to take care of her. She'd lost her whole life. So if she didn't come home with him, he wasn't going.

Silas fell in behind Red. Abby watched Silas quietly. She had a way about her of observing everything. Wade was sure the woman would be able to follow this trail back to her home without hesitation. He wondered if she had plans to do such the minute he wasn't watching. But what did "home" mean with her village wiped out?

She glanced at him, and he tipped his head for her to go next. She shrugged and started up. The trail was narrow enough that they rode single file and it was easy to stay quiet.

"Whom shall I fear?"

It was a psalm. One of Wade's favorites. The Twenty-seventh. *"The Lord is my light and my salvation; whom shall I fear? The Lord is the strength of my life; of whom shall I be afraid?" I've spent my whole life being afraid. God, I'm sorry about that man I shot. Give me peace in my soul about pulling that trigger.*

The irony was, if Wade told his pa he'd shot an outlaw, Mort Sawyer would be proud. If Wade talked about how sick it made him, Mort would be ashamed.

Everything Mort stood for and respected was completely at odds with Wade's way of thinking. And how many thousands of times had Pa made sure Wade knew what a disappointment he'd turned out to be?

Wade repeated *"Whom shall I fear?"* whenever he imagined conversations with his father, imagined rage, imagined blows. The worst was Wade's imagined blows in return. He caught himself daydreaming about venting years' worth of fury on his father.

That was the real reason it made him sick to think about putting a bullet into that brutish man. Because on a very deep level, Wade wasn't sorry. He was glad he'd shot the man. He wished he'd have killed him. Killed them all. And that bloodlust led back to his anger with his father.

A terrible sin, to imagine hurting my father. I'm sorry, God. It's driven by fear. All the anger and vengeance is based on fear. Because I know my father can hurt me. Not with his fists anymore, but his words feel like a beating. "Whom shall I fear? Whom shall I fear?"

Pa couldn't hit him. Wade was an adult. If his father, even when he was healthy, had attacked, Wade would have gotten away. He wasn't a child trapped in that house with nowhere to go. But it was so hard to leave the childish fear behind.

"Greater is he that is in you, than he that is in the world." The Bible said so. Jesus was in Wade's heart. Jesus was greater. *"Whom shall I fear?"*

Wade had stored up scriptures about fear and strength and courage since he'd become a believer. Red and Cassie had helped him search for verses that gave him strength against the things that tormented him, and now he clung to them.

And he clung also to the dream of being a light in his father's life. That would be the true test of courage. Not hitting back or shooting a bad man but speaking honestly of his love for God and of how much his father needed that love, too.

He'd already talked to his father about faith. It ended ugly. Maybe that was why he was going home now. To try again.

Wildflower Bride

After a grueling climb and descent, they approached Silas's house riding four abreast as the setting sun washed red and orange across the land. From a distance, they saw dust kicked up from a corral.

"That's Cassie. She's riding. Cassie doesn't ride." Red kicked his horse into a trot.

Wade was on Red's right, Abby next to Wade with Silas on Abby's right. They picked up the pace to stay even with Red.

Shaking his head, Wade found his first smile for a long time. "Belle must've taught her."

"My Belle knows how to train girls to handle themselves." Silas looked across Abby to smile at Red.

"But she. . .she always rode to town on my lap." Red tilted his hat back. "I kind of liked that." They closed the distance to the corral.

"There's four of you now, Red." Wade had stayed at the Dawson place for long stretches, working as a hand for Red. He well remembered carrying the baby while Red carried Cassie. The little woman was scared to death of riding. "That would've been a load for a single horse."

Wade knew that when he wasn't around, Red carried Cassie while Cassie carried Susannah with the baby on Red's back.

"She's doing good, isn't she?" Red's voice was thick with pride.

They'd drawn near enough that Wade could see Cassie twirl a rope. "Look at her with the lasso."

The noose shot out and snagged a yearling steer. Cassie's pony dug in its heels and jerked the calf off its feet. Hitting the ground, Cassie fell toward the calf, straight into the thrashing hooves.

With a cry of alarm, Red lashed his reins on the horse's shoulder, and the buckskin leapt into a flat-out run.

Wade was one second behind, goading his chestnut, charging toward the disaster.

Red pulled up at the corral and hit the ground sprinting.

Just then Cassie stood up out of the churning dust, her hands raised high in triumph.

"I did it!" Her teeth gleamed white in her dirty face as she smiled.

"Cassie!" Red vaulted the fence.

Whirling at his voice, Cassie laughed aloud. "Did you see me hog-tie that calf? I'm going to brand him then cut him. Emma's going to—"

"Belle Tanner, you get over here." Red's face turned the color of a beet. He was enraged.

Cassie had taken several running steps toward him, but she stumbled to a halt at his tone. Her arms lowered. The smile shrank off Cassie's face.

Red turned toward the group of women sitting on the fence. Wade recognized Belle and little Susannah. But the rest of the brood were strange to him—except the infant with hair the color of a carrot had to be Red's son, and he knew Belle had a brood of young'uns.

"It's Harden." Silas joined them in the pen. "Belle Harden. Try to remember that."

Wade stood outside the fence to watch the fireworks. He and Abby dismounted and shared a look.

"Belle, you promised me you wouldn't start spring branding until I got back." Silas pulled his gloves off and glared at his wife as he tucked them behind his belt buckle.

Wade whispered to Abby, "I know Belle Tanner…uh…I mean Harden, a little. Silas is a brave, brave man to talk to her that way."

Abby arched a brow at Wade.

"What'd I tell you, Cassie Dawson?" Belle climbed over the fence with economical movements, striding toward the bawling, thrashing calf. Her spurs jingled, her holstered six-gun slapped against the hip of her leather riding skirt. She released the hog-tied little guy.

Cassie nodded and marched right up to stick her nose in Red's scowling face.

Red was an easygoing man for a fact. He didn't get mad often.

Wade had only seen it a few times. But when Red's temper blew, it flared as hot and red as his hair. Wade resisted the urge to go put himself between Cassie and that anger.

Red took his eyes off Belle to face his wife. "What are you—"

"Don't you speak to me that way, Red Dawson." She jabbed him right in the second button of his broadcloth shirt. "I am an adult woman, not a child. If I think a calf needs to be thrown and branded, then I'll do it."

Red's mouth formed a hard straight line as he glared down at his wife.

His wife glared right back.

It wasn't much of a standoff, because Red quit glaring and started grinning. "You roped that calf like a real cowboy, honey. And you were riding to beat all, too. Scared me half to death, which is why I blew my stack. I'm sorry. I'm so proud of you." He circled her trim waist with one arm, yanked her against him, and swooped down to fetch himself a kiss right there in front of all of them.

By the time he quit, the whole group was clapping. Cassie had her arms tight around Red's neck and her toes dangling off the ground.

"What else did Belle teach you to do while I was gone?"

"I can't wait to tell you. I missed you, Red. And Michael learned to clap his hands."

"I missed you all something fierce." He hugged her hard then set her on the ground. With his arm around her waist, they walked together toward the gathering of children.

Silas walked over to Belle. "You promised me you wouldn't start spring work. You just had a baby."

Wade thought Silas sounded more resigned than mad.

"I didn't do a thing, Silas." Belle raised both hands to shoulder level as if it were a robbery. "Emma worked with Cassie. I gave advice and watched from the fence. I kept my promise. Besides, I trusted you with the roundup. I knew you'd be back."

Silas kissed her on the nose. "Thank you."

Belle's return kiss was much warmer. "Tanner's double the size since you left."

Silas turned to look at the baby, and they headed toward the group.

Loneliness welled up inside Wade as he watched that smiling crowd fussing over babies. Red hoisted Susannah high in the air. She squealed with laughter and yelled, "Papa's home!"

Red accepted his warm welcome-home from sweet, beautiful Cassie. Silas was welcomed just as thoroughly by that tough-as-nails Belle Tanner. . .Harden. Wade was so impressed he decided he'd try to learn the woman's new name. This husband just might last.

He looked sideways at Abby. "You want to go meet 'em all?"

Abby had been watching, too. Now she turned to Wade. Her eyes were sad, aching. He wondered if she was thinking about her Flathead village or her mother or her husband. She'd lost so much.

Soft feelings had sprung up between Abby and Wade last fall. Had she ever thought of *him* with a sad, aching look in her eyes? But why would she when she had a warrior at her side?

"Abby, when we get to my father's ranch, there's a woman there who cooks and cleans for us."

"Your mother?"

"No, my mother died a long time ago. But Gertie runs the house. She has her own private room and there'd be one for you near her. She would welcome your company. She's always been able to handle my father, and she'll teach you how, too." Wade smiled, but he didn't feel one ounce of happiness. "She could never teach me. But she spent a lot of time taking care of me after—" Wade fell silent.

Abby hesitated. "After what?"

Wade tensed and didn't answer. There was no good reason for her to go home with him. He only knew he wanted her by his side when he faced his father. "If you don't go with me, then I'll go with you, Ab. I'm not letting you just wander off alone into the

Wildflower Bride

wilderness." He said it as if he was worried about her, and he was. But he was almost as worried about himself.

"I will go as far as your ranch. If staying there suits me, I will stay until it no longer suits me."

"Thank you." Wade exhaled like a weight had lifted. He rested a hand on her upper arm and guided her around the corral to where the happy families congregated.

They saw Susannah squirming to get down. Red let her go and took the baby in his arms. Susannah went scurrying off toward some scrub brush nearer the cabin.

"Susannah, come back here." Cassie smiled at the active little girl and went after her.

Wade reached the group just as a rattling sound jerked everyone in the group around. Only one creature made that deadly rattle. Wade, Red, Silas, and Belle all drew their guns.

"Susannah!" Cassie was in their line of fire. With a wild leap, Cassie hurled herself forward, stretched flat, inches above the ground.

A rattlesnake uncoiled from the brush, launching itself at the toddler.

A dull *thud* and the snake's head stopped. Momentum carried the rattling end of the snake forward. The snake's coils twisted around her and Susannah.

Cassie hit the ground on her belly. The rattler's head was pinned to the ground by a narrow, razor-sharp knife.

Cassie shrieked and flailed at the snake. Red reached the two of them and swooped Susannah into his arms as he tried to get the bleeding snake off Cassie.

Wade, Silas, Belle, and Emma were only a step behind.

Cassie shoved at the moving snake, screaming.

Susannah started crying, frightened by her mother. Betsy and Michael bought into the noise, too.

The group extracted Cassie from the coils and comforted Susannah.

When Cassie was on her feet and double-checked for injuries, Silas looked at Belle. "Did you throw that?"

"Not me." Belle holstered her six-gun.

One by one, they all looked between each other then finally turned and looked at Abby. Wade noticed she only had eyes for the snake.

She strode toward the long, brownish-gray striped creature, jerked her knife free, and beheaded the serpent with a quick, ruthless swipe. Cleaning her blade by stabbing it into the ground, she returned it to the sheath at the back of her skirt waistband and picked up the rattler.

"Supper." She sounded satisfied. Hungry, too. "Enough for everyone to have a bite. I know how to prepare it so the poison doesn't—" She turned and looked at the others, all transfixed by the sight of that perfectly thrown knife and that long, still-wriggling snake. "What?" She glanced at the snake.

"You saved her," Cassie sobbed. "You saved my baby girl."

"You act surprised." Abby frowned as if Cassie wasn't talking rationally. "Far wiser to use the knife than your body. Do you know this snake is deadly if you let it bite you?"

Cassie flung her arms around Abby's neck.

Abby staggered back a step and held her arms out at her sides, obviously shocked.

"Uh, we'll probably just have beef stew." Wade carefully reached for the snake dangling from Abby's fingers. "Not rattlesnake. Okay?"

He didn't want to upset Abby; after all, she'd just saved Cassie's life. But he wasn't eating snake. If he'd been starving. . .maybe.

Abby, with Cassie hanging from her neck, shrugged. "Rattlesnake is a special treat, but if the meal is already cooking. . ."

Wade tossed the snake away with terrified energy coursing through his veins at Susannah's near miss.

"No, wait. Save the rattle. The children will enjoy playing with it."

"Let's wait to get the toy until Cassie calms down a bit." Wade patted Abby on her arm.

Chaos erupted as everyone rushed forward to thank Abby.

Wade caught Abby looking from one grateful person to another as they swamped her. She acted as if they were foreign creatures. More dangerous to her than the snake.

Before long, Belle had Abby at her side talking. The two were swapping advice on how to best skin a buck.

Cassie gave Wade a smile and yanked on his beard. "It's good to see you. I didn't recognize you at first. You look a fright." She gave him a quick kiss on his furry cheek then turned to go with the women.

"Keeping your knife razor sharp is the secret." Belle pulled her knife out of her boot.

Abby produced her own skinny blade. "My stone got left behind at my village."

"It's sharp." Belle admired it. "You did this with a stone? Can you show me? We've got a whetstone, but I haven't been able to get the edge I want with it. I always use my strop." Belle turned to Cassie. "Let's sharpen yours while we're at it."

Cassie produced a knife. Wade was too surprised to notice where it came from.

"You're carrying a knife now, honey?" Red, looking uncertain, pushed his hat back and scratched his head.

"Belle said I should. A woman has to be able to take care of herself." Cassie followed after the other women, Emma and Sarah included, leaving the men alone with two babies and Susannah.

"Why did you throw your body instead of your knife?" Abby asked Cassie.

Wade didn't hear the answer.

Red dropped back to walk beside Silas and Wade. "Uh. . .I don't know if Cassie should carry a knife. She might cut herself."

"Or you." Wade chuckled.

Silas slapped Red on the back.

Susannah slapped Red smartly on the ear. "I wanna knife, Papa."

Red groaned.

Silas started laughing.

The three men got along well. Which was a good thing, because without knowing exactly how it happened, they ended up being ousted from the house after supper to bunk down in the barn. Sure, the house was crowded, but Wade had a strong notion that Red and Silas would have liked to sleep next to their wives.

Maybe Wade wouldn't rush into learning Belle's new name after all.

CHAPTER 6

Abby watched the tension grow in Wade until she thought he might snap.

He looked more like himself with his hair cut short and his face clean shaven. It was easier to separate herself from the horror of her village riding beside Wade as he'd looked last fall. She did her best to turn her mind away from the death she'd witnessed. The gunshots still rang in her ears. The blood was there every time she closed her eyes. She tried to shut it down by focusing on Wade and this strange world of the whites.

She'd let Cassie convince her to don a gingham dress. It pushed up high on her legs as she rode her barebacked pony. Wade had urged her to use a saddle, but she'd refused to load the horse down with heavy leather and iron.

The closer they rode to Wade's ranch, the tighter his jaw clenched. Tension vibrated off him in nearly visible waves.

A rugged trail opened to lush valleys of grass edging along the mountain slopes. As they rounded an outcropping of rock, Wade pulled up and turned on the trail to face her. "You told me you were a believer, a Christian. . .is that right?"

Abby wondered what the man was fretting over now. She

thought of Wild Eagle and the steady way he faced everything. He rarely laughed, rarely got angry. He was a rock she could lean on. But a rock was hard, and she'd been hurt by that hardness many times. Abby felt like she knew every thought that went through Wade's head, and if she couldn't figure it out, she just had to wait a bit because he'd tell her.

"Yes, a Blackrobe lived among our people. He spent part of the winter with us, in our winter hunting grounds. He told us of the white man's God and how He'd given His life to save us. A beautiful story, a story only God would have written. Our small village embraced Jesus. As I learned more, I remembered stories my own parents had told me of Jesus and Christmas and Easter. When the Blackrobe heard me speak to him in his tongue, he let me say his white words to my people in their tongue."

"I noticed that you have been speaking English well. Would it be okay if we prayed right now?"

"Prayed? You and I together?"

"Yes. Once we round this bend, you'll see my father's house. I don't want to make a show of praying in front of the cowhands or my father. There aren't many believers among them. I'd like to go in there with another believer at my side." Wade shook his head. "I've been praying since Red came to tell me I had to go home. I should have let Red come along. He's a wise man. He fills in for the circuit rider in Divide, but he'd been on the trail a long time searching for me. He needed to get home."

"What is it you pray for?"

A humorless laugh escaped from Wade's lips. "Courage."

"Are you lacking courage? I had not noticed."

Wade tilted his head a bit. "Thank you. But when it comes to my father. . .I'm afraid of everything. Afraid of what he'll say. He has a cruel tongue, Abby. And there's more. I'm afraid of my own anger. Red told me I'm to honor my father, and I know that's true. God sets it down in the Good Book as a commandment. But my thoughts toward Pa are angry, even violent. I want to yell back at him all the angry words that I've got in my head, and I know that's a sin."

"Why is it a sin to tell him of your anger?"

"Because I picture myself screaming, 'I hate you.' And in my mind, while I yell that, I punch him and pay him back for all the years and years of hurt I suffered at his hands."

Abby pursed her lips. "Well, take out the screaming and the punching, but the rest is just honest. There can be no honor without honesty. The words are the same."

Wade looked at her as if he wanted to see inside her mind. "That's true. I could just be honest but without the fury. I see rage as a sign of strength. But that's from Pa. Truth is strong and needs no anger." He nodded his head then rode up beside her so they faced each other. "It would be a. . .a light. There is so much darkness on the M Bar S."

Wade tugged his hat off and hung it from his saddle horn, pulled away a single leather glove, and held out his bare hand. "Will you join me?"

Knowing it was what he expected for some reason, Abby took his hand. When he closed his eyes, she followed his lead.

It was a simple prayer. As he spoke quietly of his desire to be sinless and courageous, a sudden image of her white father kneeling beside her bed, holding her hand and praying with her, flickered and was gone. Was that a memory or her imagination? Was it just once, at the end of his life when he knew the family was dying? Or had it been a normal part of her day? For some reason she thought of bedtime and prayer together. But it was only an impression. There was no memory beyond that lightning-quick image of her father in prayer.

Wade finished his heartfelt words then looked up. Their eyes caught. Their hands held. A moment stretched too long and still neither of them looked away. Wade hadn't given much thought to riding together, only Abby and him, for a few hours. But as he looked at her, he knew it was well they weren't together longer.

At last Wade quietly dropped her hand. "Thank you, Abby."

They rode forward, and it was as Wade had said. The second she rounded the outcropping of rocks, she saw the massive log house. "What kind of fool builds such a house in this cold land?"

Wade turned to face her, his brow furrowed. "A fool? You're calling my father a fool?"

Not the best way to get along with Wade, but she reminded herself that she didn't want him touching her hand. She didn't want to look deeply into his eyes again. She had no wish to get along with Wade, so it mattered nothing if she insulted his home. "How many hours a day does he spend chopping wood to keep a fire going to warm such a monstrosity?"

Considering he was wound tight as a coiled rattler, that Wade managed to smile seemed akin to a miracle. "That's good for me to hear. My father does struggle to keep it warm. And even with hired men chopping the wood for it, it's never really comfortable in the winter."

"And winter lasts half the year." Abby sniffed her contempt. "Better to live in a tepee. One small fire would warm your entire home."

Wade squared his shoulders. He appeared to have relaxed a bit. Perhaps she should insult his father more. It seemed to agree with him.

"How many trees were cut down so your father could be so. . . so. . .grand?"

"Too many. My pa was never one to worry about what he took from the land, only what it could give him." He looked her straight in the eye. "I'm glad you decided not to stay with Belle."

"Your offer of a job was the only way I could think to take care of myself right now. I have nowhere else to go."

They rode up to the house, Wade on his chestnut, Abby on a roan mare.

Dismounting, Abby followed Wade up the four steps of the porch that stretched the length of this monster of a house.

Wildflower Bride

The door swung open. A woman as wide as she was tall moved with startling speed for one so elderly. She darted across the broad porch and flung her arms around Wade.

Her weight and enthusiasm nearly knocked Wade down the steps. He grabbed for a sturdy pillar and caught himself in time.

"My boy! My boy is home!"

Wade hugged the woman close, leaning his tall frame down to press his cheek on the gray head.

Abby had to wonder if Wade was correct about his mother being dead. It didn't seem like the kind of thing a man would be mistaken about.

"I heard about Pa."

The woman nodded her head but didn't speak, her face still buried in Wade's chest.

Abby came up beside Wade and watched the reunion. The longing she felt for this kind of contact was stunning. Her Salish... no...Flathead—that was the white word—mother had been kind to her, but the woman wasn't given to hugs. Her Flathead father had been as quiet as Wild Eagle. Abby had no memory of her own long-lost ma.

A fleeting image of a woman as thin as a sapling pulling Abby onto her lap was there in her mind. Was that her white mother?

Ma... Yes, thinking of the woman as Ma fit. But what other name? What first or last name? It itched inside Abby's mind that she'd so completely left her white family behind. Perhaps more would come back to her now that she had reentered the white world. As she thought of that, her anger welled up. The white world had killed her Flathead family. But now the rest of her tribe didn't want her. She belonged nowhere.

The woman pulled away from Wade, wiping her eyes on her apron. Finally, she looked up. "Mort's fit to be tied. Laid up in bed, near to thrash anyone who comes within reach. He's spitting mad that he can't move his legs. The foreman comes and takes his orders and gives reports. Besides him, I'm the only one who goes in his room. It's like trying to talk to a wounded grizzly."

Wade's shoulders slumped. Abby knew he was dreading this meeting.

"He's been shouting for someone to find you and bring you home. He won't be happy to see you, though. He'll just take more of his temper out on you, son. I'm sorry."

"I'll see him and give him a chance, Gertie." Wade slid his arm around the stocky woman's shoulders. "That's all I'll promise."

"No." Gertie's hand clamped on Wade's. "Give me more than that. We need you here, Wade. The men aren't working anymore. Most of the old reliable hands have left. And new ones have come in that. . .that scare me."

She looked hard into his eyes. Abby felt the force of the woman's will and knew this one was strong. Despite the tears and the hugs, there was an iron core in the woman.

"I can't leave your pa, and I'm afraid to stay. Afraid for both him and myself. Please promise me you won't leave, at least as long as your pa is alive. Once he's gone—the doctor says he can't live long like this—we can let the jackals take the ranch."

"Take the ranch?" Wade shook his head quickly. "It's Pa's ranch. Who's gonna take it?"

"Anyone who's strong enough, Wade. This is the West. There's no law outside the city limits of Divide. And precious little there."

"Divide's a quiet little town, Gertie."

"Not since the rustling started." Her tight bun quivered as she shook her head. "People are on edge. Mort's new hands are too quick with a gun. The old sheriff quit and moved to Helena to live with his son. The new one isn't strong enough to keep the peace. Mort either holds this place or loses it with the strength of his back and his will. And his back doesn't work anymore."

"Let's go see him."

"Promise me first."

Wade fell silent.

They stepped inside the house.

Wildflower Bride

Abby's eyes widened at the huge living room stretching to her left. A set of stairs rose up along her right. Doors opened on the left side and at the far end of the massive room. Foolish whites to close in the outside then be forced to heat it and clean it. Waste. Pride. She was ashamed of the color of her skin. "Foolish."

Wade turned to her.

The old woman did, too.

"Excuse my manners. You taught me better than this, Gertie. Let me introduce Abby. We found her along the trail. Her...uh..."

Abby saw him flounder. They hadn't discussed what to tell people. Did she want the whole world to know she'd spent years with the Flathead tribe? In the gingham dress Cassie had given her, with her hair neatly braided, she outwardly fit in with the white world, even though her soul boiled with contempt for the whites, for their violence and lust for her blond hair and their stupid, immovable homes.

"My family died." She could hear the stilted tone of her voice. She had rediscovered her white language almost completely. She wondered if one day soon she wouldn't be able to remember her Indian family just as she had forgotten her white family. How did her mind do that? Separate her from her past like this? "Wade came along and helped me. I have nowhere to go."

"I told her there would be work for her. What about it, Gertie? Could you use a hand?"

Gertie looked Abby up and down. Her eyes had the sage look of the oldest women of the Flathead village. Finally, Gertie nodded. "I can always use help. I'd be glad to have you, Abby...." Gertie fell silent, letting the phrase hang.

Abby shrugged.

"Salish." Wade gave Abby a look of apology like it was his fault that she'd been cornered into telling a lie. "Her name is Abby Salish."

Gertie nodded. But Abby saw those sharp eyes and knew the strange exchange between Abby and Wade hadn't been missed.

"Well, Abby, you might as well go on into the kitchen. No need for you to listen to Mort's poison."

Wade's arm snaked out and grabbed Abby. "No, I've told her about Pa, and she's been giving me a hard time for not honoring my father. I want her to see Mort Sawyer in action." Wade turned, challenging Abby with a look.

Abby lifted her chin. "I would love a chance to have my father back. You should appreciate him more."

A roar sounded from upstairs. "Gertie! Get this slop away from me!"

Wade arched his brows at Abby as if daring her to honor that angry man.

"Let's go meet your father."

CHAPTER 7

Once when he was a young teenager, Wade and a couple of cowhands he rode with had surprised some rustlers using a running iron on a calf. Wade's horse had been shot out from under him in the chaos. He'd used that dead horse as a shield from flying bullets.

Now he was the horse. Or at least he felt like the poor beast must have as he led the way up to his father's room with Gertie and Abby hiding behind him.

Pa's shouting got louder, maybe because they were closer, but Wade thought the rage was building, too.

Abby straggled behind. Wade already knew she wasn't one to hide. But Gertie very definitely had Wade smack in front of her.

The coward.

Wade reached for the doorknob.

"You get up here!" The door seemed to shake under the impact of his pa's anger.

"Gertie! Gertie, you're fired. You worthless—"

Wade stopped as the tirade grew more hateful. He looked behind him at Gertie's wide eyes.

"You get fired often?" Wade whispered, as if, if Pa didn't hear his voice, he still had a choice of running.

The threats and insults continued.

"About six times a day," Gertie whispered back. "Until he needs something. Then he starts in shouting for me to fetch for him."

Mort let loose a stream of language that made Wade want to cover Gertie's and Abby's ears. His own, too. But he was short on hands. Wade shook his head in disgust.

Then he noticed Abby's contemptuous expression. "This is how a man speaks to his woman? This is what passes for strength in a white man's world?"

Wade noticed she didn't whisper. He also noticed his father quit hollering.

"I'm not his woman," Gertie said.

Wade thought he saw a pained expression in Gertie's eyes. Had she nurtured dreams, ever, that Pa would marry her? He should have, Wade realized. Gertie had cared for Pa, his child, and his home faithfully for over a decade. But Wade had never seen so much as a breath of romance pass between the two.

Sucking in a deep breath, Wade twisted the knob and swung the door open. His father sat up in bed. Their eyes met.

Silence.

Wade stepped in, braced for the insults and threats. He decided to start first. Chances were, once Pa got wound up, he wouldn't hear anything Wade said anyway. "I heard you sent for me, Pa. Well, I'm here. Here to help if you'll have me, with your care or your ranch, wherever you need me."

Wade hadn't meant to say that. In fact, until Gertie's pleading at the front door, Wade had fully intended to come, listen to whatever spiteful things his pa had to say, and leave. Most likely he'd be ordered to leave. But Gertie had asked, and the sight of his pa in that bed was shocking. Pa's strength of will was still there, but he no longer had a body to back up his threats.

Pa was a shadow of his former self. He'd lost weight, his

shoulders were narrowed, his chest caved in. Jowls hung from his cheeks. His legs were as slender as twigs under the single coverlet.

"Wade?" Pa was nearly six and a half feet tall, but his prone position stole even that commanding height from him.

Bracing himself for the explosion, Wade advanced into the room.

"Whom shall I fear? Whom shall I fear?"

Wade knew exactly whom he did fear as he watched his father's expression go from surprise to anger. He shouldn't have, not according to the Bible, but he feared his own earthly father, God forgive him.

"Decided to come home, huh, like a whipped pup?" Pa's fists clenched as if he were dreaming about throwing punches.

Doing his best not to flinch, as he would have in the past, Wade prayed silently for the courage he'd gained from knowing a better, kinder Father. God in heaven was on his side. He turned as always to Psalm 27.

"The Lord is my light and my salvation; whom shall I fear? The Lord is the strength of my life; of whom shall I be afraid?"

An almost supernatural calm eased into Wade's muscles and bones. "I came home because there is a God-given commandment to honor you, Pa. I am here out of obedience to God. Now, do you want to spend the first moments we've seen each other since you threatened me on the trail last fall telling me what a disappointment I am? Or, since I'm your only living family, should we try and talk to each other?"

Pa's fists opened and closed. His jaw clenched as if he was physically trying to hold back the rain of words. It might be the first time he had ever exerted an ounce of control over his temper, and, even doubting it would last, Wade was encouraged.

"I cut you out of my will." The words were harsh, but Pa didn't shout. "If you're here to watch me die then take over my ranch, you're wasting my time."

"Good, I'm glad you did." Wade crossed his arms to cover up

the deep pain in his belly. Not because he'd been disinherited, but because he had a father who would do such a thing. "Keep it that way. Then you'll know I'm here to help, not for the money. That's settled. Now, do you want to tell me what you need done around the ranch?"

"You don't know how to run a ranch. A ranch takes strength and guts. You've got neither."

"If you're happy with your foreman, I'll just help care for you. Give Gertie a break. I also brought someone home to help. She's—"

"You'd stay to the house like a woman?" Pa roared.

The clenched jaw hadn't held.

"You're the one who sent for me, remember? You just said you don't want me working the ranch."

"I didn't say that. I said you don't know how. I said you don't have any guts. And you just took it like a weakling."

"Being cruel to your son isn't a sign of strength, Pa. It's a sign of weakness, to my way of thinking. Being kind to an old tyrant who doesn't deserve it, doesn't want it, and doesn't thank you for it—now, *that* takes strength." Wade felt his temper slipping. His pa had taught him that anger was strength, but God had taught him better. Yes, Jesus got angry, but mostly He stood right in the face of powerful people and remained calm. There was great strength in self-control.

Pa fell silent.

Wade waited.

Gertie began straightening the covers on the massive oak-framed bed.

That's when Wade looked back at Abby. She stood by the door, studying Pa with narrow eyes.

Wade reached out his hand. "Come here. Meet my father."

Abby snorted, not quietly either.

"Who's she?"

Wade turned to see his father now watching Abby.

Wildflower Bride

"Her family is dead. She needed somewhere to go. I told her she could stay here, work with Gertie."

"Now I'm running an orphanage?"

"No, you're hurt. Caring for you is more than one person can do. Gertie, you can use some help around here, right?"

Gertie grunted as she tugged on a sheet. "I've told you how things are going to the dogs around here, Mort. I've got all I can do to carry food up and down these stairs. I'm not getting my cleaning done in the rest of the house, and I can barely keep up with the laundry. I haven't planted a bit of the garden yet, and we'll be pinched for food this winter if I don't get something done. Having help will keep the rest of the house from going to wrack and ruin."

She'd always had a way with Pa that Wade couldn't understand. She didn't seem to mind his rages, his insults. She'd just soldier on, do what was asked and then some. How many times had she diverted Pa's temper and given Wade a chance to scoot into some hiding place? Then she'd come and find him and tell him to come on out. It was safe. She'd come after Wade's mother had died, and Gertie had been a mother to him in every way but blood. Of course, many times she hadn't been able to divert Pa's fury. Then she'd come and find Wade and bandage his wounds.

"I'll be dead by next winter anyway."

Abby made the rude noise again.

Pa turned his attention to her. "You got something to say, girl?"

"Wade told me you were a tyrant. I'm not afraid of a strong man. My father was strong. But Wade was wrong. I come here and see a man whining."

"Abby." Wade stepped to her side.

She tilted her nose up at Pa. "I see self-pity and stupidity. Your son comes home with an offer to help and you insult him. Your woman waits on you hand and foot and you snap at her like a yellow dog."

"She's not my woman."

Odd that Pa would think to object to that.

"I will stay here because Wade has asked me to, but I work for a fool and a weakling. Better I should tend a crying child than a man such as you."

"A weakling!" Pa punched the bed.

Flinching from the raised voice, Wade stepped closer to Abby.

"Yes, a weakling. A man in my tribe once lost the use of his legs and he dragged himself around the camp working, helping to skin deer, prepare the food. He knew it was better to work with the women than to not work at all. He refused to be lazy and worthless like you."

Gertie gasped.

Wade braced himself.

Pa's face turned a shade of purple Wade hadn't ever seen on a human being before. "You get over here, you spiteful little shrew. I'll show you worthless." Pa sat forward as if he planned to throw himself at Abby.

She laughed. "Come and get me, old man." She turned to Gertie. "Why is he in bed all day like an infant?"

Pa threw aside his blankets and used his arms to swing his legs around. They dropped, lifeless, bending at the knees. Before he fell out of bed, he stopped and looked at his legs.

Silence iced over the room.

Pa stared as he ran his hands up and down his withered legs.

Tension wrapped like fingers around Wade's neck. He glanced at Abby, every inch Glowing Sun right now, her arms crossed, her eyes too wild and fierce for a lady. But so brave. And honest, too. Wade felt his spine strengthen as if he drew courage straight from her.

At last Pa looked up, straight at Abby. "Get out of my room. Get out of my house."

"A man's house is only his if he can hold it. I have a job here and I'll keep it unless *you* actually throw me out. But I will gladly leave your presence." Abby whirled and left the room.

Wade stared after her then turned back to his father, his spine working better than usual. "I hired her. She stays." He marched out, too.

When he'd prayed to God, *"Whom shall I fear?"* it never occurred to him that God might bring someone into his life who could give him lessons. Or who could be even more fearful than Pa.

"It's that wild woman." Paddy ran into the bunkhouse.

Sid looked up from the saddle he was mending. "What wild woman?" But Sid only knew of one wild woman.

"The one Harv tried to take. She's dressed in gingham now and her hair's tied back neat, but it's her. I just saw her go into the house with a man."

"What man? The one who shot Boog?"

Boog had come riding into the ranch with them, not showing a single sign of weakness. He'd made his excuses then ridden out again, heading for a line shack to spell the men who kept watch over that far corner of the M Bar S. In truth, he was going out there to heal. But if that wild white-haired woman was here, she'd recognize Harv for sure.

Harv lay stretched out on his bunk. They'd made up an excuse about rustlers and Harv getting the worst in a knife fight. Everyone here at the M Bar S was too stupid to know the only rustlers around were Sid and his gang.

This woman could ruin everything. "We'll lay low awhile. Harv's the only one they saw, and Boog with that gunshot might have given 'em a clue. But I can just walk right in that ranch house and give Mort the report like always. It'll look wrong if I don't."

"But how long can Harv stay hidden?" Paddy glanced nervously at Harv.

Sid forced himself to think about the gold. Harv was starting to be a burr under Sid's saddle. Only that treasure kept Harv alive.

"I'll have to tell Mort about the rustlers. Then Harv'll have an excuse to stay in the bunkhouse. Maybe the woman and man are just passin' through. They'll stay the night and move on. We're not doing anything to tip our hand."

"And what if she doesn't move on?" Paddy hissed. "You know she's gotta die sometime. She can't be around Divide, let alone the M Bar S."

"Well, we know how to stage a fall off a horse, don't we? When we did it before, no one suspected a thing, not even Mort."

Paddy smiled. Then he giggled and plunked himself down on his cot. "We do know sure enough. This time, I'll come in after just to make sure she's dead. I shoulda never left Mort lying there alive. I heard a wolf pack and figured he wouldn't last the night. I didn't want anyone seeing a bullet hole in him."

"You're the man we want to dry-gulch a woman, Paddy." Sid didn't even try to hide his contempt. Paddy had his uses. There was nothing too low for the man. Nothing too dirty. He enjoyed watching people die. He'd especially enjoy killing a woman, and Sid knew he'd done it before.

Paddy didn't even react to words that would have made Boog draw his gun. Well, Paddy did react. He grinned and started humming an Irish jig.

Sid was tempted to draw his own gun.

CHAPTER 8

S o then I got a hoof right in the belly."

Cassie had talked every second since Red had come in for dinner. She hadn't scolded him yet, but he'd earned the sharp side of her tongue several times since they'd left Silas and Belle's. He remembered how quiet she'd been when they were first married. How careful to be obedient.

Those were the good old days.

After a week with Belle, Red's wife was now just looking for an excuse to yell at him.

It was all Red could do not to be ornery, just to let Cassie have her fun. Honestly, it was all pretty lightweight as far as bossiness went. His sweet little wife just didn't have a mean bone in her body.

Cassie gently wiped mashed potatoes off Susannah's face, wrinkling her nose to get the toddler to smile.

Red had added onto their little soddy, made a log house about three times the size of the first cabin. Of course three times the size was still about half the size of a normal home. They still used a cave as their bedroom and a second, smaller cave with a chilly spring running through it for a cold cellar.

Mary Connealy

"You think we need to make the house bigger, Cass honey? Does the baby keep you awake at night?" Red took the cloth from Cassie. "Here, let me do that. You've got your hands full. We could add on a bedroom like we did for Susannah and move him just that little bit farther away from us if you're tired. I wake up faster'n you at night, and I'd be able to go cheer him up most of the time."

Cassie finished with Susannah then looked at the wriggling little boy in Red's lap with a fond smile. "He is a terror, isn't he? Why will the child not sleep through the night?" She ran her hand over Michael's curls and Red felt as if she were touching him. She'd been so thrilled when the little boy had his daddy's hair.

Between her cute, newfound toughness and the way she touched little Michael, Red hated to ruin the moment. But he respected her enough to be honest. "Cassie, I've waited until we're about done eating to tell you something important."

His Cassie had a sensitive soul. She looked up straight into his eyes, knowing this was serious. "What is it?"

Red turned Michael against his chest so he could pat a burp out of him, also to stall a few seconds. He wished so much he could smooth out all of life's bumps for his wife and family. "I've. . .I've got cattle missing. Someone from the Jessup ranch stopped in every day while we were gone to do chores and check the herd. Walt, the Jessup foreman, came by this morning, not knowing we'd gotten back. He told me he found a carcass that had been butchered right on the range. Well, a cow can wander off, but Walt thinks several head are missing. It'll take awhile to run a tally, but Walt's a mighty knowing man. If he says he's worried, then I'm worried, too."

A line formed between Cassie's pretty, dark brown eyes. Red regretted laying any trouble on her, but she needed to know. "I'll do some tracking and hopefully pick up a trail and get to the bottom of it. But you need to be on guard." Then Red thought of a way he could maybe cheer her up. "You'd better always keep that blade Belle gave you close to hand."

Cassie sat up straighter as if almost hoping she'd get a chance at having a knife fight with a rustler.

Red wished he could have a long, cranky talk with Belle Tanner...Harden...for putting ideas in Cassie's head. The woman was trouble and that was a fact. Silas had his hands plumb full, and yet he seemed to be a happy man. Which Red wouldn't be if he tussled with Belle. The woman was tougher than a full-grown longhorn and twice as dangerous.

Then he thought of Wade and Abby. The way she'd stabbed that rattler then planned to eat it. Abby had also saved Cassie and Susannah.

The West bred women tough, and his wife was learning to protect herself. No matter how much Red tried never to leave her in jeopardy, he couldn't be at her side every minute of every day. But even if she wasn't as tough as Belle and Abby, well, he couldn't help thinking that, when it came to women, he'd gotten the best end of the deal.

Red stood up and, with no wasted motion, plunked Michael onto the floor then swept Cassie up and sat back down.

She giggled. "Red, what are you doing?"

Red reached out and loosened the towel that kept Susannah secure in her chair then set her on the floor so she wouldn't fall. Leaving Red free to kiss his sweet little wife thoroughly.

"I'm just letting you know I think I'm the luckiest man who ever lived." He gave silent thanks to God that he'd gotten the best of the three women and made sure Cassie knew he felt that way by the strength of his arms and the depth of his kisses.

He only quit kissing his pretty wife when Susannah's slaps on his knee and shouts of "Papa!" got his attention. He wondered how long the little girl had been whacking at him.

Cassie stood; then her knees sagged and Red supported her until she could support herself. When he was sure she was steady, he plunked Michael into Cassie's arms and lifted a fussy Susannah high over his head. She giggled as he hugged her tight and scratched her chubby neck with his whiskered cheeks.

"You know what I think we oughta do, Cass honey?"

She had that wide-eyed obedient look that Red had come to cherish because he saw it so rarely these days. "What, Red?"

"I think while we've still got a little daylight left, we oughta go practice throwing that knife of yours. I think you could teach me a few things."

Cassie's obedience faded to something much warmer and livelier. She threw her one free arm around his neck, and even with both young'uns between them, they managed to while away so much time there wasn't enough light to get any serious practice in before bedtime.

Red was just fading off to sleep when Michael woke. They'd moved his crib temporarily to the kitchen. His howl for attention was the first of what would most likely be four times through the night.

Red went to cajole the fussing baby.

He heard Cassie mumble as she dozed off, "I think another room for our son is a good idea."

Wade came into the house for breakfast to find Gertie and Abby talking and happily working side by side. "Abby, you want to come out and see the ranch?"

"I will stay and help Gertie. We have a full morning planned cleaning this monstrosity. What foolishness."

Gertie snickered. "You go on out with Wade. The hands should be stirring by now, and I'll have breakfast ready when you get back. Something tells me you'll be happier outside than in, but that doesn't mean I'm going to turn down your help."

Wade suppressed a sigh of relief when Abby turned to him, removing the apron Gertie had her swathed in. He dreaded facing the cowhands, knowing he had to earn their respect and knowing he'd never managed it before. But Gertie had said these were nearly all new hands. Maybe they wouldn't have judged him already as a weakling and a coward, a view his father openly held.

Abby hung her apron on a nail beside the kitchen door. She wore the same dress as she had yesterday and had her hair neatly braided. But she still wore her moccasins, and her braid was tied back with a leather thong. She'd packed along her doeskin dress, too.

He could also see the small raised place at her waist, in back, where she tucked her knife. It was an unsettling mix of civil and savage that Wade found wildly appealing.

"I would like to see your ranch. My father raised cattle. I have only flashes of memories from my white family, but I remember a barn with horses and a herd of sandy brown cattle with long horns."

Wade held the door open for her and she stopped to stare.

Gesturing outside, he said, "After you."

"After I what?" Her brow beetled.

Wade smiled. "I mean I'm holding the door open so you can go first."

With a shrug, Abby went outside and Wade followed her. They walked side by side toward the massive barn, one of three huge buildings his father had built, connected by corrals, all set to best block the force of the winter winds.

Wade moved ahead of her and held the door to the closest barn, the one where the horses were taken to foal or heal from injuries. They entered the warm barn. The smell of hay and horses and leather evoked a warm memory of home. He'd always loved the horses best.

As Wade came in behind Abby, he saw five cowboys. Four Wade didn't recognize were mostly loafing around, while one, a grizzled old man who had been with Wade's father for years, was brushing a mare who had a new baby foal at her side.

"Chester, hello."

The old-timer straightened and laid his brush aside. "Wade?" The old man's voice was kind.

Wade had learned most of what he knew about horses from working along with Chester. The man had a kindly way with horses and had always been patient with Wade, too.

Emerging from the stall, he came forward quickly, his hand extended. "Good to see you, boy." The man's grip was solid. He turned to the cowboys lolling about. "Come and meet the boss's son. He's here to take the reins. And about time, too."

The men stood quickly, exchanging glances. One of them, skinny with a weak chin and mean eyes, seemed unable to take his eyes off Abby. Wade could understand that—women were scarce in and around Divide, Montana. That didn't mean he wasn't tempted to punch the guy in the nose.

Then Wade noticed another one staring between him and Abby as if he didn't know which one interested him more. The man had two missing fingers on his left hand. He was broad and running to fat, with blue eyes that looked cold as death. He stepped forward in a way that told Wade this man was in charge.

Chester jerked his head at the leader of the pack of loafers. "Wade, this here is Sid Garver. He's the foreman of the M Bar S now, ever since the old foreman took off."

"Otis took off? He'd been here forever."

"He vanished just after your pa's accident, and then Sid got the foreman job."

Something in Chester's voice made Wade wary of Sid Garver, as Wade was sure Chester intended.

"Sid"—Chester turned to the scowling man—"this is Mort Sawyer's son. His pa sent word that he needed his help, and Wade came home to take up the reins until his pa gets better."

"He's not gettin' better and you know it, Chester. No man gets over a broken back." Garver tugged his Stetson low over his eyes.

Chester sniffed. "Where there's life, there's hope. Somethin' my ma used to say. As long as Mort's alive, there's a chance he can get better. Anyway, he can still rule this ranch with Wade here to be his eyes and ears."

Wildflower Bride

Garver turned to Wade. "Welcome home, boy. I heard you'd quit the country long ago. Heard ranching didn't suit you, that you'd gone looking for a life that didn't get your hands dirty."

The other men, all but Chester, laughed.

The sting of those words sapped the stiffness out of Wade's spine. He wanted to turn away, slink off and hide. It's what he'd have done before he found God. But he wasn't the same boy. He was a Christian. That might not be the same as a rough-and-ready cowhand with a quick draw, but it was a better strength, one that would last.

"Sid, that's the last time you'll call me a boy, and if I hear another insult from you, you'll draw your time and hit the road. Is that clear?" Wade stood straight, holding Garver's eyes.

"I was hired by your pa, and he'll be the only one to fire me." Garver crossed his arms.

Wade turned to Chester. "Have you finished the roundup yet?"

"Haven't even started it." Chester narrowed his eyes at the other cowhands. "And it's plumb late in the season for it."

"Okay, let's go ask Pa if early June is high time to be doing the spring roundup. You want to go in now and explain to him why it's not done? Then we'll see if Pa will back me."

Garver's beefy fists dropped to his sides. "I was starting today anyway."

"I'm glad we agree." Wade watched Garver closely as his hands swung too close to his holster. Wade noticed the man wore his gun on the left, which meant he was left-handed, the same hand that had the two fingers farthest from his thumb missing. "Is there grass in the south canyon?"

"Yep, plenty," Chester answered.

With a jerk of his chin, Wade said to the cowhands, "Let's spend the next three days bringing the cattle in there. We'll take the Lord's day off then be ready to start branding come Monday. Can you handle that, Garver? Have you got any men who'll spend their time working instead of loafing?"

"I can handle it." Garver's jaw was so tight the words were barely audible.

"Glad to hear it. I saw on my ride in that the grass is overgrazed in the west valley. Let's move those cattle first." Wade studied the man for a second longer. "Have we met before, Garver? I can't place you, but something about you is familiar."

"I've never seen you before in my life." Garver made a sudden move with his left hand, and for a fraction of a second, Wade braced, expecting the man to draw his gun. Instead Garver shoved his disfigured hand into his pocket. "Let's get cracking, men." Garver stormed out of the barn.

The rest of the hands tagged along with none of the speed and determination Wade expected to see from cowhands in the spring. Wade watched them closely, still a bit shaken by something he couldn't put his finger on. Once they were out of earshot, he turned to Chester. "We need to have a long talk."

Chester nodded. "I heard you were around, at the Dawsons' and working at other ranches, doing some cattle drives. The best hands have moved on, driven off by Garver and the sluggards he's hired."

"And it's not like Otis to up and leave. He'd stick by Pa."

"There's more, but for now it'll have to wait. I'm glad to have you home. You're dead right that we need to get hustling on the roundup. I've tried to start it, but Garver's been against me every step. And you're looking fit. I've heard you've made some good changes in your life."

"I'm glad to be here, Chester." Wade realized with a start that he was telling the truth.

Chester headed for the barn door then turned back, his eyes somber and steady. "Watch your back, Wade. There've been too many accidents on this ranch, and that includes your pa's."

Nodding his head, Wade said, "I've never known the man to fall off a horse in his life."

"I don't want the next accident to happen to you or your pretty woman here." Chester tugged his hat down low over his eyes and left.

Wade glanced at Abby, who had stood quietly through the tense meeting with Garver. He noticed she held her hand tucked in the folds of her skirt. "You can put the knife away now." He couldn't control a flicker of a smile.

"For now. But those men look evil." Abby shrugged and returned her knife to its carefully concealed sheath. "Don't be surprised if I keep it close at hand."

Chuckling, Wade said, "I'd be surprised if you didn't. Let's go see the rest of the buildings. Then we can go turn you and your bad attitude loose on Pa."

CHAPTER 9

I'm not taking orders from that whelp." Sid saddled his horse as he watched Wade and that half-wild woman snoop around *his* ranch.

"The kid wasn't supposed to ever come back." Paddy mounted as he whined. "He was long gone before we came here to work. His pa never spoke of the boy except to say he was dead to him."

Sid had only heard bits and pieces of the disappointment Mort's son had been. A lazy coward and a drunk. The only real detail he'd heard was that the falling out between Mort and Wade was final. "I heard the boy disgraced his pa until Mort disowned him. Mort sure enough announced that loud and clear."

"And here he is back." Paddy rode alongside Sid.

Sid was tempted to knock the man out of his saddle just to relieve his temper, but it would draw attention, and the four of them—Sid, Boog, Harv, and Paddy—had been careful not to appear too friendly. "And giving orders like it was his place."

It churned Sid's stomach to think he might lose the ranch if the youngster inherited it. "A kid could die as easy as an old man. And, shame though it is because she's a pretty little thing, the blond wildflower has to die, too."

Wildflower Bride

Paddy gave Sid a hungry look. "I'll take care of her, pard. I'm already watching for my chance."

"It's gotta look like an accident."

Paddy shook his head. "No, it don't. If she disappears, everyone'll just think she went back to the wild, took up with the Flatheads again. I'm tempted to keep her alive awhile, have some fun with her."

"And Harv can't be seen out now." Getting rid of one little woman wouldn't be much trouble. Sid wasn't going to wrangle over how Paddy handled it. "It's possible both Wade and the woman would recognize him."

"We can take him into Divide and leave him with the doctor. He probably oughta have his cuts seen to anyway."

"But the doc might talk. We've got the story about running into rustlers, but I'd as soon not answer any questions from the sheriff."

"Wade is walking the yard like he owns the place. He won't stay out of the bunkhouse if he don't wanna."

"Yep, we'd better get Harv to town." Sid didn't like it a bit.

What had Wade been getting at when he'd asked Sid if they'd met? Sid had only been visible over that rise for a couple of seconds and masked. But had Wade noticed the missing fingers? It wasn't possible the kid could identify him, but a cold chill ran up Sid's spine at the thought of having all those murders connected to him. They were only Indians, but Montana was haggling right now over tribal lands and forming a state. They didn't want to be seen as a lawless place. Not even outside the towns. Someone could get it in his head that even an Indian deserved justice. What was the world coming to? "Better quit talkin' now, Paddy. Put some space between us."

With a swift jerk of the reins, Paddy dropped back as they rode out to start moving the herd.

It was backbreaking work. Work Sid wouldn't do once this was his place. He'd rule his kingdom from a nice office in that big old house. Bitterly, Sid considered how to get rid of Wade and the woman, and Mort, too, while he was at it. The old man was a tough one. He was taking a long time to die.

It was past time they quit leaving it to God and took over shoving Mort into the afterlife.

Wade spent an hour rearranging the furniture in his father's study. Ready now, he carried the odd-looking conveyance Gertie had ordered from back East up to Pa's room. Wade hated the cruel anger his pa was so famous for. But Wade's days of cowering were over.

"Whom shall I fear?"

Praying for the day he wouldn't have to repeat that prayer constantly, Wade rolled the chair down the thickly carpeted hall then peeked in the slightly opened door, bracing himself for the coming war of words. And there *would* be a war and Wade *would* win it.

Pa lay on his back staring out the window. Wade was struck by the bleak expression on his father's face. Wade loved his father enough to have prayed steadily for the bitter man to find peace with the Lord. He held out little hope that his father would ever change.

But this aching sadness showed a vulnerability Wade had never before seen. God was answering Wade's prayer, but not in the way he'd expected. He wasn't giving Wade endless courage, but He might be weakening Pa's cast-iron will.

Wade swung the door and went in. His father turned. His jaw set as his eyes flickered between the chair and his son. Wade couldn't be sure which Pa hated more.

"What is that thing?"

"Gertie ordered it for you. It's a wheelchair. She said she's tried to get you to come downstairs and have a look at it."

"In case you're too stupid or blind to notice, my legs don't work. And I'll die before I let someone carry me down like a baby. It's bad enough someone had to carry me up."

"I've set up a bed for you downstairs. You're moving there. For now, I get you up and into the chair every morning. But Gertie said there are ways you can learn to swing yourself into it without help. With this thing, you can sit up, move around the main floor of the house, read, and pass the time in less miserable activities than staring out at a ranch you can no longer run."

"Get out of here."

Wade had the urge to laugh. Since it made no sense and he'd been praying for a way to deal with his father, he trusted God and laughed in his father's face. "You can't stop me. You've been wasting away up here. I'm stronger than you and more determined than you. I'll help you into the chair, roll you down the hall, then carry you downstairs, or I can just throw you over my shoulder right now. You decide."

Pa started shouting, as Wade had expected. "I can still tear you apart with my bare hands, you young pup. I'm not going to be carted around like a piece of garbage you're looking to throw in the trash."

Wade sighed. It was a long hallway. Pa riding to the top of the steps would have been easier. "I knew you wouldn't cooperate, but I could hope."

"I'll thrash you if you get near me with that thing!" Pa struggled until he sat up. "Get out! Gertie, get up here!"

"Calling on a woman for help? Never thought I'd see the day." Wade rolled the chair aside. "Gertie is out planting a spring garden. She can't even hear your caterwauling."

Coming toward the bed, Wade dodged his father's fist. The intended blow almost upended Pa. Wade grabbed him before he fell out of bed. Wade hitched his arms around the invalid, now sprawled on his stomach, and gently hoisted his pa into his arms. Grief twisted inside him as Wade realized Pa had wasted away to nearly nothing. Dragging Pa's feet, Wade backed toward the door.

The shouting hurt his ears but nothing else, so it was easier than Wade had feared it would be. He ignored the roaring and dodged the fists flying backward impotently and soon had Pa in the study, settled in bed.

"I'll crawl back up those steps the second you're gone!"

"Why, Pa? Does it make you feel better to make Gertie's job harder, running food up and down the steps? In here you've got a library. You could even get back to work, keeping the books for the ranch. Gertie's been doing it and I'm surprised you trust her. With a little practice, you could get in and out of your wheelchair, come to the dining room for supper, and even go outside once I build a ramp out the back door. The ground is smooth enough I could push you to the barn and you could check the spring foals." Wade crossed his arms and leaned one shoulder on the door frame, staring at his father's face, red with rage.

The old man's chest was heaving, his hands fisted.

"You can't walk, Pa."

"I know that!"

"But you don't have to curl up and die."

"What good is life if you don't have legs?"

"You can run this ranch again, live again. Your life isn't over."

"Yes, it is. I'm worse than dead."

Wade straightened. "Considering you've never spent one second of your life contemplating God, I'm thinking you'll be a *lot* worse off dead, because nothing you've done in this life will ever get you into heaven."

Pa responded with the kind of vile language that only proved Wade right about the state of his father's soul. "I'm going to get your chair down here and you can practice climbing into it. Or you can just lie there like you're dead while you're still alive." Wade stalked out of the room.

"You get back here, you little. . ." Pa continued his tirade.

Wade turned his mind from the sound of his father's hate. He prayed all the way up and down the stairs, wondering as he balanced the heavy wheelchair why he wanted his father to have easier access to the ranch. Between his rage and filthy language—which was now easier to hear—and the shady things going on, Pa might have been better off staying secluded.

Wade's chin came up. Would Pa want to fight for this ranch? Of course! And if Wade could turn his father's anger to something that should've made him mad for *good* reason, maybe he'd let Wade be a part of fixing this place. And maybe turning the ranch around would at least give Pa something to live for.

CHAPTER 10

Red fashioned a bull's-eye using the side of his barn and a chunk of coal pulled out of the fireplace. Then he stood and watched in painful silence as Cassie missed the whole building.

She'd been at it for a week, during the young'uns' nap time. Usually the throw was short, plowing into the ground. Red was afraid to stay too close to her, especially after the time she'd dropped it on his boot. Luckily the handle had hit, not the blade, but it had taught him not to get too close beside her. Once she'd dropped it only inches from her own foot. And she'd gotten into the habit of losing it on the backswing. So Red had to make sure he wasn't behind her because he wasn't safe there. He also didn't like to get too far away in case she stabbed herself.

So he couldn't get behind nor beside. Not close nor far. In all honesty, the safest place might be right in front of the bull's-eye. Wherever else she'd hit since she'd started knife throwing, it had *never* been close to the place it was supposed to go.

She was getting better, though. The knife was going forward over half the time these last couple of days. It almost never went so wide it missed the barn. A couple of times, starting yesterday, she'd made contact with wood, but often the knife would hit on its side then slide to the ground.

"Maybe you should step a little closer, honey. Most knife fights are pretty close up. You don't need to stay back this far." They were about ten feet away, and if anyone ever got closer to Cassie than this, Red wasn't going to wait around for her to fight. He'd take over and save the day. But since the barn was no armed killer, Red encouraged her to move up.

"But this is how far away Abby was when she killed that snake." Cassie got a mule-stubborn look on her face. She was so cute when she scowled at him it was all Red could do not to hug her.

Red didn't know how to break it to Cassie. "Abby is okay as an example to follow, but until you're a whole lot better, I wouldn't compare yourself to her. She's about the best knife thrower I've ever seen. Way better than me or Silas. . .or even Belle."

Cassie stayed right where she was, and this time she held the knife by its tip instead of the hilt and threw it like she was mad. There was a solid *thunk* when the knife embedded in the barn. Her eyes lit up like stars. "I did it!" She launched herself at Red.

Knowing not to make light of her accomplishment, plus always being happy to hold his pretty little wife, Red swung her around in a circle until she giggled. "You did great! Look at it. It's almost to the outside ring of the bull's-eye and it's sunk deep in the wood. You are such a tough cookie." Sweet cookie, too. He bent down and stole a kiss and, for a second, distracted her from practicing mayhem.

Deepening the kiss, Red heard her catch her breath, a sound that always sped his heart. He'd begun to consider just how long the young'uns would stay asleep when she pulled away and looked at the barn.

Red let her go, digging deep for patience as his single-minded, knife-fighting wife headed for the barn to jerk her blade free. "I think I've learned the secret. I've gotta be *mad* when I throw."

Since Cassie didn't have much of a temper—despite Belle's best efforts to help her develop a killer instinct—Red figured she might as well give up now. But oh no, thanks to Belle's bloodthirstiness and Abby's hostile confidence, Cassie-the-marshmallow was determined to learn knife throwing.

She was pestering him to let her help with the branding, too. So far two young children and her barnyard chores and spring garden had kept her distracted while Red branded calves at top speed. He hoped to be long done before she found a spare minute.

She squared off facing the barn and raised the knife again just as Silas and Belle and their brood rode into the ranch on horseback.

Waving to draw the Hardens' attention, Red dropped his hand when he saw a grim expression on Silas's face and an even more serious look on Belle's. This was no social visit.

Belle had Tanner on her back; Silas had Betsy riding in front of him. Emma and Sarah rode their own mustangs right behind their parents.

Silas swung down, handing Betsy to Emma, who'd come up to hold the horses. "I've got cattle missing, Red. We set out to track them and found evidence of cattle from your herd being run off, too."

The pleasure of the day faded as Red nodded. "I've been keeping a close watch, but I can't light out hunting rustlers and leave the family home."

"We were close enough to your place we turned away from the trail." Belle jerked her gloves off as she stood shoulder to shoulder with Silas. "It's pretty clear they're headed into some rugged timberland on Mort's range. Mort isn't up to hunting them down, and I doubt Wade is, at least not this soon after getting home."

Red admired Belle for a lot of things, none more than the way she stood by her man.

"Didn't you say you'd found evidence of thieves?" Cassie asked Red as she tucked her knife into a little pouch Belle had sewn to the inside of her skirt's waistband.

Red flinched, always afraid she'd stab herself in the stomach. Belle wanted the knife concealed. Red thought a nice, sturdy leather pouch *outside* her skirt would be better. Guess who Cassie listened to?

Silas pulled off his Stetson and ran his fingers through his hair to get it to stop drooping over his eyes then settled the hat back in place. "We've been snowed in, so we hadn't had any trouble until the spring thaw."

Red looked at Sarah. "Susannah should be up pretty soon. You want to go check on her for me?"

"It's been a long drive," Cassie said. "Sarah, we've got ham in the cold room."

"Eggs, too? I could make up some ham and eggs." Emma slid Tanner out of the pack on Belle's back while she balanced Betsy on her hip.

"You don't have to cook for us." Cassie looked embarrassed. "I'll make the meal. I just thought if you or Betsy were hungry you could make sandwiches."

"I'll take care of supper for all of us." Sarah reached to take Betsy from Emma.

"Emma, go help, will you? The grown-ups need to talk." Silas didn't order her. It sounded more pathetic than that. Red wondered how often Silas had any luck getting his womenfolk to mind him.

"Like any one of you is tougher'n me." Emma rolled her eyes then headed for the house with Tanner while Sarah carried Betsy.

Red shook his head. The girls would take care of supper and watch four active babies and not turn a hair. He got annoyed with Belle for a few things, like teaching Cassie to be bloodthirsty, but he had to admit the woman raised terrific—though somewhat fierce—children.

"Red and I need to talk a minute, ladies." Silas jerked his head to indicate Red needed to follow him. They'd gone one step before Belle fell in beside Silas. Red glanced back and saw Cassie directly behind him. "Belle, please let me talk to Red alone for a minute."

"No."

"Yes. This is man-to-man."

"No."

Silas stopped and frowned at Belle. "I distinctly remember you promising to obey me, woman."

"That was a long time ago."

Leaning down so his nose almost touched hers, he continued, "But your promise was *forever*."

Silas was a hard man. Red had seen that on their trek to find Wade. He rode long, never asking for a rest. He read tracks like they were the written word. He packed light and could live off the land without breaking a sweat. And now, looking as fiery as a Montana sunset, he scowled at his wife.

Red was pretty sure, if it'd been him, he'd have backed down right away.

Belle took a step forward. "I've hardly ever obeyed you, Silas. Why would you expect me to start now when you're going to talk about stolen Tanner cattle?"

"*Harden* cattle." Silas jabbed Belle in the chest. "And don't you forget it."

Red's spine tingled with fear. Not because of the warrior's gleam in both their eyes, or because he was afraid there was going to be a real live fight between these two, but because Cassie might be taking notes.

Belle caught Silas by the front of his shirt. "I never forget it. Even though I built the herd"—she pulled him down closer, but he didn't move so she ended up standing on her tiptoes— "I trained the horses and—"

"You are going to mind me!" Silas grabbed Belle by her slim waist and yanked her hard against him. "You promised, and your word oughta be good. You still want to live in that pretty house I built you, right?"

"You'd never kick me out and we both know it."

They glared at each other until Red thought the tension might snap both of them in two. Then suddenly Silas swooped down and kissed Belle. His arms slid around her waist and he lifted until her feet dangled off the ground.

Silas let up his kissing and whispered something in Belle's ear. She giggled.

Red shook his head in shock. He'd have never dreamed Belle Tanner—Harden—was capable of making such a feminine sound.

Silas whispered some more, and this time Red caught the word *Cassie*. It was low enough that Red wouldn't have heard if he hadn't read Silas's lips. Which brought to Red's mind the possibility that he was watching these two a little more closely than he should be, but it fascinated him to see Silas work his way around stubborn Belle.

With a quick nod, Belle said, "Okay, you've got ten minutes. Then Cassie and I are coming."

"Thanks, honey. And you still don't obey worth a hoot."

"Sure I do. As long as you order me to do what I was gonna do anyway."

"And you're right. I'd never kick you out of that house. I've gotten real used to having you around." Silas kissed her again, soundly.

Once her feet were back on the ground, Belle turned, strode over to Cassie, and linked their arms. "Just because we disagreed and he won doesn't mean anything I told you about how to stand up for yourself is wrong." They walked toward the house.

Red almost followed so he could hear what advice Belle was giving his sweet Cassie now.

"Let's head toward the watering hole."

Red hated to let the two women go. His life might depend on his being ready for Cassie's next round of independence. But since it was about cattle rustlers, he followed Silas.

"I just wanted Cassie away from this. I wasn't worried about Belle." Silas glanced behind him as if to check that the women were gone. Then he lowered his voice. "Okay, I'll admit I'm a little worried, but I can't let Belle know that, and my woman has ears like a nervous mama cougar. Belle gets the bit in her teeth and there's no stopping her. Here's how it goes, Red. I've found a solid trail leading into some rugged land on Sawyer's range. It was mighty bold the way they came into our valley—that gap is close to my house—and drove off about ten head of cattle. I only know it was that many because of the tracks. Then I back-trailed 'em and found a little canyon where they'd held the cattle not more'n a couple days. Then they drove 'em out and met up with another small herd, another ten cattle maybe."

"You think those came from my place?"

"I know they did because we followed the trail back this way."

"I've come up short in my tally. But we always lose a few head to winter kill. Still, it was high enough I was sure there'd been some thievin'."

Nodding, Silas went on. "If I take you with me tracking the cows, that'd leave Cassie alone here. I don't like that idea at any time, but especially not if a pack of rustlers as bold as these are close to hand. But I didn't want to leave the children at our place or here with you and Cassie. So I want Belle here and Emma. They're tough ones. They'll keep everyone safe and be better here than they would be in our cabin. 'Course, Belle is fit to be tied that I'm not letting her come along. I swear the woman would take on a whole gang of outlaws with a baby strapped on her back, and Emma and Sarah are game enough to go along. But I can't stand the thought of them in danger."

Red wondered if Belle wasn't an abler saddle partner than he was going to be. Which made it pretty easy to accept Belle's staying here with Cass.

"So I think Belle will stay behind here if we make it about Cassie, but Cassie will pitch a fit and try to come, too, if she knows it's for her own good. Which then means we'd have to take all the children."

"We might as well be taking a wagon train with us." Red shook his head.

Wildflower Bride

"We can go and leave the women and put an end to this gang once and for all."

"I'd have had it to do pretty soon anyway," Red said. "But I couldn't leave Cassie home with the young'uns. Besides, I'm pretty sure she's got another babe on the way. She hasn't admitted it to me yet, or maybe she hasn't noticed."

"How could she not know if she's expecting a baby?"

"It don't surprise me none. Cassie's led a real sheltered life."

"Keep her with child as much as possible." Silas nodded with satisfaction. "It slows Belle down some, gives me a few months off her scaring me to death busting broncs and hog-tying thousand-pound longhorns."

With a grin, Red said, "I oughta tell Belle you said that."

Looking terrified, Silas said, "You wouldn't!"

Red laughed. "Let's go join the women for a quick supper then hit the trail. There isn't room in that house for us anyway. We might as well put some miles behind us on the trail since we're gonna get banished to the barn."

"Ain't that the truth?" Silas headed for the house like a man who wasn't the least bit scared of his feisty wife.

Red followed along, deeply impressed.

CHAPTER 11

Abby worked on the house, disgusted by the time that was wasted wiping away perfectly natural dust. Didn't the land have a right to be part of every home? Strange people, these whites.

Obeying Gertie's orders, Abby ignored the shouts she'd heard from the weakling tied to his bed—or he might as well be—as she finished her assigned tasks. Turning to her own needs, she found a whetstone and sat at the kitchen table sharpening her knife. The roaring from the bedroom finally got on her nerves to the point she slapped the whetstone on the table, returned her knife to its sheath, and stormed into Mort's room.

His face was bright red. He lay on his side reaching for the strange contraption Wade had called a wheelchair, which, since it was a chair with wheels, was a fair name. His ruckus stopped and he glared at her. "Help me get into that chair."

Sneering with contempt, she said, "And will you need me to bring you warm milk and a baby's bottle to suck?"

Mort's eyes narrowed. "Get out of here. Get off my ranch. You're fired. Fired, I tell you."

"I do not work for you. Wade offered me the job and only he can fire me."

"He's paying you with my money and he has no right to spend it."

"He spoke of this money. I told him I would need food and I accepted the roof over my head, a room next to Gertie's, even though it is a roof held up by your monstrosity of a house. I refused any other money. It would be just something to carry around, another burden."

"Money isn't a burden. It makes life easier. You can buy your own roof."

"I'll build a bow and arrow and shoot a deer or two, skin them, and make a tepee. I need no money for that."

"What about food?"

"The deer that provides my home will also give me food."

Mort waved a fist at her. "What about when you need clothes? Your deerskins are on your tepee."

"I will shoot another and dry the meat into jerky so I can survive for a long while before I have to hunt again. For the cold months, I will find an animal with fur for a warm coat—a buffalo or bear. What good would money do me for that task? Why did you come to this wild beautiful land, overrun with food, clothing, all the things you need to live, then shut yourself away from it inside these ridiculous walls?"

Mort snorted like an enraged buffalo. "Help me up. Come over here. I try to keep the chair from moving but it won't stay put."

Abby narrowed her eyes at him. Their gazes locked. As if they were in a fight, neither of them broke the contact. Abby felt her temper rise, her patience shorten.

Finally, when she'd decided to just walk out, Mort looked away. "Please."

"What?"

"Please. I'm asking you *please* to help me get in my chair."

That word, *please*. It went with *thank you*. Wade had reminded her of these white men's manners. Mort said it like the word was painful to force from his lips. She realized that, to a stubborn tyrant like Mort Sawyer, saying please was an act of humility. And she knew how much a tyrant hated to ask for anything.

Her Wild Eagle had been like that. He didn't ask; he ordered. Abby was used to it, but Wade's kindness had been a surprise and a delight to her. Was this man like Wild Eagle? Would Wild Eagle have been any better if life brought him so low?

"Fine." With a deep breath, Abby rolled the chair to the side of Mort's bed.

They made several attempts to get Mort transferred to the chair, and finally, using his arms and with Abby supporting him almost completely, they made it.

Gasping, Mort finally caught his breath enough to say, "Thank you."

"You're welcome." The words came almost as a reflex, without thought.

"Can. . .can you push me to the kitchen? There's a window there. I'd like to look out over my ranch."

"Use your arms. Push the wheels. Can you not do a thing for yourself?" Disgusted and ashamed that she'd had a moment of sympathy for the weakling, she stalked out of the room.

Before she'd gotten her knife's edge to suit her, Mort was in the kitchen studying the huge piece of the earth he so foolishly claimed as his. The earth was the Lord's, given to everyone, teeming with food, fuel to burn for warmth, and beauty to soothe the soul.

White men seemed to understand none of that. What a strange breed.

"What's that idiot son of mine doing?" Mort punched the arm of his chair.

⤳❦⤳

What were these idiots doing?

Wade saddled up and met the first bunch of cattle the men drove into the yard. They'd been at it for hours and Wade should have gone out to help, but he'd made a quick trip to town instead to arrange for the lumber to make some changes to the house that would make his pa's life easier. Sam Jeffreys, one of Libby Jeffreys's mule skinner sons, usually had a few days between hauling loads. Wade needed to focus on the spring roundup, so he'd asked Libby to have Sam ride out next time he was in Divide.

With that all in order, he'd returned home to find his men just bringing in the first herd. Watching, Wade knew why it had taken so long. The herd milled and broke away.

Wade charged his horse into the fractious cattle. Chewing on dust, Wade cut this way and that to force the critters forward. It was almost as if the men here had no idea how to handle cattle or run a ranch. Or if they knew how, they didn't care enough to break a sweat trying.

The bawling cattle and the thundering hooves of Wade's horse kept Wade from thinking too much about his incompetent cowhands. When he got the herd headed in the right direction, Wade watched. He drove the whole herd with the help of about three of the old hands. A dozen other men spent their time making the day harder for everyone.

They got the longhorns herded into the lush valley. A few of them found the gushing spring. The rest waded into the belly-deep spring grass. They all settled in quickly, as Wade knew they would.

Wade waved his drovers in. He'd seen his father operate long enough to know what he needed to do. Run most of these men off, including the foreman. But that wasn't what God wanted from him. He saw some laziness but mostly incompetence. "I want you, you, you, you. . . ." Wade jabbed a finger at ten of the men. He skipped Sid Garver for now. The man had to go, but not in front of the whole crew. No use humiliating him.

"Team up, each of you. Everyone needs to learn a few cowhand tricks." Wade turned to the oldest hand. "Chester, pick who you want to work with from the men I've pointed out." Noticing

Chester's disgruntled face, Wade said, "Let's head for the high pasture to the west. It's next closest. I want to move at least three more herds today."

The men turned to ride out.

"Chester, wait a minute."

Turning his horse with only the pressure of his knees, the old cowpoke dropped back to Wade's side. "Well, you got part of it. You saw what a bunch we've got here. But instead of teaming them up with the older hands, you should have shown them the road."

Taking a quick look around, Wade made sure no one was within earshot. "I did it that way because not all of these men are no-accounts. Some of 'em are just new. I don't want to fire a man when I can teach him a skill. If I'd have run ten men off, with rustlers in the area, they might have thrown in with outlaws. They might have headed to Divide with their pay and a grudge and drunk all their money away. That'd leave 'em mad and broke, and in some men that adds up to dangerous."

"Some of these men are just bums. All the training in the world isn't gonna help."

Nodding, Wade said, "In a week I'll decide who's a bum and who's just new at ranching. The ones who don't shape up will get run off my range. Fair enough?"

"A week is too long."

With a bark of a laugh, Wade said, "I'll bet we know enough to tell who's gonna at least try to work hard by the end of the day. So maybe I won't give 'em a week."

Chester scowled. "I always knew you were soft, boy. To my way a'thinkin' you're just provin' it the first day."

"I know how to handle a horse, Chester. And I know a cowhand when I see one. Have all these men been hired since Pa was hurt? I can't believe he'd've been fooled by them."

"Sid Garver hired them. So they're loyal to him. And Garver ain't loyal to anyone but himself. Watch your step, Wade."

"Watch yours, too, old man, because I'm naming you the new foreman."

"I'm doing the job anyway; I sure had oughta get the title. And if I'm the foreman, then you'd be better off listenin' to me and just get the worst of these drovers off the property. Instead you've hurt their pride by askin' 'em to pair up like they were greenhorns. Now you'll have a bunch of cowboys carryin' a grudge."

"Maybe, but that's the way it's gonna be." Wade met Chester eye to eye. "That's the way God wants me to handle it."

Chester wasn't a bad man, not much of a talker. A grizzled gray beard, lean and brown and tough as leather. He'd never joined in the harassment of Wade as so many of the hands had. But there'd been plenty of contempt in the old coot's eyes back then. Wade had a lot to prove before the wrangler gave Wade any respect.

"I didn't understand your pa, Wade. He rode you hard, held you up for a fool, and he was too ready with the back of his hand. I have my own beliefs when it comes to the Almighty, and I can see that there's been a change in you. But I've lived long enough to be sure God ain't gonna send lightning bolts to run off a bad bunch'a cowhands. Without your pa here to rule the roost, we're all looking to you. But no one's gonna hand you the reins. You're gonna have to take 'em. And the best way would be to run off the no-accounts and the malcontents."

"Which would leave us about fifteen men short for spring roundup." Wade quirked a smile.

"Not really." Chester looked around. "If all of 'em are worthless, we're shorthanded anyway."

"I'll give you that. I'll decide soon who stays and who goes, and I'll listen to your opinions when I decide."

"I already know who I'd pick. I just hope you figure it out before it's too late." Chester reined his horse around and took off after the cowhands.

Wade rode up beside Sid, who was teamed with one of the men who'd been lazing in the barn this morning. Paddy, that was his name. An Irishman for sure with that name, but nothing about him looked Irish. He was just another Montana cowboy.

"Paddy, mind ridin' ahead? Sid and I need to make some plans."

Paddy looked as if he was planning to refuse. Something about his expression sent a chill up Wade's spine. It wasn't anger but rather vicious amusement laced with a hunger to hurt. Wade decided then and there he'd watch his back whenever Paddy was around. And if Paddy was friends with Sid, then Wade would keep an eye on Sid, too.

Especially after Wade gave him the bad news. "I'm naming Chester foreman, Sid. He knows the way things work on the Sawyer range."

Sid's eyes flashed fire. For a second Wade wondered if Sid would throw a fist. He controlled his rage. "I've been running the Sawyer range to suit your pa."

"You're nearly a month late with the roundup, Sid. That doesn't suit my father. I'll be interested to see if he knows when I get in tonight. Maybe where you're from the winter doesn't let loose of the land until now, but that just proves you don't know how we work here on the M Bar S. Stay on as a cowhand if you like. But if you have any influence on the men, you'd better tell 'em to pick up the pace, because I'll decide who stays and who goes by week's end."

Sid's brow arched. "You want me to push the men after you took away my job as boss?"

"I do. Because one of the men who may stay or go is you. And I can make decisions before week's end if I need to. I'm watching close." Wade turned away from Sid and picked out an inept pair of cowhands who had paired up with each other. Had they deliberately defied him, or were they just that stupid?

Wade rode over to find out, and out of the corner of his eye, he noticed Sid and Paddy riding together, talking up a storm.

CHAPTER 12

Abby caught herself watching out the window for Wade to come in.

Not Wade really, all of them. It was her job.

Gertie had spent the morning working endlessly in the kitchen. Along with a huge baking of bread, she'd made pan after pan of apple cobbler and a mountain of doughnuts. When a bawling, shoving herd of cattle appeared out of a cloud of dust a short distance from the ranch yard, Gertie carried the warm sugary doughnuts out to the men, and Abby hurried along behind her with two huge pots of ink black coffee.

The milling cattle, their horns long and sharp, their coats brown and white and black and red, all colors, all sizes, were shaggy and mean. Baby calves kicking up their heels in the lush grass bawled. Their mothers answered with low crooning moos as their pace sped up to the smell of water.

Abby realized that Mort Sawyer had built his own herd, but longhorns instead of buffalo. But there were no fences. How did the man keep them from heading south when the weather turned cold? Shaking her head, she searched the crowd for Wade.

He emerged from the chaos and came riding toward them.

He called over his shoulder, "Coffee, men."

All the riders began trotting their horses toward Gertie and Abby. Gertie reached a waist-high flat rock near the entrance to the canyon, set her huge tray of doughnuts on top, and pulled off the cloth towel. Abby set one tin coffeepot on the ground and the other one beside the doughnuts.

Wade swung down and fished a tin coffee cup out of his saddlebag. His eyes met Abby's, but he didn't come toward her. Instead he dropped back and waved all the men in first. They ground-hitched their horses and dove into the food.

"Why do the cattle stay around, Gertie?" Abby asked. "And why do the horses stand without being held?"

Gertie smiled. "We'll talk ranching once this mob is fed. Or maybe you oughta ask Mort. That man, grouchy as he is, knows more about running a spread this size than any man around these parts. Talking might get him to let up on his self-pity." Gertie focused on the men.

One grunted, "Thanks," and moved toward Abby.

She didn't like the intent shine in his eyes and moved close to Gertie. A quick exchanged glance between the women was all it took to keep Gertie from telling Abby to move over.

The other men took their turn speaking to her, eager to say, "Thanks for the coffee," and a few words more. She felt them all staring at her.

Wade came around the back of the flat rock and stood by her side so that he and Gertie had her surrounded.

"You want coffee?" She did her best not to glare at him. Just another man who prized her fair skin and pale hair.

"In a minute. I'll wait." Wade said no more, but Abby, despite being annoyed at Wade's nearness, realized she felt safe with Gertie on one side and Wade on the other. How could she think she'd be safe in the white man's world? Of course, she had turned out *not* to be safe in her Flathead people's world, too, now, hadn't she?

Wildflower Bride

When Wade finally got his turn, he drank his coffee while Gertie asked questions about the progress of the roundup.

"We'll have lunch in the bunkhouse. You don't need to feed this mob." He watched his men ride back to the next herd as he told Gertie about the morning. He decided to wait until the men were out of sight to make sure none of them bothered Abby.

"I've been talking to Cookie. He's got a pot of stew going, but I've baked a day's worth of bread this morning, so I'm taking that and enough apple cobbler to give every man a bite. While roundup is going on, we'll keep your bellies full."

"Sounds great, Gertie. Thanks."

Looking at Abby, Gertie said, "I need to hustle back to the house. Do you mind waiting until the men are done then bringing along the tray and coffeepots?"

Abby nodded.

Gertie did hustle. In fact, Abby didn't think she'd ever seen the older woman move so fast.

Realizing that while she'd stared after Gertie, the cowhands had swung up on horseback and headed out, she stood alone with Wade. She began collecting the pots as Wade went to his chestnut, the last animal still standing idle.

Wade tossed the reins over the gelding's head. He grabbed the pommel then paused. "If...uh...the men...ever bother you, Abby, you should let me know. I...I don't like the looks of some of them, and...well...I..."

Abby looked away from the tray she reached for. "What is it?"

"I suppose I made 'em mad. Some of 'em at least."

"What did you do?" Abby had a flicker of memory when she spoke the scolding words. She thought maybe her white mother had taken that exact tone with her long ago.

Wade dropped the reins again and stepped close. "I changed foremen. I didn't like the looks of the one we had. And a lot of the cowhands are new since Pa got hurt. The foreman looked mad enough to take my head off when I told him. But he's not runnin' the ranch to suit me nor my pa. And I teamed up my better cowhands with the ones who weren't up to snuff. I suppose I stepped on some pride with that. But it was either that or send 'em down the trail to hunt work somewhere else. Anyway, they might be mad, maybe fightin' mad, and I want you to stay well away from them."

"It suits me to stay far away from all of you." Abby tossed her braid over her shoulder. "I will gladly avoid your men."

"Well, okay then, good. I'll be going." Wade went back to his horse.

Abby turned away to gather the rest of her things. She heard the leather creak as Wade swung up. She wasn't quite able to stop herself from sneaking a look at him—lean and strong and kind—mounting his horse.

As he landed on the saddle, the horse went berserk. Exploding in noise and motion, it launched itself straight up, neighing and fighting the bit. The chestnut's head jerked back. Its head would have smashed Wade's face if Wade wasn't off balance and leaning to the side.

Stiff-legged, the chestnut landed hard. Abby heard Wade's teeth click together. Rearing and squealing, the normally gentle gelding rose up and up. It looked certain to go over backward.

Wade threw his weight forward and the horse landed on all fours. Wheeling, it lashed its heels high in the air, and the iron-shod hooves whizzed past Abby's face.

"Abby, look out!" Wade's voice roared over the shrill whistles of the maddened animal.

She threw her body backward, trapping herself against the rock.

Wade fought for control.

The horse whirled again then lunged forward. Its front hooves raked at her.

Throwing herself sideways, Abby watched as the horse missed her by inches. As she landed, she saw an arrow protruding from the sleeve of her dress, but it didn't hurt. It must have missed her arm. Without a split second to think under the hooves of the maddened horse, Abby regained her feet then timed her leap to the horse's jumps. Swift as a pouncing cougar, Abby grabbed the horse's bridle.

The horse lifted her off her feet. Her weight brought the horse back to the ground as a second arrow whipped by so close that feathers attached to it swiped her face.

With the horse still, Wade leapt from the saddle. "What are you doing?" He raced to the horse's head.

"Holding your horse." Abby gasped from exertion, pulling the horse around so its big body protected them from the arrows.

"You could"—Wade's chest heaved—"have been killed."

Abby seriously doubted it. She caught the fabric covering Wade's shoulder and dragged him out of the line of fire. "What happened to him?"

Wade's eyes flashed in temper, seemingly directed at Abby. But at her question, he turned to the horse. It stood trembling, its eyes wide with fear or maybe. . . "He's in pain."

Abby shoved the reins into Wade's hand and went to the horse's side, keeping her head low, still mindful of those deadly arrows.

"Let me do that."

"Hang on to him." Abby unfastened the cinch. An odd contraption. But there had been a saddle or two in their village. She knew how one worked.

The horse skittered sideways, and Wade dug in his heels. "What's wrong, boy? What's hurting?"

The quiet murmur of Wade's voice made Abby realize she was skittish, too. Those hooves had barely missed her. A quick look around revealed no one who might have sent an arrow her way. A glance at it protruding from her shoulder revealed markings similar to those of her people. Had someone from the Flathead village tried to kill her? What lies and poison had Wild Eagle's mother spread?

She lifted the saddle away then swept a blanket aside to

find a small, jagged rock and two heavy burrs tucked under the blanket. "Look." Scooping up the painful objects, Abby patted the chestnut's shoulder as she came to stand beside Wade.

Wade stared for two seconds then looked up at her. "There's no way I was riding all morning with those things under my saddle."

Nodding, Abby said, "Someone shoved them in while you were having coffee."

"And no one was around here except the cowhands."

"How many of them did you say had dented pride?"

With narrow eyes, Wade looked in the direction his men had ridden. "Most of 'em."

Abby couldn't quite control her sarcasm. "You've had a full day, then."

"What is that?" Wade's eyes narrowed on her arm. Quickly, his expression grim, he reached for the arrow. "You've been shot." He touched the arrow. Abby heard his sigh of relief as he realized it hadn't embedded in her skin. "When did this happen?"

"While the horse was going wild."

Wade pulled the arrow gently loose from her dress.

Abby glared at the weapon. "If I'd had my doeskin dress, that arrow wouldn't have even torn it. Why do you whites wear these..." What white word described it? "Weak dresses?" She went back to soothing the horse.

"Abby, I'd like to remind you that you're just as white as I am. Whiter actually, considering the blond hair."

Furious to be reminded, she ignored him to tend to the horse.

"Where did the arrow come from?"

Abby tilted her head in the direction the cowhands had gone. "It's got the markings of a Salish arrow, but none of my people sent an arrow my way."

"How do you know?"

"It's not their way to shoot at a woman from cover. That is the coward's way, the white man's way."

Wade stared at the rocky outcropping that the cowhands had

rounded. "It wouldn't be very hard to hide in those rocks. My cowpokes could ride right past a bushwhacker and never see a thing."

Abby looked at him. "Let's go see if the back-shooting coyote has run away."

"You can be sure he has. But he might have left some sign."

Wade fastened the horse's saddle again; the horse now stood calm and steady. Wade stroked the horse's neck, and Abby was struck by his kindness. So different from Wild Eagle.

Thinking of Wild Eagle made her remember something else. "In the madness of the massacre of my village, I remember the men getting off their horses. . .to torch the tepees and club a few of the wounded." Abby glared at the arrow. "Whoever shot that arrow at me just now might have stolen it from my village. He might be the same one who killed my family."

Wade looked as grim as death. "Could be. If that's right, he may still be after you."

"Or you. Or both of us. We both were there when I pulled off that man's mask."

Frowning, Wade reached his hand down for Abby and she swung up in front of him. It was her designated place, after all.

"If you're right and it wasn't one of your people, then who else would know how a Flathead arrow looks?" Wade asked.

"My village is. . .was solitary, and only a small group of us spent summers in that valley. Years ago my Flathead father and Wild Eagle's father defied the rest of the tribe. We would go with our tribe for the winter, but in the summer we returned to our ancestors' hunting grounds. The rest of our people live far to the south all the time, but the land is not so fair as our high mountain meadow. We hunt and fish and live quietly there. We don't run off livestock or steal horses. We have never harmed anyone, but neither do we mix with the whites or trade with them. Knowing how we make our arrows wouldn't be common knowledge."

They reached the outcropping of rock. "There's a very good

chance then that there is only one group of whites who would have access to one of your arrows." Wade swung off the horse then reached up to lift Abby down before she could tell him she'd manage fine on her own.

"The men who killed my people."

"Yes." Wade lowered her to the ground. "And I've made men angry enough that they might want to harm me here on the M Bar S, so somehow my ranch hands might have knowledge of your people. A lot of 'em are new. If they rode the mountain trails, they could have come upon your people. Their anger could explain the burrs under my saddle and even someone taking a shot at me. But why you? Why both of us together? The only thing we've done together is see that man and face your angry mother-in-law."

Abby frowned. "What is that word, 'mother-in-law'? What does it mean?"

"Your husband, Wild Eagle—his mother is your mother-in-law."

Abby nodded slowly. "But Wild Eagle wasn't my husband. We were to be wed at midsummer."

Wade stopped studying the crags above and turned to her. "You told me he was your husband. Was he or wasn't he?"

Abby shrugged then pointed upward. "He would have needed to be about there?"

Wade caught her by the shoulder and turned her to face him.

"What?" She scowled, annoyed at being interrupted from her search for a path up the steep rocks.

"Were you married to Wild Eagle or not?"

Abby tried to sort the vague meaning of his words. "We were... to be married. He had spoken for me and the marriage was coming very soon. As soon as we settled in our summer grounds."

Wade's hand stayed on her shoulder. He looked into her eyes in a way that made Abby allow his touch when she should have shaken him off. "I. . .I'm sorry for your loss. You must have loved him very much."

"Love is. . .it is not a reason among my people to marry. At least not for me. I was treated well by the Flatheads, but I was not one of them and they never let me forget it. It was not a choice for me to marry him. Even less so because of my white heritage. In fact, I am much too old by my village's standards to be marrying for the first time. And I might not have ever been accepted as a wife if Wild Eagle hadn't wanted me after his first wife died. I was given an order. Wild Eagle was to be the future chief of our village. He could have any woman he chose. It was an honor that he chose me."

The concern and kindness in his eyes drew Abby in, made her want to look closer, deeper. Her body swayed, and possibly Wade helped her along because she was closer to him. His grip, with those gentle hands, was firm and compelling.

"Abby." His voice was a whisper, so soft it seemed to come from inside her, from her own thoughts and feelings. "Do you mourn him?"

Against her will, her head shook just a bit, just enough to warm his gaze.

"Did you let him into your heart, or is there room in there for another?"

She opened her mouth to reply, not sure what that answer would be, but his lips touched hers, brushing softly as if a butterfly had passed by.

Drawing in a sudden breath from the enticement of those lips, Abby waited, watched. Then her eyes drifted closed and the butterfly returned and landed.

After seconds passed, Wade lifted his head and studied her. "I'll take that for an answer that there is room. For me."

Her eyes opened and her mind began to work again. . .and her ability to reason. She took two quick steps back and crossed her arms. "That should not have happened."

"You're right."

"You will stay away from. . . I'm right?"

"Yes, you're a guest in my home. It's not proper that such as that kiss passed between us. I will explain things to Gertie when we get home, and she will become more than the housekeeper. She'll become a chaperone. I won't dishonor you, Abby. But my feelings for you..." He looked back at his hat. "I won't ignore them either."

At the sight of Wade's bowed head, something far away and faint trickled into Abby's head. The image of her father. He'd had a way about him of protecting her, sheltering her. A flash of his face, browned from the sun, came to her mind. He was tall and wore a hat as battered as Wade's. Blond hair instead of Wade's darker shade. Then the memory widened and Abby saw her mother, too, her parents together in the kitchen smiling at each other across a table. And one other child sitting in a high chair near her mother.

"Lind. I...I think my name is Abby Lind." Abby straightened as more memories flooded in. "We lived far from here, I believe. I traveled a long way with the Flatheads. It seemed that we traveled for days on end, but I'm not sure. When their hunting party found me, my family was dead." Abby's voice broke.

"And the hunting party came..." Wade urged her to continue, saving her from that most horrible memory of being alone with her father's body. "And..."

"My father, my tribal father, took me to live with his people. Walter Lind, maybe. I think that's right."

Abby looked up. "I could find them, I believe, now that I know my father's name. And maybe I have family somewhere back East. I had an older brother. He was grown up and gone— married I think—when we moved West." Abby closed her eyes as she tried to force the memory. "Why can't I remember? I wasn't that young."

"I suppose your life with the Flathead people was so completely different than what you'd had before, there was nothing to remind you of your early years."

Frustrated, Abby exhaled hard. "Maybe that's it, but it seems wrong, sinful, that I forgot my family."

"You want to search for your brother? Maybe go back East and live with him?"

The tone of Wade's voice told Abby that he was dismayed at that news. It pulled her out of her discouragement at the blank wall where her memories ought to be.

She couldn't quite manage a smile, but her heart lightened. "I have no place in the East. Montana is too settled to suit me. There were great cities back there. I don't remember living in one, but I was told. No, I have no wish to go, but I might want to learn of my white family, let them know I am alive."

"I can help you with that. I'll send some telegraphs the next time I'm in town. If your pa bought land, or homesteaded, there'd be a record of it." Wade settled his hat back on his head firmly. "So your Flathead father took you to his village and raised you as his daughter?"

"He was a good man. But I remember now that my white father was a good man, too. I remember I loved him and my ma and little brother. It's all so vague, though, the memories and the feelings."

"You'll remember more with time, I reckon. For now, let it go. It's just upsetting you. Let's see if we can find any evidence to identify our attacker."

Abby pointed to an outcropping of rock. "He must have been up there."

"How do you figure that?" Wade lifted his hat with one hand and smoothed down his hair with the other.

Abby noticed his hair was past his collar. Belle Harden had taken her scissors to it, but she hadn't cut deeply. Not as long as Wild Eagle's, but neither was he shorn like so many whites.

He'd been living in the mountains all winter. Near enough to her to hear gunshots. Roughing it nearly as much as. . .maybe more than. . .the people in their winter hunting grounds in the Bitterroot Valley.

"The arrow was slanted downward, but not arcing down. He couldn't have been higher or lower than that ledge."

Scowling, Wade turned from where she pointed. "You got all that while you were under my horse's hooves?"

Abby snorted. "How do you whites survive in the West?"

"So were they shooting at you or me? Whoever put those burrs under my saddle couldn't have known where you'd be standing, so maybe he was hoping—"

"Hoping to blame it on the Flathead people?"

"Or hoping in the distraction of the rearing horse he'd get us both at once."

"I have done nothing to deserve murder."

"Oh, well I suppose I have," Wade said sarcastically.

"You've come home. It looks to me as if some among your people might have thought this ranch was free for the claiming with your father hurt and maybe dying."

"It's a fine welcome home, isn't it? I've only been back one day."

"And someone's already trying to kill you."

"No one tries to kill a man with a few burrs under a saddle. I've been thrown off many a horse in my day while breaking broncs. Sure, a man could die, but it's not a reliable way to kill. Most often, you just get up and walk away."

"Your father didn't."

Freezing where he stood, Wade seemed to look beyond what lay in front of him. "True. Someone could finish me off and make it look like a fall killed me."

"But that would only work if there were no witnesses."

"Like you." Wade pulled the burrs and stones from his shirt pocket and glared at them. "Someone tried to kill my pa."

"Not my people. We'd only moved to our summer grounds recently, long after your father was hurt. And now my whole village is dead or gone back to the larger tribal settlement. There are no Flatheads about to try and kill either of us." Abby raised the arrow to eye level.

Wildflower Bride

Throwing the burrs and rock on the ground, Wade stomped them with his boot. "So welcome home. It's good to be back, huh?"

"It's not my home, white man."

"Lucky girl."

CHAPTER 13

Sid missed.

He'd had a chance to end this all at one time and blame it on the savages, but he'd missed. He'd done his share of bow hunting, so he was good, but he hadn't counted on that horse being so close to her when it exploded.

Then that half-wild woman turned the horse so it blocked his next shots.

Furious at wasting the opportunity and putting Wade on guard, Sid jumped down from the rocks where they'd hidden the bow and the arrows they'd made to look like the Flatheads'. Ready for a chance to finish this and lay the blame on the Indians, Sid ran for Paddy, who waited just around the bend with his horse. They were far enough behind the cowhands that no one paid attention when they caught up to them in the mountain valley, lush with thick grass.

"We can't stick together." Sid glared at the incompetent cowhands he'd hired. He hadn't wanted trail-savvy men on the payroll, but now hiring this pack of fools and running off so many of the experienced drovers would likely cost Sid his job. And he needed to be here, on the spot, to take the reins when the old man died. . .which was going to be soon.

Paddy knew cattle, Sid would give him that. "Let's split those two up." Paddy nodded toward a pair of half-grown boys, brothers who looked to be running away from nursery school. The pair didn't know the kicking end of a horse from the biting end.

"They must have come West on the train. They don't have a lick of horse sense." Paddy snickered as he watched one of them fighting his well-trained pony when the pony was smarter than the kid. The sandy brown longhorns that dotted the flowing grassland ripped grass from the ground and chewed while the cowboys tried to get them moving.

"And try 'n' teach 'em something, Pad. Wade isn't man enough to run me off, but there are enough of the old hands left that, if Chester tells 'em to back that young whelp, I won't be able to hold on to this place." Sid grunted when one of the boys nearly fell off his cutting horse. "Maybe if we bring a few of these men along, we can put off that fight. I want Boog and Harv here backing me when that happens."

Paddy nodded and spurred his horse toward the pair.

Sid looked back to see Wade riding through the narrow canyon mouth. Sid scanned the lay of the land, figured where he'd perch to take a shot. He needed to finish this soon with the boy then take out that old he-coon Mort Sawyer. He should have shot him where he lay that night. Instead he'd left him for dead, preferring to make it look like an accident. He could have crushed his head with a rock, though. Or run his horse over the still form until there was nothing left of him.

He'd outsmarted himself that time.

Before Wade could ride up, Sid went and took one of the boys Paddy was working with under his own wing. The fool kid was game, Sid would give him that.

Silas dismounted and crouched by the half-gone hoofprint.

"The cattle passed this way for sure." Red stayed on Buck and rode forward, patting his loyal old horse to encourage him. "They had to, but it looks like a solid wall of rock ahead."

Silas swung back up. "Let's go over that area really closely. These cattle were headed somewhere."

They were surrounded by rugged scrub pines and tightly bunched groves of quaking aspen. Some still small, others much taller. They were just leafing out for the spring, and they grew like an impenetrable wall in front of the rock wall that seemed to have erupted straight out of the heart of the earth.

The ground was pebbles and stone, and if cattle had come this way, the trail had been concealed by a master. The occasional rare bit of a hoof would have been lost if Red was alone, but Silas knew the trail and had an eagle eye. They urged their horses forward as the slippery rocks underfoot gave way to the scratching branches of the scrub pines. "How did anyone get cattle to come through here?"

"Yeah"—Silas eased his sorrel forward—"through here to nowhere." Silas pointed.

"I see it. Another print." Red marveled at the skill of the man. He was good on a trail, but Silas humbled him.

Reaching down, Silas snagged a tiny tuft from one of the sharp branches that tried to claw them to a stop. He held it up. "Fur. A couple of my cattle are red. Herefords. Weirdest thing. We found Herefords in among our herd."

Silas held the fur so it gleamed orange against the brownish red of his sorrel gelding.

"Those probably are descendants of the cattle Cassie's first husband owned." Red studied the fur. "He had some dumb idea about red cattle being the future of the West."

Silas snorted. "Maybe if the land was lush everywhere and water plentiful. There are places those animals could thrive, but not out here."

"It wasn't the only dumb thing the man did."

Wildflower Bride

Silas smiled and continued urging his unhappy sorrel gelding forward.

Red saw Silas's eyes sharpen, and Red followed his gaze.

"A game trail. Right here, going. . ." Silas lifted his eyes.

The rock wall was almost sheer. Red studied it as they drew nearer. Their horses were single file with Silas in the lead, but they moved calmly forward now, no urging necessary. The stone was streaked with shades of brown.

Suddenly, only a horse length ahead of him, Silas vanished.

Gasping, Red leaned forward and saw it. The wall wasn't solid. The game trail veered into a crevice, disguised by the streaks in the stone and the overlapping of one side of the split in the rock. Red found himself in what would have been a tunnel if it wasn't open on top, nearly fifty feet overhead and less than four feet wide. It twisted and turned like a sleeping rattler. Red's throat closed in the tight passageway. There wasn't room to turn around. If this was a dead end, Red would have to back his horse the whole way out.

The scratch of hooves ahead said Silas was still making progress. Buck walked forward without hesitation.

"Silas?"

The response was only a whisper. "Quiet."

Falling silent, Red began to study the ground and saw clearly that many animals had passed this way. A hairpin turn in the canyon brought Red to Silas.

The trail widened for a few feet, and Silas waited silently. "The cattle are in here somewhere sure as you're born. All these cattle prints go in; none come out. The horses, though, go both ways."

"Must be some kind of dead-end canyon in there with enough grass to feed at least a few head of cows."

Silas nodded. "The trail coming up to this gap couldn't be that well covered if it was a big bunch."

"And there could be a back trail out, too."

Silas's eyes narrowed as he considered that. "Then why do the horses come and go this way so often?"

"We'll soon find out." Red could see ahead twenty feet before the gap twisted and went out of sight again. "What are we going to face when we catch up to these rustlers? A band of armed men?"

Silas shook his head. "They've quit covering their trail since we got inside the canyon. Tracks from four different horses. I'm thinking only two of them are in there right now." Silas pointed to a distinct print. "Those two horses walked over top of the rest. And one set is even fresher than the other. I think they've settled in for a few days, letting the cattle heal from rebranding maybe before they drive them off and make a sale somewhere."

Red's eyes met Silas's. "Do we take 'em?"

Silas was dead serious for a few seconds. Then a slow smile crept across his face. "I kinda wish Belle was here. She's a mighty fine help in a fight."

Shuddering to think of Cassie showing up, Red shook his head. "I guess that's a yes, then."

"A definite yes."

"But let's go slow." Red swung down off Buck and led the way to the next twist in the gap.

The trail narrowed and they went single file.

Red saw the first glimpse of sky ahead and knew they'd gotten to some kind of canyon. Then a chill cut through him so hard he jerked his horse backward. The poor horse danced back, and Silas had to step lively to keep from getting trampled.

"What's wrong?" Silas's voice carried, but just barely.

Red kept backing his horse, and Silas had no choice but to do the same. When they reached the wider spot, Buck backed until he was even with Silas's sorrel; then Red pulled him to a halt.

"What happened?"

Red opened his mouth. Nothing came out. Finally, feeling foolish, he said, "I just, well, honest, Si, I felt like God jabbed me in the belly with an icicle. Something told me loud and clear not to go into that canyon."

Silas stared at Red then turned to look at the passageway. At last he nodded. "If someone's on watch, we might walk right into blazing guns. Okay then, what do we do?"

Red almost heaved a sigh of relief that his gut instinct didn't bring him ridicule. He knew, though he'd be hard pressed to explain it, that God Himself had just sent him a message. A life-saving message. Emerging from that gap was walking straight into the teeth of a gun.

Silas was a man of the West, used to the odd ways of a trail. He was also a man of faith. Red had talked to him enough to know that. But not all men of faith did a good job of walking in that faith. Not all believers managed to live up to trusting God with their lives. Apparently, Silas did.

And finally, just as sure as the cold poke in Red's belly came to him, so did something else. "I have an idea."

CHAPTER 14

I have an idea." Belle quit the lassoing lesson. Cassie was getting just plain dependable with her rope. "Let's go throw your knife for a while."

Cassie grinned. "That'll be fun."

Belle almost groaned at the woman's complete lack of killer instinct. "This isn't about fun, Cassie Dawson. How many times do I have to tell you—"

"Yes, ma'am." Folding her hands meekly, she hunched her shoulders a bit. "This is about self-defense."

"*Cassie!*"

Cassie froze then scowled at Belle in such a phony way that Belle had to fight back a laugh.

"Don't you take that tone with me, Belle Harden. I've got all the...the...." Cassie's scowl faded to a frown. "What'd you call it?"

Emma was pulling her own razor-sharp knife from the sheath on her hip as she walked past Cassie heading toward the target drawn on the barn. She whispered, "Killer instinct."

Smiling her gratitude, Cassie said, "Thanks, honey. That's right. Killer instinct. I've got a lot of that."

Belle rolled her eyes, looking to heaven for mercy for this little marshmallow. How had Red kept her alive this long? Of course, Cassie had survived with her first husband, that worthless Lester Griffin, for three years. So she had to have some toughness in her.

Cassie lined up beside Emma and Belle. Emma sent her knife whizzing, and it landed square in the dead center of the big charcoal circle with the black dot in the center for a bull's-eye.

"Ouch." Cassie flinched.

"What?" Emma turned. "Did something hurt?"

"No, I just wish we could call it something besides a bull's-eye. Just thinking of that knife stabbing a poor defenseless bull right in the eye. . . I mean the bull didn't do anything to deserve—"

"I'm next." Belle cut her off, unable to stand this complaint for the fortieth time. Belle's knife hit with a dull *thud*, a fraction of an inch above Emma's. "I aimed a little high so our knives wouldn't scratch. That's hard on the edge."

Emma nodded.

Cassie squared off and drew her knife.

Emma stepped back four long, quick steps.

So did Belle. She felt there came a point when it wasn't cowardly to protect herself, and Cassie's knife throwing was—no pun intended—that point. "Act like you're mad at it, Cass."

Cassie threw with all her might, and it hit the barn. True, the knife hit on its side rather than the tip, but it was progress.

"You've got the range down. Good. Try again."

By the time the afternoon had faded to evening, Cassie had gotten the knife to stick right in the wood nearly ten times. Ten successes out of one thousand throws wasn't great, but. . .

"A journey of a thousand miles begins with a single step." Cassie jerked her chin in a determined nod.

"What's that?" Belle thought it sounded true, though.

"An old saying of my mother's." Cassie pulled her knife out of the barn.

Emma and Belle had split the chores so one of them could stay near Cassie to stem any bleeding she brought on herself. . .

and protect the children. Sarah was doing her best to keep the young'uns in the house and well out of harm's way.

"What's it mean?" Emma asked.

"It means that if I have to throw this knife wrong ten thousand times to learn how to throw it right, then it's a good thing I've gotten past the first one thousand throws today. Because I am going to learn to defend myself better."

"At that rate, considering you're just making up that ten thousand number—but still, it's a good guess—you'll be throwing your knife like a pro in ten days." Belle thought that was wildly optimistic, but she didn't tell Cassie so.

Cassie beamed. "Maybe I'll throw it two thousand times tomorrow just to speed things along."

"You've got to leave time to feed your baby."

"True, suckling a baby does slow a woman down from learning to knife fight."

Belle laughed just as Sarah called them for supper. She rested one arm on Emma's waist and the other on Cassie's. "Let's go eat."

The three happy knife wielders walked into supper together.

"I found out today Sid hadn't started spring roundup." Wade served himself some mashed potatoes.

Abby noticed Wade's casual tone, but his shoulders tensed as if he braced himself for Mort's reaction.

"What?" Mort's fist slammed on the white cloth. The heavy silverware jumped, and Gertie's water glass tipped on its slender stem. She caught it so deftly, Abby wondered how often Mort punched the table.

"We started today." Wade spoke calmly considering his father's face was so bright red. Abby wondered if a head could explode.

"It's a month late! We'll be pushing to get the roundup done in time to cut the herd and get a drive to Helena." Mort shoved against the table and his chair rolled backward. Abby hoped he stayed there, away from the breakables. But Mort rolled himself right back up to the food. "If you'd have been here, this wouldn't be happening." Mort backed his rolling chair away from the table, heading straight for Wade, who sat on his left. Lifting his fist, Mort seemed determined to throw a punch.

Wade stood, positioned his chair between himself and his father, and stopped Mort in his tracks. "You think I'm going to sit there and let you hit me? You really think I'll put up with that from you ever again?" Wade laughed.

It sounded like an honest laugh to Abby. But "ever again" sounded like Wade had known his father's fists before. There was nothing to laugh about here.

"You'd never have the guts to stand up to me if I wasn't in this chair. You're taking advantage of an injured man. You're a weakling! A little, worthless fool." Mort grabbed at Wade's abandoned chair as if he would throw it aside.

Abby flinched and glanced at Gertie. Gertie stared down at her lap, the sorrow on her face telling Abby clearly that this was something that had gone on many times before.

"I know what comes next." Wade held the chair in place with little effort, his strength far exceeding his father's. "You're ashamed to call me your son." He said the words in a singsong way as if they bored him. "I've heard it a thousand times before."

"I am! How did I raise such a coward? If you'd been here—"

"Pa, stop!" Wade's voice was clear but calm.

Abby could hear no anger in it. Only strength underlaid with kindness. But this wasn't a kind of strength she understood. Strength was Wild Eagle's skill with bow and lance. It was riding a horse, racing across the rugged hills. It was battling hand to hand and winning. It was anger and physical domination. Mort's strength seemed more familiar, except being bound to that chair stole any true strength.

"You know why I left this place and you know I only came

back because you were hurt. We've had this out."

"Don't start with your preaching."

"There'll be no preaching. You're not a stupid man. I've spoken to you of my faith and I won't speak of it again unless you ask. It's yours to accept or reject. But know this—if it hadn't been for your accident, and what I believe is my God-given duty to honor my father, I would *never* have come back."

Mort glared.

"I know what you want to say. I can see it in your eyes." Wade stayed on his feet with the chair a barrier Mort couldn't cross. "You want to throw me out. But you can't, not in your condition. Not now especially, now that you know your foreman is incompetent. So you're stuck putting up with me for now. Just as I'm stuck putting up with you. I give you news that makes you furious, and as usual you have no control over yourself. Not something I consider strength, Pa."

The truth of that resonated with Abby. Yes, much of Wild Eagle's strength had instead been simple anger, a tantrum suited more to a small child.

Wade held Mort's eyes, refusing to look away or back down. "All your temper is doing is letting our dinner get cold."

Mort's hands tightened on the chair between the two men.

The moment stretched.

Abby noticed the gravy on her potatoes had quit its lovely steaming, and she resented missing out on the savory food while it was piping hot. She could stand it no longer. "Roll yourself back to your place at the table, old man, or I'm throwing your meal out to the dogs. That's what we do in my village when the two-year-olds act up at mealtime."

Mort's head snapped around.

Wade inhaled so sharply he started to cough. It almost sounded like laughter, but that wasn't possible.

Gertie looked up from her hands, her eyes wide with fear.

Abby took a quick look at the others then glared at Mort.

"What? Am I supposed to pretend that this noise is anything but weakness? Am I supposed to respect a man who would insult and threaten his son, when his son is the only one who can save his ranch? This is some white man's game I don't know how to play, and I refuse to learn. Eat. Both of you. Now."

They obeyed her.

She expected them to, but Gertie seemed stunned. Abby ate her food quietly, ignoring everyone else. The clink of silverware on plates annoyed her as she considered with contempt the ritual involved in a meal. "How many travois does it take to move on if the water goes foul or the herd dies off in a blizzard? You could never take the house. Explain to me why you built this huge structure."

Wade looked up from his plate and smiled at her. A warm smile that reminded her of the moment that had passed between them this afternoon. And another such moment a year ago, when Wade had saved her from treacherous men. He'd done that twice now.

"It keeps the snow off our heads."

Abby rolled her eyes. "The plates, the tables and chairs, such a burden. Eat out of a communal pot. Sit on the dirt floor. Why would you box in such a huge part of the outdoors then be left to clean it and heat it and build useless pieces of furniture to fill it? Why not just leave the outdoors. . .outdoors and let God keep it hot or cold to suit Himself?"

"You told me you believe in God, Abby. That your people believed in Jesus."

"Yes, we were visited by the Blackrobes."

"Blackrobes?"

"Our word for men who came talking of the white man's God. The first such man came years ago, long before I lived with the Flathead. A man named DeSmet spent a long while with our people. We respected him greatly and embraced his teachings. Other Blackrobes have come since, including one last winter. There are many believers in the one God among my people."

"I've heard of DeSmet." Mort spoke, sounding almost polite.

Abby braced herself for his cruelty. It was nearly all she'd heard from him since they'd met.

"He walked into a hostile Sioux gathering of five thousand warriors and demanded to talk to Sitting Bull. He convinced them to sign a peace treaty when they were talking war. I never knew he'd been around here. Imagine the strength of the man—facing down Sitting Bull."

"He walked with God. That was his strength. My people told me so. My Flathead mother knew him well. She was a young girl when he lived among them. There was a greatness to him that led us to embrace his words when we would have driven off another white man. And we have passed that belief in his faith down over the years."

Mort stared at her. "You're saying you believe in this God stuff, too? You, raised as a savage?"

"You were the one who lifted your fist to your son. Neither my Flathead father nor my white father ever did such to me or *anyone* except in self-defense. You are the only savage at this table, old man."

Mort glowered at her.

"Do you now wish to strike me? Is that what makes you feel like a man?"

Mort shook his head. "I'm done with this meal and this company." Mort, his head shaggy with overgrown white hair, turned to Wade. "Move aside, boy, so I can get to bed. Been a long day, my first to be moving so much. I'm tired."

"Do you need help getting settled for the night, Pa?"

At first Abby thought Mort would shout and threaten again. His fists clenched and his face reddened. For a long, taut minute he seemed to fight a battle within himself. Mort said at last, "I might. I'll call you in later if I can't manage."

Astonished, Abby remembered that in her village she'd been taught that the elders of the tribe were to be revered. Her dealings with Mort to this point had been anything but reverent.

Wade, however, had spoken of honoring his father. Ashamed of herself, Abby watched Mort nod, his eyes downcast, as he waited for his son to politely move the same chair they'd used as a wall between them earlier. Mort rolled past that side of the table.

Laying one hand on his father's shoulder, Wade said, "I'll get things straightened out fast with the roundup, Pa."

"Thanks." Nodding, Mort headed for the office they'd converted to a bedroom.

CHAPTER 15

Belle, honey, I might need you to shoot a man."

"Now, Silas? Or can it wait until after lunch?"

"After lunch is probably soon enough. The Jessups are sending three men over. They'll sleep in the barn and watch over Cassie and the children. I need a couple of sharpshooters, though. Can Emma come, too?"

"I want to go. I'm a good shot." Cassie smiled eagerly.

Suppressing a groan, Red went to his newly bloodthirsty wife's side and slid an arm around her waist. "You are a good shot. But someone's gotta stay here with the young'uns."

"We can take the children."

Silas shook his head and scrubbed his face with his gloved hands. "No babies allowed in our posse. That's final. Belle, tell her. I'm going to get something to eat." Silas marched inside.

"You go eat, too, Red," Belle ordered. "We can't leave until the Jessups get here, so there's time."

Cassie turned, her hands fisted and plunked on her hips, as Red, recognizing a will stronger than his own, obeyed Belle. As he went in the house, he heard Cassie say, "Don't you tell me what to do, Belle Tanner."

Wildflower Bride

"It's Harden," Silas yelled from inside the house. "Try and remember her name, Cassie."

The Jessups showed up, three of the six brothers, who batched with their pa on a nearby ranch. They were a rough bunch, with no female influences to soften their manly ways, but decent men and the Dawsons' closest neighbors. They often rode over to share church services when the weather wasn't fit for them to all get to Divide.

Red was pretty sure they were believers, but he didn't kid himself that they were coming for his sermons. They liked looking at his pretty wife and two little children. The men were as fascinated by the young'uns as they were by Cassie. . .well, almost. Close enough Red hadn't had to punch anyone yet.

Despite her nagging, Red, Silas, Belle, and Emma left Cassie behind.

"I can't thank you enough for teaching Cassie to stand up for herself more." Red considered Belle to be an uncommonly intelligent woman. No chance she missed the sarcasm.

Belle worked the lever on her Winchester as her horse galloped smoothly along, the four riders abreast.

They made good time closing the distance to the gap. It had been slow going to keep up with the faint trail before, but now they knew where they were headed.

"You may not like her standing up to you—"

"She's never had much trouble standing up to me anyway. Maybe a little bit at first, but it didn't last."

"But she needs to stand on her own two feet. What if something happened to you? You want her to be trapped like she was last time, when that worthless Lester Griffin died? Forced into a marriage she doesn't want? The next time she might not get as lucky as to have a kindhearted man at the ready to save her."

"What do you want us to do, Pa?" Emma slipped her rifle into the boot on her saddle and settled in to take the long ride to the gap.

"Red's idea. Let him explain." Silas rode with Belle on his left and Emma on his right. Red was beside Belle, probably so she was handy to protect them both, trusting Emma to take care of herself.

Remembering how Belle had taught Cassie to sass him, Red couldn't bring himself to break the news of what Belle's part of this plan entailed.

"You want me to scale that mountain?" Belle stared at the sheer rock. "Emma, too?"

"This is the steepest part." Red pointed to his left. "There's an easy place to climb farther down that way." Relatively easy.

Silas pointed right. "And Emma, you can climb that tree. It'll take you up to that rock shelf." Silas raised his hand, his finger pointing almost straight upward. "From there you can get a clear view of the canyon inside. Be mighty careful when you get up there. Keep your head down. We think there are two men in there, and they're wily. They most likely are watching the gap, but they could see some movement on the rim, too."

"They had to be wily to find that gap." Belle studied the almost invisible fissure in the sheer rock wall.

A low rumble turned them around in their saddles. "And here comes the rest of my plan." Red settled his hat firmly on his head and turned to see cattle of all colors, but mostly brown with dust, tromping up the trail.

Jessups, the three sons who weren't staying to protect Cassie, herded twenty head of cattle up the trail.

"You think they'll find that gap?" Emma reined her horse aside to make way for the oncoming cattle and to help funnel them toward the rocky gap. The girl knew more about horses, cattle, and ranching than Red ever would.

"Get to climbing, girls. We'll hold the herd till you give us a signal." Silas rode with Belle to make sure her horse got tied up tight when Belle started climbing. Red followed Emma, though the Harden horses were so well trained Red suspected they'd both stand untied and riderless for hours.

As Emma stood on her horse's back and reached for the nearest branch on the twisted pine tree growing out of the rock, she said to Red, "How'd you come up with this plan anyway?"

"Well, my first idea was to dynamite the gap."

Emma swung herself up to sit on a branch then looked down at him. "That seems kinda mean hearted."

"I s'pose. But in a way, it's no different than putting those outlaws in jail. If we catch 'em, they'll be hanged or end up in the territorial prison. They'd probably be happier in that canyon."

"I didn't say it was bad, just mean. I like it. If this doesn't work, Ma and I can ride to Divide for the dynamite."

Red sincerely hoped it did work, or chances were he and Silas and the Jessup brothers wouldn't live to tell the tale. Belle and Emma would be all right, though. No one was going to get them up on those rocks. And between the two of them and Cassie, there would be three remaining Jessup men to marry.

The more Red thought about his own sweet Cassie married to one of the Jessups, the more determined he was to win this showdown.

Emma scrambled up the rock wall like a mountain goat and vanished over the rim. Red turned to see Belle swing over the top with her rifle strapped on her back.

Red and Silas rode out to meet the Jessups. All three cut from the same cloth, dark hair windblown and too long for respectability. They all were lean, running to skin and bones, with weathered skin and eyes, wise to the trail.

"Let's get this over and done." Red fell into a semicircle with the Jessups and Silas, urging the cattle forward, hoping that a sudden rush of cattle and gunfire from above would give them the seconds they needed to breach this outlaw fortress.

"We're short a couple of men, Chester." Wade looked up from the list he'd made when he went over the ranch books late in the evening.

Chester slapped leather on a feisty black mustang Wade had always admired. Chester was a steady hand, and with that bright-eyed little cutting horse under him, there was no cow that could best him. "Boog's at the line shack and Harv's in at the doc's. Sid left him because he needed some care and we don't have time for it."

"Harv's the one that came up on the rustlers, right?"

"Yep, caught a man kneeling over a calf, using a running iron. Leastways that's what Sid said. Harv wasn't talkin'. The outlaw knocked him cold. Sid couldn't get anything out of him, a description of the man or the horse."

Wade stared at his notes for a long second. "I went in to the doctor's office to talk to him and he's taken off. So that's another hand we've lost. We've been losing cattle all winter, it sounds like."

"Yep, nothing big, but more than can be explained by wolves and blizzards. And we've got more than two men missing; three of the hands you picked out yesterday as no-accounts were gone when I woke up this morning. Payday was last week. They didn't have cash coming and they didn't want to work, so why wait around?"

Wade got their names and marked them off his list. "That leaves us shorthanded, but those men weren't pulling their weight anyway. We're no worse off. I don't want to take the time to ride to Divide and hire more help. We can get by until the roundup is finished. Who sent Boog out to the line shack?"

"Sid. Bad thinking, too, because Boog's a top hand. Too fast with his gun, but he knows cattle. Did the work of two men. Harv wasn't so good. Knew the job but didn't push any harder'n he had to."

"What was my pa thinking to hire Sid?"

Chester shrugged. "You want my opinion? Your pa wasn't

right in the head when he made that decision. Sid rode in a couple of days after Mort was hurt. He went in the house and came out with the foreman job. I'd have accused him of lying about being hired except he went in that house every day, a couple of times a day, and did a lot of the heavy lifting work for Gertie."

"Pa must have just not cared after he fell. I think he's coming out of the worst of that black mood and starting to show interest in the ranch again." At least a little. Most of it rooted in anger. But Wade didn't think those words would encourage Chester.

"Whatever Sid said, Mort must have agreed to hire him. I accepted that Mort was out of his head. First because he was knocked cold. Then, when he realized his legs wouldn't work, he was half crazy. Sid knows cattle, I'll give him that, but he did a poor excuse of hiring hands and a worse excuse for bossing them. He's as lazy as the rest of this lot."

"One hard week, Chester, we'll have the cattle branded and can start cutting out the stock for a drive. We'll put them in the valley with the lush grass and let 'em fatten up then drive 'em to Helena."

"We'll have to push it to give 'em any time at all on grass before market." Chester swung up on horseback. The mustang danced and crow-hopped a little, but it was just spirit and Chester knew how to stick a saddle. "There'll be no break between roundup and cutting the herd like most years. And even if we push, there won't be as much time to fatten the cattle as we'd like."

"Sittin' here talkin' doesn't add any more days to the year." Wade finished saddling his own horse. "Let's get on with it. We're burning daylight."

CHAPTER 16

It took considerable work to get the first of those stubborn cattle into the gap.

For a few minutes—which seemed like an eternity—Red thought he'd come up with a real poor idea.

The cattle balked inside the gap. They tried to turn.

Red had worked cattle for years, though, and he knew a thing or two. He and the rest of the men kept them crowded against the rock wall but didn't push. Instead they waited, letting the herd sniff around and calm down.

When the herd was settled and quiet and a few had milled close to that narrow gap, Red began threading his way in, quietly, so as not to stir them up. He walked his horse straight into that gap without a moment's pause. He went in just a few feet and stopped and poured a small bag of corn out on the ground.

It took about ten seconds for a steer to come sniffing. He licked up the corn and followed Red straight on in.

Silas and the Jessups would work from the rear.

Red kept moving until he got to the slightly wider section of the gap and then eased to the side to let the cattle come on past him. Because others followed the first, the lead steer was pushed along, though he balked when he passed Red. Red used Buck's big body to crowd the animal forward. Dust churned underfoot as the animals bawled and slashed with their wide horns.

Choking on the dirt, Red forced the recalcitrant longhorn forward until they both pushed past the wider spot. Then Red dodged to the side and dropped back to push the next cow forward. In here they could walk three abreast. A few tried to turn and go back.

Silas pushed up beside Red, and the two of them had a few uneasy moments as the cattle wallowed in dirt they were churning up from the canyon floor until it was nearly blinding. At last they moved forward, and the rest followed, pushed by the herd. They picked up speed and began trotting as Red had hoped they would, straight into the rustlers' canyon.

A single shot rang out when the first steer charged through. Then gunfire exploded from overhead.

Red kicked his horse into the line of cattle, dodging those vicious horns. The gunfire from inside the canyon stopped before Red reached the opening. But the shooting from overhead, from Belle and Emma, rained down like hailstones. Red, Silas right behind him and the Jessups a few jumps after that, charged into the valley.

Red leaned low over Buck's shoulders to make less of a target. Eyeing the terrain, high and low, for likely lookout spots, Red brought his gun level as Buck's hooves thundered. Exploding bits of rock drew his eye to an outcropping about fifty yards straight ahead. The perfect spot to keep watch on that canyon mouth.

Judging by the boulder being battered by gunfire, Belle and Emma had seen the outlaw take a shot when the first longhorn came through. Then they'd pinned the shooter down. He must be crouched at ground level, so he'd never get a clear shot at the womenfolk. And the women made it impossible for the varmint to get a shot at Red and the rest of his posse. Perfect.

The focus of the gunfire was so exact Red knew Belle hadn't seen a threat from any other direction or she'd have aimed at one man while Emma took care of the other. It struck Red as just a bit amazing to have such complete confidence in a woman and her skill with a rifle. Amazing but true, because Red had no doubt Belle wouldn't make the mistake of being careless. But there were two men in here. Red knew it from the tracks. One had yet to show himself. Which meant he still posed a threat.

In the melee of bawling cattle and guns, Red raced his horse for cover, hearing the beating of shod hooves behind him. Swinging down, Red saw Silas alight right beside him. Silas had a look of such satisfaction as he threw himself against the rocks, Red knew the man was button-popping proud of his wife and daughter.

Red, Silas, and all three Jessups had made it into the canyon without a scratch. The women had things so well under control they hadn't even had to duck any gunfire. A quick glance told Red that none of the cattle were even wounded. The bad *hombre* who'd done the shooting had fired a single time, and he'd missed. Or maybe he'd pulled his aim when he recognized a longhorn was coming through. But that one shot had alerted Belle, and that had been the end of the shootout.

"Spread out," Silas yelled. "We can get the drop on him, if Belle hasn't filled him with lead."

The five men fanned out, slipping along the scattered rocks of the canyon entrance. There was plenty of cover in the rugged mountain canyon once they'd cleared the opening. They drew steadily nearer the rustlers' hideout boulder, each taking turns providing cover, although Belle and Emma had pinned them down so well there was no sign of a man.

At last Red found a place on the canyon wall slanted enough he could climb and get a good look at the hiding place. A lone man lay flat on his back. Red leveled his Winchester and shouted at the bloodthirsty women. "I've got a bead on him."

The thunder of bullets ended.

Red looked down on a pathetic excuse for a desperado. Bleeding, scratched to bits by chunks of flying rock. "There's only one man back here. Be careful. There's another here somewhere."

The man raised his hands. "I'm alone. No one with me. Don't shoot."

"Stay up there and keep us covered," Red hollered at his two faithful sharpshooters.

While Red kept his eye on the outlaw, the rest of them scoured the canyon, lush with grass, holding nearly a hundred head of cattle, all with fresh brands.

There was no one.

While the Jessups continued to search, Silas quickly trussed up the outlaw.

"Where's the other one?" Red asked.

"I'm alone." The man had an ugly cut on his chin, sewed up but still raw and red. He was clean shaven, except for close around his wound, and his hair looked like he'd cut it himself with a bowie knife and no mirror.

"I'm not talking to you." Red raised his rifle in what he hoped was a menacing fashion. Truth was he'd never so much as aimed a gun at a man. The thought of pulling the trigger made him sick.

Thank You, God. We ended this without any killing.

"We saw tracks from two men, so we know there's someone else."

"No!" The man's clothes were battered and slashed as if he'd gone a few rounds with a grizzly. "The tracks were just me riding two different horses."

Red didn't think so, and he wasn't about to take the word of cattle-stealing scum. "Silas, are you sure the canyon's empty?"

Nodding, Silas rose from beside the man he'd just hog-tied. "I was careful. But remember how that gap opened so you could barely see it? There could be a back way out of here just as hidden.

I found his camp. Two men have been here, but one's gone."

"Are Belle and Emma in danger? Could the other one have gone out over the rim?"

Both men wheeled to stare up at the women. The rocks the women stood on were so sheer from this side of the canyon that no one could have gotten within a hundred yards of them.

Emma waved down when they looked at her, but the girl was uncommonly smart. She kept low to the ground, never relaxing her guard.

"I've got me a family of women, don't I?" Silas blew a soft whistle through his teeth.

"They're the kind of women who can help tame a wild land and make no mistake about it." Red turned back to the outlaw and prodded the vermin with his toe none too gently. "They work their hearts out. They put in long hours in the blazing sun. They work in the bitter cold. They miss meals and get knocked around by longhorns and feisty mustangs. Then you come along and steal from the labor of their backs. You're going to hang, or if you're lucky, spend a lot of years in prison. Let's get you to the sheriff. Maybe if you help us catch your friend, and any others of your gang, the sentence won't be quite so long. The judge who comes through Divide likes a cooperative prisoner."

The Jessups rode up. Huey Jessup, the oldest of the brothers, seemed to be the spokesman for the taciturn family. "I think we found where a man went out on foot over the west rim. It'd be a scramble, but a man could make it and stay low enough not to draw attention. He couldn't pack things with him, though. He left on foot and his bedroll is still here. I found two horses and leather for both of 'em. We might find a name."

"Let's gather everything up," Silas said. "I'll start heading the whole herd out of here. It'll be slow going, but we need to drive them into Divide then put out the word that we've recovered stolen cows. The area ranchers can come in and identify them best they can through those altered brands."

Wildflower Bride

"We'll let the law sort it out." Red untied the outlaw's feet and nudged the man to stand. "What's your name?"

Glaring through mean, animal black eyes, the man refused to answer.

Red didn't wait around to try to get it out of him. That job he'd leave for the sheriff.

CHAPTER 17

I want this step fixed!" Pa's fist hammered against the door frame. "I want to get out of this house."

Wade had only moments ago strode into the kitchen out of the dark, up the three steps that formed a back stoop. He had a ladle full of Gertie's delicious chicken noodle stew ready to dump on a plate full of biscuits.

Wade lowered his plate and the ladle. He was starving, exhausted, frustrated, filthy, saddle-sore, and grouchy. Not a good time to have to handle his father. "How do we fix the step, Pa? Got any ideas?"

There, dump it back in Pa's lap. Wade figured the old man would rant and rave steadily for about ten minutes while Wade ate. No trouble tuning out the sound of Pa's yelling. Wade had become a master over the years. He returned to dishing up his dinner, his stomach growling nearly as loudly as his father.

"Someone with any brains would know that."

Abby came in with Gertie right behind her.

"Sit down and let me get that for you, Wade." Gertie immediately began flapping at him, shooing him aside.

Grinning, Wade escaped with his full plate and sat at the small kitchen table. It was a relief to not have to sit in the formal dining room and eat off china. Instead he had a tin plate and quick access to seconds. "Sit down with me, ladies. It's been a brutal day and I could stand the sound of a woman's voice or two."

"We're going to fix this door or I'm ripping the whole back of the house down with my bare hands." Pa grabbed at the door frame as if intending to begin right now.

Sighing, Wade said, "You ladies are gonna have to talk loud to drown out Pa."

Gertie gave Pa a wide-eyed look. Had he taken his nasty temper out on the housekeeper? In earlier days, after Wade's ma had died, Gertie had protected Wade to the extent she was able, and Wade had never seen Pa use his fists on her. But Pa's temper was out of control at times. Why else would Gertie be so scared?

Wade felt heat climbing his neck—temper. If Pa had hit Gertie...

"And if I can't get my own son to help me, then I'll find someone who—"

Abby laughed and jabbed a finger at Wade's plate. "You eat your food. Keep your mouth busy so we women can talk."

Pulling his thoughts from violence, Wade looked from his raging father to Gertie to Abby. "I think I'll say a prayer before I eat. Would any of you like to join me?" Prayer was what he needed very badly right now.

Pa continued shouting. Gertie stared at her entwined hands, more fearful than prayerful. Abby bowed her head.

Wade prayed quietly, ignoring his furious father, who was too wound up to even notice they weren't listening to him.

"God, thank You that the roundup is going well. Bless the hired cowhands I have. Let those who want to learn find skills here on the M Bar S that they can use all their lives. Keep us safe, help Pa get better, bless this fine food Gertie and Abby made, and let me use the strength I gain from this meal to be a good servant to You, Lord. In Jesus' name I pray. Amen."

"I've got enough money to buy and sell all of you ten times over. If you don't get this door fixed—"

"We already took a mountain of cake over to the bunkhouse. You kept the men out for such a long time." Abby braced her elbows on the table and plopped her chin on her fists. No manners at all. Wade had never seen anything so beautiful in his life. And she lived here at his house, with him.

"I'm trying to get three weeks' work done in one, and short-handed, too. But the worst of the hands quit right off, and the ones who stayed are working their hearts out trying not to lose their jobs at the end of the week. Some of them are pretty unskilled, but they're game, and they're making up with effort what they're lacking in experience."

"Stop talking and eat." Abby pointed at Wade's plate.

He couldn't help but smile at her bossy ways.

She smiled back. "I've thought that maybe we could build a ramp of dirt to the back door. Your father could be free to come and go as he pleased."

Pa quit trying to yell and jerked around to face Abby. "Really? That's a good idea."

"I may let you roll out of here then knock down the ramp so you can't get back, old man." Abby smirked at him.

Wade was appalled—and thrilled—at her disrespect. He had never dared talk to his father this way. Of course, his father had been quick with punishment, but that was when Wade was a child and had no ability to defend himself or escape.

The fear Wade battled every day, with the help of his Savior, faded, replaced with confidence that if Abby could face down his father, so could he.

"Instead of a dirt ramp, how about I have a wooden ramp built. Less work than piling up dirt. It'll be smooth and that wheelchair will roll right down it." Wade cut one of his fluffy biscuits and scooped it up with a spoonful of the savory stew.

"Quiet, eat." Abby flicked her fingers at him. "Good idea,

though. I have some practice with building. I could cut down saplings, lash them together. It wouldn't be hard." Abby turned to glare at Pa. "You could even make yourself useful and help."

Pa lifted his chin, his eyes shooting bullets.

Abby's eyes narrowed and didn't waver.

Wade watched the byplay between the two, memorizing Abby's courage and his father's impotence.

"I think we could build a special wagon without much trouble, too." Abby stared at the wheelchair. "If we tore the seat out of the buckboard and could somehow roll your chair into place, you could probably handle the reins. You could make yourself useful."

Pa slammed his fist on the arm of his chair and made a noise similar to a hissing rattler.

Wade swallowed quickly to interrupt the attack. "I asked Libby in town to send Sam out here when he's home. I thought we could widen some doorways so Pa could get to all parts of the house. Sam's a good builder. He could help with the ramp and any other ideas you've got. Pa, if you could work the buckboard, maybe you could run to Divide to pick up supplies. If we sent a list, the storekeeper would fill the order and load the wagon. You wouldn't have to get down. Your arms are still strong enough to drive. You could get out of here, see your friends."

Wade paused for a moment to consider if there was a man alive who would count Mort Sawyer as a friend. A neighbor, even a friendly acquaintance, maybe, but a friend? No one with any sense would count Pa as a friend. He had always been too ruthless to trust.

"I'm not going to town in the buckboard." Pa battled the wheelchair to roll it to the table then slugged the arms of it hard. "People would see me and pity me."

Remembering Abby's calm disrespect, Wade scraped his plate clean, chewed, and swallowed. "They probably pity you already, Pa. And you break that wheelchair, I'm not buying you another one, so calm down."

Gertie gasped.

Pa's face turned an odd shade of purple.

"Maybe if you got out, proved you can still do some work, they'd pity you less." Wade waited to see what form his pa's explosion would take.

"Probably not." Abby studied Pa as if he were an interesting species of bug. "I think they're going to pity him no matter what. But if a man were strong, strong in his guts, in his heart, he could ignore misplaced pity. Only a weakling would prefer to be useless."

Gertie slid from the table, and for a second Wade wondered if she was going to leave or maybe fly to Pa's defense. Instead she took Wade's plate and refilled it.

Good thing—he was still starving and this conversation had given him an appetite. "What do you say, Pa? Interested in any of this? The ramp? I don't know how well that chair rolls."

"The ground is hard packed. Not too many ruts, except right after a rain. He might be able to get to the barn and even do some work out there." Abby looked doubtfully at Pa. "It'd probably take a lot of strength to get out to the barn, but it might work. It'd probably be good for your arms."

"There are some rough places in the yard, but the men could spend some time smoothing them starting tomorrow. And if we built the ramp right, we could make one part slope down and a second part at the right level to roll right into the buckboard. We could have you free to ride the range in no time."

A sudden look on Pa's face had Wade regretting, just for a split second, that he'd been unkind. The hunger on his pa's face, when Wade said the word *free*, reminded Wade of the best things about his father. His willingness to work long, hard hours. His skill as a horseman and cattleman, never asking hired men to do a job he wasn't willing to do.

Pa had a brutal streak, and no amount of hard work made up for that, but Wade couldn't take away from his pa the incredible strength of will it had taken to move into this country and take and hold this land.

Wade would have called it strength of character except Pa's character was so badly, miserably flawed by cruelty. Watching now, knowing how badly Pa wanted to control his own property, Wade asked quietly, "What was it that made you think turning your fists on me was a decent thing to do?"

Pa's expression of hope and hunger faded, replaced by sullen anger. "I raised you the way my pa raised me."

Abby laughed scornfully. "And look how well you turned out. Is that your point? A broken, lonely old man in a wheelchair? With one child, a son who had left you and only now returned home, not out of love but out of duty? You call your life a success?"

All good questions, but Wade wanted to ask something else. "You mean my grandpa Sawyer hit you when you were growing up?"

"Some. When I had it coming." Pa's defiant eyes slid away from Wade's. "My. . .my ma was tough, though. She put a stop to it. Most times. But I got the message that I had to be strong. Same as I tried to teach you. But you came out weak. Weak like your ma."

"Weak because of what? She died? She couldn't turn aside your anger? She wasn't mean enough to pull a gun on you to drive you back?" Wade remembered his mother. She'd been a gentle soul, trapped like Wade. "What do you mean by weak, Pa?"

Pa scowled, and Wade saw the lines cut into his father's face by years and years of steady hate. "She was always at her Bible. Always praying. She tried to ruin you with that stuff, too. A man has to depend on himself. God respects a man who makes the most of what he's been given. God gave me strength and a sharp brain and He expects me to use it."

"You used your strength to tame this ranch land, Pa. But you also used it against me. Why?"

"I wanted you to stand up for yourself. I wanted you to grow up as strong as me. To be worthy of this ranch I built for you."

"You sit there now, in that chair, a broken man, and claim

to have had a reason for how you acted, but I don't think you really thought it through, Pa. I think you have a mean streak and you took it out on someone smaller. That isn't what I think of as strong, Pa. It sounds weak to me." Wade stared at his pa for a long time, and for the first time in his life, he saw a man to be pitied. A boy who'd been battered. A weakling who was maybe, in his own way, just as fearful as Wade.

" 'Whom shall I fear,' Pa?"

"What's that?"

"It's a Bible verse I say to myself all the time. Psalm Twenty-seven. 'The Lord is my light and my salvation; whom shall I fear?' I've spent my whole life fearing you, Pa. But no more." Wade slashed his hand downward. "Because with God, I don't have to fear anyone." Wade turned his attention to his supper.

"I—I'm sorry, son."

Wade looked up from his meal at the words he'd never heard before. He had no idea how to react to an apology from his father. He'd never gotten one before.

"It was never my intention to make you afraid."

Somehow Wade found it easy to respond to that. An excuse. The old man wasn't really taking responsibility at all. "As if the way you acted wasn't meant to frighten me? As if the fact that it did is somehow my fault?"

"No, that's not how I meant it."

"That's what you said. And you know, I think it was your intention. I just can't figure out what pleasure you got from terrorizing a child." Wade went back to eating.

"No pleasure." Pa stared at his hands, folded in his lap, subdued. Not himself at all. "But power, I guess. Some kind of satisfaction. I thought I needed to run the whole world, control every bit of it. Dominate every acre and tree and cow and rock. And that stretched to people, too. Including you. Just know that I'm sorry. I know I done wrong by you. I'll probably do wrong again, but maybe now I can at least admit it when I do."

Wade stared at his plate of cooling supper. When he spoke, it was quietly. "I appreciate the words. It isn't enough, it doesn't make up for much, but thanks for at least saying it."

After a long stretch of silence, Pa rolled to the kitchen door and opened it. "We could do it. We could fix up a ramp and adjust the buckboard. I could oversee this place again."

"Good—the sooner you take back control of this ranch, the sooner I can leave." Wade chewed thoughtfully on his biscuit.

Gertie gasped and rose from the table to begin cleaning the kitchen.

A cow lowed softly in the distance. Crickets chirped, and a night owl whooed. A cool breeze reminded Wade that summer came late up here and left early.

"I'm for it. Mort and I will start work on it tomorrow morning." Abby took her knife out of its sheath. "It will get him out of this house, and good riddance." She rose and picked up a whetstone lying on the kitchen counter, and soon the soothing rasp of metal on stone filled the silence.

The first thing Red saw when he came riding up was Cassie, running out of the house to meet him, a smile on her face and her long dark hair flying.

Red had pushed all night to get this rustled herd home, just so he could see his pretty wife. Silas and his women were agreeable, and the Jessups were too quiet to voice an opinion.

The Jessups who'd come to see to Red's place stepped one by one out of the rocks here and there, lowering their rifles as soon as they recognized Red, Silas, Belle, Emma, and the three other Jessup brothers.

It gave Red a deep pull of satisfaction to know his family had been so carefully guarded. Good men, the Jessups.

Red spurred his horse ahead so he could keep Cassie from

getting run down by the herd, but the cattle were tired after a long trek and they probably would have just walked around Red's careless little wife. When he pulled his horse beside her, he bent down and lifted her off her feet to settle her on the saddle in front of him.

"Hi." He looked at a smile warm enough to melt the Rockies in January; then Cassie flung her arms around his neck and gave him the hello kiss he'd been dreaming about. The herd headed straight for the pond south of his house while Red greeted his wife enthusiastically.

Then Cassie noticed the prisoner. "Is that man draped over the horse one of the rustlers?"

"Yep. There were two, but one got away."

"Does it hurt him to have his head hang down like that?"

Red sure hoped so. He wasn't about to forget the man had a rifle trained on that gap. "He's fine. We'll take him on into Divide after breakfast. You think we've got enough food to fill this crew up?"

"I'll start scrambling eggs and frying potatoes right now. We've got plenty." She kissed him again and said with a pert tilt of her nose, "Now take me over to the house and quit distracting me. I've got work to do."

Red loved it when she sassed him; he'd made sure she knew it, too. He rewarded that pert little mouth with another kiss.

Belle's daughter Sarah had breakfast going before Red could walk Cassie back to the house. She dished out enough eggs and ham to fill up the whole crew of them, and it was a considerable crowd. The little redheaded girl did it all with one baby on her back, another on her hip, and one clinging to her ankle.

"We're not riding into Divide with you, Red," Belle said as she drained her second cup of coffee. "We've been away from home too long as it is."

"With another rustler still on the loose, I don't like leaving my place for so long." Silas looked at Belle. "We ought to start standing a watch on both gaps into our place. We've never hired any cowhands, but maybe it's time we did."

Belle frowned. "I don't like strangers around the place. Especially men when we've got young girls."

Emma looked up from where she was wolfing her food. "Ain't no man around I can't handle, Ma." Red saw the narrow eyes and quiet determination in Emma and suspected the girl had it exactly right.

"Let's wait a few days on it, Silas. See what Red finds out about the rustler he caught. Maybe he can get the man to talk and we can put an end to the trouble without adding hired hands at the ranch."

Silas nodded. "Gonna go cut our cattle out of that herd." He rose from the table, the legs of his wooden chair scraping against the floor. "You womenfolk gonna help or sit in here having tea and cookies while I work?"

Red watched a brave, brave man leave his house, Belle and Emma right on his heels.

Silas and his family were soon heading down the trail, pushing their cattle toward home.

The Jessups found a few of their own herd, and Red cut out the ones that belonged to him. It was a smart operation, taking a few cattle at a time. Red wondered if the rustling hadn't been going on for years.

Three of the Jessups drove their recovered animals home. Red was left with around fifty head to drive into Divide.

They were ready to set out by midmorning. Cassie rode well enough now to actually help with the drive, but she had Michael strapped on her back and Red had Susannah on his lap, so the Jessups got to do more than their share of the work.

The normally three-hour ride took the rest of the day, and as they confined the cattle in a holding pen, the Jessups hit the trail in three directions to area ranches with the news that cattle had been recovered. A man was in town from the Linscott place and rode out for his boss.

Before Red escorted his prisoner to jail, he turned to Cassie. "Cass, honey, go get us a room at Grant's, okay? We'll have to stay the night in town and wait for the ranchers to ride in and sort out their cattle."

"Yes, Red." The polite obedience was like sweet balm to his soul. There once was a time the little woman would hardly say anything other than "Yes, Red." Ah, he loved remembering those days. Cassie scooped Susannah off his lap; then, loaded down with children, she skillfully turned her horse toward the hotel. Watching her reminded Red how far his wife had come since they'd married. His overly submissive, fumble-fingered little wife had turned into about the best rancher's wife in the whole world.

He noticed the knife sheath at her waist and felt a little chill of terror.

Later, Red got his family settled in Grant's Hotel and gave them each a good-night kiss, going down the row, sweeping Susannah up to eye level and listening to her giggle. Red next gave Michael a noisy smack on his drooly chin then ended with a longer kiss for his pretty wife.

"I'm going to stay with the sheriff, at least for a while. He'll need to keep watch all night, and we can spell each other."

Enviously, he watched Cassie tuck the children into bed then join them. If he stayed, he could climb in, too, and be surrounded by comfort and warmth and love.

Instead, feeling a mite sorry for himself, he went to jail.

CHAPTER 18

"Harv's in jail." Boog slipped into the small cabin Sid was allowed as foreman. Chester had yet to kick him out.

Sid looked up from his whittling. "What? How?"

Judging by the way Boog moved, Sid knew his arm was still hurting him, but no one else would have noticed. Boog wasn't a man who showed weakness.

"Someone must have tracked us." Boog positioned himself so he wasn't visible through the single small window in the shack. "I didn't stay around to learn their names. They posted marksmen on top of the canyon wall and pinned Harv down. I could see I'd never be able to pick them off from the angle I had, so I told Harv to keep his mouth shut and we'd bust him out of jail as soon as we could. Then I climbed out on foot over the west wall."

Sid felt his throat tighten at the memory of that treacherous trail. He and Boog had scouted it, knowing a way out might be necessary. But that trail was a terror. And Boog had managed it with only one good arm. He'd had to go out on foot; no horse could make the passage. Then he'd made it all this way. Sid raised his already sky-high respect for his saddle partner's toughness.

"I walked ten miles before I found a horse. I rode hard then set it loose and swatted it toward home. I hope it just goes on back and no one asks too many questions."

"So the cattle are gone, too?" The very careful cattle thieving they'd done was a prison offense, but a man could get hanged for stealing a horse. Sid steered clear of hanging offenses until he had no choice. That was one of the reasons Sid hadn't killed Mort Sawyer that night. A decision he'd regretted ever since.

"I didn't stay around to watch, but we gotta figure they took the herd." Boog wasn't so squeamish about killing, but then, he'd ridden a hard trail for a long time and was a known outlaw in parts of the West. Boog figured he could only hang once and he'd done his worst, so nothing he did now made any difference. His only goal was to stay out of the hands of the law.

Sid's pockets were empty of cash money. He'd enjoyed himself a bit too much after their last sale, with whiskey and women and poker. He'd been counting on those cattle. "Okay, give me a minute." Sid set his knife and the sharpened stick aside. "Mort's son and that wild woman are here to stay. The only way we're gonna take possession of this ranch is by getting rid of Mort and his son. Getting to that old curly wolf, Mort, took some planning, but Wade's a weakling. I can swat him like a fly."

"Don't count Mort out. He ain't dead yet, and even busted up, he's dangerous. Worse now that he's got his son to back him." Boog eased toward the window and took a long, careful look out through a crack in the shutter.

"He'll be dead soon enough. No one lives long with a broken back. As for Wade, I just need some time to set it up, make it look like an accident or blame it on someone else." Sid didn't admit that he'd tried once already and he'd missed. He didn't want to hear what Boog had to say about that. "Are they taking Harv into Divide?"

"Yep. I reckon."

"Someone there will recognize him as being a hand here. We need to get him out of there fast."

"He don't look like himself without the beard."

Sid met Boog's eyes. The two men knew each other well. Their thoughts traveled the same lines. Harv knew too much.

"Easier just to put a bullet in him," Boog said as if he was discussing the weather.

"We'd lose the gold."

"Yep, 'less'n we find it ourselves."

"Harv said it's where no one would ever find it. He stumbled on it by accident." Sid pondered. "We'll make one try for him. If we run into trouble, we won't leave him alive to talk. We need to go as soon as it's dark and bust Harv out. I told Wade you were at the line shack, the old Griffin place, so he hasn't asked any questions, but if I'm not here for work in the morning, he'll notice sure enough."

"I wouldn't mind a few minutes with the Sawyer kid. I owe him for this bullet." Boog's eyes burned with hate. He rubbed his shoulder hard as if to stir up his pain and feed his desire to get revenge for being wounded.

"You'll get your chance to pay him back."

A quiet shake of the head was Boog's only answer. "Go wake up Paddy."

"Leave him. If I go into the bunkhouse, the hands will remember we left the place."

Nodding, Boog said, "Let me get down the trail a ways and into the woods. Then you catch up." Boog left the cabin as silently as he'd come.

Sid moved furtively to the corral, saddled up, and made tracks for Divide, doing his best to keep the barn between himself and the bunkhouse until he was out of sight. If they were careful, no one would even know Sid had been gone tonight. As he rode, Sid considered that it might be time to just cut his losses and move on. Instead of riding toward Divide, he could head for Helena, hop on the train, and make tracks for Denver. Boog would probably go, but it might be best to travel alone. Sid would have done it if he had enough money to pay for the train ride. Instead he'd have to go on horseback, live off the land, find some way to make money as soon as he got to Denver, because no one lived without money in the city.

The M Bar S was going to be hard to claim now. The gold was lost if they didn't pull Harv out of that jail. Sid was probably going to lose his job by the end of the week anyway, unless he broke his back working for Wade. And working that hard for a young whelp grated until Sid wanted to start unloading his gun at someone.

This had seemed like a way to strike it rich when he'd ridden in. One old man working a huge, successful ranch. Easy pickin's. But there wasn't much easy about it now. He should just ride out, leave Boog, Paddy. . .Harv, too. Start over in California. Easy pickin's out there, he'd heard.

But he thought of Wade coming in here and taking what Sid thought of as his, and it made him mad clean through. No, he'd stay, and he'd get Harv out, too. He wanted the ranch, the gold. . . and at that instant greed took him by the throat, and he decided that he even wanted that pretty wild girl. He'd break her spirit, crush her for causing all this trouble, bringing Wade home, being in the way when they'd attacked that village. She was the only survivor, and if she hadn't been there, no one would know what had happened. The massacre, if it was ever discovered, would have been blamed on one tribe attacking another. Yes, he owed that spitfire of a girl, and he'd make sure she paid.

As he savored his hate, he felt fire for a second, fire in his soul. Painful fire telling him, not for the first time, his life fit him only to spend eternity in a burning lake.

Even knowing that, he heard a whisper from his black heart that it was his *right* to take by strength. This was the West. Strength won in the West. And he was strong. The feeling of fire in his soul had been with him for years. He remembered long ago; the first few times he'd felt it had scared him, made him doubt the path he'd chosen.

Not anymore. As he spurred his horse toward Divide, he basked in the warmth.

"Why don't you get some sleep, Red. No sense both of us being up all night." Sheriff Dean had his feet up on his desk and was rocked all the way back in his heavy wooden chair. His hands were folded over his stomach, and Red suspected that with about ten minutes of silence, the sheriff would be fast asleep. He wasn't used to much trouble here in Divide. It was a quiet little town for the most part.

Red was tempted. Of course, he'd have to lie down on the hard floor. "It's been a long day, Sheriff. I think we both need to stay alert. I'll keep you awake and you do me the same favor."

"Fine, let me get a stack of wanted posters, then."

"I thought you went through them already."

With a dry laugh, the sheriff pointed to a stack of posters knee high against one wall. There was an ankle-deep stack right beside the bigger one. "I set the ones to the side I've looked at."

"Tell me it's the short pile we have to study."

"Nope, 'course not. I've looked at the ones on the left."

Red sighed and thought of Cassie, asleep and warm and sweet. And his beautiful children. "Catching outlaws is almost more trouble than it's worth, Sheriff."

"Tell me about it. I thumbed through 'em until my eyes crossed and all the men started looking alike."

"Fine." Red got up and picked up all the posters he could get in his hands. He took them to the desk.

The sheriff sat up straight, the hinges of his chair shrieking like he was killing them. "Give me half and pull your chair up to the desk."

Red dragged his chair over, and as he got it in place, he felt a little rush of cold chill. Not from a gust of wind so much as from nerves.

"You ever had a jailbreak from this place, Sheriff?"

Shaking his head, Sheriff Dean said, "Nope. I've mostly just arrested cowpokes that drank too deep in their monthly pay. Let 'em sleep it off and sent them on their way with a scolding. Usually half-grown boys get into nonsense like that."

"You checked that the back door is locked, right? That man we arrested has a partner out there."

"Like as not his partner ran for the hills. It's a cowardly bunch that rides the outlaw trail."

"They struck me as a savvy bunch. I'll ride you out to that canyon sometime. Hard to believe a man ever found it."

"If they were real savvy, they'd be honest. Being a rustler is just plain stupid."

"Well, I'm not saying they're wise, but they just might be smart. I think we need to stay on edge all night. I'll feel better when we've had a chance to question the prisoner a little better."

"Well, he's asleep for the night. He's cut up and so exhausted from being hauled over a horse for two days that he ain't makin' no sense." Nodding, the sheriff said, "In the meantime, let's see if one of these posters looks enough like him to give us a name."

Red's neck still felt cold, like God in heaven was sending a warning. He bent over the posters but kept his ears wide open.

Sid rode side by side with Boog, and the moon was high in the sky by the time they reached the sleeping town. A light shone in the window of the sheriff's office. Sid nodded toward it. "Sheriff Dean must be keeping watch."

Boog muttered in the cool spring night, "Looks to be the only light in town."

"Let's circle around. Come in through the back. You still got that key that works on most doors, Boog?"

"I got it."

"Then let's go in quiet, get the jump on the sheriff, then knock him cold and leave him in a cell. No shooting if we can help it.

We'll be in and out before he knows we're there."

Pulling their kerchiefs over their faces, the two men circled like patient vultures. There was no sign of life anywhere in town. It was long after midnight and even the Golden Butte had closed up.

Sid saw a dim light showing under the back door of the jail. Sid had made a point to know the layout of every building in Divide he could gain access to, always planning for a robbery or escape. He silently swung down off his roan and hitched him beside Boog's gray mustang and the horse for Harv.

They moved toward the door. Boog quietly produced the key he'd filed down until it would open all but the most expensive locks. The jail hadn't bothered with expensive.

The lock gave with a single scratch of metal on metal. The door opened with an almost inaudible creak. Boog slipped in. Sid knew his saddle partner well and let Boog lead the way. The man knew more about sneakin' and thievin' than anyone Sid had ever known.

It was what Sid liked best about him.

"What's that?" The voice coming from the front of the jail froze them in their tracks.

A second later, trying to be silent, they slipped out the back, and Boog swung the door shut. He turned the lock with aching slowness, and then they hurried into the shadows, pulling their horses along. An outcropping of rocks that edged the town about a hundred feet to the south was the nearest cover. Sid led his horse with Boog right behind him and they waited.

Looking carefully around the rocks, Sid saw the back door open.

Red Dawson poked his head out. The town parson.

Sid had seen the man once, right after he'd struck Mort down and taken the job. Hard to forget the preacher with his flaming red hair. Sid had heard of the Dawson ranch, too. A well-run operation, and he knew of Cassie Griffin Dawson because the Sawyers used that fancy, neglected Griffin house as a line shack. The older cowpokes on the Sawyer place liked swapping stories about what a worthless, no-account Lester Griffin had been and how beautiful and spoiled his wife was. The stories were laced with envy that Red had gotten her and apparently taken a firm hand, because now she was the hardworking-est woman any of them had ever seen.

Boog nudged Sid then spoke in an almost silent whisper. "He's who came into the canyon and took Harv. I could look back once I got myself clear. They had two men scale the cliffs outside the canyon and pin Harv down. Sharpshooters, the best riflemen I've ever seen. Probably fought in the War Between the States."

Sid had fought in that, too. Then he'd stayed on and fought after Lee had surrendered because he'd gotten a taste for shooting men, and it suited Sid to take what he wanted. Let weaklings work for their bread.

"I wasn't on watch, or they'd have had us both. I yelled to Harv to lay low and if they caught him I'd bust him out of jail; then I ran. I saw that red hair for sure."

"Name's Red Dawson," Sid said. "He's a rancher, but he's the town parson, too."

Boog grunted in disgust. "He must be staying the night with Sheriff Dean."

"You sure it was him in the canyon? Preachers don't run with riflemen."

"This one does. Maybe he converts people by threatening to send them to Hades. It was him for sure. How could it be anyone else? You think there's any chance someone else would offer to stay with Harv, someone with bright red hair?"

Dawson, the sheriff just behind him, stared into the darkness. It was too far to see Red's eyes, but his whole body spoke of alertness. He wasn't going to let Harv go without a fight.

"Let's ease back and wait 'em out." Sid thought of the long, brutally hard day of work he'd had and another one coming tomorrow. He needed that gold. He was sick of breaking a sweat to earn a living. But to just go charging in there with guns blazing would bring the whole town down on them. "They'll be easier to take when they're asleep."

Sid and Boog faded a bit farther under the trees and settled in.

"I'll take first watch. Get some sleep. You can spell me later." Boog sat and leaned his back against a tree so he could keep an eye on the back door.

Sid dozed until Boog jarred his arm. "It's gettin' on toward daybreak. We've gotta move on the jail now or forget it."

"Let's go." Both men pulled their handkerchiefs up and eased forward in a silence so thick the hoot owls didn't even breach it.

Boog led the way back to the rear entrance of the jail. Again he unlocked the door with his filed-down key. They stepped into the quiet murmur of voices and the loud roar of Harv's snoring. Sid stayed close. Despite the narrow confines of the hall running along the front of the two cells, with Dawson and the sheriff to deal with, it was a two-man job now.

The hall was about two feet wider than the door leading to where the sheriff and Dawson sat talking. Slipping up that hall, the sight of the iron bars sent a chill up Sid's spine. He'd cheated prison so far, and he had no intention of ever spending a night in jail. If he ever found himself cornered by the law, he'd decided long ago to go down guns blazing rather than be locked in a cage like an animal.

Harv lay snoring in the cell farthest forward; the other cage was empty and its door stood slightly ajar.

Sid didn't wake him, afraid the cessation of the deep roar of Harv's sleep might be the same as sounding an alarm. Sid ducked behind the slightly ajar door and peeked through the crack between the door and the frame.

The sheriff sat there, hands behind his head, feet propped up on his desk with the ankles crossed, talking cattle. Dawson's chair was closer to Sid. He sat just inside the door, holding a cup of coffee in both hands, rocking his chair on its back legs.

Sid knew his blow to Dawson's head had to be brutally hard. Sid wanted him down and out with one quick move. Whether Dawson survived the strike or not didn't matter much. A witness could bring trouble. Then Sid would get the drop on the sheriff and tie him up. Hoping to avoid the noise of gunfire, Sid knew he'd shoot 'em both, grab Harv, and run if he had to.

Sid glanced at Boog then drew his gun and turned it so the butt end was forward. Boog nodded, understanding Sid's plan. Dawson's chair swayed as he sipped his coffee.

Raising the gun butt, Sid prepared to storm into the room and strike.

Dawson stood suddenly.

Sid whirled his gun around to take aim.

"I might as well get some sleep. It'll be dawn in a few minutes."

The sheriff lowered his hands and took his feet down off his desk. "I'll make it the rest of the night."

"Just remember he had a partner. Someone out there knows we caught him and could be looking."

"I appreciate the company. Stop by before you head out of town and we'll try and get some information out of him." Dawson left without a backward glance, and the sheriff settled back into his reclining position at his desk.

Sid and Boog exchanged glances; then, less than a minute after Red's exit, a soft snoring sound came from the front. Boog's cold eyes gleamed. He slipped through the door into the sheriff's front office.

Sid heard the dull *thud* of something hard striking flesh and bone.

Boog backed into the room, dragging a bleeding sheriff by his feet.

Enough light came from a single lantern in the sheriff's office that Sid saw the trail of blood. Vicious satisfaction uncurled in Sid to think of hurting any lawman. They were the enemy. "Harv, wake up."

Dropping Dean's feet, Boog went back up front and returned with a key hanging from an iron ring as big around as a saucer.

"Sid, that you?" Harv sat up, groggy but jumping to his feet the second his eyes focused.

With a rasp of metal, Boog unlocked the barred door.

Harv rushed out.

"Let's go. Get clear of town fast." Sid led the way. The three of them scurried through the night to the horses—they'd brought a spare for Harv from the M Bar S.

The three of them kept to the woods as they swung a wide circle around the town. "You and Boog go stay at the Griffin place. As soon as Boog is healed up, he can come back in. No one's paying too close a mind to who's there working because of Wade being back. He don't know how things were before. So no one's gonna notice you gone for awhile longer. Harv, you might need to lay low until I get shed of Wade and that wild woman he brought home."

Staring out of the thick trees of the rugged mountainside Sid studied the trail. It would split about two miles ahead—one trail well traveled, leading to the Sawyer place, and the other only a faint depression in the grass heading toward the abandoned Griffin house.

"The going gets hard in the woods from here on." Sid nodded at the tumbled stretch of slippery shale ahead. "Let's get on the trail. We won't meet up with anyone out this late."

"Hold it." Boog's quiet voice stopped Sid. "Look down the trail."

In the gray of predawn, Sid heard more than saw someone approaching from the direction of the Sawyers'. "A bunch of riders."

Harv spoke up. "I heard Red Dawson sent men out to the Sawyer place and every other ranch around. He told 'em to put out the word that he'd brung in rustled cattle and to come claim their stock. The Sawyers must be sending a party into Divide to fetch their cows."

Either Sid's eyes adjusted or the sky lightened or both, because he could make out one blazing white head in the midst of five riders. An unmistakable head of hair. That wild woman was riding with them.

"There's that woman." Harv had a hungry tone to his voice.

Sid didn't like the sound. He'd gotten to thinking of that untamed woman as his. "Keep quiet until they pass."

As the group rode closer, following the trail, Sid realized they'd come within fifty feet of where he hid with Boog and Harv. He could take them now. With Boog's gun and Harv's and his own, they could end it in a blaze of bullets, then ride to the ranch, get rid of Mort, and settle into the Sawyer place right away.

"Don't do it." Boog must have read his mind. Sid looked sideways and Boog nodded at the group of riders. "That's the saltiest bunch on the Sawyer place, and look, the woman—she heard something."

"Quiet!" Sid hissed.

The wild woman stopped. She sat on a barebacked pinto mare that few at the M Bar S ever rode because she was so feisty. The horse paused without any visible direction from that wildflower on her back, almost as if the horse had read her mind. The woman turned and stared into the woods straight into Sid's eyes.

He knew she couldn't see him. The woods were too thick, and with the barely lightening sky, the forest was impenetrably dark.

Impossible.

But those eyes. Chills sprang up on Sid's arms. Her eyes crawled over him then glanced left and right as if she not only saw him but made out Boog and Harv, too.

All three of them sat their horses motionlessly. Even their mounts seemed frozen as if they knew danger lay in the slightest movement.

At last, as the Sawyer hands left her behind, the wildflower looked forward and her horse, as if the two were one creature, started walking again.

Spooky, that woman. Seeing into the dark, maybe seeing into Sid's mind.

After the Sawyer riders vanished from sight on the winding trail to Divide, the trio stayed still.

"It's safe." Boog urged his mount forward. "Let's go."

Deciding to trust Boog, because Sid was tempted to stay hidden for a good long time, the three moved on.

"I'll be in by the weekend. My arm's almost healed up and I'm sick of sitting around. Should have spent the last few days driving those cattle south into Idaho. Now we've lost 'em." They reached the fork in the road and Boog paused. "Maybe we oughta cut out of here, Sid, and go collect that gold. It's been long enough for those Indians to bury their dead and go home."

"Forget it." Knowing he had to face a long day's work without a minute of sleep, Boog's wanting to quit fired Sid's temper. "Come back from Griffin's when you're ready, but the plan doesn't change."

Sid spurred his horse toward the Sawyer place. As he rode alone toward the spread he planned to make his own, it occurred to him that Boog and Harv were free as birds. They could sleep the day away. They could even head out and collect that gold and make tracks for California.

Refusing to look back, Sid decided this whole plan had taken too long. Mort was supposed to die outright. Arrogance had goaded Sid into letting the fall and the long cold night kill the old man. Now he needed to finish off the old man and the son and deal with that wild woman.

He'd give Boog and Harv a few more days to heal up; then it was time to make his move.

CHAPTER 19

I have no wish to see your white village, Wade. I should have stayed with Gertie."

"I'm sending a telegram to Helena asking about settlers named Lind, from back a few years. They can pass it on to land offices, and maybe we'll find where your pa lived. Don't you want to be there if we get an answer back?"

Abby scowled. She'd done more frowning since she'd come to live with the Sawyers than in her entire years with the Flathead. This long trail ride in the predawn darkness was unsettling. She'd smelled something back in the woods. Men. White men. Even riding with this group of them, she knew more were watching from the woods. But white men were always about. She'd learned to fear them, hate them, but mostly ignore them.

They'd taken everything from the Flatheads, all tribes in fact, but her people had found fertile valleys and lived in remote places. They were far from the whites who spread like a disease across this land. Until that massacre of her village, they'd left Abby's people alone in their rugged mountain valleys.

Wade rode his horse a bit closer to Abby's side and lowered his voice. "The more I think about it, the more I'm sure that arrow was aimed at you, not me."

"You don't know that."

"Or maybe they were going for both of us. If that arrow was shot by the same men that massacred your village, then they might count both of us as witnesses."

"You're just trying to scare me."

"Maybe you need to be scared. If I'm right, Abby, then we're dealing with the worst kind of yellow dog."

"You've just described all white men." Abby waited for Wade to defend his people. When he didn't, Abby felt bad about it. Wade had been nothing but kind, even sweet, so all white men except Wade.

Instead of defending his honor, he went right on pestering her to be more cautious. "We're talking about a man who'd shoot at a woman from cover. When you're in the house with Gertie, I think you're safe. A coward like that wouldn't storm the house. But that's with me and my best hands working close enough to be here in minutes. But today I have to go to town and I needed to take my best hands with me. I didn't want to ride off and leave you and Gertie without any protection. If they're really after you, then Gertie's in danger, too, as long as you're there. I couldn't ride off to town without you, so you had to come."

He'd used this same argument to nag her into going. She had agreed to come along and now she regretted it. Mainly because of that sense of being watched. "Fine, I will see this village and help drive your stolen cattle home."

His eyes narrowed as if she'd insulted him somehow, but he didn't say why, and she made no effort to coax his reasons from him or soothe his feelings.

"Let's pick up the pace now that it's light. We need to make a fast trip. The roundup is going well, but I want to get back."

As she guided her pony with her knees, Abby looked at the men, loaded down with their iron guns and their heavy leather saddles, and wondered how the poor horses stood it.

❦

"That's Tom Linscott and his drovers." Wade drew Abby's attention toward a group coming into town the same time as the Sawyers.

He and Abby and his cowhands rode into Divide just as the sun finally cleared the horizon.

"Red must've sent word to him, too. Our range butts up against the Linscotts'. Pa and Tom have been wrangling over water holes and grazing land ever since Linscott came in here nearly eight years ago. The man isn't an easy neighbor, but truth be told, Pa was always more at fault than Tom."

Abby gave the riders a disinterested look and turned back toward the corral ahead of them. Wade saw the yard full of cattle standing quietly as if they hadn't gotten out of bed for the morning yet, but he turned back to study Linscott. Wade had picked up his father's attitude toward the stubborn Swede, but now Wade was determined to be friendly if Tom would allow it. There was considerable bad blood between the families.

It was easy to resent the blond giant because Wade knew Tom was the kind of man Mort wished Wade would be. Being a Christian now, Wade admitted that the hostility he felt toward Linscott had a lot to do with jealousy, and it wasn't right.

Wade rode up to the corral just as Tom got there. Tom had a wary gaze on Wade. It was hard to look the man in the eye, remembering drunken insults Wade had hurled at him only a couple of years ago. Wade knew God had forgiven him, but he had no such hope about Tom.

"Morning." Wade swung down off his horse and wrapped his reins around the hitching post. He noticed Abby swing one leg over her horse's neck and drop lightly to the ground on her moccasin-covered feet. He saw her legs almost to her knees and looked away quickly just because he didn't want to see any more. He could not convince the woman it was important to keep her ankles covered. But proper manners or not, all the gingham in the world wasn't going to dull her skill as a horsewoman.

"Sawyer." Tom looked at Wade; then his eyes were drawn on past.

Wade glanced behind him to notice Abby striding toward them. Abby was as white-blond as Tom, and it occurred to Wade that the two would make a likely pair. For some reason that reminded him of why he'd hated Linscott. "Looks like we're on the same errand."

Linscott rode a black thoroughbred with a white blaze and white stockings on his front feet. The animal was huge and feisty, rumored to be so dangerous no one went near him but Tom, and no one else had ever been on his back. He'd made Linscott a fortune as ranches paid top dollar for stud fees. And Linscott used that fortune to buy up land and build up his herd.

As Wade stepped close, the stallion snorted and shook his head, jingling the metal of his bridle. The bared teeth were ample warning for Wade to stay back.

Linscott rode the black to a hitching post well away from the other horses and lashed the reins tight.

"Can I talk to you for just a minute, Tom?" Wade knew Linscott was a brusque, short-tempered man, a good match for his horse.

"Make it quick." Tom walked toward Wade, his spurs jingling, his stride long and impatient. He faced Wade almost as if squaring off for a shootout.

Wade couldn't blame Tom for expecting the worst, but Wade wasn't going to give the man trouble. "I spent most of the years since we've met being a first-class coyote and I'm sorry. There, that fast enough?"

Linscott's shoulders slumped a bit, and his eyes narrowed. "That's what you wanted to talk about?"

"Yep, that's it. I don't expect you to trust me after some of the things I pulled, but I've changed. I quit drinking. I'm back on the ranch with Pa. I'd like there to be peace between us. No more pushing Sawyer cattle onto your range, no more fighting about those two water holes Pa liked to wrangle over. They're yours and always have been. I'll keep my cattle away."

Linscott scowled. "I've wanted to put my fist through your face for years."

"You have a few times, if I recall."

"It wasn't ever enough." Linscott crossed his arms as if to keep his fists from flying.

"It'll take time to prove to you that I mean what I say." Wade made a point of looking Linscott straight in the eye. If there was anger, even fists, Wade intended to take it as his due. Linscott wasn't an evil man, just a grouch with a short temper. "But I do. After a time, you'll believe me, I reckon."

A soft nicker from Linscott's stallion drew Wade's attention.

"Such a good boy." Abby caressed the beast's nose, standing directly in front of the horse.

"Get back!" Wade took one step.

Tom's hand clamped on his arm like a steel vise. "Don't move!"

Releasing Wade, Tom eased himself the ten feet or so toward Abby. "Miss, step away."

Abby looked up from the horse's muzzle. "Why?"

"He's dangerous. Step slowly back."

Abby smiled then gave the stallion a kiss on his nose. "Dangerous, are you, boy? I'd say you're just looking out for yourself. I know how you feel."

She stepped away from the horse and walked toward Tom without a bit of fear or caution. She was easily within reach of the stallion's iron-shod hooves.

Wade held his breath until she was far enough away from the horse to be out of biting and kicking range.

Tom took two long strides toward her, put that iron vise of a hand on her arm, and jerked her nearly off her feet. "Are you crazy?" He dragged her about half a step before she kicked him in the back of the knee, twisted her arm loose, and rammed a fist high into his belly. Tom was flat on the ground on his back, sucking in breath like a backward scream, with Abby kneeling on his chest with her knife pressed to his neck.

It all happened so fast Wade hadn't even reacted before it was over.

"You put your hands on me again, white man, and I'll see you don't get your fingers back."

Linscott was too busy trying to breathe to do much else.

Several of the Linscott drovers turned to defend their boss.

Wade was at her side and raised a hand to Linscott's men. They might not obey a hand gesture from him, but they might hold off on shooting the woman who was threatening to slit their boss's throat. "Don't hurt him, Ab. Tom was afraid his horse would attack you. The animal's got a reputation as a killer."

"Hey, my stallion's never killed anyone." Linscott defended his horse from his position flat on his back.

"Not for lack of trying." Wade prodded Tom with his toe, not too hard, to remind the idiot that he was one swift knife slash from death. Not that Wade thought Abby would kill him. Unless she really had to. Or Tom was really stupid in what he said in the next few minutes.

"The horse never put his hands on me." Abby leaned forward and put all her weight on the knee she had rammed into Tom's chest. "He never dragged me around or shouted at me. I'd say the stallion has better manners than his owner."

"He was trying to save you." Wade knew Abby was just having fun now. The time to cut was long past.

Abby gave him a look of such doubt that Wade added, "No, really, he was."

With motions so quick the human eye couldn't follow them, Abby whipped her knife away, back into its hidden pouch. Wade still wasn't sure where exactly the woman kept the knife, and it was rude to study her skirt long enough to be sure.

Abby shoved off Tom's chest far harder than necessary, and she dusted off her knee as if Linscott had gotten her dirty.

Wade reached down, and Tom, his eyes locked on Abby, didn't notice. Wade kicked him, no gentle prod like last time.

That Tom noticed. He grabbed Wade's hand to get to his feet.

Wade pulled maybe just a tad harder than was absolutely necessary, and Tom, back to looking at Abby, almost fell over forward.

"S—sorry, I didn't mean to mistreat you. . .uh. . ." Linscott looked at Wade.

That wide-eyed fascination with Abby set Wade off. But he'd just told Tom about turning over a new leaf, so he refrained from gaining Tom's attention with his fists. "It's Abby." Wade tried for a minimum amount of good manners. "Abby Lin—"

"What?" Tom reacted as if a lightning bolt had just landed slap on him. "Abby Linscott? That's my sister's name."

"Not Lin*scott*." Wade resisted the urge to swat the man in the back of the head, just to see if he could make him blink. Tom was riveted by Abby. "Lind. Abby Lind, this is Tom Linscott."

Tom moved closer to Abby.

Abby seemed to be focused unduly on Tom, too.

Wade needed his gun.

Suddenly Tom was fumbling with something on his shirt.

Wade stepped closer. He'd have stepped right between them if there'd been room.

"Linscott?" Abby paid rapt attention to the man. "Tom Linscott?"

Tom produced a large gold pocket watch and pressed the stem winder. The watch popped open to reveal a picture. "This is. . ." Tom looked from the picture to Abby and back. "This could be you."

"Who is it?" Abby leaned close, studying the picture. She took it from Tom's hands even though he tried to hang on, but he didn't try hard. He tried like a man who was numb all the way to his fingertips. She lifted it close, and long seconds passed as she stared at the likeness. "Mama."

Barely able to hear the words, Wade leaned closer. "You recognize this picture?" Wade looked, and there was no way to deny that the woman in the picture bore a stunning resemblance to Abby.

"They died. My whole family died." Abby's eyes rose to meet Tom's. "Except my older brother. You stayed back East."

"When you all went West, I stayed behind. I had a girl I was sparking and a good job working in a lumberyard." Tom's lips curved down. "You forgot you had a brother?"

"No, not forgot. But that life seems so far away. Almost like it happened to someone else." Abby looked deeply into Tom's eyes.

"She's been living with the Flathead all these years, Tom. Speaking their language, living by their customs. She's remembering her old life only in bits and pieces."

"Indians kidnapped you?" Tom's brows slammed together. "Savages? I never knew. I never even considered you'd lived or I'd have come to save you. We heard the family died of the fever. I inherited Pa's land and my girl married someone else, so I came West."

Wade saw a flash of temper in Abby's eyes. He jumped in to head off her drawing her knife again. "The Flatheads found her alone, her family dead. They didn't kidnap her. They *saved* her. Took her and cared for her and raised her as their own." Wade added in a whisper, "She doesn't like it when you call them savages."

Tom started shaking his head. "My sister. I. . .I never thought one of you might have lived. I was t–told. . ." Tears welled up in Tom's eyes.

Wade looked around quickly, knowing Tom wouldn't want anyone to see him crying. Once the danger was past, his men had moved away. They were in the corral separating the stock.

Suddenly Tom launched himself forward and grabbed hold of Abby in a bear hug. Startled, Abby looked to Wade as if asking for help.

Wade shrugged. "He's happy to see you. Aren't you kinda happy to know you have a brother?" For some reason, Wade was extremely happy to find out Tom was Abby's brother. He didn't bother trying to decide why exactly. Of course, there was bad in it, too. Tom couldn't spark her, but he could take her home.

"Yes." With a quiet cry of distress, Abby flung her arms around Tom and hugged back. "I'm very happy to know I have a brother. Tom, I do remember you. I was so young when we headed West."

"Seven." Tom let her go, stepped back a bit, and kept his head down as he fished a handkerchief out of his pocket. He blew his nose and made a quick swipe of his eyes then looked up. "You were seven when Pa threw in with a wagon train. I was sixteen and not about to leave my best girl behind. Stubborn kid. If I'd have come, maybe I could have helped."

Wade clapped his hand on Tom's back, enjoying slapping the man a bit too much. If he wasn't careful, he was going to lose Abby because of this. "You two have a lot of catching up to do. Why don't you send your hands home with the cattle and ride out to the M Bar S with us, spend the day."

Tom suddenly bulled up, got a mean look on his face that Wade remembered well from the old days. "I'm not coming out there. Abby is coming home with me."

Wade froze. Then he melted; in fact, he got a little hot under the collar. "No, she's not."

"My sister is coming home with me." Tom dismissed Wade's comment and turned to Abby. "We'll give you a ride. You don't need a horse or anything else from Sawyer."

"She's got a job on our ranch." Wade wasn't about to let Abby ride off with anyone, least of all Tom Linscott.

"She doesn't need a job. I can support her." Tom reached for Abby.

Wade stepped between them. "I know how you live out there."

"I live just fine." Tom's jaw clenched.

Wade could see the man remembering, but just in case, Wade

reminded him. "Your cabin is falling down and your ranch hands live in it with you. She'd be more comfortable in a cave of bears. Safer, too."

"So I'll build a house." Tom's hand seemed to sweep aside the problem of where Abby would stay in the meantime. "I didn't have a reason to before this."

"Come out to the Sawyer place after the house is built. We'll talk about her going with you then." That gave Wade plenty of time to convince Abby that she needed to stay with him forever.

"No. She comes now." Tom squared off in front of Wade, turning sideways to Abby.

"It's not right nor proper." Wade took a step closer to Linscott. "At least at my place we've got Gertie. Plus, Gertie is run ragged trying to take care of Pa and cook for the hands doing roundup. We really need Abby's help."

Tom jerked back. "You don't have your roundup done yet?"

Wade thought the heat in his cheeks might be a blush. Blushing, at his age, in front of Tom Linscott, while the man swept Abby off to live with him. Could things get any worse? It was not *his* fault that he'd come home and found chaos. "No, we don't. And that's not what we're talking about. Abby's reputation will get dragged through the mud if she's out there with all of your bachelor cowhands."

"No one will say a word against my sister or they'll face me." Tom jabbed a finger straight at his chest.

"Oh, now you're going to shoot anyone who raises an eyebrow." Wade snorted. "Instead of just letting her come to the M Bar S like you should."

"She's my responsibility. She's my sister." Tom shoved Wade's shoulder.

Wade took a step forward. "You're a stranger."

"She's mine."

"No, she's not. She's mine!" Wade clenched his fists.

"Shut up!" Abby shoved herself between them, one hand flat

on each of their chests. "Just shut up!"

Dead silence reigned. She looked from one to the other. " 'She's mine'? Did I hear those words come from your lips? Both of you?"

Neither answered.

"I belong to no white man. I belong to no *man*!"

Wade watched Tom's eyes focus on Abby with confusion and fondness. Then those eyes shifted to Wade and narrowed. Wade wondered what in the world the man was thinking. "Any fool can see she can't stay out there with you."

Abby's blade flashed right under Wade's nose. "I said shut up."

Tom's narrow, dangerous eyes widened. Then he smirked. "You ever meet a man you didn't pull a knife on, baby sister?"

Wade thought it over. "I can't remember her skipping anyone so far."

Abby glared.

Tom studied Wade as if taking his measure. . .maybe for a pine box.

Wade wasn't sure what the stubborn idiot was hunting for.

Suddenly Tom's expression eased, and he shook his head and smiled. "No more fighting, Abby girl. You're a woman grown, easy to see. You can decide where you go all on your own."

"Of course I'll go with Wade. I have a job, and I don't want to live in a single house with a crowd of cowboys. At the M Bar S, I only have to put up with him and his whining yellow dog of a father."

Tom jerked a little then started to laugh. "I'm starting to really like you."

"And Gertie," Wade interjected. "Don't forget her. My house-keeper makes a perfect chaperone. Tough, no nonsense." Abby might not be getting the undercurrent here, but then, the woman was busy putting her knife away in some secret hidey-hole. Wade knew Tom got it just fine.

"But I do want to spend time with you, Abby." Tom rested

his hand on her arm, sounding as sincere as a man ever had. "I've got enough men in town to drive my cattle home. I think I'll come on out to the Sawyer place with—"

A bloodcurdling scream cut Tom off, and they all turned to face the sound.

A woman ran out of the sheriff's office. Bright red blood on her hands. "Doctor! I need a doctor!"

Wade dashed forward. He heard other feet running, all charging toward the bleeding woman.

CHAPTER 20

The sound of screaming bolted Red straight out of his chair. "Stay inside, Cass." Shouting that order, he hoped Cassie picked today to be obedient and ran.

He saw Libby before he'd gotten out the door of the diner. Libby Jeffreys, his good friend who only minutes ago had left the diner with a tray of food for the sheriff and his prisoner. Libby now staggered onto the board sidewalk covered in blood.

He sprinted toward her and almost collided with Wade Sawyer, who reached her at the same moment from a different direction. Red caught Libby's shoulders, looking for the source of the bleeding. "Wade, get the doctor for her."

"No." Libby's voice shook. "I mean yes, get the doctor, but not for me. It's Merl."

"I'll go." Tom Linscott was a single pace behind Wade. He wheeled and raced for the doctor's office.

"He's knocked cold, bleeding, maybe dead." Libby burst into tears.

Red took one more hard scan of Libby's bloody but uninjured body. Then as Seth from the general store came up beside Red, he thrust the sobbing woman into Seth's capable hands.

Wildflower Bride

"Take care of her." Red let her go and headed for the jail.

Wade beat him in the door.

The two went in to find a trail of blood leading from the single front room of the sheriff's office through the swinging door to the back room. A room where Red's prisoner had spent the night in one of the two small cells.

Red rushed to the door and swung it open to find Sheriff Dean facedown on the floor, lying in a pool of blood. The cell where Merl had locked up Red's prisoner last night stood empty, the door swung open.

Dropping to the floor, Red felt sick to think the prisoner he'd brought in had done this. Red looked up at Wade, who was kneeling on the other side of Merl, and said, "It didn't happen long ago. The blood is too fresh. I didn't hear a gunshot."

"Let's roll him over. Be careful."

Red and Wade eased the burly older man over, and he groaned. With a rush of hope, Red saw what looked like a single blow to the head, a nasty gash, swollen and bleeding into his salt-and-pepper gray hair, but not a bullet wound.

Merl's eyes flicked open, and he struggled to sit up.

"Lay still." Red pressed on the older man's shoulders. "The doc will be here in a few seconds. You're all right. Just got knocked cold."

Red prayed silently. A quick glance at Wade's moving lips told him Wade had joined in with his own prayers.

No other wound showed up. Merl reached for his head with a moan of pain. "What happened?"

"Just stay quiet. Looks like your prisoner or maybe his partner knocked you cold and escaped." Red had hoped the prisoner would talk, especially after he'd been locked up overnight.

The man didn't seem possessed of any great supply of courage, judging by the way he'd lain frozen under the onslaught of Belle's and Emma's gunfire. And if the man talked, then the ring of outlaws could be broken up for good. Now the area ranchers had their cattle back and the hideout uncovered, but they didn't have a line on the outlaws.

Frustrated, Red turned back to Merl just as the doctor hustled into the narrow hallway that ran along the front of the jail cells. Red got to his feet to make room for the doctor. He studied the little area and moved toward the rear of the building. That's when he noticed the alley door standing just barely ajar. "Wade." Red strode the last few feet and examined the latch. "They must have gotten in this way." Red stepped outside, knowing it was far, far too late. He crouched down and studied the dirt torn up with hoofprints.

"Look at this door. The knob isn't broken. They must've had a key."

"Door probably takes a skeleton key. Easy to find." Red stood and rubbed one hand into his hair. "I should have stayed all night instead of going back to Grant's Hotel to sleep. We knew he had a partner."

Wade tugged the brim of his hat low over his eyes. "Tell me how you caught him."

Tom Linscott picked that moment to round the building. Glowing Sun—no, Abby—was right behind him. Red was struck by how the two resembled each other. Not many folks had that unusual shade of white-blond hair. "The doc is taking Merl over to his office. Looks like he just got a hard blow to the head. He should be okay."

"Morning, Tom. Find any cattle of yours in that mob we brought in?"

"My men are checking. We were just in town a few minutes when Libby started screaming. She's fine, by the way. Upset but not hurt at all. This gang's been hitting us for a few head all winter. Probably gathers a few up then drives them somewhere to sell. Tough call with the brands, but it's hard to do a perfect job of covering the old ones. We should be able to identify ours."

Red looked from Tom to Abby again then shook his head to focus on what was important. "I brought in a man to the sheriff I found holed up with the cattle. He had a partner with him who got away."

Red quickly told them as many details as he could. Then they started studying the tracks. In the lightly traveled alley, they could tell which way the gang went, straight for a clump of trees that led into the rugged hills around Divide.

Abby did a better job of tracking than any of the rest of them. Finally, the ground turned to rock and the riders seemed to vanish. Frustrated, they turned back to Divide.

"At least we got these cattle." Wade slapped Red on the shoulder. "Maybe with their hideout found, they'll move on. But I hate passing our troubles on to some other ranchers. I've got to get headed for home now. We're in the middle of roundup."

"You're still doing roundup?" Red was amazed.

Wade scowled. "Yes, we're still doing roundup."

Red was sorry he'd said anything. "Send your men on home and take a few more minutes to decide if there's anything to be done about these rustlers. It won't take long."

Wade agreed.

The group headed for Libby's Diner, where Cassie was now waiting tables with Susannah hanging from one ankle and Michael strapped on her back. Red marveled at his wife. She just would not stop working.

"How's Merl?" Cassie came up with a coffee cup and a pot as Red settled at the table. Michael blinked sleepy eyes at Red over Cassie's shoulder and smiled.

"He's at the doctor's office. Doc said he's making sense and sitting up, so he'll be okay, but someone must have come up behind him, because he can't remember a thing." Red got up to relieve Cassie of her burden and also because he couldn't get enough of holding his little redheaded son. He settled Michael on one knee, Susannah on the other, and still managed to drink his coffee without burning tiny fingers. He was getting real good at this father stuff.

Wade came in next, holding the door open for Abby. A cranky-looking Tom Linscott tried to come in with Wade still holding the door, but Wade stepped in front of Tom and dropped the door in Tom's face. The two shoved at each other for a few seconds as if fighting to see who could get in the door first.

"I told you I'll start building a cabin today." Tom was talking to Abby. Was Tom trying to convince Abby to marry him?

Red's eyes slid to see how Wade was taking that. It hadn't taken any leap of great genius to see that Wade was sweet on this woman.

"Come and talk to us when it's done." Wade wasn't taking it a bit good.

"You can move out to my place in a week if we push hard." Tom ignored Wade and talked to Abby. "And we will push hard."

Abby ignored both of them and looked down at Susannah.

"She's not coming out there, Linscott. She's got a job at the M Bar S."

Red looked at Abby, obviously the object of this discussion.

"Let me help you." Abby swooped in and plucked Susannah off Red's lap and began talking to her as if there wasn't a wrangle going on behind her. . .about her.

"Why're they fighting over you?" Red jerked his head at the two men.

Abby studied Red for a few moments as if he'd asked her to explain the mysteries of the universe. "I am Tom Linscott's sister."

"You are?" Red lowered his coffee to the table, clicking it hard.

Abby rounded the table to sit straight across from Red. "It would seem so. In fact, I believe I remember him. Of course, he was much younger."

"No sister of mine is going to work for a living. And especially not for the Sawyers." Tom headed for the seat beside Abby, but Wade beat him to it. Scowling, Tom went to sit on the bench next to Red, right across from Wade. Handy—now they could glare at each other full-time.

"Are you sure of this sister thing?" Red asked.

Cassie appeared with more cups and the steaming pot. "What sister thing, Red?"

"Abby and Tom Linscott are brother and sister."

"Family." Cassie smiled at Abby. "That's so wonderful for both of you."

"She's not working for an outfit so worthless they haven't even gotten spring roundup done yet."

Abby snorted.

Tom bared his teeth.

The soft sound of pouring liquid and the chatter of others gathered in Libby's Diner weren't enough to draw Red's attention from this new development.

"He has a pocket watch with a picture of my parents." Abby's brow furrowed. "I resemble my mother closely. And I. . .I remembered. . .earlier with Wade. . .that my last name was Lind. But now that Tom says Linscott, yes, I know that's right."

"Well, I'm happy for you. Finding out you've got a family has to be good."

"Good? To have more white men wanting me? I do not see how that is good."

Red laughed.

Abby relaxed a bit from her frowning, and her eyes went to Tom, who was so busy arguing with Wade that his sister might as well have not existed.

Red had noticed the resemblance, the pure blue of their eyes, the white-blond hair. But now he saw that Tom had a lot of features similar to Abby's, a more rugged, manly version of course, but no one would be surprised to find out they were kin.

"Well, you're welcome to come out to our place." Cassie was still serving coffee, but she'd heard the end of the exchange. "I need more help with my knife throwing. Belle spent a couple of days working with me, and I've improved. But I can't seem to hit the target dead-on."

Susannah reached for the blazing hot stream of liquid Cassie was dispensing into Abby's cup. The two women moved together in a way music could have been put to it to keep Susannah from burning herself and still get done what they wanted.

The door swung open and Sheriff Merl Dean walked in with no color in his face and a bandage on his forehead. "I need a posse."

"We already tried to track them." Red stood and guided Merl, still pale and shaky, to the seat Red had just vacated. "We lost them in the foothills just west of town. Nowhere for a posse to go."

"I want to check myself. Can you three help?"

"Wade can't," Tom said with his usual cocky smirk, his only real expression except for anger. "He's still doing roundup."

"You're not done with roundup yet?" The sheriff's brows disappeared into the bandage on his forehead.

"No." Wade's stony expression didn't encourage further comment.

Red changed the subject. "Did you question the prisoner any more last night after I left?"

"No. I think I got hit minutes after you left. I don't remember anything past you saying good-bye. Figured I'd have another crack at him this morning. Are you sure you didn't find anyone in that stack of wanted posters we thumbed through?"

Shaking his head, Red said, "The man had no scars or anything else that would identify him. That cut on his chin is too new."

Abby turned on the sheriff like a hungry cougar who'd just spotted a three-legged buffalo. "Cut on his chin?"

"Right here?" Wade asked as he sat up straight and ran a finger along his jawline on the right side. Then he rose and stood behind Abby, resting his hands on her shoulders.

"Yep."

"Get your hands off my sister." Tom half rose from his seat.

Wade's hands stayed where they were. "Long beard, dark hair?"

Sheriff Dean shook his head. "His hair was dark, but short, looked like he'd hacked it off with a knife to me. And no beard."

"He could have done all that to change his appearance." Red looked at Wade and Abby. "Probably had to if his face needed stitches. What's going on?"

"I told you about the man who tried to take Abby after the massacre."

"Massacre?" Tom slammed his coffee cup on the table. "My sister was in the middle of a massacre?" He jabbed a finger at Wade's nose. "You didn't say anything about a massacre."

"I told Red." Wade dismissed Tom, which struck Red as very brave or very foolish. Tom Linscott was notorious for his bad temper and quick fists. A match in every way for that famous black stallion.

"He did tell me." Red felt the need to back his friend.

"And where exactly were you when my sister was in the middle of a massacre?" Linscott rounded the table as if to put himself between Wade and Abby, as if it were Wade's fault the girl had been in a massacre and she was still in danger. And just maybe Tom had some massacre plans of his own.

Wade, rather than backing down, which most sensible people learned to do when Linscott's temper flamed, took a step forward, lifting his chin as if daring Tom to land a fist on it.

"Shut up, both of you." Abby stood and, as if this was nothing new, shoved her way between the two men. "Red may have captured a murderer. You fight like squabbling children. We don't have time for your foolishness."

Tom jerked back as if Abby had cut *him*. Which she probably would, given time.

Wade smiled and moved out of Tom's reach. "Yes, Abby fought back and managed to cut her attacker with her knife. She got in several good slashes. I think his clothing was cut up. His face she laid open bad. He let her go and ran. She saved herself. I only came along afterward."

"That's not true. You put a bullet into one of them."

"One of them? How many men had their hands on my sister?"

Tom's face turned beet red.

"There were four," Abby said.

"You shot a man?" The sheriff's brows lowered and he glared at Wade. "You should have reported it."

Wade shrugged. "He rode off. He couldn't have been too badly hurt."

"Which means you took a shot at him and missed, of course," Tom sneered.

"This rustler I brought in could be the same man." Red ignored Linscott. Everyone was used to his cranky ways. He pulled up a chair from another table and sat by the sheriff. "And if he had four men at the village, then there are more rustlers around than we figured."

"What village?" The sheriff was looking irritated. Red couldn't blame him. The man was finding too many things out by chance that they should have reported to him from the start. And all while nursing one beauty of a headache.

"Abby was living with the Flathead in a high valley past the Tanner ranch." Wade settled back in his chair.

"It's the Harden ranch," Cassie said as she poured more coffee for them all.

All the men grunted.

"Oh, only Indians." The sheriff turned to his coffee.

"Only?" Abby turned on the man, and Red thought her hand was going for her knife. "Only Indians?"

Wade grabbed her arm. "Don't pull a knife on the sheriff, Ab. He can arrest you for it."

"He'd have to be alive to arrest me, now, wouldn't he?"

The sheriff was concentrating on his coffee and missed the ensuing struggle.

"Abby really liked her Flathead family," Red told the sheriff, hoping to avert yet another massacre. "They saved her life. Found her when her family was dead from the fever and took her in. They treated her far better than many whites have."

Wildflower Bride

"Sorry for the insult, miss." The sheriff rubbed his bandaged head. "I'm sorry about your village, too. I'd pick your village over the scum that are running these hills any day. And I'll help you catch them, too, and see them hanged for what they did to your people."

Abby quit trying to arm herself and sank with a disgusted snort into her chair. "Your prisoner destroyed my village, he and his three friends. And now he rides away from your jail cell free as a bird."

Merl lifted the coffee cup and took a long sip. "I thought I could handle him. Red stayed for most of the night, but I should have brought my deputy in, too. We've never had a jailbreak before."

Abby's eyes softened as she looked at the battered man. It reassured Red some to note that the woman wasn't always bloodthirsty.

"Maybe you oughta go home, Merl." Red studied the man's ashen face. "You look white. You couldn't stick your horse even if we did know which way to ride."

Merl sighed. "No one reported this massacre to me. Where'd this happen?"

Red, Wade, and Abby took turns filling the sheriff in.

Tom seemed bent on yelling every time one of them added a new detail.

"Try and describe these men more carefully." The sheriff looked between Wade and Abby. "Do better than heavyset, thin, masks. Think hard. Picture them. You've left a scar on my prisoner and a bullet wound in another one of them. Did they have any other marks, scars, anything we could use to identify them? Did you notice their horses? Were they branded?"

Wade considered things quietly for a time. "One of them had a funny way of holding a gun. I can't put my finger on just... Wait! His fingers, that was it. He held his six-shooter in a stiff way." Wade pulled his own Colt and checked the load to make sure the hammer was on an empty chamber. Wade pointed the gun at the ceiling and stared at his hands. "Two fingers on his left hand stuck out." Wade demonstrated. "Usually they'd be curled around the gun butt, like this."

Wade seemed to be looking into the past, trying to picture the scene. He closed his fist, his index finger on the trigger, the next three fingers wrapped around the gun handle to meet his thumb. The normal way to hold a gun. "But instead his little finger and the one next to it stuck out straight. He had leather gloves on, tight, not like the buckskin gloves you see. Normally a man would take his gloves off to handle a gun, but this one didn't. Of course, it all happened so fast, and the massacre was over. Maybe he was leaving and it was a cold morning. He didn't have time to remove his glove when they came upon me."

As they finished the telling, Abby added, "I smelled the stink of a white man in the woods this morning. I believe there were three of them, certainly more than one. Maybe it was the escaped prisoner heading north."

"You smelled a man?" Tom looked at her as if she'd sprouted elk antlers.

Red would have looked at Abby strangely, too, except Red saw right away that Tom's comment made Abby mad. So Tom's big mouth saved Red from making himself a target.

"What did you learn living with those savages all these years?" Tom asked. "It'll take me forever to teach you better."

"Teach me better?" Abby's voice got so high it threatened to shatter glass. "A white man teach me? I will fight learning the white ways to my *death*."

Cassie reached for Michael, probably to save the little tyke's hearing, and she started choking.

It took some doing before Red was satisfied Cassie had recovered enough to hand over the chubby little boy. He helped tuck the boy into Cassie's carrier on her back then kissed the child on his cheek and spared a quick kiss for Cassie, too.

Wildflower Bride

She smiled, ran one finger down Red's nose, and then went back to waiting tables.

"What do you mean a white man stinks?" Tom demanded.

Red couldn't imagine the idiot really wanted to hear Abby's answer.

Red noticed Wade's eyes followed the exchange between him and Cassie. He knew Wade envied the Dawsons' happy marriage. There'd been a time when Wade's interest in Cassie was an obsession. Wade had gotten past that when he'd put his faith in God. But Wade was lonely. He'd told Red he wanted a family, a wife like Cassie who would be gentle and funny and sweet. Then Red watched Wade's eyes go to beautiful Abby, and Red thought maybe his friend had finally found himself a woman.

"You are a fool, brother"—

Well, maybe not quite as sweet.

—"to ask me what I mean when I say white men stink."

And not really all that gentle.

Abby drew her knife and tested the blade. "Better to live amid skunks."

But she was pretty funny, Red had to give her that.

CHAPTER 21

Sheriff Dean rose from the table. "I'll ride with you partway home, Wade. Abby can show me where she thought she. . .uh. . . smelled. . .someone."

"You should bring more riders." It made Abby furious to see how the man doubted her. Her fingers itched to reach for her knife, but she knew that was getting to be a bad habit. At least the sheriff was going to check. "You'll find tracks and maybe catch these murderers before they harm more of my people or steal more of your *cows*." It sickened her to think of these brutes running free while her Flathead family lay dead.

Wade came to her side, and his hand rested whisper-soft on her lower back.

Abby wasn't sure if he was showing his support and offering her comfort or blocking her from getting to her knife. "Tell me, Sheriff, what are you really hunting for, rustlers or murderers? Would you even stir yourself from your chair if there weren't cows missing?"

"Now, miss"—the sheriff's brow beetled and he pulled his hat from his poor wounded head—"I didn't know about the village massacre. Someone has to report a crime before I can arrest someone for it."

Wildflower Bride

Abby had to admit that the sheriff couldn't arrest a man for a crime that no one had even told him about. And from the look of his bloody bandage, the lawman had his own reasons to want these men caught very badly. It wasn't all about cows.

"You and Wade didn't even bother to ride into town and tell me about it." The sheriff shifted his eyes to Wade. "I saw you in town, Sawyer. You've ridden in at least once since you've been back. You didn't say a *word* about murder."

"You don't go out to the countryside, Sheriff. And Abby's village was located at least two days' ride away from town. I didn't even consider telling you about it."

"I reckon you're right. I wouldn't have gone out to try and catch an outlaw that far from Divide." The sheriff sighed and rubbed his head. "I'm sorry to admit that's true, Miss Linscott. But I don't really have jurisdiction in the countryside. I don't worry about trouble unless it comes into my town."

It burned Abby to hear him say it, but she had to admire the man for looking her in the eye and admitting the truth. How was she ever going to find her place in this white world? Abby's eyes went to Tom Linscott. "You really are my brother, aren't you?"

"I do believe I am, Abby girl." Tom turned to Wade. "I'll be riding out to your ranch with you, Sawyer. I want to spend some time with my sister. Meanwhile, I've told my men to start building a cabin."

"She's working for me, Tom." Wade got that bulled-up look in his eye, and he had the same tone she'd heard when Wade had snarled, "She's mine," to Tom.

Insulting. Yet Abby felt a softening in her heart to have two men wanting to take care of her. She didn't need them for protection, but maybe she wanted them to care just a little.

"Come on out, though. We'd love to have you." Wade's hand stayed on her back, more firmly pressed against her spine now. Definitely support, since she suspected Wade wouldn't mind one bit if she pulled her blade on Tom.

Abby thought of Mort Sawyer and sniffed in disgust. A clear lie—Wade wasn't even bothering to fake honesty. She marveled at finding a brother, even an arrogant, unpleasant one. Couldn't she have found a better family than him? Wade would have made a better brother to her. But thinking of Wade as a brother wasn't comfortable. She didn't care to examine why.

"Come in to services on Sunday morning." Cassie gave Abby a huge hug.

Abby found herself nose to nose with the little redheaded boy on Cassie's back while receiving her hug. The boy blew a spit bubble at her and smiled. Abby smiled back. After receiving the prolonged hug from Cassie, which Abby found she rather enjoyed, she mounted her horse and they headed for the M Bar S.

Wade, Tom, the sheriff, and five others from town rode along.

"This is the place." Abby pressed her knees into the sides of her pinto and turned the horse to the wooded area by the trail. "Judging by the stench, I'd say there were three of them."

Tom shook his head a bit hard. Abby had seen dogs around the Flathead village shake themselves that way when they'd come out of the river, and yet Tom was bone dry. White men made no sense.

When Abby reached the edge of the woods, she saw immediately the tracks of three men coming out of the forest onto the trail. A trail that had been trod heavily by the cattle Wade's cowhands had driven home.

Tom and the sheriff and his men all swung down and began studying the tracks.

"They could have shot us dead, three men. We had some riders with us, but we'd have been sitting ducks." Wade rode up to her side, his eyes examining the ground. Then he looked sideways at Abby and spoke softly, his words only for her. "If these are the men who kidnapped you after the massacre and attacked us at the ranch, why did they pass up a chance to finish things this morning?"

Abby looked from Wade to the tracks and back again.

"Cowards, I'd say. They could probably have killed us all shooting from cover and not gotten a scratch, but they didn't want to take that chance. These men have proven themselves to be cowards with every move they've made. Attacking defenseless women and children, kidnapping a lone woman."

"You weren't exactly defenseless." Wade smiled at her. "I'm glad you fought them. I'm glad you hurt the man who put his hands on you."

"Are you glad you put a bullet into one of them?"

Wade's smile shrank to something grim. "It had to be done. That's not the same as being glad."

"Then that's a difference between us, Sawyer. Because my only regret is that he wasn't hurt worse and that he was gone this morning and I didn't get my hands on him in that jail cell."

"We'll never follow tracks in this rocky soil." The sheriff rubbed the white bandage on his head.

Elders were respected in her tribe, and she had to force herself to mind the sheriff. Men had pride, and Abby doubted the sheriff would thank her. But he wasn't up to chasing outlaws and that was a fact.

"Let's follow the trail back toward Divide. Study it, see if we can get a feel for their horses," the sheriff suggested.

"You don't even know it's the right men." Wade raised his Stetson and ran one hand through his hair before putting his hat back on.

"No, and that's the plain truth." The sheriff stared at the tracks. "But why sit in the woods and watch you go by? It's suspicious behavior, enough to make me wonder. I'll follow the trail back into the woods, see where it leads."

Abby watched the sheriff and his men leave. Wade, Tom, and Abby were left alone.

Wade nudged his horse forward, and the three of them rode abreast. "I didn't go into details yet, Tom, because we just haven't had time, but someone tried to kill Abby after she came to the

M Bar S. He shot an arrow at her, tried to make it look like an Indian attack."

Wade and Tom exchanged a long look that excluded her, as if they were in charge of her protection. As if she couldn't protect herself well enough. As if, when things got bad as they were sure to do with murderers on the loose, she wouldn't probably have to save herself and both of them, too. It made Abby want to bang their heads together.

"So does this have to do with the massacre or the rustlers?" Tom looked at Abby as if he was counting all the reasons someone would want to kill her.

Wade shrugged. "I don't know. I brought her to town with me today mainly because I don't like her being alone out there, even with Gertie. I think someone tried to kill Pa and make it look like an accident. I've been trying to never let her go anywhere alone. That's another good reason she should stay with me. With the house she's got some protection. At your place she'd be out in the open all the time."

"She could stay inside at my place." Cranky Tom was not a woman's dream of a brother.

"Your house is a falling down shack." Wade sounded as bristly as a porcupine. "She'd go crazy in there before the first day was over and be outside doing something."

"Don't talk about me as if I'm not here." Abby was tempted to smack them both in the back of the head.

"I've already told my men to start leveling ground for a bigger house."

"Good for you. About time. I hope you'll be very happy living there alone."

"Shut up, Sawyer. It's for Abby. And I can afford to make it real nice."

"Better make it a tepee or she'll start insulting you just like she does my pa."

Wade smiled at Abby and she shook her head. Why did her

insults to his father cheer him up?

"It won't be a big dumb house like the one you built."

"My pa built it, not me."

"But it'll have plenty of room. I've just never bothered when it was only me and my cowpokes." Tom turned and studied Abby with eyes that surprised her. Kind eyes. They didn't go with the gruff man. "I want to talk to you about our life. I'll help you remember everything. Leastways everything I know about. And that falling down shack I'm in is where you lived. It's the house Pa built before he died. I—I—" As Tom fell silent, Abby wondered what it was he couldn't say. He'd shown no shortage of words up until now.

"You what?"

"I love you, baby sister." From the strained look on Tom's face, Abby sensed that the man didn't talk much about feelings. In that way he was far more like Wild Eagle than Wade.

Abby stared, trying to absorb the words. "I remember you so slightly and all in bits and pieces. I know I loved my white family. I imagine that includes you. I would love to talk with you about the early days of my life."

Tom jerked his chin in a satisfied nod. "Good. I told my men I might be a couple days coming home, so we can really spend some time together."

"Well, have fun," Wade said. "I'm going to be busy with roundup."

Tom did a poor job of covering a laugh. "I can't believe you're not done with roundup. . . ."

Wade kicked his horse into a ground-eating gallop, leaving Abby and Tom in his dust.

"I wonder what's the matter with him?" Abby decided to ride faster, too, rather than be left with her grouchy, confusing brother.

CHAPTER 22

"Are you still here?" Wade came into the house and his mood dropped so low he'd need to get a shovel and dig for it. And he'd been cheerful a second ago. The roundup was finally done.

"You said I could stay and get to know my sister." Tom smiled, as content and lazy as a housecat. The lazy lug was sprawled in one of the kitchen chairs watching Abby and Gertie get supper.

"Did you get done, Wade?" Gertie tapped a heavy metal spoon against a pot bubbling on the massive black stove that took up an entire corner of the kitchen.

Shaking his head, Tom said, "I can't believe you're just now done—"

"Yeah, yeah, yeah, done with roundup, I know!" Wade jerked his gloves off and tossed them onto the floor below a row of elk horns. He hung up his hat and turned back to the room, running ten fingers through his hair to smooth it, and since his hands were busy, it also kept him from strangling their houseguest. Vermin could have moved into the house and been better company than Tom Linscott.

Pa rolled his chair into the room. Wade noticed that the old grouch was getting around pretty well in the contraption. "You about done with the roundup, Wade? I can't believe you're still—"

"We're done, Pa." Wade cut him off and slid his eyes between his father and the king-sized rodent who had moved in. "I haven't been nagged like this since you tried to teach me how to rope a maverick calf."

"You were hard to teach roping?" Tom rolled his eyes heavenward. "Why doesn't that surprise me?"

"I was five years old at the time. And Pa's idea of teaching was mainly yelling his head off and swinging the back of his hand. Roping lessons aren't exactly my favorite childhood memory."

Tom looked sideways at Pa with contempt. Wade's mood further deteriorated. A stubborn, short-tempered grouch like Tom Linscott knew better how to raise a child than Wade's pa. Didn't that just beat all?

"Supper's ready." Abby brought a stack of plates to Gertie, who began scooping beef stew, thick with potatoes and carrots and onions.

Working from can-see to can't-see for all this time had left Wade thin and hungry and cranky. Right now that stew smelled so good it was all he could do not to dive headfirst into the boiling pot.

He washed up quickly at the kitchen sink, and his heart warmed when Abby brought his plate first. By rights she should have served Pa first, then Tom because he was company. Abby wasn't too interested in polite ways, and anyway, it was fitting he got the first plate. He was the only man at this table who'd worked a hard day.

"Abby and I are done with your pa's ramp now," Tom announced.

Okay, so maybe they'd done a little something.

Abby put a plate in front of Pa next.

"And we got the old buckboard out and tore out the tailgate and the seat so Mort can roll right up and grab the reins." Tom watched Abby with the affectionate eyes of a brother, a grouchy brother.

Maybe Tom had done more than just a little. Wade started eating to reassure his growling stomach that his throat hadn't been cut.

"And with the ramp done, Mort can roll straight out the kitchen door onto the thing and drive easy as you please."

Fine, they'd put in a good day, then. Big deal. How many thousand-pound longhorns had they wrangled?

Tom got his food and dug right in. "And Mort took the buckboard for a ride around the yard, didn't you?"

"Sure did. Felt great." Pa sounded happier with Tom than he ever had with anything that Wade had done since birth. "I might ride into town in a few days. Oughta build up some strength in my arms first, though. Hard to get back to working when a man's been sitting around for weeks on end."

Wade sat at the foot of the table, Pa at the head. Tom was on Wade's left with his back to the wall. Gertie and Abby took up two seats on Wade's right. Abby next to Wade. He could have reached out and touched her.

Tom might have pulled his six-shooter and killed him. It was obvious the man was watching their every move. But it was nice to know she was within reach. Now if Wade could only get a few minutes alone with her, just to talk. He'd little more than exchanged greetings with her since Tom had as good as moved into the house. And he'd thought Gertie was a tough chaperone.

He sighed and continued shoveling in the stew.

"So how soon until we can do the drive?" Pa was a mighty bossy man for someone who'd been outside for the first time all spring just today. "It's almost time now."

Wade had to quit wolfing down his food to answer. "We'll leave the cattle on the closest pastures for the next week. We'll move them around so the grass stays thick for them, try and get the yearling calves fattened up before we cut the herd and drive them to Helena."

"They should have been on those pastures a month ago." Pa glared at Wade.

"Yes, they should have, Pa. Why weren't they?"

"Because you weren't here." Pa pounded the table with his fist, but the silverware didn't jump. No doubt the man would build up to that if he kept talking.

"No, because you hired someone incompetent to be your foreman. What'd you ever sign Sid on for?" Sid was still living in the foreman's cabin, too. Wade and Chester both had been too busy to evict him. But that was no longer true. Wade could see to that right away.

"He looked good to me." Pa picked up his fork and scooped up a savory helping of stew. He clearly didn't want to take any responsibility for the mess Wade had found, so having his mouth stuffed full of food seemed like a good way to stop talking. "I was hurting. If my son had been here, if you hadn't gone off in a pout—"

"Do I eat my meal here, Pa, or should I go out to the bunkhouse? It's not enough I'm working eighteen-hour days—I've got to come in and get whined at by all of you? I swear, sometimes I feel like I've got four nagging wives."

Pa slammed his fist on the table.

"You're comparing *me* to a *wife*?" Tom roared.

Gertie let her head fall back so she could stare at the ceiling. Abby laughed.

Wade wished he could get rid of Tom something fierce. But he loved having Abby here at his table. She wasn't exactly his dream woman, true. Not one bit like Cassie Dawson to be sure. But her strength drew him as well as her reckless disregard for what anyone thought of her. He needed to learn that. She could teach him. He noted that she was sitting sideways to the table, faced toward him, with her legs crossed and in her bare feet. Beautifully arched feet. He could see her ankles again, too. She had one elbow on the table, and she plucked a chunk of meat out of her stew with her hands, sucked the gravy off it, and then ate it.

He could maybe teach her a few things, too.

"Tomorrow's Sunday. Red will be in town for church services. Anyone want to go with me?" Wade looked at Tom. He'd never heard a word about believing from Tom Linscott, and he'd never seen him in church. The man was a heathen and that was a fact.

"Waste of time, church." Pa hit the table again. Wade wondered how the furniture stood up under the assault.

"I'll take that to mean you're not going." Wade expected it. In fact, he was looking forward to a day that included neither backbreaking work nor his pa's endless complaining. But as much as he wanted a day of peace, it always hurt to think how lost his father was.

"I'd think a man who's had a brush with death like you oughta figure out where he wants to spend eternity. If you ever decide to ride along, you're welcome. I'd even let you drive us."

Pa turned back to his plate with a scowl, eating with the grace of a wild dog.

"Have fun, Sawyer." Tom's refusal hurt, too. "I want another day or two here with Abby before I head home." As annoying as the other man's company was, Wade had a burden on his heart for any unbeliever.

"I'll go." Abby reached for the biscuit plate and helped herself.

Tom frowned.

Pa muttered.

Wade smiled. "Good. Gertie, you in?"

Pa stiffened visibly. Wade could see he was worried Gertie would leave.

Gertie shook her head. "Your pa shouldn't be here alone."

Wade knew Gertie refused the offer of church to keep peace in the household. But he wasn't so sure of where her soul stood with God. Not that it was his place to judge, but Gertie spoke of God and there was a Bible on a shelf in her room. But he'd never seen her read it, and she'd steadfastly refused to attend church.

Now Wade had the whole ride to town and back alone with Abby. His mood lifted.

Wildflower Bride

"I guess I'll go, too." Tom as good as tossed a bucket of brackish pond water on Wade's mood. "If Abby goes, I'll go."

Wade's sogged-up mood fell straight back down with a splat. Tom wanted to attend church. Wade should be glad of that.

One look at Tom's smirk told Wade that big brother threw in to keep an eye on his sister, not out of any desire to worship God. Well, fine. Maybe Red would say something that would drill its way into Tom's hard head.

Wade quickly washed up and headed for bed, hoping he could get enough sleep to keep going through another day.

Thank You, Lord, for a day of rest.

CHAPTER 23

Wade came into the kitchen the next day in his best black pants, wearing a black leather vest and his newest white shirt. He'd found the clothes in his old room or he'd've had nothing after his winter in the mountains.

He should count it a blessing his father hadn't dragged his clothes out onto the ground and burned them to ashes.

After he'd worked four hours on the morning chores, taken a bath in the spring, dried off, and dressed, he'd come in to shave and comb his hair at the kitchen sink.

"I've got water boiling and your razor laid out, Wade." Gertie was at the stove scooping eggs and bacon onto a plate. The house smelled so good, Wade decided to eat first and then shave. No sign of Pa or Tom. It was too much to wish they were gone for good, though.

Abby added two biscuits to Wade's plate and set a ball of butter and a dish of preserves on the table beside him.

"Gertie tells me there is a proper way to dress for church." Abby frowned but she didn't go for her knife, so Wade took that to mean she'd cooperate. "I can see that you've put on special clothes, so I must, too, then."

Wildflower Bride

A cup of coffee was added to Wade's meal by Gertie; then the two women hurried off, with Gertie talking, possibly giving Abby pointers on church behavior. No one had ever threatened to stab anyone at church before. It might be a day to remember.

Gertie and Abby disappeared into the back of the house where they slept.

The food went down fast and Wade shaved quickly, not wanting anything like a weapon in his hands lest Tom Linscott made an appearance. Could the man be sleeping this late?

Up in his room, Wade found his best Stetson, the one with the shiny silver hatband and a small feather on the side of the band. The feather made him think of Glowing Sun—Abby—as she'd been in her doeskin dress and moccasins. She was dressing in gingham and calico now, but she wore her civilization very lightly. Wade would like to see her in that beaded dress she'd had on the day he'd found her after the massacre. He'd fallen in love with her in that dress.

There was nothing left of this day, until evening chores, except to attend church and do his best to find a few minutes alone with Abby. He held out little hope he could accomplish the latter.

Abby came out of her room seconds later, her hair untied from its braid, curling about her shoulders with the shine of sunlight. She was wearing a dress Wade had never seen before. The fit wasn't perfect, but the sky blue gingham sprigged with yellow flowers made her sun-bronzed skin and white-blond hair glow like—Wade couldn't see it any other way—like a glowing sun.

Wade pulled his eyes away from Abby when Tom entered the room. He'd only brought one set of clothes, and he didn't seem inclined to go home anytime soon and clean up. "Is it time for church yet?" He sounded like a choir boy, eager, good, sincere.

Wade wasn't fooled. "Don't you have a ranch to run?"

Tom just smirked. "Good thing I got done with roundup. . . about a month ago."

Wade had no response to that fit for a Sunday morning—or any day.

They headed for the corral. The three of them, always together.

As they approached the nearest horse pen, Abby whistled to the pinto mare grazing in the far corner of the corral. The half-wild pony perked her head up, whickered, and trotted toward Abby.

She'd done the same thing the morning they'd ridden to town to inspect the herd Red brought in. Wade had to keep his mouth clamped shut. He'd ridden that pinto. It was small, but it was mean and fast. Blue blazes as a cow pony, if you could stick on her back long enough to calm her down.

Catching the pinto usually involved a fast-moving horse and a cowboy with a lasso. Now Abby had the little stinker eating out of her hand. And she hadn't lost a finger yet.

Tom's shining black stallion lifted his head, too, in a neighboring corral. Wade had taken to moving his best mares into the corral with the stallion. Maybe he'd get some good foals out of the beast.

He'd pointed out what he was doing to Tom, hoping the man would throw a fit and go home. Tom didn't seem to care one whit.

The beautiful killer whickered at Abby as if he was being slighted and moved in his pen to the closest point to her.

The mare came to her. Abby slipped on the bridle she'd rigged to have no bit. Leading the pinto out of the corral, she mounted up bareback with one supple leap while Wade was still leading his horse to the barn for a saddle.

Abby's skirts flew about, her ankles clearly visible. She batted at the fabric impatiently. "Stupid gingham dress."

Tom's stallion was busy trying to commit murder, though his heart wasn't really in it or Tom never would have gotten leather on the brute. The stallion reared toward the sky then landed stiff-legged and crow-hopped sideways. Tom hung on expertly. "Abby, you need to put a saddle on that horse."

When Wade and Abby had ridden to town to check the cattle Red had brought in, Wade had taken this same position.

Wildflower Bride

Wade had lost.

Now it gave him pleasure to stand back and watch Tom lose.

Abby made an incredibly rude noise for such a pretty woman and started for town without a backward glance.

Wade, thinking of the dry-gulchers gunning for her, raced through his preparations and was on the trail while Tom was still letting the black work its kinks out by jumping and rearing.

Wade caught up to Abby quickly, and soon Tom came along. Wade had hoped to visit with Abby on their rides to and from church. Maybe risk asking her if she might one day have feelings for him, but with Tom along that was impossible. They set a swift pace and made it to town in record time.

The church in Divide was so new it still smelled of wood shavings, but it was painted bright white, as clean as a new penny. Wade had noticed it in passing when they'd come in for the cattle, but now he could really appreciate the tight little building the town had erected.

They tied their horses to the hitching post alongside a dozen other horses and scattered buggies and buckboards. Inside were tidy rows of oak pews. The church was packed, and Wade, Tom, and Abby stood, leaning against the back wall with several other worshippers.

Church was its usual informal affair. The service was different when the circuit rider was in town. Parson Bergstrom ran a very proper, orderly service, and Wade enjoyed that well enough. But he much preferred it when Red was in charge. Red was far more casual. He had told Wade that he was working on getting himself named a real legal minister so he could perform weddings. Wade doubted Red's style would change much, though, if he got papers calling him a real live parson.

Today he talked on one of Wade's favorite verses. It was from the first chapter of John.

"'In him was life; and the life was the light of men. And the light shineth in darkness; and the darkness comprehended it not.'"

It reminded Wade so much of the dark world he'd lived in before he found his faith. Wade found light once he understood about Jesus dying for him. But Pa still lived in that dark place. And just as the verse said, he couldn't comprehend the Light. It grieved Wade to think how lost Pa was, but Wade also battled an angry, sinful part of himself. He bitterly resented the abuse he'd taken from his father's hands. It was a battle to pray for his father. A cruel voice inside of Wade said Pa deserved a terrible afterlife for the way he'd lived this one. Most of Wade's petitions for God to open his father's heart ended with Wade begging God's forgiveness for himself, not his pa.

When the service was over, Wade, Abby, and Tom stayed to visit. Abby took a turn holding Michael, but all the women wanted to hold the baby. A fair number of the men wanted turns, too.

Wade loved Cassie and Red's children, although he'd been gone for most of little Michael's life. He knew Susannah well from all his time spent at the Dawson place, so she giggled and demanded a hug as if he was a beloved uncle.

Wade hoped Tom had really listened to what Red had to say. The ruffian had seemed to be listening attentively to Red's talk and asked some good questions. Even feeling like Tom was a leech who was determined never to let Wade and Abby be alone, Wade prayed silently for Tom to hear this truth.

Standing outside the church, Wade saw a rider galloping into town on a horse wearing Tom's brand. The rider pulled his racing mount to a halt when he spotted Tom. "I thought I'd have to ride all the way to the Sawyer place. We've got trouble out at the Double L. Big Black ran afoul of a grizzly."

Wade recognized the name of the prizewinning Angus bull Tom had brought out from Kansas City at great expense. It was the first pure black breed anyone in these parts had ever seen.

Angus cattle had only just been imported into America. They were reputed to be as hardy as a longhorn but faster growing with tender meat where a longhorn tended toward gristle. Wade was skeptical. He figured some snake oil salesman had gotten the best of Tom. But Tom had a good head for ranching, and he loved to talk cattle more than any man Wade had ever known, so he might have heard of the breed somewhere, even before he came West. Wade had seen the bull a year ago, and there was no denying he was a beauty.

"Is he dead?" Tom slapped his Stetson on his head and started for the hitching post in front of the closed general store, where his black stallion stood tied. Tom had left the temperamental horse well away from the other horses.

"The grizz had him down and tore him up, but he's got a chance. You're the best hand with hurt animals, Tom. You've gotta come and come fast."

Tom jerked his chin in agreement and started to mount up. Then he halted and looked back at Abby. "Sorry, Ab. I'll be coming around again as soon as I can." Tom gave Wade one hard glare that promised swift, brutal retribution if any harm came to his sister.

Abby watched as Tom galloped out of town behind his cowhand, but she didn't look particularly sad to see him go.

Wade was outright thrilled.

The fellowship outside the church broke up with a lot of conversation about that magnificent blue-black Angus bull. Red even led them in a prayer for the big animal.

Wade and Abby rode out of town with Wade on top of the world. "Let's not go directly home, Abby. I want to spend some time away from Pa and his bad temper."

Abby gave a harsh half-laugh. "I feel no excitement to return to your father's side."

"There's a house I want you to see out here. You think my pa's place is foolish—this is even worse. But it is beautiful."

"More beautiful than the trees they cut down to build it?"

Wade laughed. "Maybe not. And definitely not now that it's abandoned. We use it as a line shack. I think it will be safe. No one can waylay us because they can't know we'd ride that direction."

When they came to the fork in the road that led toward the old Griffin place, Wade guided his horse down the faint trail. "So are you happy to have found a brother, Abby?"

Abby looked sideways at Wade, barely touching her reins, so comfortable was she on her barebacked horse. "I remember Tom just a bit. I have felt so separated from memories of my white family here in Montana, remembering back to living in the East is even more confusing. I have this image of rushing wagons and people and noise. I need to ask Tom more about our home back there, but I can tell...he's...angry that I can't remember."

"Hurt, I think, not angry. But Tom is a Western man now. He's going to cover his hurt with gruff words."

"My Flathead father was like that. Once, my little brother fell into the water and had to be pulled out. He wasn't breathing, and for a few minutes we thought he was dead. Once it was over, my father was furious. But he was scared, I know. He just saw those feelings as weak, so he covered them with stronger emotions."

"I spent a lot of my life doing that." Wade felt the warm breeze and knew that summer had come to Montana. It came late up this high and left early, but for now it was here and he enjoyed it. The season of growth gave Wade the nerve to say more about his life before he'd become a man of faith. "My father punished me every time I showed fear or cried. Pa saw that as weakness. So I became rude and insulting and arrogant to cover my fear. I managed to pick a few fights with your brother along the way, too."

Abby sat up straight. "Really? You punched Tom?"

"Well, not so much punched him. Insulted him, threatened him, but I always had M Bar S riders with me. I thought I was being brave, but I always knew they'd step in if I got into trouble I couldn't handle."

They rounded a curve that followed a rockslide at the base of a mountain. Wade could see the clump of pines that surrounded

Cassie's old house. Wade had come visiting many times before Cassie's first husband had died. There was a twisting trail up into the rocks they'd just skirted. He would lie in wait. When Griff would leave, as he did nearly every Saturday to ride to Divide to waste more of Cassie's money, Wade would go see Cassie. "This curve in the trail marks the end of your brother's property and the beginning of the Sawyer holding."

"My brother lives near here?" Abby looked around as if she expected to see a house.

"No, this is the far north edge of his ranch. His cabin is a couple of hours away, but he holds a lot of rangeland. The house is right behind those trees. It's only a few yards from a spring that never dries up, which makes it as valuable as gold. Cassie Dawson lived here with her first husband. When he died, Pa and your brother had a dustup deciding who would own it, and Pa paid a big price to win."

"Tom is so much younger than your father. I'm surprised he'd enter into a fight like that."

"He's one tough hombre, your brother. He's a respected man in these parts. Age doesn't have that much to do with earning respect."

"And you, Wade, are you a tough hombre?"

"No." Wade laughed to even think of such a thing. "Far from it."

Wade's eyes narrowed as the chimney came into view above the trees. Smoke curled up into the sky.

CHAPTER 24

"Hold up, Abby." Wade pulled his horse to a stop. "Why would we staff a line shack this time of year? The cattle are all moved close to home for the roundup."

Abby stopped beside him. Wade saw her suspicion and her unwillingness to approach the house. He decided then and there she was about the smartest, trail-savviest little thing he'd ever seen. One tough hombre for sure. Tougher than him by a long shot.

"I know an overlook where we can study the place before we ride in." Wade turned his horse and went easily to the barely existent trail. There'd been a time when he'd worn quite a path.

That old obsession and his weakness of character haunted him to this day. He knew he was forgiven. And that forgiveness helped him keep his heart open to his father. The man's cruelty had driven Wade to believe Cassie needed saving from her first husband and Red. Wade could understand and explain away the shame. But there remained a ghost of wonder that a man could be so confused and steeped in sin and still find God. That wonder urged him on after his father's soul. Pa had done nothing worse in his life than Wade. If Wade could find God and change, then so could he.

Wildflower Bride

With Wade leading, they moved to a high, well-concealed spot with a clear view of the house. Abby rode up beside him, gasped, and pulled her horse to a stop.

Wade smiled as they looked at the ridiculous, crumbling monstrosity.

White clapboard, three full stories high, stained glass windows shining from gables in each side of the roof. A second-floor balcony above a whitewashed porch, both wrapping around the whole building.

Abby turned to Wade. "Who would built such a. . .a. . ."

"Castle?" Wade suggested. "Mansion?"

She looked back at the house. Wade saw a missing board on the porch and broken windows that made him think of a gap-toothed old crone. The paint was peeling and weathered.

"A real fool of a man built this house about. . .five years ago." Wade swung down from his horse, ground-hitched it, and leaned on the massive stone that had a lower spot just perfect for spying.

"It's only five years old? Why is it. . ." Again words seemed to fail her. She dismounted and came to his side. "Who would build such a thing then just let it die?"

"A man who had no sense. Simple as that." Wade didn't want to talk about Cassie's first husband and how he'd wasted her money and left her destitute and pregnant at the mercy of the Rockies. . .a mountain range that had no mercy.

"It's a shame, though." Wade hated to see the waste, but he wasn't going to pay the money to keep up this monument to a man's foolish pride. "It's a beautiful thing. The owner hired some guy to come all the way here from Denver to build it. Shipped the building material in, too."

"Where is this foolish man?" Abby asked.

"Where most foolish men end up. . .especially in the West." Wade settled his hat lower. "Dead."

The smoke had thinned then vanished from the chimney. No

movement in or outside the house was visible. Wade studied the place then asked Abby, "What do you think?"

"No horses around. No movement or noise from the house. And if the fire has burned out already, it was most likely left from the morning meal. I'd say whoever was in there is gone."

"Can you smell them?" Wade turned and grinned at Abby.

She lowered her brows to a straight line and reminded him so much of Tom Linscott that he smiled bigger. "The only white man I smell is you."

He smelled her, too, but she made it sound like a bad thing, whereas Wade had no objection at all. "Abby, I want to ask you something important." He barely whispered the words, afraid he'd scare her away like a half-wild mountain creature. "We haven't known each other long enough, but I want this thought to be in your head."

"What is this thought?"

"Me. The thought is me. I want to be in your head and in your heart, Abby. Because you are in mine. Could you consider letting me court you? Might the day come when you could see yourself agreeing to spend your life with me?"

"Marry a white? Never!" Her words were cutting, but she didn't back away. No, in fact, his wildflower stepped a bit closer, studying him as if there was a speck of dirt in his eye and she was considering doctoring him.

And maybe she noticed a smudge on his lips, too, because her eyes went there as well.

Wade leaned down and touched his lips to hers.

Abby jumped back, reminding Wade of a startled horse. A beautiful, golden-maned. . . He shook his head. The woman was nothing like a horse.

She kept her eyes locked on his, and the little jump was only her straightening away from him. In the silence, Wade saw her fascination and fear. He decided to ignore the fear and take ruthless advantage of the fascination. He captured her lips again, and this time she wrapped her arms around his neck with the strength of a warrior.

The kiss deepened as Wade's future unfolded before him with perfect clarity. Abby, the ranch, six sons and three daughters. Maybe they'd live here. He could restore the old Griffin place. He kind of liked the idea of all the children's names starting with the same letter. Having a name that came at the end of the alphabet, Wade was partial to *A*. Like Abby. Maybe Adam, Andrew, Alan—

Abby slammed the heel of her hand into Wade's stomach.

Staggering back, Wade gasped for breath that wouldn't come. "What'd you do that for?"

"Keep your hands off me, white man." She flashed that wicked blade right under his nose.

Okay, so maybe a little early to be actively naming their children. Finally, he dragged in some air on a high whistle, and his lungs decided they'd let him live. "*My* hands?"

By way of an answer, she waved her knife close enough to draw blood if Wade made one wrong move.

Backing off would have been the sensible thing to do. Wade never had much sense. How many times had his father told him that? "You had your arms wrapped around me like a thousand feet of vine, Ab. Don't pretend like you didn't like that kiss. You may hate that you liked it. You may be surprised that you liked it. You may even want to stab me because you liked it. But you liked it just fine."

He actually heard the air whoosh past the blade as she swung the knife. For no reason on earth, her fierce resistance to something neither of them could deny made him smile. Raising his hands like a man surrendering, Wade backed away—not too far on the narrow, rocky slope, but enough to get her to lower the weapon. He still wasn't perfectly safe. The sharp, angry, downward slash of her white-blond brows could have cut him.

"Okay, no kissing. You're right anyway. You're right for the wrong reason, but I shouldn't have taken such liberties, especially without your permission. I apologize." He noticed he still had his hands up like he was surrendering and lowered them, since he wasn't giving up at all.

She sheathed her knife. When had she found time to add a hidden sheath to this dress? Did she stay up late at night planning to stab people? "Your words mean nothing when your actions presume so much. I do not want your hands on me."

Wade suspected she did, but he didn't mention that. "Abby?" He stood silently until she quit attending to her knife and faced him.

"What?" She nearly shouted her impatience.

It was with a bit of pain he gave up his dream of a perfect, gentle, Cassie Dawson–like wife. But his feelings were stronger than the dream. "I want your permission to court you."

"No." She crossed her arms that had been warm and fluid around his neck only moments ago. Now they were a flesh-and-blood fortress wall between them.

"I want to spend the rest of my life with you."

"I will never tie myself to you." Her head shook with absolute denial. "To no man."

"What are you planning to do, then?" The woman had to use her brain if she intended to get on with her life. "Stop being angry and think for a minute. You've got no home with your Flathead people now. You're the one who told me that."

Abby lifted her chin defiantly. She'd left her hair down for church, and the sunlight of it curled and danced and swayed around her shoulders and all the way to her waist, alive and beautiful in the gentle mountain breeze. "I will strike out on my own. I will hunt for deer, skin them, and build a tepee."

"I'll help you. We can live in your tepee together."

"You will *not*." With a silent stomp of her moccasined foot and a derisive snort, she went on. "I'll make a buckskin dress instead of this foolish thing I'm wearing now."

Her dress was the color of the Montana sky behind her. It brought out the blazing blue of her eyes. Or maybe the only blazing was caused by her temper.

"You can wear a buckskin dress if you wish. You had one when I found you. You brought it along to my house. Wear it. Or make another if you want. I'll find you beads if you want to add them. Sturdy clothes make sense on a ranch. I'm not trying to change you, Abby. I think you're wonderful. I wish I had half your strength."

Her arms dropped to her sides. Her jaw went slack, too. "You do? No man should look to his woman for strength."

"Why not?"

"Because it's weak."

"Jesus said, 'My grace is sufficient for thee: for my strength is made perfect in weakness.'"

Abby narrowed her eyes. "What is this? How can strength come from weakness?"

"It's a Bible verse. One of my favorites. You're strong and independent, but that's never been true of me." Wade sighed and looked at the ground. It was hard to confess weakness to anyone, even himself. But almost impossible to do it now, to this woman. He was sure he would only deepen her contempt for him if he admitted just how weak he was.

Then he remembered her graceful arms enfolding him. That wasn't him stealing an unwanted kiss. That was the two of them stealing a kiss that shouldn't have been, not between two people who weren't committed to each other and intending to marry. Wade had made that commitment. Obviously Abby wasn't ready to admit that she had feelings for him.

"I was a bad man. I shamed myself. I failed God." He shoved his hands into the back pockets of his pants to keep from reaching for her again then raised his head to meet her gaze. "My strongest sense of failure, not that long ago, was that I'd never had the guts to kill a man."

"Killers are weak. There's no strength in taking a human life. The strength comes in controlling yourself, doing right, even when it's hard." Abby's pretty brow furrowed. At least she was listening.

"Thank you. I agree."

"Unless they need killing, of course."

Wade shook his head. He was in love with a savage. It was hard to get used to. "Before I made my peace with God, I convinced myself that all the worst things in the world were strong—drinking, fighting, lying, killing." Wade slid his hands out of his pockets and wished he hadn't because now he didn't know what to do with them. He'd never felt this awkward in his life. "I lived the life of a fool because I was trying to live up to my father's standards. He called me weak, and I did terrible things to prove I wasn't."

"Your father is a foolish old man."

Nodding, Wade said, "I can feel sorry for Pa now, but that's because I've found peace, and I've found a Source of real strength." Wade raised his eyes to meet hers. "You know, I think it was easier for me, always drunk, obsessed with evil, to find God than it is for my father. I knew I was ruining my life. I knew I needed help. But how does a man like my pa ever admit he needs help? His whole life has been lived on pride and the strength of his will and his back."

"Well, his back has failed him now." Abby seemed to have forgotten wanting to kill Wade. He was thankful for that mercy. "Maybe this weakness you speak of has finally come to him. Maybe God's strength can reveal itself with your father laid so low."

"I keep hoping. I keep trying to be a light shining in the darkness of his life. But he's thrown my words back at me so many times, I feel like I'm casting pearls before swine."

"You speak in riddles." Abby shook her head. "Light shining, pearls and pigs. . ."

Wade smiled. "We got off the subject."

"What subject is that?"

"The whole reason I was glad we'd have a chance to ride together for a few hours. You say you will refuse to belong to a white man, but then what will you do?" He fell silent. Let her think for a while.

"Gertie has no ties to a man. She has a job. She belongs to no one but herself."

"So you'll be getting a job, then? Doing what? You can stay on at our ranch. But if you're going to stay there and be with me every day, see to my food and wash my clothes, then you might as well. . . marry me." He'd said it. Point blank.

Marry me.

His heart started thumping so hard he hoped she couldn't hear it.

"Wade. . ." Abby fell silent, and she stared at him as if lost for words.

Well, that might be a good sign. "No" had come easily before. "If you can't say yes, at least say you'll think about it. We'll get to know each other. I can help you hunt your deer and skin it for you to make your dresses."

It wasn't what Wade wanted, because, though she hadn't said no, she was far from saying yes. But well he remembered that moments ago her clinging arms seemed to shout yes.

"Perhaps—I don't know. It–it's true I have no home. And we get on well together."

"We do." Wade didn't mention that she'd pulled a knife on him only moments ago. He could live with an occasional outburst of mayhem if it suited Abby.

Abby stared at him as if trying to look inside his head. What was it she searched for? A warrior's bravery? The cruelty of some of the white men she'd known? He possessed neither.

She slowly leaned forward, and Wade was so busy worrying about her refusing to even give them a chance, he didn't realize her intent until her lips brushed against his. He resisted the urge to grab her. She pulled back and gave him a sad smile.

"What is it?"

"I've lost everything that mattered to me in my village. I don't know if I can be comfortable in your world."

"We don't have to live in Pa's house." He was very close to

begging, and that wasn't showing strength. "We could set up a tepee. They're kind of cold, but I'd live anywhere with you."

"Tepees are easier to keep warm than a house. No one could burn enough wood to keep your father's house comfortable."

It was the absolute truth that Pa's house was drafty and the floors were freezing no matter how huge the fire in the three different hearths. "We could build a snug cabin." Wade felt such hope that he could barely speak. She was actually talking about what their lives might be like, where they might live. "Strong log walls to keep out the winter wind but small enough that a blazing fire will warm us up like toast."

"I do like kissing you." She didn't sound all that happy about it. "It was so with my tribal parents. They were very affectionate with each other. And I remember my white parents kissing, too. That is an important thing for a man and wife, isn't it?"

"Very important, Abby. Vitally important." Wade brought his hands up to cradle her face. "May I kiss you? Will you give me permission this time?"

Abby didn't speak.

Wade didn't move. He'd never felt such closeness to another human being as they stood there, her nose almost touching his as he waited and waited until finally he heard the faintest of whispers.

"Yes."

He cherished her with his lips for long moments. He had never dared hope for so much. Or rather he'd hoped, but he'd never dared believe.

When they drew apart, he watched her with hopeful eyes and felt the breeze waft past them. Aspens quaked and danced. The warmth of the sun shone like a halo off Abby's beautiful hair. It was a beginning. She was going to give them a chance. The kissing needed to end now. It was surely the only proper thing to do.

Then her arms slipped around his neck, and Wade didn't have a proper thought in his head.

CHAPTER 25

"Honey, can we have lunch before you start stabbing the barn?" Red knew he was whining, but the woman was obsessed with that knife.

Cassie pursed her lips and scowled at him.

Red fought a smile. He knew she liked to scare him. So he did his best to act scared and begged sweetly. "I promise we can work all afternoon on making you dangerous."

"Red!"

"Oops, sorry, I mean *even more* dangerous. You're already a real tough character, sweetheart."

She smiled as if he'd offered her roses.

"But I'm starving after the ride home from church."

With a little huff, she stuck her nose right up in the air as if she were put upon mightily. "Well, all right, but don't expect me to help you with your chores."

Covering a sigh of relief to not have Cassie risking her life in the barn, Red nodded, perhaps just a bit too frantically. "That's fair. And with the herd culled, I don't have that many cattle to check. I can manage without your help."

Her eyes narrowed a little.

He gulped. "But it won't be easy. I'll miss the extra pair of hands."

Cassie had come a long way helping with chores, but often as not she did the chores with Michael on her hip and Susannah clinging to her skirt. It scared Red to death to watch her try to feed Harriet—his very angry sow—with the children in hand. To be fair, she hadn't set the barn on fire in months.

"I'll help you get the meal on, too. I won't leave it for you to do alone." Red saw that sweet smile break out on her face again.

She looked like every kind of fragile there was, with her ivory skin and her endless dark hair. The roses on her cheeks might have been painted on like those on a china doll. Her brown eyes, circled by lashes as long and soft as a mink's fur, shone with kindness. It was just the plain truth that the woman didn't have a mean bone in her body, no matter how hard she tried to be fierce. He still thanked God a dozen times a day for the precious gift of Cassie.

They ate quickly, and the young'uns, worn out by the long ride home from Divide, went down for their naps without a whimper. Well, Susannah did a little bit of screaming, but Red could see her heart wasn't in it. Michael fell asleep in his mashed potatoes.

They went outside to get to work. Red with chores, Cassie with stabbing the barn. Red stayed for a few nervous minutes, scared to death she'd somehow throw the knife and stab herself. But she was getting purely good. The knife stuck in the barn wall nearly half the time now, and the rest of the time it splatted against the barn and fell to the ground. He decided it was safe to do chores. Except for one little problem.

"I just can't get the bull's-eye, Red." Cassie went to dislodge her knife from the barn wall, right near the ground. It always hit there. Always. "How come I can't get more accurate?"

Red lifted his Stetson from his head and ran one hand through his unruly red hair before clamping his hat down to corral the mess. He studied the circle of charcoal on the red barn with the single black dot in the center. It was the pure undeniable truth.

Cassie had never made a single knife hole in the bull's-eye. Red could see where Belle and Emma had stabbed it up pretty good.

"Um—have you tried aiming higher? Maybe if you aimed at the top of the circle—"

"But that's admitting failure." Cassie crossed her arms and pouted like Susannah did when the cookies ran out. "I want to hit what I aim at."

Red deftly plucked the knife from her hand and pulled her into his arms. When he'd kissed all the pouting out of her, he rested his forehead against hers. "Have I told you lately how proud I am of you?"

Her eyes, which had fallen shut—as if the kiss had robbed her of her thoughts—flickered open. That warm gaze made Red feel like the richest man in Montana. And it was the truth—he was. Not a whole lot of money, but rich in the things that endured.

"Thank you. I love you, Red."

"Aw, Cassie, honey, not half as much as I love you." Wrapping his arms around her waist, he lifted her to her toes. Then her toes must have curled, because she was all the way off the ground. The richest man in Montana swept his ten-thumbed, knife-throwing wife up into his arms.

She giggled, and he silenced her with his lips.

Red, with a herd to check and a cow to milk, chickens to rob of their eggs and a hungry, killer sow and her ten piglets to feed, enticed his beautiful, precious Cassie into following him into the hay mow and forgetting all about throwing her knife for a long, long time.

While they passed an hour together, it occurred to Red once, briefly, that he should tell Cassie a baby was most likely on the way. She was as innocent as a babe in these matters. But he knew she'd be excited. But then he lost all track of his thoughts, too, and never got her told.

Red whistled while he milked in the dark. Rosie, his black and white Holstein who'd come West with him, kicked him to punish him for being late, but despite her best efforts, Rosie couldn't knock the smile off his face.

"We'd best have a look at that house." Wade's voice was hoarse as he pulled away from Abby, his wildflower.

She was acting purely tame just now.

He'd made his point with this kiss, and the few before. Well, honesty forced him to admit it had been more than a few. Abby was going to marry him. He wasn't going to take no for an answer.

He had a sweet feeling the answer wasn't going to be no.

With a grin, he slid his arm around Abby's waist and turned to study the old Griffin place.

Abby leaned against him.

The happiness filled his heart until it barely fit in his chest.

"I don't"—she cleared her husky throat and went on—"see any sign of life."

Wade smiled down at her. "And if there's someone sleeping there, just passing through, we'll let 'em stay."

Abby nodded then stopped cold.

He felt the tension in her body. "What is it?"

"We've had a jailbreak, cattle rustling, and a massacre within days of each other."

Wade couldn't find a single smile now. "And someone tried to kill you."

"Or you."

"Or both of us." Wade knew his woman well.

"And these bad men must be staying around here somewhere."

Wade studied the obviously recently occupied house then looked at the wild woman he'd taken up with. "How good are you at sneakin'?"

The tension left Abby's body, and she smiled and arched one brow. "I'm *real* good."

"With the stand of trees around the place, we should be able to come up on it quiet, get a closer look. I don't think anyone is there, but they may be back, so we'll be careful."

Nodding, Abby said, "Let's get the horses to a place they can graze and go check that house."

∽

Sid stirred the cool ashes and looked sideways at Boog. "It's time we get that gold."

Boog grunted as he sipped the last of his coffee.

Paddy couldn't sit still. He was on his feet, moving, twitching, pacing. "Good, good, let's go. I'm tired of sitting."

"We can find the gold and get back to the ranch. With me out as foreman and so many of the men fired or new, Wade doesn't seem to realize you and Harv are gone. Why would he? He never knew you were there."

Harv sat forward with a groan. A lazy man, Harv. Never stood when he could sit. Never walked when he could ride. Sid would be glad to get rid of his edgy, bad-tempered, do-little saddle partner.

Boog froze, so suddenly, so completely, Sid was instantly alerted.

"What?"

Boog hissed at him and slashed a hand inches from Sid's face. No one talked or moved. Finally, Boog said, "Someone's coming."

Sid grabbed for his gun.

Paddy let a tiny giggle escape. His eyes shone with a hunger to shoot someone.

Sid knew of the four of them Paddy was the one who had a real appetite for murder. The rest could kill and had killed their share. They were hard men in a hard land, and Sid prided himself on being willing do to what he needed to do. But only Paddy smiled while he emptied his gun.

They turned to cover all approaches, guns cocked, eyes peeled, every sense alert.

Chapter 26

The sharp *snap* sounded loud as a gunshot.

Abby looked back and scowled at Wade's clumsy foot, now square on a brittle stick. Then, on her belly on the ground in her foolish gingham dress, she continued sliding through the tall grass, hunting shadows to use like hiding places.

Thank heaven he'd let her go ahead. Abby stopped her forward progress when she caught herself falling back into that kiss. What had come over her? Why had she let Wade, a white man, hold her close and tempt her into believing she could be happy in his world?

He had let her go ahead with her sneaking, though. With a twinge of pleasure, she thought of how Wade had not only admitted she was better at sneaking; he'd admitted she was a master. She knew it chafed him to admit she was the better woodsman, but he'd done it. It filled up a strange, empty place in her heart to be respected like that.

Wild Eagle had certainly never conceded that she had skills superior to his. He had seen her ease her way up close enough to slap the children during games of hide-and-seek. When she was young, she was the best of all the children when they'd played at hunting. But older girls weren't included in the hunts. She'd known she could help feed her family, but Wild Eagle's pride had been too great to consider letting her come along. Instead he'd forbidden her to go along on the hunts. Ordering her to stay in the village where a woman belonged.

But truth was truth. Wade knew who was better in the woods. Now he stood there, not moving, and managed to be noisy. Abby wanted to growl at him through the knife she had clenched in her teeth. He grinned at her, apology and admiration in one sweet smile.

She looked away to keep her attention on her sneaking. Easing forward, using swells in the ground and the waist-high prairie grass to conceal her as she inched forward.

That sound bothered her but she didn't turn back. If there was anyone in the house, Wade had very possibly alerted them.

She heard another sound, much softer, the hush of iron on leather, and turned back to see Wade pull his Colt revolver and take careful aim at the house. Abby was approaching from the south. There were two windows on the ground floor and more on the second. She knew that if Wade saw someone at those windows, he'd cover her.

Protect her.

Kill for her.

Die for her.

Abby hesitated to admit it, even to herself, but she felt the same. She knew a fraction of how much Jesus must have loved her because of the determined look on Wade's face and the deep resolve she felt in her heart to protect him.

God, please let me be worthy of his love. Please help protect us both. Please, please, please don't make it necessary for either of us to kill or die.

Abby inched forward. The moving grass would hopefully be mistaken as the blowing wind. She prayed.

Wade aimed.

God, please hear the praying and forgive the aiming.

❦

Nothing. No movement. No sound. Minutes passed. Then half an hour.

Sid could see Paddy twitching with impatience. Sid wasn't far behind. He hadn't heard a thing but that one snap of a twig. "There's nothing out there, Boog."

Boog turned narrowed eyes on him, and Sid froze as surely as if he'd been hit with a high mountain blizzard. Those eyes threatened slow, painful death, and Sid had no doubt Boog could deliver that death without a qualm if it meant protecting himself.

Sid hunkered down again. His partner was woods savvy, no doubt about it. But there were animals in the woods, the wind gusted, trees sometimes had a branch snap and fall to the ground. He dropped his own vigilance and let Boog play his game.

Suddenly Boog, already taut with acute attention to the area in front of him, stiffened even more, raised his gun, and took careful aim.

❦

"Abby, get down!" Wade felt an icy chill of fear, and he had to stop her.

She dove low, invisible behind the waving grass.

Silence stretched.

Wade stared at the seemingly empty house. What had scared him? Had God Himself given that warning? Or was Wade reacting to some subtle movement at the window? A faint noise? Or was he scared of his own shadow?

There was nothing.

Then there was Abby. She hadn't gotten down at all. She'd continued forward, so smoothly that Wade hadn't noticed until she emerged from the grass right next to one of the south windows and pressed her back against the house. With a look at Wade, a smirk it had to be, she moved closer to the window as she silently took her knife from between her teeth and eased her head past the glass.

Wade couldn't believe she'd ignored him.

No, no, no. Please, God, don't let her die.

Waiting for a gunshot to end Abby's precious life, Wade snapped. He screamed loud enough to impress Abby's Flathead family at a medicine dance and charged from behind the tree. Waving his arms and shouting, he rushed the house. He could draw their fire if someone was inside.

"Wade, no!"

Boog, on his knees crouched low, suddenly reared up and brought his rifle to bear. Then he twisted his body. "Get down!"

His low, harsh order drove the three other men to the ground.

"Not a sound. Nothing! Flathead hunting party!" Boog had barely whispered, but the terror in his voice was enough to make Sid obey him without question. Boog was scared right down to his belly, and Sid had never seen the man scared before.

Not one of them moved. Sid didn't think he even breathed.

Seconds passed. Minutes.

A whisper of noise reached Sid, and he stared through the grass that surrounded their camp.

They'd been riding since before dawn, pushing hard after the gold. He'd let Boog and Harv rest at the Griffin place while he'd ridden in for Paddy and made an excuse to Chester for why they'd be gone a couple of days.

Pushing as hard as four hardened men could, they'd brought spare horses and switched saddles to keep going. They'd made good time and now were near the mountain valley where they'd killed off those interfering Flatheads.

There shouldn't have been anyone here. It had been long enough for the larger tribe to come, bury their dead, and return to the Bitterroot Valley. But Sid saw through the tall grass a group of warriors. These riders, ten in all, were armed with rifles as well as bows and knives, unlike those they'd attacked earlier.

If Boog had fired a shot, the Flathead warriors would have been all too ready to fight. It was one thing to come upon a sleeping village with only a few armed men, none of them bearing rifles. It was another to take on ten adult warriors. That was certain death.

The hunting party was far enough away and upwind. They didn't notice Sid and his gang. Pure luck, because Indians were a noticing kind of people.

Each rider had a deer slung over his saddle as the group rode up the mountain, undeniably on their way into the valley Sid had just cleared of Indians.

His fury grew in direct proportion to the terror he'd felt a few minutes ago.

The Flatheads vanished into the trees that covered the mountainside most of the way to the top, before it dropped off into the lush green bowl of a valley that hid Harv's gold.

Once they were gone, Boog turned to Sid as if he needed to work his fury off on someone. "Cleared out that valley, huh? It don't look like they're gone. It looks like there're more of 'em than ever."

"Just shut up! Give me a minute to think!" Sid saw Boog's mouth close, but it wasn't because Boog obeyed. No one ordered Boog around. So Boog must've decided to be quiet for reasons of his own. Probably doing some thinking for himself.

"Let me shinny up there," Paddy offered, his eyes bright and sick to think they could massacre again. "I'll find out how many there are. I'll count 'em and come back and report."

"They'll have lookouts, you fool!" Harv sat up, looking after the hunting party. Then, as if he'd heard something, he began scanning in all directions.

Sid controlled a snort of disgust. Of course there might be more. He'd been scanning from the moment he'd spotted the riders.

Harv was a bigger fool than Paddy.

"Let him go." Boog wasn't suggesting; he was ordering.

Sid should have called him on it. Sid was the boss. But calling Boog on anything could lead to shooting trouble, and neither of them dared fire a shot. It'd bring those Indians right down on their heads. Sid jerked his head toward the upward slope. "Go scout, Paddy, but watch your back."

Practically drooling with excitement, Paddy slipped into the heavy woods surrounding them and vanished.

Paddy was good, Sid had to admit it. If anyone could get up there, get the lay of the land and come back alive, it was the Irishman. But once he was there, if anyone was stupid enough to open fire on someone, it was Paddy. Then they'd all die.

"I've gotta make sure he doesn't do anything stupid." Practically growling, Sid stood, crouched down, and headed after Paddy.

"No one there."

Abby's terror exploded in something she felt a lot more at home with—rage. He'd run out into the open to draw fire to himself. She grabbed Wade's shirtfront and yanked so hard he stumbled forward. "You could have been killed! Are you crazy?"

Suddenly she wasn't pulling him forward. He was coming forward all on his own. His arms went around her waist and he lifted her right off the ground. "Why, Abby Linscott, you were afraid I'd get hurt."

"No I wasn't!"

"You care about me."

"I'm tempted to hurt you mysel—*mmpph!*"

Her words were cut off by Wade's lips, and her terror, flipped to rage, now flipped by this kiss to. . .to. . .God help her. . .to love. She'd been unable to resist kissing him on that overlook, but she'd held back her heart. But now it tumbled free, falling into love.

No, no, no, God. I will not be in love with this man.

It was already too late. She wrapped her arms around his neck until she might have strangled him.

The man didn't show a speck of fear as he kissed her senseless.

Then, so suddenly she thought her head might be spinning, he put her down and pushed her away. "You behave yourself, woman." Then a ridiculous grin spread from ear to ear on Wade's face. "Kissing me like that isn't proper until we're married."

Married! Married? No, no. She'd be in that stupid house with his grouchy father, surrounded by the horrible whites for the rest of her life. Wearing gingham, of all disgusting things. She'd reached for her knife several times today planning to slit the skirt up the sides like her doeskin dress, but so far she'd controlled the urge.

Abby was back to wanting to kill him. She dove at him, but he was too fast for her.

He rounded the house and was up on the porch. The only reason he got away was because her knees were wobbly from that kiss. He pulled open the mansion's door and vanished inside.

She went charging after him. Yes, he needed strangling, but she was sorely afraid if she got her hands on him again, it would be to grab another kiss.

Sid caught Paddy just as he clambered up the last of the steep rise.

Paddy poked his head over the canyon rim then jerked it back, flipped over on his back, and slid down a few feet. "Injuns, hunnerds of 'em."

Sid took one look at Paddy, his eyes wide with fear. He lay flat on his back, his arms spread a bit as if to cling to the ground.

Sid inched upward for his own look.

"Careful." Paddy's voice was hoarse. Paddy was a man who liked to kill, and he never seemed too afraid of dying himself, like the danger was a drug he was addicted to. But right now, Paddy found no fun in what he'd seen.

Slowing down, Sid picked a spot where a gnarled pine grew

only a few feet high, its long needles lying on the ground. He lifted his head the bare minimum over the ridge, slowly, careful to make no sound or sudden movement. And he saw.

The entire Flathead nation must have moved into this valley.

Before, there'd been a handful of tepees and only a few adult warriors, no guns that Sid had found when scouting. Now there were dozens of armed men. Tepees filled nearly the whole bowl-shaped valley that topped this mountain, lining both sides of the rushing stream that poured down from a higher mountain to the north.

They'd waited too long and now they were locked away from the gold. Maybe forever. The tribe might leave for winter hunting grounds, but this was no hunting party. They'd put up their tepees. Women stirred pots. The hunting party was already skinning the deer they'd brought in. Women were tanning hides, probably from yesterday's hunt. Children shouted and played along the water's edge. They were here to stay.

Sid turned just as Paddy had and lay on his back, his plans tasting like ashes in his mouth.

"There's no chance we'll find the gold. Not until they move on." Paddy said what Sid already knew, and Sid had a strong urge to slam his fist into Paddy's mouth until he shut up forever.

The gold was out of reach. Sid realized in a moment of perfect clarity that he now needed the M Bar S more than ever. He needed a place nearby to stay until the Flatheads moved on. His defeat turned to bitter determination. "Let's go. Let's get back to Sawyer's and finish what we started. This tribe'll move on come cold weather and we'll come for the gold then."

"It looked like a permanent settlement to me."

The only reason he didn't put a bullet in Paddy right then was the noise it'd make.

Sid started back to Boog and Harv fast, because one more stupid word from Paddy and even a village of Flatheads coming down on them wouldn't stop Sid from shutting Paddy's mouth permanently.

❧

"No one here. But someone's been here recently." Wade jabbed a finger at the pile of tin cans. The jagged edges of the lids looked like they'd been hacked open with a knife. "He cleared out. Nothing left. If a drifter went out hunting for an hour or two, he'd probably leave his gear behind."

"Maybe."

Wade smiled up at her. He could still see that anger when he had been reckless. Now why would a little woman who claimed to hate him care one speck about a man getting hurt?

She didn't hate him half as much as she wanted to. Of course, he'd suspected as much when she'd let him kiss her silly up on the mountainside while they watched the house.

God, I can see she cares, and I can see she doesn't want to. Help her. Help me to say the right thing. Ease her grief for her Flathead family and her hurt at their rejection.

Wade realized that Abby's rejection by her Indian world was far too similar to his rejection by his father. It was no wonder they had turned to each other. Two people alone in the world.

Despite the fact that Wade was now back at his father's house, Wade felt adrift. Abby could be his anchor.

"Enough adventure for one day. Let's be on our way." Abby crossed her arms and glared at the huge front room they stood in. A stairway swept in a graceful arc upstairs on one side of the room. Doors opened off the other side of the mammoth entrance. "This house is even more ridiculous than yours. I didn't think that was possible."

"My father's house, not mine."

"Wade"—Abby let up her glowering for a second—"how can you stand the way your father treats you? Why don't you stand up for yourself?"

"The Bible says to honor your mother and your father."

Pursing her lips, Abby studied Wade. "I know this verse, but

I don't think God asks us to let our parents heap cruelty on us. Do you?"

"I've struggled with that, for a fact. What do you think?" Wade prayed silently, wishing she'd have the answer to the question of his life—how to honor his pa.

"I think that we can honor our parents from a position of strength."

Considering, Wade shrugged. "But what does that mean, exactly?"

"Do you feel God urging you toward calm? Or do you want to fight your father, demand his respect the only way he understands, with your own anger?"

Wade crossed his arms. "I've never been able to demand a thing from Pa. He's always treated me badly and I've never found a way to change it, short of leaving."

"Then why did you come home to him?"

"You were there. He sent for me. He was dying, Red said. I had to obey that summons. I didn't expect to have to live with the old coot. I expected to be on hand to bury him."

"And now it looks as if he'll live, probably for years. Are you going to accept that and let him pour hatred on your head for the rest of your life?"

She sounded so kind. Not like his Abby at all. A fighter by nature and by upbringing, she was more likely to go for her knife than to coax cooperation out of anyone. That was one of the things Wade liked best about her.

"So you think I should. . .what? Yell back?"

Rubbing her mouth as if considering just that, finally Abby said, "You'll do as you see fit. But I don't believe it's honoring your father to let him get away with the things that make his son hate him. In fact, you're standing quietly by while your father commits a terrible sin."

Stunned, Wade could only stare at her. His heart, already soft toward the whole world, softened even more. "I think you're right."

Wade's spirits rose as he thought of his father and the hate that festered in him. It was indeed a sin for Wade to patiently accept his father's sin. He smiled. "Say, when we're married, we can build a tepee and stake it out anywhere you want. We can go up into the mountains and live off the land."

"We won't be getting m—mar—married." Abby closed her eyes tight then seemed to force them open. "I will bind myself to no white man."

Wade had to admit that was a long, long way from "I do." But he had time. "We can start out with a small tepee then work on a bigger one when the babies start coming."

Abby turned and stalked toward the door.

Before she reached it, Wade, in a strange mood of utter confidence that he was going to change Abby's mind, with God's help, followed, tormenting her for her own good. "I'm a crack shot. I'll keep us in deer meat. You can plant a garden. . . ."

Abby moved faster across the thin stretch of overgrown weeds, away from the house and him.

"I saw a really nice valley not too far from the cabin where I spent the winter. . . ."

Abby vanished behind the clump of trees, heading for the horses.

Wade decided to shut up before she pulled that knife again. And he ran in case she stole his horse.

He thought he was getting to know his little wife-to-be pretty well.

CHAPTER 27

Mort met them at the front door roaring. As usual.

"Old man—"

Wade caught her around the waist and dragged her past the beast at the door. "Ignore him, honey." He grinned at her.

She could have taken a swing at him, but it just didn't seem worth the effort.

"You know we need to work on that reflex you've got to pull your knife every time you're the least bit aggravated."

Looking down, Abby saw she had it in her hand. Reflex must be right, because it hadn't been a conscious choice. But she'd been raised to loathe and fear whites. Nothing she'd seen had convinced her to forget that raising. Except she'd learned she liked kissing one white man very much...too much. "I don't need to work on it at all. I'm very good." She tucked her weapon away.

"I didn't mean that." Wade had her nearly through the front entrance area, heading toward the kitchen. Any part of the house where they wouldn't have to listen to Mort's growling. Honestly, the man belonged in a cave. "I meant—"

"You called her 'honey'?" Mort followed in his chair. They never should have put wheels on the man.

MARY CONNEALY

Abby was going to lose the hearing in her ears if that grizzly man didn't stop roaring like a trapped bear.

"Pa, did you have a good day?" Wade talked pleasantly, quietly. Abby doubted if Mort heard him. She also doubted that Wade cared if his pa heard him. "I took a ride after church. Abby 'n' I needed some time alone. With the roundup over and the men free on Sunday, it was the perfect time."

"Sundays free, bunch of nonsense." Mort rolled his chair forward.

Abby heard the gentle rolling of the wheels on wood as Wade dragged her into the kitchen. Gertie was pulling a roast out of the oven.

Wade was planning to widen a few doorways so Mort could get around more easily. Abby was tempted to ask if he could narrow a few of them so she'd have a place to escape.

Wade dropped Abby's hand and rushed forward. With a quick grab for a thick towel, Wade protected his hands then relieved Gertie of the massive roasting pan. Abby had to admit that growing the cattle and keeping them nearby was far handier than going hunting. Except of course Wade had spent nearly every waking moment since he'd been home working with his cows, so how much easier was it, really?

Wade slid the black pan, with its domed lid, onto the top of the massive iron oven. He pulled off the lid, and a faint sizzle got louder. Steam that smelled like a lovely dream billowed from the pan.

Abby realized she hadn't eaten since breakfast, and now the sun was low in the sky. "Did you expect us for the noon meal, Gertie? I never thought of discussing it with you."

"No, Wade said you might be late. If he could get your brother to go away."

"Oh, he did, did he?" Abby's head swiveled to look Wade in the eye. He'd planned their little afternoon ride, then. Most likely with the intent of stealing a kiss. The truth was Abby had never been touched by a man in such a way. Wild Eagle had walked with

866

her, but they had been mindful of the proper distance between an unmarried man and woman. Wade had no such consideration. Or rather, he'd spoken of propriety then ignored his own dictates.

"He never mentioned it to me until after church."

Wade helped Gertie get the roast and vegetables out of the pot, and Gertie went to work turning the drippings into her wonderful gravy. Abby knew she should try to learn how Gertie made that delicious concoction, but it was hard. She'd tried once and nearly destroyed the meal. Quitting seemed wiser, but Gertie said she needed to learn.

Wade was taking a deep breath, bent over the meat, inhaling the savory smell. He straightened and grinned at Abby, unrepentant. "I didn't think you'd go, and I had almost no hope of running off your leech of a brother."

Mort bumped into Abby with his chair.

Startled, Abby jumped out of the way.

"Pa, you're a menace with that thing. If you don't be careful, I'm going to hang a bell on it so we hear you coming." Wade stepped to Abby's side, gently caught her upper arm, and pulled her out of the doorway when Abby would have preferred to snarl at the rude old man.

She wondered if their talk at the Griffin place had taken root. Wade exchanged a look with her and she knew he was thinking the same thing—how to handle Mort.

Abby gave him a barely perceptible shrug. The decision had to be Wade's. She would have been crushed to her soul if either of her fathers had spoken to her the way Mort spoke to Wade.

Abby saw sorrow in Wade's green eyes as if he pitied his father. Pity she could maybe manage. But never would she allow this old man to run roughshod over her.

Mort rolled to the head of the table then slammed his fist so hard a glass on the table toppled over. "Get supper on the table, Gertie. I'm hungry."

Gertie began bustling around.

Wade went to a cupboard on one side of the sink and took plates out.

Abby reached for her knife.

Looking over his shoulder, Wade caught her eye and winked at her, as if he knew she wanted to attack.

That calmed her for some reason. She went to the cupboard, shoved Wade aside, and took over his job.

Wade laid out the heavy pottery plates carelessly, noisily, then went to the side of the table closest to the wall, around the corner from Mort's left hand, and sat. Once he was settled, he turned to his father. "Pa, do you want me to stay on here?"

Turning with her hands full of silverware, Abby looked from Wade to Mort, bracing for a flood of cruel words.

Mort, busy centering his plate, froze. Then slowly his eyes went to Wade. "I don't—"

"I know what you're going to say." Lifting a hand, Wade stopped his father with a motion. "You don't need anyone, least of all me. You are ashamed to call me your son. I'm a coward, I'm lazy, I'm clumsy." Wade said the words in a singsong chant as if they bored him to death. "What else, Pa? I've heard it all before."

"You've never been—"

"Know this, Mort Sawyer"—Wade cut him off with a hard voice Abby had never heard before—"I am ready to leave. I don't suppose I've convinced her yet, but I have hopes of persuading Abby to marry me."

"Marry her?" Mort's white brows arched to his hairline.

"Marry me?" Abby set the cups on the table with a sharp *click* of glass on wood, the fistful of forks clattering against them.

"You're getting married?" Gertie set a platter on the table, heavy with roast beef, ringed with bright carrots and white potatoes and whole baby onions.

"Like I said, she hasn't agreed yet."

"That is an understatement." Abby crossed her arms and glared. "In fact, I've told you—"

Wade cut her off. "Whether or not I can convince you doesn't change the fact that Pa treats you terribly."

"He treats everyone terribly. I'd feel left out if he was nice to me."

"I don't treat anyone terribly. If you'd all act right, I wouldn't have to say a word."

Wade snorted.

Abby exchanged a dark look with Gertie.

"I can put up with a lot, Pa, because I see it as my Christian duty to honor you. For me, that means not letting you waste away in your bed for the last few pitiful months of your life stewing in hate."

"Now, Wade, Mort's getting better." Gertie put a bowl of gravy on the table then helped spread the utensils and glasses.

Abby chipped in setting the table.

Even Mort pulled his glass and silverware into place.

"Well, that's the problem, Gertie."

"What?" Mort roared. "Me getting better is the problem?"

With a kind expression completely at odds with his words, Wade said, "If you were going to linger a bit then die, I'd stay on for sure. Least I could do."

"Wade, shame on you." Gertie fetched a loaf of bread, still warm from the oven, and set it on a breadboard next to the roast. She added a tub of butter and a pitcher of milk.

"But since you seem to be surviving pretty nicely, and in fact it looks like you could live ten more years, I'm not going to stay on"—suddenly Wade's calm voice began to darken as his pleasant expression faded to grim anger—"if you don't find a way to get a civil tongue in your head and treat Abby and me with some respect! I'm not going to put up with it!" Shouting, he pressed both hands flat on the table and pushed himself up from his chair.

"You've been a tyrant all your life. I've talked with you about my faith and you've thrown it in my face. So fine, make that choice, cut yourself off from God. But do not think for one moment"—Wade slammed his fist on the table—"I'm going to live my life with your hate and spite! Decide now, Pa." Wade's hand slashed only inches from Mort's face. "Right now. A man with no self-control is a weakling. So have you got any control over your mouth or not?"

Silence reigned in the kitchen.

Wade breathed as if he'd just completed a long race up a mountainside. His eyes flashed with angry fire.

For the first time, Abby saw a man she'd think twice—or three times—about making angry.

Wade's breathing slowed, and he lowered himself to his chair. With a huge, razor-sharp knife, he began carving the roast.

For a while Mort was frozen, his face beet red. Mort's eyes, as green as his son's, locked on Wade's and they held in a battle of wills. Abby suspected Mort had a thousand horrible things to say, but Wade's crack about his being a weakling had obviously started a war in the old man. Finally, Mort ate in sullen silence.

No one spoke a word through the entire tense supper except an occasional "Pass the bread" or something else necessary to complete the meal.

As they finished Gertie's hot apple crisp, swimming in cream, Wade finally spoke. "It'll do no good to give me an answer, Pa. Your promises mean nothing even if you could bring yourself to make them. The next time you're deliberately unkind to me or Abby, or Gertie for that matter, I'm leaving. Chester is a good foreman. You'll be fine without me." Wade rose from the table and began gathering the dishes.

As he slipped past Gertie at the foot of the table, Mort spoke. "You're right." Mort sounded tired and defeated.

Wade turned, a wary look in his eyes. If his father had threatened him, he wouldn't have flinched, but Abby thought Wade actually looked a little scared of this version of his father.

Abby had certainly never heard this tone. From his reaction, Abby guessed Wade had never heard it either.

"I'll try. That's the best I can do." Mort's hands gripped the arms of his wheelchair until his knuckles turned white.

Abby held her breath. She'd never expected Mort to give an inch. She still didn't really believe he would admit he was wrong about anything.

"I've been wrong about everything. You've done a good job with this ranch since you've been back. I'll watch my mouth, and you can take over the ranch I broke my back building out of nothing." Mort jerked the wheels backward to roll away from the table. "While I wither up and die in my room." Mort nearly ran over Abby as he left the room.

Good survival instincts served Abby well as she stood and pulled her chair out of the way for Mort's exit. She watched him leave, and then her gaze went to Wade's. "Maybe you should go after him?"

The door to Mort's bedroom slammed so hard Wade's Stetson fell off the elk antlers by the back door.

"Better let him cool off." Gertie looked after Mort, regret plain on her face. "You were pretty hard on him, Wade."

"Yeah, and he's been pretty hard on me all my life, and you, too, Gertie. Why'd you put up with it all these years?"

A frown turned down the corners of her mouth, and from the lines on her aging face, Abby was sure frowning was something Gertie had done a lot in her life. Why had Gertie stayed? Why had she put up with Mort's vicious temper?

"I stayed to protect you." Gertie's eyes brimmed with tears. "I knew how he was to you, but I couldn't stop him. But I could be here and comfort you after it was over."

Wade looked at Gertie in silence.

The silence was too much for Abby. "You couldn't stop him? Why not? Did he hit you, too?"

"No, he's never laid a hand on me. Oh, I got the same yelling as everyone else. . .but never a fist."

"Well, I'd say you did a poor job of protecting Wade if that was your goal."

Wade gasped. "Abby, Gertie was always good to me. No one could control Pa."

"Two adults in a household." Abby sniffed. She liked Gertie, but the woman had failed Wade just as Mort had. "One of them an abusive tyrant, the other a kind and decent woman who stands by while the tyrant beats a child. You could make a case that the tyrant is out of control, even crazy. But the decent adult has no such excuse. To me, that makes the one who stands by more evil than the one who swings his fist."

Gertie lifted her chin and glared at Abby. The kindness that was usually there had vanished. "I did the best I could."

"She wasn't to blame." Wade set his plate down as if he needed his hands free to defend Gertie from Abby's unkind truth.

"The best? The best you could do is cower in the kitchen and come out with hugs and sympathy afterward? A true defender would throw herself between the child and the tyrant."

Gertie turned her face aside as if Abby had slapped her. "I was too afraid to protect the closest thing I'll ever have to a son. You're right."

"Being right in a family of whites isn't hard." Abby stepped away from the table and turned her eyes on Wade. "I can't sleep in this house of grief and anger tonight. I can't even breathe. I need the wind blowing to cool my body and the night sounds to soothe me to sleep."

"It's not safe out there, Ab."

"And it's safe in here? This home is a haven from danger? I don't think so, Wade. All the danger is locked inside with you. Your father built a fortress to keep happiness out."

"Now, Abby, just settle down and we'll talk about this."

"The time for talking is past." Abby turned toward the door.

"Don't go out." Wade rushed across the room and literally threw himself in front of Abby, blocking her from the door.

"Get out of my way."

"Calm down. It's dark and damp. Don't just go storming off.

We'll talk this through like two reasonable adults."

"You want to talk, you come outside."

"No." Wade got a stubborn look on his face that reminded Abby of how he'd stood up to his father. "You stay in. You don't get to win all the fights, Abby. A man is to be the head of the house. The Bible says so. You're going to mind me, and that's the end of it."

It was a lovely night for a walk in the woods. And Wade knew he was going for one when Abby snarled at him, dodged past him as spry as a mountain goat, and slammed the door on her way out.

He had to go after her, but first he needed to comfort poor Gertie. "She's wrong."

Shaking her head, tears welling in her eyes, Gertie said, "Maybe. I did what I was able to do for you, Wade. But we both know it wasn't enough. I was a coward. I still am one." Gertie turned and left the kitchen.

Wade was left alone. The silence was so profound he could hear his heart beat in his chest.

They'd all left him. It came to Wade then that he'd been alone all of his life. His pa had never been with him, not in any sense of affection or support.

Gertie's arms had comforted him, but only when it was too late.

Now here was Abby, a woman he wanted to marry and bring into his home, into his heart. She didn't want him, either.

Oh, she was drawn to him. Wade was sure of that. But it was against her will. If he married her, would her untamed ways just be another kind of loneliness? If he did convince her to marry him, would he spend his life bending to her will? Was that God's vision of a good marriage? His trying to keep her happy, hoping and praying she wouldn't dash off into the night and return to the life she loved far more than she would ever love him? Leaving him alone again.

She'd just this minute made that choice, and now she was in danger. There were dangerous beasts, four-legged and two-legged, outside this house. He'd lived in fair harmony through the winter out there, with a mountain and the bitter cold seemingly bent on killing him five times a day. He'd liked the barren life. The time with his Bible had been good for his soul.

And now he was back with Pa and Gertie and more confused than ever. Not about his faith. He needed the comfort of God more than he needed his heart to take its next beat. But what was he supposed to do with his life? What did God want for him?

Wade walked to the door and went out onto the back step, now a ramp sloping down to ground level on the left and a section that went straight ahead for several feet so Pa could roll right onto the buckboard. Wade went to the end of that section and sat down, his legs swinging, staring out into the night.

He prayed.

As the silence of the night embraced him, he saw a light in the bunkhouse and another in the foreman's cabin. Everyone was abed for the night. . .or would be soon. Except Abby, his Glowing Sun, who was no doubt using that confounded knife of hers to kill and skin a buck so she could build her own house.

He was an idiot to hunt for her. She was tougher than he was by far. Yes, she'd been caught by white men, twice. So she wasn't invincible. She'd been kidnapped once last year when Wade had found her while on his way to help Belle Tanner—it had still been Tanner back then, before she'd married Silas—with her cattle drive and once this spring.

But the honest truth was she'd been running from the first men, already free, and she'd been slashing away at the second man. She'd saved herself both times before Wade ever got there.

Dew had formed on the ground, and he could see footprints leading around the house as clearly as if they'd been outlined by lantern light. With a sigh, he followed them. He'd just talk to her. Find where she was sleeping.

Wildflower Bride

She'd said, *"All the danger is locked inside with you. Your father built a fortress to keep happiness out."* He looked at the house he was right now rounding and knew she was right. He could never ask her to live in this house. So he'd make sure she knew he was ready to leave. To live anywhere as long as she was with him.

Shoving his hands in his pockets, he followed her trail toward a wooded area to the north of the house, hoping she'd just gone in there to fume and cool down. He stepped into the woods and felt an arm go around his neck and a pointed blade jab into his neck.

Either someone was trying to kill him, or. . .he'd found his woman.

Or both.

"Go back inside." Abby needed some peace. She needed time to think.

"I was hoping that was you, Ab." Wade's voice worked, just barely, through her hold. He didn't try to escape. In fact, after they'd stood there a few seconds, the grip she had on him seemed less like an attack and more like she'd grabbed him to give a hug.

A hug with a knife involved, but still—

"I meant it when I said I wouldn't sleep in there tonight."

"Okay, I'm not going to try and argue. I just wanted to know where you were going to stay. I want you to be safe."

"As if I was safe inside." With a sniff of disgust, Abby let him go, sorry she'd ever touched him. Her arm was warm where it had wound around his throat. Holding her knife felt foolish. She would never harm Wade. Never.

"There are different kinds of safe, Ab. You're right—so right—about my family being an unhappy one. I don't think you can blame Gertie any more than she blames herself, but in the end, yes, I grew up in a sad place."

Abby walked deeper into the woods. The ground was rocky, but that was so everywhere in this part of Montana. She needed to find shelter but didn't worry about it. The mountains and forest would always shelter her.

She found a shattered pine tree, its stump nearly four feet across. It had snapped about ten feet up, and the massive top of the tree had fallen and was long dead and bare. The ground, piled high with the fallen needles, was soft as a feather bed. Sinking to the ground, Abby leaned back against the tree. She could sleep here as well as anywhere.

But Wade needed to go away first. Instead he slid down the trunk next to her. The tree was big enough that there was plenty of room for both of them, especially with Wade sitting so close their arms touched. "You know I care about you, Abby, don't you? I want you to stay here."

"And if I can't?" The needles gently scented with pine seemed to ease into Abby's bones. There was peace for her in the wild places.

"Then I'll leave with you. That home holds nothing for me but responsibility, Christian duty. I needed to come home and see to my father, but I've done that now. I thought for a time we could stay and be happy here, but now I doubt that. We'll go somewhere else. We can leave now, tonight if you want. Go into Divide and have a marriage blessed then head for the mountains, in the direction of your high valley. Build a small cabin, raise a garden, and hunt for food. We don't need the ranch to survive. We've both proved that."

He just would not stop jabbering about marrying her. She couldn't say yes, yet she found herself unable to say no. So she changed the subject. "You really lived in the mountains last winter?"

Wade nodded, and Abby had to look close in the dark night. With the trees overhead, even the bright moonlight and blazing stars struggled to penetrate the darkness, but Abby's eyes adjusted quickly and his sincerity was unmistakable. "I found an old miner's shack, or maybe a trapper lived there. It was probably smaller than your tepee."

"And you liked it there?"

"I—I was contented there. I needed some quiet to get over—"

It took a moment for Abby to realize he wasn't going to continue.

"To get over what?"

The sound of Wade slowly inhaling melted into the soft rustle of the wind and the cry of a hunting owl. Insects chirped in the night, and the leaves overhead sang their own quiet song.

Long after she decided he wasn't going to answer her, Wade finally spoke. "To get over—the—the sight of you—riding away from me with Wild Eagle. It broke my heart."

Now it was Abby's turn not to speak. Abby thought of how Wade had saved her from those men last fall when he was headed for work on a cattle drive for Silas Harden's family. He'd abandoned that job and stayed with her, tried to persuade her to come back with him to his white world. When she'd refused, he'd taken her to her home. And on the way, they'd come to care for each other. Abby thought of these things in the silence.

Wade reached down and took her hand, fumbling for it a bit in the dark. He pressed her knuckles against his lips.

She liked it so much it terrified her, so she wrenched away. "I can't do it, Wade. I can't bind myself to you. I've seen too much of the white men, all bad."

"No, not all bad. Not me." He moved suddenly, rising onto his knees. He caught her shoulders and turned her, pulling until she knelt to face him. "You trust me, Abby. I know you do. And my father and the trouble that goes with him doesn't have to be part of choosing me. I will go with you wherever we have to go to find a peaceful home, full of happiness. Say you want that. Please, at least tell me there's a chance. I need to hear that."

She hesitated to speak the words that he seemed to believe would bring him happiness. But there was no way for them to be happy with her dislike of all his people.

His lips settled onto hers. In the darkness, she hadn't seen him lowering his head. For this reason only, she didn't duck away. And then she couldn't. She couldn't end the kiss that she knew was all wrong for both of them.

He drew her closer, all his loneliness pulling at her own.

At last he raised his head. "You know we could find a way to be happy together, Abby. Your kiss tells me the truth even if your words deny it."

"Oh, Wade. . ." Abby rested one palm on his face. He had whiskers, bristly from neglect. She remembered her father would come in cold from checking cattle and scratch her cheek with them and she'd giggle. She'd loved her father, a white man.

"Just a chance, Ab. I'll give you all the time you need to decide if you can live here with me, or we can leave here right now if you can't bear life in this house. I'll walk away with you, not even go inside to say good-bye. We'll find a preacher and say our vows to God. I'd pledge myself to you forever."

"You offer to give up your family for me?"

"You'd be my family. We'd begin our own." Wade kissed her deeply. "Have children." The kiss came again, longer this time.

He turned then and sank back down to lean against the tree. He pulled her down, tucking her to his side. "You don't have to answer me now. I know you're still confused and grieving and angry. But say you'll give me a chance, please. Here or in the mountains or anywhere else you'd like to go."

Knowing it was a mistake, Abby rested her head against Wade's broad shoulder. Through the trees, she could see the lights in the big house. She hated that house. It represented all that was wrong with the whites. Its foolish size and the unhappy people who inhabited it. Now she was forcing Wade to do something he might regret all his life. It wasn't yet time to leave. "I will give you this time you want so badly, Wade."

His arm tightened around her, and his sigh ruffled her awful yellow hair. The light in Mort's room extinguished. Moments later, a light farther to the back of the house came on, in the room where Gertie slept. There was still a lantern burning in the kitchen; the light spilled out and illuminated the bit of backyard that Abby could see. Gertie had left the light on to guide Wade home.

"I will stay here and try to adjust to this world while I decide if I can risk a life with you."

A soft kiss on the top of her head made her smile and admit the truth. "I, too, felt my heart break when I rode off with Wild Eagle. I did not want to leave you."

His other arm came around her, and he hugged her until she thought she might have to pinch him so she could breathe. Then he laughed and pulled back enough that they could see each other. "Do you really want to sleep out here tonight? I could go in and get you a blanket."

"No, I'll come back in. But there may be times when I need to get outside, to clear my head and breathe clean air and think without the noise of your father ringing in my ears."

"I was dead serious about leaving if he speaks rudely to you again. If he is unkind, just tell me and we'll go. I give you my word."

Abby nodded, thinking he'd just put yet another burden on her. Now if his father was cruel, which he was bound to be, she would have to keep it secret unless she wanted to send Wade from the house.

They stood and Wade took her hand, his fingers sliding between hers. "Are you ready to go back in?"

She would never be ready, so why wait? "Yes."

"Do you mind if we pray before we go? I need to ask God to be with both of us."

"I need that, too." Abby took Wade's other hand, and he quietly said many things that were in her heart, but not all.

He couldn't begin to imagine all. And she couldn't begin to tell him.

CHAPTER 28

I'd like to go see Belle, Red." Cassie had Michael on one hip, and Susannah was clinging to Red's right leg singing as the two adults washed the supper dishes side by side in their new, bigger kitchen.

Cassie had tried to stop him from making it too big. Heating a large house was too much work. But Red had a stubborn streak and a bit of a temper to match his red hair. He'd pushed for more space when he'd found out Michael was on the way, and Cassie admitted she liked the children having their own room.

"Now, Cass, honey, we've been doing so much running lately I'm not seeing to the cattle like I oughta."

Cassie grinned at him. She could get the man to do anything and that was a fact. It was a power she tried not to abuse. Michael slapped her on the face and she probably deserved it. But she was determined to get her way. "We've only been to Belle's once."

"Yes, but she came here once, too."

"Not really. She and Emma went off with you. I want to talk with her about why I can't get the hang of knife throwing." It was a plain fact that no amount of practice seemed to improve her skill.

"It sticks in the wood almost every time now. You're doing great."

"But it's always too low."

Red opened his mouth.

"And no"—she wasn't listening to any more of his nonsense—"I'm not going to just aim higher."

"Why not?"

She could be stubborn, too. "Because—" It pinched to admit the truth. "Because—" So she rushed it out in one long, frustrated shout. "Because I've already tried!" She slammed a metal pot onto the counter with a loud *bang*. "I still can't hit what I aim at."

"Oh." Red subdued himself after that and picked up the pot to dry it.

"It doesn't work." She pouted. Pouting was one of the best things she'd learned since she'd gotten married. She loved the way Red teased her out of her bad mood. She could hardly sustain the down-turned lips when she thought of how sweet he was while he cheered her up. But that really wasn't why she'd started this. "Please, Red."

Susannah hollered, "Pick me up, Papa!"

"We've been to the Tanner Ranch."

"Harden, Red."

"Right, right. Sorry." Red nodded. "The Hardens have visited us here. I went hunting for Wade. Then later I had to track down the rustlers. I took the herd to Divide. We went in for church. Why, we've been gone more than we've been home. Good thing we got the roundup done early. I can't believe the Sawyers are just now finished." Red shook his head as if it was incomprehensible.

Cassie had felt sorry for Wade with the roundup still ahead of him. He hadn't been home, so it wasn't his fault, but none of the other ranchers would see it that way. "I didn't get to go with you to hunt for Wade."

"You were with Belle. I thought you liked Belle." Red swiped a bit of drool off Michael's chin with his shirtsleeve. Michael, content on Cassie's hip, swatted at his papa and giggled.

"I didn't get to go hunt the rustlers with you."

Red gave her a very dry look. "You're saying you *wanted* to be part of the posse?"

It was all Cassie could do to maintain her pout. She was really crazy in love with her husband. "I'm just saying you feel like you've been out and about a lot, but I haven't been. I want to go see Belle. A woman with a baby on the way needs the company of other women from time to time."

She stamped her foot and almost felt ashamed of herself. Reminding Red of the coming baby was very dastardly of her. He was so excited about it and so kind to her. She could barely lift a finger around the barnyard these days.

Susannah stamped her little foot and giggled.

The reminder about the baby he'd had to tell Cassie about earned her a very long, sweet kiss. The man was a marvel the way he figured out a baby was coming.

"I'm wondering which of us this'n'll look like. We've got a matched set now. Maybe we'll have a redheaded little girl or a dark-haired boy. I can't wait, no matter which it is." He kissed her again until Michael started trying to poke his little fingers between their lips.

"I can't wait either, Red. And I want to tell Belle about it."

"She probably knows."

Jerking back from him, Cassie narrowed her eyes. "How would she know?"

"I told Silas."

"Before you told me?" Cassie felt herself blush. How *had* Red figured it out?

Red just laughed in her face. "Yep, and he probably mentioned it to Belle."

She really did need to wheedle his secret out of him. The symptoms she knew of—a round belly and lots of kicking—came quite late.

"Red, I insist we go see Belle. I want to visit with her, and I'm not letting up until we do things my way. Especially now that I'm carrying your child." Cassie fluttered her eyelids a bit and rested one hand on her flat stomach. She'd win now. Red was just too sweet; he wouldn't be able to resist giving in.

"Nope. We can't. I've got too many chores."

Cassie's mouth fell open.

Red hung the last pot on the hook beside the kitchen sink then set his dish towel aside and used one finger to push up on her chin to close her mouth. "And that's final."

Michael grabbed at his finger.

"Pick me up, Papa!" Susannah put both her tiny feet on his big boot and started bouncing up and down.

Red swooped Susannah into his arms and lifted her to the ceiling.

We'll see about final. Cassie narrowed her eyes and considered which of her womanly wiles to use on her husband to get her way.

Before she could bring out her arsenal, Red tucked Susannah onto his hip. Then he plucked Michael out of her arms, bent over, and kissed her with a low smack on the lips. "How about next week? Give me that long to catch up on a few things, move the herd to better pastures, and clear the deadfalls out of the spreader dam. I'll get the Jessups to ride herd and we'll go and stay awhile so you can work with Belle and get all your female talkin' out."

Cassie grinned until she thought she might laugh out loud. "Next week would be fine, Red." She said it in her best submissive wife voice. The one Red loved.

"You're such a good, obedient little wife." He kissed her again as a reward. As if he didn't realize she'd gotten her way, as usual. "I love it when you pout, honey," Red whispered.

Startled, Cassie pulled back and glared at him.

He laughed and turned away, bouncing the children around the room, singing a silly, lilting Irish song about wearing green, while Cassie contemplated whether she was controlling her husband or he was controlling her.

Since it didn't matter, and she was going to see Belle regardless, she didn't contemplate it too long before she snatched Susannah away from him and joined in their play.

∽≫⚬≪∽

Sid pushed the men hard to get back.

Boog had seemed to be completely well, but he was pale and tight-lipped by the time they got back to the derelict Griffin house. Harv was practically asleep in his saddle.

Sid and Paddy decided to split up so no one would connect them. Paddy would ride in first, then Sid. Boog and Harv would stay away for one more week.

As long as that girl was alive, she could recognize Harv. Maybe without the beard he could get by, but Sid wasn't going to risk it. And if Red Dawson had a reason to come to the ranch, it would all be over.

The trail from the Flathead valley back to the M Bar S was brutal. It should have taken two days to cover, but Sid didn't want the men to make note of his absence. Lots of the hands had taken off for the day, with Wade announcing Sundays would be for rest from now on.

As Sid hitched his horse at the old Griffin place in the early hours of Monday morning, he felt the whole weight of the long weekend. First pulling Harv out of jail, then riding for the high valley, and now coming home. And all for nothing. They had to leave the gold behind. He ached until it felt like someone had taken a club to him.

He gave Paddy fifteen minutes to get to the ranch well ahead of him. Sid would barely beat the sunrise home. He stood watching Boog and Harv unsaddle their horses as Paddy rode off toward his bunk.

"We've got to finish this." Sid got out the makings for a cigarette.

Boog lifted his saddle off his gelding's back. "Yep. Someone's gonna identify Harv sooner or later."

"We'll do it this week," Sid said as he dumped the tobacco and rolled the fine paper, counting down the time until he could head back.

"Let's hit 'em all at once." Harv rubbed his chin. Sid could see his hunger for revenge against the wild woman. "We tried to make it look like an accident before, but why bother trying that again? With that woman dead—the only one who saw me—no one will be able to prove we had a hand in the killing."

"A lot of the hands rode off to town yesterday morning." Sid remembered the exodus when he'd gone in to get Paddy. "They went to church with Wade. That leaves Mort home alone with only his housekeeper. He's vulnerable then. We can do it next Sunday."

"Then we'll waylay Wade and the woman on the trail. Finish it in one stroke." Harv pulled the bridle off his horse and swatted his rump. The horse trotted away with a thud of hooves on grass in the small corral Mort kept up at the Griffin place.

"But let's keep our eyes open this week," Boog said as he rubbed hands full of grass on his gelding's sweat-soaked side. "If we have a chance, catch one of them out alone, we'll take it, thin the herd a little."

Harv snorted. "Herd? A cripple, a woman, and a coward. No herd to thin there. I'd like to keep that woman alive for a while, though. If I caught her out alone—" A chuckle broke up his big talk.

Sid drew on his cigarette. Harv always talked big, when he wasn't whining. He was a weak link in every job they pulled. If he hadn't grabbed that girl to begin with, no one would be able to identify him now. Harv wouldn't have cuts as good as shouting his identity. Sid did his best not to glare at the fool. He mentally repeated that Harv held the secret to a hidden shipment of gold that had been lost in that valley.

Even with the gold in mind, Sid was afraid of what he'd say. Deciding he'd given Paddy enough time, Sid tossed his cigarette butt on the ground, climbed into the saddle and spurred his weary horse toward the ranch. No roundup to face this morning. Maybe he could steal a few hours of sleep.

He'd stolen a lot bigger things in his life and paid no price.

CHAPTER 29

It almost pained Abby to admit it, but Mort was trying.

It was almost killing him. Watching Mort try to be nice was funny. He quit most of his barking. Not all, but Abby didn't say anything about the times he snapped at her and Gertie. And he was doing really well with Wade.

They sat at the table enjoying a fairly civilized supper of fried chicken. It was delicious, but Abby missed the smoky taste of a wild bird cooked over an open fire. Turning the spit was one of the first jobs she'd been allowed when she lived with her Flathead family.

Mort sat eating as if he were starved. He'd regained some muscle in his arms from rolling his chair around, and he spent enough time outside these days that he had lost that sickly pallor.

Wade always discussed the ranch thoroughly with his pa, and Mort seemed hungry for details about the preparation for the cattle drive and how the hands were doing. Wade listened to Mort's opinions, too, and seemed to respect his father's ranching skills.

When the daily report was finished as well as the evening meal, Abby reached for Mort's plate to stack it with the others for washing, but his words stopped her.

"Have I been doing well enough to suit you, Wade?" Mort turned to his son.

Abby let her hand sink back to her lap, afraid Mort might be getting ready to snap. She'd seen the uncertain hold he had on his temper at times.

"It's been a good week, Pa. I hope I've been doing well enough to suit you, too."

"You're running things right. I can see that. Or hear it at least. I can't get out like I'd like to. I know, from this week of watching. . . well, I'd like to say. . .to say. . ." Mort gave Abby a leery look.

There'd been a couple of times when, if Abby had wanted to, she could have tossed the last kerosene on the fire and burned up this family. She knew Mort feared she'd mention that now. But she had no wish to break the family apart. If that happened, it wouldn't be because of her. She'd leave alone before she left with Wade and bad feelings.

"I can—well, it's been hard. Harder than I've ever imagined. And—what you said about my own pa awhile back, I can see now how my ma protected me from him. He was angry all the time, but Ma could handle him. I saw her take his anger on herself when he'd come home mad. She'd always shoo me away. I know he hit her. I think—" Mort fell silent. "I'm sorry. I can't promise I'll never lose my temper again. But I'm going to try." Mort refused to meet anyone's eyes as he quietly rolled himself out of the room.

Wade stared after him, a longing in his eyes that Abby's heart hurt to see.

"Go after him," she whispered.

Wade looked up, hopeful and scared. "Should I?"

She nodded, feeling like she might be sending Wade away from her by encouraging him to choose to draw closer to his father. "He may be ready to talk for the first time in your life. Don't miss it."

Wade turned and smiled at her. "You're right." He came

around the table and kissed her, a hard, fast smack. "And I *am* going to marry you." He hurried after his father, following him into Mort's converted bedroom.

Abby and Gertie looked at each other in wonder. Then Gertie pressed a shushing finger to her lips, and they eavesdropped shamelessly while they cleaned the kitchen.

Wade watched his father swing himself from his wheelchair into an overstuffed leather chair that he'd always used behind his desk. It was huge and comfortable. Wade had liked sneaking in here to sit in it when he was little. Until the time he'd been caught.

Pa knew how to teach a lesson.

"You're getting good at that, Pa."

Pa looked up, startled. Then he leaned back and stared down at his useless legs. "You really think I can live ten more years like this?"

Wade shrugged. "Or twenty. I don't see why not. You seem healthy enough to me."

The tight line of his jaw was so rigid Wade was afraid his pa's teeth might crack. "I've always prided myself on being tough."

"Pride's a sin, in case you need a list."

A humorless laugh escaped Pa's throat. "I probably do need a list. I think I've done everything exactly backward in my life. And nothing more backward than the way I treated you." Pa raised his eyes until they met Wade's.

"I think this is the first time in my life you've ever looked at me without anger or contempt." Wade shook his head, and it was only his faith in God that kept him in the room. He wanted to run outside and cry.

"I think those are words God would use to judge me at the Pearly Gates. An awful thing for a son to say such about his father, that he'd never known a moment of kindness. My duty to you is to protect and love you. I failed at the second, and at the first, well, you needed someone to protect you from me."

"I agree...God would judge you harshly for that." Wade wasn't inclined to pretend a lie. He prayed silently for wisdom.

Give me the words to speak, Lord. Give me love in my heart that he beat out of me years ago.

His stomach twisted as he realized just how fully he hated his pa. Yes, an awful thing for a son to feel for a father. God would judge Wade for that.

They faced each other in silence.

"I'm not going to throw out a bunch of words now that I spent my life destroying. I'm not going to cheapen a father's love by claiming it for you, because I don't think I know what it means."

Sick to his stomach that, even now, his father couldn't say, "I love you," Wade turned to leave. The room, the house, the ranch. Everything. He couldn't stay.

"I will tell you this, boy." Pa drew his attention and Wade watched the defiant old man square his shoulders. "You're a better man than I am."

Wade gasped. He couldn't have been more shocked if his pa had slugged him in the stomach. In fact, that wouldn't have been a shock at all. "You mean that?"

Pa nodded. "I've known it since before you left. Since you got ahold of your drinking and carousing and came back here to work. I could see then you'd finally grown up. And grown into something better than I could have ever created with my yelling and hitting. I was ashamed that Red Dawson had done something I could never do."

"It wasn't Red, Pa. It was God."

Nodding silently, his father took a long time to respond. "I know that, too. But it's easier to see what's there in front of my eyes and not try to figure out some distant God that I've never seen the need for."

"Everyone needs God."

"Not me. I never did."

"You needed Him more than anyone I've ever known."

"How can you say that?" Pa shifted in his chair, his eyes furtive, not meeting Wade's now.

"Because you're so strong."

Pa jerked his chin up. "In the kitchen you called me a coward. That's a weakling. And you were right. Only a coward hits someone littler. A child." Pa rubbed his face as if he wanted to scrub away twenty years of bad memories. Or maybe, if Grandpa Sawyer was as mean as Pa, the bad memories went back much further.

No way Wade could think to deny that. "A strong man— measured by Western standards—can carve a good life out of a hard land, and you've done that. No one on earth would call you anything but strong." Struggling for the right words, Wade continued. "But that kind of strength needs to be tempered. A man that strong needs to—to put limits on himself. Or accept the limits God puts on a man."

"Like the Ten Commandments."

"Except Jesus gave us new commandments, did you know that?"

His brow furrowed. "I've never heard they threw out the ten."

"Jesus gave us two. Love God; love your neighbor. That's it. He said that if you followed those two, you'd be keeping all the rest."

"Instead I've broken them and all the rest."

"You've as good as stolen land from Tom Linscott. I told him we wouldn't run cattle on his spring anymore."

"You what?" Pa's eyes flashed, and he lurched forward. Then he caught himself. "Yes, of course we can't do that. I always knew where my land borders were. But I'd used those springs before Linscott came in and bought them."

"And you've coveted those springs, and the Griffins' water, and—"

Waving one massive hand, Pa cut in. "I've coveted everything.

Things I didn't know I wanted until someone else had them. My neighbor's land and water and wife."

That one almost flashed Wade's temper back to life as he remembered the things his pa had said about Cassie. The way Pa had tried to force a marriage against Cassie's will.

"And none of it had a thing to do with loving God or your neighbor," Wade snapped. "You didn't accept that there was any limit on right and wrong. And there was no one around strong enough to back you down. So you became a tyrant."

"Red Dawson backed me down, didn't he?" Pa looked up sheepishly, as if he was ashamed of that fact.

"Good thing he did, Pa. Good thing Tom Linscott came in and stood up for himself. You were beyond the laws of God and man before those two stepped in. I hate to think what would have happened if you'd have gotten your way and brought Cassie here. It makes me sick to think of it. That's why a strong man needs some power over him—God—or terrible things happen."

Pa looked reduced by more than the wheelchair and his weight loss. His spirit looked crushed. "Things are going to change, son."

"Like I said earlier, I'll decide if I stay or go. No assurances from you will make a bit of difference if you start in on me or Abby again."

"That's as it should be. You *are* a better man than me." Pa reached for his wheelchair and rolled it a bit, back and forth, staring at it as if there were answers in those moving wheels.

Maybe they were the answer. "Maybe God struck you down to get your attention."

"I don't think much less would have worked." Pa looked up from his chair, and Wade saw longing in his father's eyes. Longing for something better between the two of them.

"How about this, Pa? How about I fetch my Bible in here for you? For the first time in your life, you've got time stretching out empty in front of you. Days and days of idleness. Spend them reading the Bible. Hunt for the Ten Commandments and the two.

See if you can find Someone stronger than yourself. Someone you can respect enough to give Him charge of your life. You'll be a better man for it."

Pa nodded. "I want you to stay, son. I want to try and fix things between us. I promise you I'm going to try."

"It's more than I ever expected to hear from you." Yet it wasn't enough. Even though it seemed hopeless, he wished Pa could find a way to love him. "I'll be right back."

Wade ran upstairs and was back in Pa's bedroom in minutes. He handed over the heavy book. Wade had bought it new from Bates's General Store in Divide. Muriel had helped him pick it out. He'd nearly worn it out in the last couple of years.

Pa accepted the book, and then an almost-smile quirked his lips. "So you really gonna try and get that little wild woman to marry you?"

Wade did smile. He couldn't stop himself. "Oh yes."

"So have you asked her yet?" His pa caressed the Bible while he spoke in a friendly way to Wade.

It was already more of a miracle than Wade had ever dreamed of. He should have started yelling at his father years ago. "I mention something along those lines just about every day."

"And what does she say?" Pa ran his hand over the leather.

"As a matter of fact, she usually pulls her knife on me. She's done it so often I've kinda quit keeping track."

Pa chuckled. Then that wasn't enough and he laughed out loud. "I liked that girl from the moment she walked in this house and started threatening me."

"We're going to hit the place next Sunday," Sid whispered to Paddy. "We'll let Wade and the girl, plus all the hands, ride off to church. Then we'll just go in the house and finish Mort."

Paddy snickered as he nodded. "Then waylay the rest of 'em on the trail home."

Nodding, Sid stared at Wade, riding the herd, cutting out the older steers to drive to market.

"We'll be pushing cattle to Helena after next Sunday, so if we don't get it done, we'll have to make that long drive."

Paddy narrowed his eyes. "If you're taking over the ranch, you'll need to make the drive anyway, boss."

"No, I won't. I'll order the hands to go. I'll stay here and they can bring me the money."

"You'll trust this crowd to bring the money home?" Paddy stared at the half-trained cowhands Sid had so carefully hired for their incompetence and lackadaisical attitudes, so when the moment came for him to seize the ranch, he wouldn't have much resistance.

Sid snarled. He didn't, now that Paddy mentioned it, but it burned to have Paddy point out something so obvious. "Okay, then I'll go along."

"Better to let Wade take the drive. The girl will be left home with Mort. Maybe we go on the drive, finish Wade off on the way home. Lots of places for accidents to happen on a cattle drive. Leave Boog and Harv to handle Mort and the girl."

Sid rode his horse, pushing a docile, fat-bellied bunch of longhorns along toward new pasture, and considered the plan. No plan was perfect; some risk was involved in all of them. But dry-gulching Wade on the trail was no sure thing. There wasn't a good spot to shoot from cover. And walking straight into the house to murder Mort was as cold-blooded as Sid had ever been. They'd have to kill Gertie, too, because she'd be a witness, and it bothered Sid to kill the old woman. Her cookies reminded him of his ma's cooking. It made him sick to think of someone killing his ma just because she was standing beside a man who needed killing.

Maybe the drive was best, leaving the women and cripple to Boog and Harv. "We'll wait." Sid looked around to make sure no one had ridden up on his flank. "Unless I find a likely chance. We don't have to kill 'em all at once, you know. We could space it out.

Wildflower Bride

But I want this done. We've been too careful. It's time now to act."

"It's past time." Paddy had to wipe his chin.

Sid could see he was so hungry to hurt someone he was drooling. Just the kind of man Sid needed at his side.

CHAPTER 30

Abby tied the apron on around her clothes. It was a good idea to wear it. How many times had she gotten her soft leather dress stained while she worked over a cooking pot? It was a fact, though, that gingham made her skin itch. She missed her doeskin, the easy movement, the split skirt that made riding so easy. Foolish whites and their fussy dresses.

Even so, she was beginning to adjust to the ways of the white man. With disgust, Abby realized she was getting soft. Remembering Wade's confident announcement that he was going to marry her, she'd gone to ridiculous lengths to avoid being alone with him all week. She needed to figure out what was the matter with her that she could hate his kind and his skin color and his ways. . .but still like the man.

Wade wasn't like the rest of the whites. Abby knew that clearly enough. She forgave herself for her fascination because of that. She might have even considered marrying him if they could get away from the ranch and live somewhere in the mountains, away from her Indian family and his white world. He was an especially kind man—look at the way he grinned when she threatened him with her knife. Although, truth be told, she was almost certain she could never really stab him.

When had she become such a weakling?

"Time to punch down the rising of bread, Abby. Do you want to do it and shape the loaves?" Gertie smiled, and Abby felt another pang of guilt. She'd come to care about this elderly woman, too. When they worked on the house or the meals or the garden, Abby felt almost like a daughter being taught by her mother. It helped shake loose memories of her own white family, and with the memories came love. Yes, she'd loved her family. They were good people, and they'd tried to take care of her until the sickness had made that impossible. Not all whites were evil. She knew that.

The smell of the yeast and flour made her mouth water. Another thing Abby had begun to like—the easy food. Yes, there was hard work to making a meal, but the choices were plentiful and the garden was yielding a rich bounty of vegetables. The beef supply never ended, and there were chickens and eggs, ham and bacon, milk and coffee laced with thick cream. And sweets. Gertie was a hand with the sweets.

Punching the soft, puffed-up mound of dough with more force than necessary, Abby admitted the disgusting, unthinkable truth. She was starting to like this place.

Mort rolled himself into the kitchen, and Abby almost cheered up. Finally someone she really couldn't stand.

Mort was trying, Abby could see that. But he was failing—a lot. More this week than last. The man had a short temper, and he liked things done his way and right now.

So far, Abby had followed Gertie's example and kept the hard words Mort said to them from Wade, not wanting to cause the final break between Wade and his pa. Especially since Mort *was* trying. He only yelled his orders part of the time these days.

"Get me a cup of coffee and some of those gingersnaps, Gertie." Mort wheeled around the table to his place at the head.

Abby was working near that end with the dough, but there was plenty of room for the old tyrant.

"Why didn't one of you women bring them into my room?" Mort swept his hand across some flour that scattered too close to him.

Abby started kneading harder, pretending the dough was Mort's yammering face.

"You used to care that I was stuck back in there alone, Gertie."

Abby felt her temper rising. But was it really Mort, or was she panicked because she felt herself weakening to the white world?

"But now you'd let me starve to death if I didn't come and fetch every bite I eat."

Bam! Abby slugged the dough with her fists, her jaw clenched shut.

Mort jumped a little, and his eyes narrowed. "You act like a savage. You need to learn some woman skills if you're going to stay around here."

"And you're like a whining dog that used to sneak around the edges of our camp." She punched the dough again. "Worthless, begging for food but never doing the few little things a dog can do to help."

"You got something you think I should do, say it. You think I like sitting in my room all day reading Wade's book?"

Abby felt a pang of remorse over her temper. She knew Wade wanted his father to come to his own faith in God. After his outburst the other night, Wade had gone back to being patient with his father. But his father had behaved himself with Wade.

The man really didn't want his son to leave. And wasn't that a good thing? Wasn't that loving? Wade finally had a father who loved him after all these years. Abby didn't want to ruin that, and she knew she could with a word. She'd tell of Mort's behavior and announce she was leaving, and Wade would come with her. He'd follow her into the rugged mountains to her valley.

She longed to go there and live. With her Indian family gone, she'd be able to have the place to herself. All alone. Forever. No, she couldn't bear that much loneliness. She knew herself well enough to admit that. But with Wade, maybe they could make a life up there in the thin air among the mountain peaks.

"I do know something you could do, old man." Abby jammed her fingers deep into the dough.

Mort's eyes widened as she swung her hands toward him. He snatched his coffee cup out of the way just in time.

She slammed the dough onto the table in front of Mort. "This takes no brain nor skill nor legs. Knead this dough for two more minutes. Then shape it into loaves."

Mort shoved his chair back two feet from the table. "Woman's work." He might as well have spit when he said it. "You think I have no pride left?"

"Now, Abby. . ." Gertie had endless patience with this old curmudgeon. Abby knew confrontations distressed the older woman. If she hadn't known she had to leave sometime, she might have kept quiet.

Abby put both fists on the table and leaned down to Mort's face, his teeth nearly bared. She kept her jaw clenched so she wouldn't shout the next words. "If you want to be useful"—no, she wasn't shouting, more like hissing, which still wasn't good—"there are things you could do. You might not think they are worthy of your great manliness, but they would help. And there are more *manly* things we need done. There is a chair we set aside in the pantry because the leg is loose. You could repair that. Surely that is a manly pastime."

Mort's face was turning red. His breathing was loud. Abby had a sense that he, too, was struggling to control himself. He hadn't forgotten Wade's threat. And yes, he'd lashed out a dozen times this week. But Gertie had jumped to do his bidding and he'd calmed down. There'd been no drawn-out string of insults and shouts. Too bad he'd been closer to Abby this time. "I'll do any work you have for me. Don't pretend like you've asked." Mort's voice started climbing.

"Now, Mort. . ." Gertie stepped to the foot of the table, wringing her hands.

Abby knew she should stop for Gertie's sake. For Wade's sake. But the satisfaction grew. She'd been spoiling for this fight. For the first time she really knew what she wanted—to leave and take Wade with her. This would be a real chance for happiness. The only one she could see.

"Don't pretend like I've refused to help you." Mort pounded the side of his fist on the table and hit the dough, plunging his hand into the soft, sticky mound.

"Don't pretend like you've tried, old man." Abby reached for the dough and jerked it away from him.

"Please, let's not fight." Gertie took the dough from Abby, clearly hoping they'd just let her do the work.

"Always you leave women's work for us and men's work for Wade while you roll around this house like a. . .like a. . .worthless object, a child's toy on a string, making everyone's life harder."

"I want this fight to stop now. You're both being unreasonable." Gertie for the first time sounded stern.

His temper blew. "A child's toy?" Mort grabbed the wheels of his chair.

Satisfied, she gloated that she'd ignited that temper. Now he'd say words he couldn't take back. And she'd tell Wade and they'd leave.

"I want peace!" Gertie shouted and clutched her hands together as if begging.

Until now Abby had been calculating in her pokes and jabs at Mort's ego. But when Gertie said "peace," and Abby knew she meant peace no matter the cost, Abby went over the edge of her temper, right after Mort.

Suddenly she saw Gertie and Mort in a way she'd never seen them before. Peace at any cost. "That's right. That's what we've all been doing, having peace at the cost of our self-respect. Taking Mort's abuse to try and maintain some kind of peace in this house."

Abby turned on Gertie. "Is that what you did when Wade was growing up? You let Mort hit him, then rushed in and bandaged his wounds when it was over, all for peace?"

"You leave Gertie out of this, you little wildcat."

"Well, if a man hit a child I loved, any child"—Abby glared at Gertie, sorry that her temper had turned on the older woman, but not sorry she spoke the truth—"he'd have himself a *war*."

Abby knew then that she wasn't going to find a place in this house and she wasn't going to go tattling like a child to Wade, either. She'd find her beloved mountain valley. She'd find her home alone in the wild. With no man, no people, white or Indian, no peace but the peace she found in God. She ripped the apron off her body and flung it aside.

Mort and Gertie seemed frozen by her hateful words.

She stormed out of the room and was changed into her deerskin dress and moccasins and out of the house before either one of them had moved from the kitchen. The two of them were stuck in a twisted relationship of anger and placating, wounding and bandaging. For all she knew, Wade didn't have the will to leave it all behind either.

If he couldn't break free of this sickness, it was best that she found out now before she was foolish enough to fall in love with him.

She took no horse. She had only her knife and knew she could live very nicely with nothing else forever.

"We've got the herd rounded up and ready for the drive, Pa." Wade pulled his Stetson off his head and wiped his brow.

The days were long and hot now. Spring had come so late up in the mountains where Wade had wintered that he was having trouble adjusting to the full summer heat. Add to that, he'd only a few days ago finished roundup, and it didn't seem right at all.

Gertie set a glass of cool water on the table as Wade hung his hat on the elk antlers on the wall beside the kitchen door. Wade noticed her setting a plate of cookies on the table, too. She always had some on hand for him. Wade had to admit this was a more comfortable life than the one he'd lived in his mountain cabin during the bitter winter.

"Where's Abby?" She'd been avoiding him ever since Sunday. Wade had to bite back a smile. A spirited little thing, his Abby, but she'd come around.

Gertie and Pa exchanged a look, and for the first time since he'd come in, he really looked at them. Two very worried people.

Wade's head swiveled to nail his pa to the wall with his eyes. "What did you do?"

Pa got a stubborn look on his face. "I've been trying to do better; you know that, son. But that woman is just plain contrary."

"Tell me right now." His pa got a sullen look that Wade knew only too well—stubborn, mean old man. But Gertie wasn't so tough. He turned to her. "Well?"

Gertie's hands were clenched together, her eyes wide with fear. She'd always been the peacemaker in this house; Wade wondered how she could have stood it all these years. "She left, Wade."

"Left? Left for where? When?"

"We don't know. She was okay and then Mort came in. He didn't say that much, nothing that should have set her off like that, but she took exception to it."

He felt empty inside. Lost. She'd left him. Or had she ever really been with him?

"Let her cool off for a time, son. If she wants you, she'll come back. If she doesn't want to stay in the white world, you can't make her."

Turning to study his father, Wade prayed silently, wondering what exactly had happened. Pa could still bark well enough. But he'd been so much better. He'd been reading the Bible daily. Why hadn't Abby been patient and given his father more time to grow in the Lord?

Sinking into his chair, Wade stared forward, seeing his future stretched out in front of him without her. He slapped the table and stood. "No, I can't make her stay. But I can go with her."

Wildflower Bride

"Wade, you can't leave us." Gertie grabbed his arm. "We need you here."

Stopping at that familiar weight on his arm, Wade looked down at the only person who'd ever loved him all the while he was growing up. The woman who had come to him after his father's rampages and bandaged his wounds, held him, prayed with him. She did need him. He saw that now. Looking back, he saw that, in her mothering, Gertie had needed Wade as much as Wade had needed her. They were both Pa's prisoners.

If he left with Abby, he'd be abandoning the only mother he could remember. And would his father fall away from his first steps toward faith? Could Wade's actions now be directed by the devil himself to knock Pa off his path back to God? Why had Abby left? She knew he loved her. She had nowhere else in the world to belong. Wade shoved his hands deep into his hair as his thoughts chased themselves in circles.

The answer came to him quietly.

Prayer.

That was the only answer.

"I need time in prayer." Wade grabbed his hat and went outside, knowing there'd be no peace to pray in that house. There'd never been any peace.

He'd been in prayer three minutes before he knew where she'd go.

"What do you mean she's gone?" Tom Linscott grabbed Wade by the shirt collar and lifted him onto his toes.

"Get your hands off me." Wade knocked Tom's hands aside. He'd come charging into this little wreck of a cabin lined with bunks. Tom and all his hands lived in this hovel. Now Wade stood in the doorway shouting. "I don't have time for this. Abby left. She had a fight with Pa—"

"I'm going to find your father and shoot him dead." Tom

rammed his fist into his palm with a loud *smack*. "He's a complete waste of human skin. I should have—"

"Will you shut up? Fighting with my pa won't help me find Abby. I was sure she'd come here. Where else could she be?" Wade turned and strode away from the cabin.

"To town?" Tom followed on his heels.

"There's no one in town she knows at all." The sun was setting. Wherever Abby had gone, she'd spent at least one night alone in the wilderness. Wade was half crazy thinking of the danger.

"Muriel would take her in. Or Libby."

"She might have seen Libby, said hello. And she met Muriel at church, but she doesn't know them at all, and she hates whites. She'd never go to them. She'd see it as begging." Wade stopped beside his horse, ready to mount up and ride, but to where?

"How about the Dawsons'? She sat at the table with us the day of the jailbreak. Red and Cassie were both there. And you said the two of you stopped by the Hardens' on your way home, with Cassie and Red there. She knows them."

Shaking his head, Wade tried to think. His mind spun around. "It doesn't sound right. But I don't know where else to try."

"Let's go check the Dawson place first." Tom whirled and charged toward his corral. His black stallion stood there, proud, watchful.

Wade called after Tom. "I'm not going with you. No sense both of us trying the same place."

Tom stopped and turned back. "Where else then, the Hardens'?"

Wade couldn't answer that. "I'll head that way. Then I'll see where I'm led."

"Where you're led? What does that mean?"

"It means I'm praying as hard as I can for inspiration. But if she did what I'm afraid she did—"

"What's that?" Tom's eyes sharpened, reacting to Wade's obvious dread.

"Headed out to live in the mountains alone."

Clenching his fists, Tom said, "No, no one's that stupid. A woman can't live out there alone."

"Abby could. On her own she'd be fine. Your sister is the bravest, toughest woman I've ever known. She could live off that land, even in those rugged mountains. It's just that—"

"Just that what?"

"Lonely as it is up there, there are still men who might hurt her." Wade thought of the rustlers who had escaped. He thought of the men who had massacred her village. "If someone finds her before we do and gets that knife away from her, she'll be at his mercy. With all that wild country to cover, the two of us will never find her."

"There'll be more than two of us. My men and I will split up and go south and west of town, toward the Dawsons'. You go north." Tom whirled toward his horse, yelling for his men as he ran.

"Did you hear that the wild woman ran off?" Paddy sidled up to Sid at the breakfast table. Paddy heard a lot more living in the bunkhouse than Sid heard in the foreman's cabin.

"No. She's out alone?" Sid knew this might be his only chance to catch that woman. He'd been watching her all week and she never strayed farther than the garden. He'd planned to waylay them on Sunday morning, but he hadn't liked the plan any too well.

"Yep, and Wade took out after her. Mort told Chester when he went in to give the week's accounting last night."

"So they're together?"

"Nope, don't sound like it. She went without him and he went hunting her."

All their targets were separated, alone. Even Mort in the house with only Gertie was defenseless. Sid wanted to charge into that house and put a bullet in that stubborn old man. But he couldn't do that now. Too many cowhands around. The West was still untamed, but even out here there was a limit to cold-blooded murder. Killing Mort Sawyer in front of twenty witnesses was well beyond the limit. He'd have to pick a better time. For now, he had his chance at Wade and the wildflower.

"Saddle up. I'm telling Chester we're riding supplies out to the line shack."

"Are we really going there? Boog's the best tracker among us."

Nodding, Sid said, "I think that little woman wants her wild life back. And if she ever gets to that high valley and sees her Flathead tribe is there, she might just move right in with them."

"Well, then let her go. If she goes off with the Indians, our problem is solved."

"Not as long as she's out there, able to recognize Harv's face. And Wade's sweet on her. He'll be going to try and bring her back. No, we can't have her running around. This is our chance to finish Wade, too. Then we'll come back and pick our moment with Mort. If we find the wild woman first and use her to set a trap for Wade, then kill Mort, we can take over this ranch in a couple of days."

Paddy's eyes narrowed. Hunger and greed glowed like lantern light out of his beady eyes. "Let's go." He whirled to saddle up their horses while Sid told Chester his "plans" to go to the line shack.

Chester didn't like it, but Sid wasn't interested in what Chester wanted. Firing Chester was the first thing Sid planned to do when he took over.

CHAPTER 31

Abby felt as if she shed her white skin as she strode along in the early dawn.

She had days to walk to return to her high valley, but she'd learned to walk tirelessly with her nomadic tribe. And time mattered nothing to her.

No one waited. She simply needed to care for herself, only herself. The very thought was like a huge weight lifting off her shoulders. She could breathe again.

The summer day promised heat, but the early morning air had a bite to it. She loved the breeze that cooled her muscles, and she rushed along, her long legs swinging under her doeskin dress. The pretty beads she'd sewn around the neck reminded her of the quiet time spent with her tribal family, learning at her mother's side.

She was at peace.

Except for Wade.

She missed him.

At the same time, she was glad to be rid of him. She never should have allowed him to lure her with his confusing kindness and tempting kisses.

She remembered the path they'd taken from her high valley.

Her dead reckoning told her she might cut the distance by striking out straight north. But the mountains she had to pass in that direction were daunting. Better to veer west a bit and take the trail past the Griffin place, through the gap into the Harden ranch and out the other end of that. If she was careful—and Abby knew how to be very careful—no one would see her as she quietly walked home.

If she set a fast pace, the Griffin house would be an easy point to reach by dark. Abby glanced to the west and knew a storm was possible. The sky was gray and overcast, but no rain was falling so far. Rain didn't scare her. She could move along soaking wet as well as dry. She admitted to herself that if the house was empty and the night was stormy, she might set aside her contempt for the foolish house and wait out the storm.

Increasing her speed to a ground-eating lope, she smiled as her muscles stretched and became fluid. She felt at one with nature like any other wild thing running free.

As the hours passed, the overcast sky grew heavier. Abby could see rain streaking to the ground in the distance. She could run tirelessly for hours, and she picked up her pace from the comfortable lope, knowing she'd never get to the Griffin place in time but feeling pushed to hurry anyway.

At last, as the wind grew cool and the midafternoon turned dark as dusk, Abby saw the white of the house through the stand of trees. She heard the first sprinkles of rain on the trees overhead, and she made a dash for shelter. She raced under the drooping porch roof with a laugh of triumph and fell against the front door, gasping for air, turning to watch the rain. She'd beaten it. A rare victory against nature.

Suddenly the door behind her opened and she fell backward. Hard hands grabbed her around the waist, and she looked up into the evil eyes of the man who had destroyed her village. His face was nearly healed, but the cut she'd given him had formed an ugly scar and she was glad. She'd enjoy adding to his marks.

She reached for her knife, but a viselike grip on her wrist stopped her. She lashed out with her feet, but a blow to the back of her head stunned her. The world wavered. She shook her head to clear it and only faintly felt the shock of another blow.

The man let go of her, and she sank to the floor. She was fumbling for her knife, but her fingers were stupid and clumsy. Her vision seemed to narrow as if she were looking through a tunnel. The man loomed over her, scarred and victorious, holding his gun so the butt end was handy to use as a club.

As the light faded from her eyes, he smiled at her in evil pleasure to have her in his power.

Wade threw his covers off an hour before dawn.

He'd had to give up the search when darkness fell. He'd hunted the trail to Divide and asked about Abby there then ridden back to the ranch and tried to pick up a trail. Not wanting to sleep in Pa's house, he'd headed in the waning light for the Griffin place and made a cold camp in the woods, knowing he had to stop. He could ride right past her in the dark. Precious little sleep came his way for worrying and praying.

He circled, trying to pick up a trail, but none was there. Abby was too light on her feet, too woods savvy to leave a single footprint.

Chafing at the delay, he slept a short night then set out for the place that kept coming into his head. The place she thought of as home. That high mountain valley. It was so far away that if he was wrong, Wade would be wasting days in the search.

Lord, let me find her.

Darkness was catching him as he drew near the Griffin place, planning to spend the night there. A storm seemed bent on crashing down on his head when he heard someone coming along the trail. He pulled his horse to a stop and eased off the path to watch.

Red and Cassie rode into sight, and Wade came forward. Red caught sight of him and instantly put his horse between Cassie and trouble to shield her, reaching for his pistol.

Red's lightning-fast reflexes reminded Wade that his friend, for all his gentle heart and good nature, was as tough as any rancher around, and that included Pa. This was the kind of strength Wade wanted. Strength used to protect and defend rather than tyrannize and terrorize.

Red visibly relaxed as soon as he recognized Wade in the fading light. "What are you doing out here?"

Cassie leaned around her husband and smiled. "Hi, Wade."

Susannah was riding in front of Cassie, and the little girl waved and bounced as if she wanted to kick the horse into a gallop. The wind was rising and the setting sun was blanketed by gray clouds.

Letting go of his screaming tension for just a second, Wade allowed himself to smile at the Dawson family.

Michael, carried on Red's back like a papoose, whacked at his father's hat, and Red grabbed it before it fell. He did it so naturally Wade knew the child had tried that stunt many times before.

Then Wade's moment of relaxation was over. He pulled up beside Red. "Abby's run off. She had a fight with Pa last night and she stormed out. No one's seen her since."

"She was out overnight?" Cassie's fair skin seemed to pale in the sunset.

Nodding, Wade said, "Linscott's whole crew is out hunting for her. I'm riding back to the valley where we found her, hoping she went there. She's threatened to take off and live by herself in the mountains. She could go anywhere. So I'm trying to pick up a trail, but there's nothing."

Red frowned. "We're on our way to visit the Tanners."

"Hardens," Cassie whispered.

"This late?" Wade looked around. "You've got hours of riding yet."

"We got a late start. Trouble with the cattle, then a couple of other little things."

"I let Harriet out." Cassie grimaced.

Red smiled at her. "It was an accident. It could have happened to anyone."

"Big mean piggy." Susannah's eyes were wide as the full moon.

Wade could hardly stand to imagine it. That old mama sow was a killer. "You plan on trying to get through that pass tonight with the little ones? The gap into their ranch is pretty steep. You might have trouble with it in the dark."

"We almost waited until tomorrow to leave, but we finally decided we'd make it. Now, with the storm brewing, we've decided to ride as far as Cassie's old house tonight and bunk there."

Nodding, Wade said, "Mind if I ride along and stay? There's no trail to be found this late anyway."

"Glad for the company." Red smiled. "It's your house anyway."

"You're welcome to the shelter anytime you need it. You know that."

"Thanks. I appreciate it. And we can pray together for Abby."

"We'd better move or we're going to get wet." The panic Wade had been riding with all day eased a little now that he wasn't alone. Maybe he'd go as far as the Hardens and take Red and Silas along with him to search for Abby. Their help might make all the difference.

"You wanted her—now you've got her."

Sid glared at Harv. Then his eyes wandered to the still female form in the corner. She lay with her back against the wall. Her hair had mostly fallen out of its braid and now covered her face in long white curls. She had her wild woman dress on, the deerskin she'd been wearing when they'd taken her after the massacre. It even had stains on it from Harv's blood.

Sid itched for that woman. Seeing her lying there unconscious gave him a feeling of such fierce power that it was all he could do not to pull his six-gun on his gang, drive them out of the house, and have her to himself.

None of them looked eager to give her up.

Cool-eyed Boog wasn't a man Sid could read. So maybe he didn't care, but that woman was a feisty little thing. They'd watched her attack Harv after the massacre. Subduing her, dominating her, appealed to Sid, and he couldn't believe it didn't appeal to every man.

"We don't have time to fool with the woman." Nothing about Boog's voice gave anything away.

"I wouldn't have grabbed her if she hadn't come right to the door," Harv said. "I didn't have time to get out. I knew if I didn't get her under control, she'd run for help and bring a posse down on our heads."

"She wouldn't have run for help." Sid wanted to backhand Harv. "She'd have carved another notch in your face. You hit her because you were scared, not because you were afraid of the law."

The lump on the back of the wild woman's head told Sid that Harv hadn't fought fair. Not even with a woman. He'd come up behind her, knocked her cold, and tied her up while she was unconscious. Harv had a wide coward streak.

Sid had been around enough cowards that he knew to watch his back. The four of them sat cross-legged in the first room of the big house. They needed to get rid of the woman somehow and then turn to hunting Wade, but no one stepped forward and volunteered to pull the trigger, mainly because she was too beautiful a woman to want dead. "Boog, I want you and Paddy to ride toward the south."

"Now?" Paddy looked out the window. There was little light left, and the storm kept threatening, though it hadn't dropped any rain yet.

"Yes, now. This is our chance. Wade headed that way and we need to finish him."

"Who's gonna take care of that wildcat?" Boog jerked his head in their captive's direction.

"I owe her. I oughta do it." Harv looked at her and wiped his mouth.

Sid nodded. It suited him to let someone else do it. Not that he was squeamish, but he'd never killed a woman before. No sense starting now if Harv would do it. "If you can catch up to Wade and kill him, and Harv finishes the girl, we only have Mort left. We'll meet up in the morning and have that ranch in our hands by tomorrow night." Thinking about the land grab gave Sid more pleasure than thinking about the woman.

"Bury her deep, whatever you do." Boog stared at the woman's still form. "Women are mighty scarce out here. Some folks get mighty riled when someone mistreats one of 'em."

"I'll bury her deep." Harv's eyes shifted between Sid and the woman. He looked like a rat, making filthy plans.

Boog stood. "Let's get it done, Paddy." Something about the tone of his voice told Sid that Boog wanted no part of killing this girl. But as usual, Sid couldn't be sure.

Grumbling and looking at the woman with no attempt to disguise his unhappiness with the assignment, Paddy stood and left the room with Boog.

Sid relaxed when he heard the hooves of their horses pounding away down the trail.

"You know I don't want her dead, Sid." Harv stood.

Sid got to his feet, not wanting Harv towering over him. "You want her dead in the end, don't you?"

"Yeah." Harv rubbed his finger over the scar on his chin and stared at the unconscious girl. His eyes flashed as he touched his wound. "But I want her to beg to die."

Sickened, Sid was tempted almost beyond control to put a bullet in his saddle partner. But if he did, the woman would still need killing. If instead Sid turned his back, walked out into the night, Harv would do his worst and Sid wouldn't have to get his hands dirty. Harv's knowledge of where that gold was tipped the balance, even if getting to the treasure seemed impossible.

"I'm gonna go looking for a deep hole to dump her body in." Sid turned and strode from the room, forcing himself to hurry before he did the foolish things that were rattling around in his head. He almost ran off the porch, pushing himself to make a clean break from his hunger to hurt Harv, hurt the woman, hurt the whole world. It was like a thirst for whiskey and it rode Sid harder all the time.

Leave the woman for Harv.

As Sid walked away from the Griffin place, he rounded the side of the house and looked back. He could see into the room. The last traces of the setting sun found their way between two trees and the billowing clouds and sent a single shaft of light into that room. Sid saw Harv staring at the woman, and Sid stopped. His heart seemed to beat at half the speed and twice the strength as Harv slowly advanced on the woman. Swallowing hard, Sid watched Harv bend down, out of sight, but Sid could picture Harv's filthy hands reaching toward all those miles of golden hair.

With a grunt of self-contempt, Sid turned away toward the corral to saddle his horse and ride away. Give Harv some time then come back and everything would be taken care of. The wild woman who could identify Harv and bury them all would finally be dead.

CHAPTER 32

Abby'd be fine. Wade hated that she was out here alone. But she was tough. She'd take good care of herself.

Her only real trouble would be loneliness.

Same for him.

Wade thought of that long, bitter cold winter in his shack. The cold was relentless and brutal, but compared to the loneliness, it was nothing. Wade had needed that time. Maybe Abby needed some, too, but it was a hard way to live, and Wade wasn't going to even consider leaving Abby alone. She needed him whether she knew it or not.

Having Red and Cassie along cheered Wade up. With his friends along, nothing could go wrong. They'd hunt for Abby however long it took, and in the meantime, she'd protect herself, probably better than Wade could.

The trail to the Griffin place wound through woods and mountains. It was too narrow to ride abreast, so they strung out single file with Red leading, Cassie going next, and Wade bringing up the rear.

The rain was holding off, but the night was wild with wind and scudding clouds playing peekaboo with the moon and lightning and thunder in the distance.

Wade had taken Susannah in his lap, and the little one had chattered away for a long time before she'd passed out in his arms. She went from fully awake to limp between two sentences. It would have scared him if he hadn't seen her do it so many times before.

"She's sleeping," Wade whispered.

The wind was at his back and carried his voice over the thrashing limbs overhead and the soft *clop* of horses' hooves to Cassie. She looked back and smiled. Her teeth gleamed in the twilight.

They kept their horses at a fast walk. In the darkness, pushing their mounts would have been dangerous.

Wade saw a glimpse of the moon overhead as the clouds rushed across the sky. A jolt of lightning lit up the east. The thunder sounded next, but not for a long time. The storm might be going to the south. Wade could only hope.

Red's fist went up in the air, and even in the dark, Wade knew there was trouble. He goaded his gelding forward, coming alongside Cassie on the slender ghost of a trail. He caught her reins just as Red glanced back. Red jerked his chin, giving Wade his approval, and Wade pulled Cassie's horse toward a barely existent break in the surrounding woods.

"Wade, what—"

"Shh." The single sound brought Cassie's question to a halt.

The woman was too obedient for her own good, but right now Wade was thankful for it.

Red's horse disappeared off to the left of the trail. Wade went right, wishing fiercely Red didn't have Michael strapped on his back. But there wasn't time to snatch the little boy. It was just as well. Red and Cassie would protect their children, leaving Wade free to handle whatever trouble was coming.

The only problem was Wade wasn't half as good at handling trouble as Red.

When he had Cassie well hidden behind a nearly impenetrable

line of ancient oaks, Wade helped her down from her horse and urged her behind the massive trunk. He leaned inches from her ear. "Take Susannah and stay here."

Cassie was sweet and pretty. She was a city girl born and bred. But she'd lived in the West for a few hard years, and Wade saw every one of those years in her knowing eyes as she took her little girl.

"Red's got Michael, so I need to handle this. You make sure you and Susannah are safe."

Cassie caught Wade's sleeve. "Be careful."

With a quick nod, Wade left his horse with Cassie and inched forward until he saw the trail through the brush and low-hanging limbs. He wondered where Red was, knowing his friend wouldn't hide from trouble. But the man had a baby with him, and protecting that child had to come first. Wade prayed Red thought of his son first and stayed out of the action. Wade was the one without a child. He was the one who should take the risks. Even if he was killed protecting his friends, he'd leave no one behind to mourn. Not even Abby, apparently.

On that sad thought, he drew his gun with a soft *whoosh* of iron against leather, a sound he could barely hear in the rising wind. He waited, prepared to give his life for his friends. The trees danced and swayed, reaching out for him like skeletal fingers clawing at his neck. A night for danger and nightmares. A night for fear.

"Whom shall I fear?"

He wasn't afraid of any harm to him. Instead, he feared for Abby in danger. And that his friends might come to harm. His own life he would gladly, fearlessly lay down to protect them all.

As he prayed in the howling wind, Wade heard the soft whinny of a horse.

"He could be anywhere." A man's voice, high with nerves, carried over the sounds of the approaching storm.

Iron jingled. Horses' hooves clopped quietly. An eagle screamed high overhead where it soared, playing on the downdrafts.

Another voice, lower, was audible, but Wade couldn't make out words.

"She shoulda been mine!" The high-pitched voice sounded again. "I'd've liked to get my hands on all that long white hair. I'd've tamed the wild outta her." The voice droned on, complaining, making sickening suggestions. The man raved on and on about a wild woman with white hair. It had to be Abby. Some of the words were lost when the wind struck just so and carried them in another direction.

Wade didn't need to hear them. He'd heard enough to know they had her prisoner somewhere.

"I say we go back." That whining voice started again. Wade recognized it, but he wasn't sure from where. "Just 'cuz she cut Harv don't make her his. I want that wild woman."

"I don't care what you want."

Chills of terror almost drove Wade out onto the trail, gun blazing. He fought a terrible battle with his desire to charge out to confront the men. Wade knew better. Getting himself killed was no way to save Abby and no way to protect Red and his family. But still he felt his legs tense to jump forward. His hand tightened on the butt of his gun, ready to open fire.

God, they have her. Protect her, Lord. Help me find her. Get us there on time.

Two men here at least, and they'd left Abby behind with someone else. Could it be four men? Could it be the ones who'd attacked Abby's village? Knowing how vicious those men were made it harder to stay hidden.

The voices were closer. A bend in the winding trail hid the riders, but Wade knew they'd appear any second. He swallowed hard. He gripped a low branch of the tree he knelt behind, partly to hold himself in place, partly so when his chance came he could use the limb to catapult himself onto the trail.

Wait. Wait.

Wildflower Bride

The wind held him in place as if it were the hand of God. He itched to move, to act, to fight and punish, but he controlled himself, biding his time.

The lightning flashed so often the trail was lit almost constantly. An especially bright slash lit up the trail enough that Wade caught sight of a horse's nose just as it appeared from around the bend. He leveled his pistol. He wouldn't shoot, though. Instead he'd charge in once they were closer, get the drop on them, and make sure they were disarmed, with Red backing him up but staying hidden well enough to protect Michael and make sure they survived for Cassie's sake. Wade would stop them, and they'd find out where Abby had been taken. Repeating that in his head gave him hope that he could do the right thing when he was killing mad.

Suddenly, to his left, a noise scared Wade into nearly jumping out onto the trail. A swift hand grabbed his arm or he might have run forward right into the men's path.

"It's me. Hang on." Red appeared by Wade's side on foot. It took a second for the lightning to show that Red didn't have Michael. He must have circled back, crossed the trail, and given Michael to Cassie.

Wade hated the thought of Red risking his life, but the odds had just gotten a lot better.

Their eyes met. Then Red nodded at the approaching men. "Now." They rushed the trail.

"Stop right there or I'll shoot." Red cocked his gun, the sound clear and chilling in the stormy night.

The men shouted. One of their horses reared up.

Wade rushed the riders, eager to get his hands on them and beat the truth out of them, to find Abby. He caught the closest man and, from the cry of alarm, knew he'd gotten the man who'd uttered such horrible threats against Abby. Jerking the man to the ground, Wade snatched at his holster and relieved the villain of his gun.

The other horse landed four-legged, and Wade saw its back was bare. The quiet man was gone.

Wade yanked the man he held to his feet and used him for a shield, searching in the darkness for the other man. There was no sign of Red, either.

"Let go!" his prisoner shouted then began flailing his hands and feet.

To subdue him, Wade flipped his gun around and crashed the butt down on the man's head. The fight went out of him and his legs sagged. Wade crouched low, looking for the missing outlaw and now for Red. Wade didn't dare shoot at someone coming toward him because he couldn't be sure who it was in the dark.

Underbrush thrashed and snapped.

Wade heard it and turned. They were on the side of the trail where Cassie was hidden with the children. Like the seasoned rancher he was, Wade snapped the fringe from his buckskin jacket and used it to hog-tie his prisoner.

A crack of gunfire split the night, followed by a flash of light deep in the woods. A man's sudden cry of pain that Wade hoped didn't come from Red was followed by more commotion in the trees.

Wade's attention focused on a spot close to him. He quickly dragged his limp captive to the side of the trail and stashed him out of sight then rushed toward the oncoming noise. Slipping behind a tree, Wade bided his time, drawing his gun but knowing he didn't dare shoot.

A dark form leapt through the last of the cover, and Wade tackled him. The second he made contact, he was sure he had the other outlaw. They tussled, Wade searching wildly for the man's gun in the darkness. A fist slammed into Wade's face. He stumbled backward, losing his grip.

Another gunshot split the night, then another. In the chaos, Wade knew he'd pulled the trigger. Sickened, he didn't waver. He rushed toward the man. It wasn't Red, Wade was sure of it. But that bullet could have gone wild.

The man, facedown on the ground, groaned in agony.

Wade knelt and rolled him onto his back.

"You got him?" Red reached Wade's side, sounding desperate.

"Yes." Wade bound this man's legs and hands just as he had the other's.

"He fired his gun too close to Cassie. I've got to see if she's okay." Red vanished.

Scared to death, Wade saw a gun within the outlaw's reach and kicked it aside then searched the man for hidden weapons. As he frisked the attacker, he became aware of wetness soaking the man's shoulder. Blood. Wade ripped another long fringe off his jacket and bound the man as quickly as he would have bulldogged a calf.

Seconds ticked by as Wade waited, hoping and praying Red would come back and tell him Cassie and the children were okay. The time crawled.

Finally, Red emerged from the woods.

"Everything okay, Red?"

"Yep."

"You weren't hurt? Your family's okay?"

"They're fine."

"Did you shoot him?"

"Nope, I never even fired my gun."

"Then this must be my bullet in his shoulder." Wade reached for the bleeding shoulder and ripped the shirt aside. A flare of lightning revealed not one but two bullet wounds. A new one and an old one. Instantly, Wade was sure he'd put the old wound in this man near the Flathead village.

"This one was in on the massacre of Abby's people."

"How do you know?"

"Because I shot one of them that day near Abby's village, and I can see the bullet wound right here." Wade jabbed a finger at the two wounds.

"And if it's like it sounded—" Red didn't continue because it was too sickening.

Wade knew someone had to say it. "They've got Abby." Wade stood. His foot slipped, and he accidentally kicked his prisoner.

The man howled in pain in a way that struck Wade as ridiculous for such a minor bump.

Then Wade looked closer and saw a knife sticking out of the man's boot. Shaking his head in disbelief, he looked closer. He'd seen that knife before.

"Can I have my knife back?" As polite as a schoolmarm, Cassie approached Wade's prisoner. She had Susannah in her arms and Michael on her back, and she held the reins of all three horses.

Wade remembered that man's cry of pain in the woods. A sound he now realized was wrung from this man when Cassie's knife had embedded in the leather and obviously gotten some toes. Honestly, they'd made the little woman do more than her share of the work tonight, and now it looked as if she'd taken a big hand in bagging an outlaw.

Wade hoped there was a reward. "You have got yourself a handy little woman, Red."

Red reached down and retrieved Cassie's knife with no oversupply of gentleness. The outlaw howled in pain.

He handed the weapon to his wife and took Susannah. "You should get out of here, Cassie, but I can't leave Wade, and I can't let you go off alone."

"I'm fine, Red. I'll be careful."

"Like you were this time?"

"I'd say stabbing that man was real careful of me."

Wade would have laughed if he hadn't been so scared for Abby.

"This trail doesn't lead anywhere but to your old house, Cass. I'll bet they've got Abby there."

In a tearing hurry, Wade and Red made short work of dragging the two men well off the trail, making sure they were trussed up tight and had no concealed knives to cut themselves loose.

Red held Susannah and helped Cassie to mount with little Michael on her back. Then he and Wade swung up on horseback, and the three of them moved swiftly down the trail.

Wade kept hearing those men talk. Kept thinking of Abby in the hands of these brutes.

Wade took the lead this time, leaving the Dawsons to bring up the rear with their children. He set a dangerously fast pace. It was so dark now Wade could barely make out Cassie when he looked behind him.

One thing did bother him about that attack. . . . He dropped back beside her. They were far enough from the Griffin place, and the wind whipped wildly enough. He decided it was safe to talk. "Why'd you stab him in the foot, Cassie? That's a pretty small target."

There was no answer except Red's laughter. A shocking sound considering what had just happened and the danger that lay ahead.

"It's not funny, Red." Cassie sounded huffy. It was too dark to see her face and no handy lightning bolt supplied illumination, but the little woman sounded for all the world like she was pouting.

"It's a little bit funny," Red said quietly from behind them.

"It is not!"

"What's funny?" Wade asked.

"Nothing." Cassie said no more.

"Then what's *not* funny?"

But Red wasn't done talking. "She wasn't aiming for his foot."

"You don't know that for a fact. I might well have been aiming for his foot." Cassie sounded like she was trying to threaten Red into silence.

Wade's good friend Red apparently wasn't scared at all. "She was aiming for his. . .uh. . .his bull's-eye."

"You're mine, you wildcat." Harv sank his fingers deep into Abby's hair. "And I'm gonna make you pay for this cut on my face."

MARY CONNEALY

She slashed out with her knife and gave him a new cut to worry about.

Harv stumbled back.

Abby, her feet bound, dove at him. Her weight slammed into him, and she jerked his gun out of his holster as he fell backward. His cry of fear gave her a purely sinful surge of satisfaction. She flipped the gun so it faced away from the filthy pig and brought a clean, hard butt stroke down on his head.

His turn to hurt, his turn to be overpowered.

She felt the vicious pleasure of that blow. She really needed to talk with God more about this desire she had to hurt, or threaten to hurt, white men. It wasn't biblical, she was nearly certain of it.

She didn't think it was a sin to defend herself, but enjoying it was most likely not something God approved of. She decided then and there that once she was sure the stinking outlaw was knocked into a sound sleep and she'd gotten well away from here, she'd spend serious time in prayer and repentance.

He slumped to the floor unconscious on the first blow.

Infuriated that she had no excuse to keep beating on him, Abby quickly slit the bindings on her ankles and jumped to her feet. "One of your men is still around," Abby said to the still figure in front of her. She wasn't going to stand around waiting for him to come back.

Eyeing the gun with distaste, she decided there was no reason to leave it behind for him to use on her or another innocent. She took it and ran out the front door, dashing into the woods, hoping the second man wasn't watching.

The trees surrounded her. She crouched down, watchful, worried about the location of the other outlaw. The first two who'd left would be on their way far down the trail by now. But the second one was close at hand, and he'd intended to return after Harv did his worst.

The fools had tied her hands behind her back and not taken her knife. The slim weapon was hard for others to find in its

924

pouch. The stiffness of the blade was concealed by the beading, so if they searched her at all—she'd been unconscious at the time, so she wasn't sure—they'd missed it. But she'd awakened in that room and watched them through eyes opened just a slit while she'd found her knife and cut her hands free.

Then while they plotted, she prepared to make them sorry they'd touched her. These were the men who had massacred her village. The man's injured face was testimony to that, and his threats to make her pay for his scars were as good as a confession.

She would have to do some serious work on the state of her soul to find an ounce of regret in her that she'd hurt that dreadful, stinking man. But she'd do it. She promised God.

Not now but soon.

She expected no white lawman to exact justice for the murder of a village of Flatheads, so she didn't consider trying to take the men to the sheriff, even if she could have figured out a way.

Staring at the house, she tried to decide what to do. These men were dangerous, and though she'd hurt this one, he'd be fine and all four men were still free. She'd heard them plotting to kill her and Wade and Mort and take Mort's ranch. It made sense to kill her because she'd witnessed them committing murder, and Wade had seen this man's face. But Mort? What did he have to do with this? Was he just another victim, another chance to do evil?

Crouching there in the woods like a frightened rabbit didn't suit her. But what should she do? Where should she go? The forests weren't safe, and she needed to warn Wade. She could have lived in the wilderness alone. Hadn't she just proved that she was tough enough? But did she want to be this tough? Did she want to fight for her life every day?

Abby had lived through a disease that killed her white family. She'd survived a brutal massacre that finished her Salish family. She'd never been allowed time to grieve for either as she'd been torn away from both of those lives. Twice now her life had been broken into pieces. And now, with her aching head, fresh blood on her hands, and the man she now knew she loved in danger, she couldn't make a decision.

She had to protect Wade. She had to leave the white world.

God, I belong nowhere.

Wind whipped around her and laughed as if the devil himself mocked her.

She was utterly alone. The whole wide world seemed closed to her. A moment of loneliness so profound it nearly choked her held her in place. Go forward. Go back. Every choice was hostile.

Abby knew this was the lowest moment of her life. The utter loneliness sank into her bones until she knew things could never get any worse.

A crack of thunder proved her wrong.

The heavens split open and slashing, frigid rain poured down on her head.

CHAPTER 33

Hold up." Wade lifted one gloved hand.

The trail widened enough that Cassie and Red were able to come up beside him just as the rain began slashing his face. They stared at the dark house. Cassie and Red had both donned oilcloth ponchos, and the children, sleeping under the waterproof cloth, were still and comfortable. Red and Cassie looked okay, too.

Wade hadn't taken the time to pack anything. He was miserable, cold, wet, and within seconds of pure panic.

The house was dark. No sign of life anywhere.

"Let me go in alone." Wade spoke low, his voice barely audible under the sounds of the storm.

"No. Cassie, lift up your slicker and let me hand Susannah over." Red tented his poncho and shifted around to slide Susannah off his lap and under Cassie's rain gear without awakening the little girl or getting a single drop of water on her.

"I don't want you hurt." Wade's fear for Abby and guilt at putting Red and his family in danger were making him twitchy.

Turning to Wade, Red said, "Give me a minute to scout the outbuildings. I'll signal you when I'm ready. Then you go in the front, and I'll go in the back."

"No, I'm not waiting. I need to get in there. You stay back. Protect your family."

"It's all quiet now, Wade. If she's in there, she'll be no worse for a few minutes' wait. If we go in stupid and get ourselves shot, she'll be a lot worse off, and so will Cassie and the little ones."

Red was right. Wade knew it. He forced himself to do the smart thing. He nodded in agreement, keeping his eyes fastened on the old house. She was in there, maybe hurt, maybe dead. And if she wasn't in there, then where did they look?

"Cass, honey, you drop back into the woods and mind the young'uns and the horses."

"Yes, Red."

Wade tried to imagine Abby saying, "Yes, Wade," in that obedient tone of voice. It would never happen, and Wade would never care. He'd let her say anything and do anything as long as she was all right. He'd never ask for more than her safety.

The drenched horses obediently followed Cassie into the dark woods as wind buffeted them and thunder rumbled overhead.

"Stay back until you hear from me, Wade." Red vanished toward the back of the house. There was a large barn, built with Cassie's inheritance before her first husband went broke and died, leaving her alone, pregnant, and penniless in the unsettled West. Griffin also had several smaller outbuildings erected, too, so it would take time to search them all.

It took every ounce of self-control Wade had to watch and wait. He stared at that house through the nearly blinding rain, trying to burn a hole through the wall with his eyes. Was she in there? Was she hurt or dead?

God, please let us be in time.

Suddenly Wade heard a birdcall—a bird that would never be out singing in this kind of rain. Red.

Inching forward, Wade drew his gun.

Wildflower Bride

Sid stopped in his tracks.

His eyes narrowed as a shadow separated itself from the barn. Moving slowly, silently, someone slipped from building to building, searching.

Sid backed his horse well out of the man's line of sight, dismounted, and tied the animal securely.

A bolt of lightning lit up the yard at just the right second, and Sid got a good look at the man. But as he was swathed in oilcloth, he couldn't identify him. Not Harv, that was for sure.

The man came out and headed in a crouching run toward the house. A flare of light outlined the man's gun. Then a shrill whistle told Sid the rest. This man wasn't alone.

Dying was not part of Sid's plan. He felt his feet itching to take off, to run for the hills, to leave Harv to his fate. Except Harv was the only one who knew where that blasted gold was hidden.

They'd run into that house and see Harv with the wild woman, and there'd be killing trouble and Sid's dreams of gold would die along with his saddle partner.

Inching forward, Sid drew his gun.

Abby couldn't believe her eyes.

Maybe the lightning had left her addled, but she saw somebody huddled in the woods, barely visible because she was covered head to foot with a cloak. Watching closely, a long braid whipped out, and a pretty bow on the braid told Abby that this was a woman. The woman held three horses, and even deep in the woods on this black night, Abby recognized Wade's horse.

Wade was here? Abby sidled closer, hating that she lost sight of the house as she moved closer to the woman.

A high-pitched cry Abby recognized convinced her to forget being quiet, and she walked forward without concealment. It sounded like. . .a baby. And who had a baby with her every time Abby had seen her? "Cassie, is that you?"

"Abby? You're here? You're okay?"

Cassie Dawson, and from the odd wriggling and crying from under her cloak, Abby surmised that the woman had indeed brought a baby along.

"You brought a baby to a gunfight?"

Cassie's smile shone in the darkness. "We didn't set out for a gunfight. We set out for Belle's."

"So how'd you end up here?"

"Mama scary."

Startled at the little voice sounding from beneath Cassie's slicker, Abby looked closer at Cassie's little tent she'd created with her waterproof coat. "You brought a baby and a toddler to a gunfight?"

Cassie shrugged under the wind-battered oilcloth. "Here's what happened. . . ." Cassie finished her explanation quickly.

"Now I reckon I've got to go in there and save Red and Wade." Abby turned toward the house just as a ridiculous excuse for a birdcall sounded through the storm.

"I'd surely appreciate it if you would, Abby." Cassie said it like she didn't have a single doubt in her mind.

Abby didn't have any doubts, either. "You stay here."

Inching forward, Abby drew Harv's gun.

Using every bit of cover, Wade rushed the house. He paused at the porch. The minute he took the first step, the people inside would be warned. There was no way to disguise the creaking of the wood.

He caught his breath then charged up the steps. He threw open the door and swung his gun to cover the dark corners. One lump lay in the room. A human-sized lump. Wade's heart stopped beating.

"Here, Wade." Red appeared in the doorway that led to the back of the house. The frequent lightning flashes helped Wade locate his friend. Red stood alert, pointing his gun toward the floor so no wild shot went in the wrong direction. With Red watching the corners of the room, Wade rushed to the prone figure. Never had he known such terror. It made all he'd felt in his growing-up years, with his brute of a father, fade into nothingness. If this was Abby, if she was dead, then Wade would have to find a new way to live, because nothing made sense without her.

He dropped to his knees, and a helpful blaze of lightning told him it was a man. An unconscious, bleeding man. Another lightning bolt revealed an ugly scar on the man's chin.

"Where is she?" Wade shook the man. "Where's Abby?" The unconscious man didn't seem to be so much as breathing, though Wade had checked and he was alive. And considering that the man was knocked cold, Wade suspected Abby had been here. This looked like her work.

A scratching sound pulled Wade's attention from all the black niches of the room. Red had come all the way into the room, and now light popped to life as he held a match close to the still figure. Red leaned close. "This is the rustler I brought in."

Wade studied the man until he was sure. "He's the man Abby cut at the massacre."

"So it was the same gang." Red lifted the match to look at Wade. "And you said there were four of them?"

"Yep, and we've accounted for three."

Red blew out the match. He and Wade wheeled to face away from each other. The house was as silent as death. The only sound the raging storm.

The rain battered the house. Wade felt awful knowing Cassie waited in the miserable darkness. Where was Abby?

"This must be Abby's doing. Who else would cut the man then knock him cold?" Red asked.

"Unless the two rustlers fought over her and one took her."

"Maybe, but those two men we caught were fast with their guns. Figures their partners might be, too. A knife sounds more like Abby's style. I think she got away."

Wade, studying the corners of the room during the occasional lightning flash, saw something against a far wall. He hurried over and lifted up a rope, knotted but cut through. "She got loose."

"And she knocked this guy cold and ran. He's stopped bleeding, but the blood hasn't dried yet. She didn't leave long ago."

"I'm going to look upstairs." Wade headed up the sweeping staircase.

"I'll check all the rooms down here." Red's voice changed. "Wade, there was only one horse in the corral out back. If there's a fourth man—"

"There is." Wade paused, wishing Red would hurry up so Wade could be doing something.

"Then he's gone. We can hope she got away, but he might have taken Abby with him."

"Maybe he saw his partner, figured out he'd lost Abby, and took off."

"Maybe. I hope so."

Sick with fear, Wade rushed toward the stairs and was halfway up them when he heard a gun cock. He stopped and turned toward the sound, hoping Red's gun had made the noise.

A bolt of lightning told Wade more than he wanted to know. Red stood in the door that led to the back of this rambling house. The black of a gun was pressed against his neck. Wade saw the gun was held in an awkward way, with two fingers of a glove extended rather than curved around the butt.

That's when Wade knew.

Sid.

The M Bar S foreman—missing two fingers. Wade had seen that before. Sid had been at the massacre. And the unconscious man was one of the cattle rustlers, which meant Sid was one, too.

Suddenly, Wade was just as sure that Sid had caused Pa's fall.

Wildflower Bride

This man or one of his partners had shot at him and Abby with the bow and arrow. This one evil man was the mastermind behind all the trouble. He had to be stopped.

"Come out where I can see you." Sid was shorter than Red, and he crouched low like a cowering dog, so Wade couldn't get off a shot.

Wade had fired his gun twice in his life at a man. Both times it had been little more than an accident. It made him sick, still, thinking about his bullet hitting the outlaw, even knowing the man was vermin who deserved to die.

"Let him go, Sid. Abby's gone. You can't get her." She'd probably run on toward her mountain valley. Choosing a life utterly alone over a life with him.

"You think I want that wildflower? Why do you think I left her for Harv?"

Wade might be too much of a coward to shoot a man, but he wasn't a coward when it came to his own life and death. He knew he'd spend eternity in heaven, and that erased all his fear. What mattered was that Red came out of this alive. He had Cassie to care for.

Wade felt God writing a message across his heart with a fiery fingertip:

"In him was life; and the life was the light of men. And the light shineth in darkness; and the darkness comprehended it not."

No, darkness couldn't comprehend the light. But Wade could shine the light of Jesus in the darkness. He'd tried with his pa, and maybe seeds were planted that would someday grow. And maybe that meant Wade wasn't such a coward. Maybe a willingness to shine a light in dark places took a special kind of courage. And if the darkness couldn't comprehend it, as Sid couldn't now, then Wade's willingness to die to save Red took more courage than a willingness to kill.

Wade's spine stiffened. He walked down the last two steps. Then he stepped out and squared off in front of Sid, his heart on

933

fire for the Lord. The light of God was shining within him until Wade thought it might be lighting the room.

A bolt of lightning brightened the room enough that Wade could see Red's eyes. Red had both hands raised slightly above his waist, and Sid's gun was jammed against Red's throat. But Red looked calm, at peace, another source of light.

Wade knew all he needed was for that gun to aim away from Red for a split second, give Red a chance to act.

It was Wade's job to bring that gun around to bear on himself.

"Let him go, Sid." Wade was amazed his voice sounded so confident. "You're finished. We've captured your other two saddle partners, and you can't get this man out of here"—Wade tipped his head toward the unconscious outlaw—"without carrying him. Time to cut your losses. Back out of here and run."

"You've captured Boog and Paddy?"

Wade had heard of Paddy, another Sawyer cowpoke. In the darkness, he hadn't recognized him. Red had taken care of the Irishman, but Boog? That had to be the name of the man Wade had shot. Twice.

Wade swallowed hard to keep his voice steady. "Yes, we've got them. Give it up and run. We won't try and stop you."

"No, I've got too much to lose, and there's still a chance I can win. As long as you're dead." With lightning quickness, Sid turned the gun from Red and aimed at Wade.

Wade went for his gun.

Red grabbed Sid's hand and shoved up.

Sid's gun blasted the ceiling.

A dull *thud* echoed in the room.

Lightning lit up the room, and Wade saw Sid's eyes go wide into a vacant stare.

Red wrested the weapon free.

Sid's knees buckled.

As Sid sank, an inch at a time, to the floor, Abby's golden head emerged behind him. In both hands, she held the gun she'd just used to club Sid over the head. She had her knife clenched between her teeth. She was soaking wet and killing mad.

Wade had never loved her more.

CHAPTER 34

We've got to help Red and Cassie take the outlaws back to town, honey."

"What do you mean 'we'? I don't have to go."

Wade did his best not to let his exasperation show.

"Quit scowling at me, white man."

His best was apparently not very good. "Just ride with us, please, Ab?" Wade was begging. He was planning to spend the rest of his life begging, because he was planning to spend it with the stubbornest woman he'd ever known. He accepted it and looked forward to a lifetime of being overpowered. Never ever would he hear those sweet words, "Yes, Wade."

"Are you okay, Cassie, honey?" Red had brought Cassie inside to drip dry.

"Yes, Red."

That sounded so sweet, Wade felt a little like crying. But there was no use in it, like crying for the moon. He loved Abby and that was that.

They had Harv and Sid tied up, both still sleeping like babies, while they waited for the rain to stop. The other two outlaws were out in the weather, but Wade couldn't get worked up about their being uncomfortable. If they thought rain was unpleasant, wait till they felt the business end of a noose.

"What I don't understand is the massacre of your village." Red interrupted the wrangling that Wade and Abby had been doing for the last hour. He spoke calmly because he had Michael cradled in his arms. They'd made a little bed for Susannah out of a blanket that wasn't soaking wet. She'd slept through everything.

The night was wearing on and they were in no hurry to head back to Divide, especially Wade, because he couldn't convince Abby to go along.

Glaring, Wade said, "You were the only witness to what these men did to your village. You've got to come in and tell the sheriff. The rustling, the kidnapping, the assault on you will send them to jail for a few years, but they need to hang or stay locked up for life. With you as an eyewitness, they'll hang."

"No white man hangs for killing Indians." Abby practically spat the words.

Sorely afraid she might be right, Wade tried another argument. He backed her up against the wall and kissed the living daylights out of her.

She'd kept Harv's gun, tucking it in the belt of her deerskin dress. She had her knife, too.

Wade was through thinking of himself as a coward. He was holding Abby close and she was armed to the eyeballs. That made him a brave man indeed.

She wasn't shooting him, though. And she didn't even go for her knife. Instead she wrapped her arms around his neck and kissed him back like a house afire. With the tiny corner of Wade's mind that wasn't overwhelmed from the feel of her holding him, Wade realized he should have kissed her the minute Sid collapsed.

He'd wanted to, but she'd really had bloodlust in her eyes, and truth be told, he was a little scared she'd hurt him. Also, there was the knife in her teeth. That could have gotten ugly.

Red cleared his throat.

Wade came to his senses. . .or as close as he'd ever get with Abby in his life. He pulled back about two inches, no more. "How could you run off from Pa's like that?"

"Your father is an insulting, cruel tyrant. I couldn't bear another moment in his presence."

"Okay. I know how that feels. That's no excuse for leaving me."

"No excuse? I wasn't going to make you choose between your family and me. I know things are bad between you and your father, but. . .the day may come when you want to return to him, and I will never do that. And I won't make you choose me over him. You'd come to hate me."

Wade looked into her eyes and realized he could see her. The sun was rising; the darkness had turned to gray. The rain had ended. Daylight would come again. "I will *never* hate you. You didn't ask because you knew I'd come. You're making this excuse because—because you love me."

He saw the fire in her eyes. He saw her desire to be her usual blunt self and hurt him. Then he saw deeper, under the hostility, to the hurt and the fear. She'd lost so much.

"You're marrying me, Abby. We will go wherever we need to to find a home, but we'll do it together. Don't you dare make up an excuse about why it won't work. I love you and we will travel through this life together, alone in the wilderness if that's where we're happy."

As she shook her head, Wade saw Abby's fear come closer to the surface, as if she was daring to show what was in her heart. "There's nowhere we can both be happy." Her arms were still around his neck.

"I'm happy now. Aren't you?"

She flinched, tightening her arms as if her mind told her to let go of him but her body wouldn't obey. Well, he wanted all of her, body, mind, and heart. Although right now, her body felt really nice. "Abby, I can be happy by your side. I need nothing else."

Their eyes held. Wade closed the distance between them,

and this time the kiss was pure tenderness. It was a promise. She nearly crushed him with her warrior's grip, and he knew he had her promise back.

When Wade raised his head this time, she smiled. The fear was still there, but she was brave enough to face that fear.

"Um. . .I have a bona fide preacher's license. I can perform a wedding ceremony."

Wade turned to Red and smiled. Wade slid his arm around Abby's waist so they could face Red, side by side.

"I say yes." Wade looked at Abby.

"And Cassie and I can get these men to town. We left the horses with the other outlaws, and we've got horses enough to carry these two. We can manage. You can say your vows and go start your lives together anywhere you want." Red smiled. "But if you'd like to stop by our place once in a while, we'd love to see you."

Cassie came and relieved Red of baby Michael. She slipped the little tyke onto the blanket beside Susannah. "I'll be a witness to the marriage. I think you need a witness, Red. I don't think those unconscious men really count."

Red shrugged. "I've never done this before, so probably having someone witness it is a good idea. Although you'd think me bein' a witness and them being witnesses oughta be enough. I mean, I'm a parson. I should be trustworthy."

"Yeah." Wade nodded. "And why would we lie? But we'd like you to witness our wedding, Cassie." Wade looked at Abby. "If there is one. What do you say?"

Abby sighed and looked disgruntled, but that was pretty much how she looked all the time, so Wade didn't let that discourage him. It just helped him to fully accept the life he was signing up for. And if she stayed by his side, that was all he would ever ask for.

The wait was nearly unbearable. The sun rose a bit more as Wade watched Abby's heart battle her mind.

Finally, she smiled. "I say yes." Her arm around his waist tightened. "And since I can't get shut of you, I'll ride along to deliver these men and tell the sheriff my story. I want the white world to know what happened to my people. I want someone to admit that the true savages are these outlaws."

Wade jerked his chin, a happy, contented, slightly-frightened-of-his-wife man. "So how about we wait and get married in town so everyone in Divide knows I'm the luckiest man alive?"

Abby leaned against him a bit, and Wade started thinking he hadn't plumbed the depths of the happiness he and Abby could find together.

"I wouldn't even mind inviting your odious father. I'd like that horrible yellow dog to see that we are wed to each other. It will make him sick. I'd like to be watching when his stomach turns at the sight of his son's choice of a wife."

"Please, Abby." Red raised his hands as if to surrender. "All this mushy sentiment is too much for me."

"We can invite Pa, but we're getting hitched whether he shows up in town or not." Wade hooked his arm through Abby's and said, "Let's get to town and get on with starting the rest of our lives."

Their future was unplanned.

Their destination unknown.

But wherever life led them, they'd go together. Wade knew that God had at last granted him an end to his loneliness.

"Whom shall I fear?"

And here he was marrying the scariest woman he'd ever known.

And that made it official. Wade was a brave man.

"Whom shall I fear?"

Those old, painful words Wade had battled to hold close and claim as his own now sang like a blessing raining down on his new life with his wildflower bride.

Chapter 35

After the outlaws were locked up, a few Linscott hands who happened to be in town rode out to pass on the news of the impending wedding to their boss.

Wade couldn't decide whether it was best to rush the wedding before Tom could stop it or take plenty of time and make Tom sit through the nuptials.

Hands from the Sawyer place had ridden out, too.

Between locking up the bad guys and the sheriff questioning Wade and Abby, as well as Red and Cassie, the day was nearly wound down when Pa came tearing in, riding in his specially built buckboard, driving it himself.

Wade braced for his father to go on a rampage. Instead Pa was subdued. They were standing in the middle of Divide's Main Street, Pa on the high buckboard seat, Wade and Abby on the ground.

"I'd like for you to come out to the ranch and have the wedding out there, Wade," Pa said real polite-like, and Wade wondered what the old codger was up to.

"Ask her." Wade jabbed a thumb at Abby.

"Will you, Abby? And not just for the wedding, but to stay.

I know I can get in an evil mood, but we want you and Wade at the M Bar S."

"No *mood* excuses the things you say and do." Abby scowled.

Wade studied her and realized he was trying to twist his own face into that same scowl. He envied her fierceness. Once he realized what he was doing, he quit mimicking her and looked around, afraid someone had noticed.

Wade realized he was looking up to his Pa, and that didn't sit right. But it wasn't exactly easy for the tyrant to get down. He wondered how long it'd take Pa to realize just how well sitting high above everyone else suited him. "I'm not promising it'll never happen again. I'd be a liar if I did, because I know my temper too well. But just for today, would you. . .please"—Wade thought the old man sounded like he was choking on the word *please*— "come out and be married at the ranch? I'd be honored if you'd let me give you my. . .blessing."

Another word that nearly did Pa in. Wade wondered if the grouch even knew what the word *blessing* meant. He prayed silently for his father. And wished he could love him in any way except as ordered by God. Wade had serious doubts that would ever happen. But Wade was honest enough to know how far he'd come since he'd made his peace with God. If Wade could change, then anyone could. Including Pa.

"We need to send for Belle and Silas." Cassie had dismounted and stood on the street holding Susannah. "They'll want to come to your wedding."

"Uh, honey," Red said, bouncing his redheaded son on his hip. "Belle's no big fan of weddings."

"She'd probably try to stop it if she showed up," Wade told Cassie. "You know how she is. She'd think Abby needed saving."

Everyone did know.

"If I need saving, I'll save myself." Abby rolled her eyes.

"Will you come, Abby?" Pa sounded sincere. He didn't look like he was dying from speaking kindly. That surprised Wade.

Wildflower Bride

He'd have sworn it would have killed the man to be polite.

Wade looked at Abby. "You get to decide." He had a feeling those words were going to be repeated a million times in the sixty years he planned to be married to her. Wade smiled in anticipation.

A horse walked by in the dirt. A door slammed somewhere. A coyote howled in the forest near Divide, all while Abby stared at Pa.

"We'll come out and be married there." Abby somehow made that sound like a threat.

"And will you stay?" Pa didn't even ask Wade. The man had obviously figured out who was going to be in charge of this marriage.

Abby grabbed hold of the buckboard and vaulted up beside Pa. Apparently she didn't like his looking down on her.

"We will stay if Wade wishes it." Abby leaned down until her nose almost touched Pa's. "But he will go the moment I say I can't bear it. And I will go the moment he says *he* can't bear it. We'll take it one day at a time."

Pa's face turned an alarming shade of red, but he kept his mouth shut for once in his stubborn, tyrannical life and just nodded. He managed to squeak the words, "I understand," through his clenched jaw.

Wade doubted Pa's restraint would last long, but maybe, with enough prayer and an almighty, powerful God, things would change.

Red came out of the sheriff's office in time to hear that. "It'll be full dark by the time we ride out to your place, Wade. Cassie is tired. The children have had a long, hard day. Can we put it off until tomorrow?"

The delay chafed at Wade. He'd have preferred to stay out at that house where they'd taken Sid Garver prisoner and let Red speak the vows. He'd be well into married life by now if they had. A honeymoon would have commenced. Wade felt a little dizzy and hoped he wouldn't fall off his horse.

But Abby had been kidnapped today, and all of them could use clean clothes, a hot meal, and a bath. Considering he planned to live a long time as a married man, another day wouldn't hurt. Wade looked at Abby.

She smiled and nodded.

"Tomorrow, then." Wade turned to Red. "We'll go on out to the ranch and see you in the morning." Wade reached his arms up, and Abby let him catch her around the waist and lower her to the ground. She smiled at him, letting him know she'd taken his help not because she needed it but because she liked it. Liked him. Loved him.

They saddled up and were almost ready to head out when Tom Linscott came galloping into town on that brute of a stallion.

He pulled the horse to a stop a few feet away from everyone. "You're marrying Wade Sawyer, then?" Tom's question was for Abby, but he glared at Wade and Pa in equal parts.

"I am. We're having the wedding tomorrow at the M Bar S. Wade and I are planning to stay there until I can no longer tolerate it. Then we'll wander."

Tom swung down off his horse and came to Abby, taking both her hands. "You've always got a home with me, Abby girl. You know that, right? I love you. And if Sawyer ever treats you bad, I'll beat him into the dirt for you."

Abby gave Tom a hug, and for the first time Wade wondered if living with the Flatheads had really changed Abby all that much. She seemed to be a lot like her brother.

"Come out to the wedding, Linscott." Wade couldn't fight the sense of pure satisfaction that he got from marrying Linscott's sister. It felt like he was getting the better of the man for some reason. Of course, that wasn't the reason Wade wanted to marry Abby, but it was a nice little extra.

"Try and stop me." Tom mounted up and turned tail for his ranch.

Wildflower Bride

The next morning dawned clear and warm after the storm of yesterday. When he awoke rested, with the ugliness of yesterday separated from his wedding day, Wade was glad they'd delayed the ceremony. Almost.

He came down to the kitchen to find Gertie humming as she frosted a cake. The woman had obviously been hard at work for hours.

"What's all this, Gertie?" Wade came up behind the house-keeper and kissed her on her round cheek.

Gertie smiled over her shoulder and waved her frosting-coated knife at Wade. "You two are having a nice wedding dinner whether you want one or not."

Wade shrugged. "I reckon we have to eat."

He dipped a finger in Gertie's frosting bowl and she slapped his fingers, but he dodged and got away with the sweet treat.

"Breakfast's warming in the oven, Wade. Fetch it yourself." Gertie turned back to her cake while Wade slipped a plate of hotcakes out.

"Wade. . ." Gertie didn't sound playful.

"What?" Wade braced himself to hear Gertie's misgivings about Abby. His stomach twisted as he wondered how long he'd be able to stay on the ranch. Not that he minded leaving. He just wished there could be peace here.

"I just want you to know. . .I'm sorry."

Wade had done his best not to think about the things that had been said that had driven Abby, and him, away from the ranch. Somehow, he'd never blamed Gertie for any part of the abuse he'd suffered. But when Gertie said she was sorry, he knew he had to think of it.

Wade opened his mouth to say it didn't matter since he had finally taken control of his own life, but the words wouldn't come. "Why didn't you stop him, Gertie? I remember all the times you'd wait for him to work out his temper. Then you'd come to me and tend me. I thought it was love, but you were part of it. I can see that now."

"I thought of just taking you and running a thousand times. But I'd imagine him stopping me, throwing me out. You'd have been left here at his mercy." Gertie turned to Wade. "But there is no excuse good enough for my cowardice."

"I suppose, but there was more than that somehow. You weren't just afraid. You were part of it. Your care of me. . .made you—" Wade couldn't quite put it into words. "It was its own kind of power. You controlled me by being the nice one. You abused me right along with Pa by letting it happen and picking up the pieces afterward."

Gertie was silent, her lips pursed. "We weren't what a child hoped for in a family, were we?"

Wade shook his head. "Not even close."

"I can't go back. I can't do it differently, but please believe me, however badly I showed it, I did love you, Wade. I still do. As for your father, I've seen some softening in him. I think God needed to bring your pa low, break him, to have even a chance of reaching him. But watching your strength, in handling your pa, has reached me. I'm not staying home from church anymore in some worthless show of respect for Mort's feelings. I've asked God to forgive me for my mistakes, and I'm hoping someday you will, too."

Wade nodded, touched and deeply glad for Gertie that she'd found her way to God and that somehow he had a part in her finding that path. "I forgive you, Gertie. You know the sin in my past. What kind of Christian would I be if I was forgiven so much and then wouldn't forgive you?"

"Thank you, Wade. I'm sorry I was always so weak. And I'm so glad you've found a woman who will be kind and gentle with you."

Wade smiled to think of his sweet, beautiful Abby.

"I'm not wearing that fool dress you left in my room." Abby chose that moment to stride into the kitchen wearing her doeskin dress and moccasins, carrying her knife.

Gertie looked at Abby. Then her gaze slid to Wade. The two of them broke out laughing.

Wade jumped to his feet and grabbed Abby in a hug that lifted her off her feet.

"Put me down!" She scowled, but he noticed she was careful not to stab him.

"Good morning." Wade gave her a loud, smacking kiss.

"Let's get on with this wedding." She didn't smile, made it sound like she was being harassed. But it sure sounded like she wanted to get married.

"Red'll be here soon." Wade glanced around and saw that Gertie had turned her back and was now fussing with her frosting again.

Wade took a second kiss, much quieter and deeper. And Abby cooperated something fierce.

"Then we will get on with this wedding." He smiled and tricked a smile out of his woman, too.

Tom Linscott picked that moment to slam the kitchen door open. "Get your hands off her, Sawyer." Tom pulled Wade's arm away and shoved in between Wade and Abby. "You're not married yet."

"We're going to fix that very soon. Have some breakfast."

Red was none too swift getting to the ranch. Pa was behaving pretty well, but Wade was ready to strangle Tom by the time the parson showed up.

It was finally time for the wedding, and Wade practically ran to stand by Red's side in front of the fireplace in Pa's huge living room. Cassie sat in a rocking chair with both her children in her lap. Gertie sat on the sofa next to Pa in his wheelchair.

Linscott finally walked in escorting Abby, smiling down at her. "I'll give the bride away."

"That sounds good, Tom." Red smiled. "This is my first wedding. You come up on Abby's right, with Wade on her left."

"Give me away?" Abby's fingers twitched, and Wade braced

himself for her to go for her knife. "As if I now belong to Tom and will soon belong to Wade?"

"You belong to yourself, Abby." Tom took her by the arm and eased her over to Wade's side. "No one here doubts that for a single minute."

Wade watched closely. He didn't mind Abby loving her brother, but there was no sense getting overly acquainted with the cranky, blond grizzly of a man.

He'd feel a lot better when the vows were said and they could get out of there. Wade had no intention of spending his wedding night under his father's roof. Maybe they'd set up camp in the woods, where Abby was happiest. Wade liked that idea. In fact, he liked that idea so well he lost track of what Red was saying.

Red kicked him in the shin. "So do you, Wade?" Red glared.

Wade realized he was missing his own wedding. "I do. I surely do." He hoped Red had asked the question Wade was guessing he'd asked and not something dumb like, "Do you want to go check the cattle before the ceremony?"

Red smiled.

Wade took Abby's hand and she let him, so he must have had the right answer to the right question.

"And Abby, do you take this man to be your lawful wedded husband?"

Abby smiled those blazing blue eyes right at Wade and said, clear as day, loud enough for them to hear all the way back in the Flathead village, "I do."

There was more talk, which Wade mostly missed because he was lost in Abby's smiling eyes. He did catch Red saying, "I now pronounce you man and wife. You may kiss the bride."

And right there in front of his nasty, cranky pa, Abby's nasty, cranky brother, sweet Cassie Dawson, and the first-time marryin' preacher, Red, Wade Sawyer wrapped his arms around his brand-new wife and kissed her until no one in the room could doubt that he was staking a claim. And since Abby was fully cooperative,

Wade decided she was staking her claim right back.

When he pulled away, he said for all to hear, but looking at only Abby, "We'll go wherever we need to go to be happy. If it's not here, we'll search until we find it."

Abby ran one finger down his cheek and gave him the tiniest possible nod. "We'll find home in each other."

Wade knew it now as he never had before. "Wherever you are, that's where my home will be."

"And we'll have children to fill that home, whether it's a house or a tepee or we're camped under the open stars."

The thought of those children and what was involved in creating them caused Wade to remember very little of the feast Gertie had prepared. He was polite, he was sure of it. Or if he wasn't, no one pointed it out forcefully enough to get his attention, and both Tom and Pa had a whole lot of forceful they could use on him.

The wedding wore itself out. Their guests all went home, and Wade told his pa and Gertie good-bye.

He and Abby slept under the stars in the woods near Pa's house, but plenty far away. When the camp was set and a warm fire crackled in the Rocky Mountain twilight, Wade finally pulled his brand-spankin'-new wife into his arms. "Abby, this is a new beginning for us. A new life. We'll roam the mountains if it's what you wish."

"I'd like to take a few days and be alone with you, Wade, if that's all right."

Wade felt a little dizzy at the very thought. "Nothing has ever sounded as right." He pulled her close and kissed her.

"I think we will give your whining coyote of a father a chance, Wade. But I want to hunt a few deer, build a tepee out away from his home. Have a place to go when I have to either get away from him or slit his throat."

"That seems reasonable to me." Wade could not have been fonder of his wife. He wasn't sure what that said about him, but the truth was the truth.

"Maybe we can even build a small cabin. That might be better in the winter."

Wade really wasn't that interested in planning their whole future right now. The way Abby was going on, he half expected her to start pacing off the land for the building site.

"And when the children come, we might be more comfortable with four strong walls and a stone hearth."

"About those children. . ." Wade ran clean out of patience, and for a mild-mannered man who'd spent most of his life fighting fear, he suddenly was almost exploding with courage. But he wasn't a foolish man. He didn't tell her to quiet down. That was a good way to get her to draw her knife, which she most likely had with her, even on her wedding day.

He tricked her instead, distracted her, kept her mouth too busy to talk.

He made sure his feisty little wildflower bride didn't say a single discouraging word.

It was a joyful beginning to a new life that rarely included Wade's prayer of old, *"Whom shall I fear?"*

Because his prayers were now of joy and praise and thanksgiving.

And besides, if he ever was afraid, he had Abby right there to protect him.

Discussion Questions

1. *Wildflower Bride* opens with a long, dramatic action scene. Discuss how a scene like this pulls you into a book.

2. Glowing Sun was cruelly rejected by the survivors in her Flathead Village. Would they have really treated her this way? Discuss perceptions of Native Americans in history and what is realistic and what is flavored by the misunderstandings between cultures.

3. Is Wade's hostility toward his father unscriptural, or do you understand and respect his reasons for separating himself from his abusive father?

4. Have you known someone who came out of an abusive relationship? How did they deal with the abuser? Is there a limit to "honor thy father"?

5. If you've read *Montana Rose*, did you like spending time with Cassie and Red again? Has she grown as in character during the years since she was the heroine of *Montana Rose*?

6. Did you like how Abby treated Mort Sawyer?

7. Were you surprised at the relationship between Abby and Tom Linscott? Did you like that moment in the book?

8. Was Wade too easy-going? Was his complete devotion to Abby a weakness in the plot? Would you rather have had him more conflicted about loving her?

9. Discuss how Gertie, while seemingly kind and loving, enabled Mort's abuse of Wade all the years Wade was growing up. Have you known enablers? Discuss what role they play in letting an abusive or addictive behavior continue.

10. An author strives to make all her characters three dimensional, even the villains. Are the outlaws in *Wildflower Bride* interesting—even if unlikable—characters in their own right?

11. Did Wade live up to the commandment of honoring his father? How would you have treated Mort if he were your father?

ABOUT THE AUTHOR

Mary Connealy is a Christie Award finalist. She is the author of the Lassoed in Texas series, which includes *Petticoat Ranch, Calico Canyon,* and *Gingham Mountain.* She has also written a romantic cozy mystery trilogy, *Nosy in Nebraska;* and her novel *Golden Days* is part of the *Alaska Brides* anthology. You can find out more about Mary's upcoming books at www.maryconnealy.com and www.mconnealy.blogspot.com.

Mary lives on a Nebraska ranch with her husband, Ivan, and has four grown daughters: Joslyn (married to Matt), Wendy, Shelly (married to Aaron), and Katy. And she is the grandmother of one beautiful granddaughter, Elle.

Mary loves to hear from her readers. You may visit her at these sites: www.mconnealy.blogspot.com, www.seekerville.blogspot.com, and www.petticoatsandpistols.com. Write to her at mary@maryconnealy.com.